Given away with Nos. 1 & 2 of]

["Young Harkaway and his Boy Tinker."

"Jack passed his sword through the Spaniard's side."

"Tinker hopped round him nimbly, and gave him another taste of the steel."

EDWIN J. BRETT'S
ADVENTURES OF
YOUNG
JACK HARKAWAY
AND HIS BOY TINKER.

BEAUTIFULLY ILLUSTRATED.

COMPLETE.

LONDON:
HARKAWAY HOUSE, 6, WEST HARDING STREET,
FETTER LANE, FLEET STREET, E.C., AND ALL
BOOKSELLERS.

EDWIN J. BRETT'S

YOUNG JACK HARKAWAY

AND HIS BOY TINKER.

"'NOW, BOGEY, MAKE YOUR BOW TO DE COMPANY,' SAID TINKER."

No. 1.

A Tinted Picture Presented Gratis with this Number.

PRICE ONE HALFPENNY.

[PUBLISHED EVERY TUESDAY.]

YOUNG JACK HARKAWAY

AND HIS

BOY TINKER.

CHAPTER I.

YOUNG JACK ON THE MOVE AGAIN—HIS PROSPECTS.

WHAT, Jack, leave us and go on your travels alone?"

"Yes, sir."

"Sir," said his father, in surprise; "you are on your dignity about something I should think, Jack."

"No, no, dad," said young Jack, quickly, "it is not that. All I want is to cut out a path for myself—to be self-reliant like my father before me."

Old Jack pursed up his brows and looked gloomy.

"But your father before you needed to be self-reliant; he was poor in starting life, Jack. You have no need to be anything of the kind, seeing that I have all that is wanted to make you comfortable—aye, and precious comfortable too."

"I know that, dad," replied his son, "but I don't like the idea of feeling dependent even upon you."

"I can't quarrel with the feeling, Jack," said his father, "but I must object to your restlessness, no matter what the cause of it——"

"Restlessness!"

"Yes, that's it."

"It is not restlessness, dad, that prompts me to be off on my own fortunes. The desire is only prompted by the hope of doing for myself."

"The fact is," said old Jack, shaking his head, "that you are suffering, my boy, from the old Harkaway disease."

"What's that?"

"Restlessness," replied his father. "But, my boy, I know full well the inclinations of one of our race are not readily baulked. I am aware that, try what I would, you must have your own way in the end. And so you want to go to sea?"

"Yes, dad," responded young Jack; "since you put it so, I want to go to sea."

"Alone?"

"Not quite."

"Harry Girdwood would accompany you?"

"Yes."

Harry faced Harkaway senior, his face flushed.

"I shall go where Jack goes," he said, "even to the world's end."

Old Jack pressed his hand in silence.

"The greatest thing of all to Mr. Harvey and myself," he said, "was the mutual support we were to each other. A staunch comrade at your back will pull you through many a difficulty."

"So I feel, dad," replied young Jack, "and that's why I hope Harry will go with me wherever I go."

"You do?" said old Jack. "Well, then, I will see what can be done for you both."

So having reconciled himself to young Jack's wish, he set to work to further his boy's views.

A friend introduced him to the owner of a ship that was just going to set sail for the west coast of Africa, and Mr. Harkaway (how strange it seems to speak of old Jack in that formal manner) used his influence to secure the two boys appointments on board.

This was easily accomplished.

Harkaway had an idea, somehow, that at the eleventh hour young Jack would repent of his resolution, and cave in.

We shall see how far he was right presently.

The two places for the boys being secured, Harkaway wrote to them from Portsmouth to come down at once to be introduced to the captain and owner. This led to a general migration of the Harkaway family and friends.

A house was taken in the outskirts of the town, with accommodation for them all, including their numerous retinue.

And here for awhile they took up their abode.

CHAPTER II.

TINKER'S MYSTERY—HOW HIS VALET APPEARED ON THE SCENE—BOGEY MAKES HIS BOW.

PRIOR, however, to the incident just narrated—long previously, in fact, for it was sharply upon their arrival in England—it became known that there was something strange going on in connection with the black boy, Tinker.

Tinker had grown singularly mysterious.

He was observed disappearing continually, when any inquiry was made for him, into the lower reigons of the Harkaway establishment.

He had been watched, and then there came a report that he often carried off food.

"He thinks there is going to be a famine," remarked young Jack, "and he is making a store."

But this did not satisfactorily explain it.

Sunday, however, solved the mystery.

"He's got some sort of animal to feed downstairs."

"What is it ?" asked young Jack, "a coon ?"

"Or a 'possum ?"

"Or a kangaroo ?"

"What larks. We'll hunt him."

"No, 'tisn't that." replied Sunday ; "we'll have it up, and you shall see for yourselves."

So down he went with orders to Tinker.

"Yes, Massa Sunday," said Tinker, "I can brought up my animile if you like, only I must have time to make him look spry."

"All right."

"An'—an' dey won't be cross, 'case of my having the noble critter ?"

"No, no."

"Nor 'case uv my hidin' uv him on board de ship comin' home ?"

"No, no."

"All right," said Tinker, brightening up wonderfully. "Now I'll come d'reckly."

The people upstairs could hardly restrain their impatience while Tinker made his preparations.

However, at length Tinker came in alone.

"Hullo, Tinker," cried the boys, "where's the animal ?"

Tinker bowed much in the way of a ringmaster at a circus.

"De splendid animile is comin'," he said, gravely. "I hope as it'll please de company all a thunderin' big immense lot."

Tinker carried a whalebone whip in his hand which added to the ring-master appearance alluded to, and with his whip he signalled the "animile" to approach.

"Bogey."

"Oh, yah, yah," yelled something unearthly outside.

And then the door opened, and a nigger boy bounded into the room.

He tripped up over the woollen mat at the door and sprawled, but turned over on to his feet with the agility of a trained acrobat.

But the impetus with which he had regained his feet sent him over the mark, and down he went, bounding up, for the second time, like an India rubber ball.

This time he landed fairly upon his feet, and coming a dull weight, he gave a thud as he grounded, and the shock rattled all the room up.

And now the party had time to examine him.

This negro was a boy a little younger than Tinker, apparently, and not quite so tall.

He was certainly not a pretty nigger.

His mouth was huge, even for a darkey.

Such a gash, in fact, that, at a casual glance at his face, you saw little else than mouth.

His lord and master, Tinker, had provided him with hair powder, and it did not adhere to his frizzly poll, but shook over his sable face, giving him a ludicrous aspect.

Tinker had rigged him up in a novel kind of livery, composed of a variety of second-hand garments, which he had purchased at a marine-store dealer's.

He wore a militiaman's coat with a pair of huge epaulettes on the shoulders, that could only have belonged to an officer in a Christmas pantomime, an old cowskin waistcoat, and a pair of real footman's plush breeches.

The boots had been Tinker's chief difficulty, for his *protégé's* feet were of abnormal dimensions.

But he had managed to find a pair of shoes that had been owned in their better days by a celebrated performing giant, and this completed the nigger-boy's rig-out.

"Now, dear Bogey," said Tinker, giving him a gentle flick with his whip, "just make you bow to de company."

Bogey smiled—he had a deafening smile—and jerking his body forward, he scraped his right shoe back in making his obeisance.

"Drop that," cried Sunday, rushing at him. "You'll spile the carpet, you black imp."

"He could use up a carpet a day," said young Jack, grinning.

"If he was often took polite," commented Sunday.

"Ladies an' gemmen," began Tinker, who meant a speech.

"He, he, he, yah !" smiled the new nigger, in rather a loud voice.

"You iggorant beast," said Tinker, flicking him with the whip. "What you grinning like a cantankerous old dam Cheshire cat for ?"

"'Case explained Bogey, showing his ivories in an alarming manner, "'case you says ladies an' gemmen."

"Well ?"

"An' an'," explained Bogey, who could not get along for laughing, "an' dere ain't no gals."

This set the company generally off upon the giggle.

"Bery good, sar," said Tinker, eyeing his subordinate severely, "bery good, sar. Gemmen, fellers, an' pussons, dis black nigger, Bogey as I calls him, I brought ovar wid me jes' as a kinder speeches o' walley, jes' to look after me, and 'tend to de little wants of dis good-looking child."

"Ur, ur, ur, ur, yah !" grinned Tinker's "walley." "You beastly ugly, Master Tinker."

"Take dat," said Tinker.

He got it, too, in the shape of a crack on the head with a whalebone whip, which sent the darkey's hair powder flying out, but did not appear to incommode him in the least.

"So you've got a valet, Tinker ?" said Harvey.

"Yes, sar."

"And what do you want with a valet, pray ?"

Tinker drew himself up to his full height, which was not anything extraordnary, it might be mentioned.

"My walley, sar, am to look arter my own pussonal wants, sar ; dat's de use of my walley. Take dat for larfin', you nigger beast."

Bogey got it again.

Tinker promised to be a rare tyrant.

"Tell us where you picked up our friend Bogey," said young Jack.

"Bress my 'art," returned Tinker, with a supercilious air, "don't you know dat, Massa Jack ? You don't know nuffin. Why, I took de poor debil 'case he was so bressed hungry. I found him starvin', 'case he belong to dat cantankerous dam willin, Capen Morgan an' when we kill all de lot, dis poor dam ugly critter hab no grub, an' nowheres to look for any. He was so bressed fin dat I took him for a skillington, an' dat's why I called him Bogey, 'case he frightened me so."

"So you adopted him at once ?" inquired young Jack.

Tinker nodded in a condescending manner.

"Dat's it ; I took de bressed nigger into my sarvice, an' feed him on de fat ob de land, sar. Don't I, Bogey ?"

He accompanied this question with a crack of the whip, probably intended to quicken the reply.

"Yah, ha, ha!" grinned Bogey, "fat ob de land—dat's it. You don't gib too much lean."

"Iggorant beast," said Tinker, with lofty disdain ; "follow dis cleber child, and don't make a row."

* * * * *

There was, at length, no end to the ranks and grades of the humbler retainers in the Harkaway household.

"That's Mr. Harkaway's bell, Sunday," said Monday, as he sat roasting his knees before the fire in the servants' hall.

"So it is," says Sunday. "D'ye hear dat bell, Tinker ?"

"De gub'nor's bell ?" murmurs Tinker, with all the repose and languor of a Belgravian flunkey. "Bogey, you nigger, do you hear dat bell ?"

"Yes."

"Well, go, if you hear dat bell, you ebony cuss ?"

"Oh, yes, Massa Tinker," replies Bogey, grinning so as to show a sectional view of his throat ; "but I thought you was all a-gwine at oncet, yah, yah, yah!"

And Bogey tumbled head over heels out of the room.

CHAPTER III.

AT PORTSMOUTH—MR. HARKAWAY'S DOUBTS —THE GOOD SHIPOWNER.

THAT is how the Harkaway party became increased by one important retainer, the funny nigger boy Bogey—Mr. Tinker's valet, if you please.

Well, Bogey soon got to be a great favourite, and a general source of amusement all round, so that when the Portsmouth trip was mooted, nothing would do for young Jack but his boy Tinker and Bogey should go.

The shipowner was a bland, agreeable gentleman, with soft, persuasive manners, and a voice to match.

Young Jack soon got upon the right side of him also.

Mr. Murray, for that was his name, had a clerical look, and was generally taken for a parson, as he wore a white choker and a pair of gold-rimmed spectacles.

Young Jack, who was not wanting in brass, put it to Mr. Murray that they would like to take his boy Tinker and Bogey with them.

"Well, Master Harkaway," said the benevolent old gentleman, smiling, "it is not exactly usual for youngsters like you to take a bodyguard on board. But I suppose I shall have to say yes. Are they good sailors ?"

"They are pretty well up in their duties aboard ship," returned young Jack ; "they made the voyage home from Australia with us."

This was settled.

"I shall be able to introduce you to your new captain to-morrow," said Mr. Murray.

"A good seaman, you say ?" remarked old Jack.

"Captain Jem Robinson, my dear Mr. Harkaway," returned the shipowner, "is not only every inch a sailor, but he is a good man—a Christain, sir—a disciplinarian, but right, sir."

"I'm glad to hear it ; I like my boys to be with a man who knows his duty and does it."

"You are fortunate, Mr. Harkaway," said the shipowner, warmly, "in having such a captain for your boys."

"I'm glad of that."

"Ah, sir," pursued Mr. Murray, "Captain Jem Robinson is the very man of all others that I should like my own boy to go under."

"You have a son ?"

"Yes."

"Has he any fancy for the sea ?"

"No ; I wished him to go out in the 'Albatross,' I pressed the matter, in fact, when I heard of your young gentleman at first ; but my boy is not a good, docile lad like yours."

"Ahem !"

"No, no, my boy is very self-willed and fast, my dear sir—very fast, I regret to say. In fact, a boy that is used up and *blase* as most fast men of forty."

"It's a thousand pities," said Harkaway ; "why, a trip with such a man as Captain Robinson would work a radical cure."

"So I feel," returned Mr. Murray, with a sigh ; "but I've tried and tried and tried until I am tired. The 'Albatross' is such a splendid ship."

"Safe as one of the P. and O. line, I am told."

"Quite," replied the shipowner.

"The underwriters must seek your custom, Mr. Murray ?"

"I don't insure," replied the shipowner.

"Not insure !"

"No."

"How is that ?"

"As I have a great number of vessels, you see, I have an insurance fund of my own, and up to the present I have been so very fortunate with my ships, that if I did meet with losses, I should be covered for a very considerable sum out of what I have saved by not insuring my ships."

"I see."

And in truth old Jack felt precious comfortable to think that since his boys—for Harry Girdwood was but one degree less dear to him than his own son—were bent upon leaving him, they were at least going in good company, and in as stout and staunch a ship as there was afloat.

So everybody said.

They had not seen the "Albatross" as yet.

But what of that?

"He insures his own vessel," said Harkaway to all his friends and companions; "that's something like confidence, eh?"

And they were agreed all upon this point.

* * * * *

"I don't like him."

"Prejudice, my dear," said Jack. "Prejudice."

"Don't care," replied Mrs. Harkaway, "there is something in his face that makes me shudder."

"Why?"

"I don't know. But I always feel when I look at him much the same as I do when I look at an undertaker."

"That's because of his white choker," said old Jack.

"No, no," said Mrs. Harkaway. "He is an oily-tongued old rascal, Jack."

"Emily!" exclaimed her husband, rather angrily."

"Object to the expression if you like," said Mrs. Harkaway: "I can't help it. Depend upon it that anything we have to do with old Murray will lead to no good, neither to you nor I, nor to our Jack and Harry."

Old Jack turned away impatiently at this.

"Jack," said Mrs. Harkaway, seriously, "do you know what you have often said to me, scores and scores of times?"

"No."

"Yes, you do. You have often told me that I am as good as a witch—and my life upon it—this old Murray is a hypocrite."

"Why, what on earth would you do then?"

"Give up all dealings with him."

"Impossible. Consider how far we have gone in the business."

"What of that?"

"Everything of that. You can't for a mere whim or fancy throw up a whole negotiation. It would not be treating Mr. Murray fairly. Besides, ask Jack and Harry what they would do?"

And so the little argument ended.

Mrs. Harkaway was silenced, at any rate.

But was she convinced?

No.

A silent, inward voice persisted in whispering warnings anent the "Albatross" and the venerable owner.

CHAPTER IV.

LITTLE EMILY AND PAQUITA—A STARTLING ADVENTURE—YOUNG JACK TO THE RESCUE—THE YOUTHFUL SWELL AND HIS FAST TIGER—A TUSSLE AND WHAT CAME OF IT.

WHILE Mrs. Harkaway was filled with solicitude about her boy and his companion, Harry Girdwood, little Emily and Paquita met with an adventure which may as well be narrated, as it bears directly upon the future of the chief persouages in this portion of our history.

Little Emily—we call her so to distinguish her from Mrs. Harkaway; in reality she was fast losing the right to the diminutive distinction—and Paquita were rambling out of the town to catch a glimpse of the country, and discussing the prospects of their two youthful admirers, young Jack and Harry Girdwood, when the adventure alluded to occurred.

"I wish they had never got such a silly notion in their heads," said Paquita, who spoke perfect English now, but with the prettiest accent in the world.

"They are rolling stones," sighed little Emily.

"I can't think what possesses Harry to go."

"I can," said Emily.

"What?"

"Because he is tarred with the same brush as my father and Mr. Harkaway. They are ever on the move, never satisfied to be settled down in one place."

"So it is with Jack," said Paquita, "but Harry only goes because he won't desert his comrade."

"Do you think that they will be likely to come this way?" demanded Emily.

"I think it is very likely."

"Why?"

"I mentioned that we thought of strolling this way."

"Oh!"

"Ahem!"

As these young ladies reached this period of their promenade and of their conversation, they perceived two young fellows advancing towards them from the opposite direction.

They only caught a casual glance at them, and taking it for granted that they were Harry Girdwood and young Jack, they at once stopped short.

But they were both mistaken about the persons coming along.

One was a rakish-looking youth, who bore some appearance of having dined very recently and very plenteously.

His cheeks were flushed with wine, and his eyes full of mischief.

Beside him walked a young fellow, of about his own age, dressed in a tiger's livery.

Thus their relative positions were shown.

"Two luscious gals, sir," said the tiger, touching his hat, and pointing to Emily and Paquita.

"Swell," returned the master, sententiously.

"Right in our course too, sir," said the tiger with a leer.

"So they are, Chivey," said his master, "so we'll teach 'em to take up all the room, eh?"

On they came behind the unsuspecting girls.

"Well, my pretty darling, where are you going?"

And the inebriated young gentleman threw his arm round Emily's neck, and kissed her.

Like master, like man.

Tiger Chivey placed his arm around Paquita's waist, and squeezed it.

"Liah!" screamed Emily, thinking it was Jack, "how dare you?"

She was mistaken; but Paquita caught a glimpse of her tormentor, and swinging herself round, she dealt him a spanking box on the ear, that gave Mr. Chivey the news-bell for an hour or so.

"My dear," began the young gentleman, "give us another."

And the young scamp endeavoured to kiss Emily again.

"Let me go!" cried Emily, indignantly.

"Not if I know it, my pretty dear."

Emily shrieked as he pressed her closer in his arms, and kissed her again in spite of her struggles.

Suddenly the young gentleman's head was jerked violently back.

A hand at the back of his collar had done it.

He was swung round and sent spinning round and round, to find his ignominious level in the middle of the road.

"Hullo, you sir!" cried Tiger Chivey, squaring up to the new comer; "drop that game, or look out for your nob."

"Be off, you dog," said young Jack, for he was the opportune performer of this feat.

Harry Girdwood was there, and he was not in the humour to stand any nonsense.

He dropped the sprightly tiger a very ugly blow upon his cheek, and following it rapidly up with a second visitation, Mr. Tiger found himself on his back, but he was quickly up again.

Chivey ran to his master's aid, and helped him to scramble to his feet.

"Just hold my coat, Chivey, while I double up that young rough," said his master.

"Yes, sir," said the tiger, quite cheerfully.

He had his coat off very promptly, and began squaring up.

Upon these unmistakable signs of warfare the two young ladies grew dreadfully alarmed, and both hung on to young Jack to keep him from getting into mischief.

"Don't go near him, Jack!" exclaimed Emily. "Come home."

"Yes, you shall take him home, my love," said Mr. Chivey, the tiger; "when my guv'nor has done with him."

"They'll kill him," cried Emily, in great alarm.

"Not quite," said the tiger, "only spoil his beauty."

"Let go, Em," said young Jack, whose dander was regularly up by now.

"Come home," implored poor Emily. "Oh, do, Jack!"

"Here, Harry," said Jack, "just you go home with the girls, and leave me to correct this fellow."

"They'd better take him home while there's some of him left," said Chivey, compassionately, "or you will have to pick him up in little pieces."

This nettled Harry Girdwood, so he ran at Chivey, but the latter dodged him nimbly.

"Come, come, this is no place for you, Paquita, nor for you either, Emily. Come along."

"No, no."

"Jack can take care of himself, I tell you; come along."

Half-persuading, half-dragging, Harry got them away from Jack.

Now the latter was no sooner freed from their embarrassments, than the youthful scamp who insulted little Emily made a rush at Jack before he could recover himself sufficiently to be upon his guard, and dropped in two stinging blows which half-staggered him.

"That will teach you to——" he began.

But he hadn't time to finish it.

Young Jack was at him like a lion, and he "forced the pace," as sporting people say, so hard, that the adversary retreated before him half-a-dozen paces, guarding somewhat wildly.

But young Jack was not to be denied.

He pulled up short, and sparred a bit.

And then leaving an opening just to coax his man on, he feinted with his left, and shot out his right like a steam hammer.

It went right over the other's guard, and down he went.

"Bravo, old boy."

Now, strange to relate, this applause came from the tiger.

Such an enthusiast was Mr. Chivey in the noble art of self-defence, that he could not control his admiration for such a stroke.

However, he helped his master on to his legs and scraped off the mud from his back.

The shock had completely sobered the young scoundrel, and he saw now that he was in for a very doubtful job.

However, he was not wanting in courage.

So, pulling himself together, he sparred warily for wind.

Both combatants were skilful boxers, but Jack had received some very valuable hints from his professor, Dick Harvey, and he remembered now one bit of advice—to follow up an advantage sharply.

So he would not allow his adversary to get into trim again, but boring him in, he set to work at heavy play, and landed him three times in quick succession upon the face.

He drew blood now, and a good deal of it, which frightened the young ladies, you may be sure.

The unlucky young rake was restored to the tiger for his care and attention.

"I think that he has had enough, Jack," said Harry Girdwood.

"I hope you're not much hurt!" remarked Jack.

The other made no reply.

"Apologise to the young ladies," said Jack, "and there'll be an end to the matter."

"You be hanged!" cried the half-beaten young rake; "I'll smash you yet."

"Well," said Jack, coolly; "you force it on yourself, so it's no fault of mine. Now I'm ready to thrash you again."

"Oh, Jack," cried little Emily, in great distress; "don't hurt him again; look how dreadful he looks."

This goaded the object of her solicitude to fury.

"You want to get him away now, do you—you-you——"

"If you forget yourself before the ladies," said Harry Girdwood, "you'll get more than you bargain for."

"Why don't you come and help him?"

"He don't want any assistance," said Harry. "My friend Jack is enough for you."

" See the girls home, Harry," said Jack, " and then come back, if you like."

" All right."

Harry took them each by the arm and forced them away.

" This is not a sight for young ladies," he said ; " come, come. Jack can take care of himself."

In this way he got them some little distance.

And then seeing that it was no use to oppose further, they effected a compromise.

" We'll go, Harry," said Emily, " if you'll stay."

" Very well."

" But see that Jack doesn't get into any harm."

" I will."

" Go back then."

" All right."

" Now, now."

" Very well ; but you go home."

" We will, we will ; but get back."

Harry waited a bit to see them on their way, and when, casting lingering looks behind towards the scene of the fray, they had got some twenty or thirty paces, he went back to rejoin his comrade.

It was just time.

Jack's adversary had closed with him, and the tiger Chivey, profiting by the absence of spectators, was pounding away at Jack's head and back as hard as he could.

" Hullo !" cried Harry, rushing up ; " that's a nice way of fighting. Drop that, you scamp."

He seized Mr. Chivey by the collar and dragged him off, and then he kicked him viciously in the rear.

This he continued until he was tired out, in spite of the tiger's struggles.

Chivey had reason to remember this.

" A low beast of a fellow," the tiger said subsequently to his master ; " my back's like a stained-glass window, I know. He wears boots like a navvy."

*　　*　　*　　*　　*

Young Jack could take a good lot of punishment, and it appeared to have very little effect upon him, for he dropped into the work again as fresh as ever.

He popped in the blows in such quick succession, that his adversary was fairly knocked out of time.

He guarded wildly, and swung his arms about, leaving young Jack to do pretty well as he liked with him now.

" Will you apologise ?" demanded Jack.

" No."

" Take that then."

Down went the ill-advised young rake as flat as a flounder.

" That's a cooper," cried Chivey, dropping on to his knees beside his master ; " you may consider as I've chucked up the sponge."

" Does he apologise ?" demanded Jack.

" Yes," responded the vanquished adversary, in a faint voice.

" All right," said young Jack, all his enmity vanishing upon the instant. " What can I do for you ? There's my hand."

" Keep it," returned the beaten youth, sullenly, " keep it until I take it out of you when

I'm in condition ; you shall get it yet. I'll have my revenge on you."

" Brute !" said Harry Girdwood ; " you deserve your licking."

" If you want me," said Jack, tossing down a card, " you will always find me at that address ; my name's young Jack Harkaway."

" The deuce it is," exclaimed the tiger ; " here's a go."

And he whispered something to his master.

CHAPTER V.

JOVIAL CAPTAIN ROBINSON—MR. CHIVEY THE TIGER VISITS HIS MASTER'S FATHER.

NEITHER young Jack nor Harry noticed the tiger's whisper to his master.

And so, without paying any more attention to master or man, our two companions made their way after little Emily and Paquita.

And young Jack had not a trace of his late encounter to take home with him.

Brave young Jack.

Young Jack was precious lucky to escape this tussle without so much as a mark to take home with him.

When he got back, he was met at the door by little Emily and Paquita, whose expression denoted how much they had really suffered in anxiety for his safety.

" What a bad, rash boy you are," said Emily ; " how dare you go fighting like that ?"

" Now, I appeal to anyone," replied young Jack. " Was it my fault ?"

" But fighting in the streets is not gentlemanly."

" I know that," returned young Jack, " but I couldn't get out of it—you wouldn't have me turn round and run away, especially from such a miserable worm as that ?"

" Of course not, Jack."

And her looks showed plainly enough that she had too much of her parents' spirit in her to wish such a thing.

Her looks, too, showed unbounded admiration for her champion.

" I've got news for you, Jack," she said, presently.

" Good news ?"

" Yes."

" What is it ?"

" Guess."

" Captain Robinson has arrived," guessed Jack.

" That's it. Why, you're a conjuror. How did you guess ?"

" I expected Captain Robinson, that's all."

Captain Robinson came, and a jovial, red-faced skipper he looked.

And his manner was perfectly in keeping with his appearance.

A hearty, taking way he had that won every heart.

" The ' Albatross !' " he exclaimed, when questioned by Harkaway as to the merits of his vessel ; " I only wish that there was a thousand such craft afloat in these waters, none of your flash-looking, rakish craft, but a downright solid-built Englishman—one of the float-while-there's-a-plank-left-sort, and never say die."

Mrs. Harkaway made no reply.

"And what do you think of the 'Albatross,' young gentlemen?" said the skipper to Harry and young Jack.

"Can't give an opinion yet, captain," answered the latter, "until she arrives."

"What!"

"Let us see her first, sir," said Harry, "and then we'll give an opinion."

"Why," exclaimed the captain, "surely you don't mean that you haven't been to see her?"

"Couldn't very well, not knowing what part of the world she is in," answered young Jack.

"Well, I suppose that she is about a mile from here, riding at anchor, and waiting to welcome us."

"You don't say that?"

"Don't I?" said the captain shortly; "I thought I did."

"I'll go on board to-morrow, Captain Robinson," said young Jack, "with your permission."

"Of course you shall," returned the bluff captain; "and as many more of you as like to."

"I'll go too, then," said Dick.

"Welcome."

"And I."

"Welcome again, say I; and welcome all round."

And so it was settled that a party should be made up to visit the ship.

Everyone about was charmed with this model skipper, so bluff and hearty was he.

"A bold and good sailor, I should think," said Dick.

And this opinion was re-echoed by one and all.

*   *   *   *   *

Mr. Murray, the owner of the "Albatross" amongst others, was in trouble.

He had one son, as he has already mentioned himself incidentally, and this son occasioned an endless amount of trouble.

Mr. Murray knew that his scapegrace boy was somewhere about in the neighbourhood, and he sought for him far and wide.

But there was no luck.

"There is nothing for it," he said, "but to wait until he has spent his last money, and then we shall see him. He always calls when the funds run low."

But this time the scapegrace boy did not call.

He sent.

His messenger was his friend, his confidant, and—his tiger.

"Well, Mr. Chivey," said Mr. Murray, in his severest manner; "what do you want?"

"Guv'nor sent me, sir," replied Mr. Chivey, touching his forehead by way of salute.

"The governor!" exclaimed Mr. Murray, in disgust; "do you mean my son?"

"Yes, sir, just so."

"Then why don't you say my son?" exclaimed Mr. Murray, testily.

"Because he ain't my son," replied Chivey, with great promptitude.

"Bah!"

"Eh!"

The tiger's manner was most aggravating, and Mr. Murray lost his temper.

"Be off," he said, "and send your master to me."

"Can't, sir."

"Can't!"

"No, sir."

"Be off, you scoundrel. You shall not stay in my service any longer. Get out; I loathe the sight of you."

"Very sorry, sir, I assure you," returned Chivey, who looked more upon the grin than contrite, "but I'm not in your service, sir; I'm in the guv'nor's."

"Send my son here."

"He can't come."

"Why not?"

"He's on his back; got on a couple o' poultices and tincture of arniky all over."

"Tincture of what?" exclaimed Mr. Murray.

"Arniky," answered Mr. Chivey, and with a pitying air he added—"you don't know what arniky is? Why, it's a sort of lotion you put on to bruises and such."

"What on earth do you mean? Is my son ill? Has he met with an accident?"

"Why, no, you can't call it a accident, exactly," answered Chivey, coolly, while Mr. Murray was foaming; "he asked for it, and he got it, too; in fact, sir, he got more than he wanted."

"Got what?"

"A licking, sir—about as neat a licking as you ever see—a proper cove the other, a regular propper, I might say, sir, with two p's—he, he! excuse my little joke—he propped the guv'nor all over. Ding dong! one on the smeller. Tick, tick, bunged up the left peeper. Tap, tap, it came—postman's knock, here, there, an' where'll you have it next, my boy?"

Mr. Murray groaned.

"This animal will drive me mad!"

"Animal!" iterated Mr. Chivey, raising his shirt collar; "come now, I say——"

"You idiot!"

"' Compliments pass when gentlefolks meet.'"

"Where is my son?"

"Here's his address, sir."

The tiger handed Mr. Murray a very dirty card, upon which was written his master's address.

"Say I'll call."

"Very good, sir; shall I take any tin to the guv'nor, sir?"

"Say I'll call."

"Yes, sir, I heard."

"Get out."

"D'rectly, sir; but you really ought to have seen him at it. Lor'! it would have made you jump for joy—such slogging, and the guv'nor ain't bad with his fives either. But he wasn't in training like the other; the propper cove, I mean. The guv'nor he liquors-up too much, and that's a fact—makes you puffy, you know—the worst thing in the world for a chap in training; you ought to be right off your lotion. But Lor'! sir, you might as well talk to the deaf and dumb school as to Master Herbert—play!"

He broke off abruptly to catch a boot which Mr. Murray, now thoroughly exasperated, hurled at him.

He placed the boot down on the floor with great deliberation, bowed to Mr. Murray, and hitching up his collar, walked quickly to the door.

" Nice boot, sir ; good morning, sir ; I'll tell the guv'nor you're coming."

CHAPTER VI.

JOVIAL CAPTAIN ROBINSON AGAIN—STRANGE REVELATIONS ! — CAPTAIN ROBINSON'S LEECH AND HOW IT BEGAN TO SUCK BLOOD —FATHER AND SON—YOUNG HOPEFUL'S RESOLVE—THE "ALBATROSS" SAILS TO-MORROW.

" CAPTAIN ROBINSON, sir," said Mr. Murray's servant.

" Let Captain Robinson come in," said Mr. Murray.

The captain entered.

He was not quite so jovial as he had shown himself upon his introduction to the Harkaways, and he went with his owner into business at once, with scarcely so much as the usual greetings.

" The ' Albatross ' must sail to-morrow night," he said.

" And why must, Captain Robinson ?" asked the owner.

" Because the Harkaways and their friends are just about as 'cute as people say, and unless you want the whole game blown, we had better get off."

" Bah !" returned Mr. Murray, contemptuously ; " you make a grand mistake ; their confidence is unbounded, I tell you—unbounded."

" Is it ?"

" Of course."

" Then they made some very curious remarks about the depth of water in the hold for one thing."

" That's your fault, then ; you ought to have had the pumps going up to the very moment they went on board."

" So I had, but damme ! the water gets in too fast by a long way, I couldn't keep it under by hook or by crook. Besides, I've got a new passenger, an awful rich Cockney, and I want to get off before he can hear any ugly tales."

" What's his name ?"

" Figgins."

" A retired grocer ?"

" That's the party. Well, he's going to dub up handsome, and to take out a whole cargo of good things, so that I don't want to risk spoiling him, by no manner of means."

" Very well, Robinson," said the shipowner ; " only mind you don't spoil the very thing you are trying after."

" How ?"

" By raising suspicions through undue haste."

" No fear of that."

" When do you go on board ?"

Captain Robinson stared at his owner.

" Didn't you hear me ? I said, when do you go on board ?"

" What for ?"

" To take command."

" Why, you don't suppose for a minute that I mean going on board the ' Albatross ?' "

" Not going !" exclaimed Mr. Murray. " Why, how on earth then can she start ?"

" Why, I set too big a price upon my precious carcase, to trust myself on such a rotten old tub. Why, she's as full of holes as a cullender."

" But they have been caulking and painting this week past."

" Aye, up above the water line. But let her get into a bit of a sea, and it'll all wash away as clean as a whistle, and in'll come the water by the bucketful—aye, by the barrelful."

" You exaggerate the danger, I am sure."

" Devil a bit," returned Captain Robinson, " and none knows it better than you——"

" Sir !"

" Come, come, no smarming politeness with me, if you please. Why who knows all about it better——"

" The 'Albatross,' sir——" began Mr. Murray.

" Is a lovely craft—on paper—a splendid ship for the underwriters. However, we're only wasting time by going into that."

" Why on earth did you lead me to suppose you accepted the command, then ?"

" Why ? I never led you to suppose I was going. I've got a substitute all right and tight, and I shall be taken ill at the last moment, d'ye see ?"

" Who is this substitute ?"

" A pal of mine, who's in trouble, and can't show up until the last moment."

" But, if the ' Albatross ' is not under skilful command, she'll founder before she gets out of sight of land——"

Mr. Murray pulled up short.

He had said too much.

He would have given something to recall those words. Too late.

Captain Robinson leered at the owner significantly.

" You needn't fear nothing about that. Joe Deering is as good a seaman as ever sailed, only he's got into an awkward mess, and must get away, or he'd be lodged in limbo in a brace of shakes—just the fellow for a forlorn hope."

Mr. Murray winced.

" Be more choice in your expressions, Captain Robinson," he said.

" Well, that's just what it is, neither more nor less ; a forlorn hope. But there, it's no use arguing. Would you like to take a voyage in the ' Albatross ?' "

" I ?"

" No, you would not, of course. No sane man would, if he knew as much as you and I know."

" But frankly Captain Robinson—disguise apart, you think that the ' Albatross ' is——"

" Fated ? Yes, that's the word. She'll go to the bottom of the sea like a stone, and you'll land a big plum in the way of insurance, and I shall come in for my little bit as captain."

" I don t see that."

" I do, though."

" But, if you don't go——"

" Then I should consider it my duty to society to show you up."

Bland Mr. Murray smiled.

" You forget, captain, that that is a proceeding which would cut both ways."

"Not it. Catch a weasel asleep, and shave his eyebrows. I've got the ground all thoroughly prepared for myself."

"How?"

"By those letters I wrote, warning you."

"I never received any."

"I can't help that," answered this jovial captain. "I wrote 'em and had 'em duly witnessed, and copied in a letter book, and if you pretended that you never received them, why, who on earth would believe you? Besides, my refusal to go is quite enough, else why did you engage Captain Joe Deering?"

"I never engaged him."

"Who did, then?"

"You."

"Get along with you. Joe Deering will never come back to say that, and you might talk till you was pea-green without getting anybody to listen to it."

"But I——"

"Bah, sir. You try it on with a jury when you like."

Mr. Murray gasped.

"Well, sir."

"Well, then," said Captain Robinson, in his old jovial style, "it is understood. The 'Albatross' sails to-morrow?"

"I suppose so."

Mr. Murray was beaten.

The villanous captain got a little money on account and left his owner, smacking his pocket with an evident air of satisfaction.

He had reason to.

* * * * *

"That's the first of a series," said Captain Robinson. "I couldn't have hit upon a better thing. I have only got to apply my leech, and I'll bleed the old rascal just as often as I like."

And the villain walked off, looking the very picture of good nature.

* * * * *

Mr. Murray visited his scapegrace son.

He found him in bed, bandaged and swathed in lint and arnica, precisely as the Cockney tiger had stated.

His eyes were both discoloured in spite of all the remedies which had been applied.

Young Jack's handiwork was not like some of those cheap printed calicoes we hear about.

His were fast colours.

Herbert Murray's nose was swollen to about thrice its normal dimensions, and his lips were as thick as a negro's.

He rued the rashness bitterly that had tempted him into an encounter with the son and heir of the Harkaways.

"Well, Master Herbert," said his father, sternly, "this is a pretty affair."

"It's no use bullying," responded young hopeful. "I did all I knew to knock him out of time, but he was too quick, and nothing hurts him."

"Hurts him!" said the shipowner, looking up to the ceiling with an injured air; "it hurts me far more than you."

"I'd bet a penny it doesn't," responded his son, "and chance it. Chivey shall hold the stakes."

"Chivey is ready and willin'," said the tiger,

holding out his palm. "Perhaps your governor will make it a fiver."

"Cease this levity," said Mr. Murray. "Who is it you have been fighting with?" he continued, turning to his son.

"What's his name, Chivey?" demanded the patient.

"Young Jack Harkaway, sir, and a stunner at a game stand-up fight," said the tiger.

"Harkaway!" exclaimed the shipowner; "you don't mean it."

"I do."

"Why, this young Harkaway is going out in my ship the 'Albatross,' or he was going—of course now that he has been fighting with you, it is all over, and I shall lose a very handsome sum. Besides which, the fact of Mr. Harkaway's son going out in the 'Albatross' inspired confidence. It brought me passengers and freights better than any advertisement we could have hit upon. You young ruffian, you have spoilt me completely."

"Wait a bit, dad—wait a bit," said the patient.

He struggled to raise himself up into a sitting posture, and succeeded, but groaned the while at the anguish of his bruises.

"Going out in your ship, you said?"

"Yes."

"That's the ticket," observed Chivey.

"He was going; but this disgraceful affair will of course spoil it," said Mr. Murray.

"I don't see that," responded Herbert.

"Nor I, my noble governor," said Chivey.

"Silence, fellow," said the shipowner, turning round.

"Mum's the word," responded the tiger, clapping his hand over his mouth so as to make it pop.

"He didn't know me from Adam," said Herbert Murray.

"Are you sure?"

"Yes."

"That's better. I breathe again."

"Look here, dad," said the patient; "you've often said that I was a good-for-nothing lot."

"I said the bare truth."

"Well, then, I'll tell you what. You've often said you wanted to get me away from this place and from bad associates."

"I have."

"Let me go to sea."

"You!"

"Yes; why not?"

"When, when?"

"In the 'Albatross.'"

Mr. Murray started back as though he had been shot.

"Are you mad?" he exclaimed.

"I don't think so," replied his son; "ask Chivey."

"Not exactly," said the tiger, without waiting to be asked; "I am proud of him, sir; he is just about as artful a card as you'll meet with between Portsmouth and Tattersall's."

And then he shouted—

"Oh a life on the ocean wave,
And a home on the rolling deep."

"Hold your tongue, and leave the room," exclaimed Mr. Murray.

"Quite so; quick march," said Chivey.

The patient, however, winked at his tiger to

wait, and Chivey, to use his own expressive form of speech, knew his book too well to go away.

The young rake did not like being left alone with his father, for he could not hold his own so well when the shipowner took to lecturing him.

The occasional interjections of the tiger helped him out.

"Well, what do you say, governor?" said young Murray; "you have wished me dead a hundred times, I know."

"I!"

"Yes; I have caused you such a lot of worry and trouble, that you couldn't help it."

"My boy, my boy," exclaimed the shipowner, "you don't know what you are saying."

"Oh, yes, I do, and if you really want to get rid of me, why, let me sail in the 'Albatross.'"

"What for?"

"To cry quits then with that young beast who has decorated me with black and blue spots like this."

Bland Mr. Murray's eyes flashed fire at this.

"I don't object to your crying quits with him," he said, "only you mustn't go in the 'Albatross.'"

"Why?"

"Because I won't allow it. Ask anything of me you will, my boy," said Mr. Murray, speaking now with unfeigned emotion, "anything but that, and I will not refuse you."

"Give me some money, then."

"There."

And promptly suiting the action to the word, the shipowner placed two bank notes in his son's hand.

"I must go now, Herbert," he said, "but I will look in to-morrow, and if you still want to go to sea, when you are better, you shall go."

"But not in the 'Albatross'?" demanded his son.

"No, not for the world in the 'Albatross,'" said Mr. Murray, hastily.

And he vanished.

* * * * *

"Unhappy boy," exclaimed the shipowner, "he little thinks what it is he asks. The 'Albatross!' I would almost as lief see him in his coffin, for then, at least, I should know the end of him. But there I should not know what sufferings might be in store for him. My poor boy! My poor boy!"

And the old rascal actually wrung his hands in anguish at the thought.

Here was one who did not hesitate, for the sake of gain, to risk the lives of numbers of honest men, and yet who was filled with tenderness for his own son.

* * * * *

"How much do you think he has given me?" asked young Murray.

"Twenty quid, governor?"

"Right. Will that pull us through?"

"Of course it will."

"And leave us a bit to the good?"

"Yes."

"Then what do you say to sailing to-morrow night?"

"By the 'Albatross'?" asked Chivey.

"Yes."

"I'm game," responded Chivey, with a chuckle; "if it's only to take a rise out of the old gentleman who was so down upon that indentical point."

"And I mean to go, Chivey," said Herbert Murray, "to take it out of young Jack Harkaway."

"Once alone with him on board your father's own ship, you will be able to do as you like with the fighting cock."

"That's just my meaning, Chivey; I'll be master there."

"To-morrow we sail, then, governor?"

"To-morrow we sail, Chivey."

CHAPTER VII.

THE ORPHAN MAKES HIS BOW—THE LAST NIGHT ON SHORE—MISCHIEF BREWING.

THE news of the sudden departure of the "Albatross" startled our friends, the Harkaways, considerably.

Young Jack and Harry Girdwood no sooner heard the rumour, than they went straight to Mr. Murray's office to inquire into the truth of it.

Here they encountered a little old gentleman of eccentric appearance.

"Are you waiting to see Mr. Murray, young gentlemen?"

"Yes, sir," responded Jack.

"So am I."

"The same errand as ourselves, probably," said Harry Girdwood. "We wish to know if the report is true."

"About the 'Albatross' sailing to-morrow?"

"Yes."

"So do I."

"Do you go in the 'Albatross?'" asked Jack.

"Yes," returned the eccentric little man; "although my line of life has, hitherto, been cast in different places, yet I feel that I was really and truly born for the sea."

"I hope you may like it, sir."

"Sure to."

"I hope it may like you."

"Why should it not?"

"Oh, I don't know. I suppose you have been to sea?"

"Never—that is, never further than Gravesend—by water, and I have never been unwell. It is almost the sea there, you know."

"Almost like the sea," said young Jack, winking at Harry.

"And you didn't feel at all sea-sick, sir?" asked Harry.

"Not a bit, not a bit."

The two boys elevated their eyebrows, expressive of great wonderment.

"Then there is no doubt about it, sir, the sea is your proper element."

"So I believe, so I believe. Have you been to sea?"

"Oh, yes," said both at once.

"How far?"

"A long way beyond Gravesend."

"Indeed?"

"Yes, as far as Australia."

"Oh!"

The stranger eyed the two boys askance. Evidently he was in doubt upon the subject.

"Australia is a very long way."

"Well," said young Jack, stroking his chin complacently—was he trying to coax on his beard?—"it is what one may call a goodish step."

"Humph!" said the eccentric little man; "and you are going, too, in the 'Albatross'?"

"Yes, sir."

"Passengers?"

"No," said Harry Girdwood; "we are officers."

"Indeed."

"And we hope that we may be able to contribute towards making your voyage as agreeable as possible."

"That's very kind of you. The fact is, gentlemen, sometimes I am very sad; my fate I consider a hard one."

"I am sorry for you, sir," said young Jack; "but why is your fate so hard?"

"The fact is, young gentlemen," answered the old fellow, "I am an orphan."

"How sad."

"Yes, I am an orphan, but my instinct always pointed to a maritime career. My grandfather was a nautical man."

"Oh, indeed; fought with Nelson at Trafalgar, and all that sort of thing?" said impudent young Jack.

"Why, no, not exactly," answered the elderly orphan; "he was a species of nautical man—a kind of custom-house officer—what is called a tide-waiter."

Harry's eyes twinkled, and he exchanged a wink with his larkish comrade.

"That settles it, sir, in my opinion; you were, no doubt, born a sailor, Mr.—Mr.—I haven't the honour of knowing your name."

"Figgins—Mark Antony Figgins, late of Cow Cross, tea merchant. Families supplied wholesale and retail."

"Dear me!"

"The name is familiar to you?" said Mr. Figgins.

"Yes, indeed."

"I don't wonder at that," said the orphan, with conscious pride, "for our emporium was noted far and wide. We made such a show at Christmas, that it was quite the talk of the neighbourhood."

"I dare say."

"Well, well," said Mr. Figgins, after a certain lapse of time, "Mr. Murray does not appear to be coming. Suppose that we adjourn to my hotel, and leave word?"

"Where are you staying, sir?"

"At the 'Royal.'"

Young Jack pulled a very long and serious face.

"It is a good house, I believe, is it not?"

"Well, yes; only it bears a very peculiar reputation," said Jack.

"Dear me, you excite my curiosity," said Figgins. "Tell me why."

"Why, people say that—really, I can't tell you."

"Oh, do—do, pray," exclaimed Mr. Figgins. "I am most anxious to know."

"Well, then, they pretend that it is haunted."

"Ha, ha, ha!" laughed Harry Girdwood, "that is a capital joke, sir."

"We don't quite believe in ghosts in this half of the century," said Mr. Figgins.

They were leaving Mr. Murray's office, when they encountered Mr. Mole, who was just coming in search of them.

Now young Jack and Harry Girdwood had never ceased to be to the worthy old gentleman the teases which we have already known them, yet Mr. Mole could not contemplate without pain the prospect of parting with them.

"Mr. Mole," said young Jack, presenting his tutor; "my best friend. Mr. Figgins, a fellow traveller, sir," he added to Mr. Mole.

"Proud to make your acquaintance, sir," said Mole. "Hope you'll enjoy the society of my young friends. I assure you, sir, it grieves me to part with them."

"So you are about parting?"

"Yes, sir, I have been with young Jack all his life, and now have to part with him; he goes on his travels without any of his old protectors."

And the old gentleman wiped a tear from his eye.

"We were just going to my hotel to dine; will you honour us with your company?" said Figgins.

Mr. Mole was nothing loth, so off they all went. And a very jolly dinner it was.

So jolly that only a new chapter can do full justice to the particulars.

* * * * *

"Harry!"

"Hullo!"

"Don't bawl out," said young Jack, "but listen."

"I'm all ears, as our orphan might say. Drive on."

"Well, we shall soon say good-bye to our friends, Mr. Mole included, and as this will be our last night on shore, it must be a jolly one."

"It must."

"I'm on for a lark."

"I'm there," said Harry. "A lark with old Mole and the interesting orphan."

"Yes."

That poor, tender orphan was doomed to have a hard time of it with young Jack and Harry the last night they remained in old England.

CHAPTER VIII.

THE DINNER PARTY—THE HAUNTED ROOM AND THE RED RIDING HOOD GHOST—A SCRAMBLE WITH THE HAIRY GHOST.

THE bottle was circulating very freely at the headquarters of the Harkaway family.

We don't mean to imply that our young friends, Jack and Harry, were indulging; they contented themselves with plying Mr. Mole and the orphan.

To do them justice, both gentlemen wanted but little persuasion to make them merry.

Mr. Mole was on his legs for the first toast.

"Bumpers round, if you please," said the old gentleman, in his most grandiloquent style; "I give you 'The Sovereign.'"

"That's for pocket money on our voyage," said Harry, in an audible whisper to Jack.

"No, no," replied young Jack, in the same

tones ; "it's the seven and sixpence Mr. Mole owes me, but I haven't got change."

"Hear, hear ! very well said."

"You mistake me, Jack, my boy," said Mr. Mole. "I don't refer to vulgar dross, but to our gracious sovereign, one that we never want to change."

The toast was then drunk with appropriate honours.

"I have now to propose a toast which will be received with no less enthusiasm than the last——"

"Hear, hear !"

"Thank you—than the last. The health I have to propose, you will no doubt have guessed."

"Guest !" exclaimed young Jack, "he means our host."

"It sounds like a riddle, for all the world," said Harry.

"Really——" began Mr. Mole.

"I can give you a better one than that," said young Jack. "If a herring and a half cost three-ha'pence, why is Mr. Mole like a rhinoceros ?"

"Really !" exclaimed Mr. Mole, looking around him in the greatest indignation ; "I never heard——"

"Never heard it !" said young Jack. "I should think not. It's original, I assure you."

"Hear, hear !" said Harry.

"Upon my life !" exclaimed Mr. Mole, "Jack, this is too bad, and on the eve of your leaving us, really——"

"Don't mind, sir," said Jack, coolly ; "I'll forgive you. I had finished."

"You !"

"Yes, sir," said Jack, innocently ; "that was all my riddle."

"Jack, Jack," began Mr. Mole, "I'll——"

"Dear, dear me," said Mr. Figgins, greatly alarmed ; "it is all a mistake, gentlemen. You don't understand, Mr. Cole——"

"Mole, sir."

"Mr. Pole, I beg pardon. Mr. Harkaway thought you alluded to the interruption of his friend, and so he said——"

"That's it," said young Jack, "you have got it, Mr. Figgins."

"I am sure no offence was meant to Mr. Pole——"

"Mole, sir," exclaimed the old gentleman, quite exasperated. "M O L E, Mole, sir."

"How well Mr. Mole spells," said young Jack to Harry, in audible admiration.

"Wonderful man," responded Harry.

"You may call this joking," said Mr. Mole, fiercely ; "but I call it downright——"

"A glass of rum, Mr. Mole."

This brought a smile on Mr. Mole's face.

He could never refuse good liquor, so this glass stopped his indignation.

They plied him with a glass or two, and he forgot all about the burking of his speech.

"There, gentlemen," said Mr. Figgins, "now we are getting comfortable again. The bottle is there beside you, sir ; fill up and pass it, Mr. Dole——"

"Mole, sir," exclaimed the old gentleman.

"Of course, Mole, I do forget names. But I must bring my artificial memory to bear upon it."

"Do you believe in artificial memory, then ?" asked Jack.

"Yes."

"How does it work ?""

"Simple enough," returned Mr. Figgins. "For instance, here is Mr. Foal ; now I recollect I have a bad cold in the throat, on the day that I have the pleasure of meeting him for the first time. I am hoarse. Now do you see ! Hoarse—foal—see ?"

"Capital !"

"Wonderful," cried Harry ; "a grand system."

"Oh, yes," said Mr. Figgins. "Let's see what was it—oh, hoarse—foal, of course—Mokes on memory is an infallible cure for my little drawback."

"Of course," said Mr. Mole, savagely, "only my name doesn't happen to be Foal."

"Pass the decanter, Harry," said Jack.

*   *   *   *

Both the gentlemen were getting what young Jack called "nice and mellow" by this time, and Mr. Mole was indulging in his old propensity for pulling the long bow.

"Yes, my dear sir, the day I lost that right leg, I——"

"Advertised in all the papers for it," suggested Jack.

"What ?"

"Beg pardon, sir, I misunderstood," replied Jack.

"That day," resumed Mr. Mole, "I slew ten men with my own hand."

"Ten !" quoth Mr. Figgins, looking quite frightened.

"Ten !"

"How dreadful."

"Glorious, sir, glorious," said Warrior Mole, dilating on his favourite theme ; "I wasn't then the miserable old wretch that you see me now."

"Come, come, sir," remonstrated Mr. Figgins.

"I repeat it, miserable old wretch. Single-handed, sir, I kept three-and-twenty of 'em at bay ; they were demoralised, sir, demoralised, and I played at skittles with 'em, sir, damme."

Mr. Figgins was struck dumb with admiration.

"This is a most enjoyable day in my life," said he ; "most enjoyable. I shall never think of this day without associating the name of Dole with that of——"

"Sir," said Mole, rising, "my name is——"

"Norval," said Jack.

"Goodness me," murmured Mr. Figgins, sinking into his shell. "I beg your pardon. The wine is near you and time is pressing."

Time to go.

Mr. Mole was by no means firm upon his wooden pins.

"How very uneven your floor is," he said, with a hiccup, to his host.

Mr. Figgins gave him his arm, and they steadied each other.

But it was no use, and down went Mole and the orphan.

Mr. Mole was not in a fitting state to walk through the streets, and so the boys proposed that he should take a room in the hotel.

"If Mr. Bole likes to accept it," said Mr.

Figgins, "he can have one of the beds in my room. It is a double-bedded room."

"Very much 'bliged, old man," said Mr. Mole, whose utterance had become strangely thick.

"Is that your bedroom?" asked young Jack, pointing to an inner apartment.

"Yes," answered Mr. Figgins, the orphan, "that ish my b-room. I mean b-droom. Dear, how very singular I can't say b-b-bed-room."

"That's the very room I was warned against beyond all others," said young Jack.

"What for?"

"Someone declares that at certain stated intervals, a huge hairy monstrosity, half man, half beast, is seen haunting the place."

The orphan opened his eyes rather wider than usual.

"What a sniglar, I mean sing'lar shtory," he lisped.

Mr. Mole giggled.

"It's like Re-Re-Riding Hood," he said.

And then subduing his voice to a growl, he replied to himself—

"All the better to shee with, my dear. He he, he!"

"Hoh, hoh!" laughed Figgins.

Young Jack and Harry enjoyed this mightily.

"Ah," said the former; "it is all very well for you to talk like that, but you would not grin, gentlemen, if you really did see this horrible thing."

He gave a most natural shudder as he spoke.

The gentle orphan looked tipsily alarmed.

"Shertanly unpleasank," he said.

Here he became conscious of a certain thickness and irregularity in his speech, and he made a definite effort to steady himself.

"But you don't believe in anything so ridiculous as ghosts?" said Jack.

"No, no."

"Well, then, I shall wish you good night, sir," said Jack.

"Good night."

"Good night," said Harry.

Mr. Mole was beyond replying.

He was carefully tucked up, and playing a very inharmonious tune indeed upon his nasal organ.

"It's snorer, dear snorer," sang young Jack, as they descended the stairs of the hotel, paraphrasing Tom Moore, or somebody else.

They stopped upon the next landing, and gave a hearty, but silent laugh, which half threatened to choke them.

"Isn't it prime?" exclaimed young Jack.

"Jolly."

"What a rich treat the young and tender orphan is!"

"Beats Mole."

"Into a cocked hat. Oh, we'll have some good fun out of him."

"Let's get back again sharp, or we shall miss the oyster shells."

Slipping rapidly upstairs again, and into the lately vacated supper-rooms, they found the light extinguished.

Yet the reflection from the inner room—the bedroom, where Mole was snoring and Mr. Figgins was still engaged in undressing—sufficed to light them upon the nefarious project which now occupied their thoughts.

"Here's the dish."

"Hand it over."

"Gently!"

"Hush!"

Young Jack passed the dish of empty oyster shells on to his companion, who hurried noiselessly to the door and proceeded with all possible dispatch to pave the passage with them.

This done, they went downstairs, and waited in the lobby of the hotel for awhile.

*　　*　　*　　*　　*

Mr. Figgins had just completed his bed-toilet.

"What an extrorny tale that wash 'bout wooden legs and the ghosk—I mean jost; sniglar thing I can't say jhost—kost—confound the thing! gossush shivelling in m'mouth—brumgoil—mean gumboil, I sposh—Red Re-n Hood. Fancy finding wooden legs and wolf dressed up in granny's nightcap in bed jush ash you wash—blew that gumboil—jush ash you wash tumblin' in—hah! oh!"

He had scrambled under the sheets when—oh, mercies!—something hairy touched his leg.

He started back.

There, in his bed, lay a long, gaunt, hairy form, with a hideous head enshrouded in a large frilled nightcap.

Mr. Figgins gazed in horror at the vision.

Was the hideous object alive?

Yes.

It moved.

Spellbound for awhile, the old orphan presently recovered himself sufficiently to shrink backwards off the bed.

The hairy monster sat up, slowly, cautiously.

Its huge jaws opened, displaying a glistening set of sharp, white teeth, and a blood-red tongue.

Mr. Figgins gasped.

The effects of the wine were dispatched instanter with the awful fright.

He retreated from the bed.

The hairy monster advanced.

Figgins retreated to the door backwards.

On came the ghost.

"Mr. Cole—wooden legs—M-M-Mr. C-Cole! M-Mr. Coke," he stammered.

Mole snored.

"M-m-murder!" gasped the affrighted orphan.

But he had not voice enough left in him to give the alarm.

He tried to cry out, but the sound died away upon his lips.

Backwards he went, trembling and shaking, into the adjoining room.

On came the hairy form, that looked half-human, half-devilish, for Mr. Figgins perceived, to his horror, as the thing slid from the bed, that its legs and feet were long, sinewy, and covered with brownish shaggy hair.

"Mr. Dole," gasped the hapless grocer, "I want you, wooden leg Dole—my dear Dole, I want you badly. Oh, come to my help, or this monster will eat up a poor, helpless orphan."

The poor orphan did indeed want help.

Meanwhile, the hirsute visitor, grinning upon its destined victim, like some evil sprite just let loose from below, advanced with outstretched arms.

And fearfully weird-like did it look in the long white gown in which it was enveloped.

"Dole!" gasped Figgins, his voice growing fainter and fainter. "Oh, help a poor orphan."

The hairy monster hopped suddenly forward, and Figgins, with a wild shriek, fled to the door.

The monster jumped after him, and Figgins darted to the other side of the table.

Now he was near the chimney, and here were the bell-ropes.

He gave a succession of fierce jerks at the rope and a deafening clatter was heard below as the rope came away in his hands.

He rushed to the other side of the chimney.

After him bounded his tormentor, with a hop and a jump.

Figgins made for the bedroom and pounced upon Mole.

"Mr. Cole! Mr. Cole!" he yelled, dragging the old gentleman half out of bed.

"Hallo!"

"Look up! here's the devil come for you, Dole—I mean the ghost of Red Riding Hood's wolf."

Mole rubbed his eyes and stared towards the door.

There stood the awful visitor, grinning diabolically.

Mole slid from the bed, and the hairy ghost retreated.

"Go and fight it out," said Mole, not quite understanding what it all meant.

"But, my dear sir, I am an orphan and can't fight."

"Come and see what it is, then," said Mole, as Figgins took hold of his guest by the arm, and together they tremblingly advanced into the dining-room.

Gone.

The hirsute monster had disappeared.

"It must have been fancy; took too much rum," said Mr. Mole.

"No fancy," moaned Figgins. "I know I saw it, a dreadful monster with large, sharp teeth."

"Well," said Mole, "you look after him; I'll go to bed."

"No, no, my dear Dole, don't go to bed and leave a poor orphan. Ha! look, there he is coming."

"Ah, yes—oh!"

The monster had been hiding behind the window curtains, and now he suddenly pounced out upon them.

The two old gentlemen dodged away, and did all they possibly could to avoid the ghostly enemy.

But the latter was fearfully nimble.

At length, Mr. Mole was so fortunate as to drag the room door open, and out he ran, followed by Figgins.

Mr. Mole stumbled over the oyster shells, which Harry and young Jack had paved the passage with so carefully, but his wooden legs preserved him from the unpleasant consequences which his companion and host experienced.

No sooner did Mr. Figgins land with his naked feet upon the oyster shells, than it made him howl with pain.

We have all heard how a cat danced on hot bricks. Well, Mr. Figgins's terpsichorean evolutions beat the grimalkin's all to fits.

And the higher he jumped, the further his fall, and therefore the more unpleasant the consequences.

"Hah, oh!"

"Murder, murder!" he cried. "I am being cut to death with sharp flints."

Now the alarm was given generally in the hotel, and up ran waiters and porters, wildly, summoned by the clanging of the bell, and the fearful cries of the two old gentlemen.

The hubbub seemed to alarm the hairy ghost as well, for out he bolted, overturning the two frightened old gentlemen, and bounding down the stairs.

A yell of alarm came from the advancing waiters, as the hairy ghost, with long night-gown on, and tall night-cap on head, rushed precipitately at them, and overturning about three at a bound, sent, by the force of the shock, not less than a dozen of them falling head over heels down the stairs.

Shouts, shrieks, and cries of alarm.

Fearful hubbub.

And when this mob of falling men, a sort of avalanche of waiters, rolled to the bottom of the stairs, young Jack and his companions were just going out at the hotel door.

But before they got out, the hairy ghost shot past them into the street, his long night-gown torn to ribbons, and his night-cap hanging round his neck by the strings.

*   *   *   *   *

"There goes Nero!" cried Jack to Harry.

"Hasn't he had a lark with the poor orphan?" said Harry Girdwood; "and what a pile of waiters he has left on the mat at the bottom of the stairs."

"We had better get him home, and hide him away."

"Yes, let's after him, or he'll frighten some old woman or policeman to death."

"Mole and the orphan will never guess it's old Nero."

"No; but what puzzled me was, how you smuggled Nero into the bedroom."

"Don't you remember, that I went into the bedroom to wash my hands just before dinner?"

"Yes."

"Well, I smuggled him into the hotel just before that."

"On the second floor?"

"Yes."

"Hah, I see."

"I then made him get in bed, and I tucked him up comfortably in Mr. Figgins' flea-bag, fixed the wolf's mask over his face, and then went back into the dining-room to prepare for larks."

Verily, it looked anything but promising for the poor orphan's peace of mind, if he had to accompany these two high-spirited practical jokers on a voyage in the "Albatross."

There they would have scarcely any other resource than victimising the middle-aged orphan.

"ITS HUGE JAWS OPENED, DISPLAYING A GLITTERING SET OF TEETH."

Poor Figgins ! Poor orphan !
He merits our fullest sympathy, and he has it.

CHAPTER IX.

MOTHER AND SON—THE LOVE GIFTS—NEVER UNTIL DEATH SHALL PART US, AND SO FORTH — THE " ALBATROSS " WEIGHS ANCHOR.

" JACK, Jack, oh, my own dear boy, pray don't go," replied Mrs. Harkaway.

" Why, mother, what on earth has got hold of you ?"

" A horrible presentiment, my darling."

" That's very strong language, mother," said young Jack.

" Not stronger than my feelings warrant," answered Mrs. Harkaway ; " oh, my darling boy, pray be ruled by me."

" Nay, mother," answered her son, " you ask too much. I have a little of your own independence of spirit, and I don't want to have to rely upon you or my father all my life. I want to show you that I am not unworthy to bear the name of Harkaway."

His mother appeared distressed at these words.

Yet, at the same time, the sentiment filled her with pride for her boy.

The old adventurous spirit of the Harkaways burnt in young Jack's breast as fiercely as ever it had done in his father's.

Neither time nor altered circumstances could change it.

It is a saying both trite and true, that what is bred in the bone must come out in the flesh.

* * * * *

" Jack."

The speaker was his comrade, Harry Girdwood.

" Come in, Harry."

" Have you any news?" said Mrs. Harkaway.

" Yes."

" Important ?"

" Very."

" Out with it, Harry," said young Jack, impatiently ; " for goodness' sake, don't beat about the bush."

" Captain Robinson is taken suddenly ill and he can't start."

" I'm sorry for Captain Robinson," said Jack.

" And so am I," said his mother ; " only I am glad that the ship can't sail."

" Oh, but the ' Albatross ' must sail all the same," said Harry Girdwood ; " it is bound by contract to start to-night, it appears, and we must be on board before eight o'clock."

Mrs. Harkaway's spirits sank to zero at once.

" How can it sail without a captain ?" she asked.

" They have found a substitute," replied Harry.

" A good man ?"

" Oh, yes, a capital sailor, according to all accounts."

" His name ?"

" Deering."

" Well," said young Jack, " if he is only as good a sailor as the poor fellow who was to have commanded, we can't ask for anything better."

When Mrs. Harkaway had left the room, the two boys set to work about their preparations.

These were of the most elaborate nature.

They had not only all their traps and baggage to get on board, but also to make everything snug for Nero, for young Jack could not leave his faithful old monkey behind.

Nero had grown greatly attached to his young master, and one and all predicted that if Jack left him behind, he would pine away and die.

Objections were naturally raised to this ; but old Jack's liberality smoothed away all apprehensions.

Nero was not all.

There was Jack's boy Tinker to be got on board, and Tinker's new valet, Bogey.

However, all was settled to their perfect satisfaction.

And now young Jack had to bid farewell to little Emily !

* * * * *

Two young couples were walking at sunset in a retired suburb of the town.

They were all of one party ; yet they kept sufficient distance between them to prevent their conversation being overheard.

It was a tender topic upon which they were engaged.

" Jack, darling," said little Emily, " I've got something here for you."

She produced a small object wrapped in a piece of paper, and pressed it into his hand.

" Don't open it, dear, until—until you are gone."

She had some difficulty in getting this word out.

Young Jack silently squeezed her hand.

" I've nothing to give you, Em'," he said, vainly endeavouring to steady his voice, for he was in fear of shaming his manhood, " unless you'll accept this."

" What is it ?"

" My portrait. I have had it taken expressly for you. It isn't a very good one, Em', but you'll know that it is meant for me."

" It shall never leave me, Jack, day or night."

" Bless you."

" And you'll never forget this night of parting, Jack ?"

" Never—never, if I live to be as old as Methusalem."

" And never forget poor little Em' that you leave behind you and say you love ?"

" Never. Can you believe me such an utter duffer, Em' ?"

" And you'll always wear my little keepsake round your neck ?"

" Always."

She pressed his arm with a tender, trembling hand.

They had turned the corner now, and a high wall hid them from the view of Paquita and Harry Girdwood.

So Master Jack took the unwarrantable liberty of pressing her in his arms and kissing her again and again.

She did not resist, but only murmured a faint protestation.

"Oh, Jack, you've upset my hair dreadfully."

"Never mind, Em', I'll be your barber, and soon put that to rights."

"I don't mind that," returned little Emily, shooting him an arch look, "so long as you don't practise hairdressing upon any girl's head but mine."

"Never, never."

*   *   *   *   *

"If you only cared half as much for me as you pretend, Harry, you would not go away at all."

"I can't help myself, Paquita," responded Harry.

"Why not?"

"I am not like Jack."

"How?"

"I have no rich parents upon whom to rely. I feel that I ought to cut out a path for myself, dear Paquita, not to be dependent upon the dear, fond friends who have so far adopted me; now, were I in Jack's place, I should talk very differently. But how would it look for me to remain here an idler and a dependent when Jack was going?"

Paquita sighed, saying—

"I never looked upon it in that light before, Harry."

"Of course you didn't, dear. Look here, see what I have got for you."

"A crooked sixpence?"

"Yes, in two halves, each drilled with a hole. You must wear this half around your neck for my sake, Paquita."

"I will, Harry dear."

"And only throw it away when you forget poor me, and are going to get married to somebody better, better-looking and richer."

"Hold your tongue, sir," interrupted Paquita; "that will never be."

"You think so now, but you may change your mind some day."

"If you never come back, Harry, I shall die an old maid."

Harry Girdwood looked very serious at this.

"Don't make any rash vows, dear, pray don't. I might never come back, and I would not have you sacrifice your life to a memory; that would be too selfish on my part."

"Hush, Harry, don't talk like that, dear."

But why should we linger over this oft-told tale?

All that they are saying has been said a thousand— aye, a million times before, under circumstances more or less similar.

But never indeed were young lovers' vows exchanged with greater mutual sincerity.

*   *   *   *   *

The "Albatross" sailed.

Captain Deering took the command, and every movement, as well as every word that he uttered, showed him to be, as he had been eulogistically described—a good sailor.

"Huzzah!"

"Huzzah!"

"Now then, my lads, give them one more," cried young Jack, "and let it be loud enough to reach the shore."

And the men obeyed.

British sailors have certainly one speciality in which they distance all possible competition.

This is cheering.

Poor old Mole, with other friends, had bid young Jack good-bye with a choking voice, and the old gentleman was seen to wipe his eyes more than once.

And so brave young Jack Harkaway bid adieu to his country, to seek adventures, and make his way in the world with Harry and his boy Tinker.

"We're off," said a familiar voice close at hand, "s'elp my Jerusalem pony."

They turned simultaneously, showing they recognised the tones, and so could hardly have been both mistaken.

But, in the nautical get-up of the speaker, they failed to recognise the tiger Chivey.

CHAPTER X.

MR. MURRAY AWAITS HIS SON—HE GOES AFTER HIM, AND FINDS ONLY A LETTER.

MR. MURRAY waited.

His scapegrace son made no signs of life.

So he still waited.

At length his impatience and anxiety to hear from his wild and reckless boy got so far the better of his discretion, that he made up his mind to go down to his lodgings and make inquiries about him.

The door was opened by the landlady herself.

"Young Mr. Murray," she said; "do you want him?"

"Yes. I am Mr. Murray's father," said the shipowner, quietly.

"Oh, you are? Then that's right"—she took a letter out of her pocket. "Perhaps you'll pay my bill. He left here the night after you called."

"Left! Where for?"

"Can't say. This letter is to tell you."

"Give it to me."

"When you have paid up the bill," said the wary landlady, "not before."

"Give me your bill then, sharp—come," said Mr. Murray.

"Hoity toity!" said Mrs. Bouncer, "we're in a hurry, I should say."

She held out her bill, and he snatched it most ungallantly from the lady's hand.

"There's the money—never mind the receipt. Give me the letter," said Mr. Murray.

She handed it to him.

He tore it open, and read it eagerly.

As he read, the colour forsook his cheek, and he turned ashy pale.

His knees seemed to give way beneath him, and reaching out, he caught hold of the landlady to prevent him from falling.

"Goodness 'eavens!" she cried, "he's dead."

"Hullo, what's all this?" cried a deep voice.

"Old gentleman took ill; he's fainted," said the landlady.

"What does he do here?"

"He came after his son. The young gent have gone away—flew. He wrote this letter."

The policeman picked the letter off the

ground, and read it down by the aid of his bull's-eye.

It ran as follows—

"DEAR DAD,—You wouldn't give your consent, so I've gone without it. Chivey and I sail to-night in the 'Albatross' for goodness knows where.

"Your affectionate son,
"H. M.

"P.S.—Send me some tin to one of your agent fellows wherever we stop first."

Mr. Murray still remained senseless on the doorstep, while the policeman gazed anxiously at him.

Was he dead?

CHAPTER XI.

THE ORPHAN'S PRESENTIMENT—YOUNG JACK AND HARRY FIND THEMSELVES ASSISTING IN LEGAL BUSINESS—TINKER AND BOGEY HAVE A FEW WORDS—HERBERT MURRAY AND HIS VALET COME ACROSS THEM.

JACK and his comrade, Harry Girdwood, were standing on the deck of the "Albatross."

"Harry, where are you?"

"Whose voice is that?" said Jack.

"'Tis the voice of the orphan; I hear him complain," laughed Harry.

"He was woke from his slumber and comes up again," laughed Jack, finishing the poetical sentence.

It was that unprotected individual.

And the next moment the head of Mr. Mark Antony Figgins appeared slowly ascending from the hatchway.

"Oh, there you are," he said, as he caught sight of our heroes.

"What now, my noble Roman?" Jack asked.

"Don't call me a Roman, please," entreated Mr. Figgins in a piteous tone; "I don't feel a bit like a noble Roman; I am a poor sick orphan."

Most certainly, he didn't look at all like the renowned historical personage, Mark Antony, whose name he bore.

The orphan had on a white cotton nightcap.

His complexion was about as yellow as a daffodil.

His nose excepted, which looked like a small cherry in the centre of his face.

Altogether, he looked woe-begone in the extreme.

"What's the matter, old son?" asked young Jack, throwing a good deal of sympathy into his look and tone.

"I hardly know," responded the tea-dealer, dolefully, "but I don't feel very happy."

"You don't look at all well, Mr. Figgins, that's certain," joined in Harry Girdwood, with much concern.

"And I feel as bad as I look."

"A life on the ocean wave doesn't seem to agree with you," Jack remarked.

"I don't think it does. My instincts deceived me. They led me to come on board; and now I feel—oh——"

"You 'never were meant for the sea,' you feel so, so, all round your——" said Harry.

"Yes, that's just how I do feel," admitted the orphan Figgins, "and somehow I fancy I shall never see dry land again."

At this ominous opinion his listeners glanced at each other significantly.

It recalled old doubts and suspicions, but after a moment Jack exclaimed—

"Oh, hang it, Mr. Figgins, that's too melancholy; you're in the dumps."

"Your liver must be out of order," suggested Harry.

"It oughtn't to be. I've taken any quantity of blue pills since we've started."

"You look quite blue."

"And I've got the blues too, dreadfully," moaned the afflicted tea-dealer; "oh, dear, I feel I'm going."

"Well, you wouldn't have us stand still, would you?" said Jack; "we're all going, ain't we?"

"Yes, but the 'go' you mean and the 'go' I mean are two different things," whined Mr. Figgins.

"Where do you fancy you're going, then?" asked Harry.

"To pay a visit to—to—I forget what the nautical people call the person at this moment —but I know his Christian name's David."

"And his surname's Jones, isn't it?"

"Yes; that's it."

"Yes, Davy Jones; that's him. I feel I'm on my way to Davy Jones as fast as I can gallop."

"Dear, dear, that's very sad."

"It is; I am only an orphan, but don't cry for me, my dear boys."

"We won't if we can help it," said Jack, getting up a fictitious sob for the occasion.

"That's right; why should you? Though not young, I'm a desolate orphan that nobody cares for."

"Poor creature," murmured Jack and Harry, as they nudged one another, and sniffed violently in order to check a rising tendency to laugh.

Mr. Figgins was so touched with these evident expressions of feeling, that he burst into tears on the spot.

"I do feel very ill, and I'm alone in the world," he wailed.

"You're not the only one in that unhappy state," said Jack consolingly.

"I know that," wept the orphan; "but what am I to do with all my money when I die?"

"Leave it behind you for the benefit of the living," counselled Jack.

"They'll be very much obliged to you for it."

"Ah, yes!" exclaimed Mr. Figgins, "no doubt; and this brings me round again to what I want to do."

"What is that, sir?"

"Why, as I've not a soul in the world to bequeath my property to, I'm naturally anxious to make my will. Oh, dear me, this rolling ship is very unpleasant. I am afraid I am going to be extremely ill."

"Leave your fortune in favour of Mr. Nobody, eh?" said Jack.

"Oh, no; I mean to leave my hard-earned gains to society in general. I think I shall bestow it on a—oh, Lor' ha' mercy, I knew it was coming."

This abrupt deviation from the subject was caused by a sudden twinge which compelled Mr. Figgins to grasp his stomach convulsively.

"Take me below; I'm dying," he gasped, in a hollow voice, as he doubled up and sat down on the deck, and his wig at the same time.

"'Take him up tenderly, lift him with care,'" said young Jack, quoting the "Bridge of Sighs."

"He's only an orphan without any heir," supplemented Harry Girdwood, as they picked him up, and his wig at the same time.

"Carry me to my cabin, dear boys," he murmured; "and you must help me make my will. But first give me something to comfort me. A little warm brandy and—oh!—water; and another—ugh!—blue p-pill—oh, oh! I wish I had never come to sea; it looks very nice on land, but when you are on it, oh——"

In the midst of these ejaculations our heroes carried him downstairs.

Hardly had they disappeared from view when a merry black face became visible emerging from the hatchway.

It was Jack's boy, Tinker.

Having stepped on to the deck, he stood sniffing the briny with evident satisfaction.

"Golly, dat beau'ful! De smell ob de sea very oderif'rous! conglomerated essence ob chloride ob lime notink to it! do dis chile much big lot o' good arter bein' shut up down below in de fowls' air."

Having thus expressed himself, he walked to the ship's side and looked down upon the water for a few seconds.

"Massa Jack smoke, me tink Tinker hab a smoke," he said to himself.

He took a few steps, but stopped suddenly.

"Gem'lam like me got no right to wait upon 'isself," he reflected; "sartainly not; what de good o' keepin' a help?"

With this impression he went to the hatchway, and called down—

"Bogey, you nigger!"

There was no answer.

"Whar dat lazy nigger got to?" he muttered to himself.

Then after a moment, finding that his help did not respond in any way, he bawled again—

"Bogey, yer lazy, ugly cuss, why you not come when you massa call—eh?"

"I'se on de way," replied Bogey's cheerful voice from the distance.

And presently Bogey himself came shuffling up the steps on to the deck.

"Why you not come quick—quick as de 'lectric telescope, eh, you dirty-looking nigger?" demanded Tinker, in a tone of authority.

"'Cos him not a telescope, I 'spose," returned Bogey with a grin.

"Den you won't do for me, dat sartain. I shall change."

"Bery good! me do for someun else, I dessay," Bogey replied.

"What dat you say, sar?"

"Me not gwine to say it ober agin to please nobody," said Bogey obstinately.

Tinker drew himself up and looked at his rebellious help in an indignant manner.

"You dare talk to me like dat?" he exclaimed after a moment.

"Course I dare!"

"What dat you say to a gentleman, who am your massa?"

"Dere no massas in dis 'ere free country; all ekal—alike—yah yah!" chuckled Bogey, with much bounce.

"Tell you what it am," cried Tinker, in a tone of profound disgust; "you dam 'umbug, dat what you are!"

"You 'noder."

"Me?"

"Yes."

"Take dat."

"Take dat yourself!"

The two niggers—master and help—having first kicked each other's shins, next seized one another by their woolly locks.

And then for some moments they tugged away to their hearts' content.

At length they fell back on the deck with a tuft of wool in each hand.

And their irritability being somewhat appeased, Tinker said in a dignified tone—

"Dere, 'nuf ob dis! an' as your conduc' bery beastly and abdominal, I only got one ting to gib yar."

"What dat?"

"De big bag—de sack."

"De sack? What dat?" asked Bogey, with a kind of sulky curiosity.

"Ya're discharged dat's what it am!" said Tinker, in a tone so hard and stern, that it almost took the frizz out of his woolly locks. "Go back to de iggorant black an'mals I took yer from. Yar not fit to live in suspect'ble society. Take yar 'ook! go!"

The tremendous energy with which these words were uttered, recalled Bogey at once to a full sense of his disobedience.

"Don' send me 'way dis time, Massa Tinker," he said, entreatingly, falling on his knees; "me neber pull your wool agin. Let me 'top."

"No," replied Tinker, firmly; "it quite imposs'ble! De young gentleman, Tinker, say yar got to go."

"I bery sorry."

"Am yar bery, big, much, dam, tremendous sorry?"

"Orful!"

"Yar neber do it again to dis noble Tinker?"

"Neber! neber!" whimpered Bogey; "not till de nex' time."

"You quite sure on dat p'int? Neber till next time!"

"Sartain!"

"Den I forgib yar," said Tinker, magnanimously; "in token ob which, you may kiss my big toe."

He extended his foot as he spoke, and Bogey kissed that important member.

In the sincerity of his repentance he did a little more.

He bit it.

So sharply, that his forgiving master shot out his leg and knocked him flat on his back.

After a moment he said—

"You cuss nigger, I told you to kiss my toe, not bite it. Now get up an' go an' fetch me a smoke."

"Whar me get a smoke?" asked Bogey, rubbing his nose.

"What dat to do wid me?" said Tinker, sharply. "I tell you get me a smoke. Whar you get it your bis'ness."

Bogey disappeared.

During his absence Master Tinker walked up and down the deck with his hands in his pockets, whistling.

In a few moments Bogey returned.

"'Ere 'im are, massa," he said, as he handed him half a cigar.

Tinker examined it a moment with evident dissatisfaction.

"What de meanin' ob dis?" he asked at length, in disgust. "Whar you get dis from?"

"Out ob one ob de cabs."

"Cabins, sar. Why you not speak gumratical? I tell you bring me a smoke. Why you bring me half smoke?"

"'Cos I couldn't get no more," was Bogey's answer.

Tinker gave a grunt and proceeded at once to light his half smoke with a fusee.

In vain he puffed and pulled; he could get no smoke out of it; it was cracked and wouldn't draw.

Happening to turn round, he espied his help very complacently blowing a voluminous cloud from a piece of cigar that looked very like the other half of the weed he was smoking himself.

His suspicions were at once excited, and rushing to him, he collared him on the spot.

"You dam nigger tief! You ugly, big-mouf chimney pot!" he shouted, as he shook him almost out of his boots. "What you mean to rob you maasa in dis hyar way—eh?"

Bogey, caught in the fact, had no excuse to offer, and at once glided back into penitent confession.

"Beg pard'n, massa, 'im no rob notink, s'elp 'im golly, 'im habn't!" he said.

"You tell lie, 'bominal wicked lie!" cried Tinker, indignantly. "You know bery well you cut de smoke in two bits."

"Dat's as true, massa, as one and two makes six," admitted Bogey. "But den de oder 'alf war cracked."

"Yes, and dis chile got it. You keep de good 'alf yourself, you greedy-gut pig!" shouted his master, as he crammed the damaged piece half way down Bogey's throat and almost choked him. "Dere, see 'ow you like it."

Bogey didn't like it at all, and spluttered and coughed a good deal.

But at length, he compromised matters by going and fetching an enormous regalia, which he presented to the incensed Tinker.

This timely atonement pacified his master immediately.

And the two niggers the next moment, forgetting all their past squabbles, were smoking together in the utmost harmony.

* * * * *

"Chivey!" exclaimed Herbert Murray.

"Sir, to you!"

"I feel inclined for a weed."

"All right, guv'nor; I feel as though I could do a smoke myself."

"So you shall. Hand over the box."

"Where is it?"

"On the shelf yonder; there are two of those rattling regalias still left."

"Not one," said Chivey, as he held out the empty box.

"Some confounded prig has been helping himself," continued the young gentleman, irritably; "I wish I knew who it was; I'd teach him to respect the rights of property."

"Ditto! ditto!" cried Chivey, doubling his right fist and giving an imaginary double knock in the air with it. "I'd let him have a good lump of returns in exchange, for his own private smoking."

"You had better go to the steward and get another box," said his master.

"Tell him to put it down in the bill as per usual, I suppose?" said Chivey, with an inquiring grin.

"Certainly; dad pays all my exes."

The valet disappeared, and in a very brief space came back with a fresh supply.

And the pair, having lit up, went on deck.

Both Jack and Harry at the time were writing in their cabin, therefore, not seen by Murray or his servant.

Almost the first things Herbert noticed were Tinker and his valet, who were both puffing away in a state of entire satisfaction.

The young gentleman eyed them for some little time in silence, and then said—

"Who are those two ugly black brutes?"

"They belong to the Harkaway gang," was Chivey's reply.

"The devil they do!"

"Yes; that's a fact."

"I can't for the life of me understand why such abominations as niggers are permitted to exist," remarked Herbert in a tone of utter disgust.

"It's a great mistake, that's certain," admitted Chivey.

"Oh, it's a frightful error; they pollute the very atmosphere. Phew! I can smell them as I stand here."

"There's no doubt they're orful strong-flavoured."

"And they're smoking, too."

"Cigars!"

"My regalias, perhaps," said Herbert, suspiciously.

"Very like."

"If so, I'll break their ugly necks."

"Quite right and proper, sir, and I'll help you."

"Let's come a little nearer to them."

Murray and his valet approached the niggers.

"How dreadfully they stink!" exclaimed the young gentleman, as he drew near.

"Oh, taller and trotters!" cried Chivey.

The darkeys, having particularly quick ears, heard these remarks distinctly.

It was fully intended that they should hear them.

"Rader fancy dem gem'lams war deludin' to us, Bogey?" whispered Tinker, to his comrade.

"Me incline to your 'pinions," Bogey answered.

"What war it he say?"

"He say you 'tink drefful."

"Bery much great insult, and dam big lie as well," responded Tinker, indignantly.

"Ob course it am. Eberybody know we two ob de sweetest objec's in creashun."

"Dat's a fac'," exclaimed Tinker, confidently ; "gas pipes fools to us."

"Hallo! you two blackbeetles," shouted Herbert.

CHAPTER XII.

A BLACK BOY'S REPLY—HERBERT MURRAY AND HIS VALET MAKE AN ATTACK UPON TINKER AND HIS HELP, AND GET THE WORST OF IT—CHIVEY RECEIVES A COMMISSION FROM HIS MASTER AND PREPARES TO EXECUTE IT—A CHASE ALOFT—TINKER GETS A DROP TOO MUCH.

THE beetles looked round.

"Who gave you permission to smoke?"

"Neber axed no permission," Tinker replied.

"Who gib you!" inquired Bogey, in his turn.

"We don't require permission," returned Herbert, grandly ; "our colour is privileged."

"Colour notink. We got jes' the same pilliwedges as you two got," said Tinker, drawing himself up with immense grandeur.

"And pray what are you smoking?"

"De very bes' 'Avannahs, ob course."

"Ob course! Black gem'lams allays has de bes'," joined in Bogey, as he sent a stream of aromatic smoke puffing into the face of the questioner, and half suffocated him.

"Ugh, ugh, ugh!" coughed Herbert ; "ugh, ugh! you brutes."

"Uncultivated swine," exclaimed Chivey, sneezing violently.

"The fact is," continued Murray, "you have been purloining my regalias, you black brutes."

As he said this, he stepped forward, and snatched the stump of the cigar Tinker was smoking from his mouth.

"Of course, as I suspected." he cried, as he glanced at it. "What have you to say for yourself, eh, you black prig?"

"Jes' dis hyar. If you take 'way dis chile's cigar, he take 'way yourn, yah, yah!"

And with these words Tinker made a grab at Murray's weed, and got it.

At the same moment Bogey followed suit upon Chivey in the same manner.

Both master and valet found themselves suddenly deprived of their choice smokes.

"Give it up, you villain!" exclaimed Herbert.

"Drop it, you sweep!" bawled Chivey.

They made a rush at the darkeys as they spoke.

But Tinker and Bogey, being as quick as a pair of electric eels, dodged aside, and the irritated pair only dashed themselves against the bulwarks of the ship, scraping their knuckles, and almost flattening their noses in their impetuosity.

When they recovered themselves, they found the young niggers a few yards from them, puffing away at their cigars with a broad grin on their sable countenances.

"Dese hyar cigars bery much consid'rable good. We smoke dem for you 'cause dey might make you ill," remarked Tinker.

"Iss, dey am good," coolly responded Bogey, as he puffed away.

This defiance on the part of the darkeys was unbearable to Herbert Murray, and scarcely less irritating to the feelings of Mr. Chivey.

"You pair of reptiles!" cried the former.

"Scum o' the earth!" exclaimed the latter.

"There's only one way of dealing with such, and that is to crush them."

"Smash 'em! knock 'em to smithereens!" joined in Chivey ; "go it, guv'nor!"

With clenched fists, the Englishman advanced, for the purpose of inflicting condign punishment on the obnoxious blacks.

Tinker and Bogey could see their opponents were in earnest, and, quickly knocking off the ash of their cigars, slipped them into their pockets, and were quite ready to meet their foe.

The latter came sparring up in the usual orthodox English fashion.

The young blacks did not spar.

They simply waited for the attack, with their legs a little bowed, and their heads a little forward, as if inviting a punch.

The invitation was instantly accepted.

Herbert Murray and his valet made a simultaneous rush in.

The pair of woolly heads instantly bobbed down.

The blows passed harmlessly over them, whilst at the same instant they shot forward, head first, full butt, and delivering their antagonists a broadside below the belt that sent them flying as though stricken by a couple of battering rams.

The shock of the fall was so severe that they lay for a moment in the scuppers, motionless, with their breath apparently shaken out of their bodies.

"Golly!" exclaimed Tinker, after a moment, as he advanced and looked down at them, "me tink we knock 'em into what dey call de 'mortal smash.' "

"Seem like it ; dey not like what we gib 'em," cried Bogey.

"Dat sartain. Dey look for all de world as if dey was dead."

Bogey's face grew a trifle longer at this suggestion.

"What dey do to people what kill oder people?"

"'Ang 'em up by de 'eels till dere neck's stretched long as turkey cocks," Tinker explained.

Bogey was so horrified at this idea, that he made a precipitate retreat down the hatchway and vanished.

"Me go hide away," he cried.

Tinker, whose nerves were somewhat stronger, quietly re-lighted his cigar and walked forward, saying—

"Dis shild not afraid."

After a short time, Herbert Murray and Chivey came to themselves.

Herbert had had enough of Australian savages for the present, and he said to his valet—

"I shall have nothing more to do with those black brutes. Having no brains, and skulls as thick as paving stones, it's losing labour to hammer at them. I leave them to you, Chivey; you know what to do."

Chivey screwed up his features with as grateful an expression as possible, and pledged himself solemnly to "smash the pair of them," if he could.

Herbert Murray then went below, and Chivey having armed himself with a marline-spike, went forward in search of the "black brutes."

He soon espied Tinker, who was leaning over the ship's side, placidly smoking Chivey's cigar.

Grasping the implement he held tightly, he approached as noiselessly as possible, and having got near enough, suddenly sprang forward, and aimed a tremendous blow at Tinker's woolly head.

Had the stroke taken effect, it would inevitably have fractured Tinker's skull.

But fortunately the black boy caught a glimpse of his assailant just in time to enable him to drop down, and the blow fell harmlessly.

Before it could be repeated, Tinker had removed himself several yards out of harm's way, and stood with his cigar in his mouth, with his large dark eyes riveted upon his foe, as if reckoning him up, calculating the chances in his favour in case the white youth renewed his attack.

That this would be the case seemed pretty evident from the spiteful gleam in Mr. Chivey's eyes. But to put the matter beyond all doubt, he exclaimed ferociously—

"It's the guv'nor's orders you're to be smashed, yer darned dirty black puddin', an' by the livin' jingo, I'm goin' to smash yer."

"Am yer?" replied Tinker, with an inward chuckle. "Dis chile bery much 'blige for de informashun, but—yah, yah!—golly! you big bully, you got to ketch 'im fust."

"I shan't be long about that," cried the valet, as he sprang forward.

But by the time he reached the spot where Tinker had been standing a moment before he found it vacated.

The young nigger had cleverly changed places with him, and was now as far behind as he had previously been in front of him.

Clenching his teeth and knitting his brows with irritation at having missed his mark, the valet made a second rush after Tinker.

Tinker simply stepped aside, and disappeared behind the foremast.

"Ha, ha! got yer now, blackin' bottle," chuckled Chivey, as he bounded towards the mast; and having reached it, he made a slashing blow with his marline-spike, but hit nothing, for the simple reason that there was nothing to hit.

To his great surprise Tinker had vanished.

"Where the devil has the ugly beggar got to?" he muttered, in a savagely perplexed tone.

A peculiar sound over his head at that moment caused him to look up.

Tinker's ebony face looked down upon him.

"'Ere 'im am, massa, yah, yah," he grinned, as he sat composedly astride the yardarm; "'ere de ugly beggar; cotch 'im if you can, you ugly white nigger."

Chivey uttered an oath, and clutched the implement he held tighter still in his fury.

"You shall have it hot when I ketch yer," he growled.

"Yah, yah! when yar do—when," grinned the black; "dat long time fust; come along, ugly white servant."

It was most galling to Mr. Chivey's already incensed feelings to be chaffed in this way by a contemptible nigger boy, and thrusting the marline-spike into his belt, he prepared to mount the ratlines in pursuit.

Chivey flattered himself that he could climb "a trifle." And so he could.

In his earlier years he had had considerable practice upon scaffold poles, and since he had been afloat he had been aloft, and regarded his skill as little inferior to that of any sailor on board the "Albatross."

But there was no doubt that Mr. Chivey would have all his work to do to catch Tinker.

At all events, he had a certain amount of dogged determination in his temper that led him to try.

Up the shrouds he went, and was soon pursuing his way through the rigging up aloft, out of sight of those on deck.

The breeze had freshened, and the cranky, leaky old vessel rolled heavily in the waters, causing the valet to hold on like grim death as the ship, in her deviations from the perpendicular, gave him a very uncomfortable glimpse of the foaming waves beneath.

But Chivey prided himself on his British pluck, and he still kept on.

So also did Tinker; but Tinker was much more at home in his aerial position than his pursuer, and seemed, if anything, rather to enjoy it. He took delight in allowing his enemy to get very near him.

Then, as the latter extended his arm to seize him, he would suddenly remove himself.

But only just sufficiently to be provokingly close, and yet beyond reach.

Here, lying at full length, with his limbs skilfully entwined in the ropes that supported him, he would grin derisively in his opponent's face. Chivey ground his teeth fiercely.

"You infernal black flibbertigibbet!" he growled, "it's no use your trying to escape me; I'm bound to lay hold of you in the long run."

"Yah, yah!" grinned Tinker, "you hab dam long run 'fore dat, massa."

And, as he spoke, he took his cigar from his mouth, and pressed the hot end upon the back of Mr. Chivey's outstretched hand.

"Dere, how you like dat, eh?" he cried.

It was awfully startling, and raised an immediate blister; and the worst of it was Mr. Chivey dared not let go lest he should fall.

A volley of execrations burst from his lips.

During which Tinker unwound his limbs from the gear that enmeshed them, and made another move.

Chivey, growling, and rendered more furious by the pain of his burn, followed.

Tinker kept himself particularly cool, and having found a short piece of knotted rope, he amused himself by turning round every now and then and giving his pursuer a sharp tap on his knuckles.

Still the chase continued.

From rope to rope—from mast to mast, Tinker led his pursuer anything but a merry dance.

In time he found himself on the crosstrees of the top mainmast.

"Yah, yah ! Massa Piggy no come up hyar ; the white nigger 'fraid to follow dis chile hyar !" he grinned as he sat poised on his rocking perch.

But he was mistaken.

For the next moment the heavy breathing of the valet was heard, and his face appeared almost livid with his intense exertions and his longing for revenge.

He now held the marline-spike between his teeth. His eyes gleamed as fiercely as those of an angry wild cat as he gradually ascended.

Tinker evinced no dismay whatever.

He simply shifted himself a little further along the cross bar on which he was seated.

But Chivey was not to be debarred from following. With an energetic tug he pulled himself up and was soon seated astride the crosstree.

Quickly removing the marline-spike from between his teeth, and clinging firmly with his legs, he once more aimed a tremendous blow at Tinker's head.

Tinker of course dodged the blow. The iron weapon slipped from Chivey's hand and fell heavily on deck, at the feet of the solitary orphan, who, feeling a trifle better, had paused in the middle of the codicil, and crept up upon deck for a moment to get a sniff of fresh air.

The marline-spike almost scraped his nose in its descent.

An inch or two nearer, and it would probably have knocked his unprotected brains out.

"Good gracious me ! what's that ?" he exclaimed aghast, as he glanced at it apprehensively. "It must be a thunderbolt, I think."

And without making any further investigations, he crept down again as quietly as he had crept up.

Whilst this was transpiring below, Chivey was up in the maintop glaring at his intended victim.

He had again missed his mark, and Tinker, in order to put as great a distance as possible between his vindictive assailant and himself, had edged off to the extreme end of the yard.

An awfully perilous position it seemed as he sat there.

Not that he felt it so.

Although the vessel was rolling from side to side in anything but an agreeable manner.

"Yah, yah, Massa Chivey !" he cried, defiantly, "you know better dan follow me 'long hyar."

"I'll have your life, if I follow you into the next world, yer imp of Beelzebub !" hissed Chivey between his teeth.

As he spoke, he commenced crawling along the crosstree with deadly determination.

Being at the extremity of his perch, Tinker could go no further.

"Oh, golly !" he muttered to himself in a perplexed tone, "what 'im do now ?"

He looked up.

There was no way of escape in that direction, for he was already almost at the highest pinnacle of the mast.

Beneath him rolled the dark, stern waves.

Almost close alongside him was his foe, with an unmistakably murderous gleam in his eyes.

Suddenly the young negro uttered a self-congratulatory chuckle.

He had espied a rope hanging from the end of the yard on which he sat.

All his coolness returned to him in a moment.

"Come 'long, Massa Chi-ikey," he cried, ironically ; "mind you don't fall. Yah, yah ! dis infant hab to fish you out if you fall."

With an oath, Chivey extended his arm to seize him.

"Not jes' yet," exclaimed Tinker ; "dis chile off to de nex' world."

And before the valet's grasp could close upon him, he disappeared with the rapidity of a flash of lightning. He was now dangling at the end of six feet of rope, like a spider hanging by its web.

Chivey looked down at him with a look of baffled spite.

But suddenly a new idea flashed across him.

His eyes became full of evil light. He muttered, viciously—

"Yes, you black beast, the next world ; an' I'll send you there in double quick time, too !"

With these words, he cautiously glided his hand into his breast pocket and drew out a clasp knife, which he opened with his teeth.

Poor Tinker, at the end of his tether, had watched his actions.

And instinctively divining what they meant, at once came to the conclusion that his position was extremely critical.

At once he began to haul himself up.

He soon reached the yard, and grasped it.

"Tink we been playin' long 'nough now, Massa Spiv'ey," he said, endeavouring to turn the affair into a pleasant joke.

A fierce growl, and an angry chop with the clasp knife on his fingers, was the only answer he received.

Down he glided again, maimed and bleeding.

"You coward ! you big sneaking white dam coward !" cried the boy Tinker, as he looked up at the livid face of his adversary.

"You dirty nigger !" returned Chivey, with a semi-sarcastic smile, "I'm goin' to send you where such cattle always go !"

Just at that moment the ship gave a fearful lurch.

Chivey severed the cord with a slash of his knife.

Then with a wild cry of horror the hapless Tinker fell through the air over and over into the dark deep waters.

Bogey heard the cry of his master.

But his fate had been so quickly accomplished Bogey knew not what had befallen him.

As the "Albatross" rolled on her way, no trace of poor Tinker could be seen.

He was gone, indeed—it seemed—to the next world.

CHAPTER XIII.

BOGEY RECEIVES A SPECTRAL VISITATION FROM AN OLD FRIEND, WHO EXPLAINS VARIOUS MATTERS, AND ARRANGES A LITTLE PLOT FOR MR. CHIVEY'S EXPRESS BENEFIT.

CHIVEY, having accomplished his dastardly act, descended from the rigging, cautiously. No one had seen him go up. No one saw him come down.

Consequently no one suspected the deed he had committed up aloft.

Having reached the deck, the half groom, half valet, hurried below at once, and joined his master in his cabin.

With much exultation he informed the latter of what he had done.

Herbert Murray received the tidings with equal satisfaction.

Not only was his revengeful spirit gratified at Tinker's destruction, but he rejoiced at the thought of the power it would give him over his servant.

Chivey would now be a mere tool in his hands.

"Devilish well managed!" he cried, approvingly; "pity you couldn't have served the other black brute in the same manner."

"I'll do that yet," promised Chivey; "I'll pickle him in brine at the first opportunity."

"Do so," replied his master; "what are the lives of a pair of dirty niggers? Something less than nothing at all. Bring out the brandy, Chivey, and let's have a smoke."

The liquor and cigars were produced.

Not the slightest compunction or remorse oppressed them.

The fact that they were at that moment chargeable with the crime of murder did not intrude itself upon their minds.

It was only a dirty nigger that had been suddenly dispatched into eternity—what was that? Less than nothing! And so they smoked and drank to their hearts' content.

*   *   *   *   *

But there was one on board whose mind was ill at ease.

This one was Bogey.

Young Jack was also dreadfully concerned about his boy Tinker, and caused every search to be made for him.

The general opinion was that the young negro had paid — not for peeping — but climbing; and that, in his gambols amongst the rigging—of which he was very fond—he had slipped his hold and fallen into the sea.

Bogey listened to these opinions.

But he only shook his head ominously, and kept his thoughts—whatever they were—to himself.

*   *   *   *   *

It was night.

Bogey feeling in particularly depressed spirits, young Jack had given him permission to retire to his bunk early; but he could not sleep.

The ship rolled heavily; and he lay listening to her creaking timbers, that sounded like the wailings of someone in pain.

Thinking, as he lay, of his lost comrade, wondering what had become of him.

As he lay there, he was suddenly startled by a strange sound, like someone breathing almost close to him.

Sitting up, he looked out of his bunk, half expecting to see one of his white foes—Chivey for instance—with a knife in his hand, standing at his side; but he saw nothing. And still the deep respirations were distinctly audible.

"What de dooce am dat?" he muttered.

Bogey began to experience some very unpleasant sensations.

"It notink! it can't be notink! It on'y some'un in de nex' cabin," he argued with himself; and with this reflection he lay down again; but presently he heard a voice exclaim in indistinct and smothered tones—

"Bogey, Bogey!"

"What de matter? Bogey am all right," he cried, starting up once more in his bed, with a chill creeping of gooseflesh all over him.

There was no answer for a moment; and then the voice continued inquiringly—

"You dare, Bogey?"

"Iss—me—hyar!" returned the young negro, his teeth chattering audibly.

"Am you all 'lone by you'self?"

"I—i—i—iss, me—all—'lone by my—self. I wish I wasn't," gasped Bogey, the big drops trickling down his face.

"Dat right! den dis chile can come out."

"Who—am—yah?" shivered Bogey.

"Don't yah know de soun' ob my woice?"

"No—n—o! s'elp 'im golly 'im don't!"

"It Tinker dat undressing hisself to yar at dis minnit."

This was too much for Bogey.

And he shouted—

"It dam lie, it notink ob de kind. Tinker dead."

"I tell you I am here."

"If you Tinker, whar am you den?"

"In de cupboard," the voice replied—

This fact of course accounted for the muffled indistinctness of the tones of the speaker.

But Bogey was still incredulous.

And he replied—

"Dat 'noder lie! Tinker at de bottom ob de sea, and de fishes habin' dere supper off him."

Something very much like a subdued laugh was heard at this.

And presently the voice said—

"Tinker come back to see Bogey."

Bogey's superstitious terrors were becoming stronger every moment.

But he replied desperately—

"If you am Tinker, why de debbil you stop in de cupboard, eh? Why you not come out and show yourself?"

There was a slight scraping heard within the recess.

The door slowly opened a little, and a black woolly head was thrust out.

In the dim light of the ship's lantern, Bogey at once recognised his comrade's well-known features.

"Iss, iss, you am Tinker," he exclaimed; "dere not de least doubt on dat point."

The door swung open wider at this juncture, and Tinker with one stride stepped forth, and stood before his comrade.

There was something in his manner that impressed Bogey as strange.

Perhaps Tinker, in his love of mischief, was acting a part.

At all events his help was still a prey to his fears.

"Am you de real Tinker, or am you a member ob de land ob sperrits?" he asked.

"I'm de real Tinker, ole hoss, and dere no sperrits about me. Wish dere war."

Encouraged by this assurance, Bogey sprang from his bed, and grasped his comrade by the hand.

To his great joy he found him real flesh and blood.

"Oh, golly, golly!" he cried, excitedly, "dis bery won'ful, bery strawb'ry won'ful. Dey say you slip from de rope, and fall into de sea."

"So I did fall into de sea. But Massa Chivey cut de rope fust, wid him knife," explained Tinker.

"He big bla'guard. But how you get back agin hyar den?"

"Him swim to de ship's side, lay hole ob rope, pull hisself up, get through the cabin winder."

"An' 'ide yourself in de cupbord?"

"Iss."

"Why you 'ide, eh?"

"Want to sarve out Massa Chivey, dat why. 'Lectrify 'im out ob his 'leben senses."

Bogey looked at his comrade inquiringly.

"'Ow you do dat?"

"'Pear afore 'im in de middle ob de night. He tink me ghost of murdered Tinker! Gib 'em de 'orrors orful," said Tinker, in an awfully deep and impressive tone.

Bogey grinned from ear to ear.

"Golly, dat good! Dat fuss-rate good," he exclaimed.

"Me rader tink it am," said Tinker, complacently.

"But 'ow you gwine to manidge 'bout de ghost?" Bogey asked.

Tinker grinned and winked, and his head nodded like a Chinese image, as he chuckled in reply—

"Dis chile know all 'bout it."

"But dis chile don't know notink; an' 'im want to know bery much."

Suddenly he exclaimed—

"Me got it—de hidear."

"What am it, eh?"

"Why, fust you get under Massa Chivey's bed."

"'Top bit; got to git into Massa Chivey's cabin fust, 'fore 'im git under de bed," grinned Tinker; "'ow me get dare?"

"Through de door, ob course," said Bogey, looking rather indignant at the simplicity of the question.

"S'pose de door locked," said his comrade, knowingly; "what den?"

Bogey scratched his head again fretfully.

"Dunno' any oder way den," Bogey replied.

"Den I show you," said Tinker; "look hyar!"

As he spoke, he went into the cupboard.

His comrade followed eagerly.

"You see de boards there?" continued Tinker, as he pointed to the back.

"Iss, me see 'em."

"Bery good; den behind dare Massa Chivey's cabin."

"Am it, though?"

"Iss—well, dem boards moves."

"Golly! does 'em?"

Tinker pushed aside a panel, which slid along in a groove, disclosing a tolerably large aperture, which was, however, entirely filled up with what appeared to be solid wood.

Bogey noticed this at once, and exclaimed—

"You not be able to get in dere!"

"Wait bit; you see."

As Tinker spoke, he applied his hand to the wood, and, giving it a slight tug, it came away, revealing the back view of the interior of a chest of drawers.

"Golly!" murmured Bogey, in much surprise at this wonderful discovery; "you mean git inside dem drawers?"

"Ob course 'im do," Tinker replied, as with another slight pull he removed the backing of the bottom drawer.

The drawer was entirely empty.

"Dere," said Tinker, triumphantly, "dat whar de ghost gwine to be."

And in order to prove the practicability of this arrangement, he crawled in.

"But Massa Chivey not be able to see you in dere," remarked his comrade, after a moment.

"Know dat as well as you do," Tinker replied sharply; "but he able to 'ear me when I gib 'im dreful warmin' (he meant warning) out ob de key'ole."

"Ah, yes; 'im 'ear dat!" admitted Bogey, "golly, 'im be in great fright."

After a moment he said inquiringly—

"'Ow you gwine to get out?"

"Crawl out the same way I crawl in," replied Tinker, with a grin as he emerged backwards from his narrow retreat, and replaced the back of the drawers.

Bogey watched this operation.

"'Ow de ghost gwine to show 'isself?" he asked.

"Open you eyes," Tinker replied, with a chuckle; and as he spoke, he pushed the panel a little further along in its groove, until it was clear of the chest of drawers, and displayed an aperture through which the interior of the adjoining cabin could be distinctly seen, and through which a not over bulky body could squeeze itself easily.

"Dere," exclaimed Tinker, as he pointed to it triumphantly; "dat de way de ghost gwine to show hisself, and dat the way de ghost gwine to vanquish arterwards."

"Golly," exclaimed Bogey, "Massa Chivey hab de funks orful when he see you, Tinker; he go inter confluxions an' kick de buckit."

"Sarve 'im right, too," Tinker replied, as he closed the panel again.

"I say, ole hoss," said Bogey, to his comrade, after contemplating him thoughtfully for a moment.

"What de matter now?"

"You don't look bit like a ghost."

" Course 'im don't jest at present; but 'im will 'fore long. Yar go an' get me lump ob chalk."

" Anything else ?"

" Shouldn't mind some grubs as well, if yar can get 'old ob some."

" An' sometink to drink ?"

" Iss. Go fetch old Mole's bottle we brought wid us, yah, yah ! Drop ob rum do me lot ob good."

" Course it would. I git some too. As you gwine to act the ghost, it bery right and proper you liquor up wid de sperrits fust."

And with a broad grin at his own humorous idea, Bogey left the cabin.

He was soon back again with a loaf and a lump of chalk, and last, not least, a pint bottle of rum.

Tinker uncorked the bottle, and took a good swig at the spirit, which, after being drenched in the waves, he needed, if only to quicken his circulation.

He then proceeded to convert himself into a ghastly spectre.

His first step in this transforming process was to give his dusky features a coat of whiting.

" Want eber so much more, yet," said Bogey, who watched the operation with much interest. " You not more dan whitey-brown at present.

" Dat lot much too white for niggers," responded Tinker ; " niggers' ghostes not white at all."

" What colour am dey, den ?"

" Grey, excep' when de weader cold ; den dey turn blue."

Tinker, after some little trouble, contrived with the assistance of a fragment of looking-glass, to bring his face to a very ghostly hue.

Altogether, he performed his work very artistically.

He was neither too white nor too dark ; but a kind of ashy grey, much more awful to con-template.

Having finished this, he wrapped himself in a couple of sheets, tied a pillow case round his head, and his spectral make-up was com-pleted.

" You look like ghost now," cried Bogey, in an ecstasy of admiration, " dere no doubt 'bout dat. Me run fitch you big fish, den you show Chivey you come from bottom ob de sea."

Tinker, as he glanced at himself in his small mirror, could but think that he was the very cream of spectres ; and having indulged in another sip of rum, and taken in hand a large fish Bogey brought him, he sat down to wait until the moment of action should arrive.

CHAPTER XIV.

A GUILTY CONSCIENCE A BAD COMPANION—THE GROAN—THE WARNING VOICE FROM THE CHEST OF DRAWERS—APPEARANCE OF THE MURDERED TINKER—TERRIBLE PREDICTION—THE GHOST SETS HIS MARK ON CHIVEY, AND DEPARTS.

CHIVEY had been spending the evening, as he usually did in his master's company, in the intellectual pastime of smoking cigars and drinking brandy.

It was late when he reached his own cabin ; which, owing to the rolling of the ship and the liquor he had swallowed, he did not accomplish very easily.

" Phew !" he muttered, as he entered, and after several abortive efforts, locked the door and dropped the key. " I've had a reg'lar good soakin' to-night. Hang me, if I don't feel more than half—hic—screwed."

He staggered to his bed, and sat down upon it.

Looking mistily at nothing particular, with his stump of cigar between his teeth,

" My mast'r's jolly good fell'r," he soliloquised ; " a reg'lar—hic—brick ; it's pleas'r' to work—for—reg'lar—hic—brick."

He sucked hard at his Havannah stump for a moment, but could draw no smoke from it.

It had gone out.

" Confound the—hic—c'gar ! but no matt'r."

His thoughts again reverted to his master.

" How pleased Mr. Herbert was when I told him how I'd settled that black beggar. Ha, ha ! what a chase he led me through the—hic—rigging ; wonder I hadn't broke my blessed—hic—neck. Lucky had my knife in pocket—that dropped him—cut him adrift, and now he's at the bottom of the—hic—sea."

With a half-drunken chuckle, Mr. Chivey leant back on his bed, and looked in a vacant manner at his top boots.

" Now for a little drop more brandy."

But before he could drink, an awfully hollow groan made him pause suddenly, and sit bolt upright.

" What the devil's that !" he muttered to himself.

He was answered by a second groan, more hollow and deeper than the first.

He looked round him apprehensively, but saw nothing.

Again the groan was repeated.

" Somebody got—hic—stomach ache nex' door—must have. What's the matter ?—anyone ill ?" he shouted.

Another groan was returned of harrowing intensity.

" Don't kick up that jolly—hic—row," he bawled ; " go to sleep."

" Oh, oh ! me no sleep nebber no more ! oh !" groaned the voice again.

These words had a startling effect on the valet.

His hair began to bristle.

His cigar dropped from between his chatter-ing teeth.

The flask fell from his trembling hand.

He fancied he recognised the voice.

" Who speaks ?" he gasped at length.

" It am me."

" Who the deuce is me ?"

" I'm de ghost ob de deceased Tinker what you killed and sent into the next world at a minnit's notice."

" The devil you are !" shivered the con-science-stricken valet, as he rolled his haggard eyes round in search of the speaker, who was still invisible.

Mr. Chivey, who was rapidly becoming sober under the influence of terror, felt certain in his own mind that the ghost was in the chest of drawers.

"It's someone havin' a lark with me," he muttered to himself; "and yet how could anything mortal get into that drawer when it's locked?" he thought.

After an instant, he asked of the spectre—

"Where are you?"

"Dat no business ob yourn, Massa Chivey!" the spectre answered in a dogged tone.

"It is my business!" cried the valet, desperately; "I know where you are, Mr. Ghost—you're in my bottom drawer; and I'll have you out too!"

A sarcastic laugh responded (evidently from the aforesaid keyhole), and then died away in a hollow murmur.

Summoning all his resolution, Chivey sprang from his bed, and, rushing to the drawer, unlocked it and dragged it out.

It was perfectly empty.

"W—w—well, s—s—'elp me n—n—never!" he gasped, as he felt the drops of perspiration trickling down his back; "it is a—a—g—ghost of someone, perhaps murdered in this little den!"

With trembling hands he closed the drawer, and staggered back to his bed.

His knees knocking together as he staggered to his bed, but he was not allowed to remain in peace.

Again the awful voice was heard at the keyhole.

"Massa Chivey, Massa Chivey!" it called. "You have done a drefful murder, and I want you."

"W—w—what do yer w—w—want?" stammered the terror-stricken rough.

"It you I want," was the hollow reply.

"I'll fetch my master for you. I c—c—can't c—c—c—come!" returned Chivey, scarcely able to reply, and feeling strongly inclined to shriek.

"Don't want yar master, and me don't want you to come nowheres jest at present," continued the voice.

"That's all right," muttered Chivey, in a tone of relief; "go back to the next world as soon as possible, that's a good cove."

"No!" cried the spectre peremptorily; "me come up from de bottom ob de sea, purpose to haunt yar."

"Haunt me?" groaned the perspiring Chivey; "oh, Lor'! oh, Lor'!"

Then, in a kind of desperate mirth, he sang out—

"Tommy, make room for your uncle."

To which the invisible ghost replied solemnly—

"Dere no room for Tommy, nor 'um uncle neider."

"Do go away, there's a good fellow; give young Jack Harkaway a turn; I don't want you. I want to go to sleep," moaned Chivey, in a tone of despair.

"Yar nebber gwine to sleep no more. The ghost ob poor Tinker keep you 'wake ebery night. Him ghost close to you now."

"Don't, don't," gasped the valet; "I—I'm v—very s—sorry, 'pon my soul I am. Hook it, for goodness' sake, or I shall do something desperate."

There was a hollow laugh at this.

And the next moment a white object rose up slowly behind the further side of the chest of drawers.

There was no mistaking the grim, ashen-grey features of the spectre.

They belonged to the dead Tinker, and no one else.

Chivey recognised them with his eyes starting almost out of his head, and sat perfectly helpless, glaring at the ghastly face.

The ghost, with its stern, unwinking orbs, glared in return at him.

"Massa, Chivey! Massa Chivey!" exclaimed the spectre at length, in an awful tone.

"I'm he—ere," gasped the unnerved valet, wishing from the bottom of his heart he had been a thousand miles off.

The ghostly form extended its greyish-white hand, and continued impressively—

"Yar jes' got to take de wool out ob yar ears, and listen to what I say."

"Haven't g—g—got any w—w—wool in 'em," murmured Chivey.

"Den don't take it out."

"I w—w—won't."

"You mind and pay de mos' partickler inattenshun. I come all de way up from de bottom ob de sea to warn yar."

"What about?"

"Ob de drefful fate dat comin' to you and your massa."

"What fate?" inquired Chivey, a nameless terror holding him fast.

"You bote ob you goin' to de nex' world together."

"You mean to say we're a-goin' to die?"

"It's sartain you am; dat quite settled."

"And when's it a-comin' off?" asked the valet, with quivering lips and blanched cheeks.

"It not my bis'ness to name dates," responded the ghost, cautiously; "you'll know when de time come."

"And me and the—the—guv'nor's a-goin' to s—s—slope together, are we?" said Chivey.

"Yes, bote togeder."

"At a short notice?"

"Yes, bery sudden; jes' as you drop me into the sea, you be dropped."

"Anything else?" said Chivey, who having heard the worst, was beginning to grow reckless.

"Yes, when you kill dis child, him drop to bottom of de sea, and die; den de big fish come to poor boy Tinker, and begin to eat him up. Dis fish," said Tinker, holding up the one brought him by Bogey, "eat up part of Tinker leg; Tinker not like it, so him bring it you; take 'im."

And Tinker flung the dead fish at Chivey's head.

Chivey fell back half dead as the cold fish struck him across the face.

"Dat all for de present," returned the ghost, "gib you more nex' time me come."

Chivey uttered an irritable growl, and tried to rise.

But his legs failed him, and he tried in vain.

But as he pressed his hands down on the bed, they came in contact with the flask of brandy.

His semi-brutal nature had been almost cowed by his supernatural terrors, but it reasserted itself as his fingers fastened upon the bottle.

"Ghost or no ghost! man or devil, livin' or dead! here goes," he muttered; and, urged on by an impulse he could not control, he hurled the flask full at the ghost's head.

The spectre, with wonderful dexterity, caught it—not on the part intended, but in his hand.

"Yah, yah, yah!" he chuckled, with a dreadfully sarcastic grin; "it no go, Massa Chivey; notink do no harm to speckters, 'cos dey corp'ral sperrits; you better take back de bottle."

With these words he sent the flask flying through the air on its return journey.

The valet had a kind of dim consciousness of something whizzing rapidly towards him, which he made a kind of frantic effort to stop, but in vain.

The fragile article went straight to its mark, that being Mr. Chivey's forehead.

There was a crash, a wound, and a yell at one and the same time.

Mr. Chivey fell back on the bed.

"Murder! fiends! devils!" he roared, at the top of his voice.

Suddenly the cabin lamp fell off its nail with a crash, and went out.

Total darkness reigned around.

"Massa Chivey! Massa Chivey!" exclaimed the deep hollow voice; "me gwine back now to de subterranean depths ob de ocean. Adoo! till de nex' time. Adoo! adoo! ad——oo!"

The voice grew fainter and fainter, and at length died away and was heard no more; but Chivey still continued to shout "Murder!" so lustily that it distinctly caught the ears of the sailors, and a body of men came hurrying to his cabin. The door was locked.

The key not to be found.

After a brief consultation, one of the sailors unlocked it by a very simple expedient.

He put his foot through the panel.

In they got; and, lanterns being procured, they found Chivey lying on his back on the bed, smothered in blood from an ugly cut on his forehead, with the fragments of the flask around him.

The loss of his vital fluid had cooled his excitement, and he answered vaguely to the eager questions put to him.

He had been dreaming—woke up in a fright—been attacked by a nightmare.

"But how about this shivered bottle and your cracked frontispiece, Mister Chivey?" said Nat Cringle, the sailor, who had forced the door.

Chivey couldn't—or rather wouldn't—give any information on the subject, and the sailors, having bound up his wound, retired, considerably perplexed.

"He's been havin' a single combat with ole Nick, seems to me. Two to one old Nick will beat the tiger," remarked Nat Cringle to his mates.

No class is more superstitious than sailors, and at these words, they raised their eyebrows, and glanced at each other ominously.

"If so be as the devil's aboard, we'd better look out," they murmured; "it's no safe craft that he sails in."

Herbert Murray, who had strolled in with the rest, remained behind after they had departed.

"What's all this about, Chivey?" he asked as soon as they were alone.

"Blest if I can hardly tell yer, guv'nor," returned the valet, in a pained tone, pressing his hand to his aching forehead; "but it seems to me I've seen a beastly ghost. I've had a visitation."

"A visitation? What do you mean?"

"Well, then, I've seen a spectre."

"Of police?"

"No, a real live spectre."

"How can a spectre be alive?" said Murray.

"No, no, I don't mean that. I mean a dead ghost!" cried Chivey.

His master burst into a mocking laugh.

"Psha, nonsense! A case of delirium tremens."

"No, it ain't," growled Chivey, "it's Tinker—cuss him."

"What of him? He's dead."

"I know he is. And I'll take my oath I've seen his ghost to-night," cried the valet, his eyes distending with horror.

"You don't mean that?"

"I do, by all that's horrible," returned Chivey.

"What did he want?" asked Murray, recklessly.

"He came with a warning."

"Oh!"

"Yes, for you as well as for me. For both on us. We're booked."

"What for?"

"Sudden death!" exclaimed Chivey, in a hollow tone.

The mocking smile died out of his young master's face, and he said no more.

Both master and man looked blankly at each other.

Perhaps at that moment they would have rejoiced to know that poor Tinker was still alive.

CHAPTER XV.

JACK FINDS OUT BOGEY'S SECRET—HERBERT MURRAY DETERMINES TO GIVE A SUPPER—THE BILL OF FARE IS DECIDED UPON—THE SPECTRE GETS SCENT OF THE FORTHCOMING BANQUET.

YOUNG Jack was leaning over the side of the "Albatross" in deep thought, when Harry came and touched him lightly on the arm.

"Jack."

"Hullo, Harry! you startled me, for I was thinking deeply."

"What about, old boy?"

"Poor Tinker, and yet sometimes, Harry, I fancy Tinker is not drowned, for I see Bogey going about with a merry twinkle in his eyes, that denotes more mischief than sorrow."

"You're right, Jack. I have noticed Master Bogey's happy, yet strange ways lately. And look, here comes the young imp; let's question him, Jack."

"Bogey!" shouted Jack. "Come here, sir."

"Yes, Massa Jack, here am Bogey."

"I know you are here, sir, and now I want to ask you a question or two."

"Yes, sir; a tousend if you like, sir."

"Attention, Bogey," said Harry.

"Now, you lump of mischief," said Jack. "Where's my boy Tinker?"

Bogey cast down his eyes, and without looking up, replied—

"Tinker fell in de sea, sar."

"Yes," said Jack, "he fell in the sea, I know. But where is he now?"

Bogey stood before Jack, and for the first time in his life, felt confused.

"Now, Bogey, the truth, and nothing but the truth," said Harry.

"Well, sar, Tinker down below."

"In the sea?" asked Jack.

"No, sar, below in my bunk."

"Not dead?" said Harry.

"He's a ghost, sar, splendiferous ghost, sar."

"A ghost," cried Jack; "and not dead?"

"No, sar; Chivey tink he kill Tinker; Tinker haunt him and frighten him and his master's life out, ebery night, sar."

"Ha, ha, ha!" cried Jack. "Go on, Bogey, and have your game out, for the rascals deserve to be frightened for their villany."

"Yes, sar. T'ank you, sar; Chivey not go scot free. Tinker bery cleber, no cotch weasel asleep. Yah, yah!"

And away ran Bogey, to inform Tinker that he had Jack's permission to torment Chivey and his master out of their lives.

And the two blacks at once set about their preparations for an immense lark.

"I say, Chivey!"

"Yes, guv'nor, Chivey is here; what can he do for you?"

"I'm getting heartily sick of this cranky old washing tub."

"Same here, guv'nor; it's a regler nausea."

"Just look at this cabin, what a state it's in."

"Perfect state of slush, that's a fact. Looks as if it had been well mopped, and badly wiped."

"It's enough to give a fellow the rheumatic fever. See, the water is making way through; hang me if I stand it any longer."

"Don't, guv'nor. Come into my 'umble cabin. It is water tight."

"So I will, Chivey. Anything's better than a blue mouldy crib like this."

This conversation took place between Herbert Murray and Chivey a short time after the ghost incident.

The relative positions of master and servant had been almost lost sight of by Herbert Murray since he had been on board.

He treated his tiger as his *confidant*, companion and friend.

Herbert Murray having made up his mind to vacate his own cabin, had his portable traps removed to his new quarters.

But even here he felt anything but comfortable.

Although the cabin was dry, it was small, gloomy and close.

"By jingo, Chivey," he growled, "I was about drowned in the other shop; I think I shall be stifled in this."

"Oh, you'll get used to it, guv'nor, after a bit," was Chivey's cheerful reply.

But his master did not get used to it.

What could he do to relieve the monotony of his existence—to throw a little life and jollity into that gloomy, dingy hole?

At last, an idea flashed across him.

"We'll have a banquet on a small scale," he exclaimed suddenly.

"A feed, I s'pose yer mean, don't yer, guv'nor?" asked Chivey, looking at his master.

"Feed's vulgar. I prefer banquet; it sounds more aristocratic," said Herbert.

"Well, it all comes to the same thing in the end, don't it?" grinned the tiger. "A blowout's a blow-out, call it what you like."

"Can it be managed?" asked Herbert.

"Dessay it can," answered Chivey, "if we can get the steward and the cook in a line to give us tick. But—I say, guv'nor!"

"Well?"

"Supposing we can make it right, where's our guests to come from, eh?"

"Ah, true; the guests," echoed Herbert. "I forgot them."

"Must have guests to join in with us, you know. We couldn't bolt the lot ourselves."

"Not exactly. Let me see, now who is there on board we could invite?"

"There's the captain to begin with."

"Don't care about him."

"The crew?"

"Nor them."

"Nor Harkaway and his pal, I s'pose!" said Chivey.

Herbert Murray knitted his brows and looked as black as thunder at this question, but condescended no reply.

"Thought yer wouldn't cotton to them, guv'nor," remarked Chivey. "Well, then, there's only one more I know of."

"Who's he?"

"Why, that tea-dealer cove as answered to the name of Spriggins—or Wiggins, or the orphan, or something of that sort."

"Splendid. We'll have the orphan, by all means."

"Um, well—suppose we say, soup, pair of fowls, boiled ham."

"Soup, pair of fowls, boiled ham," repeated the tiger, as he made his notes in his book; "anything else?"

"Plum pudding."

"Ah, yes; must have a plum pudding. And now about wine?"

"Port, sherry, claret, and champagne; spirits we have already."

"Yes, plenty," muttered the valet, with a slight shiver, as he completed his memoranda. "I've had enough o' spirits to last me my life."

"Well now, Chivey, I leave it all to your management."

"I'll do it in tip-top style," Chivey replied.

"Don't haggle about price," continued his master; "as I never intend to pay for it, of course I can afford to be liberal."

"Of course," ejaculated Chivey, with the most knowing of winks. "Ha, ha, ha!"

After which Chivey left the cabin to make arrangements for the forthcoming banquet.

*　　*　　*　　*　　*

"Dat you, Bogey?"

"Yes, it me."

"Golly, me so glad; make haste open de door, me got something to tell you."

["Young Harkaway and his Boy Tinker."

"Jack stretched forth his hand to grasp Emily's love token."

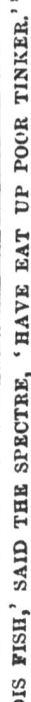

"'DIS FISH,' SAID THE SPECTRE, 'HAVE EAT UP POOR TINKER.'"

" Am it good noose ?"

" Iss ! Berry much splendif'rous good noose."

In an instant the key was thrust into the lock.

The door opened, and Tinker, with his eyes glistening like diamonds, emerged from the cupboard.

"Massa Jack know you alive, Tinker ; him asked me all 'bout you."

" That am right, Bogey ; me glad Massa Jack know Tinker not dead ; me hab had nice smoke and drop of Massa Chivey's brandy, yah, yah !"

Mr. Chivey found that his brandy and cigars vanished in a remarkably rapid and mysterious manner.

And not being able to account for their disappearance in any other way, he was compelled to attribute it to spiritual agency.

" It's that darned ghost !" he would mutter to himself.

And he was quite right—it was.

But he was perfectly willing to stand any quantity of drink and smoke to the spectre, provided it did not haunt him with his terrible presence.

Little, however, did he dream that this supernatural being had been listening with intense interest to the conversation between his master and himself, and that he knew all about their arrangements as well as they did themselves.

It was this secret he was now bursting to impart to his comrade.

" Oh, golly ! golly ! what you tink ?" he exclaimed eagerly.

" What ?"

" Massa Chivey an' Massa Muggy (he meant Murray) gwine hab supper t'morrer night."

" Dat nuffink," answered Bogey, in a slight tone of disgust ; " dey hab supper eb'ry night."

" Oh ! but dis sometink," Tinker insisted, opening his eyes as wide as saucers ; " dis great big 'normous supper. What dey call gran' blanket."

" Blanket !" echoed Bogey, thoughtfully, " dat what dey put in de beds ; dey don't eat blankets for supper."

" Tell yer dey do ! What you mean by contraflick me, sar, eh, you nigger !" cried Tinker, indignantly.

" Nebber 'noo anyone eat blanket but boa constructor, and den he choke 'isself," Bogey ventured to remark.

" Well, den, dere gwine to be great blow-up blanket to-morrer night, in de nex' cabin," said Tinker ; " and Massa Piggins invited."

" Oh, de orflan !"

" Iss. And dey gwine to hab all sort ob beau'ful grubs to eat."

" What dey gwine to hab ?" asked Bogey, his mouth beginning to water.

" Fuss dey hab soap."

" Dat nice ? What nex' ?"

" Pair ob bile fools ?"

" Golly, dat better ; bile fools bery delishus."

" Den dere ham, to eat 'long ob de fools !"

" Dat am prime. Anytink else ?"

" Plum pooddle !" exclaimed Tinker, with immense emphasis.

" Oh, golly ! golly ; plum pooddle ! dat am bery lubly." joined in Bogey, exultingly.

After a moment he asked—

" Am dey gwine to hab any wine ?"

" Iss, golly ! lots. Dey gwine to hab pork, jerry, crackit, an chilblain."

Tinker must be pardoned for his singular version of the wine list.

It being the nearest approach his memory permitted to port, sherry, claret, and champagne.

But it was perfectly satisfactory to Bogey, who grinned all over his face with astonishment.

The two darkies remained licking their lips and rubbing their stomachs for several seconds, in a kind of blissful mental reverie.

At length, Bogey, rousing himself, said wistfully—

" Couldn't we get a bit ob dis blanket for ourself ?"

" Rader !" returned Tinker, with a wink that would have cracked a walnut ; " dis chile mean hab big large bit."

' Me too," put in Bogey.

" Ob course," replied Tinker ; " you help me, I feed you."

" Me help, s'elp him golly 'im will ! What you want ?"

" Long bit ob wire, wid hook at de end ob it," said Tinker, with a grin.

" Anytink more ?"

" A fork wid long handle, d—— sharp at de points."

" Anytink more ?"

" Notink. You get me de ob'lisks what I bin perscribing to you, and we hab regler good blow-up—you see."

" What time de blanket gwine begin ?"

" Eight o'clock," Tinker answered.

And then with a chuckle of intense exultation, the lively ghost slipped once more into his cupboard, whilst his accomplice went on the prowl for the apparatus necessary to the successful carrying out of their designs.

CHAPTER XVI.

THE SUPPER COMES OFF—CHIVEY HAS A PRELIMINARY INTIMATION OF THE GHOST'S PRESENCE — THE ORPHAN COMES OUT RATHER STRONG—SPIRITUAL INFLUENCES —SPECTRAL.

CHIVEY, by means of unblushing cheek and a remarkable facility for lying, got on very well with the steward of the " Albatross."

Promising that worthy individual, on his master's part, a cheque for the entire amount due to him the moment the vessel touched land, he consented to provide all that was required for the banquet.

* * * * *

It was near upon eight o'clock.

Herbert Murray and his tiger were quite ready for supper, and in excellent appetite.

So also were two other individuals.

Tinker and Bogey, to wit, who were snugly posted at the secret panel, hungry as a couple of alligators.

Tinker had assumed his ghostly garments and whitened his face to be ready for any emergency, and he now waited anxiously the opportunity to commence his operations.

Eight o'clock struck.

The cabin door opened, and the cook entered with a tureen.

The secret panel also moved slightly at the same time, and could any human eye have been strong enough to pierce through the chest of drawers, two black noses might have been seen at the aperture sniffing eagerly.

"Dere de soap," whispered Tinker.

"Don't 'um smell beau'ful," whispered Bogey.

Herbert Murray and his tiger seated themselves at the table, which stood conveniently near the drawers.

The chair placed for their guest was vacant. He had not yet arrived.

"Where's the orphan?" asked Herbert.

"I told him eight sharp," Chivey answered.

Mr. Figgins at that moment was looking for some article of dress which had got stowed away in a corner out of his sight.

As he did not make his appearance, Herbert said—

"I'll go and hunt him up. The supper will be nothing without the orphan, Figgins."

With this, he hurried out of the cabin.

"Who's a-going to wait for orphans?" said Chivey to himself, as his master disappeared. "I ain't; I'm on my peck. Here goes."

And as he spoke, he removed the lid of the tureen, and helped himself to a plateful of savoury ox-tail.

"Ah!" he exclaimed, smacking his lips as the fragrance mounted to his nostrils, "this is somethink like, this is a fine—stop! where's the napkin? Oh, here it is. May as well do it in style. Now then," he cried, as he turned round to the table and grasped his spoon, "if there's one thing in the world I like, it's a good plate of ox-tail s——"

The word died away upon his lips.

The spoon dropped from his hand.

He gazed upon a vacant space.

Both plate and soup had vanished.

"What the devil's up now?" he muttered to himself; "I'll swear it was there a second ago."

He looked apprehensively first over one shoulder, and then over the other, but saw nothing.

An unpleasant sensation began to steal over him.

He glanced up at the dim yellow flame of the solitary cabin lantern.

"What a bad light," he growled nervously, "like a farthing rushlight in a fog. It's enough to give a cove the horrors."

With a hand slightly tremulous he poured out a bumper of sherry.

"There's nothing like a glass of good wine to steady a chap's nerves," he soliloquised, as he was about to drink.

A strange and indescribable sound caught his ear, and caused him to pause, and look once more with increased trepidation behind him. Still there was nothing to be seen.

With a fretful ejaculation he turned round again.

"Oh, hang it all!" he cried, with an attempt at recklessness; "who's afraid?"

Seizing his glass hastily, he raised it to his lips, but lowered it as quickly again in dismay.

It was empty.

"Angels an' ministers of grease defend us!" he gasped, in an awe-stricken tone, as he glared at the empty tumbler; "this d——d crib's haunted, and everything in it."

In a kind of paroxysm of terror, he made a sudden rush to the door, and threw it open, just in time to admit his master and his guest, who returned at the moment.

The sight of them somewhat restored him to himself.

"Oh, there you are, guv'nor," he said, as he wiped the drops from his forehead.

"Yes, here we are," returned Herbert Murray. "Mr. Figgins was detained by an unfortunate domestic calamity, having lost his——"

"Grandmother?"

"No, his boots."

"Poor soul!" murmured Chivey.

"I've lost all—all," murmured Figgins, in a tone of anguish. "I'm only a poor, unprotected orphan, who——"

Herbert Murray cut him short by saying—

"Let's hope you haven't lost your appetite, Mr. Figgins, at any rate."

He accompanied this inquiry with a playful slap on the back.

Chivey, who had now recovered himself, gave him another playful slap on the same spot.

"Oh, ugh!" gasped Mr. Figgins, who was startled almost out of his patent leathers; "pray don't do that; my nerves are very weak, and being only a poor orphan——"

"Yes, exactly," interposed Herbert Murray, hurrying his guest to the table; "we'll have the rest by-and-bye."

"Now, gentlemen, be seated," he exclaimed, grandly; "the banquet awaits."

They all three sat down, but instantly sprang up again with a yell, and clapped their hands simultaneously to their coat tails.

"Oh, oh, I'm mortally wounded," shrieked the orphan, writhing like a worm on a hook.

Herbert Murray looked suspiciously at his tiger, then at the seat of his chair, from which a very handsome corking pin protruded, point uppermost.

With a frown he fixed his eyes again on Mr. Chivey, who was holding his hands to his back, and like the orphan, seemed to be suffering pain there.

"Is this one of your confounded Whitechapel jokes?" he demanded, in an angry tone.

"No, 'pon my soul, it ain't, guv'nor," Chivey answered, promptly, with a very wry face, "for I'm a wictim myself. I've got the pain here," and he slapped his hands behind him.

Murray found they were all supplied with a pin apiece—and a large one it was—in each of their chairs.

They looked at each other in silent amazement.

"Who can have done this?" said Herbert, indignantly.

"Well, if I must express my sentiments," Chivey replied very seriously, after a moment, "I should say it was Figgins, the wicked orphan."

"Me !" cried the unprotected one, holding up his hands in the intensity of horror and pain. "Oh, dear, dear, dear me ; a helpless orphan who never——"

The look and tone of the innocent being were so irresistibly comic, that Herbert Murray burst into a roar of laughter, which was echoed, though cautiously, by the ghost and his confederate from behind the drawers.

" It was only a joke, my dear Figgins," said Herbert, after a moment ; "and there's one comfort, as we're all sufferers in this case, one can't laugh at the other."

" It doesn't matter much," sighed the orphan, dolefully ; "it does smart ; yes, it smarts very much, but I feel I'm destined for an early grave."

" Well, have some soup 'fore you start, anyhow, Figgins," urged Chivey, as he handed him a plateful.

" I've no appetite, and I'm afraid of my wounds mortifying," wailed the tea-dealer.

" Oh, gammon ! that soup'll set yer to rights if anythink will. Pitch into it."

The orphan did as he was desired, and considering he had no appetite, it was wonderful how rapidly the ox-tail disappeared down his throat.

" Yer find it rayther tasty, don't yer, ole Cockywax ?" asked Chivey.

" Well—a—I think—yes—very nice and relishing indeed, but my name is not Cockywax."

" Well, never mind, I'll take a glass of wine with you, Mr. Figgins," said Herbert.

" Proud and happy, I'm sure."

" Your health."

" Thank'ee ; yours."

" I'll drink with you, Figgins," cried Chivey, as he filled his glass.

" You're very kind, but I've just drank and——"

" Well, drink again."

" I'm afraid ; my wound still smarts, and my head's not over strong, and being only a poor orph——"

" Oh, come, that be blowed. Drop it, and drink. Here's wishin' some nice gal may take pity on yer helpless condition, and make yer a happy husband and the father of a dozen kids."

" Oh, horror !"

The orphan dropped his glass on the spot and fainted.

Being brought to, he asked for some port, and hoped Mr. Chivey would never say such a dreadful thing again to him.

Chivey filled him a bumper, and he drank it off.

The fowls and ham came next.

" Take a leg, Mr. Figgins ?" said Herbert.

" Thank you, if you please."

" How orful purlite you are, Figgins," said Chivey.

" Can't help it ; I was always brought up to be polite. My venerable parent—bless his memory !—never omitted to chastise me soundly whenever I committed a breach of politeness I—I—think with your permission, gentlemen, I'll drink his health."

" Cert'nly !" cried Chivey, " port ag'in ?"

" Port again, if you please."

All the glasses being filled; the company rose.

" To the health of the dear departed," said Mr. Figgins, impressively.

" The dear departed," echoed the rest.

The orphan emptied his glass, sat down, and sighed deeply.

Then, taking up his knife and fork, he prepared to set to work in earnest at the ham and chicken.

Suddenly he uttered an ejaculation—

" Why, where's it all gone ?" he exclaimed, in blank amazement.

" Where's what gone ?" inquired Herbert Murray and Chivey.

" Why, the ham and chicken," he replied ; "my plate's empty."

" So it is," said Herbert, "and—by Heaven !" he exclaimed, in a startled tone, as he glanced at his own plate, "so is mine."

" And mine, too, s'elp me wonderful !" cried Chivey, as he fell back in his chair, with his hair standing on end.

The ghost had taken advantage of the moment when the company rose, and were drinking, to slip his hand out quickly, and accomplish the feat that had such an astounding effect.

For a moment there was a dead silence, which was broken rather strangely by the orphan, who said with a slight hiccough—

" Nor'r glass—hic—port."

The wine was poured out.

Herbert and Chivey drank brandy, and then, their nerves being fortified, they commenced a search under the table.

Whilst thus engaged, a long fork was mysteriously thrust out from behind the chest of drawers and then withdrawn quickly several times.

Each time it disappeared it carried away a bottle, which it caught by its neck between the prongs.

Before the search under the table was concluded, there was not a bottle to be seen.

The remains of the fowls had also been forked away.

" There must be a trap or something of that sort," said Herbert, as he and his companions examined the floor on their hands and knees ; but there was no signs of any such thing.

It was most bewildering.

" It may be occasioned by—hic—spiritual influences," murmured the orphan, as he peered on the ground, with his coat-tails over his shoulders, and the bow of his white cravat under his left ear.

" Spiritual humbug ! Spiritual bosh !" growled Chivey, who was sore upon the subject, and sought to conceal his inward fears by a tone of bravado ; "you're tight, Figgins."

" No, my dear boy," returned that forgiving individual, "not t-tight, not 't all t-t-ight, only powerfully—hic—impressed. Let's have glass —hic—brandy."

This was readily agreed to, and the party dragged themselves once more to an upright position, but only to receive a fresh shock.

The table was cleared of everything but the empty plates and the ham.

Herbert Murray collapsed, and fell back in his chair.

His tiger turned deadly pale.

The orphan looked blandly at nothing at all, and smiled.

"This confounded place is the abode of evil spirits," exclaimed Herbert, at length, looking particularly bewildered.

"It's the devil himself, and no one else," muttered Chivey, in a tone of horror.

Just at this moment the door opened, and the cook appeared.

"Plum padden, gentlemen," he said, as he placed it on the table.

Ashamed to show the man the mental trepidation they were in, Herbert said in as steady a tone as he could—

"More wine."

"Yes, sir," the man replied, in some surprise, thinking the party must have drunk uncommonly hard, if they had emptied all their bottles.

"Shall I take away the empty bottles, sir?" he asked, after a moment.

"Ye—es, if yer can find 'em," replied Chivey, with a kind of grimly ironical mirth.

"Umph!" muttered the cook to himself as he went out; "swallered the bottles as well, I s'pose."

The events that had occurred had quite taken away the appetites of two at least of the party.

The orphan, not being impressed with ghostly fears, sat down, and began innocently enough to pick the plums out of the pudding with his fork. Herbert Murray drew his tiger aside.

"You told me not long since, you had had a visitation," he said to him in a low tone.

"Yes, from the ghost of that d——d nigger Tinker," replied Chivey, hoarsely.

"I've heard," continued his master, "that those who have been murd——"

"Oh, don't—don't, guv'nor."

"Well, then, those who have died violent deaths sometimes appear to those who have destroyed them."

"Yes, yes," groaned Chivey, in a hollow voice; "that's it. It's this cussed ghost that's doing all this. I wish to goodness the black beggar was alive again, I'd——"

A deep, hollow groan at this juncture put a stop to the tiger's expressions of remorse.

"There he is! that's his voice," he cried. "It scares me like a voice from a burying ground."

The orphan stopped picking his plums, and looked round inquiringly.

"W-w-har-rat?" he asked, in an incoherent tone. "It sounds like a groan."

Herbert Murray sprang desperately on a chair.

"I'll stand it no longer," he cried, as he hastily snatched down the lantern.

The yellow flame flickered from the tug it had received, and seemed inclined to go out.

To his horror, at that instant the ham sprang up from the dish, and began to perform as good a jig as a ham could be expected to do in the air.

"Lor' 'a' mercy, what's the matter with the ham? I'm poor helpless—hic—orphan," gasped Mr. Figgins, as he fell over the chair and all to the ground at this unearthly spectacle.

At the same moment, the dish containing the plum pudding—without any perceptible means—glided off the table, and disappeared.

Chivey uttered a cry of horror.

Herbert Murray rushed forward.

A crash and a shriek were heard.

The lantern had fallen from his hand.

The ham had stopped dancing suddenly (the hook having broken away from the wire that sustained it), and the shriek came from the prostrate orphan, on whose upturned face it came down with a tremendous slap.

Consternation prevailed.

Only a faint glimmer came from the almost extinct light.

When suddenly, to add to the horrors of the moment, the table itself became inspired with motion, and began a horrible and unnatural dance round and round, backwards and forwards.

Down the middle and up again it went, as no table ever went before.

"Oh, take me out and bury me, someone," yelled the half tipsy and horrified Chivey, as he clung to his master.

"Ghost or devil, depart," shouted Herbert Murray, hoarsely, who was like the rest, half tipsy from the effect of the port wine and brandy mixture, and he tried to kick the table.

"Murder—murder—poor helpless—orphan—hic—murder!" shrieked Mr. Figgins, as he lay on his back and did nothing. "Somebody come and pick up a poor orphan."

CHAPTER XVII.

THE SICK MAN'S LEECH—JOVIAL CAPTAIN ROBINSON MEETS WITH A DISAPPOINTMENT—UGLY THOUGHTS.

WE must now return to Mr. Murray. Our readers will remember we left him stricken down with grief at the departure of his son in the ship "Albatross."

He was borne away insensible by the policeman, and taken home to bed.

During Mr. Murray's illness his ravings were of so ugly a nature, that it was indeed fortunate no listeners were nigh, for some unpleasant rumours might possibly have got abroad else.

One day, however, the third after Mr. Murray's seizure with his illness, jovial Captain Robinson came there to inquire after him.

The doctor's orders were that no one was to be admitted to the sick room under any pretext whatever.

But jovial Captain Robinson was one of those men who will not be denied.

So up he went.

"My leech must be applied again," he muttered to himself.

He opened the door, and entered.

At the very moment he crossed the threshold the sick man was raving wildly.

"Who calls the 'Albatross' a coffin ship? I'll have the law of any man that dares disparage my property—my own boy's on her—ha! ha! And would I set my own flesh and blood afloat in a doomed hull? Liars! Heavily insured! Of course she is! Of course she is! and hark! hark! how the wind whistles, and how the waves moan and moan, before they send out their roar that foretells woe to the underwriters, and—hark! what was that?"

Jovial Captain Robinson was just a bit startled at this point.

The sick man started up in his bed, and said this so pointedly at the jovial captain, that the latter answered involuntarily—

"Which ?"

"Did you not hear ?—a cry for help! A despairing cry—a wail of agony, as the cruel waves close over the poor drowning wretch. What voice is that? Surely, I know it—yes—it is, it is my boy's."

And then the sick man cowered, in his frenzy, up in a corner of the bed.

There was something very unpleasant in all this, and the jovial Captain Robinson turned pale.

"Dead, gone, are you, my poor, foolish boy !" said the patient, with a moan, as though a settled remorse was upon him, for a matter which was no longer new.

"I have done it all—I—I—your fond, foolish, old father, that would have given my heart's best blood to save you a pang. I ruined you firstly by my want of firmness and decision of character, and lastly, by my sternness, that came so suddenly upon him. But I'll not live ! Why should I, when he's gone ? There's no reason why I should. Get me a razor, nurse ; I'll soon put an end to this. One good sharp stroke, and I'll take my head clean off ; and hark you here."

He sank his voice to a loud whisper.

"When Robinson comes to put on the screw for hush money—his leech, as he calls it—you can throw my head at him—that'll show him——"

And the sick man gave a weird chuckle at this ghastly conceit.

Suddenly he seized himself by the throat, and tried to strangle himself, but Robinson caught hold of him, and held him down.

A sharp tussle ensued, for although Captain Robinson was a very powerful man compared to Mr. Murray, yet the latter was nerved by frenzy, and he made a desperate fight for it.

At length the nurse came in, and lent a hand.

And between them they contrived to strap the wretched man down, and put him out of the way of doing himself harm.

"A lucky thing you was here, sir," said the nurse ; "I only left the room for a minute ; but I should never dare to again—never."

Captain Robinson mumbled something, and glided out of the sick room, and into the street.

The colour had left his cheek, and his jovial manners disappeared.

CHAPTER XVIII.

ON BOARD A COFFIN SHIP—ALL HANDS TO THE PUMP—NAT CRINGLE LETS THE CAT OUT OF THE BAG.

A SHORT time after our friends Tinker and Bogey had had their fun out with young Murray and Chivey, Jack and Harry were in deep conversation about the ship they were sailing in.

"Harry," said Jack, "what do you think of this ship, eh. old boy ?"

"Well, Jack, I have been thinking that although they say the 'Albatross' is such a clinker. she is certainly not famed for speed."

"Speed." echoed young Jack, "why, I call her precious slow."

"Slow." exclaimed a voice behind them ; "I call her an old crawler."

They looked round, and there stood a big sturdy sailor, one who had often touched his forelock to them in hopes they would have spoken to him.

He was six feet high, and a little bit over, and had a pair of shoulders on him that would inspire respect in the champion pugilist of England.

"That's strong language, Nat Cringle," said young Jack.

"Strong," quoth the sailor ; "is it ? Not stronger than I mean."

"Why ?"

"Why ? Because she's the slowest old tub that was ever built of sponge—a rotten old hull that ought to have been burnt up long ago."

The boys stared.

"Nat Cringle !"

"That's me, and I wish your honours had spoken to me about the ship before."

"Whatever are you talking about ?" said Harry Girdwood.

"The 'Albatross,' if you please, and few people could tell you more about it than Nat Cringle."

"I can't hear you disparage our own ship, Nat," said Jack ; "it isn't proper, you know."

"What isn't proper ? Which isn't proper, and why not ?"

"Because she is between us and Davy Jones's locker.'

"That's it," rejoined the sailor, quickly ; "that's just it. But how long will she keep us so ? That's the rub. Why, it's a downright regular conjuring trick to keep her afloat."

"Well, Cringle," said Harry Girdwood, "I never heard a man speak so yet of a ship he had just taken service in."

"Bah, they pay me well for that."

"But payment could not recompense you for risking your life." said Harry Girdwood.

"Couldn't it, though ?" exclaimed Nat Cringle. "And why not pray? Have I not often risked my life for less ?"

"Ever served ?" asked Jack.

"Of course I have," said Nat Cringle. "Seen lots of service on different stations when I was in the royal navy. I never got a scratch, and I've been in some hot jobs too ; I've been in a bit of weather, too, now and again. But when the bullets were thick as hail, and the men dropped around me like rotten sheep, I never got a scratch. I've been in three wrecks. Once I was the only hand saved. I tell you I can't come to harm, or else you wouldn't find me here, 'cause my bent ain't by no means suicidal."

"Do you really mean, Cringle," said Jack, "that you think the 'Albatross' isn't seaworthy ?"

"Bah !"

An expression of utter contempt passed over the sailor's face as he said this.

"Seaworthy ? Why, there's not a sound plank in her. It's a coffin ship."

"A what!"

"A coffin ship. Nothing more nor less," said Nat Cringle; "and old Murray's got a new line on that'll suit his book right enough—old Murray the wholesale undertaker, as we used to call him."

"But why on earth the wholesale undertaker?" asked Jack.

"Because he's buried such lots of people—more than any six undertakers have the chance of doing in their lifetimes, however brisk a trade they may drive."

"Ahem!"

"I suppose you didn't know about all this?"

"No."

"It looked oddish that you should join such a ship," said Nat Cringle; "but I supposed that there was some sort of a reason for it. Howsomever, I recommend you to keep a sharp look-out on me."

"What for?"

"When she settles."

"You don't think really that the 'Albatross' is in immediate danger?"

"Difficult to say that. But you just look how she is plugged up with goods. Low freight, you know. See how low she is in the water, and see the way she labours along. Why, she has weight enough of cargo to founder a good ship, let alone such a coffin ship as this."

Jack and Harry were more than half convinced by his earnest manner.

"Does she make much water?"

"Does she not!" exclaimed Nat Cringle; "hark at the pumps working incessantly. I have been pumping this hour or more. But you only wait until we get a little more weather, and then you'll see. You go and help work at the pumps, and see how little you can do to——"

"Work at the pumps?" repeated a voice, close by.

It was Mr. Figgins, the Cockney orphan, who had again ventured on deck.

"Yes."

"What do you mean, pray, by working at the pumps?"

Young Jack winked at the sailor and Harry.

"They are going to give the crew and passengers a dance," said he; "and Nat Cringle has been a shoemaker—he has to repair the dancing shoes—the pumps, you see."

"Dear me," exclaimed Mr. Figgins, in surprise, "how very singular the manners and customs of life at sea are."

"Very."

"You'll join in the merry dance, I suppose?" said Jack.

"No; not at present. I thought I was getting better; but when the ship rocks, I really feel the old feeling coming on."

"You're not well yet?"

"No, I have not been well ever since I came on board," replied the orphan, with a faint air of embarrassment.

"Still sick?"

"Oh, dear no."

"I thought not. You are too much of a Jack tar for that, now."

"Rather!"

Mr. Figgins had got his notions of an ideal sailor from Mr. T. P. Cooke, and other stage mariners, and as he said "Rather!" he essayed to give that well-known hitch to his trousers.

But the effort or jerk, and a heavy roll of the ship, caused a return of those unpleasant symptoms which the orphan was subject to.

So he clapped his hand to his mouth, and beat a precipitate retreat to the ship's side.

"Nat Cringle," said young Jack, seriously, "I hope that you exaggerate the dangers of this ship."

"Don't you hope anything of the kind young gentleman," said Nat Cringle, "or you'll be disappointed. I ain't exaggerated nothing. The 'Albatross' is neither more nor less than a coffin ship, and the very next storm that comes on, down she goes."

Jack and Harry looked grave.

They were no cowards.

Those of our readers who have followed them through their varied adventures, need no assertion to this effect.

"If the 'Albatross' foundered in the mid-ocean, you would have but a poor chance of saving your life."

"Who spoke of mid-ocean?" said Nat Cringle; "I didn't, for one."

"But——"

"Don't you jump at no rash conclusions, young gentleman. The 'Albatross' will founder, but not in mid-ocean, as long as I have half a chance of handling the helm. Let her have a fair run for the Spanish coast."

"I see."

"What I should like more than anything else, would be——"

"What?"

The honest tar looked anxiously around him.

"Just to run her into port, and get her condemned."

"By whom?"

"British consul and Lloyd's people."

"What for?"

"Just to pay the warmints out who traffic in honest men's lives. Don't you see, they'd lose their insurance money—aye, and they'd lose their freight too."

"What a noble notion," ejaculated Jack.

"Yes, rather tidy, ain't it?" added the sailor. "But to do this proper, we want one thing."

"What?"

"To square the skipper."

"Is it to be done?"

"Can't say."

"I should think that he's in with the owner and the other villains," suggested Harry Girdwood.

"That's just what I should like to know," said Nat Cringle, thoughtfully; "Cap'n Deering ain't no fool, he ain't. He knows his dooty—no man better—every rope in the ship, and every plank—aye, and what's more, he warn't on board six hours before he knew every man Jack of us aboard by our names. So I can't make out why he should take sarvice in sich a rotten old hull, unless there was some particular reasons for it, that no one knows about.'

"He didn't know anything about it," said Jack, positively.

Nat Cringle eyed the speaker sharply.

"Why?"

"Because he told me that he had been sent

for express to town, when it was known that Captain Robinson was too ill to go out."

" Too ill ?"

" Yes."

Nat Cringle burst out into a boisterous laugh.

" What's that for ?"

" Cap'n Robinson was about as ill as I am this 'ere blessed moment," he answered, with an oath. "Cap'n Robinson values his precious skin too much to go afloat in such a ship as the ' Albatross.' "

" But surely he meant to go."

" Never."

The boys were literally staggered at this.

"Nat," said Jack, " my father's rich, and the best man that ever drew breath. He will take in hand this rascal Murray, and punish him."

" Bless you, your honour," ejaculated the tar, quite moved ; " you're the right sort, you are."

" But I shall have to get the chance to do this act of justice," said young Jack.

" It'll come."

" But if the ship should sink ?" said Jack.

" Look here, your honour," said Nat Cringle ; " the ' Albatross ' will go down, that's a mortal sartinty ; but you stick close by me, whenever she's in trouble, and we'll sink or swim together. And I for one don't mean sinking."

" Give us your hand upon that," said Harry Girdwood.

" Here it is," said the honest tar, thrusting out a huge horny palm, " and here's the other for you, Master Jack, nearest the 'art, you know. But mum ! here comes the second mate, d—d ugly swab, betwixt you and me and the bed post !"

CHAPTER XIX.

THE YOUTHFUL SWELL NEXT TO JACK'S CABIN—THE TALE OF A CHEQUE-BOOK— THE HOLE IN THE PANEL—A SHINE ON DECK !—THE THREATENED MUTINY—JUST IN TIME.

THE youthful swell Murray was so dissatisfied with his cabin that he removed to one with more comforts, and that one happened by chance to be next to our friend young Jack.

" Chivey," said the master.

" Sir," said the man.

" Give me a soda."

" And b., sir ?"

" Of course !"

" It's all very well to say of course, sir," said Mr. Chivey ; " but the fact is the steward won't give us much more tick."

" The steward's a puppy, Chivey," said Herbert Murray ; " he knows that I am the owner's son ; tell him I must be attended to."

" Very good."

" And tell him if he makes any bones about it, I'll get him discharged from the ship, as safe as my name's Herbert Murray."

" Very good, sir."

Chivey disappeared, and young Murray waited impatiently for his return.

" I'm always thirsty," he muttered ; " should like to have S. and B. laid on by a sort of New River Company."

A merry voice in the adjoining cabin broke in upon his reverie with a snatch of a song.

" My name d'ye see's Tom Tough,
And I've seen a deal of sarvice."

" Blow his sarvice, and him too," muttered Mr. Murray Junior. " That's that beast of a Jack Harkaway, I know."

" That's him, sir."

" Hullo !"

The master turned round, and there stood the man at the door.

" What are you spying upon me for, Chivey ?" he said.

" Spying ain't in my line, sir," retorted the tiger. " I was only a-watchin' of you."

" The same thing."

" Not quite."

" Silence ! You hear Harkaway in the next cabin ?"

" Oh, I hear, sir."

And well he might, for young Jack was swelling out his voice.

" And if more you would be knowin',
I have sailed with bold Boscawen."

" He's getting on a nautical chant," said Mr. Chivey, " to make hisself believe that he don't feel queer."

" I've watched him," groaned young Murray, " and I know he doesn't ; he was rollicking about all over the ship, when I was half dead with sea-sickness, hang him."

" Don't you get impatient, sir," said the tiger, " and I can put you up to a wrinkle."

" What is it ?"

" Something extra double artful, sir. O. T. Q."

" Out with it ; you know how I hate beating about the bush !" exclaimed Herbert Murray, impatiently.

" Keep your 'air on, sir, I beg," said the tiger, " and I'll tell you all about it ; you know this ship is made up of sliding boards."

He crept up to the end of the cabin, and gently slid back a small trap.

At the same time he blew out the lamp, which was burning upon the table, so that they were in total darkness.

Through the hole they could see all that was passing.

There was young Jack seated at a desk in which were displayed a number of letters and papers on which he was engaged.

At the moment that the two spies, for they were nothing less, peeped through, Harry Girdwood was entering the cabin.

And now they could not only see, but they could hear every word that was uttered, as distinctly as if they had been in the cabin with the speakers.

" Jack."

" What now ?" said young Harkaway, looking up.

" I've been thinking over what Nat Cringle said."

" So have I ; the danger we are now in is great, for a heavy storm might come upon us at any time."

" Now supposing we got ashore off the coast yonder."

Here Herbert Murray looked nervously round

at the tiger, who pressed his master's arm warningly.

"Well?"

"I want to see Spain," continued Jack; "the land of Don Quixote and Sancho Panza and Gil Blas and Don Juan and Figaro and Almaviva, and such a lot more people we are all acquainted with in books and plays."

"That's all very well, Jack, but we are short of money."

"No, the governor gave me a cheque-book, and I have only to fill in the cheques for any amount I like, and get them cashed through any banker in any civilised city. We would have to wait while they authenticated the cheques, and there's tin for you to any reasonable amount."

As he spoke, he flourished a cheque-book in his hand.

"You must keep that in your pocket always."

"I do."

"Wrap it in an oil skin, and fasten it about your body, for if any accident happened——"

"And we had to swim for it?"

"Yes."

"It would be safe enough, and as for swimming for it, why——"

At this juncture a hoarse voice was heard giving orders on deck, and it stopped their talk.

"All hands to the pumps!"

"Hark!"

"I hear."

"Anything worse than usual, I wonder?" said Harry.

Murmurs were heard on deck so loud that the grumbling tones reached them distinctly.

Harry Girdwood ran up the cabin stairs to see what was going forward.

"The men are grumbling," said he, turning round towards Jack.

"What at?"

"This unceasing working at the pumps. They get no rest."

"All hands pump ship!" sang out the second mate.

A muttered menace was heard to come from one of the crew.

This was the signal for a low growl—low, but general.

And, as it went on, it seemed to gather force like a distant storm.

"Jack."

"Yes, Harry."

"It is getting serious. Get your pistols and let us go up on deck. The mate may want assistance."

"I'm with you," said Jack.

He dropped his cheque-book on to the desk, and sticking his pistols into his belt, up he ran.

Matters were growing serious on deck.

The wind had freshened and the glass fell rapidly, denoting that some dirty weather was to be expected.

A heavy swell had set the "Albatross" rolling, and the water was now gaining fast upon her.

The gale, which had been gradually working its way up to them, caught the ship at last with greater suddenness than they could reasonably have expected.

But Captain Deering was prompt to meet the emergency.

The upper fore and main top-sails were reefed.

The mizzen sail was furled.

The rain came down in buckets, and the men were working deep in water upon deck.

The men had deputed a spokesman to go to the skipper to ask for an extra allowance of grog.

And, surely, if any circumstances could warrant such a license, this was the opportunity to grant it.

But the captain being busily occupied, the men referred their request to the mate, a surly and ill-natured fellow, who refused it point blank.

The wind increased, and as the heavy cross sea caught her, the ship laboured and creaked, and strained continually, causing Nat Cringle to sing out, ironically, from time to time—

"There's music for you, lads!"

And as the wind continued, the ship lurched and rolled fearfully.

Now and again a heavier sea than usual would break clean over the deck, washing everything before it, and carrying the men away from the pumps to land them in the lee scuppers all in a heap, bruised and marked about dreadfully.

When young Jack and his comrade, Harry, got on deck, the crew were assembled all in a group talking to the second mate, and the conversation had grown remarkably warm.

"We've been up to our waists in water, Mr. Mackenzie," said the spokesman, "and we think you really ought to serve us out an extra allowance."

"I'm of a different way of thinking," replied the mate, who was a temperance man; "and I'll just do nae such thing."

The men murmured.

"Let us see the captain," said one.

"Aye, aye, the captain."

"Yes, yes, called a third.

"Ye'll do nae such thing," said the mate, obstinately. "Captain Deering has deputed me to see you, and——"

"Well, then, if you stop the grog, I won't go to the pumps, for one—that's flat," replied the man.

"Ye mutinous thief!" roared the mate. "I'll clap ye in irons in no time."

"Ye'd better not try it, Sandy," said the sailor, threateningly.

"Drop him overboard," suggested one of the men.

Now whether this suggestion would have been acted upon, it is not easy to say.

Before it could be put to the test, young Jack and Harry Girdwood appeared on deck, and quickly as quietly they ranged themselves beside Mackenzie the mate.

"Come, come, my men," said Jack, showing his pistols, "stand back, no mutineering here."

"We don't want to mutiny, Master Jack; we've only made a very reasonable request."

"Aye, aye," said Jack. "What is it, my men?"

"Give us some rum."

"Not a drop," cried Mackenzie vehemently.

"Down with him!" cried the sailors.

"Stand back, men!" cried Jack.

It was a very ticklish moment.

"I won't countenance anything like mutiny or insubordination," said Jack, "but put your request into more respectful language, and Mr. Mackenzie will, I am sure, listen to you, if it is reasonable."

"You're making sure before your time, then," said the mate, ungraciously.

"Sir."

"Did ye no hear what I said? Ye've no right to promise anything in my name. Ye're just a wee bit over fast, and it ill becomes ye."

"Come, come, Mr. Mackenzie, don't be vexed with me," said Jack, good-naturedly. "I spoke only for the good of the ship."

"Hold your tongue, boy."

"Will you not let the men have some grog, sir?"

"No," cried the Scotch mate, furiously; "and if you——"

"Stop, stop, sir," said young Jack, "you've no need to threaten me. I came to assist you——"

"Dom yere impudence," cried Mackenzie.

"But since you don't want it——"

"Nor you either. Go forward, you young imp, ye—ye——"

"Save your breath to cool your porridge, sir," said young Jack, coolly. "Stay here, Harry, to see that Mr. Mackenzie doesn't get into any trouble while I step aft and talk to Captain Deering."

The mate raged.

However, Jack did not wait to hear his retort.

Young Jack went straight up to the skipper at once.

"Captain Deering, may I have one word with you, please?"

"Just one, Mr. Harkaway," returned the skipper, "only be quick about it, if you please."

At this moment a deep, threatening growl was heard from the men on deck.

After a pause, the captain fiercely asked—

"Well, what is all this fuss about?"

"The men have been working like steam engines hour after hour, sir, knee deep in water, and not a man, sir, amongst them has a dry thread on him. They want some rum," responded young Jack.

"Is that all?"

"Yes, sir."

"Let them have it at once—at once. Do you hear?"

"Yes, sir."

"Off with you."

"Excuse me, captain, they have asked Mr. Mackenzie already and he refused."

"Oh."

"Well, I wouldn't ask after that, but they are grumbling and look precious ugly, but he holds out, so that I really fear some harm may come to him."

"He's a fool," muttered the captain.

And then he gave orders to the steward to serve out a grog all round.

Meanwhile, Harry Girdwood was boldly confronting the mutineers, who, awed by his pistols, hung back, hardly daring to commit the violence they had it in their minds to do. Oaths and curses were hurled at the head of the mate, but they all admired the boy's pluck, though he stood in their way.

It is doubtful, though, whether he would have been able to keep them at bay much longer, had not young Jack returned with the welcome news that they were to have the rum.

A cheer greeted this announcement, and then the steward made his appearance.

"I hope, Mr. Mackenzie," said Jack, stepping up to the mate, "that you'll not take offence at what I've done."

"If ye think to palaver me over," said Mackenzie, sullenly, "ye're mistaken. Ye think to mak' a fule o' me befoor the crew. Weel, I shall yet ha' the opportunity o' showing ye that it's no the best day's wark o' yer life to mak a fule o' Donald Mackenzie."

"All hands pump ship!" sang out Captain Deering, as soon as the men had swallowed their ram.

"Aye, aye, sir."

The men flew to work again with alacrity at this.

"Now, Mr. Mackenzie," called the captain, "tumble about, please—look lively."

The Scotch mate growled something inaudible, and moved away.

CHAPTER XX.

MASTER AND MAN—THE POSITIONS REVERSED—TIGER CHIVEY "PLAYS ARTFUL," AND HIS MASTER MAKES A VERY FALSE MOVE—THE FORGED CHEQUES AND THE SLIDING TRAP IN THE CABIN PANEL.

MURRAY and Chivey had remained all this time in their cabin.

"That Harkaway cove has left this cheque-book behind him," said Chivey.

"What then?"

"Why, by just putting my arm through this little 'ole I can get at it."

"Chivey, I forbid you to do anything of the sort."

The tiger had dived his arm through the hole in the panelling, and in the twinkling of an eye, he held young Jack's cheque-book under his master's nose.

"But I have done it, sir; look here," cried Chivey.

"Chivey, this won't do for me."

"Oh, it will for me, though. Why, with just one little lark with the cheque-book, you could pepper him nicely for all that precious sewing up he give you ashore."

"I shouldn't object to do that," returned Herbert Murray, "but I would do anything——"

Chivey interrupted his master with a cry of delight and amazement.

"My hi, and Elizabeth Martin! What a slap-up lark!"

"What is it?"

"Look here!"

He pushed the open cheque-book under young Murray's eyes, and there was a cheque already written and signed by Jack for twenty pounds.

Jack had got it ready for some purpose or other at the very moment that he had been called up on deck by the mutinous demonstrations of the crew.

"It is strange why he should leave the cheque in the book."

"Perhaps it was meant for your own especial benefit, sir."

Mr. Chivey cocked his head on one side in his own peculiar fashion.

"Whatever do you mean by that, Chivey?" asked the master.

"Only this, sir—if I could only write like you, I'd fill up every blessed cheque in the book and make presents of 'em to all the orspitals and charities and such."

Herbert Murray's eyes flashed again at this.

"By jingo! that would be a lark, and serve young Harkaway out."

"Rather!"

The tiger saw that he had got his weak and vacillating master upon the right tack, and he saw also that it would not do to press the matter unduly.

"Wouldn't that ugly young rascal stare when he found out that he had subscribed to a charity—or charities—without knowing it?"

"Would he not?" exclaimed Chivey; "only you couldn't imitate the signature near enough to match with that."

"You never made a greater mistake in your life, Chivey, than to suppose that."

"You don't mean to say, sir, that you really could?" exclaimed the tiger, with a look that combined incredulity and admiration.

Chivey knew that weak-headed young master of his well.

No one better.

He could do more with Herbert Murray with a mere look than could the latter's father accomplish by dint of praises and reproaches, coaxing and scolding, severity and leniency combined.

And the singularity of the affair was that Chivey really commanded while he appeared to obey.

Murray snatched up a pen, and wrote in imitation of Jack's signature.

Chivey gave his master an admiring glance.

"Well, there!" he exclaimed, turning his eyes upwards and seeming to address the roof of the cabin, "if he ain't just about the tallest thing out in fly coves, I wish I may die a old maid!"

"Oh, there's nothing very wonderful in that, Chivey," said his master, with an off-hand air.

"Ain't there? Why, nobody could tell but what it was young Harkaway's writing. Have a cheque out of his book, sir; you do imitate him so well."

"Yes, it ain't bad, is it?" said Herbert, taking up the pen again, and involuntarily copying the signature of young Jack Harkaway, at the foot of a blank cheque and then of a second.

The tiger looked on greatly interested.

"Beautiful!" ejaculated Chivey, "lovely. Dot the hi, sir!"

"Where?"

"In junior."

"It doesn't matter!"

"Oh, dot his hi; he dotted yours pretty smartly for you, didn't he?—ha! ha! ha!"

This was a mistake.

"What the devil do you mean by that, you impudent scoundrel?" exclaimed Herbert Murray; for this was a very sore topic to joke upon.

Chivey, with his wonted quickness, saw his error.

But he had not been able to resist the joke.

"Beg pardon, sir!" he said, saluting his master, and pulling a face as grave as a mute's, "couldn't help it, sir—no offence."

"Don't you learn to be too familiar, Chivey, or I'll give you the bag! You mustn't learn to forget your place, because I'm civil to you."

"No, sir!"

"You'll just about spoil yourself if you do, let me tell you. Now you may not earn much now——"

"It isn't to say a downright fortune, sir."

"No, perhaps not—but I shall have a pot of tin one of these days, and it will be a fortune to you, if you know how to behave yourself."

"Thankee, sir," responded the tiger. "I don't want a fortune, so long as you keep me on."

"Very well then. It entirely depends on yourself."

"Yes, sir——"

*   *   *   *   *

Chivey looked wistfully at those two signed cheques.

And as he looked, his speculative mind shot ahead into the future.

He fancied he saw in those two strips of paper the means of making himself safe—of putting his position beyond the mere caprice of his shifty young master.

But how?

This we shall see.

Meanwhile it may be well to remark that Chivey, with all his shrewdness, had yet to learn that to speculate upon the remote future was rash, seeing that if the weather did not speedily improve, the "Albatross" was likely to prove the coffin for one and all on board—for passengers as well as crew.

"Just listen, sir, what a row they are making overhead."

"That's Jack Harkaway's voice. He's coming down, Chivey," exclaimed his master, anxiously; "put back the cheque-book."

"Yes, sir."

The tiger obeyed.

And in obeying, somehow or another, the two signed cheques found their way into Chivey's pocket.

"Push to the trap."

"It's down, sir—close as wax."

"I hope they won't see it from the other side."

"Never a bit, sir."

"Then up on deck, and see what all this precious hubbub is about, Chivey."

"Yes, sir."

The tiger turned upon the cabin steps, and gave his master a parting glance of admiration.

And he disappeared up the steps on deck.

Young Murray fully believed in Chivey's adulation, and accepted it as justifiable homage.

Silly young fool!

He had just added forgery to his varied and unenviable accomplishments.

Forgery has an ugly sound; yet forgery it was.

Moreover, this crafty, cunning young man about town had left in the possession of his own wicked servant the proofs of his crime!

CHAPTER XXI.

LISTENERS HEAR BAD NEWS OCCASIONALLY.

"I SAY, Jack," exclaimed Harry Girdwood, when they returned to their cabin, "that's rather careless of you leaving your cheque-book out."

"No fear; no one came down here, they had too much to do on deck."

"True," answered cautious Harry, "but you can't be too careful with your cheque-book."

"True, but my own opinion is, that unless we look remarkably lively, the cheque-book won't be of any particular use to any of us."

"I don't think it is as bad as that," replied Harry.

"I do; the rotten old tub is as nearly waterlogged as possible. Let a few more seas break over her and down she'll go, as sure as my name's Jack!"

* * * * *

At this moment Chivey tottered down the companion-ladder to his master.

His cheeks were ashy pale, and he had not a word to say for himself; for he absolutely quaked with fear.

But his master did not want to learn the news from Chivey.

He was stretched at full length in his berth, with his ear close to the panel, and he could hear every word of the conversation going forward between Jack Harkaway, junior, and his comrade, Harry.

"Hush, listen!" he whispered warningly to Chivey.

The tiger obeyed.

And this is what they both overheard together.

"I mean to put on my cork clothing," said Jack; "get yours ready too, Harry, at once."

"Very good."

"And meanwhile, in case of accidents, I mean to scribble out a little information and stick the paper into a corked and sealed bottle."

"What's the good of that?"

"Lots," replied Jack; "if we go down to Davy Jones, it will be saying good-bye to all our friends at home, and it will show up that murderous old thief, Murray, to the world."

"But Mr. Murray's own son is on board."

"Yes."

"Well, then, nobody will believe that he sent his own flesh and blood afloat in a coffin ship."

"But he didn't know that his son was here. According to Captain Deering's own showing, the young fellow took his passage, with his servant, under assumed names, so as to dodge his father. But I'm sorry for the son," said Jack, "for he's very little chance of saving himself, and, unless the wind drops, the 'Albatross' will never float twelve hours more!"

* * * * *

"Chivey!"

Herbert Murray's voice was hoarse with terror.

"Yes, sir."

"Bring me something to drink—some brandy and water."

"I ain't got time," replied his servant; "I've got to look after myself now, and put on my lifebelt, for I mean to have a good hard try for it."

"What do the men say on deck?"

"They are getting ready the boats, and some are talking of a raft."

Herbert Murray sank back with a groan, burying his face in his hands.

Meanwhile, young Jack was writing out his statement of the case to expose the shipowner's villany.

And this being done, he enclosed it, together with a hastily written farewell to his father and mother, little Emily, and friends, in a bottle, which was tightly corked and sealed.

Then it was committed to the waves.

"Now for the lifebelts!"

CHAPTER XXII.

BETTER NEWS—THE SKIPPER MEETS AN OLD COMRADE—STRANGE REVELATIONS—THE CAPTAIN'S RESOLVE—"WE'LL DO THEM YET, BY THE LORD HARRY!"

Now, while preparations were made for dire extremities below, matters grew better above.

The wind lulled, and Captain Deering exclaimed in the fulness of his heart—

"We shall pull her through now, the rotten old sponge!"

"For the present, sir," said a voice close to his ear.

Captain Deering turned round, and there was Nat Cringle.

"Hullo, my man!" he said, biting his lip with vexation, "you oughtn't to be at my elbow to pick up every word I may happen to let fall."

Nat Cringle pulled his forelock in salute, and gave an apologetic scrape with his foot.

"All right, captain, I'm mum. Axing your pardon, I took the liberty o' speaking on the score of this not being the first nor the tightest scrape we've been in together."

"We!"

"Yes, sir."

"I scarcely remember," murmured the captain, in the voice of one diving back into the past, "and yet I should know your voice. Why, let me think."

"Don't your honour remember the 'Lively Polly'?"

Here he broke out into a snatch of a sea song—

"If you wish to know the liveliest craft that ever sailed from port,
Why, that's my Polly—the 'Lively Polly'—and she's a rare good sort."

"The 'Lively Polly'!" quoth Captain Deering; "I should think I do remember, and now, Nat Cringle, I remember you."

"Oh!"

"Nat Cringle's your name, is it not?"

"Aye, aye, sir."

"Tip me your fin, Nat Cringle," said the skipper heartily; "I'm precious glad to sail with an old comrade. Why, where have you been all these long years, old shipmate?"

"Knocking about, cap'n," replied the sailor, "up and down—oftener down than up, if the real truth be spoken."

"And so, Nat, you think the 'Albatross' will only pull through for the present?"

"Yes. sir."

"Why?"

"Your honour needn't ask that," replied the sailor, "seeing as you know all about the ship now as much as I do."

"Aye, Nat Cringle, but from the way you speak, you show me that you have known something more about the 'Albatross' than you choose to tell for a long while past."

"Not more than you, captain," said Nat Cringle. "Leastways, I suppose not, considering as you've embarked in the same venture as me."

"You suppose so?"

"Aye, aye. sir."

"Tell that to the marines. Joe," said Captain Deering. "sailors won't believe it. We all know what you believe. You know as well as possible that I only came up at the eleventh hour to take Captain Robinson's place when he was taken ill."

Nat laughed.

"When what?"

"When Captain Robinson was taken ill, I say."

"Ha, ha!" laughed Nat Cringle, grimly. "You know all about that, sir."

"What?"

"Why, about Captain Robinson's illness."

"I don't quite know what you are driving at, Nat," said Captain Deering.

There was a peculiar look in his eyes and a strange twang in his voice that told as plainly as possible that his suspicions were aroused by the sailor's manner.

"I'll tell you, Captain Deering." replied Nat. "I know, and you know too—leastways your honour ought to know—that Captain Robinson was about as ill as I am at this present moment."

"What?"

"Of course you know he was only shamming."

The skipper broke in indignantly at this.

"Do you know, Nat, what you are saying? Captain Robinson is one of my best and oldest friends."

"The devil he is!" said Nat Cringle. "Why, then, he ought to be keelhauled and have a round dozen, and be tarred and feathered and pitched overboard, the swab."

Nat Cringle's manner was so full of downright earnestness that the skipper could not mistake it.

"Do you really think, old shipmate," he said, earnestly, sinking his voice to a whisper, "that Captain Robinson——"

He paused.

He could not bring himself to put his thoughts into words.

Nat nodded.

"Yes, sir," he said, "that's just it. He knew well enough. It's all a game—a sort of play at life and death. They speculate with money for your life and for ours, and the best

news that they could hear would be that the rotten old 'Albatross' had gone to the bottom, and with her every mortal soul on board."

Captain Deering walked aft in great emotion.

After pacing the deck for several minutes he came back to where Nat Cringle stood, stock still, awaiting him.

"Nat Cringle," he said, earnestly, "we have sailed together often enough, and we have faced death too often together for there to be any deception or concealment between us."

"Aye, aye, sir."

"How came it that, knowing this, you are here?"

"Because I know very well," returned the old salt, with the same air of conviction that he had previously shown in his conversation with Jack and Harry Girdwood, "that nothing can hurt me—that, come weal, come woe, I shan't go to the bottom."

The skipper looked amazed at this declaration.

"Do you mean it?"

"Yes."

"You think that you bear a charmed life?"

"If you like to put it like that, your honour," returned the sailor, smiling, "I feel that I can't go down, else I shouldn't have come aboard the 'Albatross,' nor, in fact, any ship belonging to old Murray."

"I don't understand you quite, Nat."

"It's easy understood, cap'n," returned Nat Cringle, warming up on his favourite theme. "He gets hold of some rotten old hull that's been condemned, and dodges it up with paint and putty, and he gets a cargo in a strange port. Then he puffs it up and gets hold of a captain whose name is well known amongst the merchants and shippers, and so gets hold of passengers and cargo. The more passengers the better, you see. Well, he and Captain Robinson have worked this job together, and a nice bargain they've made of it. Captain Robinson never meant sailing in her, of course. He waits till the last moment, and then he gets hold of you."

Captain Deering here interrupted him with a boisterous exclamation.

"Do you know how he got hold of me, Nat Cringle?"

"No, sir."

"Then I'll tell you. I was in trouble up in London. I was in precious low water. My name was on a heavy bill for a poor devil who's gone queer, and they were going to nab me for it, to lodge me in limbo."

"The swabs."

"Well, I looked up my pals to help me through, and I thought of my old mate Robinson. He sent me word that he couldn't help me with money, that he was very ill, but that he could get me a ship at once, and start me off before the sharks could get scent of my whereabouts. Down I came on the sly and took ship."

"The mean, artful son of a sea-cook." ejaculated honest Nat Cringle.

"I begin to see clear now, Nat," said the skipper. thoughtfully : "and if I don't spoil their speculations, you can call me all the lubbers you can lay your tongue to."

Nat Cringle grew quite excited at this.

"Captain Deering, would your honour be offended at a suggestion?"

"Offended, Nat! There's no shame to any sailor, whatever his grade, in asking your advice, old comrade."

"Thank your honour. Well, then——"

"Your advice?"

"Put her about, and let us run for the nearest port. Have the British consul on board, and let the ship be surveyed. If Lloyds' agent gets over her after the straining she's undergone in this gale, she'll be condemned as sure as eggs is."

The skipper looked about him, and took an earnest survey of the weather signs.

"Nat Cringle," he said, clapping the old salt on the shoulder, "it shall be done. If the rotten 'Albatross' will hold together, we'll do them yet, by the Lord Harry."

CHAPTER XXIII.

A WRINKLE IN PUMPING—THE SOUNDING ROD—JACK READS THE OLDEST TAR ON BOARD A LESSON.

CAPTAIN DEERING had the men served with another allowance of grog.

And again he sang out the order so often heard in this short voyage—

"All hands pump ship!"

This time it was readily, if not quite cheerfully, obeyed.

As Nat Cringle said, the constant bending over the pumps strained their backs woefully.

"If I go on much longer," said another tar, ruefully, "damme if I shan't get as humpty-backed as King Dick in the play."

"There's a simple remedy for that, my men," said young Jack, promptly.

"What is it?"

"Rig up bell-ropes on to the pumps and you won't have to stoop."

"Bravo!"

They set to it at once.

A bell-rope is a short rope with a thimble, or iron ring spliced into one end.

The thimbles were slipped over the handles.

This done, the men tailed on to the ropes to pull the handles round.

By dint of this simple artifice the work was done quicker and better, and with half the fatigue.

When next they sounded the well, there was no abatement.

This naturally discouraged the men, who murmured ominously.

One old fellow, with grizzly hair and beard, dropped off, and swore a good round oath that he would work no more.

"She's settling," he said; and a look of dismay was seen upon most of the anxious faces present.

"I don't believe it."

"You don't believe it!" said the old fellow, fiercely. "What does a boy like you know about it? I tell you she's going down."

"I tell you, then, Norris," said young Jack, firmly, "she's doing no such thing; and if she were, why, that's no reason why you should desert your duty."

"More I don't," retorted the sailor, savagely, "only at the last gasp, and I mean to make a kick for it. As long as it's of use I was willing to pump; but now she's going down, I mean to save my breath, and not be so pumped."

Jack saw with a sinking heart that several of the men were about to follow the old sailor's example.

"Wait a bit, wait a bit," he exclaimed, eagerly, "and I'll soon show you that I'm right and he's wrong."

The old man grunted.

"Give him a chance, Norris," cried Nat Cringle. "Damme, give him fair play."

"Every time we've sounded the well for the last twenty-four hours," said young Jack, "it has gained upon us—slowly, very slowly, thanks to our hard struggle with it—yet none the less surely."

"It has."

"And that's cold comfort to give us," growled Norris.

"Well, the last time we sounded, it was stationary."

"What of that?"

"Stow your gaff!" interrupted Nat Cringle. "Damme, you're enough to make the Pope o' Rome swear. Don't you see what Master Harkaway is a-driving at?"

"No."

"Then you must ha' got your figger-'eds stuffed with sawdust instead of brains. Why, if it's a level fight now; or on last soundings, with the water, why, it's better than it was before, inasmuch and seeing as how it had us at a adwantage before."

"Nat Cringle has just said what I was trying to get at," said Jack. "Now listen."

"Aye, aye?"

"Let us have one more shy," said young Jack; "I'll take Norris's place, for we don't want any half-hearted coves this turn."

"And I'll take Marshall's," said Harry Girdwood.

"Bravo!" said one of the sailors.

The cheer was caught up readily, for the example of these plucky youngsters was the very thing to give a fillip to these poor worn-out sailors, and worn out they were and no mistake, every man of them.

"Now, Norris," said Jack, "you go and sound the well."

"Aye, aye, sir!"

In the course of a few moments back came old Norris with "a face as long as a fiddle," as one of the sailors remarked.

"A fiddle!" quoth Jack. "A bass-viol you mean."

At this they all laughed.

The old man gave his report with a precious lugubrious air.

It was somewhat serious, and Jack felt it to be so.

"Now then, mates," cried Nat Cringle; "no more palaver; but let's go in and give her a proper doing for a spell, and if we don't make the sounding-rod tell a warstly different tale in the splicing of a mainbrace, you may call me the darndest loblolliboy as ever smashed his grinders over a twel'month-old ship biscuit."

This made the men grin.

Young Jack struck up a snatch of an old song, slightly altered for the occasion—

> " 'Pull away merrily,
> Pull away cheerily,
> Send the pumps' fly-wheels all fast spinning round.
> Each try at the bell ropes,
> Heightens our well hopes,
> And the rod shall encourage us when next we sound.' "

The air was brisk and lively, and Jack's impromptu doggerel was more welcome to those hard-working tars than the Laureate's most polished stanzas would have been.

The men caught up the chorus all together.

The fly-wheels did go round as Jack sang.

"Hullo!" cried one of the sailors, "here comes old Norris again with his report."

"Jest look at his winegar mug," said another.

"Now, Norris."

"Speak up, man," said Jack.

"Out with it," cried a sailor, impatiently.

"What's the werdick?" said another.

"Well," says Norris, putting a plug of Cavendish into his cheek with aggravating deliberation, "this young fellow was right—I was wrong; and what's more, I'm not fool enough to be sorry to own myself licked by such a proper young cove."

"Bravo, Norris!"

But Norris, heedless of the approving cheer, only turned to Jack Harkaway.

"Give us your flipper, youngster," he said; "if you only live to be my age, you'll be able to take a rise out of any post-captain in the Royal Navy—aye, damme! and the port admiral into the bargain."

Jack grinned.

The men cheered.

"This is all right and proper, Norris," said Nat Cringle, who was not a little gratified with his crusty old shipmate's conduct; "but how about the well?"

"Why, you see, some folks——"

"Awast, Ned, awast," exclaimed Nat; "no yarn."

"Well, then, we've gained just four inches on her."

"Huzza!"

"Huzza!" yelled the men.

"Tune up again, Jack," cried Harry Girdwood, excitedly, "and let's have one more go."

> " 'Pull away merrily,
> Pull away cheerily——' "

"Hold 'ard, there," cried Norris, pulling young Jack away; "you take a turn at the sounding too, and let this d——d obstinate old grampus get back to his dooty."

*   *   *   *   *

Young Jack made three soundings, and reported each time.

The lad's manner seemed to fire the men with new energy every time he returned to report.

The third time he came back from sounding the well.

"How are we getting on?" cried the men eagerly.

"Why," answered Jack, grinning over his face, "you've sucked her dry as a bone. So

now I propose that we obey the good old maxim, and let well alone."

Never did these honest tars ever hear a joke so thoroughly to their tastes.

That done, Harry Girdwood made a proposition that was far from being distasteful to the crew.

"With Captain Deering's permission," he said, "I shall treat you all round to another go of grog."

"Hurrah!"

Harry went and asked permission, and what's more, he got it too.

"As you like, Mr. Girdwood," said the skipper, "but neither you nor Mr. Harkaway must ask me again to-day, for I couldn't refuse you anything. You are made of the right stuff that England's sailors are built of, and you've done more between you towards saving the 'Albatross' than any man aboard."

CHAPTER XXIV.

A BANQUET AFLOAT—"TOASTS AND SENTIMENTS"—MR. NERO IN THE CHAIR—MR. FIGGINS RESPONDS—HIS ACCIDENT WITH NERO—PANTOMIME WITH A MAMMOTH PIE—UNLUCKY BOGEY!

ALL work and no play makes Jack a dull boy.

Our Jack was a real good one to work, as we all know.

He could play, too.

Moreover, he could make others play, and enjoy his fun.

The carpenter and his mate were sent down below to the hold, to caulk and patch and trim the soft-wooded old carcase in the most dangerous places, before the water could gain upon her again, and while this was going forward, Jack and his chum, Harry Girdwood, entertained a select party, by special permission of the skipper, in their own cabin.

Jack stood treat.

It was not a very grand affair, but the honest tars thought it a banquet fit for the gods.

Jack now treated them, by the steward's aid, to a stewed rabbit and smoking hot potatoes, cooked in their jackets, some boiled pork, and pease pudding and other delicacies.

Some prime corned beef was on the festive board, too, and there was beer and grog to moisten it withal; so that the guests voted Jack a trump, and drank his health in bumpers round to an accompaniment of loud, ringing cheers.

Now amongst the company assembled to do honour to the occasion were the two young darkeys, Tinker and his "valet," Bogey, for much to Murray's and Chivey's disgust, they had by this time found out the ghostly trick played upon them by Jack's boy Tinker, but to tell the truth, they were both glad that Tinker was not killed.

Our faithful old friend Nero was seated in the place of honour, dressed in a glittering naval uniform and a grand cocked hat.

Nero did not take it for a laughing matter, we can assure you, but sat at the head of the table as grave and dignified as though he had been the lord high admiral himself.

"My Lord Nero," said Jack, filling his glass,

"DOWN FELL DISH, PIE, ORPHAN AND ALL."

"I drink to the health of the skipper, Captain Deering."

"Captain Deering!" shouted the sailor guests.

"Stop a bit, gentlemen," said Mr. Figgins, getting on his legs; "let's have Captain Deering with due honours."

"Three times three?"

"Aye, aye."

"No," cried Nat Cringle, "with nine times nine at the very least. Take the time from me, please, and all together—hip, hip, hip, hurrah!"

"Hurrah!"

"Hurrah!"

You would scarcely have thought it possible that they could be on board a ship which one and all had condemned so recently.

A ship which would, beyond all doubt, have gone down with skipper and crew, but for their manful and untiring exertions.

"And now a little one in," said Nat Cringle, waving his hand.

They responded, too, with a will, one and all.

> "For he's a jolly good fellow,
> For he's a jolly good fellow,
> For he's a jolly good fellow,
> And so say all of us,
> And so say all of us,
> And so say all of us,
> With a hip, hip, hurrah!"

And so forth, with a general chorus, *ad lib.*

Jack noticed that Nero had a knack of swinging his glass round, as he responded by gestures to the invitation to give a toast, watching all his master's movements with startling fidelity.

So he prepared.

"Charge your glasses," cried the orphan, in the pompous manner of a toast-master at a public banquet; "bumpers, gentlemen."

Jack had filled Nero's glass up, and then catching his eye, Jack waved his own glass, which was empty, round to the right, with a jerky air.

Nero followed suit.

Now Mr. Figgins was Nero's next-door neighbour, and the orphan received the contents of Nero's glass down his collar, and over his shirt front, and the glass, slipping from Nero's hand, struck the orphan in the face.

"Oh!"

"Hallo!"

"Murder!" yelled Mr. Figgins, springing up.

Nero grew frightened, and jumped on to the table at once, playing havoc with the dishes.

Mr. Figgins scrambled out of his seat, and made for the companion ladder.

But somehow or other he got the leg of a camp stool between his legs, and tripped up.

Nero jumped on his back in a jiffy, and the sailors laughed until the tears ran down their cheeks.

"Help!"

"Go it, Nero!"

"Murder! take the monster off."

"Keep it up, Nero! hi! hi!"

Nero wanted no inciting to mischief.

He was as playful as a kitten, and we verily believe that he understood fun as well as his friends and patrons generally.

"Help!" yelled Mr. Figgins; "he'll murder me!"

He grew desperate in his struggling, and scrambling to his feet, he tripped Nero over.

One desperate plunge, and he reached the stairs.

Three at a time he went up them.

But poor Mr. Figgins' troubles were not yet at an end.

At the foot of the stairs he encountered Bogey, who was descending with a huge sea-pie swimming about in a mammoth dish, full of smoking hot gravy.

The orphan was shooting up head forwards, and pressed down like an old goat butting an enemy, and he shot just under the sea-pie, and landed Bogey in the belly.

Bogey yelled.

"Oh, golly!"

Down fell the dish, pie, orphan and all—a regular smoking avalanche—that rolled along the orphan's back, while the stinging hot gravy found a channel for itself between his shirt collar and his flesh.

The result was that Mr. Figgins' underclothing was literally saturated with the luscious juice, which was unpleasantly warm.

Down he went the whole length of the cabin floor, considerably faster even than he had gone up the stairs.

Down flopped Bogey, plump into the orphan's stomach.

And up he got, "looking," as Nat Cringle said, "all ways for Sunday."

"Golly! what dis all mean?"

That was all that the astonished darkey could manage to iterate.

It had all been so sudden and unexpected.

"Oh!" groaned Mr. Figgins; "why did I leave my happy home on land to come to sea, and meet with such disasters—oh!"

The company literally yelled with delight.

Sailors are a rough lot, and there are few tars but relish practical joking.

Mr. Figgins, sitting up, with the gravy streaming down his hair and cheeks, presented such a ludicrous and deplorable figure, that it was no wonder that they laughed.

"Ha, ha, ha!"

"You may laugh," he said, ruefully, "but how would you like hot juice from a pie down your back? Just you answer me that."

"Capital!" ejaculated young Harkaway; "it must be nice."

"So sweet!" chimed in Harry Girdwood.

"But it was well done, Mr. Figgins," said Jack. "I had no idea you had got such spirits for a lark, sir."

"What!" cried the astounded Mr. Figgins. "A lark!"

"Yes. Why, you would have made an immense fortune, sir, as a harlequin in the pantomime."

"Give him a cheer."

They did, too.

"Do you mean to say," began the orphan at length, when he could succeed in obtaining a hearing, "that you think I did it for fun?"

"Of course you did," said Jack.

"But—but I assure you," began the orphan, "I——"

"Dat, sar," said Tinker, bowing at Mr. Figgins, " am awful gollopshus beastly fine lark ob yourn, sar.

> "Massa Figgins come down,
> And cracks his crown,
> And Bogey comes tumbling after.

Yah, yah, yah !"

Tinker's new version of Jack and Jill was highly applauded by one and all present.

"Dat all bery fine, Massa Figleaf," said Bogey, "but you spile dis chile's beauty."

"Bravo, Bogey !"

"And dis chile don't like it, sar, by golly, sar. Dis chile owe you one, Massa Figleaf, for dat—oh !"

"Hold your catawampus jaw, you ignorant nigger," cried Tinker, shying a hot and soft potato at his follower's head, "and listen to your s'perior hossifer ; Massa Figgins do it lubly bew'ful."

"Bravo for funny Figgins !"

"His health in a bumper round, messmates."

His health was then given with all due honours.

The poor orphan began to think that he was being made fun of.

*   *   *   *   *

"Mr. Harkaway."

"Hallo !"

"Wanted, sir."

"By whom ?"

"The captain."

"I'm there," responded young Jack, springing up.

He flew up the cabin stairs, and was with Captain Deering in half a crack.

"Sent for me, sir."

"Yes, Mr. Harkaway," said the skipper. "I'm sorry to break in upon your festivity, but duty——"

"Must be obeyed, sir," responded young Jack.

"Quite right," said the captain. "Well, then, the wind, I find, is freshening again."

"Hah !"

"Pass the word to Nat Cringle, and old—what-d'ye-call-him ?—to come up."

"Aye, aye, sir ?"

"We must keep her away. Clear away the fore-topsail," he suddenly sang out.

Then watching for a smooth chance, he gave the order to hoist away.

The sail quickly set.

The helm was put up, and the lee main braces—checked a foot or two, the object of this manœuvre being to ease the wind out of the topsail.

CHAPTER XXV.

FIGHTING WITH DEATH—A TOUGH STRUG-
GLE, AND BEATEN AFTER ALL—"LOOK TO
YOUR LIFE RAFT, AS SMART AS YOU LIKE !"

It was a moment—a good long one, by the way, of considerable anxiety to all.

It was no joke what Captain Deering was after now.

The danger of the movement precious soon made itself apparent.

The sea caught the ship abeam, and as it did so, a tremendous wave was seen curling up astern, rushing on in pursuit of the "Albatross" as if to engulf it.

Roaring like a hungry monster for its helpless prey, it came on.

"Hold fast !" yelled the captain ; "hold on for your lives, men, fore and aft."

Harry Girdwood and Jack, holding by each other, and with their disengaged hands grasping the nearest ropes they could clutch, were jerked so violently that their wrists were well-nigh dislocated, and it was marvellous indeed that they were not one and all swallowed up by the sea.

The only thing which saved the "Albatross" from instant destruction, was the fact of the bulwarks being washed away in pieces by the severity of the late gale.

The "Albatross" quivered from stem to stern !

However, as soon as the water found its way off the decks rapidly, the ship paid off quickly enough, and in the course of a few moments they were going along dead before the gale.

The force of the wind was felt much less, of course, than when they went head to it.

The sea, however, was very heavy.

Soon after this one monster wave came roaring after them astern like a mountain suddenly invested with life, and they saw that although there was not the same danger as in the previous visitation, there was a precious ugly shock to be anticipated.

It was a terrible shock this time.

Young Jack thought they were gone for a certainty.

Even old Nat Cringle avowed afterwards that he was in a thundering rage. Because why ? "He was going to get a lot more trouble to reach shore safe and sound than he had bargained for"—not that his faith in his wonderful good luck deserted him even then !

The sheets were now hauled aft, and the foresail had been loosed, and the ship shot faster through the water.

The whole topsails were now set and matters looked more promising.

Once more they had, by the prompt and skilful seamanship of the skipper, escaped a deadly peril.

But there was no rest for the hard-worked crew.

"Pump ship !" sang out the first mate ; "all hands pump ship !"

"That's a good thing," growled Nat Cringle, with an oath.

"You're right there, Nat," said a voice at his elbow.

Nat turned round.

"Ax pardon, Captain Deering," said the old salt with a grin, "but I should like to be wrung out fust."

"Help keep this old sponge afloat, Nat Cringle," said the skipper, with a fierce air of determination, "and you shall get wrung out."

"I ain't afeard——"

"Quite right," said Captain Deering, with a smile, "but help keep the ship afloat, Nat, for the sake of the rest of them, and for——"

"For what ?"

"To help pay off old scores with the owner, old Murray."

"I will, sir."

"And my friend, Captain Joe Robinson."

"Damme, that I will!" said Nat Cringle, heartily.

From that moment old Nat was all over the ship.

Lending one a hand here, and encouraging the half-drowned, shivering crew there by his cheery voice and valuable assistance.

* * * * *

"What do you think of matters now, Captain Deering?"

The speaker was our young hero, Jack Harkaway.

"It'll take us all our time to pull through unless we sight land within a reasonable time."

"Hah!"

It was enough to make the listener say "hah!"

The ship laboured and groaned ominously.

There was no possible doubt about the peril.

But the danger was not immediate.

Good seamanship and incessant labour at the pumps kept her afloat.

But Captain Deering had told those to whom he could safely entrust his views—that it was but a question of time.

"We may yet pull through," he said, "if we sight land soon, or if we fall in with assistance and get towed into port."

Eagerly they scanned the horizon with their glasses.

All in vain.

Not the faintest speck in sight wherever they looked.

* * * * *

"Nat, captain wants you."

"Aye, aye, sir."

Nat Cringle ran up on deck to the skipper.

Captain Deering was looking anxiously ahead, and so engrossed with his observations, that he did not hear the old tar's approach.

"Here I am, sir."

"What do you think now, Nat?"

"Well, I think——"

"Out with it, Nat; no palavering with me, you know."

"Well, then, I think as it's as nigh all up with the 'Albatross' as it well can be."

The skipper sighed.

"Just my notion, Nat," he said; "not that I'm going to give in yet awhile; only let us be prepared."

"Aye, aye, sir."

"For the sake of the passengers, if not for ourselves, get the ship's carpenter, and see what you can get together between you towards fixing up a big life raft."

"Yes, sir."

"That with the boats will perhaps enable us to save all."

"Perhaps, sir."

"But, hang the thieves, they'll get the insurance money then," growled the skipper.

"Not sure yet, your honour," said Nat; "let's make ourselves sure first, and then have a turn at the rotten old hull again."

"How's the well?"

"Mortal bad."

"So I feared; so look to your raft as smart as you like."

CHAPTER XXVI.

THE HARKAWAYS AT HOME—OLD JACK'S TROUBLE—THE VISIT FROM OVER THE SEA—AN UNLUCKY POSTMAN—YOUNG JACK HARKAWAY'S LAST WORDS.

WE will now return for a short time to our old friends at home.

Matters went badly with the Harkaways.

When we say the Harkaways, we mean the family ashore, and not the son and heir of the house, whom we left afloat in a coffin ship.

Not a word of information could old Jack or his friends glean to give them a hope for their darling boy's safety.

"I have behaved like a fool, Dick, for allowing my bold boy to go in that coffin ship," he would say again and again to his faithful old friend and companion, Harvey.

And it was in vain that Dick Harvey essayed to condole with, and comfort him.

"You are too hard upon yourself, Jack," Dick returned, firmly. "You acted upon cool judgment, and if you have been deceived, the fault is certainly not yours."

Harkaway and his friend Dick had just finished their walk and cigar, when they were met at the door of the house by Mrs. Harkaway.

"Oh, Jack, look at this," she said, pointing to a paragraph in the newspaper she held.

"I'll come in and read it," said old Jack; "there's no urgent reason for reading it in the street, my dear, I suppose."

"It is not a matter for smiling at, Jack," she returned.

Impressed by her manner, Harkaway took the paper, and ran his eyes down the paragraph indicated.

It was headed thus—

"MISSING SHIPS.

"The 'Albatross' has not been heard of since she sailed, on the 13th inst. This vessel has lately passed into the hands of Mr. Murray, whose bad fortune with his vessels has been a general theme for gossip of late in the shipping world. Strange rumours have been circulating about her. The owner, however, was fully insured."

The paper fell from old Jack's hand.

"Fully insured!" he gasped. "It is impossible!"

"It must be another vessel of the same name," said Harvey. "I know Murray told us that his vessels were so good he never insured."

"Look here, Jack," said Mrs. Harkaway, with a startling voice; "Murray has played us false, and I fear our poor boy is in sore peril. Oh, husband, where's our Jack?"

At this juncture a newsboy went past with a flaming placard in his hand.

"Fearful shipwreck and loss of life! All hands perished! Full and particular account —price——"

"Emily!"

Harkaway just turned round in time to catch her as she fell in a death-like swoon into his arms.

The strain on young Jack's mother's nerves was too great—she had fainted.

Some few days after the above events, a sailor came to the house to inquire for old Jack, and the latter, who was seated smoking a pipe with Harvey and Mr. Mole, gave orders to have the sailor admitted.

"You want me," said old Jack with a look of surprise.

"We picked up a bottle, yer honour," said the tar, "and inside we found a letter that was directed to you, so as soon as we got within sight of land, the captain sent me ashore with it. I made inquiries, and——"

"Where's the bottle?"

"Here."

From the cracked bottle he drew forth a letter, and handed it to Harkaway.

Mole looked at Dick, and Dick looked at Jack.

The latter had grown as pale as a sheet.

"Take something to drink, shipmate," said Harvey to the sailor; "there's brandy in that bottle; serve yourself."

Old Jack tore the letter open.

"Stop a bit," said Mr. Mole, jumping up and clapping his hand over the letter; "just take a suck at the bottle first."

Old Jack took a stiff glass of brandy, and read.

"Ha!"

The paper fell from his hands, and he sank back with a groan of anguish.

"Jack," cried poor Harvey, springing forward, and catching his old comrade in his arms, "Jack, old friend, don't—don't take on so. What is it?"

But Harkaway could not answer.

Dick picked up the letter and read.

This was young Jack's letter, which he had committed to the waves in a time of deadly peril,

"MY DEAR FATHER AND MOTHER.—The 'Albatross' is what they call a coffin ship, and we are near the end of a precious hard fight for life. Forgive your poor Jack for being so pig-headed as to insist upon leaving you, and don't waste time in regretting and mourning after Harry and I; but seek out that old Murray, and that hypocritical Captain Robinson. Take one each, dad, you and Uncle Dick, and give them a thundering good larrupping, and when you have knocked them both into a good jelly, seek out some influential man in the Great Talking House, and get him to lift his voice to get this scandalous state of things reformed. Here we are, I cannot tell you how many of us passengers and crew, all sent afloat in a rotten old tub, painted and caulked up spruce, and puffed up to impose upon poor, ignorant fools. Now, we're not gone yet, but it looks unpleasantly like going, and so in case the law can't reach these dealers in human life, I leave them to you and to Uncle Dick. I hope to come back yet, and so does Harry, who sends his love to all, if we don't. Good-bye, perhaps for ever, dear father and mother.

"JACK."

Young Jack's letter was finished rather abruptly.

His father guessed that some calamity had overtaken the ship.

But it was not so.

The simple reason was that he and Harry had been summoned by an alarm to the deck, and fearing that they might not have another chance of posting their missive, it was placed in its bottle and dropped overboard.

*   *   *   *   *

When they had finished reading the letter, Mr. Mole was observed to grow very fidgety and red in the face.

He stumped up and down the room, thrusting his hands viciously into his pockets, and dragging them out again—and then cracking his knuckles with small reports, like Barcelonas going pop!

"I don't feel very well, Jack," he said, blowing his nose hard to disguise his emotion; "I—I—in fact I shall go for a walk—good night, I mean morning, I—I'm going to bed at once."

And with this somewhat confused valediction, Mr. Mole glided quickly out of the room.

Jack stared at Dick, Dick stared at Jack.

"What's the matter with poor old Mole?" said Harvey.

Old Jack shook his head and tapped his forehead significantly.

"Going. Yes!"

"So I think."

"I think that this dreadful news has done it for the poor old fellow; he was so fond of Jack."

"I verily believe," said old Jack, wrestling with his grief. "I verily believe he would give every farthing he has in the world for those two wild boys to be here and play off their cruel practical jokes at his expense."

"I am sure he would," said Dick.

The conversation flagged now for several minutes.

"Jack."

"Dick."

"The boys have left us a legacy to punish the villains Murray and Robinson."

"I'll tell you what," said Harkaway, "you shall take charge of old Murray, and I'll look after the welfare of jovial Captain Robinson."

"Agreed."

The two friends grasped hands in silence.

Thus the compact was sealed, and now woe betide jovial Captain Robinson and the ship-owner, whenever Harkaway or Dick Harvey should come across them.

"Jack," said Harvey, coolly, "you brought home from Australia with you, a short-handled stock-whip, with a thick leather thong?"

Old Jack started.

"You don't mean to say that you will use that on the villain?"

"That's just exactly what I do mean," said Harvey.

"It shall be at your service, Dick."

So Harkaway went for the stock-whip.

If Mr. Murray could but have overheard the conversation, he would not have felt very easy in his mind.

Altogether matters looked rather ugly for him.

CHAPTER XXVII.

ARTFUL MOLE—MOLE THE EXECUTOR—HIS SINGULAR PRESENT FOR MR. MURRAY—A NOVEL DUEL—SHARP WORK—MR. MURRAY TASTES THE BITTERS HIS PROFESSION.

ISAAC MOLE went to his room and got out a pistol case. He was engaged in loading his six-shooter when his wife crept into the room.

"Evins an' erf, Ikey!" she ejaculated aghast, "what you doing thar?"

Mr. Mole looked up a bit startled, but went on loading the revolver.

"Ask no questions, my dear." he answered, "but fetch me my walking stick."

Chloe, considerably flurried, hastened to obey her lord and master.

"Which walking stick?"

Mr. Mole paused to reflect.

It was a weighty matter, and demanded reflection, for he had a regular collection of walking canes, and it was necessary for his purpose to get a good pliable stick.

"Let it be the Malacca cane, with the gold top," he said.

She returned with it in a few moments.

"Where you goin' to, Ikey?" she demanded.

"That, my dear, concerns me alone," replied Mr. Mole. "Have the goodness, for once in your life, to repress your curiosity."

"Bress my 'art——!" began the dark lady.

"Repress your curiosity," said Mr. Mole again, "for I haven't the remotest intention of telling you where I am going, or what for."

"But, Ikey——"

"Good-bye for the present, my dear; I shall in all probability return for dinner."

"I say, now, Ikey——"

But he was gone.

And very soon was knocking at Mr. Murray's door.

"Mr. Murray."

"Yes, sir."

"Take my card," said Mr. Mole, "and my compliments. I should like to have a word with him."

The maid servant went to her master, but shortly returned to say, that Mr. Murray was very particularly engaged just then, and would accept an appointment for another time, if Mr. Mole could conveniently defer his business.

"That is precisely what I can't do," returned the old gentleman. "Will you go back to Mr. Murray, therefore, and tell him that I have something for him?"

Back went the girl, and returned in a few moments.

"Master's compliments, sir, and if you would send it in by me, he would take it as a favour."

Mr. Mole smiled.

An odd smile it was—yet still a smile—of a kind.

"I can't," he said, shaking his gold-headed Malacca cane nervously as he spoke. "I must hand it to Mr. Murray personally."

This carried the day.

Mr. Mole was ushered into the shipowner's presence forthwith.

Mr. Murray sat in an armchair, before an office table, which was covered with business books and papers.

He looked up, and rose as Mr. Mole entered. But Mr. Mole had his back turned. He was apparently engaged in shutting the door after the servant.

Mr. Murray did not observe that his visitor not only shut the door, but also locked it, and pocketed the key.

"Good morning, Mr. Mole," said the shipowner; "you will excuse my refusal to see you at first, sir, but I have been ill for some considerable time, and the accumulation of business matters during that time has driven me into a corner. I cannot get the arrears of work under at all."

"I shall not detain you long," returned Mr. Mole.

"Take a seat, sir."

Mr. Mole declined.

"What I have to do is best done standing."

"My servant informs me you have brought something for me?" said the shipowner.

"Quite right."

"I am much beholden to you for the pains you have taken," said Mr. Murray.

Mr. Mole smiled.

"I have taken no pains, Mr. Murray," he answered; "it is you who will have to take the pains."

"What is it you have brought for me, may I ask?"

Mr. Mole held up the gold-headed Malacca. "This!"

"Excuse me, sir," said Mr. Murray, in his blandest tone, "but I don't quite see, even now——"

"Don't you?" said Mr. Mole, "then I will explain."

He drew a step nearer to the shipowner.

The latter shrank back instinctively.

"I am, as you are doubtless aware, the personal friend of Mr. Harkaway, and was tutor of his son, who has gone a voyage in the 'Albatross.'"

Mr. Murray winced.

"A fine ship, the 'Albatross,' sir, A 1 at Lloyds', I believe."

"Yes, sir," returned Mr. Murray, in an unsteady voice.

"Of course," said Mr. Mole, in the same strain, "a gallant craft, and you are a happy man to possess such a vessel."

Mr. Murray could not stand this.

"You will excuse the question," he said in a hard voice that had no ring in it, "but is this the object of your visit, sir?"

"Patience, Mr. Murray, patience, and you will learn."

"I must really——"

"No, you mustn't!" interrupted Mole.

"Really, I——"

"Sir," quoth Mr. Mole emphatically, and banging down the gold-headed Malacca cane between each word, on the shipowner's writing table, as if to give extra force to his speech, "I must tell my business in my own way. I say, then, that the 'Albatross' is a noble craft—'noble craft!' is the word I believe—so expressive—so romantic—so jolly Jack Tar-ish!—not a bit of a coffin ship!"

The shipowner started back.

"How dare you?" he began. "How dare you come here?"

"I came to bring you a present," said Mr. Mole, as cool as ever. "The noble craft has gone to the bottom—the gallant 'Albatross' is lying in goodness knows how many fathoms, or exactly where, but from all report, not a long way from the Bay. of Biscay."

Mr. Murray poured out a tumbler of water, and drank it off.

The interview grew warm, and he was silent.

"My murdered boy—stand still and hear me out," added Mole, sternly, "or by the Lord Harry I'll make an example of you! My murdered boy, I say—the brave young Jack found time as the 'Albatross,' was going down, to write a letter—his will I may call it—telling all he knew, all he had learnt on board since sailing, and as he was dropping into the watery grave to which you consigned him——"

"Sir!"

"He had learnt, too late, alas! the exact nature of the trade which you pursue."

"I don't understand what you mean."

"You soon will."

Mr. Murray detected something in old Mole's voice which raised dire misgivings.

So he stretched out his hand to reach the bell-rope. But before he could accomplish his purpose, Mr. Mole hopped over and brought down the gold-headed Malacca a very smart rap on his knuckles.

"Oh!"

"Stand still."

Mr. Murray bridled up at this, and stepped forth.

While only menaced with scandal, he was filled with the greatest fear.

But now that the visitor grew more demonstrative yet, his sensations changed.

He was not to say physically a coward.

Moreover, Isaac Mole with his venerable appearance, and his two wooden legs, did not look a very formidable antagonist.

"If you don't instantly quit my house," he said, shaking his fist at the visitor, "I shall put you out of the window."

"Oh, you will?"

"I will."

Mole smiled.

"That is something better," he said quietly; "up till now, you have shown that you are only possessed of the assassin's brutal instincts without having anything of such kind of courage as many of the worst murderers are known to possess."

"Scoundrel!"

"It is, at any rate," pursued Mr. Mole, who declined to be flurried under any pretext whatever, "it is at any rate refreshing to find you have a dash of something like a man in you for Jack's present—this is old Jack's present," he added, giving the walking stick a parenthetical flourish; "it is an honest good cane, and I should not like to dirty it by contact with anything so utterly degraded as I feared you would prove."

Mr. Murray grew livid.

"You, you——"

"Gently, gently," said Mr Mole, "and I'll prove myself your best friend."

"Infamous old ruffian," cried Mr. Murray.

"Thank you, I'll prove it. Jack's legacy was to have been brought by his father; I wanted the office for two reasons; first, because I looked upon it as my privilege and my right; secondly, I want you to have half a chance—we are both old men, and in addition I am a cripple, as you see; now that equalises matters, but if Mr. Harkaway had brought you his son's legacy, you would never have crossed that threshold alive!"

"So," said Mr. Murray, very white yet very determined, "assassination is your intention."

"No, punishment only," responded Mole.

"Oh!"

"Your villany may not prove get-at-able by law—may not, I say—we have to try that yet. So for fear of a miscarriage of justice, I am here to fulfil my dear, murdered boy's dying injunctions, and believe me, Mr. Murray," added the old gentleman with an odd mixture of satire and pathetic earnestness as he held out the cane, "the finest advocate in the world could never wheedle Jack's legacy into believing you were guiltless."

"You are mad!"

Mr. Mole turned up his wristband.

"We are wasting time."

"Leave the house!" exclaimed Mr. Murray, "or I'll have you dragged off to gaol——"

He slipped to the door and turned the handle.

It was fast.

"Locked!"

"As you see, my dear sir," responded Mole, quite pleasantly.

"Where's the key?"

"I have got it."

"Give it up, or——"

He made one stride up to Mole, who raised the cane.

Down it came, cutting the air with the most vicious music, and it left its mark across the shipowner's forehead and face.

Staggered for a moment, Mr. Murray made a rush at his assailant.

But the old gentleman, as cool as a cucumber still, whirled round upon one of his wooden legs, and seized Murray by the coat collar with the left hand, while with the right he banged away at his shoulders and back.

A dozen strokes were put in thus with such vigour and rapidity, that Mr. Murray was fain to wriggle himself free, and stagger across the room.

But Isaac Mole would not be denied.

He stumped after his man as fast as he could, and dropped in another or two wherever he could.

One smart cut across the face brought blood, and the shipowner, in the space of a minute, presented a very alarming aspect.

But Mr. Mole never paused to consider this.

Murray was now getting very badly punished, and it was necessary to take a serious step.

He took it.

Feinting to dart to the door, he made a sudden rush at his writing table, and dragged open one of the drawers.

Mole was after him.

Only the table between them, and he saw what it was that the shipowner was after.

He saw his hand upon a pistol, and so he whipped out his own revolver, and stretching ever the table, he thrust it into Mr. Murray's face.

"Put down that pistol," he said, in low, earnest tones ; "put it down, or I'll blow you to atoms."

Mr. Murray paused.

"Put it down, I say," replied Mole ; "in three seconds you are a dead man else—hah !"

The shipowner cowered before that revolver.

Death was unpleasantly near, and few men can face it in such proximity with anything like calmness.

He dropped the pistol.

"Shut the drawer," said Mole, sternly. "If you use firearms, so shall I, and I have first shot. I provided against such an emergency as this."

"Assassin !" gasped the shipowner.

"Not I," returned Mole, "I am poor young Jack's executor, nothing more. Lock the drawer—throw over the key, do you hear ?"

With a scowl of undying hate the shipowner complied reluctantly.

"Now I put by my pistol," said Mole, suiting the action to the word, "and we resume the thrashing."

He walked round the table after his man.

Mr. Murray waited a little.

Then he shot away.

Mole stumped after him.

Murray looked about him anxiously.

Then his glance resting upon the fire-place, he dodged a vicious cut which Mole aimed at him, and pounced upon the poker.

"Now, you old vagabond !" he said, or rather hissed serpent fashion, "we are equal."

"Not quite," said Mole, "you have a bit of the advantage ; no matter."

It was truly a most extraordinary sight.

Two men, well on in years, one with a pair of wooden legs, facing each other, armed with weapons of a more or less offensive description. It looked awkward for Mole.

Very.

A poker against a walking-cane was no fair match.

Mole had his revolver to the good, it is true, but he would not use it.

Moreover, the shipowner felt assured that he had to do with a man of his word.

So his courage rose as he advanced to meet his wooden-legged adversary.

"You shall suffer now, you villanous old ruffian !" he exclaimed.

"Indeed !" replied Mr. Mole, coolly.

The old gentleman kept a sharp look-out, and just as the shipowner drew back to deal him a desperate blow with the poker, Mr. Mole dropped in such a stinger upon Murray's hand that the poker fell from his grasp, and the knuckles were cut open.

"Now for it."

Mole pounced upon his man, and showered down such a succession of blows, that Murray, stunned, confused, and pounded into a jelly, could not offer the feeblest resistance.

"Take that," cried the infuriated Mole, pounding away, vigorously, "and that—and that, and I wish I had more wind left in me to—stay, here's one more for poor Harry Girdwood."

It was but one.

But such a one.

It seemed to lay the unhappy's man's back bare.

"And now," said Isaac Mole, readjusting his disordered dress, "I'll go home to dinner."

"You'll suffer for this," groaned the shipowner.

"That's doubtful," returned Mole ; "but there is no doubt in life that you will. Let me give you a word of advice. Keep clear of Mr. Harkaway ; I have been merciful."

Murray groaned.

"But he will have no mercy on his son's destroyer. Keep yourself under lock and key. Do you hear? For once let John Harkaway or Richard Harvey get within arm's length of you, and Heaven have mercy upon your miserable carcase. They are both young and vigorous men, not miserable old cripples, like yours obediently, Isaac Mole."

He fished out the key and opened the door.

"Don't you think to escape like that," moaned the shipowner, crawling to the bell.

"Nor you either," returned Mole, turning round, "for we mean to have the very best law that is to be bought for money, to pepper you with, and we'll see if you haven't a part more vulnerable than your body. I mean your pocket."

He went out.

But as he closed the door, an idea occurred to him, and so he pushed open the door and popped in his head.

"Your accomplice, Captain Robinson, has turned king's evidence," he said.

This was not to say the downright truth, as you know.

Yet it served for a parting shot at Mr. Murray.

With which, Mr. Mole stumped back to dinner, happy in his mind and with a ravenous appetite.

CHAPTER XXVIII.

MR. MURRAY'S MISFORTUNES—THE DOOR CHAIN—ANOTHER VISITOR FOILED—"LOOK TO IT, FOR I AM ON THE WATCH."

MR. MURRAY arose from the floor, bruised and bleeding.

Isaac Mole had piled it on pretty stiffly, and his arm fell heavily.

What was to be done ?

He would seek assistance in the town.

It would be better for him to have a sturdy man servant always upon the premises, so that if any of the Harkaway people should venture again to intrude upon him, he would be prepared to meet violence with violence.

Mr. Murray opened the door, and found himself face to face with a servant maid.

"Jane !"

"Yes," said the girl. "Are you ill again, sir ?"

"No."

"I thought I heard you call out, sir."

Mr. Murray stammered out something confusedly, and grew very flushed in the face.

"No, no, Jane, I am well enough—that is better—I am better, Jane, only pay attention to me, Jane."

" Yes, sir."

" If anyone comes to ask for me, don't admit them until I have given you orders."

" No, sir, I'll show them into the parlour, and say I'll see if you are visible or not, sir."

" No, no, no!" exclaimed the shipowner, eagerly, " you are wrong, Jane ; that is precisely what you must not do, Jane."

" What then, sir ?"

" Keep the chain up always."

" That's odd, sir."

" Hold your tongue!" exclaimed Mr. Murray, testily, " and make no reflections upon the orders I give you. Keep the chain up."

" Lor', yes, sir !"

" So that you can always keep anybody out if you don't choose to admit them. Once for all, attend to that, for I don't choose to have a parcel of insolent beggars forcing their way in and insulting me in my own house."

" I shall know that wicked old sinner ag'in, sir," pursued Jane, mentally denouncing poor old Mole ; " he's got nothing out of you, I suppose, so most likely he'll try on the seaman who was blown up, or the respectable mechanic who was whirled up on a saw mill, or, in fact, anything just to change his luck when he has his next turn ; though, I'll bet you've rayther troubled him for one while, by the way you have given it to him this time, and—bless me !"

" What is it ?" exclaimed Mr. Murray, with a start.

" You've tore your coat."

" Bah ! what of that ?"

" Nothing much, for you can get lots more ; only it's a pity to waste good clothing over such a old villain as that was ; that's all I think, sir, and—oh, Lor' !"

" What now ?"

" You've got a bruise on your face, sir."

" Hold your tongue. Bear in mind what I have told you about that door chain."

Saying which, Mr. Murray turned back into the room, and slammed-to the door.

Mr. Murray surveyed himself in a glass.

Unpleasant reflection in two senses of the expression.

His face was bruised.

His coat was torn.

Moreover, his general appearance was disordered, as well it might be by the violence of the late encounter.

Mr. Murray renovated himself at once.

A touch with the comb, a change of garments, and a little vinous stimulant steadied his nerves a bit.

" The first thing will be to get round to Harris, and make him provide me with a good big fellow as a body-guard."

He was about to remove the chain and go forth, when a knock came at the door that made him jump.

A rat-tat-tat !

Mr. Murray started back as the tall figure of a man stood in the doorway.

He recognised him, too, immediately.

Harvey !

Yes, Dick Harvey was prompt to perform his part of his contract with old Jack.

Little did he suppose that he had been forestalled.

How could he, or anyone, in fact, expect Isaac Mole to turn champion ?

Dick had been engrossed in thought after knocking, or he would have perceived that the door was open.

He gave it a push, but the chain held it fast.

" Hallo !"

Dick thrust his head in, and looked round, to find himself face to face with the very man he had come to see.

" Mr. Murray."

" I'm out," exclaimed the shipowner ; " I'm not well, and I can't see anybody."

" I'll not detain you long," said Dick, coaxingly.

" No, no ; of course not."

" One word."

" What is it ?"

" Let down the chain," said Dick.

" Impossible ; it will not come undone."

This exasperated Dick, who lost his coolness.

" You lying old villain. Can't face me, I suppose ?"

" Be off."

" You know what I come for."

" I do," retorted Murray ; " and if you are not off, I will call a policeman and have you given in custody."

" I'll wait," said artful Dick, " if you like to come out and make the charge."

" Not I," returned the shipowner ; " I'll watch until a policeman passes, and give orders, that's what I'll do."

This would not suit Dick.

" Very well, Mr. Murray," he said, " very well. Since that is your notion, I can afford to wait my opportunity."

" Wait then—wait," retorted the shipowner, " and let me caution you. I mean to invoke the law."

" You dare not," said Dick, " you dare not, and you know it. What you say is mere idle brag. Hark you, old man. If there is any justice in Providence, you will have to go afloat in a coffin ship yourself, and go down with it—experience yourself the horrors of drowning. When I hear that that has been your fate, I can perhaps forgive you. But while you are on dry land, look to your miserable self. I am on the watch."

*   *   *   *   *

" A telegram for you, sir," said the maid-servant, entering the shipowner's room.

" How you startled me," exclaimed Mr. Murray ; " there, that'll do."

He tore open the telegram, and read it down.

His face turned ashy pale, and he gasped at the sight of that paper.

And yet the news it brought was the most welcome news that he could possibly have desired.

" Here is that which would gladden the hearts of those Harkaway people if I took it to them. But no ; let them pine and languish in bitterness of spirit as I have done. That will teach them not to try on their villany again. The assassins ! No man ever yet affronted me with impunity. I'll keep it to myself, and I'll be off at once—aye, this very night, if I can get **away** from this port."

The news contained in that telegram would indeed have gladdened the Harkaways.

But before we give the reader the information upon this head, let us return to follow the fortunes of young Jack and his comrade Harry Girdwood.

CHAPTER XXIX.

THE FATE OF THE "ALBATROSS"—FOUNDERED IN FAIR WEATHER—"MAN THE BOATS"—THE ROLL CALL—THE OWNER'S SON AND HIS MAN—A POOR ORPHAN AND THE NEW BREAKFAST RELISH—OVERBOARD.

AND did the wretched old "Albatross" go down?

No.

Thanks to the admirable seamanship of her commander and to the perseverance and undying energy of the crew, to which they were in no slight degree stimulated by the example of young Harkaway and Harry Girdwood, the "Albatross" weathered the gale.

It was a precious near squeak with her.

They ran for the Spanish coast, and once they had sighted land, they never ceased firing minute guns, and they hoisted signals of distress.

They fortunately attracted attention pretty soon, and assistance was promptly rendered.

The passengers and crew were for the most part landed in other boats, but Captain Deering stuck to his post, as did young Jack.

"Let me be here while there's one plank holding to another," he said; "not that I bear the worm-eaten old hull any love, only she mustn't go down without a very big effort. I'll see her in port—aye, in dock, and have her condemned properly. Let the owners pay the piper now. They have had their sport with her and a lot of brave fellows; the owners must pay for all the work they have given us, and all the fears and qualms that we have gone through—aye, the stoutest hearts on board."

We leave you to guess how this speech was received.

A ringing cheer of assent greeted it.

And the men within earshot gathered round the skipper, more eager than ever to save the "Albatross."

They did it, too.

They worked her into a Spanish port, and then they had an official visit and examination made, the result of which was that she was condemned to be broken up.

All this was not without its effect upon young Murray, who insisted on being landed with his servant, and the ship proceeding on her journey.

But he protested in vain.

What authority had he in the matter?

It was all very well for him to say that he was the son of the owner, but he had shipped in an assumed name, and although it was pretty generally known who he was, Captain Deering professed to doubt his story *in toto*.

"You see," said the skipper, when the general inquiry was commenced before the British consul, "what he says may or may not be true,

but we ain't bound to believe a young fellow who on his own showing has shipped under false colours."

Young Murray used violent language and threatened everybody concerned, until Captain Deering frightened this style of conduct out of him by a hint at putting him in irons.

"I'll tell you what, sir," said Chivey. "You had better telegraph over to the governor, and let him get to work, or it'll be all U P with the 'Albatross,' in a brace of shakes."

"I will."

"Double quick, sir."

"Right, Chivey."

He telegraphed accordingly, and then he felt easier in his mind.

A letter was dispatched after his telegram, and this letter made his father much easier in his mind, knowing now his son was safe.

It lifted a weight of care off that unscrupulous man's mind.

It was more than he deserved, to be thus relieved, all things considered.

* * * * *

Now while the condemned "Albatross" lay off the harbour, the chief care of the captain and of those in authority was to remove the cargo, and they forgot all about the pumps.

The consequence of this may be imagined.

One night, when they had just turned in, young Jack, who was uncommonly sleepy, was aroused by Harry Girdwood with a very uncomfortable announcement.

"Hark, hark, Jack!"

"What?"

"The sound of rushing waters."

"Listen again."

Jack aroused himself with a bit of an effort, and sure enough he did catch the sound of rushing water.

"What does it mean?" demanded young Jack.

"Why, I'll tell you what," returned Harry. "The rushing sound of waters means the ship 'Albatross' is going down to her grave."

Young Jack sat bolt upright in his berth at this.

"I believe you're right, Harry. The coffin-ship is doomed, but, thank the Lord, not in mid-ocean."

He glided out of the berth and slipped on his trousers in less than a minute.

"I'm off on deck, old boy; come along."

And suiting the action to the word, he flew up the companion ladder.

Harry Girdwood was not slow to follow on deck.

"Whose watch is it?" demanded Harry, as he appeared on deck.

"Mackenzie's, your honour," was the reply.

"Where is he?"

"Below."

"He's a fine officer to set an example."

The rushing sound of water became louder and louder.

"I'll rouse the skipper," said Jack.

"Right, Jack; be quick."

Young Jack soon had Captain Deering upon deck.

The skipper was a thorough sailor, and he took in the whole situation at a single glance.

"Who is the officer of the watch?" he demanded.

"Mr. Mackenzie, sir," replied a sailor.

"Where is he?"

"Below."

"Call him up."

"He ain't exactly fit to come, your honour," was the reply.

"What?"

"He's took too much spirit in his water, your honour."

The skipper frowned.

"I'll make an example of Mackenzie."

However, it was waste of time and of words to take any more notice about him just then.

"Pipe all hands."

Nat Cringle came up now and made his way to the side of Captain Deering with considerable alacrity.

"We haven't got many minutes, your honour," he said, "before the 'Albatross' will swallow up every stick and scrap as she goes down."

"We must be smart then," cried the captain.

"Aye, aye, sir."

"All hands to the boats."

The order was given.

Now the "Albatross" was well manned and excellently ordered—far better than such a rotten old hulk ever deserved to be; and everything was got about with the quiet discipline that one might expect to observe on board a man-of-war.

A boat was lowered and filled rapidly.

"Pull ashore," cried the captain, through his trumpet, "pull smart, and two of you bring the boat back at racing pace; we may want you."

"Aye, aye, sir."

The orders were given promptly enough.

Captain Deering told off the different persons to the boats, and all went very well until young Murray and his man Chivey, who were anxiously awaiting the calling out of their names, caused some confusion by pressing forward.

For there were still a score or more of passengers on board.

"Stand back," exclaimed the skipper sternly, "or you shall remain till the last on board this sinking ship. Stand back, I say."

"But, captain——" began Herbert Murray.

"Utter a word, or do anything to impede us now," returned Captain Deering, "and I'll have you thrown overboard."

"Oh, what a orful beast," said Chivey.

But he had spoken just a shade too loud, and it was overheard by one of the horny-fisted tars, who gave the tiger what he called an admonisher, but what Chivy designated "a back hander on the smeller, that put my two peepers into mournin'."

"Stand back, stand back," cried the second mate; "keep the gangway clear."

Mr. Figgins, who had been awaiting his turn with what patience he could muster, anxiously looked around at them for help.

He tried to quiet himself at such a critical moment, and put on an appearance of calm.

He nodded at the skipper, and smiled in the sickliest manner imaginable, and tried endless artifices to call the captain's attention.

But no use.

No one took any notice of him.

Captain Deering went steadily on, calling out the names one after the other, and got everything much more forward by his quiet, calm manner of going to work than any excitement or bustle could possibly have done.

"Ahem!" said Mr. Figgins, at length, "I am not very well, I thank you, captain—I am still here."

"Barclay!"

"Here."

"I am on deck, you see," murmured the orphan. "My name is Figgins, sir, and I am an orphan."

"Fenton!"

"Here."

"Figgins?" said the orphan, eagerly; "dear me, I thought you said Figgins, captain."

"Charlton!"

"Here."

"Frampton!"

"Here."

"Here!" said the orphan, in a faint voice, stepping forward. "I think you said Figgins that time."

"Stand back!" cried one of the sailors, dragging the orphan back by the collar.

"Dear me," exclaimed Figgins, in distress. "I made sure that the captain said Figgins."

"No, he didn't."

"Grant!"

"Here."

"Dear, dear, dear," exclaimed the orphan, unable any longer to conceal his fears, "whenever will my turn come?"

"It won't come at all," returned the sailor, "unless you keep quiet."

"What do you mean by that?" faltered Figgins. "Pray, captain, let me get in the boat. I shan't take up much room, you know; I'm only a poor orphan."

"You'll go down to the bottom with the few as remain on board, I expect," remarked the sailor.

"Oh, Lor'! oh, Lor'! why was I born?" moaned Figgins. "Oh, it's dreadful to go to the bottom of the sea, and never come up again."

"And you won't come up again unless it's in the form of shrimps," said Jack.

"Shrimps!" almost shrieked Mr. Figgins.

"Yes," said young Jack, who was bound to have his lark under any conditions whatever, "we shall probably hear of you, sir, under another form altogether. Shrimps are notoriously fond of dead bodies, particularly the body of an orphan."

A hollow groan greeted the awful speech.

"It would really be a novelty," pursued the remorseless Jack; "fancy the Figgins-flavoured prawn."

"Or the orphan potted shrimp paste," observed the equally remorseless Harry Girdwood; "the new breakfast relish."

"Don't, I say."

"Don't what?"

"Don't talk so. I hate such fearful levity."

"Mr. Figgins," said the youthful Harkaway, in a deep, sonorous voice, "such a fate would immortalise the name of Figgins."

"And hand you down to posterity," added Harry Girdwood, in the same key, "as a benefactor to mankind and——"

"Breakfast tables, with the Figgins shrimp paste."

"Thank you very much," replied the orphan, "I've no desire for fame."

"Fame, sir," replied Harry, "fame is your lot, desire it or not—but hold tight, or you'll be overboard, sir."

"Bromley !" sang out the skipper.

"Here."

"French !"

"Here."

"Oh, Lor' !" cried Mr. Figgins ; "I'm a gone man."

"Figgins !" sang out Captain Deering. "Figgins !"

The orphan tried to shriek out a reply, but his tongue clove to the roof of his mouth, and he was dumbstruck.

"Figgins !"

The orphan's lips moved, but not a sound came.

"Confound him !" ejaculated the captain ; "pass on, next one—Jefferies !"

"Here."

At this moment Figgins found his voice, and shrieked—

"Here I am, captain. Figgins, the orphan, is here !"

And he dashed forward, in a frenzy of fright at being passed over.

"Then why the devil don't you answer to your name ?"

"Over with you," said Nat, who stood by.

"Dear, dear," said the orphan, "what a remarkably awkward ladder. Someone, help me."

"Now, look sharp."

"I hope I shan't fall overboard—oh !"

The words had barely passed his lips, when he stumbled and fell.

Down he dropped, touching the boat and falling into the water.

But the men dragged him out.

"Mind the shrimps don't get at you, Figgins !" cried young Harkaway.

"Oh," groaned the orphan, as the boat rowed away, "never was it my fate before to go down such a remarkably awkward flight of steps."

"But, damme !" cried one of the tars, "you didn't go down the steps. You preferred dropping into the water and sousing us all with the splash of your darned carcase."

"Don't be so impatient, my good man," said the orphan. "Consider, I was never meant for a sailor."

"Bah !"

"I don't like the sea, and I beg you——"

"There, stow your gab !"

"Dear me, how very violent," said the orphan. "Oh, I wish I was in smoky London again."

"Mr. Figgins !" shouted Harry Girdwood.

"Yes."

"Think of the new-flavoured prawn."

The orphan was drenched to the skin, but in spite of his drowned-rat appearance, he could afford a little laugh now.

So he put on a sickly smile.

"Perhaps you don't know I'm only an orphan, my good men," he said to the rowers, plaintively, "and it's my belief that there's a special providence ready to rescue the poor orphan from a watery grave."

"Special fiddlestick," returned a tar ; "why, it was Dick Bean as lugged you out by the starn o' yer blessed slacks."

"Orfin be blowed !" ejaculated another demonstrative old salt ; "jest smarm a lollipop into the orphan's gills to stop his jaw !"

"Dear, dear me," said the orphan, "what dreadful manners you men of the sea have. Oh, you make me shiver."

CHAPTER XXX.

THE LAST ON THE MUSTER ROLL—THE SKIPPER'S HEADER—DAVY JONES'S LOCKER.

CAPTAIN DEERING continued to call out the names steadily still, although every moment increased the peril of those on board.

"Jack, old fellow."

"What is it ?"

"We shall have to swim for it, after all," said Harry.

"I don't think so."

"I feel sure of it," said Harry ; "let us get on our cork jackets sharp."

"It is not far to swim," said Jack, "but there is no harm in taking precautions ; there may be harm in neglecting them."

"Very well."

Down they went.

Now Jack, in donning his cork jacket, forgot to replace his locket—Emily's parting gift—and so he had to put it on over the jacket, a chance which, strangely enough, led to a singular mishap, as we shall presently see.

They were on deck in three minutes.

"Binks," said the skipper.

"Binks," cried the mate.

"Where's Binks ?"

No response.

"He has sneaked into one of the first boat-loads, perhaps," suggested someone.

"No, he ain't," returned Nat Cringle. "Binks is as drunk as an alderman down below, along o' Joe Sprunt and Mr. Mackenzie."

"The time grows short," said Captain Deering, uneasily ; "they'll be drowned if we aren't sharp."

"Girdwood," sang out Captain Deering.

"Here."

"Drewitt."

"Here."

"Will no one go and warn these men ?" said young Jack. "I'm not going to leave the ship, and see them dragged down with it without an effort to save them."

"Harkaway," called out Captain Deering.

No reply.

"Harkaway."

"Harkaway ! Where's Harkaway gone to ?"

"Below."

"Call him," cried the captain, anxiously.

"Harkaway !" yelled honest Nat Cringle, who had taken a wondrous fancy to young Jack ; "for the Lord's sake come up."

"Cringle."

"Here, sir."

"Over with you."

"And you, captain?"

"I remain here till you are all off."

"I'll just see after Master Harkaway, sir."

"Nat Cringle," replied the skipper, sternly, "you must obey orders, or you'll be answerable for the lives of these men.   Over with you."

Two men remained ; one of the mates and a sailor.

They forced Nat Cringle over the side.

But the honest old tar never ceased yelling for Jack Harkaway.

The cries resounding in all directions were deafening.

In the boat just pushed off the voice of Harry Girdwood could be heard above all. calling to his rash young comrade in wild despair.

"Now, Briggit."

"Here, yer honour."

"Over with you."

"And you, captain?"

"Confound you !" roared the captain. losing his temper now that he had saved his crew by his coolness and presence of mind ; "over with you."

"After you, yer honour."

"D—n you for a mutinous thief. She's rocking under our feet, I tell you.   Over with you ; the ship is going down fast."

The "Albatross" was giving her final kick.

"Pull clear of the ship—pull hard—pull—pull, I say. Lay down to it, or you'll be sucked down."

The men gave way and pulled with resolution, with the instinct of discipline strong upon them rather than fear. But for the word of command, which the skipper cried out so clearly, they would have stuck there, heedless of the danger of being drawn down in the vortex, so that they could have been near their bold, lion-hearted skipper.

Captain Deering's task of peril was not yet over.

Seeing the boat clear of danger now, the captain threw off his top coat and ran along the deck to yell down below after Jack.

"Harkaway !" he cried. "Harkaway. Come up ; the last boat's gone. Hah ! too late."

He cast off what clothing he could, and bounding up to a point of vantage, he took a long, vigorous dive just as the treacherous old "Albatross" settled and went down.

CHAPTER XXXI.

DARE-DEVIL JACK—IN THE DEEP TROUGH OF THE SEA—THE CORK JACKET PLAYS ITS PART WELL.—MR. TINKER AND HIS VALET "GO TO LARN UP ALL PERTICKLARS."

"WHERE is Jack?" cried Harry Girdwood. "Pull back, I say. Don't desert him."

"There goes the skipper," cried Nat Cringle. "Hurrah !"

This was at the moment that Deering took his desperate header.

The men caught up the cheer one and all.

"Pull back, pull back," said Harry Girdwood, despairingly. "Don't let us desert like curs the bravest, boldest heart that ever beat in a sailor's breast."

"Don't listen to him, men ; Harkaway had his chance ; let him drown, he's not of any use

to us. Pull away, or we shall all be drawn under the sinking ship," said Murray.

"Hold your mag," said Harry, dropping his hand heavily upon the speaker's head. "Jack is worth a thousand of your wretched sort."

"Why should we endanger all for the sake of one?" cried Murray. "He chose to go and play the fool after those drunken men."

"Silence, you heartless young swab," exclaimed Nat Cringle. "Half a word more to that tune, and I'll drop you overboard."

"There's someone climbing the rigging, I think," said one of the sailors. "Look there."

"It's young Harkaway."

"No, no, it is not Jack," said Harry Girdwood, almost in tears. "Poor Jack has gone down."

Alas ! there was no hope for him now.

Meanwhile, Captain Deering was seen breasting the surface of the water, and pushing along with a vigorous side stroke.

*   *   *   *   *

When young Jack got down below, he found two of the crew hopelessly drunk, and the Scotch mate in a scarce better condition.

"This is a hopeless case," exclaimed young Jack.

The mate was not quite so far gone as the two unfortunate men to whom he had set so bad an example.

"Mackenzie," cried Jack, shaking him.

"Eh ? Whose watch ?" muttered the mate.

"The ship's settling, I tell you," cried Jack. "Wake up."

"Ugh !" grunted Mackenzie ; "it's not my watch, I tell ye. I ken verra weel when——"

And then he lay back and snored again.

Jack cried out in despair—

"The fool ! He's lost ! Hah ! what's this here? The very thing."

A bucket of water stood just handy, so Jack whipped it up and dashed it over the mate.

"Darn yer imperence !" cried Sandy, waking up and making a grab at young Jack.

Just then the voice of the skipper was heard calling him wildly to come up.

"Let go, Mackenzie," cried Jack, struggling with desperation.

But the mate was a gaunt, strong fellow. and young Jack stood but a very poor chance in a tussle with him.

"I'll crop yer ears for ye, ye whelp of Satan !" hiccoughed the Scotch mate.

"Too late, too late." cried the skipper up aloft. "Jack, Jack, where are you?"

The words sounded like a death knell in young Jack's ear.

He fought fiercely with the drunken mate, and, wriggling himself half out of his clutches, sent him staggering back, but before Jack could get fairly off, Mackenzie was after him again, and grabbed at him.

He was a little short, but he chanced to get hold of the locket and chain—little Emily's parting gift—and held Jack momentarily a prisoner, but holding on to the hand-rail with the energy of despair, our hero kicked out desperately, and sent the mate reeling back.

Up he flew on deck.

The captain had already taken his leap for life.

The ship sank fast.

Jack's peril was deadly.

He looked about him.

His only chance was the rigging.

Young Jack climbed like Nero himself, so up he went hand over hand into the shrouds, as the ill-starred "Albatross" quickened her pace downwards.

Even now he did not turn sick or faint-hearted, as may be guessed by the following characteristic speech—

"That beast Mackenzie has grabbed Em's locket."

He reached the crosstrees, and gave a sharp look around him as he calculated his chances.

The whirlpool which the sinking of the huge carcase caused, was of alarming dimensions.

Spars, chips and coops, and sundry floating things which had been thrown overboard at the last moment, were drawn into the vortex already.

And this told young Harkaway his danger.

It was not difficult to see it.

"Well," said young Jack, resolutely, "it is my only chance for life. Here goes."

He set his teeth, poised himself for a moment upon the crosstree, then swinging back, he plunged boldly forward into the air.

Heaven!

What an eternity it seemed to our brave young hero, that brief passage through the air!

Down, down he went, seemingly to the ocean's bed.

Then, having regained—well, scarcely his presence of mind, but rather having strong instinct of self preservation—he struck upwards, and with half a dozen vigorous strokes he reached the surface—reached air and light.

The cork jacket now played its part well.

Where would young Harkaway have been else?

Probably at the bottom of the sea.

And there would have been an end to the adventures of young Jack Harkaway and his boy Tinker at once.

Brave young Jack did not mean to cry a go yet.

He stuck to it manfully, and as he breasted the surface of the water, a singular phenomenon manifested itself.

He had not felt the influence of the sinking ship while under, yet now that he was on the surface, and on the limit of the whirlpool's eddies, he felt the strength of its influence.

It was desperate work now.

He set his teeth, and plunged on.

Yet he felt that in spite of everything, he made little or no progress.

As fast as he got ahead, the fierce strength of the whirlpool drew him back.

It was indeed well for him that he had not reached the surface earlier.

He felt this instinctively, and taking a long, deep draught of air, he ducked his head, and plunged below the surface once more.

A dozen vigorous strokes, and he shot up again.

Then he was safe.

"Now for a good, long, steady swim, Jack, old boy," he cried to himself.

Then turning over on his back, he took it easy and looked about him.

"That was a narrow squeak," he said. "But I wish that that beast of a Mackenzie had not prigged my locket."

He was a good swimmer, but there came a time, when even he was tired out.

He turned over and had a swim.

The shore looked a desperate way off.

"I shall never be able to reach shore all that way off," he said. "But 'never say die' is my motto, so here goes."

Young Jack caught sight of a boat presently, and he hailed it.

"Hollo—ho! Help—ho, ho!"

The effort took all his strength, and he gasped again.

Thanks to his cork jacket, he did not go under, but by now he was powerless to help himself.

But on board this boat there were two persons who had heard the cry.

Moreover, both of them had recognised the voice.

"Oh golly, dat's Massa Jack," said one of the persons. "I'se gwine to larn up all perticklers."

And with no more ado, the speaker, who was a nigger, tumbled over into the water.

The other person was likewise a darkey.

"You may consider dis infant dere, Massa Tinker," said the other person, peeling hastily.

He dived over too.

These two darkeys, who were, need we say?—Tinker, and that gentleman's valet and major-domo, Bogey, were quite as much at home in the water as they were upon land, and they thought no more of trusting their ebony carcases to the waves than we should think of eating our dinner.

They played up all kinds of pranks in the water, and could keep under, seemingly, any length of time.

It was a comical race.

Every now and again, one or the other would bob up and squint at his fellow countryman.

Then they would shoot along again.

"Look, Bogey," cried Tinker. "Yah, yah; dere he am, dis child soon hab him."

At length they got within range of poor young Jack.

He was floating, thanks to the corks, but insensible.

When they were within range, they dived simultaneously, and then shooting upwards, came to the surface at the self-same moment, one on either side of young Jack.

"Oh golly, Bogey," cried Tinker; "dis infant am awful glad he got hold of good Massa Jack."

And so the two niggers, master and valet, towed young Jack up to the side of the boat, and then with great difficulty they got him into it.

CHAPTER XXXII.

BOGEY IS COMMISSIONED TO RUB MASSA JACK'S LITTLE TUMMY.

"Be golly, him look pale!"

"Ole your blessed tongue, nigger!" said Tinker, authoritatively; "an' rub him little tummy."

"Yes, massa."

"Poor fellar!" said Tinker, sadly; "him bery uncommon poorly."

"Dis chile make him tummy warm," remarked Bogey, "an' den he'll get all right, massa."

So saying, he rubbed away now more vigorously than ever.

The efforts of the two faithful darkeys soon told, for Jack opened his eyes.

"Tinker," said he, with a sigh.

"Yes, sar, dat am dis good-looking child."

"Where am I?"

"Hyar, sar, 'long wid Tinker and Bogey."

"Where's here?"

"In de boat, sar."

"I remember now, Tinker."

"What you remember, sar?"

"That beast of a Mackenzie prigged my locket."

Tinker looked puzzled.

Then shooting an inquisitive glance at his master, he made up his mind.

The trials and dangers had turned "him bressed head."

"Mackenzie, sar," he said, seemingly indignant, "did you say Mackenzie, sar?"

"Yes."

"Well, sar, punch him head."

"I mean to if he's afloat," returned young Jack; "but I fear he's gone down."

This being off his mind, young Jack lapsed into a sort of semi-somnolency.

"Bogey."

"Yes, massa."

"Rub him tummy, you ugly waggibone."

"Yes, massa."

"Keep a-rubbin' ob him till he get all ober warm like."

"Yes, massa."

And he went to work at a rare rate, too.

Well, the result of this was that when they got ashore, young Jack had so far recovered that he was really very little the worse for his leap, and his dive, and his protracted immersion.

The boat grounded just about three or four minutes before another boat came on shore.

And in this boat was Harry Girdwood, just returned in bitter despair at what he thought Jack's death.

He looked so pale and haggard that one could scarcely believe it to be the result of grief alone.

Young Jack ran to greet him.

"Why, Harry, old man, what is the matter?"

Harry Girdwood looked puzzled.

"Jack."

"Yes."

"Is it you?"

"Why, yes. unless I am very much mistaken. I don't think I am anyone else than young Jack Harkaway."

"Why, Jack, my dear old boy, how did you get here?"

"Partly by swimming, partly by floating, and partly in the boat, while Bogey rubbed my little tummy to bring me round."

While Jack was urging on his wild career shorewards, the other boat in which Harry Girdwood was drafted off, had been hanging about the wreck to pick up anyone who might have been overboard and had the good luck to get clear of the vessel.

But they were singularly unfortunate.

A third boat had picked the skipper up, while they remained even ignorant of his fate as they had been until now of young Jack Harkaway's.

*   *   *   *   *

"What, young Harkaway," cried out a manly voice; "give us your grappling iron, Master Jack, for. damme, Nat Cringle longs to touch your flesh."

"With all my heart, Nat Cringle," cried young Jack; "give us a grasp."

His example was followed by all round.

And young Jack had his right hand well-nigh wrung off.

"I had all my work to do," said young Jack, "to get free of that drunken old Mackenzie."

And thereupon he related all that had taken place on board during his vain endeavour to rescue the mate from the wreck.

"I only hope as he's saved," said Nat Cringle, "for if I meet him ashore. I'll make small biscuit of him in the turning of a marlinspike."

That Nat's resolve was highly approved of was duly attested by the salvos of cheers from the sailors which greeted his speech.

"Well," cried Jack, "I hope we shall meet him, for confound the brute! he's prigged a locket my little sweetheart gave me at parting on shore."

CHAPTER XXXIII.

THE ORPHAN'S INFIRMITIES—JACK GIVES HIM A LESSON IN SPANISH.

"HERE comes the skipper."

"Hurrah, here he comes."

Captain Deering saw Jack, and he came running up to the spot to greet him.

"Egad, Master Harkaway, you've had a narrow escape this time," he said.

"And you too, sir."

"Yes, Harkaway," replied the skipper; "a closer shave than I should care for every day. I might not always come off, d'ye see?"

Just then a sick-looking gentleman came up with his head tied up in a white handkerchief.

"Oh, Captain Deering," said he, "I congratulate you, indeed I do. After what young Harkaway told me of those nasty shrimps, I feared you had gone to the bottob."

"So I had, Mr. Figgins," returned the skipper, with a grin, "and I came to the top again as quick as convenient."

"It was dearly all over with be, too, captid."

"Oh, no," returned the captain, "you were soon picked out, and you're not much the worse for a sousing. Salt water doesn't hurt any man."

The orphan gave a groan and a grunt of impatience at this.

"Doesl't it leither? Why, I've got a cole id by dose that'll last be for a fortdight."

The doleful expression of the orphan's face made the skipper laugh outright.

"Not so bad as that, Mr. Figgins, I hope."

"BUT HARRY GIRDWOOD WAS AT HAND, AND A PISTOL BULLET CRASHED THROUGH THE BULL'S SKULL."

"Isl't it ?—but I know it is. I wish somebody else had got my cold in his nose," returned the orphan.

"You may think yourself very fortunate there were no shrimps here to seize upon you, when you tumbled in the water : but you can easily get over your cold, Mr. Figgins," said young Jack.

"Oh, Mr. Jack."

"How do you feel, Mr. Figgins?"

"I'm very bad iddeed, Bister Jack ; I wish some kind person would take care of me, for I am only an orphan."

"Oh, we'll take care of you, but you must get over your cold first. Take a tubfull of gruel with a candle in it, sir."

"A what?"

"A candle ; I don't mean to eat the candle altogether."

"I should thick dot."

"You only have to drop the candle in the gruel, while it's nice and hot to melt it a little and rub yourself all over with it."

"Get alog, you're chaffig. I wish you good evedig, Baster John."

"I'm only Master John on Sundays, Mr. Figgins—Jack on week days, please."

"Jokid apart," said the orphan, "gruel isl't a bad thig for a cole, oly I cal't thig how I shall get od with these Spadiards."

"Easy enough."

"What's the Spadish for gruel, Jack?"

"Bilstickas sauce," responded young Jack, promptly.

"Dear be. Ad—ad—jokid apart, a caddle isl't half a bad thig for the dose."

"You're right."

"What's the Spadish for caddle, cub dow?"

"Fardendippa," answered young Jack.

"Fardeddippa."

"Yes."

"What a sigular lagwidge Spadish is, Baster Jack."

"Very. Remember that Spanish people are very proud and ceremonious."

"All right, I'll be cerebodious with theb. I shall get to the hotel and off to bed ; good dight."

"Well, good night, Mr. Figgins, and don't forget your Spanish, for remember you are a young and tender orphan, with no one to look after you, and the Spanish people like to use their knives on unprotected English orphans."

"True, true. Oh, I wish I was at home."

And as he went up the beach, he kept repeating it to himself—

"Gruel, bilstickas sauce. Caddle, fardeddippa, good for the nose and a cold."

CHAPTER XXXIV.

AT THEIR TRICKS AGAIN—THE COCKNEY WAITER — A SURPRISE — POOR ORPHAN FIGGINS.

"JACK, what do you think of this place?"

"Well, Harry, not half bad diggings up to the present. There is only one drawback as far as I can find out as yet."

"What is it?"

"The Carlists."

"Those rascals are never here," exclaimed Harry.

"Yes, they are : rather strong, too."

"Are these people all Carlists then?"

"To a man."

"Pheugh! I say, Jack, old boy, that's rather hot."

"Oh, there is nothing much to fear until the other scoundrels come and bombard the town."

"The deuce they will. Why, Jack, we have run ourselves into some danger."

"Very great danger, from what I hear."

"Well, this is a precious rum go," said Harry Girdwood. "However," he added, with a merry twinkle in his eye, "we can stand to it, and it won't prevent us making the most of Mr. Figgins' terror when we pile it on him."

"Oh, our poor orphan will be in for a good thing," said Jack, chuckling aloud at the bare anticipation ; "but it must be very carefully done."

"Very."

"I'll work up to it with tales of the Carlists' atrocities—make out that they're everything that's awful—cannibals included."

Poor Figgins !

Hapless orphan !

He was destined to suffer now for the amusement of our two young scapegraces.

* * * * *

They went up to have a look at Mr. Figgins, and they found him in his room in bed, struggling in an overwhelming sea of difficulties.

"You feel more yourself now, Mr. Figgins," said Harry Girdwood, "now that you have on your nightcap."

"I do certainly feel easier."

"You would of course," said Jack, eagerly. "And did you try the gruel and the candle?"

"I couldn't."

"Why not?"

"Couldl' bake eb udderstal."

"We'll manage that for you," said Harry Girdwood, tipping Jack the wink.

"Of course, anything to oblige Mr. Figgins."

"Thak you, oh ! thak you, youg geltlemal," responded the grateful sufferer ; "but, oh, why did I ever come to sea? I was never intended for a sailor. Oh, dear !"

"Poor thing. Shall I ring the bell?" said Jack.

"Oh, I wish I could hear a London muffin bell ; that would be music to me."

Harry rang, and up came a spruce young waiter.

"Waiter," said Jack, in his most Spanish air.

"Senor."

"*Candeloza por el nosa del' olda-cocka-waxa.*"

The waiter looked considerably puzzled.

"*Candeloza, senor excellenza?*"

"*Si,*" said young Jack, "don't you understand? *Candeloza—fardendippa por el nosa dell' ancienta-buffa.*"

"*Por taller sua snuffboxa,*" explained Harry Girdwood, gesticulating violently.

The waiter looked on aghast.

"He doesl' cobrehed," exclaimed the invalid, in despair ; "waiter."

"Senor."

Mr. Figgins sat bolt upright and pantomimed violently at the waiter.

"Caddle—udderstal? Caddle, tallow-wick, light, fat to rub ol by lose, udderstal?"

" Oh !"

That was all the waiter could say in his wonder.

" Now he understands," said Jack, winking at Harry.

" Mr. Figgins' Spanish is better than ours."

" Oh, dear, no, sir," responded the waiter, with a mirthful twinkle in his eye and in purest Whitechapel English ; " about the same, sir. Didn't know you was English, sir. Old gent wants a taller candle to rub on his nozzle. I see, sir. I'd no notion that you was a-getting at me, sir ! I'm from the East of London, bred and born there."

Off he ran, leaving Master Jack and his companion rather more astonished than the waiter himself had previously appeared.

*   *   *   *   *

" Well !" exclaimed Harry Girdwood, " that has rather taken it out of us."

" Rather. Who would have thought of seeing a London waiter here ?"

" Let us go and find the Cockney waiter and see what we can do with him."

" Come along."

They found that Cockney waiter and they bribed him.

And they plotted in the most shameful manner against the orphan Figgins' future peace of mind.

Of this more anon.

For the present we must limit ourselves to saying that some unhappy moments were in store for the poor gentleman with the cold in his head.

CHAPTER XXXV.

A STROLL IN AN ORANGE GROVE—THE VINE-YARD—THE HARKAWAY BLOOD IS UP AGAIN —AN AWKWARD MESS.

" LET'S go and have a look about the town," said Jack.

" With all my heart," responded Harry Girdwood, " but let us get some information first of the Cockney waiter."

Trimmer, the Cockney waiter, had lived there for years and knew everything about everything and everybody.

He was well acquainted with the country around, and he directed them to the most interesting places to visit.

" If you turn to the left when you get outside," said he, " you will come to the orange grove—the best walk in this part—and beyond that you get to the vineyards, and they are downright awful stunning."

" You are so emphatic and forcible," said young Jack, " that I shall be off at once."

" All right, sir, but keep clear of them Carlist fellows ; they're as proud as Lucifer, and they haven't a stiver to spend ; they live upon olives and garlic, and there ain't, so to speak, a clean shirt in the army."

" I'll be careful."

" That's right."

" And if any of them Carlist fellows speak to you, only bow and walk on."

" We will."

 *   *   *   *   *

It would have been as well if they had followed out the injunctions of the Cockney waiter literally.

But out of sight, out of mind.

They were no sooner in the orange grove than they forgot all about the Carlists and the waiter, and, in fact, about anything for the time being, but the delicious perfume of the enchanting scene through which they were passing.

" What a Paradise, Jack !" exclaimed Harry.

" Elysium," was Jack's rapturous reply.

" It smells like all the perfumers of Bond Street boiled down."

" Delicious !"

" What a thousand pities that our foggy old climate won't grow such a treat as this."

" It is. But then our foggy old climate doesn't grow Carlists and garlic and dirt and brag and lies so prolifically as this beautiful place."

" That's true, old wet-blanket," said Jack. " Old England isn't half a bad place, after all, in spite of its fogs and rains and coughs, colds, catarrhs, rheumatism, and the rest of it."

" Ugh !" growled Harry, " couldn't you rake up a few more reproaches for the land of your birth ?"

Young Jack's response was brief and expressive—

" Pickles !"

Then, after a moment, he said—

" Let's change the subject."

" When will the divers begin their operations ?"

" To-morrow, if what Captain Deering says is true ; the vessel is already on the spot, you know."

" But I am told that only one of the divers has come over up to the present."

" What of that ?"

" A great deal."

" Why ?"

" How can he begin alone ?"

" Easily enough."

" It must be precious dangerous, I should say."

" Why more dangerous for one than for several ?"

" Why, if two are together and one is not well—if any accident happens, the other could give the signal to haul up."

" True, there must be great danger attendant upon deep sea diving."

They walked on for some distance in silence.

" Harry."

" Yes."

" I'm going to confide in you, old man, only I want you first to make me a promise."

" I will."

" You won't laugh ?"

" I'll look as serious as a whole bench of judges."

" Well, the fact is, that in the under steward's cabin of the ' Albatross ' is something which I wouldn't lose for a hundred pounds—no, nor for a good many hundreds."

Harry stared.

" What is it ?"

" You're going to grin.'

" Not I."

"Well, it is a—now don't get on that beastly guffaw, Harry. Em gave me a locket before I left, with a lock of her hair in it—bless her! and the drunken brute Mackenzie made a grab at me as I was escaping up the companion ladder, and tore it off my neck."

"What then?"

"I want it."

"You can't get it."

"I'll go after it."

"Bosh! Do you think you would please Emily by risking your life on such a job?"

"No, but I don't mean to go home without it."

Harry Girdwood looked anxious at this.

He knew too well the determination of the Harkaways one and all, and he knew that all the arguments he could use would not turn young Jack from his purpose.

So he tried to effect a compromise.

"You have only to try and tip the diver who's there already."

"I'll try it."

*   *   *   *   *

They had now emerged from the orange grove.

Beyond, they came to an enclosed ground with a high wall lining the side of the path on their right.

They had to pick their way along here, for the road was below the level of the path, and a recent heavy rain and bad drainage combined had left the road in a sad mess.

They picked their way along in single file, keeping up close to the wall.

In this way they progressed for some distance, when a man was seen to turn a corner sharply and advance towards them.

Now this man could very well have retreated to the place from whence he had emerged and allowed them to pass.

But he was a haughty, ill-natured fellow, and he made straight up to the two lads with a sternly defiant air, and waited for them to move aside for him.

So they came to a full stop.

The stranger was a young, tall, dark man, handsome enough to look at, and seemingly a military officer.

He paused a moment, looking down upon young Jack, who stared back coolly enough, for it wanted a very big man indeed to abash a Harkaway.

"*Maledicion!* give way, boy," ejaculated the Spaniard, furiously.

And lunging suddenly forward, he seized hold of Jack and whirled him round off the path into the mud, ankle deep.

Now this was not the sort of thing that young Jack could relish, or he would not have been the son of his father.

Before you could say Jack Robinson, or, indeed, give utterance to an infinitely more brief exclamation, he sprang forward and seized the Spaniard by the leg, and gave it a mighty tug.

The effort was so sudden that the officer could not save himself, and he went sprawling in the mud.

The Spaniard made a rare noise and bluster, and used a lot of very alarming expressions, or rather expressions which ought to have frightened the very soul out of the two boys if they had understood a word of them.

But beyond a good many *Carambas, Carajoe,* and *Maledicions,* they did not understand much.

He shook some of the mud from his garments and made a rush at Jack, but the latter dodged the don and met him with a good old English one, straight from the shoulder.

"I'll have your heart's blood for that," cried the Spaniard, taking out a card and throwing it at Jack.

Now the latter understood the action, although he could make nothing of the words, and this was a species of invitation which one of his hot-blooded race could not refuse.

"It's a challenge," exclaimed Harry, in alarm.

Young Jack produced his card and wrote upon it the name of the hotel at which they were staying.

"What are you about?" cried Harry Girdwood. "I'm not going to have anything of this kind; you shall not meet this man in combat."

"You can't help it any more than I can," returned Jack, coolly. "At your service, senor, when you please," he added, with a bow to the Spaniard.

The latter bowed in return, and curling his moustache fiercely, he strode away, shaking his fist in the air.

CHAPTER XXXVI.

THE CHALLENGE—A PROFESSIONAL DUEL-LIST—TRICKS OF FENCE—JACK AND HIS MAÎTRE-D'ARMES.

"WELL, Jack, this is bad. What would your poor father say if he knew about it?" said Harry Girdwood, utterly dismayed; "it's a dreadful job."

"A rum go, isn't it?"

"A rum go," cried his companion. "Oh, Jack, Jack, whatever will you do?"

Jack stared.

"Do? What would you do?"

"It is not right you should fight this Carlist brute. I should bolt."

"Bolt," echoed Jack. "Yes, I think I see myself; why, Harry, you old fibber, to say you'd bolt. Why, you would have wanted to fight it out then and there."

"It is madness, Jack. I tell you that this meeting must not take place."

"Now don't be obstinate, Harry," said Jack, angrily. "What, would you have me turn coward before this bully? No, Harry, no wretched Spaniard shall have the chance of saying that he frightened young Jack Harkaway."

This closed the conversation.

They walked back to the hotel in utter silence.

"Let us look at his card," said Harry Girdwood.

This was the first word spoken between them.

Jack handed over the card.

"Don Gil Perez."

"He's a pretty don," said Harry.

Young Jack turned to his friend and silently held out his hand.

"Come, come, Harry, old man," said he; "we mustn't have any bad feeling over this job."

Harry returned his grip with heartiness.

"Ill feeling, Jack!" said he, with deep emotion. "Heaven forbid that anything should make ill-feeling between you and I."

The Cockney waiter came in just then with a card on a salver.

"A gent is a-waiting below, sir," said he, with a mysterious air; "a Carlist officer, I should say, sir, by the looks of him."

Jack took the card.

"'Don Miguel Basten.' Whoever is that?"

"Someone from the other don, I suppose," said Harry.

"By jingo!" said Jack, with a laugh, "the Spaniard means fighting; well, I'll fight him, and he shall find young Jack Harkaway is a true Boy of England."

"Will you see this gentleman, sir?" asked the waiter.

"Of course. Show him in," replied Jack.

"Yes, sir."

"And come back with him, waiter," said Harry.

"Yes, sir."

"We shall want you to interpret for us."

"All right, sir."

A moment after the waiter returned, ushering in a Spanish officer.

Don Miguel Basten was a fine, soldier-like man, well advanced in years, with close-cropped grey hair, and a thick grey moustache.

He doffed his cap on entering, and bowed low to the two lads.

"Will you say that it is Senor John Harkaway that I wish to see?" said he to the waiter.

"This is Senor Harkaway, capitan," replied the waiter, waving his hand towards Jack.

"Impossible; he is only a boy. It must be his father I have come to see."

This was translated to Jack, who had, however, given a pretty shrewd guess at what was meant.

"No. Tell Don Miguel Basten that my father is in England, and that I am the person."

This was duly translated by the waiter.

"It is very strange," said the officer. "The Senor Harkaway is very young."

"Yes, senor."

"Ask him if he comes from Don Gil Perez," said Jack.

"Gil Perez?"

"Yes."

"Do you know him, sir?"

"Slightly."

The waiter put on a frightened look, which they could not very well understand.

"Si, si," said the Carlist officer, with a nod of intelligence at Jack. "I have the honour to come on behalf of Don Gil Perez."

"At your service, senor," said Jack, bowing politely.

"Tell the young English gentleman," said the officer, "that he has gravely affronted Don Gil Perez, and that no apology is possible."

The waiter looked aghast at this message.

"My hi, sir," he exclaimed, "this is a precious go. Why, you've been and had a rumpus with the most notorious duellist and the very worst bully in the Carlist army. Oh, my!"

Jack smiled.

"He says that no apology is possible."

"I never intended an apology."

The waiter looked more frightened than ever.

"Translate that, do you hear?" said Jack, sharply.

"But, sir, consider; this Don Perez is a dreadful man with all weapons, and——"

"Do what I tell you, or leave the room," said Jack.

He obeyed.

The officer pursed his brows.

"I did not mean that," he said. "I meant that it would be impossible for us to accept an apology. But the senor is very young——"

"Old enough to take my own part," responded Jack.

"Very good," said Don Miguel. "Then, with the deepest regret, I have to arrange the preliminaries."

"As you please, sir."

"Your weapons?"

"Yours, senor?"

"Sword or pistol?"

"I am equally good, or bad, at both," replied young Jack. "I'm not in the habit of fighting duels. So if Don Miguel Basten will make all the arrangements for us, he may consider them as accepted in advance."

This was translated by the waiter.

"One word before we go any further," said the officer, who had been eyeing young Harkaway with considerable interest. "I said an apology was impossible. Now, my principal is a noted duellist, a dead shot, and one of the keenest blades in the army of his Catholic majesty. In consideration of the Senor Inglese's youth, I will undertake to insist upon an apology being accepted, if Senor Harkaway will make one."

"Impossible," returned Jack, hastily. "I am an Englishman, senor, and hold my honour as dearly as any Spaniard born."

"Senor," returned the officer, "your courage does you honour, and I wish this painful task had devolved upon anybody but me. Swords, then, at six in the morning."

"Where?"

"In the valley beyond the church."

"I will be there, senor."

"Is this young gentleman your friend?" asked the officer, bowing to Harry Girdwood.

"Yes."

"I shall have the painful honour of meeting you both, then," said the Spaniard, bowing once more. "Before I go, young gentleman," he added, advancing a step towards Jack, "allow me the pleasure of shaking hands with you, for you are a brave lad."

"With great pleasure," returned Jack, courteously.

They shook hands, and Don Miguel Basten, after looking once more at Jack, bowed himself out.

*   *   *   *   *

"Well, I'm jiggered!" exclaimed the waiter. "You've been and gone and done it, Mr. Hark-

away, you have. Oh, how you'll get run through, sir."

"Is it such a very poor look-out for me, then?" asked Jack, with a smile.

"You may as well say your prayers and order your coffin, sir, that's all."

"You're a nice Job's comforter," laughed Jack.

"Why, this beast of a Gil Perez has spitted about a dozen within the last month; he's, without exception, the one cove, sir, that you ought to have avoided. He's a devil, sir."

"I can't help that; it's done and can't be undone now. You can't unnerve me by any talk, so don't try it on."

"Don't say that, sir. I'd give a year's perks, sir, to see you lard him well, the Spanish beast, but there's no chance of it."

"What do they understand by swords?"

"Rapiers."

"I wish it was broadsword—cut and thrust."

"Why, sir?"

"I know the exercise."

The waiter thought for a moment, and then burst into a laugh.

"That's not half a bad idea, sir. Take your sword with you. The choice was with you; you said swords, but you didn't stipulate what kind. Insist upon your cut-and-thrust cove, and Don Gil Perez may be took at a disadvantage. Oh, what larks it would be to see a young English gentleman like you spit this brute of a Spaniard."

"Do they never fight with anything but rapiers?"

"Not often. I've seen many a duel, sir; two or three with the cut-and-thrusters, but they're blessed awkward at it. They have only one cut and one guard, as far as I can see."

"Do you know it?"

"Oh, yes. I can show it you in half a crack, and proud I am of the honour, sir."

"You seem up to a great many things," said Harry Girdwood. "How did you learn this?"

"I've been in the army here, sir."

"The deuce you have."

"I was in the army in England, and my time was out, so I came travelling here with my master, poor chap; he was an officer in my regiment, and travelling here on half-pay when he got the fever in Cadiz and it took him off. That's three years ago. I was left without any resources, so I enlisted in the national army for three years. When they was up, I came on here, and, being hard up, got a billet here as waiter."

"What an extraordinary career," exclaimed Jack. "I never heard of a soldier being waiter before."

"What's the odds as long as you're happy? I don't care much for the place, but it's vittles and drink, besides occasional pickings, an' so I manage to grub along."

"Well," said Jack, "now for this famous guard."

The Cockney soldier-waiter got a walking stick, and showed them several tricks of fence.

"If you don't mind a slight sabre-cut on the shoulder, you can spit your man like a herring."

"How?"

"This way. They cut down thus—it's a vicious cut, meant to break your guard—you mustn't attempt to parry it, but jump in under it. You're nimble enough, I see, a good deal more so than Mr. Bully Gil Perez. Run in sharp as soon as you're engaged, and you have him as safe as eggs is eggs. Oh, my eye! I should be glad."

Jack appeared to be satisfied, but Harry was less confident.

"Very well," said Jack. "Now we'll get to bed, for I want to be up at five. I shouldn't like to be late, or go on the field sleepy at all. Stay, in case anything should happen to me, here's a trifle to remember me, for you seem kind."

The waiter put back young Harkaway's hand firmly, but politely.

"Not to-night, sir."

"What! You're not proud."

"Not I, sir," returned the waiter. "Pride wouldn't well become one who lives upon tips. No, sir, good luck to you. Wait till the job's over and then double it."

"That's a bargain," said Jack.

"That's business," said Harry Girdwood, laughing, in spite of himself, for his heart was as heavy as lead.

"Good night."

"Good night, gents, both of you. Rise with a steady hand and stout heart, and may good luck attend you in the morning."

"Amen to that!" said Harry Girdwood, fervently.

CHAPTER XXXVII.

THE DUEL IN THE VALLEY—THE FACE-GUARD AND HOW IT TOLD—STRUCK HOME—THE ENGLISH DIVER.

A KNOCK at the door.

"Come in."

"Five o'clock, sir."

"So soon?"

Jack had slept like a top.

Poor Harry Girdwood had hardly closed his eyes the livelong night, and when he had snatched a little fitful slumber, he had dreamt dreadfully.

His visions were all of men slain in single combat.

Fierce Spaniards slaughtering inexperienced duellists, and these pallid men stretched upon the ground, with the life-blood oozing slowly from gaping wounds.

Such were the visions which poor Harry had, and he was not sorry when the time arrived to be moving.

Young Jack sprang from his bed and slipped into his garments as hurriedly as possible. Harry Girdwood followed suit.

But he failed to display the same alacrity in his movements.

Slowly and fearfully he prepared for this terrible business.

"Look sharp, Harry."

"All right, Jack, my dear boy."

Harry did not believe that there was much chance for his brave comrade; yet such as there was, he wished him to profit by to the uttermost; and so he tried with all his might to disguise his own unpleasant feelings upon the matter.

At length they were ready to start.

"Harry," said Jack, earnestly, "tip us your fin, old man."

Harry silently extended his hand.

"Come, come, old sobersides, you mustn't be down-hearted, or I shall go into action with a heavy heart, and that won't improve my chance."

"I'm as cheerful as I can be, but you wouldn't have me feel downright happy, Jack, would you ?"

"I tell you what, Harry, I'm as good as a hundred dead men yet. I've a presentiment that I shall pull through this job as I have many a worse one before. I don't fear the bully Spaniard."

"No, Jack. Keep your pluck up."

"Now, Harry," said Jack, "when you are quite ready."

"Now."

"Come on."

"You have nothing to say, Jack, before we start ?"

"No."

*   *   *   *   *

They were first on the field.

However, they had not long to wait, for in less than three minutes, Don Gil Perez was seen advancing, leaning upon the arm of two brother officers, Don Miguel Basten and a stranger.

Close upon their heels came two more men.

The first of them was the waiter from the hotel.

The other was a thick-set, pale-faced man, with a sort of semi-sailor cut about him.

The former saluted Jack and his companion with the grave dignity peculiar to the Spanish people.

The latter advanced towards Jack and Harry, saluting them as they approached.

"I thought I'd like to look on and see fair play, sir," said the waiter, touching his hat. "I am not a bad swordsman, and if there should be foul play on the part of these dons, I'll stand by you, sir."

"Thank you, and who have you brought with you ?" said Jack.

"A fellow countryman of ours. The diver who has been sent for to go down to the 'Albatross.'"

"Indeed," said Harry Girdwood, turning to the diver. "So you are an Englishman ?"

"Yes, sorr," replied the diver, "an' it's proud I am of that same, sorr."

"Well, we won't say English altogether," said Jack, smiling, "a Briton, at all events."

"Yes, sorr."

"Dublin ?"

"County Galway, sorr, at your sarvice," returned the diver, with a salute.

"And have you come to see fair play, too ?"

"Ye may say that, an' be jabers, I'll see it ; the murtherin' bosthoon. Give half a worrd, sorr, an' I'll wire into the lot of 'em at oncet."

Jack laughed.

"There's no need for that at present, thanks," he said ; "he's trod on the tail of *my* coat at present. You can wire in when I've had my turn."

"You're a fine boy, anyhow," exclaimed the diver, in undisguised admiration. "I hope as there'll be little left of the omadhauns for me to pound away at by the time you've done with 'em."

"I'm only going to fight with one of them," replied Jack, with mock gravity ; "there'll be plenty for you to peg away at afterwards."

"Hurrah !" cried the Irishman, "that's balm to one's feelings, anyhow."

The others drew near.

Don Gil Perez had divested himself of hat, cloak and coat, and he stood ready in his shirt sleeves.

Jack speedily followed suit.

Harry Girdwood handed Jack his weapon.

Then it was for the first time that Don Miguel discovered the difference in the swords, and he at once interfered.

"Senor Harkaway understood that the combat was to be with sabres, Don Miguel," said the waiter, pretending to interpret.

The notorious duellist curled his lip scornfully when this was told him.

"The English boy is laughing at us," he said. "He only wants a pretext to save his skin."

"No pretext, senor," replied the waiter, promptly. "Senor Harkaway remarks that the gentleman beside you wears a sabre. He says, too, that any weapon is indifferent to him."

"The sabre be it then," said Don Miguel ; "and let him consider he has not five minutes to live."

The officer who had accompanied them handed Don Gil Perez his sabre, and the latter cut the air viciously with it to try its temper.

"He looks as if he'd like to make sassengers of the whole biling of us," said the diver, with a comical grimace.

They were now about to give the signal to engage, when Don Miguel advanced to his principal's side, and said something to him in a low tone.

"A brave lad, you say," returned the duellist, coarsely, "and spare him ? Bah ! he has sought it, and he must pay the penalty. His mother's tears should not save him now. I will have the English dog's life."

He hoped that his adversary would hear it, and that this gentlemanly speech would serve to unnerve him for the combat.

But he just forgot that Jack did not understand a word that was said.

The military Cockney waiter did, however, and he turned away in disgust.

"Beast !" he muttered.

"Ready ?"

"Yes."

"Remember your face-guard, sir," said the waiter, quietly. "Hold your elbow low, keep the hilt of your sword straight between your eyes. He's a powerful and wicked brute. If he tries to break down your guard by mere force, don't attempt to parry, but leap aside, and give him your point—not too high, for I don't think you could get it into him about the chest."

The honest waiter's meaning became apparent after the contest was over.

You will see how.

"On guard !"

The swords clashed, and the Spaniard began by a desperate down cut, which Jack, remembering his instructions, leapt aside to avoid, and boring suddenly in, down went the brutal duellist with a gasp.

"Hit!" cried the waiter.

"Spitted, by jabers!"

"*Caramba!*"

"*Maledicion!*" cried the wounded combatant.

And staggering up, sword in hand, he made a step forward as if to cleave his young adversary to the earth, but ere he could reach him, Jack passed his sword through his side. The Spaniard, with a groan, tottered, and fell again in a deathly faint.

Jack at once dropped his sword, and ran forward.

"I hope he is not badly hurt," he said, dropping on one knee by the side of the wounded man.

The officer whose sabre Don Gil Perez had borrowed for the combat proved to be a military surgeon.

He examined the wound, and speedily relieved all anxiety upon this head.

"An ugly wound. Care and rest only required," he said.

"I'm heartily glad of that," said Jack, with a deep-drawn sigh of relief.

Having assured himself of his principal's safety, Don Miguel Basten beckoned the waiter to his side.

"Tell the young Inglese from me that he has conducted himself like a brave lad—that he is an honour to his name and to his country, and that if he wants a friend while here, he may count upon Miguel Basten."

"I will, senor."

"And tell him also that the sooner he is away from this place now, the better it will be. I wish the brave boy well."

This was translated to young Jack, who bowed his acknowledgments, and having resumed his jacket, started with his friends towards his hotel.

CHAPTER XXXVIII.

THE VICTOR'S RETURN—BULL RUNNING—THE ORPHAN IS IN TROUBLE AGAIN.

HARRY GIRDWOOD was now radiant with smiles.

"What did I tell you, Harry?" said the successful combatant.

"There's a sweet little cherub that sits up aloft. You know the rest."

"I do."

"An illigant fight," said the diver, "but the fun was precious soon over."

"Come home with us," said Jack. "You're going down to the wreck this morning?"

"Yes, sorr."

"I can give you a job."

"Can you, though? Ye're good at giving jobs, your honour, axing yer pardon. Ye've give that mossoo don a job in the stummick that'll want a deal of mending."

"Well, the beast deserved it, but now let us come to breakfast," said Harry.

"With all my heart, yer honour."

"I've not done a bad morning's work either,"

said the military waiter. "I did well to make my bargain last night."

"You did," said Jack, "and I'll treble the tip, my boy, for you're an honest fellow, and a true Englishman. And now for breakfast."

And a capital breakfast it was, although rather foreign in its elements, to which young Jack and Harry Girdwood sat down on their return from the duel.

Need we say that being blest with healthy English appetites, they did ample justice to it?

"What is that fellow doing over the way?" said Harry, when the edge of his appetite was pretty well blunted.

As he spoke, he pointed to a very shabby-looking Spaniard, who was plastering some gaudy strips of coloured paper to the wall of a house opposite.

"Looks like a bill-sticker," replied Jack.

"Then let him beware."

The two youths continued to watch him till he had almost covered the side of the building with an immense advertisement which, being at least ten times as large as anything else of that kind in the town, was evidently some announcement of great importance.

"Waiter," shouted Jack, ringing the bell.

"Yessir, comin', sir," responded the English attendant. "Some more wine, sir? We have very nice garlic and donkey sausages, sir, if you would like some just to finish off with, or will you take some holives, gemmen?"

"Pah! nothing of the kind. We want to know what that big bill is about."

"A bull-fight—sir."

"A bull fight, when?"

"At two o'clock to-morrow, sir."

"They don't advertise it long beforehand," observed Harry.

"Beg pardon, sir, they have had smaller bills out for a week or more."

"Shall we go, Harry?" asked young Jack.

"Don't much care about it, after all I've read on the subject, but I suppose being in Spain, we must do as the Spaniards do. How far is it to the arena?"

"Half a mile, sir; you can't mistake the road; all you has to do is foller the crowd; and if yer consciences should be uneasy, gemmen, remember this 'ere bull-fight is for the benefit of the hospital of San Carlos, so you'll be doin' good to the poor by going."

Now it may be taken for granted that all Spaniards are fond of their national pastime of the bull-fight, but it is also a fact that in all towns where such sport is supported, there is a number of poor people who are unable to pay for admission to the arena. Therefore, for the gratification of these humble folk, it is customary to exhibit the bulls publicly the day before the fight.

This public exhibition of the animals takes place in the following fashion.

The bulls having been driven down from the mountains, are pastured in some meadows belonging to the authorities, till the evening before the fight, when they are driven thence through the chief streets to the stalls, or torril, of the arena.

All the lower classes go to witness this gratuitous exhibition—called the *encierro*—to speculate on the qualities and condition of the animals, and the prospect of their showing good sport.

These ragamuffins of the town also contrive to make a little sport for themselves, for they yell like fiends, flutter their tattered cloaks, throw stones, and freely use their cudgels on the semi-savage cattle, which thus get a nice foretaste of the tortures that await them.

But to return to Jack and Harry.

By the time they had finished their breakfast, the sun was so powerful that they did not care to venture out, so they read, lounged, and dozed till the afternoon, when the sound of an unusual concourse of people in the street drew them to the window.

"What's up, Jack?" asked Harry.

"Can't say, old boy, unless it is another revolution. Ask the waiter."

The question having been put, they received the explanation given above; and being informed that the bulls would probably pass in front of the hotel, they drew their chairs out to the balcony to witness the fun.

"Look at that fellow, Harry," said young Jack, pointing to a man, whose coarse hair was visible through the crown of his broad hat, whose scanty jacket betrayed his want of shirt, whose breeches were woefully tattered, but who, nevertheless, wore his cloak gracefully draped over his shoulder, with as jaunty an air as though he had been a grandee of the bluest blood.

Both lads burst into loud laughter at the sight of this figure.

"A fourth-rate Don Quixote," exclaimed Harry. "Ha, ha, ha! his dignity is wounded by our merriment."

The object of their mirth hearing the sound of laughter, looked up, and perceiving that they were laughing at him, scowled most ferociously.

Of course this only increased the mirth of our hero and his friend Harry.

"He'd make the fortune of any East End theatre," exclaimed Jack. "See, there's an attitude for you."

The man was shaking his fist and (although the lads did not understand him) evidently swearing most furiously.

Finding this no use, however, he threw his cloak over his shoulder and stalked away.

"Jack, do you know that fellow?"

"Not I. Do you?"

"I've seen him before, I feel certain, but I can't remember where or when it was. He looks like a villain."

"He be hanged! don't puzzle your brains about him, Harry, but look out, for here come the bulls."

The roars and shouts of the crowd were deafening as the four fine animals came along the street.

One was deep red or dun in colour, another a light grey, and a third black and white.

These three went along tolerably quiet, but the fourth was a fierce-looking brute, with narrow flanks, deep chest, a tangled mass of hair over his eyes, and a skin black as night.

On seeing him the multitude at once saluted him as El Diablo, *the devil*, and a devilish temper he exhibited certainly.

"Bravo!" shouted the multitude, and, by way of response, the bull turned and made a savage rush at one fellow.

The crowd shrieked and swayed backwards, and some of the weaker were trodden under foot.

"By Jove! old fellow, this is dangerous work," exclaimed Jack.

"They want a few of our Australian stock-driving friends here," responded Harry.

Now it so happened that in the crowd was no less a person than our old friend the orphan.

Mr. Figgins had gone out, not to see the bulls, but to look at the town and pick up an idea or two as to how his trade was managed in the native home of the orange.

Luckless Mr. Figgins! he managed to get back into the main street just as the black bull El Diablo made his rush.

With head down, and eyes blinded by the shaggy hair that fell over them, the savage brute charged in a direct line along the street, the people opening out and crowding into doorways so as to form a clear course.

The course was cleared, but the orphan was left, like the dog that always appears on an English racecourse, and the bull getting an indistinct view of him, uttered a deep roar and charged at him headlong.

Away flew the orphan at full speed, the bull pursuing, but a glance over his shoulder soon convinced him that he could not escape by swiftness, so he turned sharply and tried to dodge the infuriated animal.

"Oh, dear, oh, dear," said the orphan; "I thought I travelled for pleasure, but this is anything but fun for me. Oh, you horrid beast; oh, oh!"

The bull was too quick for him, and in a moment threw Mr. Figgins on a huge heap of vegetable refuse, cabbage leaves, and such like, that had been swept out of the market place.

Into this heap of rubbish he sank deeply, but he had sufficient presence of mind to throw a few of the cabbage leaves over him, so as to conceal his body from the savage creature, otherwise he would certainly have been gored.

Not seeing his enemy, but discovering some cabbage leaves that were not quite rotten, the bull began to feed upon them.

"Save me! Save a poor orphan. Help, help, help!" shouted Figgins from beneath his verdant coverlet. "The brute is devouring me."

Loud shouts of laughter came from the crowd, and El Diablo, warned by the sound that he had more than one enemy, turned, tossing his head, pawing the ground, and apparently selecting the next object for his attack.

"Look at our orphan friend," exclaimed Jack, who had been laughing as loudly as any one at Mr. Figgins' mishap.

"Bravo! orphan. Well done, bull," shouted Harry. "Tell the bull you are a poor orphan, Figgins, and he won't have the heart to touch you."

The orphan had ventured to peep out from his hiding-place, and seeing the tail of the bull turned towards him, prepared to steal away.

With the greatest caution he removed the leaves, crept from his hiding-place, and darted down the street, towards the hotel.

He had gone perhaps fifteen or twenty yards when El Diablo, turning round—probably for another mouthful of cabbage—perceived his enemy running away.

Another loud roar, and with tail erect, the bull gave chase.

"Oh, mercy! why did I ever leave my happy home in London?" shrieked Figgins, dodging the bull and turning back. "Save me, someone. Oh, I shall feel his horns in a moment."

"I must save him; he is in real danger now," exclaimed young Jack. "Here goes."

And snatching up the sabre with which he fought the Carlist, he took a flying leap from the balcony, just as the hapless orphan, in his fright, ran past the hotel.

"Bravo, viva!" shouted the crowd, as they saw Jack safe on the ground, sword in hand, place himself between the bull and the flying man.

The monster paused a moment on seeing his new foe.

But a moment after, he charged with redoubled violence, not at the orphan this time, but at our hero.

Now young Jack had read of the style in which a Spanish matador slays his bull, and in his usual dare-devil way, resolved to show the people that an English lad could do the trick.

So, as the bull all but reached him, he stepped nimbly aside, and drove the blade of his sabre between the bull's shoulder and ribs.

Snap!

The blade parted at the hilt, and Jack, although he struck furiously at the brute, was knocked down and stunned.

"Have a care—have a care," shouted the people, as the bull, in spite of its wound, half turned, and went down on its knees to finish the brave English youth.

But Harry Girdwood by this time was close at hand, and ere the sharp-pointed horns could pierce our hero's body, a pistol bullet crashed through the skull of El Diablo, who, with a dull, hollow moan, fell dead.

"The bull's killed. Bravo!" shouted the crowd, as they closed round.

Then rose shouts for wine, brandy, and water for young Jack.

Some of the latter was given him first, then a drop of brandy, and our hero was once more on his feet.

"Thanks, old fellow," said Jack, warmly, pressing Harry's hand. "I am all right, now; is the bull dead and the orphan safe?"

"Oh, Master Jack," cried the orphan, running up; "you have saved my life; you are better than a mother to me, my dear boy."

"I was doubtful whether I should be in time," said Harry. "But are you sure you are not hurt, Jack?"

"No bones broken. Nothing but a bruise or two, and that we are both used to by this time."

"Look, Jack, how the mob is getting round us; let's get back to the hotel."

"All right. But what are these fellows grumbling at?"

The temper of the crowd seemed to have undergone a sudden change, and instead of applauding the gallantry of the two English lads, the people began to abuse them.

"They have slain the best bull," shouted some.

"Better that fifty English should have been gored, than we deprived of our sport," said others.

"Knock 'em down," cried an English voice. "Kill 'em; they're only English spies."

Jack looked round, and thought he caught sight of Chivey.

Cudgels were flourished in a very threatening manner, but in the midst of the uproar, an officer of the municipal authorities, who had provided the bulls for the show, came up.

"You are foreigners, senors?" said this man, in broken English.

"Yes," responded Jack.

"You have slain the best of the bulls provided by the council of the town for to-morrow's show, and must, therefore, pay the sum of two hundred dollars at once."

"What for?" demanded Jack, bluntly.

"The cost of the animal is one hundred and fifty dollars, and the council imposes a fine of fifty dollars on anyone who interrupts or prevents the public sports."

"I'll see the council hanged first," exclaimed young Jack, indignantly. "What, pay two hundred dollars because my brave friend here saved my life? You go to Bath and learn how to shave pigs."

The majority of the mob could no more understand Jack's speech than he could theirs; but they guessed from his manner that it was nothing very complimentary.

"What says the islander?" they roared.

And when the municipal officer translated our hero's words, they grew furious.

Knives were brandished as well as cudgels, and there arose a savage cry of—

"Death! Death to the English!"

"Give it 'em; run 'em in again," cried the voice of Chivey from the background.

Now young Jack was not one of those who, on receipt of a blow, say—

"If you do that again, I'll strike you."

But his practice was, when fighting seemed necessary and could not be honourably avoided, to put in the first blow—which he looked upon as being a good way towards winning the battle.

So now finding himself menaced, he wasted no time in words, but rushing at one fellow, snatched away his cudgel, and with it instantly knocked down another of the mob.

Harry Girdwood immediately followed suit.

"Wire in, Jack."

"Go ahead—but keep cool—don't lose your nut."

So back to back they stood defying the mob.

The municipal officer drew his sword, but Jack, without any ceremony, knocked it out of his hand with such force that the blade snapped.

"There, old man," cried Jack; "get a better sword when you again stand before a Boy of England."

"Look out, Jack. They are drawing knives," said Harry.

"The cowardly villains; why, they are a hundred to one, now. We are in for it, Harry, old boy; only keep on cracking Spanish nuts as long as you can lift your stick."

Harry responded by dropping a weighty blow on the head of a ragamuffin, who was pressing in upon them, with a knife only half concealed in his tattered coat sleeve.

"Take that, you dirty thief," he said, addressing his fallen foe, who not being quite stunned, had sense enough to roll away among the feet of his friends.

The others, seeing the resolute attitude of the two youths, drew back a little, not quite relishing the encounter.

"Cowards," exclaimed a gruff voice from the back, "are you going to be beaten by two boys?"

Jack guessed at the meaning of the words, and shouted out—

"If the gentleman in the background wants anything, let him come forward, and I will be most happy to oblige him."

Which words were translated for the benefit of the unseen speaker by the municipal officer, who remained on the scene of battle, though he prudently kept out of the reach of Jack's cudgel.

There was a slight commotion in the crowd, and a burly fellow, a butcher by trade, pushed his way to the front.

He had in one hand a heavy cudgel, and in the other a long knife, used in his business.

"He's a toughish customer, Harry, so keep the crowd back as well as you can, while I have a crack at him. Oh, if dad and Uncle Dick were here, we'd soon make short work of them."

So saying, Jack made a step forward, and at once knocked the knife out of the rascal's hand, who roared with pain.

"At wrestling, boxing, or singlestick I am your man," said Jack; but before he could give his adversary a specimen of either art, the crowd closed in upon them.

Jack was unable to use his cudgel, but he struck out with his hands and made the eyes of more than one Spaniard blacker than nature intended them to be.

"How goes it, Harry?" he found time to ask.

"Plenty to do and not much to get for it. Ease off a little, if you can, and let us get back to back."

"Right," and knocking down a man in front of him, so as to make room, young Jack placed his back to Harry's, and there they stood defying the whole mob.

By this time the butcher had recovered his courage and his knife.

He was just meditating another onslaught, when on the outskirts of the crowd was heard a loud shout.

"Hurroo! Ould Ireland for ever! Faugh-a-ballah! Clear the road, ye dhirty spalpeens, bad manners to the loikes of yez!"

"Here's Whitechapel to the fore, mates; mind yer eye," said another voice.

"Will ye trid on the tale of me coat? Come out o' that now and foight, ye ill-lookin' thief o' the worrld."

And then there were shrieks and curses as the English waiter from the hotel and his friend, the diver, forced their way through the crowd.

"Hurrah for Old England!" shouted Jack and making a dash forward, he hurled to the ground the only Spaniard who stood between him and his friends.

"Safe, Mr. 'Arkaway?" asked the waiter.

"All right, thank you," responded our hero, picking up his cudgel.

"Mr. Girdwood all right?"

"A slight cut on the arm—nothing worth mentioning."

"One more charge, lads, and victory is ours. Now, all together."

They made a charge forward, and the Spaniards scattered in every direction, shouting as they ran—

"Death! Death to the Inglese!"

"Hot work while it lasted, gemmen," observed the waiter; "but, Lord, them fellows is no use whatever. They lives on garlic, and the strongest thing about 'em is their breath. They ain't got no more biceps than a black beetle."

"Be the holy piper," exclaimed the diver, "I belave I've killed one of the ugly gossoons. Get up, ye murtherin' villain," he continued, tickling the prostrate Spaniard's ribs with his toe, "get up and tell us if ye're dead enough to be afther wantin' a coffin."

The man was not dead, for he started to his feet, and drawing a knife, hurled it at the Irishman.

The missile hissed past his head, and stuck quivering in a door behind him.

"Death to the English!" shouted the man, as he started off at full speed down the street.

"Bad cess to ye!" shouted the Irishman, shaking his fist, half inclined to follow, and yet restrained by what he thought his duty— viz., a determination to protect our hero.

"That was a narrow escape," observed Harry Girdwood.

"A miss is as good as a mile, sorr. But I'll be afther knowin' the blackguard again if I meet him, and——"

The man gave a vicious flourish to as elegant a shillelagh as ever grew in the county of Wicklow to express what would happen when he did meet that Spaniard.

"But where is Mr. Figgins all this while?" asked Jack. "We had better look about for him, for if those fellows get hold of him, they will carve him up in no time."

CHAPTER XXXIX.

THE ORPHAN FIGHTS A SINGLE COMBAT— SUPPER—A GRANDEE OF SPAIN APPEARS ON THE SCENE.

BUT where was the luckless Mr. Figgins?

Our friends looked up the street and down the street.

There may have been orphans in view, but if so, they were of Spanish descent; Mr. Figgins could not be seen.

Inquiry was made at the door of the hotel, but he had not been seen there since the morning.

"Come along; let us look for him," said

Harry. "If he is in trouble, we must help him out of it."

"Begorra!" exclaimed the Irishman, "it's me opinion that the gentleman cannot take care of himself at all, at all."

"He has never been brought up to help himself much in the fighting line," said Jack, "and you know it can't be learnt all at once."

"Thrue for ye. Howly saints! miny's the time I had me head broke before I knew how to prevint it."

"Hark!" said Harry. "Unless I am very much mistaken, that's his voice."

"Voice, d'ye call it? Shure, an Oirish pig under a gate has a more iligant voice."

Paying no heed to the Irishman's disparaging remarks, Jack and Harry rushed off in the direction of the sound.

Turning an abrupt angle, they beheld the object of their search.

Mr. Figgins was standing in a doorway.

In front of him was an old Spanish woman, armed with a dagger, with which she made furious thrusts at the orphan, all the while cursing him in the choicest Spanish.

The orphan parried her blows as well as he could, all the while bellowing for help at the top of his voice.

By a lucky stroke of his stick, he managed to knock the dagger out of her grasp.

But it was a case of out of the frying-pan into the fire with him, for the old woman, rushing in, seized him by the head, tore his hair, and buffeted his face at a furious rate.

The waiter, however, coming up behind, seized her by the wrists and dragged her away to the other side of the road, when, seeing that the odds were very much against her, she departed, not without bestowing a back-handed blessing, in the choicest of Spanish Billingsgate slang, upon the English nation generally.

"Where is he? Where is the monstrous brigand with whom I have been fighting for an hour or more?" said Figgins, catching up his stick and brandishing it very near the Irishman's head.

"Bad cess to yez! Put down that twig, or I'll be afther killin' ye. Put it down, ye spalpeen."

Mr. Figgins dropped his stick as if it was red hot.

"Brigand!" exclaimed Jack, shaking with laughter. "Why, it was an old woman, and I am surprised you should be so ungallant as to strike one of the fair sex."

"Not a brigand?"

"No."

"Then my eyes have deceived me—but that is not to be wondered at, as my eyeglass is smashed. Oh, Master Jack, I must once more thank you. But are you certain the bull is dead?"

"Dead as a doornail," answered Jack; "and you have to thank Harry as well as me for your safety."

"Gentlemen," said the orphan, "I thank you very much. I had the misfortune to be left without a parent's guidance many years ago, but I have been taught to be grateful, and to prove my gratitude by something more than words, allow me to invite you all to supper with me at—let me see, it's five o'clock now—how will nine o'clock suit?"

"Admirably," said Harry and Jack.

"These two gentlemen will join us, of course," continued the orphan, pointing to the waiter and the diver.

"Will a duck shwim!" exclaimed the diver. "An' d'ye think an Oirishman will iver turn his back on good 'ating, dhrinkin', foightin', or iny other koind of fun? It's there I'll be, shure enough, yer honour."

But the waiter said, when appealed to—

"Much obliged, I'm sure, sir, but I'm honly one of the servants, and should be out of place a-setting down with you gemmen."

"Nonsense!" exclaimed Jack. "For once we'll dispense with all notions of etiquette. As we have fought together, so we'll sup together."

"Very good, sir—honly I thought as how, perhaps, some might object."

"Not at all," responded the orphan and Harry.

"Then, that bein' the case, I had better get in and order the feed."

"Certainly," replied Figgins, "and mind that everything is of the very best. Get as many English dishes as you can."

"Trust me, sir. I and the cook is great pals."

"Mr. Figgins," said Jack, as the waiter moved off, "will you permit me to bring a friend with me?"

"Certainly. A gentleman, I presume, for I am very nervous in ladies' company."

"Oh, yes," responded Jack, "a Polish nobleman on his travels—Count Nerowski by name."

"I shall be delighted to see him. He, he, he! I am getting to be quite at home among the aristocracy. Well, good evening, gentlemen, for the present; don't forget nine o'clock, for my terrific combat has made me very hungry."

The orphan walked away.

"Sorr," said the diver, "I'll wish yez good evening for the presint."

"You'll come to supper?"

"Be aisy about that same, sorr. I only want to put on me most iligant clothes, so as not to disgrace the gintleman."

"Very well; but we shall expect you."

"Jack," said Harry, as they stood together in front of the hotel, "who is this Polish nobleman?"

"One who can climb a pole better than either of us, and we are not altogether lubbers."

"What do you mean?"

"Count Nerowski is our old friend Nero, with a tail to his name as well as to his body. By-the-bye, how did he get ashore?"

"Jumped into one of the boats along with the men."

"By-the-bye, Harry, did you see that beast Chivey in the mob?"

"Yes, Jack, I caught sight of the young villain for a moment. We must be on the look-out for him and his master. But what is your little game, Jack?"

"Only a lark."

"No harm, I suppose?"

"Not a bit ; old Nero will get a good supper, and we shall have some harmless fun."

They strolled up and down the verandah for some time, and at length resolved to go and dress for supper.

Their own costume required little alteration, as they said that if the dress of a British sailor was not good enough, they would not alter it to suit anyone's taste, but to equip Count Nerowski in a costume suited to his high rank was no such easy work.

After some trouble, however, they managed to get him rigged out in a pair of black trousers, white vest, across which a blue and red ribbon was tied sashwise, and a black dress coat.

But as for getting the count's feet into boots, or his hands into gloves, that was a matter none of them could accomplish, so they allowed his hands and feet to remain uncovered.

"Mr. Figgins, allow me to introduce you to his excellency Count Nerowski," said Jack, leading that distinguished foreigner into the supper room.

Nero bowed in imitation of his master, and chattered at the orphan, who of course did not understand.

"I am very delighted to make the acquaintance of your noble friend, but he is a strange-looking person," he said to Jack, on the quiet.

The company being assembled, supper was served, the orphan taking the head of the table, and Count Nerowski facing him, that being the dark end of the room.

For a time all went well, and the company enjoyed themselves.

When the cloth was removed, a few toasts were proposed, and Harry Girdwood gave "The health of our esteemed friend, Mr. Figgins."

They all stood up to drink the toast.

"Good Heaven ! what is the count doing ?" exclaimed Mr. Figgins.

"Bravo, Nerowski," shouted Jack.

The count, wishing to pay all honour to his host, had mounted on the back of his chair, where he held on by one foot, while with the other he lifted a glass of wine to his lips.

In his right hand he held a cigarette, in his left he waved a cambric handkerchief.

The diver, the waiter, young Jack, and Harry Girdwood screamed with laughter at this performance, but the orphan, being near-sighted, and Nero in the dark part of the room, was really frightened.

"Help your friend down, I pray, Mr. Harkaway. If he should fall and get hurt, I should never forgive myself."

"Don't be alarmed, sir ; he very often goes on in this style."

"But what's he doing ?"

"He's now imitating the celebrated marble group entitled 'Ajax defying the Vaccination Act,'" said Jack, gravely.

"It is most extraordinary. I wish I had my eye-glass, or the room was lighter, for I can hardly see him so far away."

Nero sat down, and having, by accident, wetted his pockethandkerchief with champagne, gravely squeezed out the superfluous moisture as he had seen sailors and washerwomen do after rinsing their clothes.

"That's another of his illustrations." observed Jack, "copied from a bronze group be purchased at St. Petersburg."

"Indeed. May I ask the name of it ?"

"It represents Neptune washing a paper collar at the public fountain of Cecropia."

"You surprise me," exclaimed Mr. Figgins.

"So you do me," said Harry, trying to keep from laughing.

As for the diver and the waiter, they roared again.

How long the fun would have lasted, is uncertain ; but a Spanish waiter entering, called out the English one, and that for a time interrupted the conversation.

"I shall not be away long. gentlemen." said the English waiter.

He had not left the company but a few moments, before Jack thought he heard a strange sound.

"Hark !" exclaimed Jack, "what sound is that ?"

"What is the matter, old man ?" asked Harry.

"I thought I heard a groan."

"Nonsense."

"Be gorra ! there it is again," said the diver.

They all listened attentively, and in a few seconds heard a faint sob like the gasp of a dying man.

Jack at once rushed out, followed by Harry and the Irishman.

There, in the corridor, lay their humble friend the English waiter, his life blood streaming from three stiletto wounds in the body.

"Alarm the house ; murder's been done !" shouted Jack.

The landlord and servants soon came flocking to the place, and the unfortunate man, being laid on a bed, medical aid was sought.

At the British consulate was an English medical man, and he being informed of what had happened, quickly appeared on the scene.

"Is he alive ?" asked Jack.

It was some minutes before the doctor answered—

"He still breathes, but his life hangs by a thread, and if he recovers, it will be more through the aid of Providence than my medicine. But who did this ?"

That no one could tell.

The Spaniard who called the wounded man out had left him talking with two men—those men had disappeared, and no one knew who they were or whither they had gone.

CHAPTER XL.

MR. MURRAY HAS A SECOND EDITION—DICK'S SUBSTITUTE FOR AN ACT OF PARLIAMENT —MR. MURRAY STARTS FOR SPAIN.

SOON after Mr. Murray read his hopeful son's telegram, of which we have already spoken, he made preparations hurriedly to start.

He dreaded every hour of his life to come across the wooden-legged warrior Mole. or Jack Harkaway, or Dick Harvey.

"I must be careful," he thought.

He got hold of a shipping advertisement sheet, and selected a vessel which was to start at an early date.

At length, being perfectly satisfied that the coast was clear, he sallied forth.

He was so disguised that very little of his countenance remained visible.

"I'm in luck," he said to himself; "the Harkaway people are not on the watch."

He was mistaken. Night and day they had been, one or the other of them, on watch by the shipowner's house, until the wretched man was in fear of his life.

"A brutal, murderous lot, these people," he said; "a villanous crew those Harkaways, and they would think no more of taking one's life than of cracking a nut."

Barely had Mr. Murray made this very singular simile when bang came a thwack upon the top of his head.

"Oh, oh!" he cried.

And a thousand sparks flashed across his eyes.

"You old beast!" exclaimed a voice in his ear, which sounded familiar.

Mr. Murray, momentarily dazed by the blow, looked round, and there stood Dick Harvey.

The shipowner was aghast at the sight.

Dick carried a stout ash stick.

"How dare you stop me in this way, ruffian?" said Mr. Murray, looking anxiously about him as he spoke.

"How dare I?" exclaimed Dick. "Why, for decoying young Jack Harkaway and his comrade, Harry Girdwood, on board your coffin ship. The law doesn't call this murder, so what I have got to do is not legal. But punished you must be all the same, and shall be, without witnesses."

Mr. Murray suddenly plucked up courage for a very brief moment, and made a desperate rush.

But before he could get any distance, Dick Harvey was after him.

"Stop that," cried Dick, grabbing at his shoulder. "You can't get out of it now. You brought it on yourself, and you must take punishment from my hand and this stick."

Mr. Murray had bought himself a jack-knife, a big one, for the voyage, and so, as the handiest weapon of defence, he whipped it out and stood at bay.

For a minute they stood facing each other, Dick poising his stick in his hand, ready to run in and make play, Murray crouching and watching the faintest movements of the enemy with great eagerness.

Dick advanced.

"Keep off," cried Murray; "I don't want your blood upon my head."

"I'll take my chance," said Dick, still advancing.

Now he shot in closer, and when old Murray brandished his weapon rather wildly, Dick dropped him a stinger on the hand, and down went the knife.

"Murder!" yelled Murray. "Oh, oh!"

"Cry away," said Dick, cheerfully, as he laid on his blows with a lavish hand.

"Help, help, murder!"

Bang! thwack! came down Dick's stick.

"Ruffian!" gasped the shipowner.

"There," cried Dick, "one more."

Mr. Murray felt the crack, and sank upon the ground with a groan.

"Now," said Harvey, "now, Mr. Murray, you may pause before you venture upon any more of your infamous exploits; when you want to speculate again in sailors' lives, and play at legalised murder, just you reflect on this."

Dick shook the stick before old Murray's eyes.

"Think," said Dick, sternly, "of the wretchedness you have made in many a home—as you are a father, think of the desolation wrought upon the Harkaways by your villanous conduct."

"My own boy, my darling Herbert was on board the 'Albatross,'" said Murray, looking up.

"Then the greater old villain you!" ejaculated Harvey, with indignation.

"You have used me cruelly," said old Murray, rubbing his bruised parts.

"Not half so badly as I ought to have done."

"But I will try and forgive; I will try and repay you with comfort; yes, news to make you happy."

"How?"

"Listen. Will you tell Mr. Harkaway that his boy is safe—safe and sound on the Spanish coast?"

"Never."

"He is, I swear. I have a telegram from my son."

"Where?"

"Here."

"Give it me."

"No, no," returned old Murray, clapping his hand over his breast pocket. "I am hastening now to take ship to fly over to my boy—my dear, rebellious, disobedient darling."

"Let me look."

Like a man in a dream, Dick Harvey read the telegram which old Murray handed to him.

"Safe ashore. 'Albatross' condemned in port to be sold."

"Good Heaven!" thought Dick, "if this is true, what joyful news for Jack and Emily."

"It is true," said Murray. "I have a heart, much as you may doubt it, and I would not now trifle with a father's feelings—no, not for all the mines of gold, I swear."

There was no mistaking the miserable man's earnestness now.

"He is sincere, if ever a man was," said Harvey.

He was right.

A change had come over Mr. Murray's feelings.

"Why on earth did you not tell me before?" said Harvey; "all might have been spared—all—all."

"I tried to speak; you would not listen," replied Mr. Murray, groaning over his bruises.

"Where are you going to now?" demanded Dick. "Speak without fear; I shall put your answer to no evil use."

"I am going on board to-night," returned Mr. Murray.

"Go at once, then. I will hasten to inform Harkaway of young Jack's safety."

That night Mr. Murray slept on board.

The next morning, at an hour after daylight,

the ship "Harpy" weighed anchor and carried the shipowner towards his scapegrace son.

Let the most favourable winds fill the sails of the good ship "Harpy," we doubt if she will very speedily reach the port where the "Albatross" lies fathoms low, foundered in fair weather.

CHAPTER XLI.

MR. MURRAY—ON BOARD THE SHIP "HARPY" —THE BITER BIT—MORAL REFLECTIONS.

THE good ship "Harpy" stood out at sea ready for the Spanish coast.

From the first, however, she had encountered heavy weather, and she strained and creaked as she ploughed her way through the boiling sea in a way that would have made a nervous mariner quake.

But Mr. Murray was too full of the happy anticipations of once again pressing his wild and disobedient son to his heart to think of the perils afloat.

Let the wind roar and the ship be knocked about ever so much, not a bit did he heed it.

When they had been a few days afloat, there were signs of uneasiness amongst the crew that should have made him think seriously.

But he never questioned them, nor did he take any notice whatever, until the steward came to him with a long face and broached the subject of the extreme stress of weather.

"It'll be a precious narrow squeak, sir, for us if we ever see land again."

"Do you think that the ship is in any danger?" asked Murray.

"Do I think?" returned the steward. "Do I know! Why, our chance of seeing land again in this ramshackle old cockboat is about as small as it well could be. A good ship would have a bad chance now, but a patched-up old hull like the 'Harpy's' hasn't the ghost of a chance, and that's my candid opinion, sir."

"Good Heaven!" cried old Murray, in fright.

"Yes, sir," continued the steward, "I fear we are doomed for a watery grave."

"I was given to understand that the 'Harpy' was a capital little ship. Ah, and in excellent condition."

The steward chuckled grimly at this.

"You was, was you?"

"Yes, by the people at the brokers who chartered her."

"I thought so," remarked the steward, gravely.

"But why, my good man, why?" asked Mr. Murray, anxiously, and beginning to feel dreadfully frightened.

"Why, I believe the owners are rascals, and ought to be trounced for trapping poor devils on their coffin ship."

Mr. Murray gave a start of utter dismay.

A coffin ship!

"You, you don't mean to say you think this?"

"Yes, I do, though."

"Good Heaven!" cried the ship broker, falling back with horror.

"Hold steady, sir; but that's just about the size of it," pursued the steward.

Mr. Murray gave a hollow groan and staggered back, half fainting.

He had been already punished by the flight of his boy, and now he was crowning the fulfilment of his destiny by sinking in a coffin-ship in mid-ocean.

*   *   *   *   *

It would be impossible to describe adequately the thousand and one conflicting thoughts which fled through his mind.

Was this indeed to be the end of everything?

His very soul quaked.

His punishment had come.

He walked up and down in the greatest restlessness and anxiety, vainly endeavouring to calm himself.

The hand of fate was upon him.

He jumped up and made for the deck.

He found out the first mate and questioned him about the vessel.

"Well, sir," said the mate. "all I can say is we ain't gone down yet, that's all, though how long I may be able to sing the same tune is quite another matter."

"Do you look upon the 'Harpy' as doomed then?" he asked.

The mate nodded.

"That's about it, sir."

"Then what preparations are you making to meet the calamity?"

"None."

"What?"

"We ain't got preparations to make. When the time comes, we shall take to the boats. As many as can get in, will get in, and the rest——"

"Yes, the rest?" demanded the shipowner, eagerly.

"They'll have to shift for themselves."

"Good Heaven!" ejaculated Mr. Murray. "Is it possible that proper precautions aren't taken by the owners?"

"The owners? There are plenty of owners like them; they send out rotten ships that they know must go to the bottom of the sea. What are the lives of sailors and passengers to them, sir? They are simply murderers, and when their time comes to die, they will be punished here and hereafter for their black deeds."

Mr. Murray staggered back a sad man.

Oh, how he feared death, and above all death in a coffin ship at sea.

"Is there no hope for the 'Harpy?'" asked the shipowner once more.

The mate shook his head.

"Is the danger immediate, do you think?"

"There's a bare chance, if we come across assistance. But you can turn in in safety to-night, for the wind has dropped, and there's no fear of an accident yet awhile. But it's only a question of time."

With a heavy heart, the man that had caused so many deaths at sea went below to his berth.

He tried to sleep, but he was a long time dropping off, and then his slumber was of a fitful, unhealthy kind.

"'YOU ARE CHARGED WITH BEING A SPY IN THE PAY OF OUR ENEMIES!' SAID THE OFFICER."

CHAPTER XLII.

ATONEMENT—ALONE IN THE DARK—STRANGE VISITORS — A NAMELESS TERROR — THE "HARPY" STRIKES — THE SHIPOWNER'S DYING STRUGGLES.

THE swinging lamp in Mr. Murray's berth grew strangely dull, and in the dim, uncertain light, the shipowner felt ill at ease.

A vague uneasiness fell upon him—a dread of unknown danger.

And presently, in his half-dreaming state, there appeared in the corner of the cabin a singular figure.

From the first moment that his glance rested upon this strange visitor, the shipowner felt that it was a familiar presence, and so he watched with singular interest the movements of this figure.

It advanced slowly, and without appearing to walk.

It was more like a gliding motion with which it progressed.

And, in this way, the figure advanced to the side of Mr. Murray's berth.

Never a word did he speak.

When he was close beside him, the shipowner, who was, until now, apparently tongue-tied, found his voice.

"What do you want?" he demanded, in a constrained voice.

The figure made no reply.

A grave nod of the head was his sole acknowledgment of the shipowner's question.

And now Mr. Murray observed, as the man bowed his head in solemn recognition, that water dripped from his hair and beard, which were matted, seemingly, by long immersion.

"What do you want here?" exclaimed the shipowner, suddenly. "I know you. You are Captain Rocket."

"I was," returned the strange visitor, in a hollow voice, "known by that name."

"I knew it," gasped the shipowner; "and you were once the captain of my vessel, the 'Sea Bird.'"

"I come to warn you," said the spectral figure.

"What is that water and seaweed that drips from your long hair?"

"It is part of my shroud," returned the figure.

The shipowner essayed to make answer.

But his tongue clove to the roof of his mouth.

"Your what?" he managed at length to articulate.

"My shroud."

"Then you are not a living, breathing man like me?"

The figure shook its head mournfully.

"I am what you have made me, Murray," it answered, in hollow, sepulchral tones, "through sending me out in your coffin ship. I have risen from my watery grave, to which you have sent me, to warn you."

"Of what?"

"To-morrow."

The shipowner gave a sudden cry of alarm.

"What mean you?"

"Beware to-morrow," returned the strange visitor. "The fate, to which you so heartlessly condemned me and many others, shall be yours. An eye for an eye—a tooth for a tooth."

A nameless dread filled the unhappy shipowner at these awful words.

"Go," he cried, piteously. "Go, and leave me. Why do you come to torment me now?"

"Because you condemned me to a watery grave—I who never wronged you or yours. Because, for vile unhallowed gains, you waited and waited hourly for the news that I had perished with the 'Sea Bird.' It is one year ago this very night that I and a poor helpless crew went to our watery grave from your rotten ship. Yes, I and everyone on board."

"Everyone?"

"Yes, men and boys all lost for your gain."

"It is false," cried Mr. Murray, starting up in his berth. "It is false, I say; it was through no fault of mine," retorted Mr. Murray, "that you and the crew were drowned."

"Whose, then?"

"The owners from whom I bought the ship."

The figure shook his head gravely as before.

"You know well that you, and you alone, are responsible. For you it was who trafficked in honest men's lives to secure your own vile gains. Many's the ship, and many's the crew that now lie fathoms deep in the ocean, sent to their early graves through your villany; therefore, prepare for your doom to-morrow."

"It is all false you tell me. I shall not perish to-morrow. Begone!"

The strange visitor shook his head in the same solemn manner as before.

"You may never learn the truth from other lips than mine," said the shade of Captain Rocket; "but listen. Never more shall you look upon the face of your son again."

"Begone. Out of my sight, devil," yelled the shipowner, worked up into a regular frenzy by now; "out of my sight."

The figure stood still.

"Begone, devil!" exclaimed the wretched man; "I know you now. You are an evil spirit who has taken the form of Rocket to torture me, but I defy you."

But still the pale figure of the dead captain stood there.

And now his rage was succeeded by a deathly fear.

A nameless terror crept upon him once again, and he cowered in his bed.

"Heaven rid me of this horror," wailed the unhappy man.

He closed his eyes to shut out the fearful spectacle, and on opening them, a minute or so later, it was gone.

Yes, vanished!

But only to be replaced by many figures of boys and old sailors.

"What do you want?" faltered the shipowner.

"Beware to-morrow," replied the shadows, in a hollow chorus.

"What of to-morrow?" demanded Murray, eagerly.

"To-morrow you will expiate your crimes, for the many murders you are guilty of in sending us poor souls to sea in your coffin ships," was their reply.

"But how—how?" cried the shipowner; "tell me how, if I am to perish."

"You will be punished by the fate to which you remorselessly condemned our wretched selves. Your bones shall rot in the bed of the ocean."

"It's false," faltered the shipowner, trying in vain to put on a bold front.

"It is true," returned the shade of one poor boy, solemnly.

"If it is not true," said the other figures, in the same measured and hollow tones, "why are we here?"

"As surely as we speak, Michael Murray, you shall never see another sunset. You are on a rotten ship, and you are doomed for a watery grave."

The frightened shipowner essayed in vain to speak.

He could not articulate, try as he would.

He cowered again in his berth to shut out the sight of the spectres, and muttered a prayer, and when he had done this, he found voice to articulate—

"Heaven rid me of the presence of these dreadful spirits."

"We must be gone," said the spectres. "We have warned you; now prepare for your death."

Their shadowy forms melted rapidly.

They were gone.

Mr. Murray struggled to rise from his berth; but something appeared to hold him back, powerless to move hand or foot.

So desperate became his efforts that he lost himself completely in them, and lapsed into insensibility.

*   *   *   *   *

Tossing about on his pillow.

Moaning, groaning, and sighing alternately, keeping time, as it were, to the warning creaking of the vessel, and the ominous roar of the elements without.

Presently he opened his eyes and looked about.

There he was in his cabin. The oil lamp had gone out.

"Where are they?" he murmured, rubbing his eyes, and glancing about him in fear. "Captain Rocket and the drowned sailors. I say, where are they?"

All gone!

A sudden light dawned upon him.

"I was dreaming," he cried, "dreaming—only a dream, after all. But, oh, how horrible! I fell asleep brooding over the steward's croakings of evil, and so have conjured up that horrible vision. But what a relief to find that it all means nothing! It can mean nothing."

The ship received a sudden shock, which threw Mr. Murray from his berth.

"What was that?"

It felt as if she had struck.

As Murray regained his feet, the vessel quivered from stem to stern, as if from the shock she had encountered.

Filled with dire forebodings, he made for the deck with all despatch, and as he reached it, he was dazed with a sudden and vivid flash of lightning.

Recoiling for a moment, he walked on, after holding by the ropes and bulwarks to steady himself, and—

Where was the crew?

Where was the captain?

Not a soul in sight!

He passed his hand across his eyes and stared about him.

"I am still labouring under the effects of this dreadful nightmare, I suppose. How strangely real!"

"Hark!"

A distant growl of thunder rolled on after the tempest-tossed ship, gathering force as it came, and bursting with a deafening crash close overhead.

Then followed a second flash of lightning, and in that lurid glare which momentarily illumined the boiling sea for miles around, the shipowner saw something that chilled the very marrow in his bones.

Two heavily-laden boats tearing through the waves, now perched mountains high, now diving down into the deep trough of the sea.

He guessed the whole truth now at a single glance.

The crew of the "Harpy" had deserted her and taken to the boats.

Aye, to a man.

He was left alone.

Alone!

Oh, fearful word.

Alone to encounter the fearsome perils of that awful night.

"Help, help!" he shouted, with sudden energy. "Do not desert me. Cowards—miscreants—murderers! Do not leave me alone to perish, like a rat in a trap?"

In vain did he cry.

In vain did he shout.

The roar of the wind and the waves drowned his voice.

"Hark again to the thunder!" he shouted again.

His own voice echoed back to him, borne on the wind, seemingly in a mournful cadence, as though he were singing his own funeral dirge.

He looked about him frantically.

Not a hope!

He kicked against some loose spars as he ran forward, and then with wild energy he set to work to lash himself to one with a rope.

But before he could accomplish this—a last faint hope—the "Harpy" gave signs of settling down to her fate.

He felt the ship sinking beneath him, and then he sent up a piercing shriek.

Ha! what are they rising from the waves? Sailor boys and men, with pale, ghastly faces pointing at him.

Look! they are dead men and boys—his victims—drowned at sea.

A piteous cry for mercy comes from the shipowner.

A wail of despair.

And in his frenzy he seemed to hear the voices of his vision reminding him of their warnings.

"What mercy did you have upon others? The mercy you showed them shall be meted out to you!"

He groaned in despair.

Oh, for a hope!
Oh, for the faintest glimmer of a hope!
None—none!
The ship was settling rapidly.
He knew it. He struggled to his feet.
But, weighted as he was with the spar to which he had been fastening himself, he could do nothing.
"It will never float. I shall be drawn down in the vortex."
He now fought frantically to cast himself loose.
He looked about him for a knife—for anything, to cut the rope.
He remembered then that he had provided himself with a large jack-knife, and that he had lost it in his encounter with Harvey.
He fought and struggled as the vessel went lower and lower.
Then the "Harpy" gave a fearful lurch; then heeled up; then plunged down head foremost.
A dreadful despairing shriek came from the unhappy man, and he was silenced for ever.
But the thunder continued to growl, the wind kept up its piteous moan.

CHAPTER XLIII.

MR. CHIVEY GROWS ANECDOTAL AND UN-
PLEASANT TO THE ORPHAN IN PARTICU-
LAR.

THE duel between young Harkaway and the Spanish officers was one of those tales which are called in French—
"*Un secret de Polichinelle*—Punch's secret—otherwise a secret that goes from mouth to mouth like wild-fire."
And so did this spread.
The successful issue of it was talked over with a chuckle by all the English, as you may imagine.
Yet stay.
Not all.
There were two persons who did not chuckle at all.
These were Herbert Murray, who was waiting to hear from his father, little knowing the dreadful fate that had overtaken that wretched man, and Mr. Chivey the tiger.
"A very likely tale, Chivey," said the master.
"Very," said the man.
The master meant it ironically; but the man, who delighted in aggravating the master, chose to pretend to take it literally.
"That Harkaway would run a mile if he saw a drawn sword in the hand of a Carlist soldier," said young Murray.
"Not he," returned the tiger, "he's a regular Tartar. But I never thought that he was half such a dab with the skewer as he is with his fives."
"No humbug, Chivey."
"Well, sir, we know he is a dab with his fives, don't we?" he said, stroking his chin complacently. "I've seen a bit or two in my time. I've had the gloves on with some pretty warm members, but bless my 'art, I never see a cove fib away half so pretty as he did at you. You looked like a rainbow when he'd done with you, sir."

"You're a beast, Chivey."
"But he was wonderful quick. Ding, dong, all over the shop at once. Tick, tick, where'll you have it next?"
"Chivey, I'll——"
"The awful way he must ha' made you see fireworks, sir. Beastly hard knuckles, I should think, sir."
"If you don't hold your tongue, Chivey, I'll send you packing with a flea in your ear."
Mr. Chivey sulked.
"S'pose I mustn't speak now—might as well be in the Penitentiary—or the ha'penny tentiary, if that's a wuss place."
"Hold your tongue; here comes that old fool of a Figgins."
"The orphan, sir?"
"Yes."
Mr. Figgins approached with a nod of recognition, and stopped to chat.
The gruel and tallow candle difficulty had been got over. Mr. Figgins was materially improved in health to-day, having got over the fright of the attack of the bull.
"Good morning, young gentleman," he said.
"Good morning," responded Herbert Murray.
"It's a singular thing, sir," said Chivey, touching his hat, "but just as you come up, we were talking of figs."
Mr. Figgins changed colour slightly at this remark.
"Why singular?" demanded the orphan, curtly.
"Oh, nothing, sir," returned Chivey, with another salute; "only you used to deal in 'em, sir, I believe, didn't you?"
"Ahem! Yes, I certainly did. There is nothing dishonourable in trade. I am proud of my commercial origin. I——"
"Hear, hear!" said Chivey.
"I did deal in figs amongst other articles of colonial produce."
"I've seen that line up somewheres," said Chivey, placing the tip of his forefinger to his forehead. "I'm quite certain we are old pals! Now where is it I have met you?"
After a pause, the orphan said—
"I am not ashamed to own that I have traded in figs."
"And uncommon nice trading, too," said Chivey; "only I should wolf all the profit up if I was a grocer and kept a shop."
The obnoxious words "grocer" and "shop," made the retired tradesman writhe.
Why should his humble origin be cast in his teeth here, far away from Cow Cross, and the scenes of his early struggles?
"I never see you, sir," said the tiger, with the same innocent air, "but what I think of that pious grocer, who used to call to his 'prentice—'Sammy, when you've sanded the sugar, and birch-broomed the tea, and horse-beaned the coffee, come up to prayers.'"
"That's a very stale anecdote, Mr. Murray," said the orphan; "is your servant general entertainer as well as boot polisher?"
"He takes liberties, Mr. Figgins," returned Herbert Murray, who was enjoying the orphan's uneasy looks. "Great liberties. You must learn to know your place, Chivey."
The tiger touched his hat in all humility,

YOUNG JACK HARKAWAY AND

but with a merry devil in his eye all the while.

"Don't be cross ; no bones broke," said the tiger.

"No."

Chivey was in high spirits and a mischievous humour.

"Ah, Mr. Figgins, sir," said Chivey, with something very like a sigh, " I remember your shop in Cow Cross well."

Mr. Figgins gave a start and a look of dismay.

The shop in question—although he called it an emporium—was really a very humble establishment.

"I think I can see your little drum now, sir. The smashed dates with the tupp'ny ticket on 'em, and the fly-blowed sugar."

"Ahem! Fly-blown, Chivey!" said Murray ; " that's a scandal."

"Oh, no, sir. Mr. Figgins will bear me out, won't you, Mr. Figgins? I used to know all your stock, sir, better than you knew it yourself, sir, when I was a kid. I used to go and flatten my blessed nose, sir, against your window, and get right down ravenous at the sight of your biscuits, although they wasn't too fresh-looking."

"Come, come," said Murray, who was obliged to speak so as not to burst out laughing, " the biscuits weren't fly-blown as well."

"Wasn't they, though?"

"No, no," said Mr. Figgins, indignantly, " certainly not. Fly-blown, indeed."

"Well, sir," said the tiger, " I don't like to contradick, but all I knows is that I cert'n'y thought you'd upset the black pepper over 'em myself."

"Ha, ha, ha!" laughed his master, at this.

Mr. Figgins looked very red in the face.

"And then the cheese, sir," said Chivey, seriously, " a peculiar sort o' mottled soap cheese that used to hang on hand a long while as a rule——"

"It is false," said Mr. Figgins. " Really, Mr. Murray, I——"

"And then," continued Chivey, heedless of the orphan's indignation, " it used to be jobbed off to the beershop next door ; that was Shiny William's perks."

"Shiny William?" said Murray. " Who's that?"

"Shiny William was the waiter as had to wait on the cabbies and other gents that used the house."

"But why Shiny William?"

"I think it was because of his shiny coat, sir," continued the tiger; "it had wore that smooth with age and grease, that you'd ha' took it for mackintosh."

"Ha, ha!" laughed his master ; "so that was Shiny William, Mr. Figgins's friend?"

"Yes, sir. Mr. Figgins remembers him well."

"Indeed, I don't," retorted the retired grocer, looking as though he would like to have thrashed the tiger.

"I thought you would, sir, on account of the tale of one of the parties as used the house."

"What was that?"

"He went in one day for some bread and cheese, and says he—'Here, Shiny William,

serve us up a slice o' beeswax and a buster.' 'Yes, sir,' says Shiny William ; 'and, mind, none of old Figgins's mottle mind.' "

"What did your elegant friend mean by beeswax?" Mr. Figgins demanded.

"Why, cheese, sir," continued Chivey. " Well, he cuts open the loaf and out pops a little mouse. Shiny William looks as if he'd been struck by lightning, but the other party took it quite cool. 'Here, Shiny William,' he says, 'sarve this up next turn. I wants bread and cheese. I didn't ask you for a sandwich.' "

"Ha, ha, ha!" laughed his master.

But Mr. Figgins never moved a muscle.

"I am glad, Mr. Murray," he said, " that you enjoy your servant's anecdotes. That one was stale when I was a child."

"I've seen staler things in a certing little shop down Cow Cross way. Eh, Mr. Figgins?" said Chivey.

"Sir," said the orphan proudly to young Murray, "I called on you not to be insulted by your servant, but to speak to you of the great bravery of young Jack Harkaway—how he fought a duel and beat his man, and after that how he saved my life from a mad bull ; but I see you do not understand noble deeds, and I wish you good morning, sir."

With that the orphan placed his hat on his head, and beat a retreat.

CHAPTER XLIV.

OFF TO THE BULL FIGHT—THE ORPHAN IN TROUBLE AGAIN—CHIVEY'S DISGRACE AND FIGGINS TRIUMPHANT.

THE bull fight that had been so extensively advertised and eagerly looked forward to was postponed.

As already related, young Jack and Harry had slain the best bull.

Therefore another bull, young and fierce, had to be procured from the mountain pastures, and it was some days ere that could be done.

During that time our hero was delighted to find a great change in the condition of his friend, the English waiter at the hotel, who had been stabbed, out of revenge, by some of the Spanish people, whom he had struck down when protecting young Jack from the mob.

The wounds that at first looked so deep and dangerous speedily healed ; in three days he was able to sit up, and by the time the new bulls were brought into the town, he could get about.

So on the day when at length the fight was to take place, he went out with young Jack, Harry Girdwood, the orphan, and the Irish diver.

They managed to get very good seats in the front row, but the pleasure of Mr. Figgins was considerably marred when he found he had for a neighbour the hateful tiger Chivey.

"Ugh!" he muttered, " I am surprised that they allow servants to sit in the best parts of the house."

Chivey heard the remark.

"They don't let no tradespeople come here if they knows it, Mr. Figgins, so you had better dry up, or I'll split on you ; but I say, old boy, what's the price of soap?"

"Begorra, young man," said the diver,

turning fiercely towards Chivey, "ye'd better be keepin' yer own company."

"Oh, and is it all the way from ould Ireland you have come to tell me that same, my Lord Pat? Ah, sure now!"

And Chivey put his finger to his nose and winked at the Irishman.

"By the holy poker, I'll sarve you as your mother did when you was an ugly baby, if you say another word."

Chivey was silent for a time, but he resolved to play a trick or two with the orphan before the sport was over.

By this time the whole of the seats were occupied, and the people began to signify their desire that the fight should at once commence.

Several of the people in the cheaper parts of the house recognised our hero, and threats were freely uttered, but as the British consul was present, and a British frigate was expected to call at the port in a day or two, they confined themselves to threats, and did not venture upon any act of violence.

Presently there was a great shout of applause, as two officers of the municipality came into the arena, and, after saluting the authorities, proceeded to open the large gates on opposite sides of the arena.

"Bravo!" shouted Jack; "the show is going to begin."

"Ain't they fine fellows?" said Harry, as from one of the gates there entered a band of mounted men (picadors), while at the other appeared a number of foot men (matadors and chulos).

"The best show I've seen for a long time," said the waiter. "There'll be some good sport."

Suddenly the shouts of applause were turned into groans and yells of disapprobation as a very seedy-looking individual entered the arena.

"Who is he?" demanded Jack and Harry in a breath.

"The *verdugo*, the common hangman. A lot o' them vagabonds shouting knows they'll have to pass through his hands some time or other, either to be scragged, or branded as galley slaves, so they're takin' it out of him aforehand."

Quite unmoved by the execrations so lavishly heaped on his head, the hangman bowed in a most humble manner before the state box of the authorities, and the key of the torril, or bull pen, was thrown down to him.

He then departed to give admittance to the first bull.

"That is Julian Sanchez, the best picador in the province," said the waiter, pointing to one who urged his horse in front; "he is a bold man."

At that moment the first bull rushed into the arena.

Dazzled by the bright sunlight after being in a dark stable so long, the bull stood hesitating for a minute, but it was only for a minute, and then with head lowered, it dashed at Sanchez.

But the lance of the picador glanced from the shoulder of the bull, which instantly dashed one of its horns into the chest of the horse.

A stream of blood poured from the wound, and the spectators shouted—

"*Brava!* Well done, bull."

"I say, Harry," said young Jack Harkaway; "I don't think this cruel sport would go down in old England."

"No, Jack, I think not; but look at that noble horse, how he trembles with fear."

As Sanchez drove his spurs into the flanks of the poor wounded animal, it tottered and fell, while the bull rushed across the arena to attack another picador known as El Gato, or the Cat.

This man received his enemy with a powerful thrust of the lance, but so vigorous was the onset of the bull that El Gato was thrown from his horse, the wooden shaft of the lance bending up and rebounding like a steel spring.

Again there were loud shouts of applause.

"This is no child's play," said Jack, as the chulos bounded forward, waving their cloaks to divert the bull's attention from the overthrown picadors.

El Gato's horse was fairly tossed in the air and came down dead, but Sanchez managed to stop the small wound in his animal's chest with some tow, and having dragged him to his feet, again mounted, and watching his opportunity, made a deadly thrust with his lance.

The bull sank down, made a feeble attempt to rise again, and then rolled over in the dust. Loud applause was bestowed upon Sanchez, who hastily acknowledging the plaudits, rode out of the arena.

"He seems in a hurry to be off," observed Jack.

"That's to keep possession of the horse," replied the waiter. "You see the town finds the steeds, and the picador, if he kills a bull, is allowed to keep the horse—if it has been wounded."

"Well, I would not give much for that horse," observed Jack.

"What d'ye think o' this here fun, governor?" said Chivey, to the orphan. "Beats cockfighting, don't it?"

And Chivey, passing his arm round the orphan, inserted a large pin in his side.

The orphan jumped up with pain, and looked at a lady sitting next to him, being in doubt where the pin came from.

"Pray address your conversation to your equals and friends," said the orphan, haughtily, turning to Chivey.

"Blest if you ain't a precious sight too lofty," retorted Chivey. "I'll bring you down a peg or two afore I've done with you."

Figgins was just about to retort when the trumpets sounded, and another bull dashed into the ring.

Two picadors were almost instantly overthrown, and one of the chulos only saved his life by vaulting over the barrier, in which the bull's horns made two nasty holes.

"Bravo, toro!" shouted the people.

"Bravo, toro!" shouted the orphan, standing up and clapping his hands.

Chivey saw Mr. Figgins thus excited, and seeing, as he thought, the chance of a good lark, bobbed down under the outstretched legs of the hapless orphan, and endeavoured to pitch him over the ring, but Mr. Figgins did not feel disposed to go over among the raging bulls, and caught hold of the first thing he could to save himself, and that happened to be Mr. Chivey's collar.

"Here, I say, let go, you old ass," exclaimed the tiger.

"Drag me up, you bloodthirsty murderer," shouted the orphan.

"Bravo, Figgins; stick to him," said Jack.

"Like grim death to a deceased African," added Harry.

"Here, somebody come and help me; the old orphan's pulling me over."

Figgins stuck to Chivey, who, being unable to release himself, was dragged over into the arena.

"Another bull, another bull!" shouted the people. "Look out for danger."

The attendant hangman in the pens heard the shouts, and thinking the beast last released had been killed, released another.

"Look out, Figgins," shouted Jack.

The orphan had only just time to scramble to his feet when he found one of the fierce beasts close upon him.

Figgins dodged, and then sped round the arena at his best pace, Chivey keeping close to him, his hair standing on end with fright.

Both bulls were now in pursuit and rapidly gaining ground.

In a few minutes more they must be trampled down and gored, if help did not arrive.

Suddenly Mr. Figgins bethought him of what he had seen the chulos do, and drawing out a red silk pocket-handkerchief from his pocket, he dropped it over the bull's face, and then dodged aside.

"Bravo, Inglese," shouted the people, as the bull was diverted from his course by the fluttering bit of silk.

Mr. Figgins looked round, and just caught sight of Chivey, as that unfortunate tiger was sent flying up in the air by one of the bulls.

"Good Heaven! he'll be killed," remarked Figgins.

But he had no time to make inquiries on the subject, for his bull having got rid of the handkerchief, returned once more to the charge.

"Help him, some of you," shouted Harry, "or he'll be gored to death."

Jack would—unarmed as he was—have jumped down into the arena, had not his powerful Hibernian friend restrained him.

"Aisy, sorr; it's no use, for what can ye do at all, at all? Shure your friud the orphan must be afther takin' care of his own bones. Begorra, an' he's got some of 'em broke now."

This latter exclamation was caused by the orphan getting a sudden and violent lift, which sent him flying in the air.

"Cowards!" shouted Jack, shaking his fist at the professional bullfighters who had crowded together in the gateway.

"It's the divil's own luck he has," exclaimed the Irishman. "Look at him now."

And truly it seemed so.

For the orphan had fallen with his legs astride the bull's back, and seizing the animal by its mane, clung on as tight as could be. He held on firmly.

The bull had never been treated that way before, and rushed round the arena like mad, the Spanish picadors and chulos applauding

what they considered the pluck and skill of the Englishman.

"Bravo! bravo!" shouted the people. "Look at the daring rider."

The second bull being in the way, was overthrown by the infuriated beast ridden by the orphan, and applause redoubled, but the British consul at length managed to make the professionals aware of the real state of affairs, and they entered the arena for the purpose of slaying the bull.

A matador, or swordsman, claimed the preference, and armed with a long sword, approached.

The man was either very nervous or he did not know his business, for instead of killing the bull at the first thrust, he made half-a-dozen blows without inflicting a mortal wound, though he managed to inflict a great deal of terror on the orphan, who thought that each stroke was intended for his own heart.

"Oh! Help, help! Don't let the murderer slay a poor orphan," cried Figgins, still holding on to the mane of the bull as he dashed wildly round the ring.

"Get down and pitch into the man with your fists," exclaimed Jack.

"Take the sword from him and kill the bull yourself," said Harry.

Meanwhile, the people were getting very impatient, calling the man thief, and other opprobrious names, but still applauding the orphan.

Presently, however, the bull fell, and the orphan rolled in the sand, but the luckless matador was ordered off to prison.

"A la carcel!" they shouted.

And he was dragged away to gaol.

The orphan, after taking one last look of dismay at the bull, and seeing the coast clear, clambered over the barricade and rejoined his friends, who by this time had almost had enough of it, and were preparing to leave.

"Oh, yes, let's get home."

The orphan willingly acceded to their proposition to adjourn to the hotel.

He had to endure a vast quantity of applause from the people, who still thought he had entered the ring on his own free will to fight the bull.

Jack, although he disliked Chivey, could not refrain from making some inquiries, which brought the intelligence that the tiger, though much bruised, had no bones broken.

And so ended the bull fight.

CHAPTER XLV.

CHIVEY'S PRACTICAL JOKE—WHAT CAME OF IT—HERBERT MURRAY PAYS HIM OFF—DIAMOND CUT DIAMOND—THE ARREST.

THE day after the bull fight, Chivey and his master were in the town, the tiger feeling very stiff and sore.

They were conversing together when a Spanish officer approached and gave Chivey a stiff military salute.

The tiger returned it with his own peculiar jerky greeting, the forefinger up to the brim of the hat.

"Senor Harkaway, I believe?" he said, in broken English.

Chivey tipped his master the wink.

"D'ye hear that, sir?" he whispered. "He takes me for Harkaway. Shall I have a lark with him?"

"What for?"

"Just to see if we can't pay out that Harkaway fellow."

The officer still stared and awaited their reply.

"I asked if I had the honour of addressing Senor Harkaway?" he said, looking rather serious.

"Yes—oh, yes," returned Chivey, "I am Senor Harkaway. What is your pleasure, young man?"

The Spanish officer bowed.

"I did not mean you," he said, "but this gentleman," pointing to young Murray.

"Oh, no," said Chivey; "I'm the fellow they call Harkaway, and that young man is my servant—my tiger."

The Spanish officer opened his eyes in wonder.

"Tiger!"

"Yes."

"That is a strange name for a servant," he said.

"We swells all have our tigers," said Chivey, stroking his chin, and looking the greatest toff imaginable.

"You insolent vagabond!" exclaimed his master.

Chivey winked.

"Keep it up, sir, keep it up. We'll have no end of a lark with this Mossoo Don Tickletoby. Perhaps he's going to invite us to dinner."

The Spaniard, while they were talking, had walked away into a low building hard by, which was used by the Carlists as a guard-room, and at this juncture he emerged from the door-way, followed by a file of soldiers.

"Hullo!" exclaimed Chivey, "what the doose——"

"Senor Harkaway," said the Spanish officer, drawing his sword with a flourish, "you are my prisoner."

Chivey started back.

"Come, I say, old cove, this——"

"You are my prisoner," repeated the officer.

"Prisoner! What for?" demanded Chivey.

"You are charged with being a spy in the pay of the enemies of Spain, of his majesty the king, and the enemies of the cause of order and of religion."

"That's quite enough for your money," said the tiger, with a doleful look, "but you've altogether mistook your party, for I ain't a enemy to nothing or nobody."

"That you'll have to prove," said the officer.

"But, I say, governor, don't go and——"

"Fall in," said the officer, peremptorily.

He waved his sword, and the file of soldiers advanced, closing up before and behind the miserable joker, Chivey.

"Quick march," said the officer.

"It's all a mistake," cried Chivey, in desperation. "I ain't Harkaway at all, I tell you. Harkaway's another party altogether, not anything like so good-looking as me. Oh, captain, do listen to a cove."

The officer was obdurate, and the soldiers, at a sign from him, began to hustle the tiger off towards the barracks.

"Oh, major!" implored Chivey, dolorously.

"Away with him," said the officer, melodramatically.

"Colonel!" ejaculated Chivey, "do listen."

The officer relented a little at this.

He was a sub-lieutenant, and it was not unpleasant to be addressed as colonel.

"Well, sir?"

"I tell you, colonel, I am only a poor cove. I ain't a swell. I ain't Harkaway at all, sir. Oh, no; never, sir, not me. I only said it for a lark. Ask my governor there."

The officer looked from one to the other in doubt.

"How can I believe you?" he said.

"Look at my innocent mug," said Chivey, dolefully; "ask my governor."

"Governor?"

"My master," explained the luckless joker.

"Why, you said he was your servant," said the Carlist.

"No, no; you ask him."

"Well, sir," said the officer, who was getting considerably puzzled between the two of them, "what do you say?"

Herbert Murray owed his impudent tiger a rub for his insolence.

Here was the opportunity for paying it off.

"He spoke the truth at first," said he; "I am his servant."

"I thought as much," said the Carlist officer; "away with him. This prevarication will do you no good, sir."

They marched him off to the door of the guard-room.

Here Chivey grew desperate.

"At least, general," he cried, in despair, "allow me to have my servant with me."

"Insolent scoundrel," exclaimed his master.

He would have fled, but the officer gave the word, and two of the soldiers brought him back.

"You want him with you?"

"Yes."

"If I go in with you, Chivey," said Herbert Murray, between his teeth, "I'll discharge you from this minute."

Chivey was not to be influenced by threats.

"Wants to lock me up," said Chivey to himself. "Perhaps he thinks I know too much for him. Well, well, I'll teach him to try his larks on with me."

*   *   *   *   *

They were taken into the guard-room, and formally handed over to the Carlist military authorities.

They were driven rudely into a cell, and there left to reflect upon the unpleasant habit of practical joking.

"Chivey."

"Yes, sir."

"This is a nice thing you have done for us."

"'Twasn't my fault," groaned the groom. "You had on'y to back me up when I told him who we really was."

"You're taken up as a spy, and I suppose that you know what the punishment for that is in war time!"

"Not I."

"They'll put your back against a wall, and six or eight men will fire into you."

Chivey gave a very hollow groan on hearing this.

"Oh, Lord—oh, Lord," he cried, "I wish I was back in Whitechapel."

CHAPTER XLVI.

THE NEW DIVER AT THE WRECK—COME AT LAST—BETTER LATE THAN NEVER—DOWN YOU GO.

MEANWHILE Jack Harkaway junior, all unconscious of the danger which he ran of being imprisoned, was gone with Harry Girdwood to witness the operations of the divers at the spot where the ill-fated "Albatross" had gone down.

They pulled out in a small boat towards the sloop, which was riding at anchor close by the scene of the wreck, and as they got in sight, a sudden gleam of sunshine appeared to strike the waves by the sloop's side.

"What was that?"

"The diver's helmet. He's just gone down."

They pulled sharply out, and soon they were alongside the sloop.

There was a number of people on board, watching the proceedings with the greatest curiosity.

The mechanical appliances attracted great attention.

The air-pumps, and the men on the platform beside them, whose duty it was to watch for the slightest signal of the venturesome diver, now fathoms deep in the sea.

The rounds of the little ladder lowered from the ship's side to the water, fixed the attention of our two youthful adventurers.

"Look down there, Jack," Harry Girdwood remarked, pointing to the ladder.

"I see."

"The 'Albatross' has gone down in twelve fathoms."

"Look! see those air bubbles rising just beyond the ladder."

The huge helmet of the diver appeared; then the body of the adventurous fellow emerged from the water, and he looked up the little ladder.

A horrible amphibious monster it looked, with the huge head and glass goggle eyes, the rude, ungainly limbs, and the lethal weapons fastened to the leathern girdle he wore round his loins, an axe on one side and a long-bladed dagger upon the other.

He looked armed to do battle with the marine demons below the waters.

As soon as the diver reached the deck, he was tended by two or more "valets," who removed the lead collar from his shoulders and the metal plates he wore to give his body the necessary weight to make his way through the water.

And when the huge helmet was removed, and the diver's jovial face was seen, it was quite a relief to all.

The diver went below to make his report, and when this was done, Jack questioned him eagerly.

"Did you go down below?" was his first question.

"No, Mr. Harkaway," returned our old friend the diver; "progress wasn't as easy as you might suppose above here."

"Why's that?"

"The 'Albatross' has got jammed between two or three big rocks, and the knocking about that she has received has sent all the rigging and such like all over the deck—in fact," he added, with a grin, "I had to axe my way everywhere."

"Now a word with you, my friend diver," said Jack. "I mean to go down with you next time that you descend."

"Never."

The diver evidently looked upon it as a very serious job.

"Why not?" said Jack. "I want to go below. You don't seem to care to go and get my locket I spoke of to you."

"I don't like meddling with dead men anywheres," said the diver, "but least of all under the water."

"Why?"

"They have got such a horrible look; they bob about with the motion of the water, and look as if they were living—ugh!"

And the burly diver, who was ready to fight half a dozen Spaniards, shuddered again.

"Well," said young Jack, "I don't care for such sights myself, but I have a purpose in view, so down I go with you."

The diver demurred.

"I should get into trouble for taking you down."

"Taking me down! Come, I like that. Why, you speak as if I were a child. You can't prevent my going if I choose to go. Besides, everything is favourable for the job. Your mate hasn't turned up, you say, and I can go down in his diving dress."

"Yes."

"Once inside the helmet, I defy anyone to tell whether it is Jack Harkaway or Tim—whatever his name is."

This closed the discussion most effectually.

The diver had nothing further to oppose.

Young Jack found a pretext for remaining on board.

The moment for the experiment approached, and the professional diver passed the time in giving his pupil all the necessary instructions.

One recommendation—a prime one—remained in his mind, happily.

"Four tugs at the air pipe means 'Haul me up.' Do you mark?" said the diver. "And when you are twelve fathoms down below the air and light, you are apt to forget nearly everything. Whatever you do, don't forget that—don't forget that, Master Harkaway, as you value your life."

"Four?"

"Four," repeated the diver, seriously.

"All right," said young Jack. "I'll not forget that."

A little later on, the diver and his mate emerged from their cabin with their helmets on.

"Hullo," said the captain of the sloop, "I didn't know that your mate had come over."

"Yes, cap'en," said the diver, "here he is at last."

"That's hearty," said the skipper. "Well, the water's as smooth as a millpond—nothing could be better, so lose no time, my lads."

CHAPTER XLVII.

THE HORRORS OF THE DEEP—YOUNG JACK VISITS THE DEAD MEN BENEATH THE WAVES —A PERILOUS VOYAGE.

It is no wonder that the captain of the sloop failed to recognise our Jack.

It would have been surprising, indeed, if he had.

Let a person who had never seen a man in diving costume, come upon him for the first time, and it is very sure that he would not have believed it to be anything human.

Jack's limbs, swathed in surplus clothing, were double their usual size, and more ungainly and awkward a fashion than one can conceive.

On his shoulders was a kind of plate made of white metal, edged with copper, into which was screwed a waterproof jerkin, enclosing both front and back.

Besides this, there was a deal of india-rubber about him, and leaden-soled boots, which weighed not less than ten pounds apiece.

Young Jack had heard of divers being attacked by sharks; but as soon as he had looked at himself in the looking-glass through the glazed goggle eyes of his helmet, he could not believe it possible that the boldest fish that ever swam would dare tackle such a formidable-looking monster.

"No, no," said Jack, to himself, "they would shoot away for their lives at the sight of such a horrible-looking thing as this."

Once by the ship's side, the huge and crushing weights of lead were fastened upon his shoulders, and the shock was so sudden, that young Jack was about to kick up a rumpus, when a sort of glass box was fastened over the mouth of his helmet, and screwed tightly on.

He was ceasing to breathe.

This awful sensation Jack never forgot; but, happily, it was but of momentary duration, for the air-pumping apparatus was set to work, and supplied him with the vital fluid.

The signal was given to descend the ladder, and now began the most painful part of the ordeal, for young Jack felt the weight of the garb and accoutrements dreadfully, so much so, in fact, that he could scarce move one leg before the other.

In addition to the air pipe, there was a string which was meant to guide the diver towards the ladder, in case he should lose his way under water.

However, Jack, by a strong effort of will, got down the ladder, and after a certain time, he missed the action of the air upon his head, and then he knew that he was under water.

What a journey it seemed.

Never did he forget it.

But the longest journey comes to an end, and at length he touched the bottom, where, to his intense relief, he found the other diver awaiting him.

The first remarkable thing was the wondrous power of the water upon him, notwithstanding the enormous weight of his body and accoutrements.

He was swayed backwards and forwards, and was forced to hold on to the ladder to keep himself steady.

The diver nodded his helmet gravely, and the effect was most weird and fantastic.

He gave Jack a pat of encouragement, and held out his hand, but this was no use, for the amateur diver dare not for awhile let go the ladder.

He saw the seaweed waving fantastically about at his feet, and the fishes swam about him, circling round and round, apparently very much interested in what was going foward, and all seemed wondrous strange.

Suddenly a tap on his shoulder reminded him that he had not come here to make observations upon such matters as these, but for serious business.

He let go the ladder, steadied himself by an effort, and shuffled along until a dark, shapeless object impeded his further progress.

It looked like some dead monster of the deep, ugly and confused in outline, so dire had been the work of wind and wave upon the wreck of what had once been a goodly ship, though not in our experience.

This was all that remained of the "Albatross."

The two divers groped their way along the vessel until they came to a breach, through which they mounted, the professional diver leading the way with infinite care and pains, for now the most dangerous part of their work had indeed commenced.

The air tubes upon which they depended for life itself, were in great peril of getting twisted in some projecting parts of the wreck, or snapping by a sudden jerk.

A motion of his companion's head showed Jack the way that they had to go to seek the forecabin, in which the unhappy mate Mackenzie was to be found.

Now began the most terrible part of the ordeal, for Jack had to perform the rest of his explorations alone.

He groped on, never pausing to think, and well it was, for he would never have accomplished his self-set task if he had.

He reached the cabin stairs, and then, with infinite pains, he managed to get down, for the action of the sea had already worn away the woodwork in every direction.

Down the stairs he went, groping along, and then——

Oh, Heaven!

There he was.

Mackenzie was in the same position, as nearly as possible, as when Jack had last seen him in life.

Death had overtaken him, apparently, in his drunken stupor.

Jack looked at the dead man.

He had got hold of the handrail with his right, and of a low beam with his left hand, the nearest objects at which he had clutched when young Harkaway had kicked him off in sheer desperation at the last moment.

So life-like, so real it all looked, that young Jack was filled with a ghostly dread as he looked upon the scene.

Nevertheless, his glance rested upon the hand which clutched the beam, for, hanging from his fast-clenched fist, he perceived the fragment of a chain.

This was attached to the locket—little Emily's parting gift.

The object of young Jack's perilous adventure.

The grim figure of the Scotch mate bobbed up and down as the amateur diver approached, filled with awesome dread.

Oh, that was a terrible time for the bold boy.

But he had set himself a task, and it must be gone through.

This stern resolution had carried him through many an undertaking, and it should aid him to bring this to a successful issue, come what might.

It wanted all his resolution now, however, let his will be ever so strong.

With closed eyes, Jack stretched forth his hand to grasp Emily's love token.

The first contact with that cold, dead flesh sent a thrill throughout his entire frame, which he never forgot until his dying day.

However, he kept to it with desperate resolution.

The dead man's grip was fast on dear little Emily's locket, and he failed to loosen the hand of the corpse.

He felt for the dagger at his girdle.

The thought of using a knife upon a dead body fathoms low beneath the sea was horrible indeed.

But better not be there at all than recoil before anything now.

Emily's last love gift he must regain.

He drew the keen blade across the dead man's fingers.

He clutched the prize and——

Horrors upon horror's head accumulate.

The maimed corpse slowly sank in the water, and its arms clasped Jack's legs around. Fixed and fascinated at the sight, young Jack remained there spellbound.

His senses appeared to have left him, for he knew not how long he thus remained, when a hand was placed upon his shoulder.

The diver had come in search of him, alarmed at the long delay.

The spell was broken.

Guided by the diver, he groped his way up the cabin stairs and along the deck of the wreck, when the signal was given to haul up.

It was a miracle, indeed, that young Jack ever reached the surface alive.

But fearsome as was the recollection of that voyage on the ocean's bed, he never regretted it.

He had gone through a terrible adventure.

But he had accomplished his purpose.

He had recovered his locket, little Emily's parting love gift.

CHAPTER XLVIII.

AIR AND LIGHT—THE RECOGNITION—" SENOR HARKAWAY, YOU ARE MY PRISONER "—" ON WHAT CHARGE ?"—A DESPERATE FIX.

ON reaching the deck of the sloop the helmet was taken off, and then a startled cry burst from several of the bystanders, but the loudest voice was Harry Girdwood's.

" Jack," he cried, " why, what a blessed dance you have led me."

" How ?" cried Jack, innocently enough.

" How ! Why, you traitor. Why the deuce didn't you tell me about this?"

Young Jack leered at his faithful comrade, and burst out laughing.

" I'll tell you why, old man," he said ; " it is because you wouldn't have let me go."

" That's right enough," said Harry Girdwood. " I swear I wouldn't. But what with your duels, your bull fights, and diving, I never know when you are safe. You keep me in a continual ferment, Jack."

" Never mind, old man."

" What is diving like ?"

Jack shuddered.

" Dreadful."

" How dreadful ?" demanded Harry.

" The sensation of going under is beyond description, and the sights you see below are things likely to haunt your dreams for a long —long while. But ugh ! don't let us talk of it. I have got back my locket, and now, Harry, I should like to forget that horrible journey if I could."

They went ashore as soon as they could, and as the boat grounded, they perceived that something unusual was going forward.

The beach was lined with soldiers; in the midst of whom were two persons that they recognised at once.

One of these persons was young Herbert Murray.

The other was Chivey.

Now the excitement of the latter was curious to witness as soon as he saw who were the occupants of the boat.

" There, there !" he exclaimed, in a voice which both Jack and Harry Girdwood heard distinctly, " that is Harkaway — that one there."

Jack was the first to leap ashore, and advancing to the soldiers with all his old boldness, he said—

" Yes, I am Jack Harkaway—and who wants Jack Harkaway ?"

" I do."

He turned round as one of the officers advanced from the file of soldiers.

" You want me, senor captain ?" said young Jack. " Indeed."

" Yes, sir."

" For what purpose ?"

" I have to arrest you."

" On what charge ?" exclaimed Harry Girdwood.

" That of being a secret agent of the enemy —in other words, a spy."

" Why, this is madness."

" It is serious earnest you will find," returned the officer.

" It is impossible to bring such a charge against me."

" Not impossible, for you find the charge is brought. My earnest wish is that you may manage to clear yourself ; if not, death will follow. Fall in, please. Left wheel—march."

CHAPTER XLIX.

JACK IS TRIED—CONDEMNED TO DEATH—HANGING IS THE DOOM OF A SPY—THE CARLISTS' JUSTICE—JACK'S FRIENDS RALLY ROUND—NO GO—THE SIGNAL FROM THE FORTRESS-TOWER—AN OLD NOTION REVIVED.

JACK never quite understood what took place at the examination which he underwent.

A shifty sort of mock trial took place, in which the prisoner was condemned and sentenced to be hanged.

"Well, gentlemen," said young Harkaway, boldly, "you have had it all your own way, and now perhaps I may be allowed to say a word or two to the court."

The president of the court martial, as this peculiar tribunal was styled, bowed his head gravely to Jack.

"Speak," he said, "but be as brief as possible."

"I will," replied Jack; "if you dare to carry out this wretched sentence, you will have to answer for it."

"To whom, pray?"

"England."

"We don't tremble at the power of England."

"Which only shows your thoughtlessness," replied the prisoner, boldly; "for such an outcry would be raised throughout the length and breadth of the land by the murder of an English lad by Carlists that your very cause will be imperilled, and you will be put down, as sure as my name's Jack Harkaway."

The president of the court laughed ironically.

"The lad does not put small value upon himself," he said.

"Why, you see," retorted Jack, boldly, "if I were some obscure poor devil's son, you could perhaps afford to murder me for chastising one of your comrades' insolence."

"Hah!"

"Silence."

"He dares insult the court," cried another officer, springing up and looking fiercely at Jack.

"Well," said young Jack, "from all appearance that is not a feat requiring any great amount of courage."

"*Carramba!*"

"There can be no mistake about the motive, whatever the pretext may be. And remember, gentlemen, that in that unfortunate affair I was not the aggressor. Don Gil Perez insulted me first and challenged me after—I struck in self-defence—and much as I may regret the matter, it must be borne in mind that he forced it upon me—that I had no choice but to fight. He fell as I might have fallen but for my own proverbial luck standing by me as usual."

"That has nothing whatever to do with the present charge."

"You have no evidence," said Jack.

"There you are wrong. We have ample evidence, and, moreover, there are some of your fellow countrymen who give most important testimony against you."

"What! Confront me with them, at least," said Jack, desperately.

"The case is fully substantiated without them," was the reply. "The sentence of the court you know. Remove the prisoner."

The soldiers closed up, and laid hands upon young Jack.

"Stop," said he; "before you go to extremities, let me warn you that I am English born, that my government doesn't allow its subjects to be shot with impunity; so beware."

Jack was hurried away to gaol.

Harry Girdwood was fortunately at large, and he set to work desperately to get Jack set at liberty, but this was not easily accomplished.

The captain of the "Albatross" went straight to the Carlist generals to make representations respecting the injustice of the sentence, but no less to his surprise than indignation, they turned a deaf ear to him.

In vain did he storm and threaten.

The only notice taken of this was to menace him with sharing young Harkaway's fate.

"Joe Deering, my boy," said the skipper to himself, "that would never do. No; you mustn't get clapped into limbo, or you'll not be able to lend the boy a hand."

He went off with Harry Girdwood to the residence of the British consul, and that excellent official being found at home, immediate steps were taken to secure young Jack's release.

"Jack Harkaway again!" said the consul, with a stare.

"Yes."

"Why, that hot-blooded young countryman of ours is always in hot water, it seems to me. When the 'Albatross' foundered and everybody else was taking to the boats, he was down below and had a narrow escape of drowning."

"Well, that can't be said to have got him in hot water, anyhow," suggested Harry Girdwood.

"Well, no," resumed the consul, with a smile. "He must have found it precious cold."

"And damp."

"And damp, as you say, young gentleman—it is one of the attributes of water. Well, no sooner is he out of that job than he gets into a duel, and pinks his man."

"Don Gil Perez is not dead," exclaimed the skipper, anxiously.

"No; only very bad. Well, next he is the cause of killing a prize bull, then frightens us all by going down in a diver's dress, and now he gets himself locked up and——"

"Now," said the skipper, with a long face, "he is condemned to death."

"To death," said the consul. "We live in ticklish times here, and must be prompt. They think no more of taking a man's life then of rolling a cigaretto."

"The savages," exclaimed Harry; "these Spaniards are——"

"About as bad as Englishmen, Frenchmen, Germans, or any other people in time of war."

"Here we are at the Carlists' head-quarters," said the skipper.

"I will go in alone," said the consul. "I don't want to begin by exasperating them. They are as proud as Lucifer, and we must go through certain forms, or we may sacrifice our dashing young Harkaway by our imprudence."

They waited in considerable anxiety for the consul's return.

At length he came.

The first glimpse at his countenance was anything but reassuring.

"Well, what's the verdict, sir?" demanded Harry Girdwood, eagerly.

"Mr. Jack Harkaway has been tried as a spy and convicted."

"And his sentence?"

"He is to be hanged."

"Good Heaven!" exclaimed the skipper; "how awful."

"Nothing can save him."

In what state of mind they walked away, we leave the reader to imagine.

Harry Girdwood was heartbroken.

As they turned round the citadel, skirting the edge of the moat, a shout from above attracted their attention.

Looking up, they saw someone at a narrow grated window waving a hand.

"Is that meant for us?"

"Listen."

The sound came clearer this time, and they made it out—

"A Harkaway, a Harkaway to the rescue."

Harry Girdwood gave a cry of delight.

"It's Jack."

Jack's war cry served to rally them immediately.

They nodded, waved handkerchiefs, and shouted back to encourage the prisoner.

"Captain Deering," said Harry, "we must get him out of that. Shall I write home to Mr. Harkaway?"

"No," said the consul, "that will not help, and would only frighten the family. We must see what we can do to save the boy."

"We will save him," said Harry.

"Yes," said the consul. "But how? That's the rub."

They stood looking up anxiously at the fortress.

It was a desperate place to think of effecting a rescue from.

A deadly height to descend.

A fearful wall to scale.

Anyone attempting to climb down, would be dashed to pieces beyond the slightest possibility of doubt.

The captain of the "Albatross" gave a shout.

"I've got it," returned the skipper. "Do you remember, Master Girdwood, that yarn you told me about the Harkaways' adventures in New York, when your big monkey Nero did something wonderful there at a fire somewhere?"

"Yes, yes," exclaimed Harry Girdwood, excitedly.

"Well, then he's only loafing about here at the hotel, frightening the women, and Mr. What's-his-name, the orphan, or gorging himself on nuts and oranges, till he's losing his graceful figure; let us make the beggar work."

"Bravo for Nero," shouted Harry.

"He'll do it," said the skipper.

"Hurrah for Nero; he only wants putting in the right road to see his master, and he'll reach him. Hurrah—hurrah!"

But now we must return to have a word with the poor prisoner, young Jack Harkaway.

CHAPTER L.

JACK IN LIMBO—UNWELCOME NEWS—THE COMMUTATION OF HIS SENTENCE—A SOLDIER'S GRAVE—A QUESTIONABLE HONOUR.

"STONE walls do not a prison make,
Nor prison bars a cage,"

sighed Jack Harkaway, junior, as he looked about his new residence; "but, with all due deference to the poet, they do contribute to keep up the illusion."

The stone walls of Jack's place of confinement were uncommonly thick.

The bars were both thick and close together, and firmly imbedded in the stone work of the window.

The window itself was a good nine feet from the floor.

As soon as Jack heard the door of the cell fast bolted upon the outside, and the echoes of the gaoler's footsteps die away in the distance of the long stone-paved corridors without, he looked wistfully at the window.

"I shall have a shy at that," he said half aloud.

Nine feet up.

No hold.

The wall built of solid blocks of stone—not brick, to enable a dreary prisoner to pick out the mortar mayhap, and thus by patience and perseverance secure a hold by which to mount.

Jack went up, however, after hard labour and risk.

Once he got the slightest hold upon the iron bars, he hung on like grim death, raising his whole body up, and getting a good perch on the narrow casement.

What a distance down it was to look.

It made him dizzy.

"I could get those bars out all right enough," he said, testing the fastenings as he spoke. "But how the deuce could I get down there then?"

How indeed?

"They have left me nothing to escape by," he said to himself, "no bedclothes."

For the matter of that there was no bed.

Well, here young Jack stuck, perched up like a poor little bird fluttering his wings against the bars of its cage. He saw three persons go past along the edge of the moat below.

"That one is Harry!" he exclaimed, "it is, and that is Captain Deering; but who is the third person? I wonder if they are here upon any business. Oh, they must be; Harry! ho! ho! Ho! ho!—ho! ho!"

An answering shout came up to him from below.

"Hurrah!" exclaimed Jack. "they can see me."

They shouted again and again, and presently a faint semblance to words of encouragement came up to him.

"Wait and watch!"

"I will—I will," returned young Jack.

"Hope!"

"They said 'Hope,' I'm sure," exclaimed the prisoner, excitedly: "rather. 'Never say die,' is the Harkaway motto."

In his excitement Jack did not notice that there was someone in the stone corridor outside his cell door.

It was, in fact, only when the door was swinging open that he heard it, so absorbed was he in the prospect below.

Then with a look of alarm, he dropped from his perch, and in his hurry he came a very hard cropper on the flags.

However, Jack was no milksop; so he scrambled up and rubbed his bruises, just as the new comer entered.

Jack looked round, and to his surprise discovered that, instead of being the military gaoler, it was one of the officers who had been a member of the court that had condemned him.

This officer spoke English fairly well.

"Prisoner," said he, "I come to inform you that a modification has been made in your favour, in regard to the sentence pronounced upon you."

Jack bowed. But he said nothing.

"All brag and bounce these Dons," he thought. "I was certain that they would never dare to put a British subject to death."

He was making certain a little too soon.

"You have had the honour of crossing swords with one of us," said the Spaniard, loftily, "and it has therefore been decreed that the act has so far ennobled you, in spite of the disgraceful character you have acquired, and which has caused you to be justly sentenced to die."

Jack bowed again.

"What a precious old wind-bag this fellow is," he said. "What is he driving at, I wonder?"

The news he was to learn would be communicated quite soon enough for Jack.

He need not be impatient to hear it.

"The honourable court which tried you has decided that you shall be spared the humiliation of dying by the hangman's hands."

"I didn't expect to——"

"You are to have a soldier's death—a warrior's grave. At daybreak to-morrow you will be conducted to the ground by a file of soldiers. Don Gil Perez will himself command the firing party."

The officer bowed haughtily, and made his exit, leaving the prisoner dazed—bewildered—stupefied.

"Am I dreaming?"

No; the gloomy walls, the frowning bars above, the dreary prison, were dreadful realities.

It was no dream.

"Do they really mean that they will dare to murder me in the name of justice?" he exclaimed, aloud.

There was small doubt of this.

They would dare anything.

Poor Jack felt precious unhappy now.

"That fellow meant it," he said to himself; "there was a murderous look about his eye. Harry, my boy, you will have to be smart in your movements if you wish to save your old chum Jack."

He thought of home now that he was in a really serious dilemma, and wondered if he should ever see his mother or his Emily any more.

"I wish dad and Uncle Dick were here. Oh, if I could but send to them," he said, to himself, again and again; "they would find some way out of this job for a certainty. But I fear that poor Harry won't carry enough weight to make these thieves and murderers take any particular notice."

He sighed and sang to kill dull care, but his heart was heavy as lead.

"There's a sweet little cherub as sits up aloft
To keep watch o'er the life of poor Jack.'

"No, no, my cherub has shifted his moorings, and scudded away; I'm left to my fate this time. What will poor old Sobersides say? What will they say at home?"

CHAPTER LI.

NERO'S MONKEY TRICKS AND WHAT CAME OF THEM—THE TALE OF A KNOTTED ROPE—THE SENTRY'S SHOT—IN THE MOAT—HARRY GIRDWOOD'S ESCAPADE—CATCHING A TARTAR—POOR DON!

"THAT sits up aloft."

Happy thought.

He would have another look from his perch in the grated window.

"It is a tough job getting up," grunted the prisoner, quaintly, "yet I managed to come down pretty fast too."

However, he was up again quick enough.

"I wish it was no further to drop outside than it is here," said Jack, looking down into the cell; "I'd be out then like a bird."

"I'm a sweet little cherub, perched here up aloft,
But I can't save the life of poor Jack——"

"Hallo!"

What was that?

A strange squeaking sound, which was almost familiar to his ear, sent the blood from his cheeks.

"How strange," he murmured. "How wonderfully like——"

He peered through the bars as far as he could.

The squeaking noise came again.

And now he caught a glimpse of some huge hairy object on the wall a little to the left, and about twelve or fourteen feet below the window.

"Nero!" gasped the prisoner. "It is, it is Nero."

Nero it was too.

Toiling up a wall nearly perpendicular, with scarcely a hold for his paws—we beg his pardon—his hands, and helped but slightly in his progress by the huge iron drain pipe which descended from the roof to the moat, the faithful Nero was fighting manfully—it would perhaps be more appropriate to say monkeyfully—with the difficulties besetting his task.

"Nero."

"Tweek!" responded Nero, quite joyfully.

The sound of his master's voice gave the faithful animal fresh courage and renewed strength.

He toiled onward.

Painfully slow was his progress.

But up he went.

"Brave Nero," said Jack, coaxingly, "good

Nero. Come along, come along. Hold tight, good Nero."

"Hah !"

He shot out his hand, and caught Nero by the paw.

The assistance came exactly in the nick of time.

Nero was getting used up, and at the very moment he got assistance from his master.

A moment more and he was up perched on the casement, holding tight on by the bars.

"My good Nero," cried Jack, again and again, quite overjoyed at this meeting with his faithful dumb follower.

Nero squeaked his responses to his master's greeting, and looked as happy as you could wish, and he scratched away merrily at his ribs in sheer glee.

"Hullo !" exclaimed Jack. "Whatever is this ?"

A satchel fastened to his side by a strap across his shoulder.

Nero thrust the satchel up to Jack, and eagerly opening it, he found first of all the following note hurriedly written by Harry Girdwood.

"DEAR JACK,—We are waiting and watching below. Take the file out of Nero's bag, and get through the bars quickly. There is a ball of string in the bag. Make one end secure above, and lower the other to us, where we are hiding in the moat just underneath. That is why you have not been able to see us before. We will fasten a thick knotted rope to the end of your string, and you can haul it up. Time presses. Keep your nut cool, and lose no time.

"HARRY."

"God bless you, Harry," cried Jack, fervently. "What an ungrateful beast I was to doubt your wit as well as your good will."

He dipped into Nero's satchel, and brought out the ball of string, a file, and a small phial of oil.

First to lower the string.

The end was made fast to one of the iron bars, and the ball dropped down.

A few seconds passed.

Then the string was gently tugged.

It had reached the moat.

"Now for the bars."

They wanted no filing.

Yet the file proved remarkably useful, for with its pointed end, he contrived to pick away the cement bed of the bars and loosen them in their sockets.

Once he had got one of them away bodily, the rest was easy.

The string was pulled again from below.

Ready !

They had fastened the knotted rope on to it.

So Jack hauled up.

In a very little while he had the rope up and the top of it fastened securely to the grating of the window.

"Now, Nero," said his master, "down you go first."

Nero got out and slid down the rope at a rattling pace.

Then Jack followed suit.

Suddenly from the moat there came a cry of alarm.

Captain Joe Deering and Harry Girdwood were hiding, as the latter had said in his note, in the moat just beneath the spot where Jack's prison window was situated high up aloft.

And as they watched Jack's progress down the knotted rope, the skipper saw a soldier appear on the rampart immediately below the further bastion.

The soldier stared again at the odd spectacle of a human figure swaying about in mid air upon the frail support of a rope.

Then apparently guessing what it meant, he brought his rifle up to his shoulder, took deliberate aim and——

The skipper yelled.

Bang went the rifle, but the soldier was probably put off his aim by the cry, and the ball whistled harmlessly by.

"Make haste, Jack !"

"I'm there," responded our hero.

And down he scrambled, and was caught in the skipper's arms.

Meanwhile there was a devil of a hubbub going on within the fortress.

Drums beating, a bugle sounding the alarm, and guns firing.

Jack found them in their very damp hiding place, and a hurried council of war was held.

"That sentry has spoilt us," said Deering. "We shall all be laid by the heels, every mother's son of us."

"I fear so," said Harry Girdwood, despondingly.

"Wait a bit."

"What shall we do ?"

A harsh, grating noise reached them and gave them an uncomfortable turn.

"You guess what that is, I suppose ?" said the skipper.

"No."

"Nor I."

"I should say it is the drawbridge being raised."

"I don't believe they are movable," said Jack.

"They are. Hark ! there goes the other one up."

"Then we are trapped."

"I fear so."

"What's to be done !"

Bugle calls and drum alarums went off just the same as ever.

Continentals of all countries have a great weakness for military noises—they share with the dusky aborigines of America and of Africa, the fancy for letting their warriors kick up as much of a shindy as possible.

These Carlists distinguished themselves greatly, therefore, by the row they made.

Now this place was like many of the old fortified towns upon the Continent; it had its citadel surrounded by a double moat.

Bad luck for our friends this.

Forts and fortified towns have been long ago proved useless in modern warfare, and moats only serve to yield up death-dealing miasma, however advantageous they might have been in the days when they fought with bows and arrows, and slings, and catapults, and poured

"DOWN HE SCRAMBLED, AND WAS CAUGHT IN THE SKIPPER'S ARMS."

hot lead and such trifles from the battlements upon besiegers below.

But in Spain you know they are a century or two behind the age; Bryant and May have been worsted in a tough fight with flint and steel and tinder box; and moats and drawbridges still flourish in fortified towns.

Worse luck for Jack Harkaway and his companions.

"What's to be done now?" asked Jack, doubtfully.

"Hanged if I know!" said the captain.

"Separate," suggested Harry Girdwood. "We shall all be taken of a heap if we don't."

"Good!"

"I'm off this way," remarked Captain Deering.

"And I'm going to the left," said Jack, gliding off as he spoke. "Off you go, Harry."

Harry Girdwood popped up his head.

No one was about.

The coast was clear.

He scrambled up on to the ground above, and sheltered from observation by some dwarf shrubs (which had been allowed to grow unmolested, although against the elementary rules of such kind of fortifications, so long had the works of the old citadel and its surroundings fallen into disuse), he gained the second moat.

Here he dropped gingerly down and made for the driest part he could find.

Then up he went on the other side, and staring about him, made a dash for the town.

Now before he had got half a start, there was a cry raised from a low-roofed house, little more than a hut, and a man ran out in pursuit.

He yelled out something at Harry which he did not at all understand, nor did he wish to, and made the pace very hot.

Harry Girdwood looked over his shoulder at his pursuer.

Only one.

"I'm not going to bolt away from one man," he thought. "The Dons would never leave off bragging."

So being artful, he let the man catch him up without appearing to stop for him, and then just as the man dropped his hand upon his shoulder, Harry swung round, and dropped the Spaniard a stinger on the face.

The fellow saw fireworks, and staggered.

He "carajo'd" and "caramba'd" all over the place and drew a knife.

But Harry dodged the knife, and dropped in his British weapons straight from the shoulder.

It was all over very quickly, and the Spaniard, being utterly unused to such unceremonious treatment, laid down on his back, and bellowed for help.

"Good morning," said Harry, giving him a farewell kick upon his seat of honour.

Off he bolted.

This Spaniard ever after vowed that Englishmen were worse than savages.

Never in all his life had he caught such a Tartar.

It is really very unpleasant to think that he should have run so hard after what he got from Harry.

Poor Don!

CHAPTER LII.

THE GRAVE—MARTIAL LAW—NERO'S EXPLOIT, AND WHAT CAME OF IT—BRITISH TARS TO THE RESCUE—FLIGHT FROM SPAIN.

WHEN Harry Girdwood got to the hotel, he met Captain Deering quietly smoking a cigar upon the threshold.

He stared and rubbed his eyes at this like a dreamer newly awakened.

"Hallo!"

"I'm glad to see you safe out of that little job."

"And I you," responded the still puzzled Harry. "But how the deuce did you manage to get here so quickly?"

"I sneaked along and then turned my coat inside out, pulled my cap well over my head, and crawled up out of the moat by some unlucky chance near the guard-house. It gave me a twinge, I can tell you, when I found myself scrambling up close under the belly of a horse. On the horse was seated an officer, who was sniffing all over the shop for me, I suppose, and there was I just under his sniffer. I saw a chance, and before Mister Don Officer had time to look down, I lugged hold of him, pulled him out of the saddle, pitched him into the ditch, and put myself in his place."

"Bravo, captain!"

"Wasn't half bad, was it?" said Deering, complacently.

"It was immense," exclaimed Harry. "But how did you get off without being molested?"

"I rode quickly off."

"But the officer—surely he made a rumpus?"

"Well, no," returned the skipper, drily; "he went down head first, and as he fell on nothing particularly soft excepting his head, he lay very quietly just where he dropped, while I dug my heels into the horse's ribs and galloped off."

"Bravo!"

"Well, as soon as I got some distance away, I reined in my fiery steed, turned him round, scrambled out of the saddle, and sent him flying back riderless towards the fortifications. Then, to provide against accidents, I loafed about here looking as much as possible as though I had been occupied in loafing for the entire day. And I think I may say that, bar accidents, I have established about as neat an *alibi* as any Old Bailey lawyer could wish for."

"Well done. Now I'll just change my togs a bit, and return to you."

Harry soon returned, and then they looked anxiously about: firstly, for poor Jack, and secondly, to see how the passers-by might regard them.

A patrol passed by, going to relieve guard evidently.

The officer of the watch eyed them keenly, for all the English residents from the wrecked "Albatross" were objects of suspicion.

But the lazy, lazzaroni looks of Captain Deering and his companion quite put them off the scent.

"We are safe enough," said the skipper; "they are evidently quite off the scent."

"They are," said Harry Girdwood; "and I only wish we could say as much for poor Jack."

"He may be safe enough yet," said the skipper.

"I begin to feel uncomfortable about it."

"Wait."

"We must."

"It is very likely that he has had to skulk down in the moat for a very long while, and will only be able to creep out of his hiding-place after dark."

"Let us hope we shall soon see him."

But no such luck.

Before long the Cockney military waiter brought them news.

News which confirmed their worst anticipations about poor young Jack Harkaway.

"He was surrounded in the moat, it seems," said the waiter, "and although he fought like a tiger-cat, according to the soldiers, he was, of course, powerless against a mob of armed men."

"And what is done with him now?" demanded Harry.

"He is taken back to prison, and to-morrow morning at daybreak, if nothing interferes to save him, he will be——"

He paused.

"Be what?" demanded Harry, breathlessly.

"Shot behind the chapel," was the waiter's reply.

Shot!

What a fearful sound that word had.

"Oh, Captain Deering," exclaimed Harry Girdwood, in the greatest distress, "surely there is yet some means of saving my poor, dear Jack. What can be done?"

"There is but one thing now," returned the skipper.

"And that is?"

"Wait till daybreak," said Captain Deering, "and then be there in as strong force as we can muster."

"That's a poor chance."

"I don't know that. The firing party will not be very strong."

"Perhaps twelve."

"Well, and what's twelve Spaniards?" exclaimed the captain, with the true British contempt for foreigners.

"What's twelve Spaniards?" remarked Harry, drily. "Why, about a dozen, I suppose."

"Well, with half-a-dozen Englishmen with good stout cudgels," said Captain Deering, "you shall see what'll take place."

Harry Girdwood was inspired by the speaker's confident air, notwithstanding his gloomy forebodings.

"Let us get in and muster our forces at once," he said.

"Good."

"I've got to beat up Nat Cringle to begin with."

"He's the sort. Let's get one or two of those tough old tars, and we shall have some real sport with the Dons."

"You will find I and the diver will not be far away, sir," said the waiter.

"Glad to hear it," said Harry.

Well, they matured some sort of a plan of action, but whether it was good or bad can only be learnt by reading further on.

*　　*　　*　　*　　*

Daybreak.

A dull, drizzling morning, with the sun struggling in vain to peer through the mist.

Behind the chapel, the spot appointed for the tragedy to take place, a grave had been recently dug.

It was situated just at the base of a tree, a long, drooping branch of which hung over into the grave itself.

This was where they meant to put young Jack Harkaway out of the world.

This spot was quite deserted now.

Not a sign of a soul in sight.

Surely young Jack's friends were astir?

Unless they were, there would be but small chance for him.

We shall see.

The chapel bell struck five, and then it tolled on a dismal knell as the regular tramp of the military was heard.

Then there appeared two soldiers walking along with their muskets under their arms, the muzzles pointed to the ground.

After them came the prisoner, young Jack, with form erect and a firm step, although the pallor of his cheek showed that he was far from being insensible to the solemnity of the situation.

Beside young Jack walked a priest, crucifix in hand, and exhorting the prisoner, with great earnestness, to die in the good faith.

Jack pretended to listen, but his thoughts were very far from the subject of the holy man's words.

Moreover, he could not understand a single syllable that was spoken, for the priest only spoke Spanish, of which Jack was ignorant.

They took the prisoner up to the edge of the grave, and placed him in position there.

Oh, what sad thoughts passed through the boy's mind at that moment.

Father, mother, Dick Harvey and his wife, little Emily, his sweetheart—all, all came before his mind's eye.

"And shall I die thus?" thought young Jack. "Far away from all I hold dear. Oh, it is horrible."

And the brave boy's courage for a moment left him.

The soldiers, at an order from the sergeant, grounded arms and waited.

Waited for what?

For somebody to arrive apparently.

Presently the prisoner's curiosity—for curiosity he certainly did feel upon this subject—was gratified.

A measured tramp was heard, and four soldiers appeared, bearing a litter, upon which reclined, pale and almost done to death, Jack's wounded adversary, Don Gil Perez.

Jack started, in spite of himself, nor could he repress a slight exclamation of surprise.

It was then true that this vindictive scoundrel had worked his destruction, in revenge for being worsted in the encounter with his gallant boy opponent.

"Halt!" said the wounded officer.

The litter was placed by his orders near the spot where the prisoner stood.

"You have to die," he said, in broken English, and speaking with difficulty, while his eyes glistened with fiend-like viciousness; "to die for venturing to play a villain's part, to die as a spy, although we have been merciful, and not decided to string you up like a dog, which is the fitting punishment for such as you."

Jack turned upon him with a look of ineffable scorn.

"I don't fear death, Don Gil Perez," he said, "for I come of a brave race, and have been taught to face death long ago. But you must not think that you will escape the fruits of your crime. This assassination will cost you and your party dear."

The officer smiled then in a sickly, sardonic way.

"You must brag on the brink of the grave," he said.

Jack gave him a defiant look, and snapped his fingers in his face.

"You are a very good witness," he said, "that I can do something as well as brag. Give me a sword, coward, if you dare, and stand before me."

The wounded man flushed purple at the taunt.

He scowled at the defiant Jack and gave the word of command.

"Fall in !"

The soldiers pressed into position.

"Attention ! Make ready ! Present——"

Jack's heart stood still. An awful moment was this indeed for luckless Jack, tottering, as it were, upon the threshold of the world to come.

Suddenly there was a scrambling sound in a tree overhanging the grave, and some large object flopped down out of the thickest part of it, plump on to the litter occupied by the wounded officer.

Don Gil Perez was canted out by the shock, and his strange assailant danced around him like a redskin in a fit.

Jack stared again.

Then the impulse to laugh became irresistible. He burst into such a fit of merriment that the soldiers were staggered.

They had met courageous men on the field who took peril lightly.

But seldom had they seen a doomed wretch—a mere boy—laugh in the very teeth of the firing party.

"Go on, Nero," cried Jack, pointing to the grave, "shove him into here—throw him in !"

The gesture accompanying young Jack's words gave him an inkling of his meaning, for Nero made a rush at the officer, and rolled him fairly over into the grave.

At the same moment the firing party were suddenly attacked in the rear. A desperate crack from a heavy stick brought the sergeant to the ground, and a few flourishes of the same formidable cudgel, dexterously landed upon their heads, made two of the soldiers drop their muskets.

"Hurrah ! Nat Cringle !" cried the prisoner, joyfully. "I'm in it !"

He was, too, in half a crack.

The soldiers were taken completely by surprise, and did not stand half a chance, notwithstanding their weapons and their discipline.

They were all disarmed in the confusion which prevailed.

The only one of them who had managed to keep hold of his musket was attacked in the rear in the most unmanly way by Nero, who tore out his hair.

This one dropped his musket, and fled, roaring lustily for help.

Now the sergeant, having recovered from the effects of the first surprise, turned to show fight, but Captain Deering covered him with one of the muskets, while Jack disarmed him.

Nat Cringle and two of his mates secured the rest of the firearms, and then they turned to retreat.

"Now for the beach," cried Captain Deering. "Sharp's the word, or the fool that bolted away howling will be back with all the army."

"Off we go."

They divided the spoil—the muskets of the soldiers—fairly between them, so that one should not be unduly encumbered by the weight, and then they made a good quick run for it.

But before they had got two or three steps, the disarmed soldiers made a show of pursuing them.

So Harry Girdwood and Nat Cringle turned round to menace them with their own guns.

"Stir a peg, you Spanish brutes, and I blaze away, damme !" said old Nat.

They all fell back before the pair of muskets, and the party got off to the beach.

"Tell us what we are coming here for, Captain Deering ?" said Jack.

"To get afloat safe and sound," was the reply; "for this place'll be too hot to hold us, after that job."

A long boat was ready waiting for them, so in they got and shoved off, just as a strong detachment of the military came pelting down to the beach at the *pas gymnastique*.

The soldiers swore and shook their fists after the receding boat; but the Englishmen made but one reply, and this was only by gesture, which goaded the military to fury.

But the crowning insult was offered by Nero.

That valiant monkey sat astern, taking a two-handed sight in addition to putting his tongue out at the soldiers.

"Give it 'em, Nero."

Nero caught a flea to show his appreciation of his master's words of encouragement, and carried on all sorts of antics.

"Look out," exclaimed Nat; "they're going to fire at us."

It looked like it.

They had brought up their muskets to the "present."

Quick as lightning Captain Deering and Harry Girdwood, who had half anticipated this, had their muskets ready to reply to it.

"Two can play at that."

"Bang !" went a couple of shots. One whistled harmlessly over their heads; the other struck the boat just below the water line, and so being nearly spent by the water, did no damage.

"Take that," cried Captain Deering ; and blazed away.

One of the soldiers was seen to stagger and fall.

"Hit him, by jingo !"

Two more shots from the boat threw the soldiers into confusion.

"Soon silenced their batteries," said Nat, grimly.

"Pull hard," said the skipper ; "their next move will be to send boats off in pursuit."

"Let them come," said Jack.

"Rather ; let us get on board sharp, for I for one have had all the fun that I can wish for out of these murdering thieves."

Boats were launched from the beach—no less than three—and these were quickly filled with armed men.

But the fugitives had a good long start, and moreover, the rowers were old salts, well up to their work ; most of them had served in the Royal Navy, and could put the steam on without flurrying themselves at all.

They were soon on board the English vessel waiting for them, where Captain Deering had secured passages for all, and Jack received a hearty welcome from many friends he did not expect to see on board.

But for the lucky accident of this vessel being there, the gallant and audacious rescue of young Jack would have been useless ; for the Spaniards were mad over the job.

"Hullo," said the commander of the vessel, to Deering ; "are those boats coming after you ?"

"Yes."

"We've weighed anchor. So slope's the word. If we stop any longer, we shall have to sink those boats with a shot from our little deck gun, and that's what I don't want."

They worked the ship smartly enough, the men from the "Albatross" aiding, and they were precious soon a good distance out at sea, scudding along with full sails set, and a favourable wind.

The orphan, the English waiter, and the diver were all eager to shake young Jack by the hand. Lucky Jack !

CHAPTER LIII.

MASTER AND MAN AGAIN — OSTENTATION, EXPLANATION, RECRIMINATION — HOW CHIVEY SHOWS HIS CARDS—UGLY WORDS PASS—THEY COME TO AN UNDERSTANDING—WHAT CAME OF IT.

As the ship faded away in the distance, bearing Jack Harkaway junior and his triumphant colleagues to newer climes and fresh adventures, there was a whole mob of disappointed and defeated men upon the beach.

And amongst the mob were two English lads, who were as full of disappointment as any of the Spaniards.

One of these English youths was Herbert Murray, the other was his groom, valet, confidant, his *fidus Achates*, and his most dangerous acquaintance, Chivey.

"These are English," said one of the soldiers, when it became apparent to all that the pursuit was a failure ; "let us arrest them."

And arrested they would have been but for the lucky accident of one of the soldiers present knowing all about them, and interfering on their behalf.

"They are Englese," said the soldier, "but they have been assisting us against the assassins that have escaped."

And so Murray and Chivey got off.

But they soon got tired of being in this place, "stranded," as Mr. Chivey elegantly expressed it, "for want of the dibs."

The master complained, and the man found the means of satisfying him with money.

Now when Chivey produced the funds, his master never dreamed of asking him how the money was obtained, or where it came from.

But he was destined to learn a very unpleasant truth about this at a most unexpected moment.

"This isn't half a bad place, Chivey," said young Murray, after a grand dinner they had just regaled themselves with.

"Not when you've got the tin," said Chivey, "and lots of it."

"Well, we've managed pretty well as far as that's concerned," returned young Murray.

"We !"

"Yes ; we," said his master. "Why, you must have been spending some of your own wages that you had saved up."

Chivey turned up his nose.

"Don't talk muck," he said, contemptuously.

"Chivey !"

"Hallo !"

"Learn to know your place better. You presume upon my good nature, and if you don't reform, why——"

"Well ?"

"Why, I shall have to send you about your business."

Chivey put on a serious air.

"Yes. You might send me away," he said. "You might, I will say that, but the question is, should I go ?"

Herbert Murray had just been drinking enough to get on his dignity and feel outraged at this.

"Chivey, you'll have to go," said young Murray, sternly, "and the sooner the better."

"With all my heart," responded the groom, quite cheerfully. "Would you like me to change the other cheque first, perhaps ?"

There was something in his manner which made his master turn round at this.

"Do what ?"

"Change the other cheque."

"What cheque ?"

"Why, young Jack Harkaway's cheque, that you forged."

Murray turned purple, then deadly pale.

Chivey pretended not to notice it.

"Chivey," said his master, after awhile.

"What is it now, my sweet and pleasant ?" said the groom, insolently.

"What do you mean by that stupid speech about forging ?"

"Well, I don't call that so stoopid ; it's only the literal truth."

"Don't talk rubbish," said Murray.

"Well," said the tiger, "I ain't what you can call a downright university scholard, but

I'd bet a good lump level that you can find it in any dictionary. Forgery—to write another cove's name."

Herbert Murray had been flushed and excited before, but he was suddenly as sober as a judge now.

"That was only a foolish freak, when we were on board ship with Harkaway, Chivey," he said; "you know that, and no one could call such a thing as that forgery."

"I don't know that," returned the tiger, coolly. "It would be transportation all the same if you was nabbed for it."

"Don't be a fool, Chivey," said Murray.

"Look here now, Murray," exclaimed the tiger, "I'm not going to stand your cheek—do you hear? I ain't going to stand your cheek, so don't you go and try it on."

"Scoundrel!"

"Drop that," said the tiger, wagging his forefinger warningly at his master. "Drop that talk; I ain't a-going to stand it, I tell you. We ain't the friends we was, Murray, and I warn you that if you ain't more respectful, I'm just likely to cut up rusty."

There was no mistaking the meaning of these words, there was no further concealment between them.

When young Murray made an egregious ass of himself, it was solely the result of his silly pride and vanity in showing Chivey how well he could imitate young Jack's handwriting.

"Do you mean to say, Chivey, that you have cashed one of those——"

"Forged cheques?"

"Well, yes," said young Murray, gulping it down.

"Of course I did," returned the tiger; "where could we have got the money to live upon else? I watched Harkaway, and found out the place where he got his cheques cashed, and I passed the one you forged."

"You are a fool, Chivey."

"Why?"

"Because the utterer of a forged cheque is just as guilty as the forger."

"Bosh!"

"You make inquiries," said Murray. "It would be for life with you."

Chivey did not like this.

"Don't you go trying to drag me into your mess, if you please; don't you try that on, Murray. You gave me the forged cheque to get cashed. I am your servant, just bear in mind, a poor ignorant fellow, without no education. All I'd got to do was to go and get the coin for your forgery——"

"Hush!" exclaimed Murray, with an uneasy glance at the door.

"Oh," cried Chivey, raising his voice, "I ain't afraid for anybody to hear me; I'm as hinnocent as a unborn babe, I am. Let all the world know if you like."

Murray winced.

He walked up and down the room thinking the job over, while Chivey, lolling back in an easy chair, surveyed him lazily through the thick fumes rising from his cigar.

"I've got him on the grand hop!" thought the tiger; "he won't try it on again in a hurry."

He arose languidly, and tossed the end of his cigar into the fire.

"I'm going for a stroll, Murray," he said, pulling up his collar; "I shan't be long. By the way, just pull the bell, and order coffee for me."

Murray bit his lips in silence.

"Didn't you hear me, Murray?" said Chivey, louder.

"Yes."

"Then why the deuce don't you ring the bell?"

His master swallowed this, too, and rang.

A servant came, and stood waiting his orders.

"Well, Murray," said the tiger, "why don't you order?"

"Coffee in the garden for one."

"Yes, sir."

"No; for two," said Chivey.

"I don't want any," said his master.

"Oh, yes, you do. Coffee for two," said Chivey. "That'll do."

The servant bowed, and left the room.

"Murray."

"Well."

"Give me a weed. Yours are better than mine."

His master lifted up his arm as if to strike, and then threw his cigar case over to his tiger.

"That's rude," said Chivey, stooping to pick it up, "very rude. I'll not stand that sort of thing. There's nothing like coming to an understanding. We shall be better friends for it. A match; do you hear? Thanks. Follow me to the garden, and take your coffee. Make haste; I don't like cold coffee."

And he lounged out.

CHAPTER LIV.

CHIVEY HEARS GOOD NEWS—HIS RESOLVES—HE PUTS ON THE SCREW AGAIN—"RULE OF THUMB"—THE LONELY WALK TO THE GRAVEL PITS—CHIVEY TREADS TOO HARD—THE WORM TURNS AND STINGS HIM—SOMETHING LIKE MURDER.

HERBERT MURRAY heard the retreating footsteps of his servant die away in the distance.

Then he jumped up, and paced the room like a wild beast in a cage.

"What an ass—what an idiot have I been," he exclaimed, "to be caught in a trap by such a paltry scoundrel! My father warned me against him again and again—a low, cunning thief! But I must keep down my rage and disgust. I'll show him no mercy when I get my chance, and I shall get it, that I am certain of. The sooner the better—the sooner the better."

He shook his fist at the room door, as if it had been offending him, when there came a knock.

The door opened, and the servant who had answered the bell before appeared there.

"You are to go down to the garden, if you please, to your coffee," he said.

"I'll come."

"Very good, sir."

Herbert Murray clasped his hands in a feverish manner, and hurried off to his room.

Here he locked himself in.

Dropping on his knees before his portmanteau, he routed out a revolver from the bottom of it.

"Loaded in every chamber," he said, as he examined it hastily. "It may be useful. Who can say?"

He concealed it in his pocket, and walked down to the garden, where he found Chivey lounging in one chair, with his feet on another, while he lazily sucked at his cigar.

"At last," he said. "You have taken your time to think about coming."

The studied insolence of his manner goaded Murray to fury.

He felt inclined, momentarily, to kick over the traces, and defy his impudent servant.

But Herbert Murray was too great a coward for that.

"Take a seat," said Chivey, slowly, dragging his legs off the chair, and pushing it towards Murray with a lazy, languid air.

Herbert Murray sat down in silence.

"Come, come, Murray," said Chivey, "drink your coffee. I can't stand no sulks."

"Very good," responded his master.

And he drank the coffee as he was bidden.

Chivey's contempt for Herbert Murray increased fourfold from that moment.

"Just order some chartreuse for me," said he, sharply; "do you hear?"

As he raised his voice, Murray lost patience.

He grew rather pale, and turning to his servant, said, in a tone indicative of self-restraint—

"Be careful, Chivey, be careful, I tell you."

"What for?"

"If you put too much on to me, I may thrash you."

"You?"

"Yes. Be more civil."

"As for thrashing," said Chivey, "I don't know that you could. I don't believe you would ever have had enough pluck to try it on, if you thought I would stand up to you. I have stood your bullying long enough. I worked this job especially to get you under my thumb. You may as well know it now. You dropped into the trap like a lambkin—well, what is it now?"

He broke off because Murray, with an ejaculation of disgust, jumped up and walked out of the garden.

Chivey burst out into a loud and boisterous laugh.

"But where's he gone to, I wonder?"

He did not feel quite at ease upon this score, so he got up, and went in search of his master.

"The gentleman asked the way to the gravel pits," said a man, at the door of the hotel, in reply to Chivey's inquiries.

"What can he want there?" muttered Chivey to himself.

He would go and see.

He did not like the idea of Herbert Murray being too far away, so he was just starting off in pursuit, having first inquired his way, when the British consul came up, and stopped him.

"You are Mr. Murray's servant, I believe?"

"Yes, sir."

"I want him."

"He's out, sir."

"When will he be back?"

"He'll not be long, sir."

"I must see him as soon as he comes. I have some bad news for him, and wish to break it gently."

Chivey pricked up his ears at this.

"Nothing very bad, I hope, sir?"

"Indeed it is."

"I wish you would tell me what it is, sir. I shouldn't like my poor master to know anything very bad too suddenly."

The consul gave Chivey a sharp glance.

"Are you discreet?"

"Of course, sir."

"Well, then, your master's father is dead."

"Dead?"

"Yes."

"When? How did you know it, sir?"

"He went down in the 'Harpy' on his way hither to join his son, if we can believe the papers."

"How dreadful," exclaimed the tiger, looking inexpressibly shocked. "I'll go and seek the guv'nor, sir."

"But be careful," said the consul.

No sooner was Mr. Chivey out of sight and hearing of the consul, than he executed a boisterous double shuffle to a mirthful accompaniment of his own.

"The old boss has snuffed it, has he?" he said to himself. "We must be worth coin now—a bag of money. It is more than ever this child's game to keep a tight hand over Herbert. Now for him."

He made his way with all despatch to the gravel pits to which he had been directed, and here surely he came upon his master, Herbert Murray.

Orphan Herbert.

Remorseless young scoundrel that he was, Chivey never thought of this with the least feeling of pity for his master.

"I must keep my fist on him hard," said Chivey, again and again; "rule of thumb is my motter."

He walked on hurriedly, for he felt more anxious then ever to come up with Herbert.

A barren, desolate-looking part was that surrounding the gravel pits, several miles from any signs of a human dwelling.

"This is the sort o' place," said the tiger, to himself, "that I should like to have had that young Jack Harkaway fellow—all alone—no witnesses, and his hands tied. Ah, yes, his hands tied by all means. I never see such knuckles as that beast has got. They're just like iron, and they've got such a beastly low way of finding out a feller's sore spots. I should like to give him toko; and yet I could almost forgive him when I look back to that awful doing which he gave Herbert. What's that? It's him."

Yes, there was his master sitting upon the ground by the edge of one of the deepest of the gravel pits, peering down into its depths moodily.

A book lay open at his side, as though he had been reading in this dreary spot.

Chivey chuckled.

"He's got a royal hump on him," said the tiger. "Took a dose o' doleful. I hope he won't go and commit susanside. Oh, no," he added, "he ain't got the pluck."

He approached.

"Murray," said Chivey, in his coarsest manner.

Herbert looked up at the sound of his voice.

"What do you want here, Chivey?" he said. "I don't wish to be intruded upon."

Chivey grinned.

"Do you hear?" continued Murray.

"Oh, yes, I hear."

"Then leave me."

"Oh, you are a treat, you are, and no error."

"Do you hear what I said?" replied Herbert. "Go away."

"Come now, I tell you what it is, Murray. I ain't going to have you so cheeky. So come, jump up."

Herbert Murray bent his head lower yet.

Chivey could not see the strange expression of his face, or he would not have pushed matters any further.

Herbert's face was deathly pale, his lips were bloodless. This young man had been well educated and passed his boyhood amongst people from whom he had learnt to feel occasionally something like the instincts of a gentleman.

Evil courses and dissipation had led him into the follies we have seen him commit.

Chivey, his tiger, was more than anyone responsible for Herbert's lapsing into such evil ways.

How a youth decently brought up could have fallen into the error of making an associate of such an illiterate, ignorant youth as this Chivey, is not easy to understand.

"Do you hear me, young fellow?" said Chivey, imperiously,

Herbert Murray never heeded his words.

"Come, I say."

And there the tiger made the mistake.

He ventured so far as to give his master a gentle reminder with the tip of his boot.

Murray sprang up with a cry like that of a savage beast just wounded, and he fell upon his insolent servant.

Chivey gave a cry of alarm.

He would have fallen back.

But too late.

Herbert Murray had not voice for words. Passion choked him.

Holding his traitor servant with one hand, he hammered at him with the other, until his strength, and not his will, failed him.

Then, gathering up his force for a last effort, he seized him with both hands and hurled the unfortunate tiger from him with such desperation that Chivey fell half stunned and bleeding on the ground.

"Murder!" he cried faintly, "murder, help!"

Herbert whipped out a revolver from his breast pocket.

"It isn't murder yet, devil," he hissed at him between his fast-set teeth; "but that's coming next."

"Help!"

Herbert cocked the revolver.

"Mercy!" cried Chivey, wildly; "oh, sir, do have mercy."

His master laughed.

"Oh, sir, do have mercy on a poor cove. I never did you no harm. I've been a good servant to you, and I will be again."

"No, you'll not," retorted Herbert Murray, "never again."

This quiet retort made Chivey quake from top to toe.

"Mercy," he gasped.

"Take that," said Murray.

He thrust out his pistol and pulled the trigger.

Click. But no report.

He was wrong when he had pronounced it loaded in every chamber.

One was empty, and this was the very one.

"Confusion!" he exclaimed, with an oath.

He cocked it again, while Chivey was up and creeping fearfully backwards, facing his foe.

Herbert Murray followed him up with outstretched hand.

Unsuspectingly Chivey was backing on the brink of the deepest gravel pit.

"Die," said Herbert Murray, thrusting the revolver forward.

"Hah!"

The tiger scrambled back.

A moment more and he was over the precipice and had fallen backwards down that fearful height.

A wild, despairing cry he gave as he fell.

Murray drew near.

A low, hollow groan came up from the bottom of the pit.

Then all was still.

Dead!

"He's gone," said Herbert Murray, turning deathly white; "it is no fault of mine. He brought it on himself. He's dead, and I am free."

CHAPTER LV.

MOURNING THE ORPHAN—HIS APPARITION—CRUEL HOAX—RETALIATION—HUNTING FOR RUNAWAY SLAVES—TARRING AND FEATHERING—MAMMOTH BLACKBIRDS.

WHILE the events just related were occurring in the obscure Spanish port, Jack Harkaway, junior, and his friends were on their way down the Mediterranean.

A lucky escape it was for them, one and all.

"I'm very sorry," said Jack, upon the following day, "that we have missed our old friend the orphan."

"Poor old Figgins!" returned Harry Girdwood; "I should have liked him with us too."

They felt the want of some sort of a butt, be it remarked, to supply the place of genial lying, bragging, affectionate, old Isaac Mole.

Figgins, the self-styled orphan, just filled this place admirably, with one or two characteristics which were new.

*　　*　　*　　*　　*

Now, while Jack and Harry Girdwood were talking over the loss of poor Figgins, Tinker and Bogey were seated astride the hatchway leading to the fore-cabin.

They were serious as judges, and Tinker was

reading his dependant a fine moral lesson, when suddenly Bogey looked over the stairs and stared as wildly as if he had seen a ghost.

"Look hyar, Massa Tinker," he whispered.

"Whar?"

"Down dere."

"Ugh—ugh—u—up!" grinned Tinker, with difficulty repressing his mirth. "hyar's gollopshus, catawampus, thunderin' great larks, ugh —up."

"What is it, Tinker?" demanded young Jack.

"Hush, sar; hold your blessed tongue, sar, d'ree'ly or sooner."

"Well!" said his master. "that's polite."

"A gemman's coming up. sar. Oh, my! sich larks."

He appeared as though about to be convulsed again with laughter, and rocked about so upon his perch that Jack thought every minute he would fall.

"Oh, sich larks!" repeated the black lad. "You nebber guess what."

"What larks do you mean?" asked Jack. "I believe you have been drinking, you rascal."

Tinker looked supremely offended.

"No, sar."

"You have."

"Not a drop, sar," protested the darkey.

"I've half a mind to give you a good thrashing," continued Jack.

Tinker slid off his perch sharply, and got just a safe distance away.

"Thrashin' nebber good, sar, allus miserable dam bad, sar. Only good for Bogey."

"No, 'tain't," said the person most nearly concerned. "Bewful ting for my s'perior hossifer; berry bad ting for Bogey."

"Quiet, you ugly brack niggar," said Tinker. "Hyar comes Massa Orfin."

Mr. Figgins came slowly and unsuspectingly up the hatchway.

He was not thinking of anything in particular, nor did he notice either the black boys or our hero, young Jack Harkaway, who was standing close by with his friend Harry Girdwood.

In fact, although the orphan possessed some amount of Cockney shrewdness—he must have had some wit to have been a successful trader in London—he was, just at that moment, in a state of mental abstraction, very favourable to the perpetration of a practical joke.

Half a dozen more steps, and he was at the top of the companion ladder.

As Mr. Figgins stepped on to the deck, the two mischievous niggers seized the tremulous orphan in the rear.

"We arretht you, sar," exclaimed Tinker. "We am all pirates, and yea must walk de bressed plank or be strung up."

They seized him by his garments, and threw him on his hands and knees.

He roared loudly.

"Murder!" cried Mr. Figgins; "he'p! I'm done for!"

"What are you doing with Mr. Figgins?" exclaimed the captain.

The others tried to tip him the wink.

But the captain was not very much alive to fun, and he failed to see what it meant.

Mr. Figgins, on hearing a friendly voice, looked up.

And then he learnt that instead of being surrounded by pirates, it was only the mischievous Tinker and Bogey larking.

Jack was standing close by, and with him was Harry Girdwood, grinning all over their faces.

The orphan disliked ridicule greatly.

He changed colour and looked rather sheepish, and then he got up a faint grin, as if to join in the fun.

"I'll take it out of those two young devils," he said to himself, as he sneaked off to his cabin. "Only let me get half a chance, and I'll worry them."

He kept his word.

*   *   *   *   *

They had been through the Straits of Gibraltar some time, and were sailing lazily along the Mediterranean, when one day they were becalmed off the coast of Tunis.

While there a sudden disturbance arose on shore, and it became known on board that a number of slaves had escaped, thanks to the common sense of a few English residents there.

Boats were put off, and a search ordered on board the ships riding at anchor along the coast, for those slaves were the property of the Bey of Tunis himself, and his highness was not the sort of man to tamely submit to a loss.

Tinker heard the matter discussed, and he naturally enough for a gentleman of colour, took a very lively interest in it.

The orphan Figgins was there to communicate with them.

"Well, Bogey," said he, wishing to have some fun with them. "if they do send on board here to search for their slaves, they are very likely to insist upon taking you or Tinker."

The latter pricked up his ears.

"Not exactly," said Tinker.

"Oh, I don't know." said Mr. Figgins, seriously; "we mustn't be too sure."

"Dey couldn't take dis chile."

"It is not a question of that, Tinker," said Figgins; "as for their power to take you, there isn't much doubt about that. The only thing is, would they be merciful? I am inclined to think not."

"What?"

"Dey can't take me," said Bogey, looking very frightened. "I'se not one eb dere niggars."

"That doesn't matter; all niggers are alike— all black cattle."

Tinker shot at the speaker an indignant glance.

"I'll gib you black cattle," said he to himself.

"The fact is, Bogey," said the orphan. "I don't want them to come here and get hold of you, for if the captain did give you up——"

"He wouldn't."

"Oh, yes, he would."

"Nebbah!"

"You're wrong there. He'd sooner give you up than get into any mess with the big-wigs here. and if he does I shall miss my retaliation."

"Your what, sir?"

"Tallyashun," said Bogey. "What the debil dat, sar?"

"My chance of paying you out for the tricks you have played off on me."

"Yah, yah!" guffawed the two of them in chorus. "We have larks wid you and hab more yet."

"Very funny," said the orphan, with a vicious look. "Well, I mean to tar and feather you for your larks."

Tinker pretended to look very frightened, and Bogey, taking the cue from his master, made an extravagant show of shaking at the knees.

"Oh, Massa Figgins, you so big and strong sar—an' so berry fine man, sar. You no hurt de poor niggar, sar?"

"You'll see," said Mr. Figgins; and he walked away.

He went below, and bribed two of the sailors for some purpose or another, which only transpired later on.

* * * * *

One of the crew came running up to where Tinker and Bogey stood by the cook's galley, chatting with him and sniffing the steam that arose from a savoury stew.

"Tinker," cried the sailor, "you've only got time."

"What for?"

"Just bare time; for they'll be on deck soon."

"Who?"

"And as for trying to put them off, why, it's no more use than nothing. Nat Cringle says that the skipper's sure to give you up, the pair of you. He daren't refuse. Of course they'd do justice to your memory. But before they could find out as you weren't theirs, you'd be bowstrung, or something of that kind."

Tinker looked utterly dismayed as the sailor went on, and as for Bogey, he was ready to give way now at the knees, much as he had shammed to do before Mr. Figgins.

Just at this moment Mr. Figgins came up hurriedly, and seemingly in a state of considerable alarm.

"Oh, my poor fellows," he exclaimed, in a state of great alarm apparently; "here they come."

"Who?" cried Tinker.

"Where?" said Bogey.

"Is dey many?"

"Twenty men, armed to the teeth, to capture runaway slaves," returned Mr. Figgins.

"Oh, golly!"

"All with scimitars, big enough to cleave an elephant in two."

"Oh, Jerusalem!" gasped Tinker; "how offul."

"Drefful," ejaculated Bogey; "beastly offul, drefful."

"What shall we do?"

"There is nothing for it," returned Mr. Figgins.

"Only to die or go into slavery," added one of the sailors.

"Mussy on us!" cried Tinker.

"Oh, Massa Figgins, do save a poor miserable cove, an' I'll bress you. Oh, do, sar. I'll nebar hab no larks ag'in wid you, sar; s'elp me golly, sar."

"You promise, Tinker?" said Mr. Figgins.

"Oh, yes, sar."

"Swear, then."

"I don't like to, sar."

"Swear, I tell you. Do you know what an oath is?"

"Yes, sar."

"Then swear."

"If I must, sar."

"Certainly you must; I insist upon it."

"Well, den, you'se a dam tief, a ugly old orphan, blarm yah; you, you——"

"Stop, stop," cried Mr. Figgins; "that's not the sort of swearing I mean. I want you to take an oath that you will never again behave so disgracefully to me."

"I swear dat, sar."

"Good; then I'll try and save you, Tinker."

"An' me, sar?"

"And you, too, Bogey."

"Bress your 'art, Massa Figgins; you'se a good sort."

"I hope so. Now down with you below. Go with him," he added, pointing to the sailor, "while I stop here and put them off if they insist upon going below."

Off went the two darkeys with the sailor.

After a few moments the orphan went after them, and getting to the hatchway, he shuffled about a good deal, and made a rare lumbering noise with his feet, so as to make it sound as though there were a whole host of people moving about.

Then he ran nimbly down the companion ladder into the cabin, where Tinker and Bogey shivered up in a corner, hiding behind two big barrels.

"Look out," exclaimed Mr. Figgins, in a whisper; "they are coming."

"Who?"

"The Tunisians, in search of their slaves, who have escaped."

"Golly!"

"Dey ain't gwine to come down hyar!" said Bogey, anxiously.

"Yes; hark! Here they come."

"Oh, golly, Massa Figgins," cried Tinker. "I'se a dead un. Do go fetch Massa Harkaway."

"I have no time to find him. Where can I put you?" said Mr. Figgins, looking about him for a hiding place. "Why, here you are; creep into this barrel, both of you. In you go."

Tinker obeyed with the greatest alacrity.

He was closely followed by his man Bogey.

But before Tinker had got to the full length, there came a cry from the barrel that would certainly have betrayed them had the search party from land been near at hand.

"What is it?" exclaimed Mr. Figgins. "You'll ruin all."

"Dere's suffin all wet and sticky inside dat bressed barrel," said Tinker.

"Sticky?"

"Yes; orful."

"What is it?"

"Dunno, sir; smell like tar."

"How unfortunate," said the orphan, with a sly look at the sailor, who stood beside him. "Out with you, creep into the next. Quick, for your life."

"I'm in."

"So's me."

They scrambled in on all fours, and Mr. Figgins clapped on the head of the cask.

But even this did not appear to satisfy them, for Tinker's voice was heard in loud complaint.

"What is it now?" said Mr. Figgins.

"Dis barrel is chock full ob feathers, sar."

"Well, they can't hurt you."

"No; but dey's sticking to us 'ca'se ob dat oder muck—de tar."

"Well, what of that? Hush! I hear them coming."

Surely enough, the heavy tramp of foot-steps was heard on deck.

Then down the companion ladder three or four sailors came, led by Nat Cringle.

They kicked up a rare hullabaloo, and one of them snapped a pistol.

Then they seized hold of the barrel in which the two niggers were concealed, and gave it a roll backwards and forwards, after which they departed.

"Now," ejaculated Mr. Figgins, knocking off the lid, "now's your time. Fly, for your lives."

Tinker scrambled out and got up the companion ladder somehow, closely followed by Bogey.

Having very little clothing on, they were covered with feathers from head to foot.

The first barrel had been carefully coated with tar, so that turn which way they would, they could not escape it.

The second barrel contained the feathers of a dozen fowls and ducks, and these stuck to our dusky practical jokers in a way they had never counted upon.

On reaching the deck, they found themselves faced by nearly the whole of the passengers and crew, and they were greeted with a perfect storm of laughter.

They saw that they had been the victims of a hoax, and they turned to retreat.

But, alack, the ladder was blocked by Mr. Figgins, Nat Cringle, and the rest of the sailors who had participated in the fun.

"Whatever are these funny-looking objects?" said Harry Girdwood, coming on deck with young Jack.

"New specimens. Mammoth blackbirds," cried Jack, laughing at Bogey and his boy Tinker as they ran about, not knowing where to hide themselves.

CHAPTER LVI.

HOW TINKER DISTINGUISHED HIMSELF—AN ALARM—THE SHARK—TINKER DOES A DEED OF DARING.

TINKER looked quite crestfallen.

"We look like birds moulting; but keep up your pecker, massa," whispered Bogey.

"Whatever have you been up to?" asked Jack.

"I'll tell you," said the orphan, beaming with satisfaction at the success of his exploit. "They were in a dreadful fright of being taken away by the Tunis people, who were hunting after the runaway slaves, and so they disguised themselves as a pair of geese."

"Ha, ha, ha!"

"You laugh, Massa Jack," said Bogey, rue-fully. "You no like for to be in such a bressed pickle yourself."

This made them laugh more boisterously than ever.

"Stop a bit," said Harry Girdwood. "Here's a riddle for you."

"Out with it."

"Why are Tinker and Bogey like the champions of the Thames and Tyne?"

"Because they handle their skulls so well," said Jack, promptly.

This was greeted with a perfect yell of laughter, as Tinker and Bogey were scratching furiously at their woolly heads.

"No," said Harry; "it's because they feather so beautifully."

"Ha, ha, ha!"

Mr. Figgins laughed louder than all the rest together.

Bogey, who was very sensitive to ridicule, made a desperate effort to get down below again.

But this the assembled company would not allow.

He tore ferociously at his itching skin.

"Oh, golly!" he cried out in despair, "what shall I do to get off dese bressed feathers?"

"I'll tell you how, Sambo," said one of the sailors.

Bogey turned eagerly to the speaker.

"How?"

"Go to the cook's galley, and get him to pluck you in the regular way."

"Ha, ha, ha!"

"I'll tell you another way," said Nat Cringle.

"Out with it."

"Let's draw up two lines, and give them a fair run down the middle while we souse 'em with water."

The orphan was standing very close to Tinker enjoying the fun. Tinker saw him, and at once made a rush, clutching him round the waist.

"I'se got yar, Massa Orphan," he said; "now, I gibe you some of my tar and feathers—make you look like old goose."

And Tinker began to rub himself against the orphan.

The next moment they rolled over and over together on the deck, the orphan each time getting plenty of Tinker's tar and feathers, and each time screaming loudly for help.

At last Jack, amidst much laughter, managed to pull Tinker off.

Tinker then gave a sharp look about him, meaning to make a run for it.

But there was no escape.

They were too well encompassed to get off.

In almost less time than it takes to tell the tale, buckets were brought and passed round.

Then there was an opening made in their ranks, and Tinker made a sudden rush.

He was not quick enough, however.

Two of the buckets were emptied over him as he flew, and Bogey got the contents of three more as he followed his master.

"Reserve the rest till they come back," said Jack.

But they did not come back.

Tinker made one desperate rush to the first

vacant space at the ship's side, and without more ado, sprang up on to the bulwarks.

"Dis de way I'se gwine to wash dem dam fedders off !" he shouted.

And overboard he leaped.

A cry of alarm was raised.

But before a second cry could be uttered, Bogey was after him.

In an instant the adventure was robbed of its comic aspect.

Alarm was depicted upon every countenance.

The cry was raised—

"Man overboard !"

"Lower boats."

"Aye, aye, sir."

Old Nat Cringle and another well-disciplined man—old salts who had served in the Royal Navy—set to work promptly and methodically, without any of that wild hurry-scurry which defeats itself.

Two boats were very promptly lowered.

"There's no danger for Tinker," said Jack. "He swims like any fish in the sea."

"And as for Bogey, he could live for a week in the water," added Harry.

Everybody had rushed over to the side of the vessel, and all eyes were straining eagerly after the two negro boys.

But no signs of them were visible at present.

"They don't seem to come up very quickly," said Jack, anxiously.

Mr. Figgins was precious ill at ease now.

This desperate conclusion to the fun quite spoilt the joke, and he would have given something never to have had a hand in it.

"Dear, dear !" he exclaimed, "I hope no harm will come to the poor boys."

His distress of mind was so genuine that Jack Harkaway took pity upon him, and did his best to reassure him.

"They had a good deep dive," said he. "It's no joke—a jump from the side here. But I'll wager that they are only taking a second dive, just to frighten us."

But now the boats were lowered, Nat Cringle and another sailor in one, and three sailors in the other.

They pulled away from the ship some little distance, until a welcome cry came from one of the boats—

"There they are !"

"Where ?"

"Out yonder, ever so far."

"I see them," cried Jack.

"Tinker ahoy !" shouted Nat Cringle. "Bogey, you waggybone, come back."

"Tinker !"

Tinker was seen swimming lazily along with one hand, whilst with the other he was busily engaged upon his feathers, which stuck to him with remarkable pertinacity.

"Tinker."

Tinker was within hearing now.

"I'se comin'," he answered, "when dese bressed fedders all off."

It was a curious sight to watch the antics of the sable pair in the water.

They both could do just as they liked in it, and the way they paddled round each other, and trod the water with their feet while they picked the feathers off each other's carcase, was a regular side-splitting sight.

Suddenly a cry was raised which sent a thrill of terror through every frame.

"Sharks !"

"Drop that, Small," cried Jack Harkaway ; "that's no joke."

"That it ain't, sir," replied the sailor, "but a born fact ; look there."

Jack followed the direction in which the sailor pointed, and then he perceived a huge white shark playing about under the ship's counter.

"Shark !" shouted Jack, with all his force.

"Den be golly, Massa Harkaway," replied Tinker, "you tar and fedder him."

"Into the boat with you !" yelled Jack, wildly ; "sharks, I say."

Every instant he expected to see the monster turn and dart in the direction of the unhappy negroes. But strangely enough the shark did not appear to notice them.

As soon as the word "shark " was spoken, a Yankee sailor named Biles, bolted down below and reappeared laden with a strong chain and hook, upon which was fixed a huge morsel of fat pork.

Besides this, he carried two other pieces of meat.

The pork bait struck the water.

Then the Yankee sailor threw over one of his pieces of loose bait, a little nearer to where the shark was swimming about.

The monster of the deep struck after it as it sank, and snapped it up.

Then he shot out after the next piece, and Biles gave a sudden tug at the line he had affixed to the chain.

"Hooked him," exclaimed Biles ; "hurrah !"

The interest now was clean gone from Tinker and Bogey, who were safe, and centred in the white shark, who had just swallowed Mr. Biles's bait in the mildest and most unsuspecting manner imaginable.

Now, as soon as the shark felt the hook, he made a desperate plunge to get free, and had not the line been a precious stout one, it would never have stood the shock.

As it was, however, it held out bravely.

Biles played with him a bit, and let him run out a good distance.

Then he tightened his rope, and began to haul in.

Mr. Shark objected, but the Yankee would not be denied.

"He's getting bad," said one of the bystanders ; "I wouldn't like to be near him now."

Tinker, it would seem, entertained quite a different opinion, as we shall see.

As soon as he got alongside, he scrambled up on deck like a monkey and ran off down below.

"There goes Tinker," laughed Jack.

In the space of a few minutes, back came Tinker, carrying a freshly-ground cutlass.

Jack saw him, and stepped forward in some alarm.

What could he mean ?

Was he about to wreak vengeance upon Mr. Figgins ?

He feared so.

"Now, sir, what is this for?" asked Jack, sternly.

"I'se gwine to take a walk wid Massa Shark."

Tinker then sprang up on to the bulwark, and waved his cutlass as he called out very loudly to the orphan—

"Now, Massa Figbox, I'se gwine to show you how to carve up shark for table. If you got de pluck, jist you come and tar and fedder him."

Then with a wild, derisive laugh, and before anyone could interfere to stop him in his mad freak, over he plunged again sword in hand.

The water was clear and translucid, and they could see fathoms down.

But Tinker went clear out of sight.

They watched eagerly for his reappearance, but a sudden and violent plunge of the shark drew off their attention.

"Look out," cried Biles.

Just then the shark shook all over again as if suddenly palsied, and the water was dyed red all around him.

Then Tinker suddenly shot up to the surface upon the other side of the shark, swimming with his left arm, while in his right hand he waved the cutlass dripping with blood.

He had contrived to keep under long enough to plunge the cutlass thrice into the monster's belly.

The third time up to the hilt it went, and Tinker had a bath of blood.

The shark had had enough.

It rolled over, and then lay flat and motionless upon the water.

Tinker had done for him.

"Bravo, Tinker!"

A dozen voices caught up the cry, and Jack's brave boy Tinker became the hero of the hour.

CHAPTER LVII.

NEWS FROM HOME—STRANGE TIDINGS—ROBBERY—"AYE, AND FORGERY, TOO!"—PRECAUTIONS—ON AGAIN—THE TURKISH PORT—DARE-DEVIL JACK—A PROMISE OF ADVENTURE ONCE MORE.

A RIGHT pleasant cruise they had, and we would fain linger with them as they pursue their way up the sunny Mediterranean. But we must bear in mind how great is the work before us, and how small is the space remaining at our disposal, and resist temptation.

Let us push on, then.

Malta was the most important station on their way, and this was because sundry passengers were expecting letters there from home.

Amongst the number was Jack Harkaway.

Letters from home!

Welcome, indeed, were they to everyone on board.

And they who hoped for some sign from those they had left behind, and found not a line, were naturally sadly crestfallen and disappointed.

Any but the veriest egotist might surely think of those that are far away.

A few short lines, however hastily written, may send a thrill of joy through the heart of the absent one.

It is cruel, then, to neglect such a duty under the plea that you "are such a bad correspondent," or that you "detest writing letters."

The worst pretext of all is, perhaps, the one which is the most frequently made—"I haven't had time."

The very slowest of slow correspondents can find time to idle away some scattered moments of his or her busiest day.

Never mind if your orthography is weak enough to cause you to run a muck at a "bee."

No matter if your pothooks and hangers are execrable.

Send the absent and expectant ones a scrawl.

Let them be able to decipher no more than the bare address, it will cause them a feeling of pleasure, be assured.

Well, Jack Harkaway and his friends were among the lucky ones.

There were letters for Jack and for Harry Girdwood.

Jack's first.

His will tell a tale for itself which should not be without a certain interest for the faithful who have followed his fortunes up to the present.

Jack comfortably seated himself, broke the seal, and began to read the letter from home.

And this is the letter which old Jack Harkaway had written to his hopeful son.

"MY OWN DEAR JACK,—Since receiving your first letter, I have written to you twice. Your dear mother has likewise, and although we have heard from you twice, your letters contain no acknowledgment of ours. What does this mean? Can our letters have miscarried? We fear so. Need I go over the old ground, my dear boy? Need I say how wild with joy we were to receive your first letter, and to learn that you had escaped the peril which the deliberate villany of old Murray had placed you in? This is the fourth letter to you.

"Now it is very remarkable that you should not reply, because my letters both alluded to a matter which should certainly have claimed your attention. I allude to your extravagance. This, my dear boy, is a new weakness, and one which should be nipped in the bud. When you draw cheques for four hundred pounds at once, it is high time to reflect upon what is going forward, upon how far you may be allowing yourself to be led away by persons who are either thoughtless or unscrupulous. And I certainly feel it my duty to mention the fact, as habits of extravagant expenditure are likely to grow upon one, and at some time or other there comes, however great your fortune, an imperative necessity to put on the skid and pull up; this would be attended with painful feelings of self-sacrifice. I hope that an early date will bring on an acknowledgment of this letter, and the assurance that both yourself and Harry are well and happy and not too wild.

"Your affectionate father,

"J. H."

Jack was astounded. What could it mean?

He ran away after Harry Girdwood as fast as his legs would take him.

Harry had received letters, too, from England.

One of these was in a lady's handwriting, and he was eagerly reading it when his friend exclaimed—

"Harry."

"What is it, Jack?"

"Read that."

He placed his father's letter in Harry's hands.

Harry read it down, but on coming to the four hundred pounds question, Jack's comrade was surprised.

"What does that mean, Harry?"

Harry pondered a long while over this before he spoke.

"There is but one explanation possible," said Harry.

"And that is?"

"Villany. Forgery."

"Good Heaven, Harry!" exclaimed Jack, "it is impossible."

"What other explanation can you give me?"

"None."

"Now, Jack," said Harry, presently, "let us be practical. How could any stranger draw upon your credit?"

"Only with my cheques," replied Jack; "but the honest truth is that I have never examined my cheque-book for some time."

"Then we must examine the cheque-book at once," said Harry.

Jack soon had his cheque-book before him.

"It looks all right," said Jack. "Here's the last cheque that I drew."

"Go through it, Jack," said the more thoughtful Harry.

Jack soon discovered several cheques had been abstracted.

"What can this mean, Harry?" cried Jack, aghast; "who has done it?"

"Do your suspicions rest on anyone, Jack?"

"No."

*   *   *   *   *

"I tell you what, Jack," said Harry. "we can't trace it now, that is as clear as daylight. But the first step is to write home."

"Yes."

"Note down the numbers of the stolen cheques."

This was done.

"Now, in addition to this, write home that every cheque you draw in future will bear some mark or sign in addition to your signature."

"Good," said Jack. "I'll put your initials—H. G."

"That will do as well as anything else."

"Now then to write home."

The robbery of the cheques had been cunningly contrived.

They never suspected the real culprits.

But the numbers of the cheques being sent home, nothing was easier than to trace them.

Each cheque reached the London bankers with several endorsements which would enable them to go right back to the original negociator of it in Spain.

There was a chance then of the crime being punished. We shall see the result.

*   *   *   *   *

The vessel made no more stoppages of any importance until they came to a port not a thousand miles from Lagos.

Here they cast anchor.

"I know the English consul here," said Captain Deering, "and he is a man of some distinction. He is likely to stand well enough with the pasha to make matters pretty comfortable for us while we stay here."

"That sounds like business, Captain Deering," said Jack. "I should like to go over the place."

"The pasha is sure to invite us. The only one word of recommendation I have to offer you, Mr. Harkaway, is that no mention be made of the harem."

"Why?"

"The subject is tabooed, according to Turkish etiquette."

"Oh, crikey! what fun we could have among 'em, then," said Jack.

"And they might have fun with you," replied Captain Deering, significantly.

"What sort?"

"They have various diversions with the too curious," returned the skipper. "Bowstringing is a favourite pastime, impaling is another."

"And so we can't see the harem?" said Jack.

"Not only can't see it, but you must not mention it."

"That is the most unlucky thing of all."

"I was wrong in saying you could not see it. You can see the outside of it. There, that large window, before which dangles a palm-leaf mat as a sunblind, right upon the edge of the water—that is the saloon, answering to the drawing-room, in which the beauties of the seraglio assemble."

"I should like to have a peep," said Jack, anxiously.

The skipper pulled a precious long face.

"No nonsense, Master Jack," said he, seriously. "It would cost you your life."

"Rather a long price to pay for a peep, captain."

"Yes, Jack, take my advice, and do not risk your life by attempting to annoy the Turks."

*   *   *   *   *

"Harry," said Jack some time afterwards.

"Well, Jack?"

"Tinker and Bogey are in the boat already."

"I'm afraid it is rather risky, Jack, after what Captain Deering said."

"Then don't come."

"If you are going."

"I am."

"Then so am I. Where you go, Jack, I'll go. I don't mind danger; I don't quite think it right to rush into it for sheer foolery, but I'm blowed if you shall go alone."

"Stow your palaver then," said Jack, with a grin, "and over you go."

The old Harkaway temper was in him.

The spirit of adventure was too strong within him to be resisted, no matter what the danger might be.

CHAPTER LVIII.

A MOONLIGHT ADVENTURE AFLOAT—THE
BLACK BOATMEN AND THEIR MYSTERIOUS
CARGO—A SACK FOR A COFFIN—THE AS-
SASSINATION—THE DEATH CRY—TINKER
THE AVENGER—HOW HE SET TO WORK—
RETREAT.

IT was a bright moonlight night, so they resolved to go ashore.

Tinker and Bogey rowed, pulling hard, and
Jack steered, while Harry Girdwood stood up
in the boat, and gave all the necessary directions.

"Let's make for the creek up beside that
palace," said he, pointing to a dark inlet on
the right ; "that's our best chance."

"Hush!"

They rested awhile upon their oars in silence, for from the pasha's palace came a warning sound.

A gong sounded in the distance, then came
the grating of a heavy gate, and forth from
the creek came a boat.

Now in this boat were two men, turbaned
black fellows of sinister aspect, who were
bringing a strange-looking burthen out to
sea.

In the boat was a sack, filled to the neck
with something which riveted their attention,
in spite of its outline being so confused and
indistinct.

"What's that they have in the sack?"
whispered Harry Girdwood.

"Hush!"

"They don't see us."

The palace cast such a black shadow in the
strong moonlight, that where our friends were
in their boat, they were almost invisible.

Their presence was unsuspected by the new-
comers, who pulled out into the open, and
then proceeded to complete the object of their
journey.

They shipped their oars, and each took an
end of their strange burden.

Then on a given signal the sack was hoisted
up, and——

A piercing shriek rent the air.

There was no mistaking the direction from
whence it came—the sack.

"Did you hear that?"

"Yes."

"What does it mean, Jack?" whispered
Harry.

Jack's answer was a single word, but expressive.

"Murder!"

"I believe it is."

"What shall we do?"

"We could never save the poor wretch,
whatever we did, and we should only get into
trouble uselessly."

"Hush!"

Another shriek, louder than before.

A muttered curse or two came from the boat
where the tragedy was being enacted.

The sack was hoisted up, and then pushed
over the boat's side.

A dull, heavy splash.

All was over.

A creepy, crawly feeling seized the occupants
of the boatload of spectators of this crime, and

Harry Girdwood shivered as he said in a whisper—

"It sounded like a woman's voice, I
thought."

"So did I," replied Jack ; "but you could
hardly tell, muffled as the voice was."

"Murdered a gal," quoth Tinker. "I'se off,
Massa Jack, to Charlestown after 'em."

"Brave Tinker!" cried Jack, "you can do
little good."

But as he spoke, Tinker dropped over into
the water.

He shot down under the water, and struck
out at a great pace for the boat containing the
assassins.

He was alongside of it in a crack, just as the
two coloured villains in the boat put out the
oars again to row back.

He made a sudden grab at the nearest of
the oars, and wrested it out of the rower's
hand.

Then, before the two could recover from
their surprise, he sprang at the edge of the
boat, and jerking on it with his whole weight,
over it went.

The next instant all three were scrambling
in the water together.

The assassins raised a terrible hubbub, that
soon brought assistance from the palace.

Lights were seen flashing to and fro, and an
alarm gong was heard beating.

"Jack."

"What now?"

"Sharp's the word."

"Good."

"Where's Tinker?"

"I don't know. We must wait for him."

"Yes ; if we don't, he'd be bowstrung before
many hours are over."

"Unless he is lucky enough to get
drowned."

"Tinker, hallo!"

"Hist! Tinker, Tinker," cried Harry Girdwood.

The young negro's lithe form was soon seen
shooting, eel-like, through the water, and soon
he was dragged into the boat.

"Tinker, you vagabond, you've ruined
all," said Jack.

"Yes, sar."

"And as soon as we get back, I'm going to
have you tied up, and give you a dozen."

"Cakes, sir?"

"No, lashes."

"Golly!" cried the negro, "that's luck for
dis chile. What's I been doing?"

"You have spoilt one of the best adventures
we could have had."

"And I spile them vagabonds' beauty, sar.
No vi'lence, sar ; Tinker only rub the boat's
scull agin the nigger's skull—rader hard, sar,
like, and, oh golly! Massa Harkaway, you
should heerd 'em squirm and squeal."

"I did, and so did they hear them in the
palace. The game's up for to-night, and all
through you. We must try again to-morrow."

Tinker sulked.

"I thought you allus liked, Massa Harkaway, to pay out dem dam catawampus, thundering, immense thieves, sar. I should like to
spifflicate de whole bilin', sar."

"YOU HAVE TAKEN YOUR TIME ABOUT COMING,' EXCLAIMED CHIVEY."

"Did they see you?"

"Dey too frightened, sar," grinned the darkey.

"What could they have taken you for?" Tinker.

"De debil," suggested Bogey, promptly

"Very likely," said Jack. "Tinker's not unlike him."

"Well, sar, you ought to know; I don't keep sich company myself, sar, and can't say."

The boats from the palace were seen issuing from the water gate at the side. with lanterns at the bow of each boat ; so the adventurous party pulled back as fast as possible to the ship, deferring the visit till next day, then to make it in a more regular if less exciting manner.

CHAPTER LIX.

JACK GETS INTO HOT WATER—A MORAL LESSON, AND HOW HE PROFITED BY IT— ALL'S WELL THAT ENDS WELL.

THE matter was not ended here. however.

When they got on board, there was a very serious reception awaiting them.

Their project had been discovered and be- trayed to the skipper by some officious noodle, and Captain Willis was not a little alarmed.

The consequences might be very serious.

So the captain had Jack and Harry Gird- wood up, and gave them a word or two of a sort.

"We wish to preserve the most friendly re- lations with the people here, Mr. Harkaway," said he. severely ; "and this sort of adventure is not calculated to achieve our object."

Jack did not attempt to deny what had oc- curred.

"We have done no harm," he said ; "we were simply cruising about when we saw murder done. We arrived too late to prevent it, but Tinker was pleased to take it upon himself to avenge the murdered woman, for a woman it was, as we could tell from her shrieks as the sack went under and stifled them for ever."

The captain was somewhat startled at this.

"Is this true?"

"I would have you know, captain, that I am not in the habit of saying what is not true."

The captain bowed stiffly at young Jack's rebuke.

"I don't wish to imply anything else," he said ; "but before you get too high up in the stirrups, young gentleman, remember that I command here. Remember that in your own thirst for excitement. you act in a way likely to compromise me as well as everybody on board. You are not wanting in a proper appreciation of right and wrong. Before you add anything worse to the present discussion, reflect. The injured air which you are pleased to assume is out of place. I leave you to your own reflections, young gentleman."

And so saying, the captain turned away and left him.

Jack's first impulse was to walk after the captain. and fire a parting shot.

But Harry Girdwood's hand arrested him.

"Don't be foolish, Jack," said he.

"Let go. I——"

"Don't be foolish, I say, Jack," persisted Harry Girdwood. "Do you know what you are saying?"

"Are you siding against me?" exclaimed Jack.

"In a general sense I am not against you, but I can't approve of your replies. You had no right to retort, and I shouldn't be a true pal, Jack, if I spoke to your face against my convictions."

Jack sulked for a little time.

And then he did as the captain had advised.

He reflected.

He was very soon led back to the correct train of thought, and being a lad of high moral courage, as well as physically brave, he was not afraid to acknowledge when he was in the wrong.

Harry Girdwood walked a little way off.

Young Jack—dare-devil Jack coloured up as he walked to Harry and held out his hand.

"Tip us your fin, messmate," he said. with forced gaiety. "You are right, I was wrong, of course."

He turned off.

"Where are you going?" demanded Harry.

"To the captain."

"What for?"

"To apologise for being insolent."

Off he went.

"Captain Willis."

"Do you want me, Mr. Harkaway?" asked the captain.

The chief mate was standing by, and Jack did not feel that he had so far offended as to have to expiate his fault in public.

"When you are disengaged, Captain Willis, I would beg the favour of half a word with you."

"Is it urgent, Mr. Harkaway?" he asked.

"I have been refractory, Captain Willis."

A faint smile stole over the captain's face in spite of his endeavour to repress it.

"I will see you below presently," he said to the mate. "Come down to me in a quarter of an hour or so."

"Yes, sir," said the mate.

"Now, Mr. Harkaway, I'm at your service," said Captain Willis, walking forward.

Jack grew rather red in the face at this.

Then he made a plunge, and blurted it all out.

"I have been an idiot, Captain Willis, and I want you to know that I thoroughly appre- ciate your fairness and high sense of justice."

"Now you are flattering me, Mr. Harkaway," said the captain.

"Captain Willis," said impetuous Jack, "if you call me Mr. Harkaway, I shall think that you are stiff-backed and bear malice."

"What a wild fellow you are," said the captain. "Why, what on earth shall I call you?"

"Jack, sir," returned our hero. "John on Sundays and holidays, if you prefer it, just as a proof that you don't bear any ill feeling to a madman, who has the good luck to have a lucid interval, and to apologise heartily as I do now."

The captain held out his hand.

Jack dropped his into it with a spank, and grasped it warmly.

"Don't say any more on this subject, Mr.—I mean, Jack," said the captain, smiling, "or you will make me quite uncomfortable."

And so the matter ended.

Jack could not be dull for long together.

He plucked up his old vivacity, and went off to Mr. Figgins' cabin.

"I must go and give the orphan a turn," said he.

CHAPTER LX.

TURKISH CUSTOMS—JACK GIVES THE ORPHAN A NOTION OF WHAT HE MAY EXPECT—MATRIMONIAL WEAKNESSES—PASHA BLUE-BEARD—THE SORT OF MAN HE IS—HIS EXCELLENCY'S VISIT—MR. FIGGINS IS SPECIALLY INVITED—HOPES AND FEARS.

JACK found Mr. Figgins in his cabin, squatting on a cushion cross-legged.

Tinker and Bogey were attending upon him.

Since their desperate dive into the sea, and the adventure with the shark, the two darkeys and the orphan had become fast friends.

"Hullo, Mr. Figgins," said Jack, in surprise, "what's going forward now?"

"Only practising Turkish manners and customs," returned Mr. Figgins, quite seriously. "I mean to go ashore to-morrow, and make some acquaintances; I shouldn't like to appear quite strange when I got ashore. When in Rome——"

"You must do as the Romans do," added young Jack.

"Yes; and when in Turkey," said the orphan, "you must——"

"Do as the Turkeys do," concluded Jack.

"Precisely," added the orphan. "That's it."

"You are practising to smoke the long hookah to begin with."

"Yes—no—it's a chibouk," said Mr. Figgins. "That is all you have to know, I believe, to make yourself thoroughly well received in Turkish polite society."

"Everything," responded Jack, "with a hook—ah!"

"I didn't feel very comfortable over it at first," said the orphan, "but I'm getting on now."

"There's one danger you are exposed to on going ashore."

"What's that?"

"Any gentleman having the slightest pretensions to good looks is nearly always obliged to get married a few times."

Mr. Figgins stared aghast at this.

"A few times?"

"Yes."

"But I'm an orphan."

"No matter; it's a fact, sir, I assure you," said Jack, gravely.

Mr. Figgins looked exceedingly alarmed.

"If I could believe that there was anything more in that than your joking, Mr. Jack, I should be precious uncomfortable."

"Why?"

"Because my experience of matrimony has been anything but pleasant already," responded the orphan.

"You have been married, then?" said Jack, in surprise.

"Once."

"Very moderate that, sir," said Jack. "You are a widower, I suppose, then?"

"I suppose so."

"You are not sure?"

"Not quite."

"Ah, well, then, it won't be so bad for you as it might."

"What won't?"

"Marriage."

"I beg your pardon, Mr. Jack," exclaimed the orphan; "my experience of the happy state was anything but agreeable with one wife. Goodness knows how long I should survive if I had, as you say, several wives."

"Don't worry yourself, Mr. Figgins," said Jack, "but it is just as well to be prepared."

"For what?"

"An emergency. You don't know what might happen to you in this country."

Mr. Figgins looked really very anxious at this.

"I don't well see how they can marry a man."

"That's not the question, Mr. Figgins. You could refuse. It would cost you your life for a certainty."

The orphan nearly rolled off his cushion.

"What!"

"Fact, I assure you," said Jack, gravely.

"Explain."

"You will be expected to pay a visit of state to the pasha."

"Yes."

"That is the greatest honour on landing for a stranger."

"What is a pasha?"

"The governor of the province, a regular Bung."

"Well."

"Bluebeard was a pasha, you remember."

"No, no," interrupted the orphan, delighted to show his historical accuracy. "Bluebeard was a bashaw."

"It is the same thing, another way of writing or pronouncing the identical same dignity or rank. Well, you know that polygamy is the pet vice of the followers of Islam."

"Oh, it's dreadful, Jack."

"The greater the man, the greater the polygamist. A pasha has as many wives as he can keep, and more too. The pasha of this province is not rich for his rank, and for his matrimonial proclivities."

"Lor'!"

"How many wives should you suppose he has?" asked Jack, with an air of deep gravity.

"Don't know," replied the orphan, quietly.

"Ninety-eight living."

Mr. Figgins jumped up and dropped his chibouk.

"Never."

"A fact," asserted Jack, with gravity.

"Why, the man must be a regular Bluebeard."

"You've hit it, sir," responded Jack; "that's the sort of man he is."

"Well, that is all very well for the Turks and for these old sinners the pashas, but I am an Englishman."

" This is the way it will most likely be done," continued Jack. " On your presentation to his excellency the pasha, you are expected to make some present. The pasha makes a return visit of ceremony, and leaves behind him some solid evidence of his liberality."

" Well?"

" Well, but the very highest compliment that a pasha can pay you is to leave you one of his wives. He generally makes it an old stock-keeper, something that has been a good thirty years or so in the seraglio."

Mr. Figgins took the liveliest interest in this narrative.

He was growing rapidly convinced of the truth of Jack's descriptions of these singular manners and customs of the country in which they were.

Yet he eyed Jack as one who has a lingering doubt.

"Ahem !" said Mr. Figgins, " I don't think that I shall join you on your visit ashore in the morning."

" We'll see in the morning," said Jack ; " it's a pity to put off your trip for the sake of such a trifling danger as that of having a wife or so given to you."

" It's no use," said Mr. Figgins, " my mind is fully made up ; I shall not visit the pasha."

" It will be taken as a grave insult to go ashore without paying your respects to his excellency."

" I can't help that," returned the orphan, resolutely ; " I won't visit him."

" Mr. Figgins," said Jack, in a voice of deep solemnity, " these Turks are cruel, vindictive, and revengeful. The last Englishman who refused was, by order of the pasha, skinned alive, placed on the sunny side of a wall, and blown to death by flies."

" Surely the Turks are not such barbarians," said Mr. Figgins.

" You'll find they are. They'd think no more of polishing you off than of killing a fly."

If that rascal Jack intended to make poor Mr. Figgins uneasy, he certainly succeeded very well.

Mr. Figgins looked supremely miserable.

" Good night, Mr. Figgins. Think it over."

" I tell you I——"

" Never mind, don't decide too rashly. Pleasant dreams."

" Pleasant dreams," said the orphan. " I shall have the nightmare."

The orphan's pillow was haunted that night by visions of a terrible nature.

He fancied himself in the presence of a turbaned Turk, a powerful pasha, who was sitting cross-legged on an ottoman, smoking a pipe, of endless length, and holding in his hand a drawn sword—a scimitar that looked ready to chop his head off.

Beside this terrible Turk stood five ladies, in baggy trousers, and long veils.

No words were spoken, but instinctively the orphan knew that he had to decide between the scimitar and the quintet of wives—wall-flowers of the pasha's harem.

Silently, in mute horror, the orphan was about to submit to the least of the two evils, and choose a wife.

Then he awoke suddenly.

What an immense relief it was to find it only a dream after all.

" I don't quite believe that young Harka-way," said the orphan, dubiously ; " he is such a dreadful practical joker. But I won't go on shore, nevertheless. It's not very interesting to see these savages, after all ; they really are nothing more than savages."

And after a long and tedious time spent in endeavouring to get to sleep again, he dropped off.

But only to dream again about getting very much married.

*　　*　　*　　*　　*

He slept far into the morning, for his dreams had disturbed him much, and he was tired out.

When he awoke, there was someone knocking at his cabin door.

" Come in."

" It's only me, Mr. Figgins," said a familiar voice.

" Come in, captain."

Captain Deering entered.

" Not up yet, Mr. Figgins?" he said, in surprise. " We've got visitors aboard already."

" Dear me."

" Distinguished visitors. The pasha and his suite."

" You don't say so ?" exclaimed the orphan, sitting up.

" Fact, sir," returned the captain. " It must be ten years since I last had the honour of an interview with his excellency."

" You know him, then, Captain Deering?"

" Rather. Been here often. Know every inch of the country," said the captain.

" What sort of a man is the pasha?" said the orphan, thinking of Jack's statement.

" Oh, a decent fellow enough, unless he's riled," was the reply.

" Do you speak the language?" said the orphan.

" Like a native."

" Is he as much married as they say ?" demanded Mr. Figgins.

The captain smiled.

" His excellency has a weakness that way ; but," he added, in a warning voice, " you must not make any allusion to that."

" I won't see him," said Mr. Figgins. " I don't intend to visit him."

" But I have come to fetch you to pay your respects."

" Where ?"

" Here, on board, in the state saloon."

" But——"

" Make haste, Mr. Figgins," interrupted Captain Deering. " It is no joke to make a pasha wait. Look alive. I'll come and fetch you in five minutes. Up you get."

And then Captain Deering departed.

Mr. Figgins was sorely perplexed now.

But he arose and began to dress himself as quickly as possible.

" After all," he said to himself, " it is just as well. I should certainly like to see the pasha, and this is a bit of luck, for there's no danger here at any rate, if what that young Harkaway said was true."

He went to the cabin door and shouted out for Tinker.

"Tinker !"

"He's engaged," answered Captain Deering, who was close by.

"I want him."

"He's away, attending his excellency in the saloon," returned Captain Deering.

"Bogey then."

"Bogey's there too."

"Never mind."

"Are you nearly ready ?"

"Yes."

"Look sharp. I wouldn't have his excellency put out of temper for the world; it would be sure to result in the bowstringing of a few of his poor devils of slaves when he got ashore again, and you wouldn't care to have that on your conscience."

Mr. Figgins very hurriedly completed his toilet.

"What a fiend this wretched old bigamist must be," he said to himself. "I'm precious glad that young Harkaway warned me, after all. I might have got into some trouble if I had gone ashore without knowing this."

"Stop," said the captain. "Have you anything to take his excellency as a present ?"

This made the orphan feel somewhat nervous.

It tended to confirm what young Jack had said.

"It is, then, the custom to make presents ?" he said.

"Yes."

"What shall I give ?"

"Anything. That's a very nice watch you wear."

"Must I give that ?"

"Yes. His excellency is sure to present you with a much richer one—that's Turkish etiquette."

This again corroborated Jack's words.

Yet it was a far more pleasant way of putting it than Jack had thought fit to do.

Mr. Figgins only objected to a present of wives.

Anything rich in the way of jewellery was quite another matter.

"On entering the presence, you have only to prostrate yourself three times ; the third time you work it so that you just touch his excellency's toe with your lips."

"I hope his excellency's boots will be clean."

"His excellency would not insult you by letting you kiss his boot. No boot or stocking does he wear."

Mr. Figgins made an awfully wry face at this.

"Ugh ! I don't like the idea of kissing a naked toe."

"You'll soon get used to it," said the captain, cheerfully, "when you've kissed as many pashas' toes as I have. Hold your tongue—here we are."

He pushed open the saloon door and ushered Mr. Figgins into the presence of his excellency.

CHAPTER LXI.

MORE ABOUT CHIVEY AND HIS MASTER—THE FATAL PIT—IS IT THE END ?—ARTFUL CHIVEY AND THE ARTFULLER NOTARY— DIAMOND CUT DIAMOND—HOW THE TIGER PREPARED TO SPRING—HERBERT MURRAY IN DANGER.

BEFORE we proceed to describe the orphan's presentation to that arch polygamist, the Turkish pasha, and the remarkable results of that interview, we must look around and see if we are not neglecting any of the characters whose eventful careers we have undertaken to chronicle.

We are losing sight of one at least, who has a very decided claim upon our attention.

This person is none other than Herbert Murray.

The reader will not have forgotten under what circumstances we parted company with this unscrupulous son of an unscrupulous father.

Goaded to desperation by his villanous servant, Herbert Murray turned upon the traitor and hurled him down the gravel pit.

Then the assassin walked away from the scene.

But ere he had got far, his steps were arrested by the sound of a groan.

A groan that came from the gravel pit.

"Was it my fancy ?"

No.

Surely not.

There it was again.

A low moan—a wail of anguish.

Back he went, muttering to himself—

"Not dead ?"

He went round nearly to the bottom of the pit, and peered over.

There was Chivey leaning upon his elbow, groaning with the severity of his bruises, and the dreadful shock he had received.

"You've done for me, now," he moaned, as he caught sight of his master.

"No ; but I shall," retorted the assassin.

And he took a deliberate aim with the pistol.

"I expected this," said Chivey, faintly ; "but remember murder is a hanging matter."

"I shall escape," retorted Murray, coldly.

"But you can't," said Chivey, with a grin of triumph, even as he groaned.

There was something in his manner which made Murray uneasy.

"Twenty-four hours after I'm missing," gasped Chivey, "your forgery will be in the hands of the police ; they can get you back for forgery, and while you're in the dock of the Old Bailey, if not before, to stand your trial for forgery, they will have a clue to my murder."

His words caused Murray a singular thrill.

"What do you mean by that, traitor ?" he demanded.

"Mean ? Why, I know you too well to trust you. I tell you I have taken every possible precaution," retorted Chivey, "so that you are safe only while I live. I know my man too well not to take every precaution. Now," he added, sinking back exhausted, "now, my young sweet and pleasant, fire away."

Murray paused, and concealed his pistol.

Was it true about these precautions ?

Chivey was vindictive as he was cunning.

He had shown this in every action.

"Supposing I spare you?" said Murray.

"You can't," retorted the tiger; "I'm done for."

"So much the better."

"So you say now," returned Chivey, his voice growing fainter and fainter. "Wait and remember my words—I'll be revenged."

He gasped for breath.

Then all was still.

Was he dead?

Murray trembled with fear at the thought.

The words of the revengeful tiger rang in his ear.

And he strode away.

Silent and moody as befits one bearing the brand of Cain.

* * * * *

Chivey was far from being as badly hurt as he at first appeared.

He had no bones broken, his worst injuries being a few bruises and a very unpleasant shaking.

But Chivey was artful.

He thought it best to keep quiet until Herbert Murray should be gone.

Chivey struggled up on to his knees.

Then he began to crawl along the sand pit.

Progress was difficult at first.

But he persevered and got along in time.

"If these bruises would only let me think how further to act," he muttered to himself, as groaning, he crawled back to the town.

"Senor Velasquez," he said to himself, as a happy thought crossed him. "Senor Velasquez is my man for a million."

He paused to think over the ways and means, and a cunning smile deepened on his face, as he gradually made up his mind.

"The worst of this is that I must have a confederate," muttered the young schemer. "No matter, there is only one way out of it, and I must make the best of it."

Senor Velasquez was an obscure notary.

Chivey had made a chatting acquaintance with the notary in the town, the Spaniard speaking English with tolerable proficiency.

"What is the nature of the secret you hold *in terrorem* over your master?" demanded the notary, when Chivey at length reached his office.

Chivey smiled.

"I said it was a secret, Mr. Velasquez," he answered.

"But if you seek my advice about that," the notary made reply, "I must know all the particulars of the case."

"Oh, no."

"Oh, yes."

"Why?"

"How can I advise if you keep me in the dark?"

Chivey leered at the Spanish notary and grinned.

"Don't you try and come the old soldier over me, please," he said.

"Old soldier?" said Senor Velasquez, in surprise.

"Yes."

"What is 'old soldier?' What do you mean by that?"

"I mean, sir, the artful."

"Is this English?" exclaimed the notary.

"Rather."

"Well, I confess I do not understand it."

"Then," said Chivey, getting quite cheerful as he warmed into the matter, "I think your English education has been very seriously neglected, that's what I think."

"Possibly," said the Spaniard. "I only learnt your tongue as a student, and am not well grounded in slang."

"More's the pity."

There was a spice of contempt in Chivey's tone which appeared rather to aggravate Senor Velasquez.

"You are too clever, Mr. Chivey," said he, "far too clever. Now you want to keep your secret, and I shall guess that your secret concerns——"

He paused.

"Who?" asked Chivey.

"The young man whose letters you employed me to intercept."

The tiger looked alarmed.

"I mean the young Senor Jack Harkaway."

Chivey looked about him rather anxiously.

"Don't be so imprudent, Senor Velasquez," he said. "You are a precious dangerous party to have anything to do with."

"Not I," returned Senor Velasquez; "I am easily dealt with. But those who would deal with me must not be too cunning."

"You don't find nothing of that sort about me," said Chivey.

"What is it you require of me?" demanded the notary, getting vexed.

"He's a proud old cove," thought the tiger.

So he drew in his horns and met the notary half way.

"You are just right, Mr. Velasquez," he remarked. "It does concern Jack Harkaway."

"I knew that."

"Now I want you to give me your promise not to tell what I am going to say to you, nor to make any use of it without my express permission."

"I promise. Now proceed, for I am pressed for time."

"I will," said the tiger, resolutely.

The notary produced paper and writing materials.

"My master, Mr. Murray, has attempted my life," began Chivey, "and this is because I am possessed of certain secrets."

"I see."

"He is at the present moment under the idea that he has killed me. Now what I want is, to make him thoroughly understand that he does not get out of his difficulty by getting me out of the way, not by any manner of means at all."

"I see."

"How will you do it?"

"I will go and see him."

Chivey jumped at the idea immediately.

"Yes, sir, that's the sort; there's no letters then to tell tales against us."

"None."

"Get one from him, though, if you can," said Chivey, eagerly; "something compromising him yet deeper, like."

"I will do it," said Senor Velasquez. "And what will you pay for it? Give it a price."

"Thirty pounds," returned Chivey, in a feverish state of anxiety.

"I'll do it," returned the notary, with great coolness.

CHAPTER LXII.

HOW SENOR VELASQUEZ PLAYED A DEEP GAME WITH CHIVEY—DOUBLE DEALING—HERBERT MURRAY'S CHANCE — "HARKAWAY MUST BE PUT AWAY"—A GUILTY COMPACT—CHIVEY IN DURANCE VILE—THE SICK ROOM AND THE OPIATE—AN OVER-DOSE—THE NOTARY'S GUARDIAN—THE SPANISH GAROTTE——"TALKING IN YOUR SLEEP IS A VERY BAD GAME."

SENOR VELASQUEZ was anything but a fool.

Chivey was not soft, but he was not competent to cope with such a keen spirit as this Spanish notary.

Senor Velasquez walked up to the hotel in which Herbert Murray was staying, and the first person he chanced to meet was Murray himself.

"I wish to have a word with you in private, Senor Murray," said the notary.

Murray looked anxiously around him, starting "like a guilty thing upon a fearful summons."

The bland smile of the Spanish notary reassured him, however.

"What can I do for Senor Velasquez?" he asked.

"I begged for a few words in private," answered Velasquez.

"Take a seat, Senor Velasquez," said Herbert Murray, "and now tell me how I can serve you," after entering his room.

The notary made himself comfortable in his chair.

"I can speak in safety now?" he said.

"Of course."

"No fear of interruption here?"

The notary looked Murray steadily in the eyes as he said—

"I was thinking of your officious servant."

Herbert Murray changed colour as he faltered—

"Of whom?"

"Chivey, I think you call him—your groom, I mean."

"There is no fear from him now," said Murray, with averted eyes; "not the least in the world."

Senor Velasquez smiled significantly.

"Your man Chivey," resumed the Spanish notary, "has confided to me a secret."

"Concerning me?"

"Yes."

"The villain!"

"Now listen to me, Senor Murray. You have behaved very imprudently indeed. Your whole secret is with me."

Herbert started.

"With you?"

"Yes."

Herbert Murray glanced anxiously at the door.

The notary followed his eyes with some in-ward anxiety, yet he did not betray his uneasiness at all.

"He was speaking the truth for once, then," said Murray. "He had confided his secrets to someone else."

"Yes."

Herbert Murray walked round the room, and took up his position with his back to the door.

"Senor Velasquez," he said, in a low but determined voice, "you have made an unfortunate admission. If there is a witness, it is only one; you are that witness, and your life is in danger."

The notary certainly felt uncomfortable, but he was too old a stager to display it.

Herbert Murray produced a pistol, which he proceeded to examine and to cock deliberately.

"That would not advance your purpose much, Senor Murray," he said, coolly; "the noise would bring all the house trooping into the room."

Murray was quite calm and collected now, and therefore he was open to reason.

"There is something in that," he said, "so I have a quieter helpmate here."

He uncocked the pistol and put it in his breast pocket.

Then he whipped out a long Spanish stiletto.

"There are other reasons against using that."

"And they are?"

"Here is one," returned the notary, drawing a long, slender blade from his sleeve.

Murray was palpably disconcerted at this.

The Spanish notary and the young Englishman stood facing each other in silence for a considerable time.

The former was the first to break the silence.

"Now, look you here, Senor Murray," said he, "I am not a child, nor did I, knowing all I know, come here unprepared for every emergency—aye, even for violence."

"Go on," said Murray, between his set teeth.

"You have imprudently placed yourself in the hands of an unscrupulous young man."

"I have."

"And he has proved himself utterly unworthy?"

"Utterly."

"All of that is known to me," said the notary, craftily. "Now you must pay no heed to this Chivey."

"I will not," returned Herbert Murray, significantly, "though there is little fear of further molestation from him, senor."

Young Murray little dreamt of the cause of the notary's peculiar smile.

"Your sole danger, as I take it, Senor Murray, is from your fellow countryman, Jack Harkaway."

"Yes."

"Then to him you must direct your attention. Where is he?"

"Gone."

"Where to?"

"Don't know."

"I do then," returned the notary, quietly; "and it is to tell you that that I am here. I have all the necessary information ; you must follow him."

" Why ?"

" To make sure of him," coldly replied the Spaniard.

" How ?"

Velasquez spoke not.

But his meaning was just as clear as if he had put it into words.

A vicious dig with his stiletto at the air.

Nothing more.

And so they began to understand each other.

* * * * *

Senor Velasquez, the notary, was playing a double game.

From Herbert Murray he carefully kept the knowledge that Chivey still lived.

And why ?

That knowledge would have lessened his hold.

The cunning way in which he let Herbert Murray understand that he knew all, even to the attempt upon Chivey's life at the gravel pits, completed the mastery in which he meant to hold the young rascal.

He arranged everything for young Murray.

He discovered for him the destination of the ship in which Jack Harkaway and his friends had escaped, and he procured him a berth on a vessel sailing in the same direction.

" Once you get within arm's length of this young Harkaway," he said ; " you must be firm and let your blow be sure."

" I will," returned his pupil.

" Once Harkaway is removed from your path, you may sleep in peace, for he alone can now punish you for forgery."

" I hope so."

" I know it," said Velasquez.

So well were the notary's plans laid, and so luckily did fortune play into his hands, that forty-eight hours after his interview with Murray, he had that young gentleman safely on board a ship outward bound.

Now Herbert Murray had passed but one night after that fearful scene by the gravel pit, but the remembrance of it haunted his pillow from the moment he went to bed to the moment he arose unrefreshed and full of fever.

And yet he was setting out with the intention of securing his future peace and immunity from peril by the commission of a fresh crime.

The ship was setting sail at a little after daybreak, and it had been arranged that Senor Velasquez was to come and see him off.

But much to his surprise, the notary did not put in an appearance.

Eagerly he waited for the ship to start, lest anything should occur at the eleventh hour, and he should find himself laid by the heels to answer for his crimes.

* * * * *

Chivey was supposed to be hiding.

In reality he was a prisoner in the house of Senor Velasquez, and he knew it.

The notary was an old man, and he suffered from sundry ailments which belong to age— notably to rheumatism.

An acute attack prostrated the old man, and held him down when he was most anxious to be up and doing.

And the night before Herbert Murray was to set sail, he lay groaning and moaning with racking pains.

His cries reached Chivey, who lay in the next room, and he came to the sick man's door to ask if he could be of any assistance.

He peered warily in.

In spite of his groans and anguish, the old notary was insensible under the influence of an opiate.

Chivey crept in.

On a low table beside the bed was a lamp flickering fearfully, and a glass containing some medicine.

Beside the glass a phial labelled laudanum.

Something possessed the intruder to empty the contents of the phial into the glass, and just as he had done so, the sufferer opened his eyes.

" Who's there ?"

" It's me, Senor Velasquy," said the tiger. " You have been ill——"

" What do you do here ?" demanded the notary, sharply.

" You called out. I thought I might be of assistance."

" No, no."

" Then I will go, senor," said Chivey, " for I am tired."

" Stay, give me my physic before you go."

Chivey handed him the glass.

The sick man gulped it down, and made a wry face.

" How bitter it tastes," he said, with a shudder.

" Good night, senor."

" Good night."

* * * * *

Chivey did not remain very long absent.

The heavy breathing of the notary soon told him that it was safe to return to the room.

The business of the morrow so filled the mind of the old Spaniard, that he was talking of it in his sleep.

" At an hour after daybreak, I tell you, Murray," he muttered. " The berth is paid for, paid for by my gold. You follow on the track of your enemy Harkaway, and once you are within reach, give a sharp, sure stroke, and you will be free from your only enemy, seeing that you have already taken good care of your traitor servant."

Chivey was amazed, electrified.

Did he hear aright ?

" At daybreak !" he exclaimed, aloud.

" Yes ; at daybreak," returned the notary in his sleep.

After a pause, the sleeper muttered—

" What say you ? If Chivey were not quite dead ? What of that ? How could he follow you ? He has no funds. The only money he possessed I have now in my strong box under my bed."

Chivey was staggered.

" Is Murray going to bolt, and leave me in the power of this old villain, I wonder ?" he muttered.

He broke off in his speculations, for the notary was babbling something again.

" ' The Mogador,' " muttered the old man,

speaking more thickly than before as the opiate began to make itself felt : " the captain is called Gonzales. You have only to mention the name of Senor Velasquez, and he will treat you well. He knows me."

He muttered a few more words which grew more and more incoherent each instant.

Then he lay back motionless as a log.

The opium held him fast in its power.

" Now for the box," exclaimed the tiger, excitedly.

Chivey tore open the box, and lifting up some musty old deeds and parchments, he feasted his eyes upon a mine of wealth.

A pile of gold.

Bright glittering pieces of every size and country.

And beside it thick bundles of paper money.

" Gold is uncommon pretty," said the tiger, " but the notes packs the closest."

Bundle after bundle he stowed away about his person, regularly padding his chest under his shirt.

" Now for a trifle of loose cash," he said, coolly.

So saying, he dropped about sixty or seventy gold pieces into his breeches pocket.

His waistcoat pockets he stuffed full also.

Then he pushed back the box into its place under the bed.

" The old man still sleeps," he said to himself, looking round at the bed.

He was in a rare good humour with himself.

" Ha, ha ! I am rich now," said Chivey. " Thank you, old senor, you have done me a good turn. May you sleep long."

He gave a final glance about him and made off.

*   *   *   *   *

A distant church clock tolled the hour of midnight as he gained the seashore.

He was in luck.

Not a soul did he encounter until he reached the beach, when he came upon two sailors, launching a rowing boat.

" ' Mogador ?' " he said, in a tone of inquiry.

" Si, senor."

" That's your sort," said Chivey. " I want to see Captain Gonzales."

" Come with us, then," said one of the sailors.

" Rather," responded the tiger ; " off we dive ; whip 'em up, tickle him under the flank, and we're there in a common canter."

The sailors both understood a little of English.

In very little time they were standing on the deck of the " Mogador."

And facing Chivey as he scrambled up the side, was the master of the ship, Captain Gonzales, to whom Chivey was presented at once by one of the sailors.

" Senor Velasquez has sent me to you, captain," said the ever ready tiger.

" Then you are welcome."

" He told me to give you that," said Chivey, handing the captain a pair of banknotes ; " and to beg you to give me the best of accommodation in a cabin all to myself."

" It shall be done."

" And above all not to let Mr. Murray know of my presence on board when he comes."

" Good."

" I am going on very important business for Senor Velasquez, captain," pursued Chivey, with infinite assurance ; " as you may judge, for he values your care of me at one hundred crowns to be paid on your next visit here."

" Rely upon my uttermost assistance."

" Thank you," said Chivey, with a patronising smile ; " and now I'll be obliged to you to show me to my berth."

" Here," cried the Spanish captain. " Pedro—Juan—Lopez. Take this gentleman to my private cabin."

The " Mogador " stood out to sea bravely enough.

Chivey was there.

Herbert Murray was there.

But the latter little suspected the presence of the former.

Herbert Murray, in fancied security, was reclining on deck upon some cushions he had got up from below, smoking lazily, and looking up at the blue sky overhead, when Chivey, who had been looking vainly out for an appropriate cue to make his reappearance, slipped suddenly forward, and touching his hat, remarked in the coolest manner in the world—

" Did you ring for me, sir ?"

Herbert looked up just as if he had seen a ghost.

" Chivey !"

" Guv'nor."

Herbert Murray stared at his villanous servant.

But villanous as Chivey was, Herbert Murray never thought a bit about that.

His heart leaped to his mouth, and he was overjoyed to find him there.

" Oh, Chivey, you vagabond !" he ejaculated. " I'm so awfully glad to see you."

" One touch of nature makes the whole world kin."

There's a lot of truth in that trite and homely old saying.

For one little phrase from the guilty Herbert had come so straight from the heart that even the villanous tiger was touched immediately.

" Look here, guv'nor," said Mr. Chivey, " I don't think you are half so bad as I thought. My opinion is that you are not half as bad as some of 'em, and that the ugly job up at the gravel pits was all of my provoking. I bear no malice."

" You don't !" exclaimed his master, quite overjoyed.

" Not a bit."

" Shake hands."

Chivey obeyed.

And they were faster friends than ever after that.

But what about Senor Velasquez ?

What about all their compacts with the villain ?

For the time they were of no use to that plotter, whose plans had, up to the present time, failed.

CHAPTER LXIII.

THE ORPHAN IS PRESENTED AT COURT—IS
A BIT NERVOUS—LESSONS IN THE TURK-
ISH LANGUAGE—MANNERS AND CUSTOMS
—THE PASHA OF MANY WIVES—AN OFFI-
CIAL PRESENT—BOWSTRINGING—AN EXE-
CUTION—HORROR! THE ORPHAN'S PERIL,
AND WHAT CAME OF IT.

HAVING got Chivey and his master together
again. we now travel to the Turkish coast to
be in the company of young Jack and his
friends.

The orphan had been roused from his slumbers to be presented to the pasha of that province.

His excellency the pasha had done them the
honour to pay them a visit of ceremony on
board ship, and was seated in great state surrounded by his suite in the best saloon.

After the chief personages on board had been
presented, his excellency had, according to
Captain Deering, desired to see that distinguished personage, Mr. Figgins, *alias* the
orphan.

And now the orphan stood trembling outside
the door of the saloon.

"In you go, Mr. Figgins," whispered Captain Deering.

"One moment."

"Nonsense."

"Just a word."

"Bah!" said the captain, with a grin;
"you aren't going to have a tooth out. In with
you."

He opened the door, gave the timorous
orphan a vigorous drive behind, and Mr.
Figgins went in the august presence.

The pasha was seated—it would be irreve-
rent to say squatted, which would better express it—upon a cushion that was, as Paddy
says, hanging up on the floor.

His excellency was in that peculiar, not to
say painful attitude which less agile mortals
find unattainable, but which appears to mean
true rest to Turk or tailor.

The pasha rejoiced in a beard of enormous
dimensions, a grizzled dirt-coloured beard that
almost touched the cushion upon which he
sat.

A turban of red and gold silk was upon his
venerable head.

And beside his excellency upon a cushion
were laid his arms, weapons of barbarous
make, thought the orphan.

A scimitar, curved *à la* Saladin, two long-bar-
relled pistols, with jewelled butts, "as though
they were earrings or bracelets," the orphan
said to himself, a long dagger with an ivory
hilt and sheath, and a piece of cord.

"That's to tie them together with," mentally
decided the orphan. "One might as well travel
with the Woolwich Arsenal or the armoury from
the Tower. Barbarous old beast."

"Now," said Captain Deering, "tuck in
your tuppenny, Mr. Figgins; bow as low as you
can."

The orphan put his back into an angle of
forty-five with his legs.

"Lower."

"Ugh!"

"A little bit more."

"Lower," said Captain Deering, in an
agonised whisper. "We shall all be bowstrung
if his excellency thinks us wanting in respect."

The orphan thus admonished made a further
effort, and over he went.

Head first!

There was such a chattering, such horrible
sounds going on, as Captain Deering scrambled
after the unfortunate orphan, that the latter
thought his time was come.

The captain dragged him to his feet, however.

Then the presentation was proceeded with.

"His Excellency Ali Kungham Ben Nard-
bake," cried a dignitary standing beside the
pasha, with a voice like a toastmaster.

"Good gracious me!" exclaimed the orphan,
"all that?"

"That's not half of it," said Captain Deering.
"To the faithful, he is known as well as Sid
Ney Ali Ben Lesters quar Nasr ed Bowstrung
and Strattford Bustum."

Mr. Figgins was greatly alarmed at this.

"Powerful memories his godfathers and god-
mothers must have had," he murmured.

Beside the pasha stood an official, with a
beard of extraordinary length.

"Who's that?"

"Hush!" whispered Deering; "don't speak
so loud."

"Who is he?" again asked the orphan,
sinking his voice.

"The one with the beard?"

"Yes."

"His name is Whiska Saïd Mahmoud Ben
Ross Latreille," returned Deering.

"Dear, dear!" murmured the orphan, in despairing accents, "I shall never——"

"Ease her, stop her!" cried a familiar voice
in Mr. Figgins's ear, "you've got it in a knot."

It was Nat Cringle.

All was hushed.

The bearded official looked at the pasha,
who nodded.

Then drawing his sword, he signed to two
of his men, and Nat Cringle, looking dreadfully
frightened, was bustled off behind a curtain
which had been rigged up across the saloon
just at the pasha's back.

"What are they going to do?" asked the
orphan, his teeth chattering in alarm.

Captain Deering was so much affected at
this stage of the proceedings that he covered
his face with his pocket-handkerchief.

"Poor Nat!"

"What is it?" faltered Mr. Figgins, faintly.

"Did you not see the cord taken away with
Nat?" demanded the captain, in a funereal
bass.

"Ye-es."

"Then, hark."

Mr. Figgins did hark, and an awful sound
reached him from behind the curtain.

It was more like the expiring groans of a
hapless porker in the hands of a ruthless
butcher, than anything else you could com-
pare it to.

A fatal struggle was going on behind the
curtain.

Groans and dying wails were heard for
awhile.

Awful sounds.

Then all was still.

" Oh, what is it ?" murmured the orphan, in distress.

" Squiziz Wizen, the pasha's executioner, has dealt upon poor Nat Cringle."

" What !" gasped Figgins.

" Bowstrung," returned Captain Deering.

The orphan turned faint.

Then he turned to the door, and would have fled.

" Oh, let me go home," he cried. " I don't feel happy here."

But Deering stayed him.

" You must not go, Mr. Figgins," whispered Captain Deering.

" Why not ?"

" His excellency is about to address us."

The pasha coughed.

" *Quel est votre jeu ?*" demanded his excellency.

" What does he say ?" asked Figgins.

" Batta pudn," continued his excellency, with a gracious air ; " also bono Jonni."

" He says you may present whatever you have brought," whispered the captain.

" I've brought nothing," returned Mr. Figgins.

" Nothing ?"

" No ; I forgot."

" Thoughtless man," said Captain Deering. " Take this."

He thrust a parcel of brown paper into his hands.

" What shall I do with it ?"

" Place it on the cushion before his excellency."

Mr. Figgins complied.

" Luciousosity," said the pasha, looking upon the offering greedily.

Then he clapped his hands vigorously three times.

The minister appeared, leading two veiled ladies.

The pasha made some remarks in his own language, which Captain Deering was commissioned to render into English.

" His excellency, recognising your generous offering," said he, " presents you with the choicest gifts of his seraglio, two wives. You must cherish them through life."

The orphan's countenance fell at this.

The capital punishment of poor Nat Cringle was as nothing to this.

" Tell him I'd rather not take two," he whispered to Deering.

" Why not ?" ejaculated the latter.

" I wish to live single."

The bearded minister approached, leading the two veiled beauties.

" Oh ! oh, dear," groaned the poor orphan.

He placed a gloved hand of each upon Mr. Figgins's shoulders.

Then, upon a given signal, they threw their arms around the orphan and hugged him, while a violent cachinnation was heard.

" What a lovely smile," said Captain Deering. " Did you hear it ?"

" Oh ! Please don't," cried the orphan.

He struggled to get free.

But the beauties of the seraglio held him tight.

The orphan grew desperate, and jerked himself out of their clutches.

But in the tussle down he flopped on the ground again.

" Infidel dog !" roared the pasha, venting his wrath in English, " barbarian and idolater, thou shalt die !"

Thereupon, Captain Deering dropped down beside the orphan, and sued for mercy.

" Be merciful, O great prince !" he cried. " Have pity on your humblest slave. His heart is filled with gratitude."

The pasha growled some reply that was indistinct, but which, to the startled Figgins, sounded like the rumbling of distant thunder.

" Oh, what shall I do ?" moaned the orphan. " Oh, somebody take me home."

" Silence," whispered Captain Deering. " Prostrate yourself as they do. Bury your face and be silent, until his excellency bids you rise. He may then overlook it."

Mr. Figgins scarce dared to breathe.

There he lay, with his face upon the ground, humbly awaiting the stern despot's permission to move.

*   *   *   *   *

He waited long—very long.

While he waited thus, a strange commotion was observed amongst the pasha's suite.

The chief officer removed his turban and beard, and—wonderful to relate !—beneath it was the laughing face of Harry Girdwood.

He winked at his august master, who hurriedly removed his turban and beard as well.

And then the pasha bore a marvellous resemblance to Jack Harkaway the younger.

They helped to drag off each other's robes —for beneath their Turkish garments were their everyday clothes.

The veiled beauties of the harem were disrobed.

Beneath their veils and feminine attire they were familiarly garbed, and a glance revealed them to be Tinker and his body-guard Bogey.

" Now then, Mr. Figgins," said Nat Cringle, " wake up."

The orphan looked up in amazement at the sound.

" Nat Cringle !"

" Hullo !"

Mr. Figgins looked about in wonderment.

Facing him was Jack Harkaway, sitting upon a camp stool, and beside him stood his constant companion, Harry Girdwood.

Engaged in conversation with them was Captain Deering, and the subject of their conversation appeared to be the orphan himself.

The Turkish soldiers and people generally forming the pasha's suite had disappeared, and in their places were several sailors, some of whom appeared to be considerably amused at something.

When Mr. Figgins sat up and looked about him, he muttered—

" What's all this ?"

" A very serious case, Harry," said Jack, gravely.

" Very."

" A case for the doctor."

" What do you mean ?"

"These habits of drinking grow upon one," said Harry Girdwood, sadly.

"I don't understand," faltered the orphan.

"Shall we help you to bed, sir?" asked one of the sailors compassionately.

"Never!" cried Mr. Figgins, with majesty.

"Oh, yes, do," said Harry.

But nerved to desperation, the orphan tore himself away from them, and darted to the door.

"I shall go and report upon these outrageous doings to the captain of the ship," he said, drawing himself up.

"Here's the captain himself," said a good-natured voice behind him. "And now, what can he do for you, Mr. Figgins?"

The orphan turned.

There was the captain.

"Mr. Figgins," said the captain, with a serious air, and shaking his fore-finger at him, "you have been indulging very early in the day."

"What!"

He could endure no more.

With a cry of disgust, he dashed past the captain, and scrambled up the stairs on deck.

Once there, he shot like a race horse along the deck, and gaining his own berth, he locked himself in.

But even here he could not shut out the ringing laughter of the incorrigible practical jokers.

Mr. Figgins, as you may guess, was seen no more that day.

* * * * *

Upon the day following the events just related, Jack received letters from home.

And among them was one which created no little excitement amongst the nearest friends of Jack Harkaway.

"Do you think it probable that he'll come?"

"I shouldn't wonder," said Harry Girdwood.

"I should like to see his dear old face again," said Jack.

"I'll bet a penny that we shall see him here yet; if not here, at least at our next stage," said Harry.

"It would be a rare treat to talk with some-one who had seen our dear folks at home."

"It would indeed. I hope he will come."

And who did they hope would come?

Can you not guess, reader? No.

Then read on, and you will learn who it was and what were the reasons which were to bring a friend from home roaming to this distant shore to meet Jack and his friends.

CHAPTER LXIV.

THE SAPIENT DOCTOR MUGGINS CAME IN HASTE—IMPEDIMENTS IN THE WAY OF THE PRESCRIPTION—DWELLS ON ARTIFICIAL LIMBS—OLD REMINISCENCES — THE TORMENTOR.

READER, we will return for a little time to our old friend, Mole, in England.

Mr. Mole was sad.

For so many years of his life had old Isaac Mole led a wandering career, that he found it exceedingly difficult, not to say irksome, to settle down to the prosy existence which they had all dropped into.

He never complained, it is true.

But he fell into a sort of settled melancholy, which nothing could shake off, and even grew neglectful of the bottle.

His friends grew anxious.

They wished him to take medical advice.

He resisted all persuasion stoutly.

So they had recourse to artifice, and invited an eminent medical man to their house as a visitor.

And then under the guise of a friendly chat, the doctor took his observations.

But the peculiar ailment, if ailment it could be called, of Isaac Mole, completely baffled the man of science at first.

It was only in a casual conversation that, being an observing man, he discovered the real truth.

"Our patient wants a roving commission," said the physician to himself.

And then he communicated his own convictions to old Jack.

"I scarcely believe it possible, doctor," said Jack.

But the doctor was positive.

"Nothing will do him any good but to get on the move; I'm as sure of that as I am that he has no physical ailment."

"What's to be done then?" demanded Harkaway. "He can't travel alone."

"I don't know that," said the doctor; "he's hale and wiry enough. The only difficulty that I can see, is Mrs. Mole."

"I'll undertake to get over that," said Jack.

"You will?"

"Yes."

"It is settled then," said the physician, with a smile.

"Good."

"What would do him more good than all the physic in the world, would be to send him after your son."

"My Jack!"

"Yes."

"Impossible. Why, Jack is *en route* for Turkey."

"What of that?" coolly inquired the doctor.

"Consider the distance, my dear doctor."

"Pshaw, sir. Distance is nothing nowadays. It was a very different thing when I was a boy. Take my word for it, Mr. Harkaway, our patient will jump at the chance."

"He's very much attached to my roving boy."

"I know it," returned the doctor. "Never a day passes but he speaks of him; I declare that I never had a single interview with Mr. Mole, but that he has managed somehow to turn the conversation upon your son and his pranks."

"Oh, Jack, he has played him some dreadful tricks."

"Yes," returned the physician dryly, "and so has Jack's father, by all accounts."

"Ahem!"

"And yet I really believe that he enjoys the recollection of the boy's infamous practical jokes."

"I believe you are right," responded Harkaway.

A day or two later on the doctor was seated with Mr. Mole.

"Mr. Mole."

"Doctor."

"Your health must be looked to. You'll have to travel."

"How, doctor?" said Mole.

"Young Harkaway is in foreign parts, and his prolonged absence causes his parents considerable uneasiness, and you must go and look after him."

Mole's eyes twinkled.

"Do you mean it?"

"I do. When would you like to start?"

"To-day."

"Very good. The sooner the better," said the doctor.

Mr. Mole's countenance fell suddenly.

An ugly thought crossed him.

What would Mrs. Mole say?

"There is one matter I would like to consult you on, doctor."

"What might that be?" demanded the doctor.

"My wife might have a word to say upon the subject."

"I will undertake to remove her scruples," said the doctor.

"You will?"

"Yes. She will never object when she knows how important your mission is."

"Doctor," exclaimed Mr. Mole, joyously; "you are a trump."

A delay naturally occurred, however.

Mr. Mole could not travel with his wooden stumps, his friends one and all agreed.

No.

He must have a pair of cork legs made.

The doctor who had been attending our old friend knew of a maker of artificial limbs who was a wonderful man, according to all accounts.

"Yes," said Mole, "cork legs well hosed will——"

At this moment a voice tuning up under the window cut him short.

"He gave his own leg to the undertaker,
And sent for a skilful cork-leg maker.
Ritooral looral."

"That's Dick Harvey. Infamous!" ejaculated Mr. Mole.

"On a brace of broomsticks never I'll walk,
But I'll have symmetrical limbs of cork.
Ritooral looral."

"Monstrous!" exclaimed Mr. Mole; "close the window, sir, if you please."

It was all very well to say "Close it," but this was easier said than done.

Dick Harvey had fixed it beyond the skill of that skilful mechanician to unfasten.

The aggravating minstrel continued without—

"Than timber this cork is better by half,
Examine likewise my elegant calf.
Ritooral looral——"

"I will have that window closed," cried Mole.

He arose, forgetting in his haste that he was minus one leg, and down he rolled.

The artificial limb-maker lunged after him, and succeeded with infinite difficulty in getting him on to his feet again.

"Dear, dear!" said Mr. Mole. "No matter, I can manage it."

He picked up the nearest object to hand, and hurled it out of window.

CHAPTER LXV.

HOW THE ORPHAN BECAME POSSESSED OF A FLUTE.

BUT we must leave Mole for a time, and return to our friends on their travels.

When next they landed at a Turkish town, Mr. Figgins went to a different hotel to that patronised by young Jack, whose practical joking was rather too much for the orphan.

But they found him out, and paid him a visit one morning.

After the first greeting, Mr. Figgins was observed to be unusually thoughtful.

At length, after a long silence he exclaimed—

"I can't account for it, I really can't."

"What can't you account for, Mr. Figgins?" asked young Jack.

"The strange manners of the people of this country," answered the orphan.

"Of what is it you have to complain particularly?" inquired Jack.

"Well, it's this; wherever I go, I seem to be quite an object of curiosity."

"Of interest you mean, Mr. Figgins," returned Jack, winking at Harry Girdwood; "you are an Englishman, you know, and Englishmen are always very interesting to foreigners."

"I can't say as to that," the orphan replied; "I only know I can't show my nose out of doors without being pointed at."

"Ah, yes. You excite interest the moment you make your appearance."

"Then, if I walk in the streets, dark swarthy men stare at me and follow me till I have quite a crowd at my heels."

"Another proof of the interest they take in you."

"Well, I don't like it at all," said the orphan, fretfully; "and then the dogs bark at me in a very distressing manner."

"It's the only way they have of bidding you welcome," remarked Harry Girdwood.

"I wish they wouldn't take any notice of me at all; it's a nuisance."

"Perhaps you'd like them to leave off barking, and take to biting?"

"No, it's just what I shouldn't like, but it's what I'm constantly afraid they will do," wailed the poor orphan.

There was a slight pause, during which young Jack and his comrade grinned quietly at each other, and presently the former said—

"I think I can account for all this."

"Can you?" asked Mr. Figgins. "How?"

"It all lies in the dress you wear."

"In the dress?"

"Yes; you are in a Turkish country, and although I admit you look well in your splendid new tourist suit, cross-barred all over in four colours, I fancy it would be better if you dressed as a Turk during your stay here."

"A Turk, Jack?"

"Yes; now, if you were to have your head shaved, and dress yourself like a Turk," said Jack, "all this wonderment would cease, and you would go out, and come in, without exciting any remark."

Mr. Figgins fell back in his chair.

"Ha-ha-have my head sha-a-ved, dress myself up li-like a Turk ?" he gasped. " You surely don't mean that ?"

" I do, indeed," replied Jack, seriously.

" What ? Wear baggy breeches, and an enormous turban, and slippers turned up at the toes ! What would the natives say ?"

" Why, they'd say you were a very sensible individual," remarked Harry. " Don't you remember the old saying ?—'When you're in Turkey, you must do as Turkey does.' "

Mr. Figgins reflected for a moment.

" And you really think if I were to go in for a regular Turkish fit-out, I should be allowed to enjoy my walks in peace ?" he asked, at length.

" Decidedly," answered his counsellors, with the utmost gravity.

" Then I'll take your advice, and be a Turk until further notice," said the orphan ; " but there's one thing still."

" What's that ?"

" My complexion isn't near dark enough for one of these infidels."

" Oh, that won't matter," said Jack ; " only slip into the Turkish togs. Go in for any quantity of turban, and they won't care a button about your complexion."

" Very well, then, that's settled ; I'll turn Turk at once. But must I have my head shaved ?"

" That's important," said Jack.

Having made up his mind on that point, the orphan at once put on his hat, and taking a sip of brandy to compose his nerves, he sallied forth, directing his steps to the nearest barber's.

On his way thither he attracted the usual amount of attention, and when he reached the barber's shop, he found himself accompanied by a select crowd of deriding Turks, and a dozen or so of yelping curs, shouting and barking in concert.

The barber received him with the extreme of Eastern courtesy.

" What does the English signor require at the hands of the humblest of his slaves ?" was the deferential inquiry.

" I have a fancy to turn Turk, and I want my head shaved," explained Mr. Figgins, nervously ; " pray be careful, since I'm only a poor orphan, who——"

Before he had time to finish his sentence, he found himself wedged into a chair with a towel under his chin.

The next moment his head, under the energetic manipulation of the operator, was a creamy mass of lather.

" Be sure and don't cut my head off," murmured the orphan, as he watched the razor flashing to and fro along the strop.

" Your servant will not disturb the minutest pimple," said the barber.

With wonderful celerity, the artist went to work.

In less than two minutes the cranium of Mark Antony Figgins was as smooth and destitute of hair as a bladder of lard.

Then followed the process of shampooing, which was very soothing to the orphan's feelings.

At length, the operation being completed, the barber bade the orphan put on his hat—which from the loss of his hair went over his eyes and rested on his nose—and left the shop.

His friends—the mob and the dogs—had waited for him outside very patiently.

If his appearance had been interesting before, their interest was now greatly increased.

A loud shout welcomed him, and he proceeded along the street under difficulties, holding his hat in one hand, with the crowd at his heels.

Straight to the bazaar he went.

Here he found a venerable old Turkish Jew, who seemed to divine by instinct what he wanted.

" Closhe, shignor, closhe," he cried in broken English. " Shtep in and take your choice."

Before the bewildered orphan knew where he was, he found himself in the interior of Ibrahim's emporium.

Here a profusion of garments were displayed before his eyes.

Having no preference for any particular colour, he took what the Jew pressed upon him.

In a short time his costume was complete, consisting of a pair of ample white trousers, and a blue shirt, surmounted by a crimson vest, secured at the waist by a purple sash, and on his feet a pair of yellow slippers of Morocco leather.

The turban alone was wanting.

" Be sure and let me have a good big turban," urged Mr. Figgins.

Ibrahim assured him that he should have one as big as he could carry, and he kept his word.

Unrolling a great many yards of stuff, he formed a turban of enormous dimensions of green and yellow stripe, which he placed upon the head of his customer.

" Shall I do ? Do I look like a native Turk ?" asked the latter, after he had put on his things.

" Do ?" echoed the Jew, exultingly. " If it ish true dat de closhe makes de man, you vill do excellent vell, and de people vill not now run after you."

Mr. Figgins having settled his account with the Hebrew clothier, and paid just three times as much as he ought to have done, went out again with considerable confidence, looking as gaudy in his mixture of bright colours as a macaw.

" No one will dare to jeer at me now," he persuaded himself.

But he was mistaken.

Hardly had he taken half a dozen steps when his brilliant costume attracted great notice.

" What a splendid Turk !" cried some.

" Who is that magnificent bashaw ?" asked others, as he strutted past.

No one knew, and upon a nearer examination it was seen that the " splendid Turk " and " magnificent bashaw " was no Turk at all.

Indignation seized upon those who had a moment before been filled with admiration.

" Impostor, unbelieving dog !" shouted the enraged populace. " He is an accursed Giaour, in the dress of a follower of the Prophet."

At this, a fierce yell rose upon the air.

"Down with the wretch !"

"Tear him to pieces !"

"Let him be impaled !" cried the multitude.

With these dire threats, the angry crowd rushed towards Mr. Figgins, headed by a short, fat Turk, who was particularly indignant.

The luckless orphan, anxious to avoid the terrible doom that was threatening him, rushed away in an opposite direction.

The Turks are not, as a rule, remarkable for swift running.

Mr. Figgins, whose pace was quickened by the dreadful prospect of a stake through his body, would have easily distanced them.

But unfortunately, his green and yellow striped turban, dislodged from its position, fell—as his hat had previously done—over his eyes, and almost smothered him.

He tugged away at it as he ran, in order to get rid of it.

But all he succeeded in doing was to loosen one of the ends.

Gradually the turban began to unwind itself, the end trailing on the ground.

The Turk in pursuit caught up this end, and grasping it firmly, brought all his weight to bear upon the fugitive.

Suddenly the hapless Figgins began to feel strong symptoms of strangulation.

The next moment, a sharp jerk from the burly Turk pulled him to the ground.

But this saved him.

No sooner was he prostrate on his back than the turban slipped from his head, and he was free.

Springing to his feet, he darted off at a speed which no human grocer could ever have dreamt of.

He was soon far beyond pursuit.

All he had lost was his green and yellow striped turban.

But the loss of that, though it somewhat fretted him, had saved his life.

He found himself in a retired spot, and no one being near, he sat down to reflect and recover his breath.

"What a country this is," he thought; "pleasant enough, though, as far as the climate goes; but the people in it are awful ! What a lot of bloodthirsty, bilious-looking wretches, to be sure ; ready to consign to torture and death a poor innocent, unprotected orphan because he happens to be of a different colour from themselves !"

So perturbed were the thoughts of Mr. Figgins that he was obliged to smoke a cigar to soothe himself.

But even this failed to quiet his agitated nerves.

His mind was full of gloomy apprehensions.

"Where am I ?" he asked himself. "How am I to get home ? I shall be sure to meet some of the rabble, and with them and the dogs I shall be torn to pieces. What will become of me—wretched orphan that I am ! What shall I do ?"

Hardly had he uttered these distressful exclamations when a prolonged note of melody caught his ear.

"Hark !" he said to himself, "there is music. 'Music hath charms to soothe the savage breast,' says the poet, and it seems to have a soothing effect upon my nerves."

The strain had died away, and was heard no longer.

Mark Antony Figgins was in despair.

"Play again, sweet instrument," he cried, anxiously, "play again."

Again the sweet note sounded and again the solitary orphan felt comforted.

"It's a flute ; it must be a flute," he murmured to himself, as he listened. "I always liked the flute. It's so soft and melancholy."

The grocer had a faint recollection of his boyhood's days, when he had been a tolerably efficient performer on a penny whistle.

Just at this moment the mournful note he heard recalled the past vividly.

So vividly, that Mr. Figgins, in the depths of his loneliness, fixed his eyes sadly on the turned-up toes of his leather slippers, and wept.

As the melody proceeded, so did the drops pour more copiously from the orphan's eyes.

And no wonder, for of all the doleful tootooings ever uttered by wind instrument, this was the dolefullest.

But it suited Mr. Figgins's mood at that moment.

"It's a Turkish flute, I suppose," he sobbed ; "but it's very beau-u-u-tiful. I wish I had a flute."

He got up and looked round, and found himself outside an enclosure of thick trees.

It was evidently within this enclosure the flute player was located.

As the reader knows, there was nothing bold or daring about Mark Antony Figgins.

But now the flute seemed to have inspired him with a kind of supernatural recklessness.

"I'd give almost anything for that flute," he murmured to himself. "I feel that I should like to play the flute. I wonder who it is playing it, and whether he'd sell it ?"

The unseen performer, at this juncture, burst forth into such a powerfully shrill cadence that the orphan was quite thrilled with delight.

"A railway whistle's a fool to it !" he cried, as he clapped his hands in ecstasy. "Bravo, bravo ! Encore !"

Having shouted his applause till he was hoarse, he walked along by the side of the wall, seeking anxiously for some place of entrance.

At length he came to an open gate.

A stout gentleman—unmistakably a Turk—with a crimson cap on his head, ornamented with a tassel, and a long, reed-like instrument in his hand, was looking cautiously forth.

It was evidently the musician, who, having been interrupted in his solo, had come to see who the delinquent was that had disturbed him.

The enthusiastic Figgins had caught sight of the flute, and that was sufficient.

Forgetting his usual nervous timidity, he rushed forward.

"My dear sir," he exclaimed, "it was exquisite—delicious ! Pray oblige me with an-

"'HELP!' EXCLAIMED MR. FIGGINS; I AM DONE FOR.'"

other tune—or, if you have no objection, let me attempt one."

As he spoke, the excited Figgins stretched forth both his hands.

The owner of the flute, who evidently suspected an attempt at robbery, quietly placed his instrument behind him, and looking hard at Figgins, said sternly—

"What son of a dog art thou?"

To which Figgins replied mildly—

"You're mistaken, my dear sir; I'm the son of my father and mother, but they—alas!—are no more, and I am now only a poor desolate orphan."

The tears trickled from his eyes as he spoke.

The Turk did not appear in the least affected.

"What bosh is all this?" he asked, after a moment, in a hard, unsympathetic tone.

"It's no bosh at all, I assure you, my dear signor," replied Figgins, earnestly; "the fact is I heard you play on your flute, and its sweet tones so soothed my spirits—which are at this moment extremely low—that I am come to make several requests."

"Umph!" growled the Turk; "what are they?"

"First, that you will play me another of your charming airs, next, that you will allow me to attempt one myself, and thirdly, that you will sell me the instrument you hold in your hand."

The Turk glared for a moment fiercely at the proposer of these modest requests, and then politely wishing the graves of his departed relatives might be perpetually defiled, he replied curtly—

"First, I am not going to play any more to-night; next, I will see you in Jehanum * before I allow you to play; and thirdly, I won't sell my flute."

With these words, he stepped back into the garden and slammed the gate in Mr. Figgins' face.

"I shall never get over this," Figgins murmured to himself, gloomily; "that flute would have cheered my solitary hours, and that ruthless Turk refuses to part with it. Now, indeed, I feel my peace of mind is gone for ever."

His grief at this juncture became so overpowering, that he leant against the door, and in his despair hammered it with his head.

Suddenly the door burst open, and the distressed orphan, in all his brilliant array, shot backwards into some shrubs of a prickly nature, whose sharp thorns added to his agonizing sensations.

"Will anybody be kind enough to put an end to my misery?" he wailed, as he lay on his back, feeling as though he had been transformed into a human pincushion.

He was not a little surprised to hear a familiar voice exclaim—

"Lor' bless me! dat you, Massa Figgins?"

Glancing up, he espied the black face of Bogey looking down upon him.

"Yes, it's me," he answered, in a wailing tone; "help me up."

"Gib me you fist," cried Bogey.

* The abode of lost spirits.

Mr. Figgins extended his hand, and the negro grasping it, by a vigorous jerk hoisted the prostrate grocer out of his thorny bed, tingling all over as though he had been stung by nettles.

Bogey was quite astounded at the transformation in his dress.

"Why, Massa Figgins, what out-and-out guy you look!" he exclaimed; "whar all you hair gone to?"

The orphan only groaned.

He was thinking of another h-air (without the h), the air he had heard on the Turkish flute.

Just at that moment the too-too-too of the instrument sounded again.

Figgins stood like one absorbed.

All his agonizing pains were at once forgotten.

"How sweet, how plaintive!" he murmured to himself; "too-too-too, tooty-tooty-too!" he hummed, in imitation of the sound.

Bogey heard it also, and involuntarily put his hands on his stomach and made a comically wry face.

"Whar dat orful squeakin' row?" he asked.

"Hush, hush!" exclaimed the orphan, holding up his hands reprovingly, and turning up his eyes at the same time; "it's heavenly music; it's a flute, my boyhood's favourite instrument."

"Gorra!" muttered Bogey; "it 'nuff to gib a fellar de mullingrubs all down him back and up him belly."

He looked towards Mr. Figgins, and seeing him standing with his hands clasped looking like a white-washed Turk in a trance, he said—

"What de matter wid yer, Massa Figgins? Am you ill?"

"That flute, that melodious flute, that breathes forth dulcet notes of peace," murmured the orphan, in a deep, absorbed whisper. "I must have that flute."

Bogey felt a little anxious.

"Me tink Massa Fig getting lilly soft in him nut; him losing him hair turn him mad," he said to himself.

"I must have that flute," repeated the grocer, in the same abstracted tone and manner. "I should think it cheap at ten pounds."

Bogey, on hearing this, opened his eyes very wide.

He thought he saw a chance of doing a profitable bit of business on his own account.

So, after an instant, he said quietly—

"Good flute worth more dan ten pound; rale good blower like dat worth twenty at de bery least."

"Yes, yes; I'd give twenty willingly," murmured the wrapt Figgins.

"Bery good," said Bogey, as he instantly disappeared through the gate.

The orphan remained waiting without.

The "too-too-tooing" was going on in the usual doleful and melancholy manner, and guided by the sound, Bogey crept forward till he came in sight of the performer, who was seated in a snug nook in his garden playing away to his heart's content; or, as the negro supposed, endeavouring to frighten away the birds.

Bogey took stock of the stout player and his flute.

Creeping along in the shrubbery till he had got exactly opposite to the flautist, he, in the midst of the too-too-tooing, uttered an unearthly groan.

"Inshallah!" exclaimed the Turk, stopping suddenly; "what was that?"

"It war me," groaned the hidden Bogey more deeply than before.

"Who are you?" faltered the musician, hearing the mysterious voice, but seeing no one.

"Me am special messenger from de Prophet," Bogey replied.

"Allah Kerim! my dream is coming true. Is it the Prophet speaks?" gasped the Turk, his olive cheeks turning the hue of saffron.

"Iss, it de profit bring me here," returned Bogey, truthfully.

"What message does he send to his slave?" asked the old Turk.

"He say you make sich orful row wid dat flute he can git no sleep, an', derefore, he send me to stop it. You got to gib up de flute direckly."

The teeth of the half-silly musician were chattering in his head.

His optics rolled wildly from side to side.

Just at this crisis Bogey, with his eyes glaring and his white teeth fully exposed, thrust his black face from the foliage.

"Drop it," he cried, with a hideous grin.

He had no occasion to repeat the command.

With a yell of terror the horrified Turkish gentleman, who was really half an idiot, and was just then away from his keepers, let fall his instrument from his trembling fingers, and starting up, waddled away from the spot as though the furies were after him, while the special messenger of the Prophet quietly picked up the flute with a chuckle, and retraced his steps to the gate.

Here he found Mr. Figgins.

He could scarcely believe his eyes when he saw the negro with the precious instrument in his hand.

"The flute, the flute!" he cried, "the soother of sorrow, the orphan's comforter. Let me clutch you in my grasp. Oh, it brings back my boyhood's days."

As he spoke, he rushed forward eagerly to seize the treasure.

But Bogey stuck to it.

"Money fust, Massa Figgins," he said, with a grin; "twenty poun' am de price, yah know, an' dis a fuss-rate blower. Too-too-too, tooty-tum-too," he sounded on the instrument.

The orphan was frantic.

"I haven't twenty pounds with me," he exclaimed, excitedly, "but I'll pay you the moment we get home, and five pounds over for interest. You know I'm well off, and am also a man of my word."

Bogey did know this, and was not afraid to trust him.

"Well, den, dere de flute," he said; "but don't begin too-too-tooin' till we git good way off, else p'r'aps de gem'l'm wid de red cap hear and send a dog arter de speshal messenger of de Prophet."

Mr. Figgins pledged himself not to blow a note till they were a mile from the spot at least, and on the strength of this promise, Bogey gave him up the instrument.

But no sooner did the excited orphan find it in his possession than he forgot all his promises, and putting the flute to his lips, he at once commenced "The Girl I Left Behind Me," in the most brilliant manner—so brilliant indeed that it reached the ears of the owner inside, and, as Bogey had shrewdly suspected would be the case, the latter began to have some slight suspicions that he had been done out of his flute by an impostor.

Very soon his voice was heard calling his dogs, and almost immediately loud barkings were heard.

"Run, run, Massa Figgins, or de dogs tear yah to pieces," shouted Bogey.

"They may tear me limb from limb," returned the orphan, "but they shan't rob me of my flute."

And without taking the instrument from his lips, off he ran playing "Cheer, Boys, Cheer," as he hurried along.

The next moment out rushed several gaunt-looking animals and gave chase to the musical Figgins, urged on by their mad master, who was following them.

Bogey waited for him at the gate.

As he came forth puffing, grunting, and blowing, the negro put out his foot, and over he went on his nose.

"Go back, massa bag breeches," cried Bogey, fiercely.

He added to the effect of his words by applying a switch he carried to the fat hind-quarters of the Turk, who was glad to scramble in at his gate on all fours, and shut it to keep out the "special messenger" and his cane.

When Bogey came up with Mr. Figgins, he found that usually timid personage with his back against a tree. doing battle with his canine foes, who were making sad havoc with his Moslem garments.

"Bravo, Massa Figgins," cried Bogey, as he rushed in among the yelping pack, "we soon get rid of dese heah."

With this he laid about him with such energy that the Turkish dogs, utterly bewildered, dropped their ears, and tucking their tails between their legs, slunk howling away, whilst the triumphant orphan accompanied their flight with a lively tune on his flute.

Accompanied by Bogey, Mark Antony reached his quarters in safety.

He then promptly paid the price of his instrument, and at once set himself steadily to practise, to the great horror of all in the house.

*   *   *   *   *

A week passed. Then the following conversation took place between young Jack Harkaway and his comrade Harry Girdwood.

"I say, old fellow, are you fond of music?"

"Well, it all depends what sort of music it is," Jack replied.

"What do you think of Figgins' instrumental performance?"

"Well, I think it's an awful row."

"So do I; but he doesn't seem to think so."

"No; he's always at it; all day long and half through the night; he'll blow himself inside his flute if he goes on at this rate. I consider it comes under the head of a nuisance."

"Most decidedly," said Jack, "and, like other nuisances, must be put a stop to."

"All right; let's send for him at once."

Bogey was summoned and dispatched with a polite message from young Jack, that he would be glad to speak to him.

On receiving the message, he repaired at once to the room where Jack and Harry Girdwood were located, preparing another practical joke for the benefit of the orphan.

Mr. Figgins took his flute with him, and too-tooed all the way till he reached the door of Jack's room.

For Jack and Harry, it should be mentioned, had followed the orphan to his new abode, and secured rooms in the same house.

He entered.

"Sit down, Mr. Figgins," said Jack.

Mr. Figgins sat down, nursing his flute.

"I have sent for you," Jack commenced.

"Ah, I see, you wish for a tune," cried the orphan, with much hilarity, as he put the flute to his lips and began to play.

"On the contrary," cried Jack, quickly; "it's just what we don't wish for; we should be glad if you'd come to a stop."

Mr. Figgins opened his eyes with astonishment.

"Come to a stop," he echoed; "is it possible that you wish to stop my flute? Why, I thought you liked music."

"So I do," Jack replied, dryly, "when it is music."

"And isn't my flute music? Are not its tones soft and sweet and soothing to the spirits?"

"We have found them quite the reverse," Jack assured him; "in fact, if you don't put away your flute, you'll drive us both mad, and then I wouldn't like to answer for the consequences—which might be awful."

Mr. Figgins looked aghast.

"The idea of such exquisite music as my instrument discourses driving anyone mad," he exclaimed at length, "is past belief."

"You may call it exquisite music, but we call it an awful row," Jack replied, candidly, "therefore have the goodness to shut up."

The orphan drew himself up and clutched his flute in a kind of convulsive indignation.

"I object to shutting up, Mr. Harkaway," he exclaimed, determinately; "in fact, I will not shut up. In this dulcet instrument I have found a balm for all my woes, and I intend to play it incessantly for the rest of my existence."

"You'll blow yourself into a consumption," said Harry Girdwood.

"Well, if I do, I'm only a poor orphan whom no one will regret," returned Mr. Figgins, a tear trickling down his nose at the thought of his lonely condition; "I shall die breathing forth some mournful melody, and my flute will——"

"You can leave that to us as a legacy, and we'll put it under a glass case," said Harry.

"No; my flute shall be buried with me in the silent grave."

"We don't care what you do with it after you're dead," returned Jack, "but we object to being annoyed with it while you're alive."

"Oh, you shan't be exposed to any further annoyance on my account," said the orphan, rising grandly; "I and my flute will take our departure together."

With these words he left the room, and very shortly afterwards quitted the house.

* * * * *

Mr. Figgins being determined to keep apart from the Harkaway party, gave up the rooms he had taken, and after some search found another lodging in the upper chamber of a house in a retired part of the town.

Here he determined to settle down, and devote himself with more ardour than ever to the practice of his favourite instrument.

* * * * *

It was night.

Mr. Figgins was in bed, but he could get no sleep.

Curious insects, common to Eastern climes, crawled forth from chinks in the walls and cracks in the floor, and nibbled the orphan in various parts of his anatomy till he felt as if the surface of his skin was one large blister.

"What a dreadful climate is this," he murmured, as he sat up in bed; "nothing but creeping things everywhere. Phew! what's to be done?"

He reflected a moment.

"I have it!" he exclaimed, "my flute, my precious flute, that will soothe me."

Hopping nimbly out of bed, he dressed himself in his European costume, seized his instrument, and began a tune.

He had been playing all day long, and the other lodgers in the house were congratulating themselves on the cessation of the infliction, when suddenly the instrumental torture commenced again.

"Too-too, too-tum-too, tooty-tum, tooty-tum, too-tum-too," went the flute, in a more shrill and vigorous manner than ever, whilst a select party of dogs, attracted by the melody, assembled under the window and howled in concert.

In the chamber next to that occupied by the infatuated Figgins lodged a Turk, Bosja by name.

Bosja, in the first place, had no taste for music, and particularly detested the sound of a flute.

Secondly, he was suffering from an excruciating toothache, and the incessant too-tum, too-tum, tooty-tum-too—with the additional music of the dogs—drove him mad.

He was sitting up with his pipe in his mouth, and a green, yellow-striped turban pulled down over his ears, trying to shut out the sound, but in vain.

"Oh, oh! Allah be merciful to me!" he groaned, as the irritated nerve gave him an extra twinge.

"Too-too, too-tum-too, too-tum, too-tum, tooty-tum-too," from the orphan's flute answered him.

"Allah confound the wretch with his tooty-tum-too!" growled the distracted sufferer; "if he only knew what I am enduring."

But this Mr. Figgins did not know.

Probably he would not have cared if he had known, and he continued to pour forth melodious squeakings to his own entire satisfaction

At length the patience of Bosja was utterly exhausted, and he summoned the landlady.

"What son of Shitan have you got in the next room?" he demanded of her, fiercely.

"I know very little of him," returned the mistress of the house; "only that he is a Frankish gentleman, who dresses sometimes as a Turk, and has lately come to lodge here."

"He is a dog, and the son of a dog! May his flute choke him, and his father's grave be defiled!" growled the irascible Turk; "tell him to leave off, or I will kill him and burn his flute."

The landlady went at once and tapped at the door of the musical lodger.

There was no response save the too-too-too of the flute.

"Signor!" she called, after a moment.

"What's the matter?" inquired Mr. Figgins from within; "do you wish me to come and play you a tune?" and he then continued "too-too, tooty-too."

"The gentleman in the next room objects to the sound of your flute."

"Does he?—tooty-too, tooty-too."

"Yes; and he begs you'll leave off."

"I shan't!—tooty-tum, tooty-tum, tooty-too. I intend to play all night."

The landlady, having delivered her message, went downstairs.

Mr. Figgins still continued to blow away and the agonized Bosja to mutter curses not loud, but deep, upon his head and his instrument.

But patience has its limits, and Bosja, never remarkable for that virtue, having sworn all the oaths he knew twice over, at last sprang from his bed, and dashing down his pipe, rapped fiercely at the wall.

"What do you want? Shall I come and play a few tunes to you?" inquired the orphan, placidly pausing for an instant.

"You vile son of perdition, stop that accursed noise!" shouted the Turk.

"Too-too, tooty-too."

"Do you hear, unbelieving dog?"

"Tooty-too—yes, I hear—tooty-tooty-tooty-too."

"Then why don't you stop?"

"Because I intend to go on—too-tum-too—all night."

"But you're driving me to distraction."

"Nonsense: go to bed and sleep—tooty-tum, tooty-tum, tooty-too. You will like the beautiful flute in time."

"But I can't sleep with that infernal tooty-too in my ears, and I've got the toothache."

"Have it out. You'll feel better."

This cool irony on the part of Mr. Figgins was like oil poured upon the fierce temper of the irascible Bosja, and he shouted loudly—

"If I hear any more of that diabolical 'tootum-too,' I swear by Allah I'll take your life, and give your body to the crows and vultures."

"Ha, ha!" laughed the reckless Figgins. "Tooty-tum, tooty-tum, too-tum——"

But before he could finish his musical phrase, the maddened Bosja had seized his scimitar, and rushed like a bull at the partition.

The partition was thin, the Turk was burly and thick, and he plunged through head first

into the orphan's apartment, to the no little surprise and dismay of the latter.

It was quite a picture.

Bosja waved his weapon over his head; Mark Antony Figgins hopped upon the bed and wrapped himself tightly round in the clothes, clutching his flute to his side.

For a moment the pair stood glaring at each other.

"Your flute, vile dog, or your life," shouted the Turk.

"I object to part with either," cried the orphan. "Go and have your tooth out, and be happy."

Down came the scimitar with a swish in the direction of his head.

But the grocer had quickly withdrawn it beneath the clothes.

Not to be thwarted, however, in his vengeance, the burly Bosja swooped down upon the heap, and dragged them up in his grasp, the orphan included.

"Now I have you," he cried, as he seized the obnoxious flute.

"Give me my instrument, infidel," shrieked the orphan, as he threw off the blankets, and clung to the flute with desperation.

At the same moment, he recognised the green and yellow-striped turban on the head of the Turk.

It was Bosja into whose hands it had fallen, when Mr. Figgins was escaping from the mob.

"That is my turban," he cried, as with one hand he dragged it from his enemy's head, with dauntless vehemence, and bringing his flute down with a smart crack on the Turk's bald pate.

The Turk, who was much more of a bully than a hero, was quite confounded at the excited energy which the Frankish lodger displayed. Dropping his scimitar, he then had a struggle for the flute.

Round the room they went, pulling and hauling.

At length, lurching against the door, it burst open.

The combatants now found themselves on the landing.

Here the struggle continued, till, at length, giving a desperate tug, the flute came in half, and Bosja fell backwards, head over heels, down the stairs, with the upper joint of the instrument in his hand.

The landlady, who thought the house was falling, came hurrying to see what had happened, and found the Turk lying in a heap at the bottom of the stairs, with the breath almost knocked out of his body.

It took some time to bring him to himself.

It was just as he was recovering there was a loud knocking at the street door.

On opening it, a body of Turkish soldiers appeared drawn up in front of it.

"What is the cause of this disturbance?" inquired the leader of the troop.

Bosja quickly gave his own version of what had happened.

Of course, it was highly exaggerated.

He, a true believer, had been assaulted, robbed of his turban, and thrown downstairs by a rascally dog of a Giaour, who lodged in the room next to him.

This was quite sufficient to arouse the indignation of the officer, and, with three of his troop, that functionary ascended to seize the delinquent.

But, on reaching the room, it was discovered to be empty.

"The Frankish hound laughs at our beards," said the officer. "He has escaped by the window."

And such had been the intention of Mark Antony Figgins.

But not being accustomed to such perilous descents, he had found himself baffled in his flight, and was now perched on a ledge, half way between the window and the ground, unable either to proceed or to return.

He was soon espied by the soldiers, and a shout announced his detection.

A ladder was quickly procured, and the luckless orphan very shortly found himself a prisoner.

"What dirt have you been eating?" demanded the officer, sternly.

"I haven't been eating dirt at all," returned the indignant Figgins, "but I believe that fat Turk has swallowed half of my flute."

Bosja came forward at this with the missing portion in his hand, and handed it to the officer.

The orphan made a snatch at it, but received only a box on the ear from the officer.

The other half of his cherished instrument was wrested from him, and he marched off to the lock-up until the case could be tried on the morrow before the bashaw.

CHAPTER LXVI.
HOW THE FLUTE ADVENTURE TERMINATED.

THE morrow had come.

Hearing that a Frank was to be tried, the court was crowded.

At the appointed hour Mark Antony Figgins, looking particularly doleful, was conducted from his cell to the presence of the administrator of the law.

Osman, the ruling bashaw, although a Turk, was a regular Tartar to deal with.

He administered plenty of law, but very little justice; if the latter was required, money was the bashaw's idol, and it must be handsomely paid for.

As soon as the parties were brought in, the judical potentate eyed them sternly for some time.

Then he said—

"Which is the plaintiff?"

"I am," exclaimed Bosja.

"No; I am," exclaimed Mr. Figgins.

"What bosh is this?" cried the bashaw; "you can't both be plaintiffs."

"Most high and mighty, he robbed me of my turban and knocked me downstairs," affirmed Bosja.

"No, your worship; he robbed me of my turban and stole half my flute," protested the orphan.

The official dignitary frowned and shut his eyes reflectively.

He foresaw that he had a case of unusual intricacy before him, and he was thinking how he should deal with it.

After a moment he opened his eyes, rubbed his nose profoundly, and sneezed.

All the officials imitated their superior by rubbing their noses and sneezing in concert.

The uproar was tremendous.

Order being at length restored, the bashaw fixed his eyes upon Bosja, and said to him—

"Let me hear what you have to say."

"It is this. Your slave last night was troubled with the toothache, and retired to his couch. The pain kept me awake, and just as I was going to sleep——"

"Stop!" cried the bashaw; "you say that the pain kept you awake, and then you say you were going to sleep. You couldn't be awake and asleep at the same time."

A hum of applause ran round the court at this sagacious remark.

"He speaks the words of wisdom," murmured some.

"What a lawyer he is," whispered others.

"I had been awake for some hours," explained Bosja, "when the pain lulled a little, and I began to doze."

"Well, you began to doze, and then?"

"Then I was disturbed by a dreadful squeaking noise in the next room."

"A rat?"

"No, your highness; a flute."

"That was my flute, your worship," cried the indignant orphan; "whose dulcet tone he calls a dreadful sque——"

"Silence, dog," shouted the bashaw.

"Silence," shouted everyone else.

"Continue," said the judge to Bosja.

"I endured the dreadful sound as long as I could, until the anguish of my tooth became so great I could bear it no longer, and I sent a civil messenger to the Frank yonder to cease."

"And he complied with your request?"

"Not he, your mightiness. He played all the louder, and the dreadful noise he made nearly killed me."

"I was in my own room, your worship," interposed Mr. Figgins, "and had a right to play as loud as I liked."

The bashaw here referred to his vizier.

"What says the law?" he asked, in a low tone. "Does it permit a man to do what he likes in his own room?"

The vizier scratched his nose and reflected.

All the officials scratched their noses and reflected.

After a moment the vizier replied—

"It all depends, most wise and illustrious. If the owner of the room be a true believer, he may turn it upside down if he please, not else."

"Good; and this flute player is an infidel—a dog."

"I beg your pardon, sir, I'm a retired grocer," put in Figgins, who overheard the remark.

"Silence," growled the bashaw; "go on, plaintiff."

"Well, your highness," continued Bosja, "I continued to get worse and worse under this dreadful 'too-tooting,' until at last, driven to desperation, I sprang from my bed, and hammered at the wall, imploring him to be quiet."

"And he still refused?"

"He did, your mightiness."

"And you ?"

"I was imploring Allah to soften his unmerciful heart, when suddenly he burst through the partition, which was thin——"

"No, no, no, your worship," interrupted Mr. Figgins, vehemently, "it was he who burst through, not me."

"Silence," cried the bashaw ; "dare not to interrupt the words of truth."

"But they're not words of truth, your worship ; they're abominable—false."

"Silence, dog," shouted the potentate, crimson with anger.

"Silence, dog," echoed the rest of the judicial body.

"Continue, plaintiff."

"Well, your highness," went on Bosja, " he then seized me violently, tore my turban from my head, and endeavoured to thrust his diabolical 'too-tooing' instrument down my throat."

"To which you objected ?"

"Strongly, your highness. I seized the flute in self defence, and it came in half in my hand, and he then dragged me from the room, and with gigantic strength, hurled me backwards down the stairs."

"Allah Kerim, it was a mercy your back was not broken," exclaimed the bashaw.

"I feel sore all over, your highness," said Bosja, ruefully, "and fear I am seriously injured."

"And the culprit was endeavouring to escape, was he not ?" asked the judge.

"He was, your mightiness, when my soldiers discovered him clinging to the wall," replied the officer of the soldiers.

"Wallah thaih. it is well said."

The bashaw conferred again with his vizier for a moment. and then, turning towards the luckless Figgins, who found himself changed from the plaintiff into the defendant, he said to him sternly—

"And now, unbelieving dog, what have you to say ?"

"Only this." the orphan replied, without hesitation ; "that that witness has uttered a tissue of abominable lies."

"I have spoken naught but the truth," exclaimed the unblushing Bosja, solemnly. "Bashem ustun, upon my head be it."

"Well, let us hear what account you have to give," said the bashaw, to the defendant.

"My account is very simple." said Figgins. "I was playing my flute, when that Turk insisted on my stopping. I considered I had a right to do as I liked in my own apartment, and refused."

"You had no right to do as you liked."

"What, not in my own chamber that I had paid for ?"

"Certainly not."

Mr. Figgins shook his clenched fist fiercely in the air at this extraordinary declaration.

"There's neither law nor justice here," he cried, indignantly. "In England——"

"You're not in England, dog," shouted the bashaw, "you're in Turkey."

The orphan felt painfully at that moment that he was.

"I don't care how soon I'm out of such a miserable den of thieves and rogues," he said.

"What does the fellow say ?" demanded the bashaw, who did not quite understand all the orphan said.

"He says his face will be whitened by the rays of your highness's wisdom, the like to which he has never before seen," the vizier interpreted.

"Umph !" growled his superior.

Then addressing himself once more to the defendant, he said—

"Go on."

"Well, in the midst of my practice that fat Turk burst through the partition of my room, scimitar in hand. The first thing I saw on his head was my turban, which I lost a week ago. I seized my own property——"

"Inshallah !" shouted the bashaw, "this fellow is telling the same story as the other. He is laughing at our beards and making us eat dirt. I'll hear no more."

" But, your worship——"

"I'll hear no more !" shouted the judge. I find him guilty on all points."

" But my flute——"

" Your flute is forfeited."

The orphan uttered a cry of despair.

" My flute that cost me twenty-five pounds only a week since," he wailed. dolefully.

The bashaw pricked up his ears at these words.

A man who could afford to give twenty-five pounds for a flute must be possessed of property.

The scales of justice quivered whilst he whispered to his vizier—

"This Frank is rich. is he not ?"

"Heaven forbid that I should venture to dispute your highness's opinion. Most of his countrymen are so." the subordinate replied.

" Let us see."

Looking towards the agitated grocer, the bashaw said, in a modified tone—

"The law pronounces you guilty. Still, in our mercy and clemency, we incline to show you favour. Your flute, for which it seems you paid twenty-five pounds, is forfeited ; but, for another twenty-five. you may redeem it."

The orphan was dreadfully indignant.

" What !" he cried, "pay twice over for what's my own property ? I won't pay another farthing, you pot-bellied old humbug."

"What does he say ?" asked the bashaw of his vizier ; "does he consent ?"

The interpreter turned slightly green with dismay as he stammered in reply—

" He expresses himself utterly overpowered by the—the—splendour of your highness's magnificent condescension ; but—a—a—at the same time he is not at the present moment able to a—avail himself of it."

" You mean to say he has not sufficient funds—is that it ?"

"Yes, your highness."

The disappointed bashaw uttered an angry grunt, and looking savagely at the prisoner, said to him—

" Since you can't pay, you must——"

" I can pay." shouted the orphan, in a furiously indignant tone ; " but I won't."

The bashaw grinned at him like a fiend, and demanding the flute to be handed to him, held it up before the eyes of the whole court.

"Be witness all," he exclaimed, "that yonder obstinate Frank despises our clemency, and refuses to redeem this flute, his property."

"That flute is not his property, it is mine," cried a voice from the crowd.

At the same moment a portly Turk, in a red fez cap, pressed forward.

He was recognised at once as Kallum Beg, a Turk of distinction, but who at times had to be treated as a madman.

"That flute is mine, O noble bashaw!" he repeated.

The judge winked and blinked, and seemed greatly perplexed at this unexpected declaration.

"Yours?" he echoed, at length.

"Yes, your highness. I was robbed of it a week since."

"And that lying son of Shitan told us he bought it for twenty-five pounds."

"So I did," protested the orphan.

"Silence!" roared the bashaw, "you have made us eat nothing but dirt. You know you stole it."

Then turning to the rightful owner of the instrument, he said to him—

"Kallum Beg, the flute is yours. Still, as you contradicted me in the open court, declaring it to be your property, when I had declared it to be the property of another, you are fined fifty sequins."

The Turk grunted, and shrugged his shoulders, for each of which offences he was instantly fined an additional fifty sequins, making a hundred and fifty. There being no appeal, the fine was paid and Kallum Beg received his flute.

"And now," continued the bashaw, "let that unbelieving dog receive twenty strokes of the bastinado, on the soles of his feet."

In an instant the orphan was jerked off his legs, and placed flat on the ground.

The executioner stepped forward, and having removed his slippers, flourished his cane.

"Begin," cried the judge.

Swish fell the bamboo upon the orphan's naked feet.

The pain was so exquisite that the victim shrieked "Murder!" at the top of his voice.

The bashaw grinned from ear to ear.

"Perhaps the prisoner would rather pay than suffer," he said, after a moment.

"Yes, yes, I would," cried Mr. Figgins, desperately; "a great deal rather. How much?"

"Ten sequins a stroke. A hundred and ninety sequins in all."

"I'll pay the sum. Oh, why did I ever leave delightful London?" said the grocer.

"Raise him!" said the bashaw.

The victim was lifted up, and a messenger dispatched with a note to young Jack Harkaway to forward the orphan's cashbox.

In a short time the man returned, and the box was at once handed over to the bashaw, who having received the key, helped himself at once to double the sum he had demanded.

"Now I suppose I'm at liberty," said Mr. Figgins, glancing wistfully at his cash box.

"Not just yet," returned the grasping judge, who having the money in his possession, was resolved to appropriate as much as possible. "I'm inclined to think that you have been unjustly accused. I therefore permit you as a particular favour to avenge yourself upon Bosja. You must fight with him, kill him if you can, and I shall not hold you responsible."

The orphan looked unutterable things at this permission, whilst Bosja, who was a great coward at heart, turned all manner of colours.

"Your mightiness——" he began.

But the bashaw cut him short.

"You are fined fifty sequins for speaking when you are not spoken to," he cried; "treasurer, collect the money."

But Bosja had not a single coin left.

"Then he must go to prison," said the judge, sternly; "but not till after he has fought with the man he has falsely accused."

"I've no wish to fight. I want to go home," exclaimed Mr. Figgins.

"You're fined another fifty sequins,' remarked the bashaw, blandly; "for not wishing to fight when I say you are to fight."

Whilst the judge dipped once more into the cash-box, the executioner went for weapons, and shortly reappeared with a couple of enormous scimitars, which he placed in the hands of the combatants.

A dead silence fell upon the eager crowd, who longed for the fight to commence.

"Are you ready?" demanded the bashaw.

"N-n-n-no, I'm not," faltered the orphan, whose ferocity had entirely disappeared with the loss of his flute; "I'm not a fighting man, and I don't like fighting with swords—I might get hurt. I would rather forgive Mr. Bosja than kill him."

His opponent evinced his satisfaction at this humane proposal by a ghastly smile.

But his tongue stuck to the roof of his mouth with terror, and he said nothing.

But the bashaw was not to be thwarted in this manner.

"It is my will that you fight," he said, in a determined tone; "and fight you must or each find a substitute."

The combatants strained their eyes eagerly amongst the crowd.

But no one volunteered to take their places.

Suddenly Mr. Figgins caught sight of a black figure that was pantomiming to him very eagerly in the distance.

A flash of joy rushed across his troubled spirit.

It was Tinker.

He could judge by his actions he was ready to take his place, and therefore he exclaimed aloud—

"I've found a substitute."

"Where?" demanded the bashaw, looking intensely disappointed.

"Here de dustibate," shouted Tinker, in reply; "make way, you whitey-brown Turkies, an' let de rale colour come forrards."

As he spoke, he elbowed his way through the crowd till he reached the space in front of the seat of justice.

Here he shook hands with Mr. Figgins, and nodded as familiarly to the bashaw as though he had been a particular friend of his.

"What son of Jehanum is that?" growled the bashaw, scowling fiercely at Tinker.

"He is my substitute," exclaimed the grocer.

"Is he? And do you know what you must pay to be allowed to make use of him?" asked the bashaw.

"No, you old thief, I don't," said Figgins, softly; then aloud—"how much?"

"Two hundred sequins," said the judge.

"Oh, certainly," assented the orphan; "no doubt you intend to empty my box before you let me go."

This restored the complacency of the bashaw, who, having by this last demand used up all the grocer's cash, finished by taking possession of his cash-box to carry it away in.

Having locked it safely up, he cried—

"I wish to be amused. Let the fight commence at once."

Tinker received a scimitar from the hands of Mr. Figgins, and flourished it gaily round his head.

Bosja, who could not afford to pay for a substitute, made a great effort to pull himself together for the strife, but he looked very white, and his teeth chattered audibly.

"Now, slaves, begin," exclaimed the judge.

Tinker gave a semi-savage yell, just to encourage his opponent, and then, with a most ferocious grin on his dark face, he sprang forward.

Bosja, scared out of his wits, struck wildly at random.

His scimitar came in contact with nothing but air, whilst Tinker gave him a slight prod with his sabre's point in the region of his baggy breeches.

Bosja felt it, and believing himself seriously wounded, uttered a doleful howl.

The crowd applauded.

Tinker hopped round him as nimbly as a tomtit or a jackdaw, and presently gave him another little taste of his steel.

Bosja, fully impressed with the idea that he was bleeding to death, began to grow desperate.

Grasping his scimitar more firmly, he rushed in at his sable antagonist, but Tinker, by a skilful manœuvre, locked his hilt in that of his foe's weapon, and wrested it from his hand, following up his advantage with a smart tap on Bosja's skull with the flat of his blade.

This was a settler for the Turk, who, under the pleasing conviction that his brains were knocked out, uttered a piteous groan, and fell fainting on the ground.

The spectators did not appear to relish the defeat of their countryman, and loud murmurs of discontent burst forth, in the midst of which the bashaw rose.

"Stop the fight, and arrest the murderer," he cried.

Several of the soldiers and a few of the spectators advanced with alacrity to obey the order, but Tinker suddenly delivered one of his startling war whoops and flourished a glittering scimitar in each of his hands.

Everyone stopped.

It seemed prudent to do so, for the negro grinned and gnashed his teeth like a dark demoniac, as he sharpened his weapons one upon the other, preparatory to some deadly work of destruction.

Having performed this operation, he cried—

"Now de amputashun goin' to begin!" and uttering another terrible yell, dashed in amongst the guards.

The soldiers, astonished and appalled, dropped their weapons and fled from the court, calling upon the Prophet to save them from the wild fiend.

Having got rid of the soldiers, Tinker tripped up Kallum Beg, and wresting his flute from his hand, helped that worthy individual to creep out on his hands and knees by the wholesome stimulant of the points of his two scimitars.

Next he sprang amongst the spectators, shrieking and flourishing his weapons.

What with the clash of the steel and the hideous outcry he made, the Moslem crowd were beside themselves with terror.

Struggling, shouting, and declaring that the devil himself was let loose among them, they fought, and scratched, and pulled off turbans, and tumbled over each other till they reached the door.

The court was cleared.

All but the bashaw and his principal ministers, who still congregated round the judgment seat, blue with terror.

"Seize him! seize the imp of Jehanum!"

"Allah preserve me!" cried the potentate, who was holding on tenaciously to the vizier.

But the vizier made no attempt to obey his superior.

He was clinging to another vizier, imploring Allah to preserve him.

Up sprang Tinker, yelling and waving his sword.

"'Ssassinashun! spifl'cashun! strang'lashun to de 'ole lot ob yah!" he shouted.

The officials did not wait to be operated upon.

"Look after the cash-box," gasped the bashaw, as he waddled down the steps.

The rest followed, forgetting everything but their own personal safety.

The cash box was left behind.

Tinker pounced upon it.

"'Ooray!" he shouted, triumphantly; "him got de flute and de cash-box as well. Cock-a-doodle-doo!"

Quick as lightning he rushed to the door.

At the entrance he encountered the bashaw, who had discovered his loss.

"Son of perdition, give me my property," he cried.

Tinker gave it him immediately—on his head.

The effect was stunning.

Down went the "Cream of Justice" and the "Flower of Wisdom" senseless to the ground.

Tinker sprang over him, and hurried away with the swiftness of a deer.

The orphan had long since taken his flight.

But, to his great joy, he received from the brave negro not only his coin, but what he prized more—his flute.

CHAPTER LXVII.

MR. MOLE'S LETTER—A TRIP ASHORE—THE TURKISH BAZAAR—A MUSSULMAN SLIPPER MERCHANT—WONDER ON WONDERS—BY THE PIPER THAT PLAYED BEFORE MOSES, AN IRISH TURK.

IT is now high time to give Mr. Mole's letter which threw young Jack Harkaway and his friend Harry Girdwood into such a state of excitement.

Here it is verbatim.

"MY DEAR BOY JACK.—The prolonged silence you have kept has rendered your absence a matter of serious moment to us all here, and to me more than all; I can bear it no longer. I intend to come in search of you and see for myself what keeps your tongue tied. Ah, I mean to rout you out and to give a sharp eye to your shortcomings. Expect me then soon, for I hope to run athwart you, yardarm and yardarm, as an old salt we once knew used to say.

"Believe me, my dear Jack,
"Ever sincerely yours,
"ISAAC MOLE.

"P.S.—I am told that the native liquors where you are staying are more cheering than inebriating in their effects. This will suit me capitally; but as you and your companions may find sherbet rather thin diet, I shall bring with me a bottle or two of something with a more decided flavour."

"I tell you what," said Jack to his comrade Harry, "we shall have to look out for poor old Mole. We must send word back by special courier, that he may know what direction we have taken."

Messages were sent by sure hands to the different stations which they had made upon their journey, to guide Mr. Mole to the place Jack and Harry were stopping at.

"Meanwhile my only recommendation is, young gentlemen, that you don't get yourselves embroiled in any way with the native folks here any more. The Mussulmen are fierce and fanatical, and the least provocation may make them burst out into wildness."

The speaker was Captain Deering, and the occasion of it was the eve of another projected trip by Jack Harkaway and Harry Girdwood.

"We shall be careful, captain," said the latter.

"Of course," said Deering, with a merry twinkling in his eye; "you always are."

"Always."

"There's not much to fear, captain," said Jack, lightly.

"Oh, yes, there is," responded Deering, quickly; "very much."

"How?"

"Why, very little will provoke a Mussulman when he has to deal with a Christian."

"But no one would be indelicate enough to show a want of respect to their religious scruples," answered Harry.

"I don't see how we can interfere with them at all," said Jack. "Why should the question of religion be raised?"

"Not by you," returned Captain Deering,

"but by them, for they will at any time unite to fall upon an unlucky Christian if opposed to a Mussulman in a dispute, should the Turk choose to invoke their aid against the unbelievers, as they stigmatise the Christians."

"Well, captain," said Jack, who jibbed at being lectured, "you need not fear for us; we shall be careful enough."

"No doubt, Master Jack," returned the captain, drily. "You're a mild spring chicken, you are; it is only that wild, rampagious companion of yours that I want you to look after."

Saying which, he left the two boys to their own devices.

"That's a nasty jar," said Harry, with a chuckle.

Tinker and Bogey were their only companions.

Jack and Harry had taken the orphan once more under their protection since his narrow escape from the trial he had passed through with the bashaw, and hearing from the orphan the description of the Turk he had bought his dress from, they resolved to pay him a visit.

In the bazaar there were Turks, Greeks, Armenians, Arabs, and a motley collection of coloured people.

The Turkish dealers sat at their stalls, pushing trade in a taciturn manner, speaking little, it is true, but when they did make a remark, it was to tell lies with earnest gravity about their wares.

"If you could only speak Turkish as glibly as you did to Mr. Figgins," said Harry Girdwood, "you should go and cheapen a fez for me, Jack."

"I could manage that, Harry," replied Jack.

"No, no," said Harry; "remember what the poor orphan suffered through buying his Turkish dress."

"Bother that," returned Jack. "Let's go and have a lark with that chap selling the slippers."

"Be careful."

There were several slipper vendors present.

Jack picked up a pair of slippers and inquired the price.

The dealer gave him an odd look.

Jack looked round to Harry Girdwood for assistance.

"I can't help you," returned Harry. "Ask him again."

"What's the figure, old Turkey rhubarb?" asked Jack, bowing as if paying the merchant a compliment.

The Turk replied with the same gravity.

"He don't appear to understand," said Harry Girdwood. "Try him in St. Giles's Greek?"

"What's the damage for the brace of trotter boxes, old Flybynight?" demanded young Harkaway, looking as solemn as a judge.

The Turkish merchant repeated the price in his native tongue, and they made no progress in their deal.

While they were thus engaged, who should come into the bazaar but Nat Cringle, and with him their old friend the Irish diver?

"I'll put it to him. Mayhap he'll understand me. What an illigant ould thafe it is," said the diver, when he had waited some time for a reply.

"Why don't ye answer, ye dirty ould spalpeen ?" he demanded, after a pause. "Be gorra, av ye don't sphake, I'll give ye one wid my twig."

Saying which, he flourished his shillelagh before the slipper merchant's face, and then gave him a smart tap on his head.

The grave old Turk then found his tongue, and the reply was such a startler, that the four travellers were knocked off their moral equilibrium.

"Tare and 'ounds, ye blackyard omadhauns! Ye thavin' Saxin vaggybones! av ye'd only thread on the tail av me coat, so as to give me a gintlemanly excuse for blackin yer squintin' eyes, I'd knock yez into next Monday week, the blessed lot av yez !"

The four visitors stared at each other in wonder.

They had not a word to say for themselves.

No wonder that it took their breath away.

The Irish diver was the first to find his tongue.

"By the blessed piper that played before Moses, here's an Irish Turk !"

"Stop that !" ejaculated the slipper merchant ; "av ye call me names, I'll have a go at yez av ye was as big as a house."

"Ye're Paddy from Cork," retorted the diver.

"Niver," protested the merchant, stoutly.

"Get along wid yez," retorted the diver, ye Mahommedan Mormonite ; now I'll take short odds to any amount up to a farden that that brogue came from Galway. Tell the truth, and shame the ould gintleman as shall be nameless."

The Turk had an inward struggle, and then he confessed. He was an Irishman, settled for some years in Turkey.

"But devil a word must ye say. Ye'll spoil me shop entirely," he said, "av the folks hereabout takes me for a Christian gintleman, and I shall be kilt intirely."

CHAPTER LXVIII.

PADDY MAHMOUD PLAYS THE PASHA—LOCAL STATISTICS—VISIT TO THE KONAKI—HOSPITALITY VERSUS AL KORAN.

THE Irish Turk contrived, after some talk, that our friends should procure an entry into the palace of the pasha.

"Back stairs infloonce, me boys," said the Irish Turk, with a wink, " is an illigant institooshn, and is jist as privlint here, sorrs, as it is in St. James's or at the castle."

"How do you work it ?"

"I have my own particular pals, which shall be nameless, at the pasha's palace."

"Officers?"

The Irish Turk looked very demure and replied—

" Not exactly officers ; officeresses, ye understand."

"You're a terrible Turk, Paddy," laughed young Jack.

"When shall we be able to get over the palace ?" demanded Harry Girdwood.

"Come to me in the course of to-morrow afternoon," said the Irish Turk.

"We will."

* * * * *

This arranged, they strolled through the bazaar, trading and bartering with the dealers, and making an odd collection of purchases, to take home as curiosities.

But of all the curiosities, the most remarkable was perhaps a pair of real Egyptian mummies, which they discovered in the possession of a shrewd and greedy old Arab.

" We shall have quite an extensive museum," said Jack.

"Blessed if I care to see a brace o' stiff uns on board," growled Nat Cringle.

"We shall not for the present take them on board," said Jack ; "we shall first take them to our rooms. We shall find some use for the mummies, eh, Harry ?"

"I believe you, my boy," said Harry. "We'll name the mummies Mole and the orphan. Ha, ha !"

Well, that same afternoon, as agreed upon, young Jack and Harry Girdwood presented themselves at the residence of the Irish Turk, Paddy Mahmoud Ben Flannigan, as the boys had christened him.

They had got themselves up *à la Turc.*

Tinker and his attendant Bogey were also suitably attired.

They found the Irishman seated upon the floor with his legs under him.

He arose as the guests entered, and advanced to greet them politely.

"Make yourself at home, gentlemen," he said, "and say what'll ye take before we get along."

Jack tipped the wink to his companion.

" I'd like a little nip of something to cure the belly-ache," he answered slily.

" Ye can have that same," responded their host.

He went to a cupboard, and produced a stumpy, but capacious bottle, and three glasses.

"Whatever is that ?" said Harry, in affected surprise.

"A drop of the crater," responded Paddy Mahmoud, pouring it out.

" Here's your health," said Harry Girdwood.

The two lads nodded at their host, and sipped.

The Irish Turk tossed off his whisky at a gulp.

" When shall you be ready to go up to the palace ?" asked Jack.

"All in good time," returned the host. " In the first place, it is not called the palace."

" What then ?"

" The Konaki."

" Konaki !"

" That's it. Now I'll show you exactly how to conduct yourselves when you are presented at court," he said.

Three servants entered, carrying three pipes, each of the same size, and each having jewelled amber mouth-pieces.

The servants drew themselves up like automatons, each placing his right hand on his heart.

The next moment they were inhaling their first draught of some wonderful tobacco, the host keeping up the traditional Turkish custom of puffing half a minute or so before the guests.

When they had puffed away in silence for some little time, the servants returned.

One of them carried a crimson napkin, richly embroidered with gold, thrown over his left shoulder.

And others carried a coffee tray, upon which were cups of elegant filagree work.

Each of the guests were presented with a cup of coffee—not very nice according to our notions, being thick, unstrained and unsweetened.

Yet the Turks are considered the only people who really understand the art of making coffee.

This disposed of, the servants retire.

"Now," says the host, "that's just what ye'll have to do when you go up to the Konaki, to be, so to spake, presented at coort. When you go visiting his excellency the pasha on any business, no matter how pressing it may be, you mustn't speak of it until the pipes and the coffee have been got through. You have only to observe this little customary bit of etiquette, and all will go on merrily as a marriage bell."

"Have you ever seen the pasha yourself?" asked Jack.

"Often."

"What's he like?"

"Every inch a gentleman."

This rather surprised them.

"Now let's come off, and you sha see over the Konaki."

CHAPTER LXIX.

THE JOYS OF THE SERAGLIO—A GROUP OF PEEPING THOMASES — THE CIRCASSIAN SLAVES—TINKER AND BOGEY ARE IN FOR IT—THE ALARM—ATTEMPTED RESCUE—AWAY WITH THEM—THE IRISHMAN TELLS A FEW WHITE ONES TO A PURPOSE.

THE slipper merchant had selected a favourable moment for their visit to the Konaki.

The pasha—or to speak more correctly, the pasha's deputy, for it was the deputy that had imposed upon the poor orphan—was absent from the house temporarily, and so they were able to walk about whither they listed, thanks to the back-stairs influence of which their friend and guide had boasted.

The head of the pasha's household was the person to whom they owed this unusual privilege.

There was not a great deal to see in the Konaki now that they were there, and their visit would probably have been cut very short had they not been attracted by sounds of distant music just as they were upon the point of leaving.

"What's that?" said Jack.

"That's from the seraglio," returned their conductor; "some Circassian girls that have just been sent as a present to the pasha are very clever dancers, it is said."

Jack pricked up his ears at this.

"Come on," he said, moving forward briskly.

"To this seraglio?"

"Aye."

"Why, you rash boy," said the Irish Turk, with a frightened look, "do you know what you are talking about?"

"Well, yes, I think so," said Jack; "dancing Circassian girls and the seraglio was the topic of the conversation, unless I am wandering in my mind."

"Faith, ye must be mad," said the Irishman, gravely; "why, they'd think hanging too good for any man that even looked at the harem."

"So should I," returned Jack; "I've no wish to be hanged; it's too good for me. Come on."

"Don't be foolish; it's death, if we're caught."

"All right," said Jack, cheerfully; "it's sure then that we mustn't be caught, but I don't mean to miss the chance all the same."

The Irishman resisted stoutly.

But Jack was more obstinate than he was, and so the Irishman was forced to yield a point.

"I know where there's a gallery that overlooks the harem, and you can see all the fun of the fair without being observed."

"You seem to know the place very well," said Jack.

"Very."

"But of course you have never been to this identical gallery before?" said Jack, innocently.

"Never—never."

His eagerness to impress this upon them told its own tale.

"I should think that's true, Jack," said Harry, demurely.

"Oh, yes, quite," said Jack, winking at Harry.

The Irishman led the way along a paved passage, at the end of which was an arched entrance to an apartment, closed off only by a heavy curtain.

"You see that curtain?" whispered their guide.

"Yes."

"That's the harem."

"Come on, then," said Jack, eagerly.

"Stop, stop!" exclaimed the Irishman. "The other side of the curtain are two——"

Before he could complete the sentence, the curtain was dragged aside, and two armed negroes appeared.

Their appearance was sudden and startling.

Each carried a drawn sword, a scimitar of formidable size.

They looked about as ugly customers as you would wish to see.

"Two eunuchs," whispered the Irishman, "they are guarding the seraglio. Come away."

"Ugly enough for heathen gods," whispered Harry Girdwood.

The two eunuchs stood like statues on guard.

The slipper merchant said something to them in Turkish which appeared to satisfy them.

"Massa Jack," whispered Tinker, who was one of the party, tugging at his young master's sleeve, "Massa Jack."

"What now?"

"Dat one ob de beasts what chuck de pusson in de water alive in de sack, sar."

"What!" ejaculated Harry Girdwood.

"Fack, Massa Harry," said Tinker, stoutly. "Guess I know dat ugly brack niggar, sar, a tousan' mile off—beast!"

"Come on. Don't appear to notice them," said the Irishman. "It's awkward work now.

If they had half a suspicion, they would drop on us right and left, and not leave a limb on either one of our blessed bodies."

He led the way until they came to a gallery that overlooked the seraglio.

Their leader now warned them to keep silent.

In the chamber below were about a dozen Turkish ladies, all unveiled.

They were all gorgeously attired, and lolling about in indolent attitudes, as if life were an indescribable bore to them.

Upon a square fringed carpet in the middle of the room a Circassian girl of rare beauty and perfect symmetry was gliding through a graceful dance, to a low, melodious measure, which another girl of her own country was chanting.

The dance resembled nothing that Jack and Harry had seen before.

As she turned round, the shawl she waved was made to describe a series of circles.

And then, as she came to a sudden stop, it fell around her in graceful folds, and she looked like a very beautiful sculptured figure.

But before you could fairly admire her graceful form and beauteous face, she had bounded off again in the mazy dance, to the intense gratification of the idle lookers-on.

"What do you think of that?" whispered the Irishman.

"Lovely," returned Jack, enthusiastically.

"Beautiful," added Harry Girlwood. "What would little Emily say, Jack, if she knew you were looking with loving eyes at that little beauty?"

The mention of little Emily's name made Jack silent for a minute or two.

Presently he asked—

"Are these professional performers?"

"The dancer and the singer are two out of three Circassian slaves that have been sent to the pasha as a present during his journey. He will be pleased with the new acquisition when he returns, although one has met an untimely end."

"Slaves! Is it possible?" said young Jack.

"Rather, my boy."

"What will they do with these slaves?"

"Various things. Perhaps keep them to amuse the ladies of the harem, as you see now; perhaps make them beasts of burden; perhaps make more wives of them. His excellency is not particular to a wife or two."

"He's a beast!" said young Jack; "and I should like to kick him."

"Gently, gently; it's the system of the country, dear boys, nothing more."

"But," said Jack, "when you speak of the Circassian girl being sent as a present to the pasha, do you mean the real pasha or the deputy? For this Turk is the one that cheated the poor orphan out of his money."

"This is only the deputy; I mean the pasha himself," returned the Irish Turk. "The deputy would like to appropriate the slaves himself."

"Do you think so?"

"I know it, and he does not mind what you would call murder now and then."

"Perhaps that would account for what we saw in the bay, for the horrible business with the sack."

"More than likely," said the Irish Turk, gravely. "But a slave, more or less, even if it's a lovely girl, doesn't count for much in these parts."

The boys gave a shudder.

They were not used to hearing murder discussed in such a cold-blooded fashion.

"Tinker," said Jack, by way of changing the topic suddenly, "do you think that you or Bogey could dance like that girl?"

"Go an' dance like dat," he said contemptuously. "Me an' dat nigger dance a lot better, sar. Bogey!"

"Wall!"

"Over wid you."

And then, to the surprise and dismay of all the rest, the two darkeys vaulted over the balustrade and dropped into the room beneath.

Had a bombshell fallen into the midst of the ladies of the harem, they could not have been more surprised.

There was a half-stifled shriek from one, and they all flew into a corner, where they stood huddled up together for protection.

But Tinker and his man were not at all put out by these strange demonstrations upon the part of the ladies.

"Bogey."

"Yes. Massa Tinker."

"We'll jest take de floor togeder and show dem female gals what de poetry of motion is like."

"Yah, yah!" grinned Bogey; "go it, my hunkey boy."

And they did go it.

There was not much of the poetry of motion about it, their dance being of the breakdown genus.

And to tell the truth, the ladies appeared more frightened than pleased with the darkeys' extraordinary evolutions.

The double shuffle excited wonderment.

When Bogey and Tinker brought down their respective hoofs with a bang, great alarm was manifested.

By degrees, however, they appeared to grow more accustomed to the eccentric evolutions of the young negroes, and presently one of them laughed aloud at the quaint capers the boys were cutting.

This set them all laughing, and the mirth of the ladies was at its height, when certain alarming sounds were heard without.

"By the holy fly," ejaculated the Irishman, "there's a row in the house, and our frisky black boys'll lose their lives if they don't watch it."

"What's the matter?" demanded young Jack.

"The deputy-pasha is back," whispered the Irishman, in evident anxiety. "He has discovered the presence of strangers in the house. He's coming along here with his guards, and there'll be the very devil to pay."

"What, about Tinker and Bogey?"

"They're dead as door-nails. There is an unwritten law which sentences any man to death who violates the sanctity of a Turkish harem."

"Why don't they run out?" inquired Harry, anxiously.

"What for To be cut down by the armed

eunuchs. No; better take their chance where they are."

"I'm not going to leave them to die," said Jack; "I'll have a shy for it, if——"

"Hold your tongue," interrupted the Irishman, anxiously; "but look, what the dooce are the girls up to with your black boys?"

Tinker and Bogey laboured under a very great disadvantage.

They could neither understand nor make themselves understood by the fair creatures by whom they were surrounded.

However, they managed to glean that they were in danger, and that a temporary haven of safety was to be found in an inner room beyond the curtain facing the chief entrance, which was guarded by the two eunuchs.

They were bustled into that apartment by the ladies of the harem to a chorus of excited whisperings.

"Whatever are they going to do?" whispered Jack.

"Silence, not a word. Look there!" said the Irish Turk.

The heavy drapery before the chief entrance was drawn aside, and in marched the fierce-looking Turk, that had tried to rob the orphan and his cash box, closely followed by the two eunuchs, who stood sentry at the doorway.

"Now, there'll be the devil to pay," whispered the Irishman.

Osmond, the ruling bashaw for the time, had heard that strangers were within the palace, and he hurried there with all speed.

When first he was apprised of this, his greed excited him, for some of the chief sweets of his office were the presents.

The deputy-pasha was ready to accept as many as he could send.

"Strangers are present," he exclaimed, addressing one of the favourite ladies; "now, by the beard of the Prophet, the intruders shall suffer!"

"What intruders?" said the lady.

The deputy-governor made towards the curtain.

But before he could enter, the lady with whom he had been talking placed herself in his way.

"Stand aside——"

"Restrain your temper here," returned the lady; "his excellency would not be pleased to hear of this."

These words appeared to cool the ferocity of the deputy-governor a little.

"Let the strangers come forth then," he growled.

"It shall be done."

She passed to the further chamber.

A few moments later the curtain was dragged aside, and the two fair Circassians came forth, each leading a veiled girl by the hand.

Strapping girls they were too; but so closely veiled that it was impossible to see what their features were like.

"Were these the strangers?"

"Yes."

The deputy-governor glared at the new comers, and then dismissed the Circassian girls.

They refused to go at first, upon which he grew rabid with anger.

"Your sister Selika opposed my wishes once," he said, with cruel significance; "she will never oppose me more. Begone!"

They tremblingly obeyed the tyrant.

This done, he sent the two armed eunuchs off with a wave of the hand.

*　　*　　*　　*

"What's up now, I wonder?" whispered Jack.

"Wait."

The Irishman had an odd suspicion.

And his suspicion was very soon realised.

*　　*　　*　　*　　*

"Remove your veil," said Osmond, the deputy-pasha, peremptorily.

But he might as well have addressed a stone wall.

The tyrant waited a moment.

Then he seized one of the girls and dragged her aside, tearing down her veil as he did so, and——

Oh, what a roar!

A wild ejaculation of disgust escaped him, for the face under the veil was black.

Black as night, with huge, saucer-like eyes, and a huge mouth wearing a grin that was alarming.

"Yah, yah! don't you like me, old man? Tink I do for you? Yah, yah!"

And Tinker stood with his tongue out, grinning at the fierce Turk.

The deputy-governor, enraged, made a rush at poor Tinker, and gave him a spiteful, if undignified back hander.

"Golly!" cried Tinker. "Cantankrous immense beast, old Turkey."

"Oh!"

Just then the tyrant was greeted with a stinging spank on the side of his face, and turning round, there was another negress—as he thought.

Or was it the same?

It looked the very identical face and form.

"Yah, yah!" grinned Bogey.

The deputy-governor looked round with a puzzled air.

"Yah, yah!" grinned Bogey, again.

"Yah, yah!" shouted Tinker, poking his fist into the ribs of the Turk, and nearly doubling him up.

The Turk heard the derisive laugh, and he felt the tingling of his ear and the poke in his ribs.

So he dashed at Bogey first.

Bogey feinted and dodged him.

But his petticoats got between his legs, and over he went sprawling.

The Turk sprang after him, and if Tinker had not been there, goodness knows what would have been the result.

But Tinker was very much there.

He bobbed his head and shot straight forward, landing his deputy-excellency fairly in the stomach, with his bare woolly pate.

"Ugh!" gasped the Turk, and down he went.

Bogey no sooner saw him there than he hammered into the Turk's figure head in the most violent and ungentlemanly way.

Jack and Harry Girdwood laughed until the tears ran down their cheeks.

"Begorra," whispered the Irishman, "it's better than a pantomime, but some of us will suffer."

* * * *

ከሁ one end of the adventure promised to be serious.

The fierce Turk grew frightened, and he called for assistance.

In came the armed eunuchs ready for slaughter.

"Good-bye to your boys," said the Irishman, in a whisper.

"Not if I know it," returned Jack; "I'm on in this scene, old man."

"I'm with you, Jack," cried Harry.

Jack was in danger. Over went Harry to help him.

The fierce Turk was filled with wonder and dismay; the enemies appeared to drop from the clouds.

"Now, old big bags," said young Jack, saucily, "come on, and see how a Boy of England can fight."

The words were not intelligible to the Turks, but the gesture was thoroughly understood.

There was a gong bell close beside the deputy-pasha, and one tap on this sufficed to bring a whole mob of armed men into the room.

"Seize these Franks!" exclaimed the tyrant, still holding his hands round his sides in pain; "they have earned their fate. Let it be swift. Away with them—oh, I am nearly killed—away with them!"

They resisted stoutly enough, fought like tiger-cats; but what was the use?

None whatever.

The Irishman waited to hear an ugly order given anent bowstringing, and then he came downstairs, and made his way artfully (so that his presence in the gallery overlooking the seraglio might not be suspected) to the corridor, where he once more discovered the two armed eunuchs on guard, looking like ebony statues again, and as calm as if they had never taken part in the short but stirring scene just described.

"I wish to see his excellency the pasha," said he, "for I came here conducting two young Englishmen, of great distinction, who brought some rich presents to his excellency."

One of the men went in, and brought out the tyrant.

To him the Irishman repeated his tale with an extravagant show of respect and deference.

"Are these the two Franks?" demanded the Turk.

He gave the word as he spoke, and out from the seraglio marched Jack and Harry Girdwood, their arms tightly bound to their sides, between a strong escort of armed men.

"Yes, excellency," answered the Irishman.

"Then they have been there," returned the deputy-pasha; "you know what that means?"

"They have erred through ignorance, your excellency."

"Then," replied the Turk, with vindictive significance, "within an hour they will grow wiser. Away with them!"

And the prisoners were all marched away.

"Begorra," muttered the Irishman to himself, "it's all up."

But he never relaxed his efforts for all this.

"Pardon, O excellency," he said, "but these young gentlemen who have offended through ignorance, being princes of the royal blood of Britain, their continued absence will lead to serious inquiries, and——"

"They shall die like dogs if they are kings," growled the deputy-pasha.

"Let me entreat humbly that you await the return of his excellency, for these Franks are but savages, and the least slight, even to their princes, would bring their ships of war along our coast; the town would be razed to the ground."

"Ships of war!" responded the deputy-pasha.

"Yes, excellency," continued the Irishman, with a frightened air, seeing the slight advantage he had got now, "the ship they came in is now nearing the coast. It is well within range, with the cruel engines of war these barbarians use. I tremble for the Konaki."

"They would never dare——"

"Pardon, they would dare anything. The death of the two princes of the blood royal would be the signal for the first shot, and then good-bye to us all."

The deputy-pasha paused.

The Irishman eyed him askance.

"Begorra!" he muttered to himself, "that ought to be sthrong enough for him. Them boys have made me tell enough lies in ten minutes to last a Turk himself a lifetime. Be jabers, I've pitched it sthrong with a purpose. He who hesitates is lost. He is thinking better of it."

The Irishman was right.

"I will reflect," said the Turk, with a dignified air; "I may not spare their lives, but possibly await the return of his highness the pasha."

The Irishman was dismissed.

He bowed and retired.

CHAPTER LXX.

OSMOND AND LOLO THE SLAVE—THREATS AND DEFIANCE—THE CIRCASSIAN'S DOOM—OSMOND EARNS HIS REWARD.

THE three Circassian slaves had been sent as a present to the real pasha, Osmond's master, by some friendly Algerian prince, and, arriving in the absence of the pasha, the deputy had cast greedy eyes upon the rich prize.

Finding all his authority was lost upon the Circassian girls, who stoutly refused to be persuaded, he grew vicious.

Nothing was positively known, but the tragedy which Jack and Harry Girdwood had witnessed hard by the water-gate of the Konaki, coupled with the recognition of the two eunuchs by Tinker as the two assassins whom he and Bogey had capsized into the water, made matters look altogether very suspicious indeed.

The few threatening words which Osmond had muttered to one of the fair Circassians, too, should have told their own tale.

"TINKER HOPPED ROUND HIM NIMBLY, AND GAVE HIM ANOTHER TASTE OF THE STEEL."

The Circassian girls had endeavoured to screen those luckless negroes, Tinker and Bogey, for had they not led the boys into the presence of Osmond disguised as girls?

Here, then, was a pretext for further ill-usage of the unfortunate slaves.

The girls were brought into the tyrant's presence.

"Stand out, deceitful and faithless slave," he said, addressing one of the girls; "you are accused of treason to the pasha, and you know your fate."

The girl addressed made no reply but by a bold, defiant glance.

"You are to die," said Osmond, watching the effect of his words as he spoke.

The girls did not move nor utter a word.

"You know now my power," he went on to say in a low tone. "You have one chance of life yet; would you know what that is?"

He waited for an answer.

He waited in vain.

The proud Circassian girls did not deign to notice him.

"You remember what I told your sister?" he said. "Reconsider what I said, and it may not yet be too late."

"We do not need to speak again," returned one of the girls. "What we have already said is our resolve."

"Death!" hissed the Turk, between his teeth.

He eagerly watched for the terror his words should have produced.

"Sooner death ten hundred times," returned the Circassian proudly, "than acknowledge you for our master."

"You have spoken," exclaimed the Turk, fiercely.

He struck a bell, and one of the armed eunuchs entered.

"Remove these slaves to the cells as I told you; there they will remain until nightfall. You understand me?"

The man placed his finger upon his lip—a sign of implicit obedience—and the Circassian slaves were removed to prison.

They were doomed!

Another tragedy was planned—the sequel to that which Harry Girdwood and young Jack had witnessed almost as soon as they were upon the Turkish coast.

The cord and sack were once more to play their part.

And could nothing avert their fate?

Their peril was extreme—greater even than that of the English lads and their faithful followers, Tinker and Bogey.

* * * * *

"This is a pretty go," said Harry Girdwood, dolefully, as he looked round him.

His tone was so grumpy, his look so glum, that Jack could not refrain from laughing.

"Grumbling old sinner," said he; "you're never satisfied."

"Well, I like that," said Harry. "You get us into a precious hobble through sheer wanton foolery, and then you expect me to like it."

"Now, don't get waxy," said Jack.

Tinker and Bogey did not understand the full extent of their danger.

They sat at the further end of the same chamber, grinning at their masters, and, if the truth be told, rather enjoying the dilemma which they were honoured by sharing with them.

Their masters would be sure to pull them all through safely.

Such was his idea.

As soon as they had been left alone in their prison, the boys had made a survey, and Jack pronounced his opinion, and his determination with the old air of confidence in himself.

"They're treating us with something like contempt, Harry," he said.

"How so?"

"By not guarding us better than this," was the reply.

"I don't quite see that, Jack; the door would take us all our time to get through."

"Perhaps," returned Jack, "but look at the window, and just tell me what you think of that?"

The window, or perhaps we had better have said hole in the wall—for glass or lattice there was none—overlooked the sea.

They were in the part of the Konaki, known as the water pavilion.

There was a drop of thirty feet to the water.

Thirty feet.

Just think what thirty feet is.

About the height of a two-story dwelling house.

"Supposing we get through there," said Harry Girdwood, "we should never be able to swim all the way out to a friendly ship."

"My dear old wet blanket," returned Jack, "I got you into this mess, and I'll get you out of it."

"I hope so."

They watched anxiously for a friendly ship.

At length their vigil was rewarded with success.

A big ship sailed into the bay with the British colours flying at her masthead.

They almost shouted with joy at the sight.

"That's a deuce of a way off," said Harry Girdwood.

"About a mile."

"A mile is a precious good swim," grunted Harry.

"So much the better. These villanous old Turks won't be suspicious, and a mile isn't much for either of us, I think. I don't mind it, and we can answer for Tinker and his prime minister."

"Dat's so," said Bogey, grinning from ear to ear. "Yah, yah! Me and Tinker swim with Massa Harry and Jack on our backs."

At dusk they matured their plan of action.

Tinker could float on the water like a cork, and was the swiftest swimmer of the four.

Tinker was, therefore, lowered as far down as they could manage, and then allowed to drop into the water.

It was a drop!

"Fought dis chile was gwine on dropping for a week, sar," said the plucky young nigger, subsequently.

However, once he was on the surface, and got his wind well, he darted through the water like a fish.

They watched his dusky form until they could see him no more.

"Now, Bogey."

"Ready, sar."

He was lowered and dropped the same as Tinker, and speedily was upon the latter's track.

"Now my turn," said Jack. "I shall go in for a header."

"Don't," said Harry. "You'd never come up alive if you went down head first from this height."

And Jack was dissuaded from this purpose.

He squeezed his body through the aperture.

"Give me your hand, Harry, while I look over."

His comrade obeyed, and Jack was able to see about him.

Now on his left, not more than ten feet down, was a large doorway, with a flap similar to the doors on the water-side warehouses, in London, from where the stores are lowered and raised from the barges by means of an iron crane.

"I wonder what place that is?" said Jack; "if I could only reach it, my fall would be very considerably broken."

He had a try.

They fastened their two scarves together, and Harry, making himself a secure hold above, lowered Jack, and the latter swinging backwards and forwards twice, dropped the second time fairly on the ledge.

It was a perilous hold.

But Jack was only second to Nero in monkey tricks, and he held on in a most tenacious manner.

Swinging himself up, he pushed his way into a dark and gloomy place.

A low vaulted chamber, dimly lighted by a flickering oil lamp.

"Where am I now?"

Before he could look further to get an answer to this question, he was startled by the sound of footsteps.

What should he do?

Leap out?

Or should he wait?

He decided to wait.

He crept up into a corner, the darkest he could find, and there, with a beating heart, he awaited the progress of events.

He had not long to wait.

Two dusky forms glided spectrally into the place, one bearing a lamp.

With this, they looked about, and Jack, with a sinking at heart, recognised the two eunuchs again.

"What devilment are they working now?" thought Jack.

They flashed the light just then upon the objects of their search.

Two huge sacks lay upon the floor.

Jack but imperfectly discerned what they were but a sickening dread stole over him, as the two eunuchs raised one of the sacks from the floor, and bearing it to the window, while its contents writhed and struggled desperately, hurled it out.

A stifled groan.

A shriek.

A splash.

Jack could hear no more.

He was about o dart out from his hiding-place upon those black-hearted wretches. when a third person stepped into the chamber.

He said something to the two men—a few sharp words in an authoritative tone—and they retired.

Jack recognised the voice in an instant.

It was Osmond.

"What is he up to now?" muttered Jack, to himself.

A scene of intense excitement followed.

The Turk unfastened the cord which fastened the neck of the second sack, and dragged it open.

Then, raising the sack on end, he proceeded hastily to drag it down, revealing in the dim light the well-remembered form of one of the Circassian girls.

"Lolo," said Osmond, "I come to give you one last chance."

"I defy and despise you!" said the girl.

"Reflect."

"I have."

"You know well, as I have seen again and again by your looks, that I do not hate you ——"

"Would you have me love the murderer of my sister?"

"Silence, slave!"

"I fear not your menaces," retorted the brave girl; "you must have seen that. The triumph is yours now—mine is to come."

"When?"

"Hereafter. Murder is against your creed as it is against mine. Do your worst."

Jack listened.

Osmond seized the girl by the wrist.

But she twisted herself free from his clutch without any particular effort.

Thereupon the Turk, with a growl of rage, drew his sword, and would have cut her down.

But Jack could stand no more.

Bounding forward from his hiding-place, he seized the uplifted hand and wrenched the sword from his grasp.

Then, without a word, Jack struck the man with the flat of his sword upon the back of the head.

The Turk sank to the ground with a hollow groan.

It was all so momentary that the beautiful Circassian girl looked on as one in a dream.

Hearing footsteps now, Jack ran to the doorway and peered out.

"Quick!" exclaimed Jack. "Lend me a hand, or we are lost."

She could not understand his words, but his meaning was plain enough.

They pulled the body into the sack as quickly as possible.

Then they hastily tied the cord around the neck of it.

This done, Jack extinguished the lamp.

There was no time to be lost.

He took the girl by the hand, and pulled her back into the nook where he had been hiding, just as the two villanous eunuchs entered the chamber.

The two eunuchs came slowly along the corridor.

Finding the place, as they thought, deserted, they simply raised the sack from the ground, thinking the body of the young Circassian girl was in it, and bore it to the opening.

One swing, and over it went.

As it fell, a hollow groan came from the sack.

The two men stared at each other aghast, and looked over the opening.

But before they could utter a word, a stealthy form had crept up behind them, and with a vigorous drive, hurled them both over after the sack.

A wild, despairing yell, and the waters closed over these wholesale butchers.

CHAPTER LXXI.

LOLO'S GRATITUDE AND JACK'S DELIGHT—THE SIGNAL—UNEXPECTED TURN OF LUCK—A FAMILIAR VOICE—WHO IS IT?—"SURELY! NEVER!"—READ AND LEARN.

"THAT'S a good job done!" said Jack, looking after the wretches he had pushed over.

The fair Circassian burst into tears now that the peril was over.

Falling upon her knees, she seized Jack's hands and pressed them to her lips.

She poured out a long string of thanks in the most eloquent language.

Although the language was so far wasted upon Jack, he could not fail to comprehend her meaning.

"There, there," said Jack, squeezing her hand in reply to her caresses, "don't take on so, my dear girl. The danger's over now."

But was it?

They had yet to get away.

Jack was no worse off than when in his prison ten feet higher up, it is true.

But what of Lolo?

How was she to manage?

While he was cogitating over this, he heard a shrill whistle from below.

He ran to the window.

"Hist, Jack!" cried a familiar voice from the water.

"Hullo!"

"Drop down, Jack," returned Harry's voice. "Here I am, in a boat, as snug as a domestic pest in a railway wrapper."

Comic and tragic were so jumbled up in this startling series of adventures, that Jack scarce knew whether to laugh or to cry.

He did neither.

There was a rope close handy upon a sack—its destination had certainly not been to save life—and Jack, with the quickness of thought itself, fastened it round the Circassian girl's waist.

She understood his meaning, and lent him all the assistance she could.

Once at the window, he fastened it securely, and proceeded to lower it down.

She looked down the dizzy height, and slightly shuddered.

And then, before trusting herself down, she threw her arms around her young preserver's neck, and embraced him tenderly.

"Bless you," said Jack, with emotion. "If I only bring you safe through this, it will be the proudest day in my life."

Now for it.

It was a perilous moment, for the poor girl could not help herself in any way.

But she was lowered in safety.

"Look out," said Jack, in a good loud whisper; "I'm coming now."

"Look sharp, then," called out Harry. "I smell danger."

"Make haste, dear boy," added a familiar voice.

The sound thrilled Jack strangely.

He was so full of the present adventure and its perils, that he could not give much thought to the voice now.

Yet it rang on his ears as of old days.

"You're nearly down," said Harry Girdwood. "Drop now, old fellow."

Jack obeyed.

As soon as he reached the boat, he was seized in the arms of the Circassian girl, Lolo, who hugged him as if she would never part with him again.

"Now, my love," said that same familiar voice, "when you've done with that boy, I should like to have one touch at him. What do you say, Jack, my lad?"

"Heaven above!" ejaculated Jack, "why, it's Mr. Mole."

"Right, dear boy," returned Mr. Mole. "Isaac Mole himself, turned up in the very nick of time. God bless you, Jack."

"And you, too, sir. How are they all at home? My mother, my——"

"There, there," interrupted Harry; "we'll have the family history when we're fairly out of musket shot range. If they find out anything, they'll pot us off as easily as shooting for nuts at a fair."

"All right," said Jack, laughingly. "Pull away."

"Pull away, boys."

"Aye, aye, sir."

They had a good boatload, yet they moved through the water pretty smartly.

* * * * *

The vessel which had anchored in the bay, and which showed the British ensign at her mast head, was the identical ship that our old friend Mr. Mole had come in.

The messages that they had sent back to the different stations upon their journey had been successful in guiding Mr. Mole aright, happily enough.

They had barely cast anchor, when Mr. Mole had been lowered in a boat, his intention being to come ashore, and get information, if possible, regarding the object of his cruise.

But little did he think of picking up his information in the water.

Yet such was the case.

When half way to shore, they came upon Bogey swimming swiftly along.

A few words of hurried explanation sufficed, and the astounded Mole had the boat pulled flush up beneath the windows of the Konaki, first rescuing Harry Girdwood and then Lolo the Circassian girl, and Jack, as we have described.

CHAPTER LXXII.

THE PICNIC—FIGGINS AGAIN IN TROUBLE.

AFTER Jack had placed the beautiful girl in safety, he arranged for Mr. Mole to tell him the news from home.

"Your dear father and mother are in a woeful state about you, Jack," said Mole.

"Why?" asked young Jack.

"I don't like beginning with reproaches, my boy," returned Mr. Mole, "but I must, of course, tell you. Your little extravagancies have been troubling your father a great deal."

"I can throw some light on that subject," replied Jack. "I have been robbed. Cheques have been stolen from my book, and my signature forged."

Mr. Mole looked grave.

"Is this the fact?" he asked.

"Of course. However, we need not go further into that just now. Give me the news. How is Emily?"

"Very well in health, but spirits low—sighing for her Jack," said Mole, wickedly.

"Did she tell you so?" demanded Jack.

"Not exactly, but I can see as far through a stone wall as most people."

"Yes, sir, I believe you can," said Jack. "That is about the limit of your powers of observation."

"Ha, ha!" laughed Mr. Mole. "But I know how to comfort Emily, dear girl. She'll be quite resigned to your prolonged absence when she gets news of you. I have already written home to explain the odd circumstances under which I met you—that you were shut up in some dark room with a lovely Circassian girl, and that you subsequently rescued her, and how very fond of you the lovely Circassian seems, and—"

"I wish you would only meddle with affairs that concern you, Mr. Mole," said Jack, stiffly. "I don't want you to furnish information to anybody about my movements."

"Very good," replied Mr. Mole, "I won't, then. I thought I might send a second letter, to say that I was quite sure you did not care a fig for the lovely Circassian."

Jack thought that this might be a desirable move, and so he tried to square matters a bit.

"Do so, and I will be your friend," he said.

"Consider it done," exclaimed Mole. "I like you as I did, and do your father, but I must have my joke."

*   *   *   *   *

The perilous adventures which our friends had encountered on their expedition did not deter them from further enterprises.

Only two days after the events just recorded, Jack's party set out on a pic-nic excursion, to examine the beauties of the surrounding neighbourhood.

It was not towards the desert that they directed their steps this time, but in the opposite direction.

Mr. Figgins, upon this journey, showed his usual talent for getting into scrapes.

On passing under a group of fine fig trees, nothing would suit him but he must stand upon his mule's saddle in order to reach some of the fruit.

As he was still not high enough to do this, he made a spring up and caught one of the lower branches, to which he clung.

Suddenly the mule, we know not from what cause, bolted from underneath, leaving the luckless orphan suspended.

Mr. Figgins soon relinquished the search in his anxiety for his own safety.

He saw beneath him a descent of some ten feet, and at the bottom a dense bed of stinging-nettles.

How was he to get down?

Dropping was out of the question, for it would be like a leap into certain torture.

However, Harkaway called out to him to hold on, but not so loudly as Figgins bawled all the while for help.

Meanwhile, Bogey and Tinker had started after the escaped mule, which they found some difficulty in capturing.

When it was at length secured, the animal was placed in his former position under the tree, and firmly held by the two negroes.

"Now let yourself down, Figgins," cried Jack; "drop straight and steady."

Figgins tried his best to obey.

When he let go the branch, it rebounded with a force that threw him out of the perpendicular, and instead of landing upon the mule's back, he fell and landed on the bed of stinging nettles.

The orphan roared lustily—as indeed well he might—for, besides being shaken by the fall, the pain he soon felt in every portion of his frame exposed to the nettles was excruciating.

When the party emerged from the forest, a scene of unusual beauty broke upon their vision.

"This is a charming spot," observed Harkaway.

"And just the thing for a picnic," added Harry. "I vote we halt under those trees and begin operations."

Hampers were then unpacked, bottles uncorked, and application made to a pure stream of water which flowed near the spot.

At length all was ready.

Poor orphan, the first mouthful he took seemed to consist of cayenne pepper.

The cup of water, to which he naturally applied for relief, also appeared to have been tampered with, for it tasted as salt as the briny ocean itself.

Next, and also naturally, he drew forth his pockethandkerchief, but ere he could carry it to his mouth, dropped it in haste and with a cry of horror, for it contained an enormous frog, which, in its struggles to escape, fell plump into his plate.

Mr. Mole laughed loudly, whereat Mr. Figgins was naturally offended at the schoolmaster, and began to suspect that it was he who had been playing these practical jokes upon him.

Bogey and Tinker, the real promoters of the orphan's discomfiture, observed this with great inward mirth, but they soon afterwards got into a little trouble themselves.

Harkaway, turning suddenly round, discovered the two black imps making sad havoc with the sweets.

"You young scoundrels," shouted Jack, angrily grasping his riding-whip; "take your fingers off that jam pot immediately."

"I was on'y a-openin' it, sar, ready for de company," exclaimed the unabashed Tinker.

"What's that you have in your hand, Bogey?" proceeded Harkaway, alluding to something which the darkey was hiding suspiciously behind him.

"Only a bit o' bread I brought in my pocket, sar," was the reply.

"Show it us, then, directly, sir."

Bogey accordingly produced a crust from apparently a loaf of the week before last, but while doing so, Jack's sharp eyes detected that the nigger dropped some other eatable, in his hurried endeavour to ram it into his pockets unseen.

"There, our large currant and raspberry tart!" exclaimed Harkaway. "You artful monkey, I owe you one for this, and I mean to pay you now."

Darting at them, Jack just managed to give Bogey and Tinker a cut each on the shoulders with his whip as they nimbly scampered off, both bellowing as though they were being murdered.

But rapid as was the action, Nero saw an opportunity in it whereof he took advantage, for he pounced upon the well-bitten tart, and bore it away in triumph.

This episode, however, was soon forgotten, and Mole began to relate adventures of himself which would have done credit to Baron Munchausen, while Figgins, not to be outdone, told wonderful stories of high life in which he had been personally engaged.

CHAPTER LXXIII.

OF THE DEADLY QUARREL AND MORTAL COMBAT BETWEEN MOLE AND FIGGINS.

"ONE day," began Mr. Figgins, after a pause, "I was driving along Belgravia Crescent with Lord—bless me! which of 'em was it?"

"Pernaps it was Lord Elpus," suggested Harkaway.

"Or Lord Nozoo?" said Girdwood.

"Are you sure he was a lord at all, Mr. Figgins?" asked Mole, dubiously.

"Mr. Mole," said the orphan, indignantly; "do you doubt my veracity?"

"Not a bit," answered the schoolmaster, "but I doubt the *voracity* of your hearers being sufficient for them to *swallow* all you are telling us."

"Well, gentlemen," pursued Figgins, turning from Mole in disgust, "this Lord Whatshisname used to have behind his carriage about the nicest little tiger that ever was seen——"

"Nothing like the tiger I saw in Bengal one day, I'm sure," broke in Mr. Mole, in a loud and positive tone. "Come, Figgins, I'll bet you ten to one on it."

The orphan rose to his feet in great indignation.

"Isaac Mole, Esq., I have borne patiently with injuries almost too great for mortal man throughout this day. I consider myself insulted by you, and I will have satisfaction."

"Well, old boy, if you just mention what will satisfy you, I'll see," said Mole.

"Nothing short of a full and complete apology."

"You don't get that out of me," the schoolmaster scornfully retorted. "Preposterous. What. I, Isaac Mole, who took the degree of B.A. at the almost infantine age of thirty-four, to apologise to one who is——"

"Who is what, sir?" demanded Figgins.

"Never mind. I don't want to use unbecoming expressions," said Mole. "You wouldn't like to hear what I was going to say."

The orphan was so angry at this that, unheeding what he was doing, he drank off nearly a tumblerful of strong sherry at once.

This, coming on the top of other libations, made the whole scene dance before his bewildered eyes.

He began to see two Moles, and shook his fist, as he thought, upon both of them at once.

"I d—don't care for either of you," he exclaimed, fiercely.

"Either of us? For me, I suppose you mean?" said the tutor.

"Which are you?" asked Figgins.

"Which are who?" retorted Mole.

"Why, there are two of you, and I wa—want to know which is the right one," said Figgins.

"I'm the right one. I always am right," said Mole, aggressively. "You don't dare to imply I'm wrong, do you?"

"Won't say what I imply," answered Figgins, with dignity; "but I know you to be only a——"

"Stop, stop, gentlemen," cried Jack. "Let not discord interrupt the harmony of the festive occasion. Mr. Mole, please tone down the violence of your language. Mr. Figgins, calm your agitation, and give us a song."

"A song?" interrupted Mr. Mole, taking the request to himself. "Oh, with pleasure."

And he struck up one of his favourite bacchanalian chants—

"Jolly nose, jolly nose, jolly nose!
The bright rubies that garnish thy tip
Are all sprung from the mines of Canary,
Are all sprung——"

"There's no doubt upon their being all sprung, anyhow," whispered Harkaway to Girdwood. "Stop, stop, Mr. Mole," he cried, at this juncture. "It was Mr. Figgins, not you, that we called upon for a song."

"Was it?" said the schoolmaster. "Very good; beg pardon. Only thought you'd prefer somebody who could sing. Figgins can't."

Figgins again looked at Mole, as if he were about to fly at him.

But the cry of "A song, a song by Mr. Figgins!" drowned his remonstrances.

"Really do'no what to sing, ladies and gen'l'men," protested Figgins. "Stop a minute. I used to know 'My Harp and Flute.'"

"You mean 'My Heart and Lute,' I suppose?" said Jack.

"Yes, that's it. And I should remember the air, if I hadn't forgotten the words. Let's see. Stop a minute, head's rather queer. Try the water cure."

Whereupon Mr. Figgins staggered to the adjacent brook, and, kneeling down, fairly dipped his head into it.

After having wiped himself with a dinner napkin he rejoined the party, very much refreshed.

"Tell you what, friends, I'll give you a solo on the flute," he said. "Something lively; 'Dead March in Saul' with variations."

And without more ado, he took up his favourite instrument, and prepared to astonish the company.

If Mr. Figgins did not succeed in astonishing the company, he at least considerably astonished himself, for when he placed the flute to his lips and gave a vigorous preliminary blow, not only did he fail to elicit any musical sound, but he smothered and half-blinded himself with a dense cloud of flour, with which the tube had been entirely filled.

Bogey and Tinker, as usual, had been the real authors of this new atrocity, but Figgins felt convinced that the guilt lay at the door of Mole, on whom he turned for vengeance.

"Villain!" he cried, "this is another of your tricks; it's the last straw. I'll bear it no longer; take that."

As Mr. Figgins spoke, he struck the venerable Mole a sounding whack over the bald part of the cranium with the instrument of harmony.

Mole sprang upon his legs with astonishing alacrity, and, seizing Figgins by the throat, commenced shaking him.

A ferocious struggle ensued, among the remonstrances of the spectators, but, before they could interfere, it ended by both combatants coming down heavily and at their full length on the temporary dinner-table, and thereby breaking not a few plates, bottles, and glasses.

Helped to rise and seated on separate camp-stools, some distance apart, the two former friends, but now mortal foes, as soon as they could get their breath, sat fiercely shaking fists and hurling strong adjectives at each other.

"I'll have it out of you, you old villain!" cried Mole.

"And I'll have it out of you, you old rascal!" shrieked Figgins.

"We'll both have it out," added the tutor, "and the sooner the better. Name your place and your weapons."

"Here," answered Figgins, pointing to an open space before him, "and my weapon is the sword."

"And mine's the pistol," said Mole. "I'll fight with that, and you with your sword."

"Agreed," said the excited Figgins, quite forgetting the impracticability of such an arrangement and the disadvantages it would give him.

Figgins had a battered sabre of the light curved, Turkish make, and Mole rejoiced in the possession of a very old-fashioned pistol.

Mole gave the latter to Girdwood, who volunteered to be his second, and who took care to put nothing in more dangerous than gunpowder.

"Now we're about to see a duel upon a quite original principle," cried Jack to his friends. "I don't think either of them can hurt the other much. I'll be your second, Figgins, my boy."

"All right. I take up my position here," cried the orphan, stationing himself under a tree near the brook.

"I shall stand here," said Mole, stopping at about half a dozen paces from him.

The orphan looked as though he intended to bolt behind the tree if Mole fired.

"Well, Master Harry, don't be in a hurry," said Figgins. "I am not quite ready, are you, Mr. Mole?"

"Oh, yes," said Mole, "I am ready."

He fully intended to blow the orphan's head off the first fire.

"I'll give the signal to fire," said Harry. "Now, are you ready; one, two, three!"

Mole's pistol-shot reverberated through the copse, but, as a matter of course, it did not the slightest harm to Figgins, who, however, thought he heard it strike against the sabre which he held in a position of guard.

It now began, for the first time, to strike the orphan that this novel mode of fighting was very awkward for himself, for how was he to get at his enemy?

At first he poised his sword as if about to fling it at him, then moved by a sudden impulse he rushed forward, with a cry of vengeance, and began attacking Mole furiously with some heavy cutting blows.

Mole, as his only resource, dodged about and caught some of these blows upon his pistol, but judging this risky work, he took up his stick and used it in desperate self-defence; thus dodging and parrying, he retreated while Figgins advanced.

Once Mole managed to get what an Irishman would call "a fair offer" at Figgins' skull, which accordingly resounded with the blow of his weapon.

Half stunned, the orphan plunged madly forward and took a far-reaching aim at the old tutor.

He, in his turn, dodged again, but his wooden legs not being so nimble as real ones, he stumbled over some tall, thick grass, and fell backwards into the stream.

Jack, thinking matters had gone far enough, caught the orphan's foot in a rope, and bent him so far forward that he overbalanced himself and fell on top of Mole, and both tumbled into the water together.

The alarm was given, and they were both drawn out, "wet as drowned rats," but not quite so far gone.

They were, however, entirely sobered by their immersion.

A small glass of brandy, however, was administered to each, to prevent them catching cold, and some of their garments were taken off to dry in the sun.

Mole, the tutor, and Figgins, the orphan, wearied out with their exertions, soon fell fast asleep.

CHAPTER LXXIV.

A TREMENDOUS RISE FOR MR. MOLE.

THE quarrel between the two had been so far made up, that when they awoke from their *siesta*, and the fumes of the alcohol had subsided, neither of them seemed to remember anything about the matter.

The party got safely home without encountering either robbers, snakes, wolves, thunderstorms, or any other dangerous being or foes whatever.

The next day, however, commenced for Mr. Mole an adventure which at the outset promised to form an exciting page in his life.

He was walking through the streets and bazaars of the town, Jack on one side of him, Harry on the other, though the reader, at first glance, would probably not have recognised any of them.

Harkaway and Girdwood presented the appearance of Ottoman civilians belonging to the "Young Turkey" party, whilst the venerable tutor stalked along in full fig as a magnificent robed and turbaned Turk of the old school.

It had become quite a mania with Isaac to turn himself as far as he possibly could into a Moslem.

He had taken quite naturally to the Turkish tobacco, and the national mode of smoking it through a chibouque, or water-pipe.

But in outward appearance Mr. Mole had certainly succeeded in turning Turk, more especially as he had fixed on a large false grey beard, which matched beautifully with his green and gold turban.

He had again mounted his cork legs, and encased his cork feet with splendid-fitting patent leather boots, and Mole felt happy.

"They take me for a pasha of three tails, don't you think so?" he delightedly asked his companions.

"Half a dozen tails at least, I should say," returned Jack, "and of course they take us for a couple of your confidential attendants."

"In that case, I must walk before you, and adopt a proud demeanour, to show my superiority," said Mole.

So whilst Jack and Harry dropped humbly in the rear, he strode forward with a haughty stiffness of dignity, which his two cork legs rather enhanced than otherwise.

"Holloa!" exclaimed Harry, suddenly; "who's this black chap coming up to us, bowing and scraping like a mandarin?"

He alluded to a tall dark man, apparently of the Arab race, but dressed in the full costume of a Turkish officer, who, dismounting his horse, approached Mole with the most elaborate Oriental obeisances, and held out to him a folded parchment.

Mole took the document with a stiff bow, opened it and found it to be a missive in Turkish, which, notwithstanding his studies in that direction, he could not for the world make out.

But unembarrassed by this, he turned to Harry Girdwood, and making a gesture, indicating his own inability to read it without his spectacles, motioned him to do so for him.

"Good Heaven!" exclaimed Harry, in amazement. "It is the imperial seal of the Sultan. Mole, old man, you have been mistaken for a pasha."

"Is it possible?" cried Mole; "but what does it say?"

"Imperial Palace, Stamboul.
"In the name of Allah and the Prophet.
"To his Excellency Moley Pasha.

"This is to certify that, in consequence of the lamented death of Youssouf Bey, Pasha of Alla-hissar, I am commanded by our sublime master to appoint and instal you into the said government of the city and province of Alla-hissar. Therefore you are commanded at once to proceed thither, under an escort which will be in readiness at the door of your hotel at five o'clock in the morning, after you receive this. Given at the Sublime Porte by Ali Hussein Pasha, Grand Vizier to His Imperial Majesty the Padishah."

Mr. Mole turned pale with anxiety.

"This is very serious," he exclaimed; "but I fully expect to become a king before I die, but in this case, what shall I do?"

"Why, become a pasha," said Jack; "it will be worth your while. We'll give you our assistance."

"But how am I to answer the messenger?" asked Mole.

"No necessity to answer him; make signs that you obey the sultan's mandate; you know how they do it."

Mole accordingly folded the firman again, placed it to his forehead, and then to his heart, bowing all the time with the most profound respect.

The messenger evidently quite understood, for he bowed too, and rode away rapidly.

"That's what you call having greatness thrust upon you, eh, Mole?" said Jack.

"I don't much care about it," answered the tutor; "I don't believe I shall be able to carry out the character of a pasha. It's a dangerous game."

"Nonsense," said our hero; "if they choose to make a mistake, it's their look-out."

"I shall find it a mistake when I come to be bowstringed, or hanged, or shot, or something of that kind," said the tutor; "but, Jack, my dear boy, I depend upon you to pull me through."

"No fear," answered Jack; "you're a great man, Mr. Mole, and no doubt the authorities, becoming aware of your merits, have really made choice of you as the governor of the pashalik."

"But they must know I'm not a Turk," objected Mole.

"That doesn't matter," said Jack; "not only Turks, but Greeks, Americans, Italians, French, all sorts of people are in power in this country."

The excitement of the moment and the influence of some spirituous liquid he had taken before starting, so far bewildered Mr. Mole's intellect, that he actually accepted Jack's explanation.

"Hang it, I will be pasha," he cried, "and risk all. Haven't I got the sultan's own firman?" and he flourished that important document round his head in the most defiant manner.

"That's right," said Jack; "keep up that spirit, and you'll make your fortune. Remember, first thing to-morrow you are to be conducted to your seat of government; the guard of honour will be at the door of your hotel at five o'clock, you will reach Alla-hissar about ten, and to-morrow morning you'll begin your public duties."

"What will your father say, Jack, when he hears of this? But I hope you won't desert me, my dear boys," said Mole, imploringly.

"We'll go with you," answered Harry.

"Rather!" acquiesced Jack. "We'll never leave you, old boy."

The remainder of the day was spent by Mole in the further study of Turkish.

These exertions were fatiguing, and Mr. Mole was tired when he retired, as he expressed it.

He was not long falling asleep, and dreams of glory, power, and magnificence, filled his slumbers.

He was just dreaming he had been elected sultan when he was suddenly and rudely awakened by a terrible knocking at the door.

Mole started up, and was told that he must prepare in a great hurry, for the escort had already arrived.

The tutor, still half asleep, looked out of the window, and in the day dawn he discerned a small body of horsemen at the door of the hotel.

Mole felt that he could never get into those elaborate Turkish robes without assistance; luckily at this juncture, young Jack put in an opportune appearance, and offered to help him.

"You'll have to make haste, pasha," said our hero; "strikes me you've rather overslept yourself. Where is your beard?"

"Here it is," returned Mole; "but why didn't some of you wake me before? I was so busy dreaming that I was sultan, and—that's right, my boy, help me on with the cork legs and boots, that's the worst difficulty, and then all these things, and lastly the turban and beard."

"I'll get Harry to help me," pursued Jack; "you'll have proper attendants when you are installed in the palace. Remember what we agreed upon last night; we are to pass off as your two sons, under the names of Yakoob and Haroun Pasha."

"Just so," said Mole; "but I expected a larger escort than those half a dozen men there. I would not go through this, my boy, if I thought future history would not give me a glorious page."

"Oh, don't fear, sir, this will be something grand for you; at the gate of the town you will be met by a regular guard of honour."

With the combined assistance of Jack and Harry, Mole was fully invested with his Oriental robes, with which he stumped down stairs as gracefully as a moving bundle of clothes.

His escort consisted of six spahis, most of them black, and headed by the messenger of the day before.

"Jack, my dear boy," said Mole, "at last my time has arrived to become a great man in the eyes of the world."

"Right you are, sir," replied Jack. "On you go, my noble pasha."

As soon as Mole was mounted, the chief spahi gave the word, and the imposing cavalcade set off at a quick trot.

In two hours they had arrived at the primitive and sequestered town of Alla-hissar.

CHAPTER LXXV.

THE GREAT MOLEY MOLE PASHA.

SUCH an important event as the arrival of a new governor naturally caused a great deal of excitement among the worthy inhabitants of the remote town.

They came out in crowds to greet him, headed by all the inferior functionaries, and a military guard of honour conducted him to the old castle, which had been fitted up as a sumptuous official residence.

Two things puzzled his new subjects; the fact of his arrival being two days before the appointed time, and the circumstance of the new pasha, who was apparently a Turk, returning their greetings through an interpreter.

However, none had any doubt of the reality of his appointment, and the production of the sultan's firman at once made the old cadi, or magistrate, who had been temporarily put in command, give way to his superior.

Briefly let us explain these circumstances.

It was another hoax, and a most daring and gigantic one, on the part of Jack and his friends, upon their long-suffering tutor.

Having ascertained that the town of Alla-hissar was actually waiting for its new governor, the real pasha, who was to arrive from Constantinople in two days' time, Jack and the others hit upon the idea of making the situation the basis of a grand practical joke.

The *firman* was of course a forged document, written by the old interpreter, who was in the plot, and the Turkish officer who had presented it to Mole, was no other than our friend the diver.

The waiter, the orphan, and the two nigger boys had also effectually disguised themselves, and became members of Mole's escort.

A skilful combination enabled them to carry out the details of their plan with such success as to deceive not only Mole himself, but the simple pastoral folks of Alla-hissar itself.

Moley Pasha, as he now styled himself, was in all his glory.

"This is a proud day," he observed to Jack, as he gazed round on the handsome residence provided for him. "Little did I imagine that old Isaac would ever live to come out in all the glories of an Oriental magnate. Jack, we must let your dear father know of this."

"We will, sir; but now let us congratulate you," answered our hero. "The more especially as you've promoted us to such high positions."

Moley, the pasha, now retired to his private apartments to rest until the hour arrived for his first council.

During this time, he was coached up by the old interpreter, and by his aid, Moley Pasha found himself able to receive the reports and congratulations of subordinates in the government, and to try several cases brought before him.

After three hours of arduous public duties, the pasha and his friends retired to his private apartments, which were fitted up with every Oriental luxury.

"By Jove!—I mean by the Prophet!" exclaimed the new potentate, "I am getting on like a house on fire ; but I am still mortal, and need refreshment, not having had anything to speak of to-day, beyond a cup of coffee with a dash of brandy in it."

Dinner being served up (in the Turkish style) the pasha grew still more enthusiastic.

"Yes, this is a delightful life," he said ; "it only wants the presence of lovely woman to render it perfect. Now if Mrs. Mole Number One or Number Two or Three were here——"

"Oh, I forgot," suddenly broke in Jack, looking very serious. "That reminds me, there was one most important subject I had to speak to you about. The late pasha had thirteen wives."

"How awful," exclaimed Mole. "But what is that to do with me?"

"A good deal ; they are now left, by his sudden death, desolate widows, and it is expected that you, as his successor, should take them under your protection. They go with the premises, like the stock and fixtures of a business."

"Heaven above! you don't mean that?" exclaimed Moley Pasha, becoming much agitated, and pausing ere he quaffed a goblet of champagne, which he drank under the name of sparkling French sherbet.

"It's quite true, though, isn't it, Abdullah?" turning to the dragoman.

"It's true as the Koran itself," returned Jack. "Every pasha of Alla-hissar must have thirteen wives."

"Good Heaven! what'll Mrs. Mole say!" exclaimed Mole, in great agitation ; "hang it, you know, this will never do—Isaac Mole with thirteen wives. I always thought I was very much married already, quite as much as I want to be."

"Unless your excellency agrees," continued the interpreter, "I won't answer for the consequences."

"I have had three wives already, and now you wish me to take thirteen. I'd sooner resign my government at once," exclaimed Mole.

"Impossible!" returned the dragoman ; "it is death to resist the sultan's firman."

"Powers above! what a situation am I in?" exclaimed Mole, in increasing dismay. "I find it's not all roses after all, being a pasha, but thorns, stinging nettles, and torturing brambles. But about these thirteen widows, Abdullah? Who and where are they, and what are they like?"

"They are at present in a house not far from here," was the reply ; "five of them, it seems, have been the widows of the pasha before last, and they are rather old ; six belonged only to Youssouf Pasha, and are middle-aged."

Mr. Mole responded with a deep groan.

"The other two," proceeded Abdullah, "are fair Circassians in the very summer of youth and beauty."

Moley Pasha uttered a profound sigh.

"Ah, that's much better."

"I expect they will be here soon, at least some of them," said Abdullah, the interpreter.

The subject then dropped for a time, and the great Moley also dropped—asleep, from the combined effect of the pipe, the coffee, and the wine.

He was suddenly awakened by Abdullah shouting into his ear—

"May it please your excellency, they've come."

"Who—who?" gasped Mole, in fearful terror ; for he had just been dreaming of the rack and the bowstring.

"The noble Ladies Alme and Hannifar, widows of the late lamented Youssouf Pasha," was the reply.

"Gracious mercy!" exclaimed the persecuted Mole ; "they've come to claim me, perhaps to bear me off by main force.

"Ho, there, guards ; stand round ; not without a struggle will Isaac Mole surrender his liberty as a single man, that is, as a married man, but not—Heaven, my brain is growing utterly confused in this terrible position. Where's that boy Jack?"

"Their excellencies Yakoob and Haroun Pasha are both gone out," was the response.

"Then, Abdullah, I command you to stand up in my defence. Come here."

The old interpreter approached with a low bow.

"Write on two pieces of card the words—'Admire Moley Pasha, but touch not him.'"

"In Turkish?"

"Turkish and English, too."

"Pasha, to hear is to obey."

At this moment a young negro attendant announced—

"The Ladies Alme and Hannifar are impatient to be admitted to your sublime presence."

"Let them wait; it will do them good," cried Mole, desperately. "Have you written it, Abdullah?"

"One moment, your highness," was the reply. "There," he added, finishing up with an elaborate flourish ; "all will understand that. And now what am I to do with them?"

"Fasten one notice on my back, and the other on my chest," answered Mole, "so that the ladies may understand and keep at a respectful distance. That's right. Be still, my trembling heart. Now you can admit them."

The negro drew aside the curtains of the chamber, and two female forms of majestic height and proportions, in gorgeous Oriental costumes, but closely veiled, entered.

They made a very graceful salute to the pasha, and were walking straight up to him, when he sprang backwards, and leaping upon a high sofa, turned his back to them, not in contempt, but in order that they might read the Turkish inscription thereon inscribed.

Then he turned and pointed to it on his breast in English.

Far, however, from being struck with awe and covered with confusion, the ladies were highly amused and laughed consumedly.

"What are they smiling at?" asked Mole, somewhat indignantly.

"Only at the felicitous ingenuity of your highness's idea," answered the interpreter, pointing to the placards.

"Well, I hope they understand, and will

abide by it," said Mole, venturing to step off the sofa.

But the moment he did so, the foremost, who, he understood, was the Lady Alme, and was certainly of an impulsive disposition, sprang forward as if to embrace Mole.

"Save me!" he cried. "To the rescue, guards, attendants, Jack, Harry! Where can they have got to? Help, help! Mrs. Mole, come to the rescue of your poor Mole."

The old interpreter, with some dexterity, flung himself between them, just in the nick of time to avert from Mole the fair Circassian's effusive greeting.

"'Tis our Eastern custom," explained the dragoman. "Her ladyship is only expressing her delight at beholding her new lord and master."

"Tell them I am nothing of the kind, and I have got a wife in England," answered the pasha.

Abdullah did so, whereupon the ladies set up a series of piercing shrieks and lamentations.

"What in the world's the matter with them?" asked Mole, greatly dismayed.

"They are desolated at the thought of having incurred your sublimity's displeasure."

"Tell them that they had no business to come unless I sent for them," said Mole.

"They say, O magnificent pasha, that, hearing of your arrival, they have come hither in the name of themselves, and the other eleven ladies of his late highness's harem, to know when it will be your princely pleasure to bid them cast aside the sombre weeds of widowhood, and——"

"There, cut it short, dragoman; do you mean that they really expect me to marry the whole lot of them?"

"Precisely so, your eminence; even now the most reverend imaum of the town is ready to perform the ceremonial."

"He'll have to wait a long time if he waits for that," cried Mole; "thirteen wives, indeed, and these you say are the youngest of the lot. I suppose they have no objection to allow me to behold the moonshine of their resplendent features. That's the way to put it, I believe, old man."

Abdullah answered—

"It is against Turkish etiquette to unveil before the solemn ceremony has been performed; nevertheless, their ladyships consent to remove one of their veils, through which you may behold their features."

Alme and Hannifar accordingly threw back their outer black veils, and appeared with the white ones underneath.

Mole scrutinized them as well as he could, but he took very good care not to go too near.

"And so, Abdullah, you tell me that these two are the youngest of the whole lot?"

"Indeed, they are, your eminence; famous beauties of pure Circassian descent; each originally cost five thousand piastres, and they surpass the remainder even as the mighty sun doth the twinkling stars."

"Then all I can say is," returned Mole, "that I shudder to think what the eleven others must be like. Just tell the Ladies Alme and Hannifar that, as far as I can see, from here, I don't think much of them."

"I will put your message more mildly."

And having spoken to the ladies again, he said—

"Their ladyships are enchanted to find so much favour in the eyes of your excellency."

"Thirteen wives," mused Mole, scarcely heeding the last reply. "It is preposterous—though nothing, it seems, compared to some of the Turkish grandees. But fancy old Isaac Mole—ha, ha! really it's quite amusing. Why, the mere marrying so many would be a hard day's work, Abdullah."

"The ceremony would be slightly wearisome, your highness."

"Yes, but I should require thirteen wedding rings—ha, ha, ha!—the idea of thirteen wedding rings being used at once, and by one man."

"Don't let that be any objection," said Abdullah; "for the ladies tell me they have come provided with exactly the number of rings requisite for the purpose."

Sure enough, Alme detached from her fair neck an elastic band, whereon were strung thirteen bright gold rings.

Mole was fairly staggered by this determined preparation on the part of the irresistible enslavers.

"They mean to have me," he gasped. "I see how it is; they come here with the intention of dragging me to the late pasha's mansion, and marrying me by main force."

"It looks like it," answered the interpreter, "for I find that they have brought with them a dozen of the harem-guard, fully armed."

"Then I am indeed lost," cried Mole. "But no, I'll die game. Here, help, guards, soldiers, fly to the rescue of your pasha. Oh! Mrs. Mole, where are you now? Your poor Mole is in danger."

As Mole uttered the piteous lament we have recorded, both ladies made a combined charge at him, with a wild shriek and a sudden outburst in Turkish, which might have been either a chorus of endearments or of reproaches.

Alme got behind him and flung her arms around his neck with such vigour that he was nearly strangled, Hannifar attacking him in the same way from the front.

In the pressure of this combined assault he was powerless; struggle as he would, he could not detach himself from their overwhelming embrace.

His cries for help were smothered.

His turban was knocked over his eyes.

He could feel the placards being torn from him, and himself being hauled hither and thither by the ladies who seemed fighting for the sole possession of him.

At length, by a gigantic effort, he freed himself and raised a cry of alarm that might have aroused the dead, but in that effort, he stumbled and fell on his back over a pile of sofa cushions.

Roused by his cries, the military and body guard of the pashalik rushed in, and the whole house was in an uproar.

When Mole had been again uplifted to his feet, and was gasping forth confused explanations, he perceived that the Ladies Alme and Hannifar had mysteriously levanted.

CHAPTER LXXVI.

THE SUDDEN RUIN AND UTTER DOWNFALL OF THE GREAT MOLEY PASHA.

THE ladies' absence was a great relief to Mole. He devoutly hoped that he had for ever got rid of the thirteen widows of his late lamented predecessor.

About an hour afterwards, when Mole was striving to calm his irritated feelings with a cup of coffee and hookah, Jack and Harry arrived, as they said, from a walk round the neighbouring country, looking as innocent as any of the lambs they may have met on the finely-grassed hills.

This innocent look was remarkable, because, as the reader has probably suspected, they had really been concerned in Mr. Mole's recent adventure.

In short, Jack had been the Alme, and Harry the Hannifar, of the domestic scene we have described, the Turkish dress and the ladies' custom of keeping veiled, immensely assisting them in the imposture.

"Whatever has been the matter here?" asked Jack. "As we were coming along, we heard a dreadful row outside, and saw a large body of troops bolting off in a deuce of a hurry."

"Oh, my sons," replied the pasha, in a tone of paternal pathos, "sore hath been the wretchedness and distress of your afflicted parent. I wish you had been here, then it could not have happened. I'll tell you all about it."

Jack and Harry Girdwood had sufficient self-command to listen with unmoved countenances to Mr. Mole's account of the adventure, and even to express great surprise and alarm at the harrowing details.

"Shall I write home to Mrs. Mole for you, sir?" said Jack.

"For the Lord's sake, no," cried Mole, in dismay.

Then they tried their best to frighten the old tutor, by suggesting various deadly schemes of vengeance, which it was very possible the ladies of his late highness's seraglio might form against Moley Pasha.

"You must never go out without a strong body guard," said Jack, "for at any time they may have you seized and borne off to the harem."

"And you'll have to take care of yourself even at home," added Harry, "especially with regard to the food you eat, for in Turkey, those who owe a grudge think nothing of paying it out in poison."

"Gracious Heaven! don't talk in that way," cried Mole, "you quite make my blood run cold. I think—I hope—I can trust my guards and my new attendants."

"I hope so too," replied Jack, shaking his head in grave doubt. "But you must always bear in mind that treachery is one of the commonest vices of the East; you can't be too careful."

"Oh, Allah, Allah!" exclaimed Mr. Mole, who had slipped naturally into a habit of using Turkish interjections; "what a life it is to be a pasha. I used to think it was all glory and happiness, but now I find, to my grief, that—if this sort of thing goes on, I shall bolt."

It being now far advanced in the evening, the pasha, wearied out with the cares and excitements of the day, retired to rest in the Turkish fashion, half-dressed, and upon a kind of sofa.

His cork legs, of course, were carefully taken off first.

In this Jack and Harry assisted him.

Moley Pasha went to sleep and to dream of bowstrings, scimitars, and various painful forms of execution.

The next morning, however, he arose more hopeful, and fully resolved to show himself a vigorous and successful ruler.

In his sumptuous seat in the divan, or hall of audience, Mole began to feel like a monarch on his throne, and signed his decrees with all the triumphant flourish of a Napoleon.

It was in the height of this power and glory that there arose a sudden consternation in court.

Murmurs arose, shouts, mingled with the tramp of many steeds, were heard outside.

"What's the matter?" asked the pasha. "Who dares to make a disturbance and disturb the pasha? Officer, command silence."

A deadly stillness fell upon the assembly.

For some few moments one might have heard a pin drop.

But distant shouts in the streets, and the tramp of horses recommenced.

The interpreter and Harry and Jack, who stood on each side of the pasha, exchanged meaning glances, which partook much of alarm.

Consternation could be perceived on **every** face in court.

It was evident that something serious was about to occur.

"Whatever is the meaning of this?" cried the pasha, who himself seemed to feel no suspicion and alarm. "Abdullah, go and see what it means."

The old interpreter at once hurried to the door.

Jack and Harry, as if impelled by resistless curiosity, followed him.

Karam, the chief of the guard, did the same, and many of those about the court followed in a now excited and expectant group.

At this moment, the shouts outside grew louder and fiercer.

An angry consultation, in which half a dozen at least were engaged all talking at once, could be heard, and then Karam, the chief of the guard, came rushing back with a face full of dismay.

"Your highness——" he gasped.

"Well, Karam, what's the matter?" asked Mole.

"A grand officer, who calls himself Moley Pasha, the same name as your excellency, is outside with a body of troops, and insists upon admission."

Mole started from his seat, and almost immediately sank exhausted with fright and horror.

He saw now the peril in which he stood, and devoutly wished he were safe at home, and in the arms of Mrs. Mole.

"A—pasha—calling himself Moley!" he exclaimed. " What does he want ?"

" He declares he has been appointed to this government by the firman of his imperial majesty the sultan, and that you—you—pardon, your highness—are an impostor."

Mole now knew the worst.

It was all up with him now.

But desperation inspired him with an artificial courage ; he resolved to die game, and keep it up to the last.

"Tell the so-called Moley Pasha," he exclaimed, "that he is the impostor. Here, guards, stand round me, and defend your rightful governor."

The soldiers wavered.

They began to fear that all was not quite right.

Karam, the captain, also hesitated in enforcing the commands of Mole.

At this moment the scale was turned by Abdullah, the interpreter, rushing into the hall, and thundering forth, to the utter amazement and consternation of Mole—

"Down with the impostor, my friends. We have all been deceived by this usurper, who has forged the sacred signature of our mighty sultan."

Shouts of " Down with the impostor !" now resounded on all sides, and a rush was made to drag Mole from his seat.

Poor Mole, he was entirely defenceless.

Jack and Harry did not return ; probably they had been secured by the enemy.

Mole gave himself up for lost.

He was surrounded by an infuriated crowd, still shouting " Down with the impostor ! Death to the infidel who dares to wear the colours of the blessed Prophet !"

It seems, indeed, that the luckless Mole would have fallen a sacrifice to Lynch law, but at this moment the real Moley Pasha, with his troops, entered the hall, and at once commanded the infuriated crowd to stop, and relinquish their victim.

"Now," said the real Moley Pasha, "bring before me the stranger who has so audaciously assumed my title and dignity."

Poor Mole, now a trembling "prisoner at the bar," was brought, bound and guarded by soldiers, before the magnate whom of late he had defied.

" Prisoner," said the pasha, sternly, "what do you dare to say for yourself in defence of the crime you have committed ?"

Mr. Mole, in the deepest fright and humility, made shift to stammer in Turkish—

" I don't defend it at all ; I—I was egged on to it by that young Jack Harkaway."

"What's Harkaway ?" now inquired the pasha.

"The youth who came with me, and passed as my son, Yakoob, and his friend Harry Girdwood, or Haroun Pasha."

"Ah ! two more impostors ; bring them forward," said the pasha.

Search was made for Jack and Harry, but they were nowhere to be found.

In the confusion they had contrived to make good their escape.

"Well, we must make an example of the chief offender," said the pasha. " Prisoner, I find you have some difficulty in expressing yourself in our language, which alone should have stamped you as an impostor. I suppose you speak French ?" he added, continuing his interrogation in that language. " I command you instantly to point out any other accomplices in this villanous fraud."

" The interpreter, Abdullah, your highness," said Mole, glad to be avenged upon that worthy.

Here Abdullah came forward, making a gesture of disgust, and turning up his eyes in pious horror.

"Inshallah ! what lies do these dogs speak ?" he exclaimed. " I swear to your highness, by the Prophet that I knew not, suspected not, till this moment that he was other than he seemed."

" You rascally old villain ! you deserve bowstringing for this," cried Mole.

" Peace !" sternly cried the pasha. " Show me the forgery you dare to call the firman of his sublime majesty, the sultan."

Mole instantly produced the unlucky document.

The real Moley Pasha instantly compared it with his own.

"An impudent forgery !" he exclaimed, turning to the cadi of the town, who had now arrived, and was much amazed and dismayed at what had occurred.

"Pardon me, I entreat, your excellency." said the old cadi. " I trust you will let this accusation go no further. In any case, my associates in office were quite as much to blame."

" 'Twas this Frankish magician who has befooled us with his spells," said several of the town officials.

And they pointed at Mole with fierce and vengeful gestures, which made him feel certain that his life would be sacrificed to their vengeance.

" I doubt whether it was witchcraft or mere folly," said the pasha, who was much more enlightened than most of his audience. " It seems to me that this giaour is very probably the dupe of others. But, in any case, he must not go unpunished. Prisoner, your crime is proved, and I sentence you to——"

He paused.

Mole fell on his knees.

"To a week's imprisonment in the first place, which will allow time for further inquiries to be made, and, if necessary, to communicate and receive our sublime master's commands on the matter. Till then you will be kept in solitary confinement, on bread and water, and closely guarded."

" Mercy !" Mole found tongue to exclaim. " I trust—I implore that your highness will at least spare my wretched life, for I declare——"

"Away with him," interrupted the pasha.

So the unhappy Mole was taken off in chains to his dungeon, bread and water, and horrible anticipations of his ultimate fate.

CHAPTER LXXVII.

MOLE IN "THE DEEPEST DUNGEON"— HOPES OF RESCUE.

THE unfortunate Isaac Mole was now reduced to a position unprecedented even in his varied career.

He was placed in the "deepest dungeon" of the old castle, which was used as the town gaol, in a cold stone cell all to himself, and a couple of fierce-looking bashi-bazouks to watch him.

Bread and water—both of the stalest—constituted poor Mole's only fare, and his lodging was literally "on the cold, cold ground."

The constant fear of a terrible doom haunted him.

It was the third night of his incarceration, and about the middle of the night Mole was kept awake by his own depressing thoughts, together with the gambols of the rats that infested the dungeon.

Suddenly the deadly stillness was broken by a sound outside, which much agitated him.

"Ha, what sound is that?" cried Mole; "yes, oh, joy, it is the sound of a flute."

Could he mistake that note?

Who could make such melancholy strains but the desolate orphan—the melodious Figgins?

Had Figgins, forgetting all past differences and animosities, come to soothe Mole's captivity, in this manner, or—horrible thought!—was it a strain of malice or revengeful triumph that emanated from the long-suffering and tortured instrument?

But the flute did not long continue playing, and Mole conjectured that it was only a signal to which he was expected to respond.

He had no mode whatever of doing so, excepting a melancholy whistle, which, however, served its purpose.

Through the bars of the prison, which were far too high up for him to reach, a small object suddenly came crashing, and very narrowly did it escape falling upon the prisoner's nose.

Reaching out his hand in the dark, Mr. Mole picked it up, and found it to be a stone wrapped in paper.

He knew at once that it must be a written message from his friends outside, and again he whistled as a signal that he had received it.

A few triumphant notes on the flute responded to this, and then all was silent again.

How impatient Mole was for daylight, that he might read the letter.

But it was many hours to that yet, and sleep he found impossible.

At length, a faint streak came through the bars of the gloomy dungeon.

Mole, with some difficulty, dragged himself under this light, straightened out the paper, and read thus—

"ISAAC MOLE, ESQUIRE,—You are not forgotten by your friends, who much lament your misfortune. We very narrowly escaped being caught and served in the same way. We have, through Captain Deering, got hold of the British consul, to whom we have represented the affair to be only a practical joke, not deserving of a severe punishment. So we hope to get you off with a fine, which we will undertake to pay, whatever it may be. Therefore, keep up your pecker, old man, and believe us to be

"Yours, truly as ever,
"JACK AND FRIENDS."

"Cool, after the way they've served me," was the tutor's mental comment upon this message: "but the question is, can the British consul, or any other man, get me out of the clutches of these ferocious Turks?"

The next night, Mole was able to sleep.

But his sleep was suddenly and fearfully interrupted.

An awful and confused noise, shouting outside, flashing lights through the bars, the clash of arms and the hurried tramp of men, indicated that the prison was the scene of some warlike commotion.

Mole started up in a state of great alarm, and struggled towards the door of his cell.

"Oh, dear, oh, dear!" cried poor Mole, "this is dreadful. Oh, if I was only a boy again. I would stick to Old England, and never leave it. There, they are at it again. Oh, dear, why did I leave Mrs. Mole?"

The noise was as if there were a mutiny or outbreak of some kind.

Nearer and nearer came the sound of footsteps, louder and louder sounded the clashing of arms, and the clanking of chains.

A shout of triumph sounded just outside his cell door, and amidst a volley of interjections in Turkish and Arabic, he fancied he could hear English shouts of—

"Hurrah! boys, we shall do it. Open every one of the doors, and set them all free."

Two heavy bolts were shot back outside, the heavy key was turned in the lock, Mole's cell door was opened, and in a burst of torchlight entered groups of armed Bedouin Arabs.

Mole shrank back in a corner.

These ferocious Moslems had doubtless come to murder him in hot blood.

In reality their object was quite different.

The event that had happened was not an outbreak within the walls of the garrison, but an inbreak of those whose purpose was to rescue the captives.

Jack and Harry had the day before put up at the encampment of some friendly Arabs, who became more friendly still when they found their guests liberal in respect of coinage.

One of the Arabs had a brother in prison awaiting the pasha's further orders of punishment, so they were anxious to help Jack and release the Arab chief.

Jack and Harry, being informed of this, thought it would be an excellent opportunity for the escape of Mole, who was incarcerated in the same gaol.

The party set out in the middle of the night.

They soon reached the prison.

Darkness befriended them.

The first step was to gain admission into the outer yard or enclosure.

This they did by suddenly setting upon the two warders outside, and, before they could give the alarm, binding, gagging, and disarming them.

Then, mounting one of the sentry-boxes, Jack and Harry, being the lightest and most agile members of the party, contrived thus to get over the gate, and drop down inside.

Here, with great labour, they forced back the ponderous bolts, and the Arabs poured into the building.

The alarm was taken, and the old castle of Alla-hissar, as it was called, was all in an uproar.

Gaolers and soldiers, utterly taken aback by this sudden onslaught, made but ineffectual resistance.

Ere they could grasp their weapons and put themselves in order of defence, the Bedouins were on to them, striking them down, forcing away their keys, and ill-treating them in proportion to the resistance to the attack they made.

"Tell me, slave," thundered the Arab chief, to one of the gaolers, "in which cell my brother Hadj Maimoun is confined?"

"In—in No. 6," answered the man, trembling for his life.

"Art thou sure? Deceive me, dog, and thou diest," continued the chief, threateningly placing the muzzle of his pistol to the man's forehead.

"I swear, by the holy tomb of Mecca."

"Enough; and which is the key?"

"It is numbered, great lord; see here, No. 6."

"And the cell lieth——"

"To the right yonder. I will lead your highness thither."

"Do so, and if you attempt to deceive us, not the fiend himself can save you from my revenge. Come on, friends; Hadj Maimoun shall be free."

A wild shout of triumph rose from the Arabs.

In a few moments they had reached the cell indicated, where a young Arab, in heavy chains, looked up at their entrance.

The chief recognised his brother.

"Strike off these chains, villain!" the Arab then commanded the gaoler.

The chains dropped off the young Arab, whereat his friends raised another triumphant shout—

"Allah, Allah, Allah! Glory be to the Prophet. Hadj Maimoun is free."

By this time the prison was fairly in the hands of the victorious invaders.

One man, however, managed to slip out, and made the best of his way to the town to rouse the pasha and other officials.

CHAPTER LXXVIII.

THE RESCUE OF MOLE.

MR. MOLE'S place of incarceration would have been difficult to find in that large rambling old building, had not Jack, by similar threats to those of the Arab chief, forced one of the gaolers to tell him the number of the cell.

Armed with this information and a bunch of keys, Jack made his way to the deepest dungeon, followed by the rest.

Mole's cell was the most remote, and therefore the last they came to.

"Mercy, mercy! don't kill an unfortunate prisoner, who has got three wives somewhere about the world, and a lot of little black and white children to look after!" cried Mr. Mole, still confused by the tumult around him, and the ferocious aspect of the new comers.

"Kill you, Mr. Mole; why, we've come to let you out," said the foremost of the group, and he flung back the cowl of his Moorish cloak, thereby revealing to Mole the startling fact, that instead of a murderous Arab, it was young Jack Harkaway.

Harry was close to him.

A very few words now revealed to Mole the actual state of affairs.

"Oh, my boys, my boys," he exclaimed, "what I have suffered all through you. But still, Jack, my boy, I was not afraid of them. No, my boy, I intended to have fought to the last, and I have no doubt I should have killed a dozen or two of 'em."

"No doubt, sir; but let us get out of this," said Jack. "Come on."

"But my hands are fastened with these heavy chains," said Mole.

"Bring a hammer and a chisel, you fellows," called out Jack, "and we'll have 'em off in no time."

The ex-pasha was therefore operated upon, and in a few minutes the chains were off, and Mole was nearly a free man—not quite free, however, for by this time the whole neighbourhood was up in arms; the pasha had been roused in a hurry, and mustering his troops, had hurried off to the gaol.

"We shall have to fight for it, lads," cried Jack, drawing his Arab sabre; "we must cut our way through them, or we're lost to a certainty."

The Bedouins were prepared to follow their leader to the death.

The chief Zenaib, with his brother, Hadj Maimoun, led the desperate enterprise, and the numbers of their followers was now increased by all the escaped prisoners.

As they came rushing out, they were opposed by twice their number of well-armed troops, whom they had to cut through as best they could.

It was a desperate conflict.

Hand-to-hand, cut-and-thrust, bullets discharged from pistols and muskets, fierce charges with bayonets, continued for half an hour.

The confusion was dreadful, the noise deafening, numbers of men killed and wounded on both sides making the result far more tragic than our hero and his companion had ever anticipated or desired.

The prisoners fought to secure their liberty, the Arabs out of hatred to the Turks, while Jack and Harry, with no particular animosity against either party, now fought desperately in self-defence.

They received several severe cuts, and in a short time got entirely separated from their friend Mole.

He, meantime, half propped up against the wall, was valorously holding out against his former gaoler, who was trying to recapture him. At length, the Arabs, finding it impossible to break their way through so large a body of disciplined troops, fell back, and their destruction would have been inevitable.

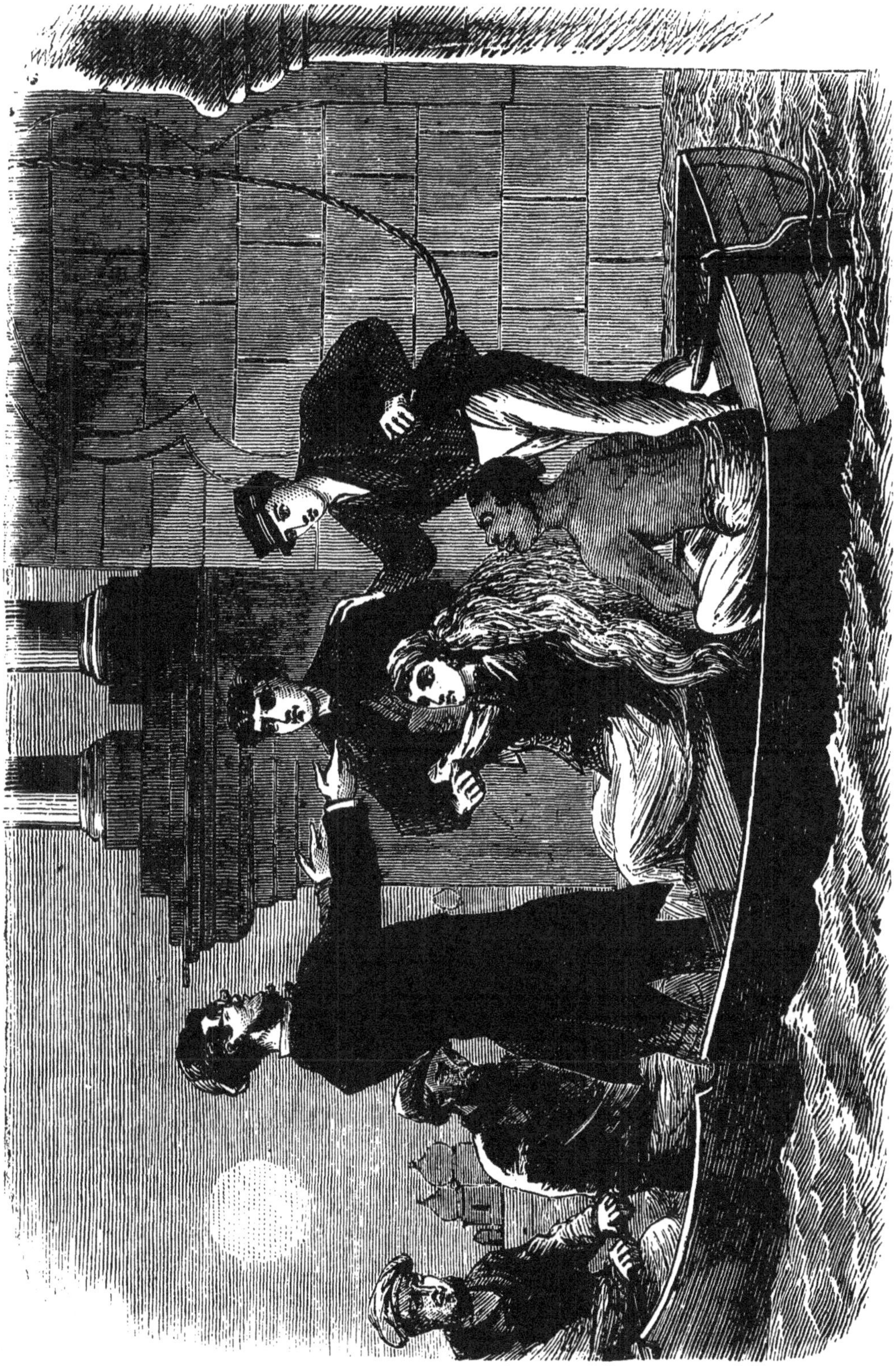

"'HEAVEN ABOVE!' EJACULATED JACK, 'WHY IT'S MR. MOLE.'"

But, at this moment, one of the half-escaped prisoners called out that he had discovered a back entrance, on the other side of the building, through which they might all make their exit.

The Arab chief accordingly ordered an immediate retreat.

The Turkish soldiers, seeing this manœuvre, gave chase to them, whilst others were ordered round to intercept their flight at the back.

Jack and Harry having returned to Mole, took him between them ; each one holding an arm, they got along as swiftly as the cork legs and feet of the *ci-devant* pasha would allow.

But as ill-luck would have it, on emerging from one of the alleys, they met the detachment of Turkish soldiers, who at once rushed upon them.

The whole three gave themselves up for lost.

Mole at length stumbled, and fell heavily to the ground.

"Save yourselves at once," he groaned. "Don't mind me; I'm done for, I can't get a step further. Oh, dear, and my head's all bleeding from that sword cut. Run! Make haste, my dear boy ; the wretches are firing at us!"

Reluctantly the two youths obeyed the instinct of self-preservation, by letting go the hands of the old tutor, and turning round, they immediately dived into one of the adjoining alleys.

It was just in time, for at that moment, two musket balls whizzed so close to them that the difference of a mere inch would have been certain death.

It was a narrow escape for them ; but once out of sight of the soldiers, they finally reached a place of perfect safety, and after all, as Harry remarked—

"A miss is as good as a mile."

Meanwhile, Mole's catalogue of misfortunes were still being added to.

Picked up, bleeding and exhausted, by the soldiers, he was instantly taken before the officer commanding the troops.

Several Arabs, a few Turkish soldiers, and two of the gaolers had been killed, and there were many wounded men that required attending to.

The commander had enough to do in restoring matters to order, therefore he left the punishment of Mole to his lieutenant.

"Remove all the prisoners, for the present, to the guard-room," said the lieutenant. "When I open my council at noon in the divan, bring them all before me."

"Your excellency's word is law," answered the head gaoler, bowing.

The lieutenant turned his horse, and, followed by his body-guard, rode home in a very ill temper.

An hour or two's rest, however, and the soothing effects of pipe and coffee, had somewhat restored his equanimity by the time he re-entered the divan.

Punctually at noon, the prisoners were brought before him by the head gaoler.

"Let me see," said the lieutenant, referring to the document, and checking off the captives as they were identified ; "horse stealing, highway robbery, drunkenness, assault—yes, I have resolved what to do. As these offences seem comparatively light, and as our prison is for the present inefficient, I shall order all these men to be punished with the bastinado."

"There is one more," said the lieutenant. "This, I find, is the wretched Frank who dared to personate our great pasha."

"Nothing escapes your honour's penetration," answered the vizier.

"Such a crime deserves a heavier punishment. However, when his turn comes, give him twenty-five blows."

"It shall be done, illustrious governor," was the response.

And forthwith were summoned the two burly officials whose unpopular duty it was to administer castigation.

One bore a stout rattan, the other several pieces of strong rope.

The frame to which they were to be lashed was then brought into the room, it being the lieutenant's intention that the punishment should be administered in his presence.

The first prisoner was then seized and his slippers—stockings not being worn by the majority of Turks—taken off.

He was then bound hand and foot, and securely tied to the frame.

The two executioners then took it in turns to administer ten heavy blows upon the bare soles of the criminal.

At the first blow, the "patient" set up a howl, which seemed but to increase the vigour and energy of the "operator."

It was indeed a terrible sight for any person of sensitiveness to see a human being—though deserving—suffer in this manner.

Mole, however, didn't feel any anxiety on that score, and he made up his mind to do the brave and noble Englishman, for he knew that they might hammer away at his cork soles for ever, without hurting him much.

What troubled him was the probability that they would take his stockings off, and discovering the insensate nature of his "understandings," order him some other and more deadly punishment.

So, after the infliction of seeing several men suffer, with various degrees of bravery and cowardice, and all variety of groans and contortions, Mole heard himself called up for similar castigation.

He had, in the meantime, thought of a *ruse.*

Then, marching up boldly to the lieutenant, he addressed him—

"I know I fully deserve your dreadful but just sentence, and quietly will I submit myself to the torture ; but, I entreat you, do not compel me to remove my stockings, which, among my countrymen, is considered the deepest degradation, and never inflicted, save upon criminals sentenced to death."

"H'm!" said the lieutenant, somewhat moved. "For my part, I would just as soon suffer the infliction with bare feet as through a thin layer of stocking."

"But my feelings as an Englishman," pleaded Mole.

"Well, be it as you wish. Take off your

shoes only ; but, Hamed, remember to give it to him a little harder, to make up for the stockings."

" Great lieutenant, I will obey. The force of the blows shall be doubled."

At this moment, Mole saw the eyes of Tinker fixed upon him, and he should yet get help.

Mole then submitted himself resignedly to the hands of the torturers.

Binding him like the others, hand and foot, they tied him to the frame, and the chief castigator, rolling up his sleeves, proceeded to belabour Mole's soles with terrific energy.

The blows sounded fearfully loud and sharp, and each was given with such vigour that even the framework creaked under it.

But the victim showed no pain or terror.

He did not cry out, nor flinch in the least, nor strive to mitigate the pain by twisting about.

Thus ten heavy blows were given, and the inflictor paused.

A murmur of astonishment ran round the assembly.

" Truly the Frank hath wondrous strength and courage," exclaimed the lieutenant.

" Englishmen are generally brave," said an old Turk ; " but I never knew one who would silently undergo such pain as this."

" Make the next ten blows harder."

The second man, therefore, in his turn, rained down upon the inanimate soles of the ex-pasha, such fearful blows as resounded through the place, and made many spectators shudder.

But still the victim neither flinched nor cried out.

" *Bismillah !* this is truly wonderful, that a giaour so old, so grey, so apparently feeble, should thus bear so terrible a punishment. Harder, Selim. Now do you not feel it, prisoner ?"

" Of course I feel it, great pasha ; it even tickles my beard," replied Mole ; " but Heaven hath given me power to withstand this terrible torture, and the high spirit of an Englishman forbids me to cry out."

" I could scarcely have believed it, did I not behold it with my own eyes," said the puzzled lieutenant. " Selim, a little harder."

" Your eminence, the tale of blows is fully counted," said the man, laying aside his cane.

" Five-and-twenty already ? I was so interested with the prisoner's fortitude, that I didn't count them. He has not suffered enough yet ; give him five blows more."

" I am ready," said Mole, stroking his false beard. " Remember, an Englishman fears not pain. Strike away."

And he stretched out his cork legs to their full extent.

Five blows more were given, but had no more effect than the previous ones.

" By the holy Kaaba ! but this amounts to a miracle," exclaimed the lieutenant. " I shall begin to respect the infidel for his heroism. Hamed, give him ten more blows ; no, make it twenty, and do you, Selim, assist. That will be fifty ; just double the amount of the sentence. If he flinches not this time, he will deserve being let off altogether."

And in truth, it would, under ordinary circumstances, have wanted well-nigh the strength of Samson or Hercules to endure such torture as now came upon the schoolmaster.

Hamed and Selim, each armed with a heavy rattan, rained down alternately thick and fast, a shower of blows upon Mole's wonderful feet, which even shook the room, but still couldn't shake Mole's resolution.

He writhed not, nor uttered cry, and showed not the faintest sign of giving way.

On the contrary, he jeered at the men.

" Bah ! see how an Englishman can bear pain," exclaimed Mole.

And to the intense astonishment of the Turks, he plucked out a good-sized handful of hair from his beard and threw before the officer.

" Allah is—ah !"

And the Turk stopped in the midst of his speech to spit out a second handful, which Mole, with good aim, had thrown into his mouth.

" Wonderful !" exclaimed the bystanders, as Mole tore away at his false beard till he had nearly stripped the framework, while the tormentors worked away at his feet with redoubled energy.

" Stop, stop," cried the pasha, for the men in their energy had exceeded even the fifty blows without knowing it, and seemed to be going on *ad libitum*, " stop ; unbind and release the prisoner."

The two men, who were bathed in perspiration through their exertions, accordingly removed Mole's bonds, assisted him to his feet, and helped him put on his shoes.

" Prisoner," said the lieutenant, " your heroic conduct this day has won my deepest admiration. Be seated, and rest your poor feet, and then tell me something of your history."

" My poor feet will still support me, therefore I will not be seated, but standing thus," said Mole, stamping his cork feet on the ground, " will show you something wonderful."

CHAPTER LXXIX.

MOLE PASHA ASTONISHES THE NATIVES STILL MORE—THE ORDER OF THE GLASS BUTTON.

" I AM all attention," replied the lieutenant.

" I come from a land," said Mr. Mole, with a grandiloquent flourish, " where we despise physical suffering."

The august Turks around were filled with wonder and with admiration for the speaker.

After what they had witnessed, they were prepared to credit Mr. Mole's most extravagant assertions.

" Would you have some further proof of my great courage ?" demanded Mr. Mole, folding his arms and striking a defiant attitude.

" Brave man, what more can you show us of your courage ?" was the reply.

" Behold !" cried Mole.

The whole assembly eyed Mr. Mole's movements with the greatest curiosity now.

" Bring me a dozen sharp implements, such as swords, knives, daggers, etc., etc."

They were brought to him, and he then laid them down in a row upon the carpet.

The first was a needle of the dimensions of an ordinary bodkin.

Next this, was a small iron skewer.

After this came a long-bladed dagger knife.

And finally, there was a cut-and-thrust sword of alarming dimensions.

"You shall see now," said Mole, sternly, "how I can despise such trivialities as your bastinado."

What was he about to do now?

In solemn silence, Mr. Mole bared his right calf, then requested the company of his black servant Tinker, who was still in the hall.

The request was granted.

"Tinker."

"Yes, Massa Mole."

"Go and fetch me——"

Here he sank his voice to a whisper, and the rest of his instructions were heard by no one save the darkey, for whom they were intended.

In the course of a few moments, Tinker returned and passed something slyly into Mr. Mole's hand.

It was a small sponge in an oil-skin bag.

Yet it appeared to be saturated with something, to judge by the way it was handled, for Mr. Mole slyly put it in his pocket.

Mr. Mole then took up the smallest of the row of implements just described.

"Behold what an Englishman can do!"

And then to the amazement of the spectators, he thrust the needle into the thick part of his calf.

A quiet smile played about the corners of his mouth.

But no sign of the slightest suffering.

"Judge how much your bastinado can affect me," he said, with superb disdain.

"Allah be praised!" ejaculated the Turk; "wondrous man."

"Behold," pursued Mole, picking up the skewer.

He passed it fairly through his calf, and stood there with his foot firmly planted on the ground, gazing about him like another "monarch of all he surveyed."

"Look again."

And Mole took up a large nail, and hammered it into his foot, so that he was pinned to the floor.

"Allah be praised!" again shouted the Turks.

"One more proof," he said, disdainfully.

He picked up another dagger, and pushed it resolutely into the ill-used leg.

At the same time he held the calf with his left hand, in which he concealed, with considerable dexterity, the sponge which Tinker had brought him.

Blood now trickled slowly through Mr. Mole's fingers, and ran down his legs and feet.

A thrill of terror passed through the assemblage.

"Yet another proof," exclaimed Mole, grandly.

"No more, no more," exclaimed the Turk.

Mole withdrew the nail from his foot, and the dagger from his leg, and seizing the sword, he thrust it with ferocious energy into the other mutilated leg.

He pressed his hand to the wound, and the blood flowed out in a small torrent, while the spectators groaned.

Mole looked around him proudly—defiantly.

Had he just conquered on the field of Waterloo, he could not have shown a greater apparent belief in himself.

He smiled sardonically as he bound up the wounded legs with his scarf.

Mr. Mole here nearly spoilt his exhibition of his marvellous power of endurance, for pricking his finger accidentally with a pin, he sang out lustily, much to the astonishment of the Turks.

But he was lucky to recover himself in time before the Turks could divine what had occurred.

"You must invent something more violent than any punishment I have yet seen here, if you would subdue the soul of Isaac Mole."

And he strode along with the air of the heavy man in a transpontine melodrama.

The marvellous exhibition of endurance aroused the phlegmatic Turk to real enthusiasm.

"Mole Pasha," he exclaimed, "you are a great hero. I shall seek an audience of his highness the Sultan, and beg of him for you some mark of distinction, perhaps even to confer upon you the distinguished order of the glass button."

"The glass bottle would be more in your excellency's way, Mole Pasha," suggested Tinker.

And henceforth when Mole walked abroad, the population was aroused.

"Behold the bravest Frank that ever lived," they said. "He is a great hero."

CHAPTER LXXX.

THE SNAKE IN THE GRASS—THE POISONED DAGGER.

As young Jack was sauntering through the streets of the town one day, he fancied that he was being followed by a man who was dressed in a semi-Oriental garb, but whose head was shaded by a broad-brimmed hat.

Jack was not given to fear without a cause, yet he certainly did feel uncomfortable now.

At first he thought of turning round and facing the man sharply.

But this, he reflected, might lead to a rupture.

A rupture was to be most carefully avoided.

He was determined, however, to assure himself that he was followed.

With this view, he made a circuitous tour of the city.

Still the man was there like his very shadow.

"This is unendurable," muttered Jack.

So he drew up short.

Grasping a pistol, which he carried in his pocket, with a nervous grip, he waited for the man to come up.

But the man did not come up.

He disappeared suddenly, at the very moment that Jack was expecting to come into collision with him.

How strange!

Jack was not conscious of having an enemy—at least, not one in that part of the world.

" Very strange," he muttered ; " very strange !"

And brooding over this episode, Jack wended his way thoughtfully homewards.

*   *   *   *   *

" Hah !"

Crossing the very threshold of his residence, Jack was suddenly and swiftly assaulted.

The same semi-oriental figure had stolen stealthily up behind him, and with a murderous-looking knife dealt him a sharp, swift blow.

Jack bounded forward, and turned round pistol in hand, but so nearly fatal had been the blow that Jack's coat was ripped down the back.

" Hah !"

The assassin was marvellously nimble ; although Jack made a dart after him pistol in hand, meaning to wreak summary vengeance upon him, the ruffian contrived to vanish again—mysteriously.

Strangely disturbed by this, Jack went home and related to his friends what had taken place.

" This is a rum go," said Mr. Mole ; " you have been mistaken for somebody else."

" So I suppose," returned Jack.

" What's to be done ?" said Harry Girdwood.

" Lodge information with the police at once, I should say," suggested Mole.

" By all means."

" What was he like ?"

" I could scarcely see," was Jack's reply, " for he was gone like a phantom."

" Perhaps it was a phantom," suggested Harry, slyly.

" I should be half inclined to think so," said Jack, " if I hadn't received this solid proof that he was flesh and blood."

Saying which, he turned round and displayed the back of his coat, ripped open by the assassin's dagger.

" Well," exclaimed Mole aghast, " that is cool."

" I'm glad you think so," returned Jack, " for I can tell you it was much too warm for me."

" Well, we shall soon leave this wretched place, I hope," said Mole, " for I don't feel safe of my life. I am expecting every day to be had up again before the pasha."

" We must always be on the watch now," said Harry Girdwood ; " constant vigilance will be necessary to avert danger."

*   *   *   *   *

Let us follow the movements of the would-be assassin.

The secret of his sudden disappearance was really no great mystery after all.

Darting round the first corner so as to put a house between himself and Jack's pistol, he found himself suddenly seized by a vigorous hand, and dragged through an open doorway.

" Let go," hissed the assassin, fiercely, " or——"

He raised his long-bladed knife to strike, but before he could bring his arm down, the dagger was beaten from his grasp.

" Now," said the stranger, planting his foot firmly upon the knife, " listen to me."

" You speak English," said the assassin, in surprise.

" Because you spoke English to me," was the reply ; " until then, I took you for one of us."

" What do you want with me ?" demanded the Englishman, doggedly.

" Not much," returned the other, speaking with great fluency, although his foreign accent was strongly marked. " I have saved you from the consequences of your failure. Had my friendly hand not been there to drag you out of sight, your young countryman would have shot you."

" Well," returned the assassin, surlily, " I owe you my thanks, and——"

" Stop—tell me would you like to succeed in this in spite of your late failure ?"

" Yes."

" Then I will give you a safe and sure method."

" My eternal thanks," began the foiled ruffian.

The stranger interrupted him.

" Reserve your thanks. Tell me what you can offer if I help you."

" Money !"

" How much will you give to see your enemy removed from your path ?"

" I will give a good round sum," returned the Englishman, eagerly.

" Name a sum."

He did.

A good round sum it was, too.

" Now, then," said the Turk, producing a small phial containing a pale greenish fluid. " Observe this."

" Well ?"

" Anoint your dagger with this. Scratch him with it ; let your scratch be no more than the prick of a pin, and he will be beyond the aid of mortal man."

" Is this sure ?"

" Beyond all doubt. " Would you have proof ?"

" Yes."

" Wait here a moment."

The Turk left the room, and presently he appeared carrying a small iron cage.

" Look."

He held up the cage, and showed that it contained two large rats.

" Now," said he, " remove the stopper and dip your dagger's point in."

The Englishman obeyed.

" Now, prick either of the rats ever so slightly."

The Englishman pushed the point of the dagger through the bars of the cage, and one of the rats came to sniff at it—probably anticipating a savoury tit-bit to eat.

Moving the dagger slightly, it barely grazed the rat's nose.

But it sufficed.

The poor beast shivered once, and sank dead.

" What do you say now ?" demanded the Turk.

" I am satisfied," replied the Englishman.

" Now, before you go," said the Turk, " I will give you a hint. The slightest scratch will suffice, as you see."

" Yes."

" Dip two ordinary pins in the poison, and send them by letter to your enemy. Place them so that in opening the envelope, he will probably scratch his finger."

The Englishman's eyes sparkled viciously.

" I will, I will."

" Let me know the result, and should you want my aid, you will note well the house on leaving so as to know where to return."

" Yes. What is your name?" demanded the Englishman.

" Hadji Nasir Ali," was the reply; " and yours?"

The other hesitated.

" Don't give it unless you feel it is safe," said the Turk.

" There's no harm in your knowing it," returned the Englishman. " My name is Harkaway."

" Hark-a-way?"

" In one word."

" I see. Farewell, then."

" Farewell."

And the interview was concluded.

* * * * *

" That letter is a splendid dodge. Look out, Master Jack Harkaway, look out, for I mean to cry quits now, or my name is not Herbert Murray," muttered the Englishman, as he walked away.

But how Herbert Murray had got to Turkey requires some explanation.

It will be within our readers' recollection that after his unsuccessful attempt on Chivey's life, and the adventure of the groom with the old Spaniard, Murray found himself on board the same ship as his groom.

He resolved to make the best of this circumstance, as it could not now be altered.

A few days after leaving the Spanish coast they put into one of the Mediterranean ports, and there heard that young Jack and his friends had gone on to Turkey.

" I'll follow them!" exclaimed Murray. " I can do as I like now the governor's gone and I've plenty of tin, so look out for yourself, Jack Harkaway."

Murray's ship was delayed by adverse weather, but at length reached port, and Herbert had scarcely put foot on shore, when he beheld young Jack, the object of his deadly hate, walking coolly down the street smoking a cigar.

This so enraged Murray that he hastened to disguise himself in Oriental attire, and then made the attempt on Jack's life which we have related.

* * * * *

That same night a man was found dead on the threshold of the house in which Jack Harkaway and his friends resided.

How he had died no one could imagine, for he had not a scratch on his body.

Yet, stay.

There was a scratch.

Just that and no more.

In his fast-clenched hand was found an envelope addressed to Mr. John Harkaway, and on a closer examination a pin's point was seen sticking through the paper.

This had just pricked the messenger's hand.

So slightly that, had not the tiny wound turned slightly blue, it would have entirely escaped notice.

* * * * *

Jack was now aware that he had in Turkey a deadly enemy, but who he was he could not yet tell.

When the men of skill assembled around the body, they were puzzled to assign a cause of death until one of them suggested it was apoplexy. So apoplexy it was unanimously set down for.

There was no more fuss made.

The man was only a poor devil of a Circassian, who got a precarious livelihood as a public messenger. So they

" Rattled his bones
Over the stones,
Like those of a pauper whom nobody owns."

And meanwhile, his murderer went his way.

" Fortunate I gave the name of Harkaway to that old professional poisoner, for they will never trace this job to me."

There was, however, one result from this using of Jack Harkaway's name which Herbert Murray certainly never contemplated.

But of this we must speak hereafter.

* * * *

In spite of his knowledge of the fact that he had enemies following his footsteps, our hero would not remain in the house.

" I am quite as safe in the street as here," said he, in reply to Harry Girdwood's representations of the danger he ran, " and I am sure, old boy, you would not have me show the white feather."

" You never did that, and never will; but you need not run into unnecessary danger."

" ' Thrice is he armed who has his quarrel just,' and his revolver well loaded. Ta-ta! I am just going to stroll down to this Turkish substitute for a post office, and see if last night's steamer brought any letters."

So Jack strolled down accordingly, and found a letter for him.

His heart beat with joy as he recognised the handwriting, and he hurried home to read it.

On breaking open the envelope, out tumbled a beautiful carte de visite portrait, a copy of which we are able to give, as we still thoroughly retain young Jack's friendship and confidence.

He kissed it till he began to fear he might spoil the likeness, and then placing it on the table before him, began to read.

And this is the letter—

" DEAR JACK, — *You very naughty boy. Where have you been, and why have you not written? I have a great mind to scold you, sir; but on second thoughts, I think I had better leave the task of correcting you to your parents, who, perhaps, have more influence with you than I have. You don't know, dear, how anxious we have all been about you. Poor Mr. Mole has started in search of you. Have you seen him yet?—and if you don't write soon, I shall feel obliged to try and find out what has become of you, for I almost begin to fear that some fair Turkish or Circassian girl——*"

" The deuce!" Jack thought; " she can't have heard anything of that affair yet. If

Mole has written, the letter could not have reached England on the 20th of last month."

Then he continued—

"——has stolen your heart, and Harry Girdwood's too. Why, poor Paquita always has red eyes when she gets up. So, darling Jack, do write at once, and cheer our hearts. I can't help writing like this, for I feel so fearful that something has happened to you. So be a dear, good boy, and send a full account of all your doings to your father, and just a few lines to

"Your ever faithful and affectionate

"EMILY.

"P.S.—I was just reading this over to see if I had been too cross, when your father came in with a photographer, who took my portrait without my knowing anything about it. Do you think it like me, sir?"

Then followed three or four of those blots which ladies call "kisses."

CHAPTER LXXXI.

MR. MOLE AGAIN OUT OF LUCK.

HERBERT MURRAY, attended by Chivey, was strolling down the principal street of the town, smoking his cigar, thinking how he could yet serve out young Jack, when he suddenly saw, on in front, the figure of an elderly man, who appeared to walk with difficulty.

He made such uncertain steps and singular movements, as he hobbled along by the aid of a stick, that the effect, however painful to him, was ludicrous to the on-lookers.

"Why, blest if it ain't old Mole, the man who came to bid young Harkaway and his friends good-bye when we sailed," cried Chivey.

"Or his ghost," said Murray.

"I'll have a lark with him, sir," said the tiger, laying his finger aside his nose, and winking knowingly. "You see!"

And walking nimbly and on tiptoe behind the old man, he soon caught up to him without his knowing it.

Murray halted at a little distance, ready to behold and enjoy the discomfiture of Mole.

The reader must be informed that the venerable Isaac was then experimenting upon a new substitute for those unfortunate much-damaged members, his cork legs.

An American genius, with whom he had recently made acquaintance in the town, had induced Mole to try a pair of his "new patent-elastic-spring-non-fatiguing-self-regulating-undistinguishable-everlasting cork legs."

The inventor had helped Mr. Mole to put on these formidable "understandings," and given him every instruction with regard to their management.

"They'll be a little creaky at first," said the American; "nothing in nature works slick when it's quite new, but when you get 'em well into wear, they'll go along like greased lightning; now try them, old hoss."

Creaky indeed they were, for they made a noise almost as loud as a railway break; but what was even worse was that the Yankee had failed to inform Mole of the fact that the "new patent" etc., were only fitted to act perfectly on a smooth surface.

Now the roadway, or footway—for they are all the same in those old Turkish towns—are the very reverse of smooth, being principally composed of round nubbly stones.

Consequently Mole's locomotion was the reverse of pleasant.

Chivey crept up behind the old schoolmaster, and seizing an opportunity and one of his legs, gave it a pull, which caused Mole to roar with fright.

Down, of course, came Mole on the nubbly pavement, but Chivey didn't have exactly the fun he expected, for instead of his getting safely away, Mole fell on him.

"Oh, it's you, is it? You, the bad servant of a bad man's wicked son," exclaimed the angered tutor; "it's you who dare to set upon defenceless age and innocence, with its new cork legs on? Very good. Then take that, and I hope you won't like it."

Whereat he began pommelling away at Chivey.

Chivey roared with all his might, till a small crowd of wondering onlookers began to collect.

"What do you mean by daring to assault my servant in this manner?" asked Murray sternly, as he came up.

"He attacked me first," protested Mole; "and it's my belief you set him on to do it."

"How dare you insinuate——" began Murray, and he violently shook the old man by the collar.

But there was more spirit in Mole than Herbert was prepared for.

By the aid of a post, the old man managed to struggle to his feet, and leaning against this, he felt he could defy the enemy.

"My lad," he said, "it's evident that you didn't get enough flogging when you were at school, or you'd know better manners; I must take you in hand a bit now, sir, there!"

With his stick he gave a cut to the palm of Murray's hand, just as he was wont to do to refractory pupils in the old days.

Murray was livid with rage.

Chivey, now rather afraid of Mole, didn't interfere.

"Come on, if you like, and have some more," said Mole, and shaking his stick at both of them, he again urged on his wild career.

Very wild indeed it was, too.

Mole's patent legs, which outwardly looked natural ones, were indeed self-regulating, for they were soon utterly beyond the control of the wearer; they seemed to be possessed of wills of their own; one wished to go to the right, the other to the left.

Sometimes they would carry him along in double quick march time, and anon halt, beyond all his power of budging.

Of course the boys of the town were attracted by the stranger's singular movements, and began to hoot and jeer.

The merchants were interrupted at their calculations, the bazaar keepers came to their doors, long pipe in mouth, to see what the "son of Sheitan" was about.

Mole was red in the face with such hard work.

"Confound the Turks," he cried; "why don't they make their roads smoother? Oh dear, I wish I could manage these unhappy legs; there they go."

By this time the crowd had become unpleasantly dense around him.

"Out of the way, un-Christian dogs," cried Mole, flourishing his stick round his head; "I'm an Englishman, and I've a right to—hallo! there it goes again."

For here his left leg took two steps to the right, and he came down with all his weight upon the toe of a white-bearded Alla-hissite.

"Son of a dog," growled the old Turk, as he rubbed his pet corn in agony; "may your mother's grave be defiled, and the jackass bray over your father's bones."

"I really beg your pardon," began Mole, but just at this moment his right leg was taken with a spasmodic action, and began to stride along at a furious rate, creaking like mad.

Mole lost all control (if he ever had any) over his own movements, and was carried forward again, till he came where Herbert Murray and Chivey, having made a *détour*, happened to be just turning the corner of the street.

"Stop me," yelled Mole, as he flourished his stick over his head; "my spring legs are doing what they like with me. I have no control over them. Oh, dear, they are at it again."

Chivey, undeterred by his recent castigation, thought he would repeat the trick, so, when Mole came up, he, by a dexterous jerk, turned him round as on a pivot.

He was thus stopped in his forward course, but this didn't check the action of his clock-work legs, which now scudded along as swiftly as before, into the very heart of the yelling crowd.

The result was rather bad for the Turks; they went down like a lot of ninepins before Mole's railway-like progression.

"A mad Christian," they cried; "he is possessed with a devil; down with him."

The perspiration streamed from Mole's face; he felt that if the spring-work in his new cork legs did not stop, he should die.

At this moment a body of women approached, closely veiled.

Their *yashmaks* obscured all but their eyes, which could be seen to open wide in wonder at the extraordinary behaviour of the red-faced giaour.

Two of the younger and slender ones fell with piercing screams before Mole's impetuous charge.

A third, a stout woman of middle age, stood her ground, and Mole, before he could stop himself, rushed into her arms, and floored her.

The scream she gave surpassed in loudness that of all the others put together; and brought up several ferocious-looking Turks, bent on condignly punishing the outrageous conduct of the mad Englishman.

"Death to the giaour; down with him!" roared the excited crowd.

What fate he would have suffered we dread to think, but he found an unexpected deliverer in the person of the old white-bearded Turk, whose corns he had trodden on.

"Defile not your hands with the blood of the unbeliever," he said; "but take him before the cadi to answer his conduct."

"To the cadi, to the cadi!" was now the cry.

"Hear me," said Mole, astonishing himself by his proficiency in Turkish; "I am not to blame, but at all events, take up those two other Englishmen who assaulted me."

He pointed to Murray and Chivey, who had by this time got into a dense crowd of Turks, whom they were elbowing in an angry manner.

"Take all the infidels before the cadi," cried the Turks.

Herbert Murray and Chivey were accordingly seized, and the whole three borne off to one doom.

The cadi was seated in his divan, administering justice, as was his custom, in the open air.

His style of doing so was summary, but vigorous.

"Let the giaour, who has unwarrantably assaulted the true believers, receive one hundred lashes," he said; "or pay fifty pieces of silver to our treasury."

"I haven't got the money," said Mole.

"Then receive the punishment," said the cadi.

This time there was no ceremony used; two negroes bound Mole, pulled off his shoes and stockings, and exposed to view the new patent steel clock-work legs.

"Allah, what have we here?" cried the cadi. "Is the Christian enchanted, to be half man, half machinery?"

"My lord," said Mole, "if you'll only permit me to speak, I'll explain all.

"Having lost my legs in the wars, helping the Turks to beat their foes, I have been induced to try as a substitute this new invention, and behold, the legs were enchanted, and I had no control over them."

"Allah kerim! Can this be?" exclaimed the cadi.

"That was the whole reason of my conduct, your excellency," pursued Mole; "otherwise, I would perish sooner than have attacked true believers. But these infidels," he added, pointing to Murray and Chivey, "first attacked me, as many here may bear witness."

"If that be so," said the magistrate, "we will remit your sentence on payment of fifty sequins."

"Gladly would I pay the sum if I had it," said Mole; "but I haven't."

"Search him," cried the cadi.

Mole was searched, but the investigations of the officer could not bring to light a greater sum in his pockets than a bad sixpence and a battered fourpenny-piece.

"Little enough," grumbled the cadi, pocketing the amount; "but as it is all you have, I consent to take it. We must have it out of the other infidels; they too are English, and look rich. Bring them before me."

Herbert Murray and Chivey were accordingly examined.

Mole gave evidence as to their assaulting him, though they utterly denied doing so, but Mole's statement being backed up by several believers who had witnessed it, the judge declared both guilty, and sentenced them to the bastinado.

"Me bastinadoed!" exclaimed the indignant Murray. "I'd have you know, sir, that I'm an Englishman of rank, of influence, of property, and——"

"Of influence, eh? Very good; then you'll have to pay a fine of five hundred sequins," cried the cadi, exultantly.

"I swear that I haven't——"

"Search the infidels," cried the cadi.

The officers did so, and altogether twenty-five pounds, in gold, notes and silver, were found upon Murray and Chivey.

With an audible chuckle, the cadi took possession of it all.

"There," he said; "so now go in peace, all of you; and if I find you making another disturbance in the town, it will be bastinado and gaol, as well as a fine. Go, infidels, and remember the grand Turk."

CHAPTER LXXXII.

THE CONSPIRATORS—THE DEED—THE FALSE INFORMERS.

THE walls of Alla-hissar gleamed in the noontide heat.

The air was heavy with sleep, which weighed upon all living things, and made them seek shelter from the burning sun.

All was still in the city.

It seemed as if the spirit of death brooded over all the habitations.

Yet there were some awake at that dreary hour.

Gathered together at one of the principal houses in secret conclave were some of the chief Turks of the province.

In spite of the heat, the heavy curtains covered the doorways.

The door was shaded, and the assembly spoke in subdued tones.

At length Ibrahim Bey, a grave old Turk, subtle and resolute, arose.

"It is sacred then, friends," he said, looking round at the assembly; "the deed must be done, and the hour is at hand."

"Such is the will of Allah," was the reply of the conspirators.

"'Tis decided then, that Moley Pasha, our new governor, has, since he has assumed power, done all he could to destroy our old customs, and introduce the manners of the infidel Franks, therefore he must die."

"He must die," murmured the assembly,

"Allah's will be done," said old Ibrahim, turning up his eyes piously; "but by whose hand shall the blow be struck? Who will take upon himself the dangerous deed?"

Up rose Abdullah, the interpreter, formerly of Mr. Mole's party.

"I will do it," he said, in a firm voice; "he dies ere another hour has sped. I will risk the deadly danger, if you will guarantee, that if I succeed, I shall be rewarded."

"That is but just," said Ibrahim Bey. "Should it be his sacred majesty's pleasure that I succeed Moley, a post of honour shall be the guerdon of your bravery."

"I accept the terms," said Abdullah; "I know a secret way into the palace, I have a disguise and a dagger; doubt not my courage for the rest. Wait here, my friends, and ere another hour strikes, I shall return to say the deed is done."

He glided from the room, leaving the others wondering at the cool audacity with which he undertook so desperate and criminal a deed.

The angel of sleep had spread her wings over the seraglio of Moley Pasha.

The veiled beauties of the harem had retired to their luxurious rooms.

The pasha slept soundly and peacefully.

Well for him had his dreams warned him against the peril that hovered over him like a black shadow.

For the form of a woman, tall, thin, closely-veiled, glided along the passages of the harem.

Her steps gave forth no sound, and she disturbed not the sleeping servants.

She glided like a smooth serpent, or an invisible spirit; her presence was unseen, unfelt, unsuspected.

She enters the inner chamber where lies the unconscious pasha.

She bends over him, she draws forth a knife, slender, tapering to a point almost like a needle.

The pasha still slept on, the fountain outside made sweet music, heard through the curtains and windows.

A smile played upon the pasha's lips.

He was dreaming, perchance, of the rosy bowers and the dark-eyed *houris* of Paradise.

Suddenly the knife descended, there was the flash of a moment, while it hovered like a hawk over its quarry, the next instant it was buried in the pasha's heart.

A deep groan was the only effort of expiring nature.

The fiercely flashing eyes, and a part of the face of the murderer were now exposed; the dress was that of a woman, but the form and features were those of Abdullah the interpreter.

For a moment he stood gazing on his deed, then lifted some tapestry which concealed a small door, and disappeared.

*   *   *   *   *

What cry was that which startles the seraglio from its siesta?

What combined lamentation disturbs the whole palace with its harrowing intensity?

All the inmates of the establishment have been rudely awakened from their slumbers.

It was the pasha's favourite wife who had broken in upon the privacy of her lord, and she had found him dead.

Dead, plainly by the assassin's dagger, but what assassin, none could even suspect.

None could conjecture by what means any stranger could have obtained entrance and exit.

Then arose that dreadful wail of despair, that beating of breasts, and tearing of tresses.

The news soon spread, and the whole town was in a fever of commotion.

Who had done the deed ?

Who was to be Moley Pasha's successor ?

The conspiraotrs played their parts well.

Ibrahim Bey pretended to be terribly amazed and shocked ; he refused to be placed at the head of affairs until the sultan's will should be known, and he offered rewards for the discovery of the assassin.

A council, consisting of Ibrahim and others, was now established to temporarily rule the town.

A grand funeral, at which all the dignitaries of the place attended, was given to the unfortunate pasha, the evening after his assassination.

The same night arrived a firman from the sultan, proclaiming Ibrahim Pasha of Alla-hissar.

Such is the perilous nature of power and dignity in Eastern lands.

Ibrahim at once appointed Abdullah his vizier, and gave all the other conspirators important posts.

Several perfectly innocent men were arrested and hanged on a pretended suspicion of having caused the late pasha's death.

At the first divan held by the new pasha, two Englishmen were announced, who were said to be the bearers of important evidence about the murder.

They were admitted accordingly, and proved to be no others than Murray and Chivey.

"Christians, you are welcome," said Ibrahim, through his new vizier. "Allah in his wisdom hath sent you hither, wherefore discover your knowledge."

Murray bowed, and seated himself upon a chair pointed out to him by the pasha.

Chivey, as a servant, wasn't honoured with a seat, whereat he murmured, half to himself—

"Well, they might let a cove sit down, and if they offered us a drop of something cool this hot weather, it wouldn't come unwelcome."

Reclining on his divan in the old Turkish style, and smoking his *hookah*, Ibrahim listened to Murray's communication.

"It may already be known to your excellency that there is in your dominions a young scapegrace of an Englishman, named Jack Harkaway. He has surrounded himself with many doers of evil, worse even than himself, amongst whom is an old scoundrel, formerly a schoolmaster, who, though he has lost both his legs, still continues to go about, and get into mischief."

"The audacious giaour who dared to impersonate Moley Pasha ?" asked Ibrahim.

"The same," continued Murray. "Well, I have received proofs that it was this Harkaway and his friend who murdered the real Moley Pasha."

"Shade of Eblis !" exclaimed Ibrahim, pretending to be much shocked. "This must be seen to ; Christian, proceed."

"Harkaway was once my friend," continued Murray, "and it is quite against my will to speak against him ; but my love of justice is above all other considerations."

"Christian," said Ibrahim, "proceed."

"In the harem of your illustrious predecessor," said Murray, "there lately resided a Greek girl, of exquisite beauty, named Thyra, a pearl of delight, a peri of Paradise, and she was bewitched by this Harkaway, who, how we know not, penetrated within the sacred precincts of his highness's harem, and stole her away."

"Vengeance of Allah ! but he deserves death !" exclaimed the pasha, half rising, and his eyes flashing with anger.

"But, your eminence, to make his crime complete, he committed another ; he stabbed the pasha to the heart."

"By the sword of the prophet, he dies !" exclaimed Ibrahim ; "but what proof hast thou of all this ?"

"I can bring several witnesses to the truth of what I say," said Murray. "If any other proof were wanting, Thyra, the pearl beyond price, disappeared from the palace the very day, the very hour of the pasha's death, and she is now at the residence of Harkaway and his friends."

"Please, your worship," here broke in Chivey, "if you'll let me have my talk, I'll prove it, as sure as eggs are eggs."

"The giaour's servant entreats your highness to listen to the words of truth," was the way in which the astute Abdullah translated this appeal.

Chivey gave his evidence, a story carefully concocted between him and his master, and to this was added the confirmation of several natives of the town, men who would swear black was white, for a dollar or two.

Of course, old Mole was represented as Harkaway's chief adviser, and his aider and abettor in the late pasha's death.

This story, of course, did not really impose upon Ibrahim Pasha ; he knew more of the actual facts than Murray could do, but it served his turn to pretend to believe it, so he thanked Murray for his information.

Abdullah (the real assassin) was so profound a dissembler, so utterly devoid of conscience, that he put down, at Murray's dictation, the names of the innocent Harkaway and his friends, remarking calmly—

"I think we have got hold of the right criminals at last."

"We will send and have them arrested at once," said Ibrahim. "Vizier, let these Christians be rewarded for their information by a purse of gold, and despatch an armed force to the lair of those English dogs, who have slain my lamented predecessor. And, vizier, don't forget, whatever you do, to bring the beautiful Thyra to me."

"Pasha, to hear is to obey," said Abdullah.

"Ha ha ! I think we've done for the Harkaway party this time," said Murray gleefully to Chivey.

"It was a capital dodge, I must say," answered Chivey, " although my belief is that Ibrahim Passher is an old rascal, and knows who really did for the last governor."

"Keep all such suspicions to yourself," said Murray.

In a short time the captain of the pasha's guards, with a detachment of troops, marched out to arrest our hero and his friends.

The news spread like wildfire that the murderers of the late pasha had at length been discovered.

CHAPTER LXXXIII.

JACK HAS TO STAND A SIEGE.

AND how far were Jack Harkaway and his friends really guilty in this matter?

It was indeed true that Thyra, the beautiful Greek slave before alluded to, had fled from the harem of the late pasha.

But this had nothing at all to do with his assassination.

No doubt Thyra cherished a strong attachment for young Jack, having found a refuge in the same house.

She could not overcome it.

"I throw myself upon your protection," she said. "If I returned to my master's, my fate would be instant death, but that would be preferable to live without you, and be for ever separated from you."

Jack was much embarrassed.

He told her, gently as he could, that her love was hopeless.

"Oh, do not say that," cried Thyra, bursting into tears. "Do not send me away; I'm ready to be your slave, and obey your every word."

Jack consulted with his friends under this difficult and delicate condition of affairs, and they all agreed that Thyra must not be given up to the pasha.

An hour afterwards, the report of his murder made matters still more serious.

But he never dreamed that any suspicion of the actual crime would be turned against himself.

It was therefore agreed to keep Thyra in close concealment, until an opportunity offered to get her back to her friends.

The house occupied by Harkaway and his friends, was, like most Oriental edifices, built for endurance.

The walls were thick and strong as those of a castle.

The doorway was narrow, and led into a square courtyard or garden, and with a fountain in the centre.

Into this yard most of the rooms opened.

The windows facing the street were mere loopholes.

The roof was flat, and in the evening formed a favourite lounge, approached by a flight of steps, from one angle of the court.

It is necessary to be particular in describing the house, that our readers may fully understand what follows.

Jack Harkaway was one morning in the courtyard, near the centre, with Harry Girdwood, looking at a heap of curious weapons, which they had purchased when roaming about the bazaars.

"Why, we've got quite an armoury here," said Harry Girdwood. "It's a pity we haven't got some fighting to do to use them."

"I mean to make the place into a kind of fortress," said Jack. "Here, Bogey."

"What you after, Massa Jack?" asked the nigger, appearing instantly.

"Go and take charge of the gate, and don't let anyone pass in or out without my order."

"Right you are, massa; me keep him safe as a sentrybox," answered the darkey.

And he started off to take up the post assigned to him.

Jack next summoned Tinker.

"Serve us up our dinner here under the trees," said Jack; "and be quick about it, you rascal, or——"

"Understand puffeckly, massa," responded the black. "To hear yer is to obey yer, as dese Turkeys say. Yah, yah!"

It was very pleasant to sit down to their repast under the refreshing shade of the trees.

Of course Mr. Mole and the orphan, as well as Thyra, the waiter and the diver, were summoned and came at this juncture.

The orphan and Mole appeared arm-in-arm.

Mr. Mole had a black bottle in one hand and a tall glass in the other.

He looked very jolly, whilst the orphan appeared rather melancholy, for his flute had got slightly cracked.

"Have a drop to raise your spirits," said the schoolmaster, filling him a brimmer, and fairly forcing it into his hand.

The orphan could not refuse so pressing an invitation.

He drained the glass, and as it came upon the top of several more, its effect upon him was not inconsiderable.

Intending to walk straight to the table, he walked, instead, extremely "slantindicular," till lurching up against the fountain as he passed it, he stumbled over its ledge, and fell with a splash into the middle of its basin.

Mr. Mole, with the best intentions in the world, rushed to his companion's rescue.

Before Mole could reach the orphan, his patent legs being still uncontrollable, and his head unsteady also, he fell backwards, smashing his wine bottle on the stones of the courtyard.

The scene was certainly ludicrous, and elicited much laughter from the spectators.

They, however, helped the orphan out of his accidental and very unwelcome bath, which, though it had drenched him, had also sobered him.

Mole was also assisted to re-assume an erect posture, and in a short time, both of them were sufficiently recovered to take their places at the table.

Mole and Figgins seemed somewhat struck by the warlike appearance of the place.

"What are you going to do with all that cutlery?" inquired Mr. Mole.

"Perhaps you mean to set up in the scissors trade?" suggested the orphan.

"You'll see by-and-bye, old man," answered our hero. "We shall find 'em useful, perhaps sooner than you expect."

"Oh, dear! I hope not," exclaimed Figgins. "I'm sure I don't want any more fighting; I have had more than is good for my health."

The waiter now took up his accustomed duty of attending on the guests.

The diver, at Jack's request, summoned Thyra, whose classic features, slender form, and Eastern garb, were well in keeping with the scene around.

A seat of honour was kept for her at the *al fresco* banquet, to which Jack gallantly conducted her.

No one could doubt her love for him, for it

shone out in her slightest action, her very words, and look, and tone. It seemed a pity that he could not return it, otherwise than by studied politeness and consideration.

To be at his side, to hear the sound of his voice, was her greatest happiness, and made her forget all other dangers and troubles.

When towards the conclusion of the meal, Jack proceeded to—

"Fill high the bowl with Samian wine,"

and hand it to Thyra, it was to her a moment of supreme pleasure.

Her dark eyes sparkled, her soft cheek flushed, and her jewelled fingers trembled as they held the crystal glass, filled with what, for his sake, and independent of its own nature, was to her as the nectar of the gods.

"Hark! What noise is that?" asked Jack, with such suddenness, that Thyra spilt some of the wine ere it could reach her lips.

There was indeed a sound in the street like the blended hum of many voices, and tread of many feet, each moment becoming louder.

"Perhaps it is some procession," said Harry Girdwood.

"Or a march round of the troops before the new pasha," said Mole. "Oh, how I pity him."

"No, there's something up more dreadful than that, I am sure," exclaimed the orphan. "Oh, this terrible country. I'll go home to-morrow if they'll only let me."

"Here, Tinker, you black son of a gun; go up on the roof, and see what's the matter," said Jack.

The nigger ascended as nimbly as a monkey.

At that moment a thundering knock came at the outer gate.

"What you want?" asked Bogey, still acting as porter.

"Open, in the name of the pasha," said a stern voice outside.

Bogey replied not, but ran in to his master.

Tinker and he arrived breathless at the same moment.

"Awful lot o' soldiers—Turks—outside, big guns and swords, massa," said Tinker.

"Wants to come in here, too," added Bogey. "Hark! Oh, ain't they giving what for at the door? They're at it again, a-hammerin' away."

And the thundering knocking was repeated louder than before, and a stern voice demanding Thyra, the slave.

"Just as I feared," cried Jack; "they've found out where Thyra is, and have come to drag her back."

"Oh, powers of Heaven, protect us all!" she exclaimed, nervously clutching Jack's arms. "Am I unfortunate enough, dear Jack, to have brought you into this great peril? I entreat you to save yourselves by surrendering me; only do me one favour; let one of your number shoot me dead as soon as I am in the enemy's hands."

"Impossible, dear Thyra!" said Jack. "Do you think, as a Boy of England, it is possible for me to act in that cowardly way? No; we must make a gallant resistance. Surely we are well prepared; here are arms enough for all. Where's the Irish diver?"

"Here, your honour, ready for any row that's goin'."

"Mr. Mole, you can handle a gun," said Jack; "here is one that will just suit you."

The waiter and the orphan were also accommodated with weapons, but the orphan thought he would rather load the guns than fire them off.

"Quick! get all the movables, and place them against the gate," said Jack. "With its own strength, its bolts, and bars, and keys, and a barricade behind it, we can defy this band of Turks, or the sultan himself."

All gave a cheer at these defiant words, and proceeded with their impromptu fortification with great vigour.

"I'll go up on the roof and reconnoitre," said Harry.

And dangerous as was this duty, he proceeded to it with great alacrity.

In a few moments he came down, with much consternation on his face.

"This is a bad job, Jack," he said; "worse than I thought."

"How?" asked our hero.

"We are accused of murdering the pasha, as well as carrying off the young Greek girl. There are over a hundred of the pasha's troops on guard outside, with that scoundrel Abdullah at the head of them, and thousands of wild Moslem fanatics, thirsting for our blood."

"I will go and see for myself," cried young Jack.

"For Heaven's sake, don't," said Harry, restraining him; "it will be certain death, for you, as our leader, are the particular object of their animosity."

Thyra's entreaties were even more pressing.

She threw her arms round Jack's neck, and earnestly entreated him not to risk his life.

"Dear Thyra," cried Jack, "you shall not be taken. I will and must protect you."

He sprang up the stairway, and was soon on the roof.

It was a sight indeed to appal the stoutest heart.

As far as the eye could reach was an excited crowd, restless, furious, and thirsting for vengeance.

In the front were a body of troops, in the Turkish uniform, led by the captain of the guard, by whose side could be recognised the sinister countenance of Abdullah.

They caught sight of Jack Harkaway.

He was recognised.

A shout burst from a thousand throats; a deep, angry cry, like the roar of a tempestuous sea.

Thousands of eyes flashed upon him—the eyeballs gleaming white from out of the dusky skins.

"The murderer of the pasha!—the despoiler of the harem!" they cried. "Death, death to him, and all the Christians!"

Jack endeavoured to parley with them; but it was useless, until silence was obtained by the commands of the captain of the guard and Abdullah, who called out to Jack—

"Resistance is useless; surrender at once, or I will not answer for your life."

"If you want me, you must come and fetch me," returned dauntless Jack.

"Your blood be upon your own head, then," said Abdullah.

The captain gave the word of command, and the battering, for a while suspended, was recommenced upon the door below.

CHAPTER LXXXIV.

THE SIEGE—THE ESCAPE—A DESPERATE RUSE.

JACK now left his dangerous elevation, and returned to his friends.

"Quite as bad as it can be," he said; "there's nothing for it but to make a desperate resistance, and to die game."

The yells and shouts of the crowd outside were like the combined roar of a large herd of wild beasts.

The blows became more furious on the door.

It quivered beneath the repeated shocks; but its own strength, and that of the fastenings, and particularly the barricade behind it, still defied the efforts of the besiegers.

Suddenly the hammering ceased, the yells of the crowd subsided.

Then came a volley of musketry.

They were firing at the door.

The volleys came thick and fast; the woodwork, strong as it was, began to be penetrated by the bullets.

It was clear the place would soon be untenable.

Should the besiegers enter, all hope of escape would be over.

"At least, we'll return their fire," said Jack.

The windows in the wall facing the street were mere loopholes.

At each of these, Jack commanded one of his men to take his stand, and pick off the enemy with the rifle.

It was a dangerous game, but it served its purpose.

Several of the besiegers fell before the well-aimed shots of the besieged.

The Turks began to think that they were being opposed by a considerable force of well-armed men.

Their own shots failed to reach the highly-placed and narrow windows, which were now so many portholes for the fire of the besieged.

The captain and Abdullah accordingly ordered their troops to fall back.

The excited crowd gave a yell of disappointment.

"I do believe we've defeated them, after all," cried Harry Girdwood.

But it was only a lull in the storm—a fatal presage of overwhelming disaster.

The Turkish commanders now resolved to make certain of victory by bringing up a cannon.

If, by this means, their troops could once effect an entrance—and this was almost certain—what could stop their progress?

What were Harkaway's mere handful of men against the thousands they would have to encounter?

Once more, and at greater peril than ever, Jack went on the housetop to reconnoitre.

He laid himself down flat that he might not be seen, but yet contrived to take a rapid glance of the position.

The house was detached on three sides; the fourth side was built against the wall of a mosque.

Upon those three sides the building was entirely surrounded by troops.

The only chance of escape would be by the mosque.

But how was this to be effected?

The wall of the sacred building rose high above that of the house.

Jack raised himself to examine it more closely.

A flash—a report—and the whiz of a bullet told him that he was observed.

A volley followed from all sides.

It would therefore be impossible for his party to raise a ladder, and thus escape from their own roof on to that of the mosque.

Jack, the bullets whistling thickly around him, managed to crawl unhurt to the trap-door and again descend into the courtyard.

"Well, Jack, what think you of the situation now?" asked Harry.

"Desperate, indeed."

"They gave you a very warm reception, my boy," said Mr. Mole.

"It will be warmer still when they capture us," said Harkaway.

"Oh, gracious, gracious! how shall we ever get out of this? Oh, dear! oh, dear! I wish I was in London once more," cried the orphan, wringing his hands.

His distress contrasted strongly with the calm, self-possessed demeanour of the beautiful Thyra at this time of supreme peril.

"There is but one thing we can do," said Jack.

"What is that?" asked Harry, anxiously.

"Break through that wall and get into the mosque; that's the only side of the building which isn't surrounded."

"But it is impossible to pierce such a wall as that," said Harry.

"We'll try, at all events," Jack responded. "Come, boys," he added. "one last desperate effort, and we'll baffle 'em yet."

The waiter and diver understood in a minute.

Hurriedly they collected the tools—pickaxes, crowbars, chisels, and hammers—and they all set to work on the masonry.

But their momentary hopes soon subsided.

The mortar had, in the course of ages, become even harder than the stone itself.

It was impossible to make any impression upon it.

When they saw this, disappointment was depicted upon every countenance.

Jack flung down, in sheer despair, the chisel with which he had attempted to break the mortar.

As the implement fell upon the stones of the courtyard, Thyra's quick ear noticed the peculiar sound.

"It is hollow beneath here," she exclaimed, eagerly.

Again testing the floor in the same way, they became convinced that she was right.

There were probably vaults beneath this

courtyard, and this stone concealed the entrance to them.

Animated by this fresh hope, the party now worked away, and in a few minutes had lifted the ponderous flagstone.

A flight of rude steps, leading down into utter darkness, was discovered.

"As I thought," cried Jack, "these are vaults; we may baffle them after all. Bogey, run down immediately and see what they are like."

Bogey hesitated not a moment, but skipped down the rude steps and disappeared.

The others waited his return with great anxiety.

At this moment, a shout of triumph was raised by their enemies outside.

It signified that the cannon had been brought, and that the attack would soon recommence.

The hope of escape was still of the very slightest.

In a few moments Bogey returned.

"Well?" asked Jack.

"All cellars, massa, goin' along—oh, miles and miles under de earth, all dark, 'cepting a bit of light that comes here and there through little holes in de roof. Plenty of room to hide all of us, sar. Oh, golly, won't de nasty Turks go mad?"

"Hurrah! down you go immediately," said Jack. "Now then, ladies first. Harry, I commend Thyra to your care. Take her down."

"I cannot, will not leave you, dear Jack," she cried, desperately clinging to our hero.

"No, no; I will soon be with you. For Heaven's sake, Thyra, do not hesitate now, or we shall all be lost. Go quietly; it is my wish."

Thyra resisted no more, but with Harry's assistance descended the steps into the vault.

"Now, Mr. Mole, down you go," said Jack. "Here, Figgins, you take his legs and go first, or they'll be running away with him again. Tinker, follow behind, supporting his head."

But Mr. Mole objected to this arrangement.

"What! do you think I'm an infant, to need carrying?" he said, with offended dignity. "No, though I have got patent self-controlling cork legs, I can walk down by myself."

And to prove this, he began jauntily descending the steps.

But the next moment he lost his footing, and with a cry, tumbled right down to the bottom, on to the body of the unfortunate orphan.

Luckily, it was not very far to fall, and Mr. Mole was very little hurt, though Figgins got the worst of it.

"Now, boys, down you go," cried Jack. "Hark! they are battering down the gate with artillery."

At that moment a ball tore through the doorway, shattered the top of the barricade, and at length lodged in the solid masonry.

Yells of triumph broke from the Turks.

"Quick! Tinker, Bogey, for your lives!" cried Jack.

"Is it that we are to desart ye?" cried the Irish diver. "No, Mr. Jack, I'll see you down first."

"Please make haste," said Jack, almost imploringly. "Of course I shall save myself; but I'm the captain, you know, and I mustn't leave the ship till the last."

Thus reassured, the rest descended, and no sooner was the last safe in the vault, than Jack Harkaway shut down the stone in its place, thus closing the opening.

Then he hastily laid earth in the interstices round it, and tried to efface all signs of its having been recently removed.

With equal rapidity, he gathered up the crowbars, chisels, etc.

All this time the firing continued.

The door would soon give way, and the enemy pour into the courtyard.

Was our hero mad, thus to remain behind while his friends escaped?

No.

His conduct was part of a desperate and deep-laid design.

He saw that if he had followed them in their rapid flight, the Turks would be sure to perceive that the stone had been removed, and this would at once enable them to discover the retreat of the whole party.

By remaining outside, he could restore the stone to its original appearance.

And this he had now done.

But his own safety?

He had thought of that, too.

Wild and desperate as was his scheme—one that required far more than ordinary courage to accomplish—gathering up the tools, he re-entered the house, and rapidly ascended to his own room.

Here, from the window, he could perceive how much the crowd of enemies had increased outside.

He was almost shaken off his feet by another discharge of artillery.

But every second was precious.

Hastily Jack robed himself in the ordinary garb of a middle-class Turk—for he had plenty of Oriental garments—bound a turban round his brows, and rubbed his face all over with a chemical powder, which greatly darkened his complexion.

He quickly stained his eyebrows a deep black, with henna.

None of his friends could now have recognised Jack Harkaway.

But how were his enemies to be deceived and eluded?

Having completed this hasty transformation, Jack descended the stairs.

He looked out into the courtyard.

A third discharge of artillery had now broken down the door, and the troops were rapidly clearing away the obstacles before entering in a body.

Loud were their shouts of triumph, and Jack recognised the countenance of Abdullah, lit up by a savage satisfaction.

But a glance sufficed.

Jack then retired into the smaller garden at the back, where he completely concealed himself under some thick shrubs.

In a few moments, the troops were all over the yard, probing and seeking in every corner.

Just as Jack had calculated, the soldiers were followed by a wild helter-skelter of Turks, of all ages and conditions, fanatical Moslems, who were ready to raze to the ground the accursed house where the Christians had taken refuge.

The soldiers were considerably surprised to find no one.

They sought in every room in vain, to their intense disappointment.

Abdullah's fury was terrible to witness.

Speedily the whole house was filled with a motley Turkish rabble.

In this fact consisted Jack's safety.

Seeing the moment when a number of the Turks were passing his hiding-place, he stepped out and mingled with them.

In the confusion, nobody noticed him.

In appearance, he was just like a score of other wild Turkish youths who were in the throng, shouting lustily " Death to the Christians !" in which cry Jack joined with great vigour.

The crisis of his danger was now over.

He had only to follow the movements of the crowd, and join the first group who, tired of their search, went back through the gate.

This soon happened, and amongst those disappointed Turks, Jack Harkaway was not for a moment conspicuous.

Mingling now with the crowd outside, Jack soon found an opportunity of slipping down a side lane, and reaching the suburbs of the town.

He was free, his disguise still protecting him.

He now increased his speed, making towards the desert.

For there dwelt the tribe of Arabs with whom he was friendly, who hated the new pasha as much as the old one, and who would be sure to extend their assistance to the gallant young Englishman, and enable him to rescue his friends. They received him kindly.

Jack told his story—in which they were all powerfully interested—but they told him that nothing could be done until the chief returned.

In the meantime, our hero was so overcome by excitement and fatigue that a deep sleep fell upon him, despite his efforts to keep it off.

CHAPTER LXXXV.
ADVENTURES IN THE VAULTS—NEW FRIENDS —JACK AGREEABLY SURPRISED.

WE must now follow Jack's friends in their subterranean flight.

They were, in fact, the remains of some ancient and long-disused fortifications, of far greater antiquity than the edifice which had been built over them.

Light and air were only admitted by small gratings on the sides of the roofing, which was about level with the ground outside.

As soon as the party had got over the confusion of their hurried concealment, Harry Girdwood took the lead.

Their greatest distress was the loss of Jack Harkaway.

That he was not with them soon became evident.

And that being shut outside would be certain death to him, seemed equally so.

Thyra could by no means be consoled.

Her grief at this separation from Jack took the form of intense and violent lamentations.

She declared that had she known that Jack would thus be left outside, no consideration would have induced her to enter the vaults.

In her frenzy of despair and her love for him, she resolved to go back and perish with him.

But all her efforts were inadequate to raise the stone which had already resisted the greater strength of Harry Girdwood.

As soon as the Greek girl could be in the least degree pacified, the party proceeded through the vaults, Harry reminding them that they were by no means out of all danger, but that further on some other outlet, or at least more secure retreat might be discovered.

It was a great drawback that they had no lamp or candle, but Tinker had a box of matches, and by lighting one of these at every few yards, they were enabled to gain some idea of the place they were in.

In this way they penetrated a considerable distance, till, arriving at a kind of wide underground room, the party rested awhile.

Harry Girdwood now proposed to go and explore the further portion of this subterranean region.

Leaving, therefore, the others resting, he took the box of matches, and entered the further passage.

He soon found a low rugged opening, from which another passage branched off.

Going through this, Harry was almost sent falling on his face through making a false step, for he did not see that this passage lay more than a foot lower than the other.

Then he struck one of his matches, and by its light perceived that this passage was lower, narrower, and more rugged and winding than the rest of the vaults, and seemed to have been hewn out of the earth, rather than built in it.

" Perhaps this leads to a cave," he thought, " inhabited by robbers or wild beasts. In that case I shall come off badly. I ought to have brought Bogey with me ; he's ugly enough to frighten anybody. Never mind, here goes."

And grasping his cutlass in one hand, and in the other a piece of lighted paper, which he had twisted into the form of a torch, Harry Girdwood marched manfully on.

Grazing his head against a jutting piece of rock reminded him that the passage was growing very small, and it behoved him to stop.

Suddenly Harry stopped.

He heard voices.

He saw the gleam of a light at the end of the passage.

He was apparently approaching some robbers' lair. Here was a fresh peril.

But there was still time to draw back from it.

No ; urged on by curiosity, Harry determined to see and know the worst.

In a few moments that curiosity was gratified.

He came to a point where the narrow, winding passage terminated, leading out into a lofty, rugged vault, fitted up in rude imitation of a room.

Here, seated upon the floor in a group were about a dozen men, all armed, and by their

EDWIN J. BRETT'S

YOUNG JACK HARKAWAY AND HIS BOY TINKER.

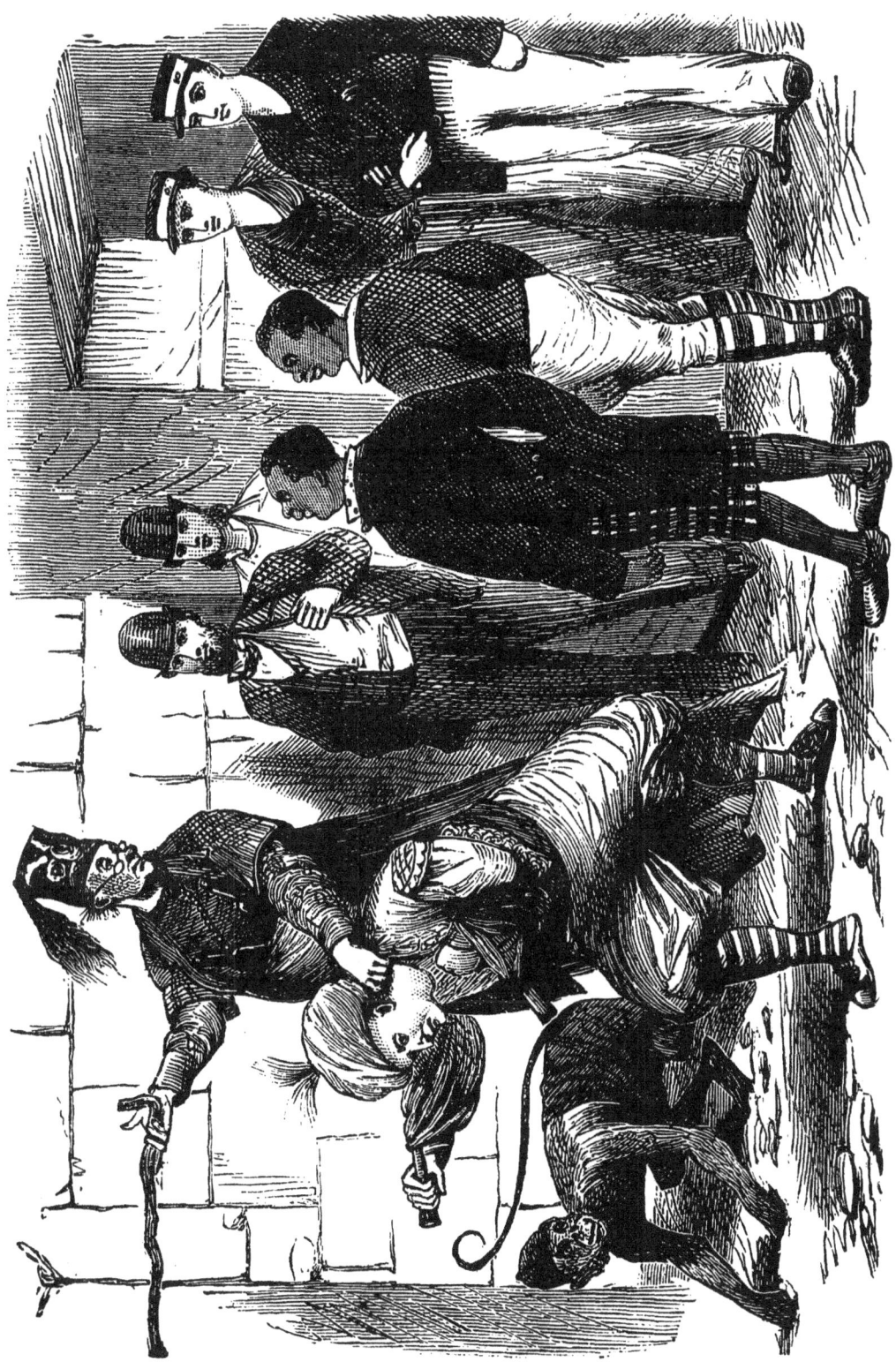

"THE CROWD LOUDLY CHEERED THE WOODEN-LEGGED PASHA MOLE."

No. 12.

PRICE ONE HALFPENNY.

[PUBLISHED EVERY TUESDAY.]

dress and appearance evidently Bedouin Arabs.

Harry was at once reassured.

He knew that the Arabs were enemies to the Turks.

The sharp eyes and quick ears of one of these sons of the desert soon "spotted" the stranger, and before he could resist or retreat, gave the alarm.

Two of them seized and secured him.

Harry now feared that his curiosity would cost him dear.

Questioned by their chief, Harry, by dint of words and signs, explained what had occurred.

The Bedouins became at once friendly.

They were ever ready to help even the unbelieving Christians against the still more hated Turks.

Two of their number were therefore told off to accompany Harry back.

By the aid of a torch, the three soon found their way to the rest of the party, who were astonished and alarmed at the ferocious appearance of their intending deliverers.

Indeed, the waiter and diver drew their weapons and prepared to offer resistance, but Harry stepped forward and explained that the Arabs were friends.

Thyra, who could speak perfectly both Turkish and Arabic, acted as interpreter, and gave a full account of all that had occurred, which seemed to impress the Bedouins greatly.

The beauty of the speaker produced a powerful effect upon the young and gallant chief to whom Thyra particularly addressed herself.

"Oh, brave sheikh!" she exclaimed, "hasten to assist the young Englishman whom I love, and who has fallen into their hands while so generously saving his friends."

"Lady, more beautiful than the peri of the gate of Heaven," replied the chief, Kara-al-Zariel, "I and the warriors of my tribe will protect thee and thy friends."

Thyra knelt and kissed the hem of the Arab chief's garment in humble gratitude.

He raised her from the ground.

As he did so the deepest admiration shone from his dark and luminous eyes.

But Thyra felt love only for young Jack.

"We were even now debating how to attack the Turks," said the Arab, "for Ibrahim is our enemy; but from thy words it would appear that they are strong and many, and armed with the weapons of western science. In the desert we fear neither men, nor kings, nor armies, but in the cities our strength availeth not."

"But you will at least fly to the assistance of brave Jack?" implored Thyra.

"It is too late; already the castle is in the hands of the pasha's men, and your friend, doubtless, is their captive."

"But you will rescue him?" entreated Thyra; "promise us that."

"I promise to make the attempt, fair maiden," answered Kara-al-Zariel; "but it must be by night and by stealth."

"That hope gives me comfort," exclaimed Thyra.

"Thou seemest greatly to love this Frankish youth," observed the chief, bending his dark eyes upon her; "if so, he is much to be envied."

"Gallant emir," said Harry, addressing Al-Zariel at this juncture, "is this cave safe from the entrance of our common enemy?"

"Safe as the top of Caucasus, as far as we are concerned," the chief answered. "The Turks know not of these vaults, and if they did, would not venture here to be at our mercy. It was through these vaults that we intended to enter and take the town by surprise."

"But where does the other end lead to?" asked Harry.

"Into our native desert, where its opening is concealed by a dense shrubbery," replied Al-Zariel. "We have often found these caves very useful in our excursions against the Turks. But you and your friends shall accompany us to our tents, where the Turks will be bold indeed to seek you."

Harry thanked him for this generous offer.

This arrangement having been made the party quitted the caves by means of a narrow path leading between two walls of high rock.

Two of the chief's men, disguised as Turks, were left behind to enter the town and keep an eye upon the condition of affairs there.

The chief of course took command of the party.

He seemed to make Thyra the especial object of his care.

It was evidently a case of "love at first sight" towards her who had been, with equal suddenness, smitten with Jack Harkaway.

And both attachments were equally hopeless.

In some parts the path was so narrow that it was with difficulty they could squeeze through it.

This rugged path proved particularly difficult to Mr. Mole, whose head was, as usual, not entirely free from the fumes of alcohol, and whose ungovernable legs still insisted upon going all ways but the right one.

But his Arab friends occasionally assisted his progress by prodding him in the back with their long spears, a species of incitement he could well have dispensed with, but which they insisted upon affording.

The poor orphan, too, was, as usual, bowed down with weight of woe.

"Oh, what a cold I am having!" he exclaimed, pathetically, feeling for his pocket handkerchief. "It's tumbling into that fountain that did it. Oh, dear, what shall I do? It will be my death, I know it will."

Such was the burden of his lament, which greatly amused the others, especially Bogey and Tinker.

They were now on the edge of the desert some distance outside the walls of the town.

The Arab tents could be faintly descried in the distance.

They had still some distance to walk in order to reach them.

The road, however, was now plain and easy, consisting of the usual flat desert sand.

On nearing this encampment, they were challenged by a Bedouin sentinel, but the chief, stepping forward and explaining, the whole group were of course readily admitted.

The black and white camel-hair tents dotted the plain to a considerable distance, and numerous horses and camels were picketed round.

One of the principal Arabs having conferred with Kara-al-Zariel, he went back to his English guests, saying:

"Christian friends, I will now show you what will cheer your hearts even more than the flesh of lambs or odour of pure bread. Behold!"

And throwing back the curtains of the tent he exposed Jack Harkaway, attired as a Turk, peacefully sleeping upon a rude couch.

The astonishment and relief of mind experienced by our friends at this discovery cannot be described.

Their joy at finding Jack safe was equal to their wonder how he had escaped.

But what words will denote the ecstacy of Thyra?

With a cry of delight she ran towards him, and kneeling besides his couch, poured forth thanksgivings to Heaven for his deliverance.

This caused some jealousy to the noble chief, who now began to perceive how passionately the "Pearl of the Isles," as he called the beautiful Greek, was enamoured of the youthful Briton.

"Stay," he said, as Thyra passionately impressed her lips on the brow of the sleeping youth. "Stay, or you will wake him. The Christian sleeps the slumber of the weary; disturb him not, and his waking will be all the more joyous."

"Thou sayest right," answered Thyra. "If he is happy, sleeping or waking, 'tis not for me to intrude upon his happiness. But I will sit here and watch his slumbers, that I may be the first to greet him when he wakes."

"You mustn't do anything of the kind, miss," interposed the waiter. "Girl's can't live upon love, though you seem inclined to try at it, and as we've got a nice supper awaiting us at that tent, Mr. Girdwood insists upon your coming to join us."

With some difficulty Thyra was induced to assent, and again left the object of her idolatry sleeping in blissful unconsciousness of her presence.

A short time, however, only elapsed before, either awakened by some outward sound or disturbed by some dream, young Jack started up, much confused and puzzled to find himself in this strange place.

Then he remembered the events of the day.

"Holloa! what's that?"

Could he believe his eyes, or was it possible that, beyond the group of Bedouins sitting feasting around the camp fire, was another group, among which the figures of Harry Girdwood, of Mole, and of Thyra were conspicuous.

It must be a dream.

Jack leapt to his feet, fixed his eyes on the group, and now recognised also Mr. Figgins, the Will-'o-the-Wisp forms of Bogey and Tinker flitting about and waiting on the others.

Now convinced, Jack rushed out of his tent into the larger one.

A perfect storm of welcome greeted him, and mutual surprise and delight were exhibited by all.

Thyra was beside herself with joy.

"Oh, dear Jack," said she; "I thought never to see you more."

"How did you get away from the Turks?" asked Harry Girdwood and two or three of the others in chorus.

Jack told his story, and in turn listened to his companions' adventures, and there were mutual congratulations upon their escape.

Never in all Jack's wanderings was there a happier occasion than this re-union.

CHAPTER LXXXVI.

THE GREEK GIRL'S FOREBODING—A BATTLE WITH THE TURKS.

THYRA slept little that night.

This could not be because she was unwearied in frame, for the toils, anxieties, and dangers of the day had been sufficient to exhaust far greater strength than hers.

It was not that she had not much cause now for anxiety of mind.

Jack was safe—that to her was the first consideration, and all his friends, including herself, had been rescued by his cleverness from the more imminent perils that beset them.

But her soul was in a state of great agitation; dark, melancholy thoughts, which would not be chased away, continually oppressed it.

This interfered with the blissful visions, the roseate castles in the air which she was so prone to build, and of which Jack Harkaway ever formed the central figure.

If she could win his love, and accompany him to England—a grand and mysterious region which she had all her life longed to see—Thyra thought the climax of happiness would be reached.

But still she felt a terrible presentiment that, not only would this never be accomplished, but that some dread and imminent fate was hanging over her.

"To-morrow," she murmured, "the hand of destiny will lie heavily upon me; there is a voice within that tells me so."

And this melancholy condition continued throughout the hours of darkness.

She looked out of her tent.

All around her slept.

Even the sentinel had fallen asleep beside the camp fire.

The air was laden with the chill breath of night, but the stars were fading and the first gleams of dawn were breaking through the eastern mists. At such a time the appearance of the vast desert was especially gloomy and depressing.

Thyra turned her gaze in the direction of the town.

What cloud was that coming thence, and advancing along the plain towards the camp?

The Greek girl strained her eyes to penetrate the mist; in this she was assisted by the growing light of the morn.

Presently the cloud shaped itself into recognizable distinctness.

It was a mass of armed men.

The Turks were marching on their track!

Thyra's terror for a moment kept her spellbound.

This onset boded destruction to herself and

all her friends; above all, to him she loved best.

Involuntarily she uttered a cry of alarm, which at once aroused the whole of the camp.

The Arabs sprang to their feet, and seized their arms.

In an instant all was commotion.

Kara-al-Zariel heard that beloved voice, and in an instant was at Thyra's side.

"What has alarmed the Pearl of the Isles?" he asked, in the poetic phraseology of his race.

Thyra stood with dishevelled hair, and dilated eyes fixed upon the approaching army, at which she pointed with trembling fingers.

"Look! look!" she exclaimed, "they are coming—the Turks are upon us!"

Kara-al-Zariel followed her gaze.

He saw the cloud; he knew the danger.

"To horse!" he thundered. "To arms! every son of the desert, and every Christian guest!"

Instantly the horses were untethered, and the riders mounted; armed men assembled on foot, and every warrior appeared in readiness.

Jack Harkaway and his friend Harry, by this time familiar as old soldiers with these sudden calls to arms, soon answered the summons; and the rest of their party, on hearing the danger, were not backward in preparing for it.

There were in the encampment a large number of fleet Arab steeds, more than were actually required by the tribe, but the chief, like many of his race, dealt largely in horse-flesh.

This was particularly fortunate on the present occasion, for their Christian allies could also be mounted, and if overwhelmingly outnumbered by the enemy, could save themselves by flight.

All the more experienced warriors were now sent to the front, to face the first shock of the coming attack.

Kara-al-Zariel led a beautiful steed to Thyra.

"Mount, sweet maiden," he said; "this steed is one of my fleetest. Go, ride on towards the sea, for our enemies are coming fast upon us, and this is no place for thee."

Thyra mounted, but steadfastly refused to take flight.

"Thinkest thou, O chief, that I will fly from this danger?" she said scornfully. "Never! I will escape with my best friends, or perish with them."

In vain the emir persuaded her to seek safety at once.

"To perish or to fall again into the hands of the licentious Turks," he said; "remember, rash girl, these two terrible fates menace thee."

"If I am killed," responded Thyra, "it is the will of Heaven; but ere I become a captive to the Turks, the dagger shall end my life."

Her resolution being evidently fixed, the Arab chief ceased to persuade, but resolved, throughout the coming fight, to do all he could to shield her from danger.

On came the enemy's forces.

The light was now sufficient for it to be perceived that they consisted of a large and well-armed body of Turkish cavalry.

They were led, as before, by the captain of the guard, and the truculent vizier Abdullah.

It was through the later's acuteness that the vaults beneath the castle had been discovered, and conjecturing that the fugitives had escaped thus, he had traced them into the desert.

He, therefore, organized an expedition to set out and surprise them in the camp.

Abdullah's plans were deeply laid.

He wished to capture the Greek girl, that he might curry favour with the Pasha Ibrahim by presenting her to him.

He was resolved to secure and punish Harkaway and the other Christians, to turn away every public suspicion from himself and Ibrahim, as to the late pasha's assassination.

After that, it is exceedingly probable that the unscrupulous interpreter meant in some way to destroy Ibrahim, and set up as pasha himself.

These subtle treacheries are common under the corruptions of Oriental rule.

The vizier intended to take the Arabs by surprise, and he would have succeeded in this, had it not been for Thyra.

Instead, therefore, of finding a sleeping encampment, he found the whole tribe up in arms, and ready to receive him.

Other tactics were therefore necessary, but Abdullah believed that his own superiority in numbers would ensure victory.

As the Turkish regiment approached, they spread themselves out, their object being to surround the force opposed to them.

On came the Turks.

Their sabres flashing and clashing.

The steeds neighing.

The sands of the desert rising up in clouds beneath their thundering tread.

Arrived within a short distance, the two armies halted and surveyed each other.

Then a trumpet sounded to parley, and a messenger rode forward to communicate with the Arab chief.

"To the Emir Kara-al-Zariel," said the soldier, "thus saith the great Lord Ibrahim, pasha of Alla-hissar. Whereas, though thou hast been often a rebel against his highness's lawful authority, yet will he pardon thee all past misdeeds on condition that thou shalt give up the Frankish men and the Greek woman, who are accused of the secret murder of his late highness, Moley Pasha. Refuse this, and no mercy will be shown to thee or to thy tribe."

"Tell thy ruler or his officers," thus replied Kara-al-Zariel, "that I refuse his proffered pardon; that Ibrahim is an assassin and usurper I despise and defy; that I will never deliver up to his hands those who have sought my hospitality, and that I and my tribe, and my guests, will resist him and his, to the death."

This rebuff was sufficiently conclusive.

There was nothing now but to commence the fight.

Shots came forth from the midst of the mass of Turkish horsemen, and were promptly answered from the muskets of the Arabs.

The battle cry of the Bedouins rang out clear in the morning air.

The first rays of the sun now lit up the plain, piercing the clouds of mist and desert dust, and gleaming upon the rapidly-moving blades and barrels.

Now shone out the white *naiks* of the Arabs and the red caps of the Turks.

The Ottoman cavalry pressed with terrible force upon the Bedouins, whose old-fashioned long guns were inadequate to compete with the modern European rifles of their foe.

But on each side the bullets tore through the ranks and laid low many a gallant warrior.

The fray soon became a fierce and close one.

A fight, hand to hand, muzzle to muzzle, and sword to sword.

One slight advantage was on the side of the Arabs.

They and their horses were quite fresh, while the Turks and their chargers were wearied with a long and difficult march.

Our friends did not forget they were Englishmen, and upheld the honour of their country in the personal bravery they showed upon this occasion.

Jack Harkaway and Harry Girdwood hewed their way right and left among the Turkish horsemen.

They were like mowers among the corn, their sickles sharp, and their harvest heavy.

Soon shone the morning sun brightly upon this scene of strife.

The Turks, from their numbers, could relieve their comrades when they became tired.

The Arabs had no such advantage.

They began to thin terribly.

But still they fought on with unbated vigour, and succeeded in preventing the enemy surrounding their encampment, and enclosing them in.

Kara-al-Zariel was ever in the thickest and most perilous part of the contest, encouraging his men with his presence.

He performed prodigies of valour, and his long hiltless Arab sabre was stained deeply with the blood of his foes.

The diver and the waiter both showed themselves skilful and valorous in fighting, and if Mole and Figgins failed to distinguish themselves so much, and preferred the more modest and retiring rearguard of the army, we must consider the weak nerves of one and the wooden legs of the other.

Bogey and Tinker were in their element, and their African blood spurred them on to deeds of bravery sometimes even approaching barbarity.

Thyra, stationed on horseback in the rear, had in her a spirit of heroism, which of her own will, would have led her to the very front of the battle.

But the entreaties of the chief and of Jack induced her to restrain her valour, and remain in a position of comparative safety from which she could see all that went on, and discharge a pistol when she saw a chance of bringing down a foe.

But by degrees the Arab ranks were broken.

Their numbers were fearfully diminished, and no efforts of theirs seemed to make any perceptible diminution of that of the enemy.

So the chief resolved upon a retreat.

But ere this could be effected, the Turks succeeded in placing a large contingent in a position to intercept them.

"We must cut through them, or we are lost," exclaimed the chief.

The war-cry of the Arabs was again raised.

They dashed at a portion of the living ring that surrounded them.

They cut their way through the circling mass of steel.

CHAPTER LXXXVII.
STILL THE BATTLE RAGES.

AT that moment Kara-al-Zariel's horse received a mortal wound, and sank beneath the chief.

He fell heavily, and narrowly escaped being trampled to death by his own advancing men.

But procuring another steed, he again led the van.

Jack Harkaway had already had two horses killed under him.

He was disfigured by blood and smoke, and dizzy with weariness and excitement, but he still fought like a lion, for it was for life.

The task of breaking through the Turkish ranks was a terrible one.

Many Arabs fell dead in the desperate attempt.

As fast as gaps were made in the ranks of the enemy, they were filled up by fresh men.

The horses trampled upon the weary limbs of the wounded.

Into this wild *mêlée* Jack plunged, closely followed by his friend Harry.

Our hero struck down a gigantic Turk, fired a revolver into the face of another, and gave a cut right and left with his sword.

Taking advantage of the passage thus made the other Englishmen rapidly followed their leader.

Thyra was led by the waiter and the diver, while Mole and Figgins mutually assisted each other.

It was amid shots falling like hail in every direction, and menaced by killing blows from heavy sabres that this retreat was made.

Thyra performed another act of heroism at this juncture.

A Turkish sergeant, on foot, fired straight at her as she passed.

By the width of scarce an inch, the bullet missed piercing her brain, but she answered it by a shot which sought and found the heart of the Turk, and he fell dead instantaneously.

In this way all the Englishmen got through the ranks of the foe and joined the chief.

The rest of the Arabs followed, but they had a hard task to do so, for the enemy now overwhelmingly outnumbered their reduced force.

But our friends were not to escape even thus easily.

The Turks made fresh and vigorous efforts, not only to prevent their retreat, but to effect their capture.

Seeing the peril they were in, Jack called to Thyra and said—

"My good girl, you have acted with heroic bravery, but our danger is now greater than ever, and you must quit this scene."

"Never, dear Jack, whilst you are imperilled," she firmly replied.

"But you can aid me more that way than by staying," he said. "Listen, yonder is the sea, not more than two miles off. There is an English ship in the bay ; its gallant sailors will not fail to assist their countrymen in distress. Go to them at once, your steed is swiftest of all. Ride, ride for your life, dear girl."

Thyra needed no further urging.

"I will bring assistance to you," she cried, " or perish in the attempt."

She turned her steed, and was off in a minute at lightning speed.

On came the Turks, now headed by Abdullah, for his comrade, the captain of the guard, had been desperately wounded.

"We must capture them !" he cried to his men. "Forward, men ; death or victory."

Jack and his men saw that resistance was useless against so overwhelming a force.

Flight was the only chance remaining to them.

Yet they could not give in without some attempt to punish their enemy.

Jack levelled his pistol at the vizier's head, but by a dexterous movement he avoided the shot.

"Yield, Christian dogs !" he thundered. "Yield to might and right, for your capture or death is inevitable."

"You do not know us Boys of England," cried Jack. "We may be taken dead, but while a breath of life remains, we will never surrender to black-hearted Turks."

The vizier answered by ordering his men to surround the Christians, which they did their best to accomplish.

But by an agile movement, Jack and his friends suddenly turned and galloped off.

It was not in the direction of the sea, for retreat was at present cut off that way, but across the desert that they fled.

"Forward !" cried Abdullah. "They must not escape us."

For a considerable time this chase continued, till the English, by " doubling " again, changed the direction of their flight, and made towards the sea.

Hope arose within their hearts, for they saw a considerable number of well-armed English sailors, led by Thyra, coming towards them.

A few minutes' galloping joined them with these welcome allies, and this reinforcement enabled Jack again to defy the Turks.

The latter drew rein, and stood for awhile in hesitation.

This unexpected turn of affairs evidently disconcerted them.

But 'ere their horses could be put in motion again, Jack and his party were upon them, backed by their new allies.

The impetuosity of their charge was for a moment irresistible.

They bore down all the Turks before them.

The Turkish troopers recoiled as from the flight of a rocket.

Jack rode on like a hero of old.

His hair streamed in the wind as he darted through the air on his noble Arab steed.

His eyes flashed fire, and struck awe into each foe that approached him.

But he soon found himself surrounded by his enemies. Abdullah, who was at their head, cast himself upon Jack. Their horses were driven on their haunches by the force of the shock.

Half a dozen sabres at once circled round Jack's head.

Abdullah made a lunge at him with his sword, which would have proved the death of Jack had not Harry Girdwood at that instant caught the thrust upon his arm.

Poor Harry ! His devotion to his friend had cost him dear.

He reeled, and would have fallen from his saddle, probably trampled to death, had not Bogey, at the risk of his own life, caught him and led his horse apart from the thick of the battle.

Burning to avenge his friend, Jack struck with all his force at Abdullah's head.

The interpreter received the blow upon his sword, which, proving the stronger of the two, Jack's weapon snapped in the clash, and he was left weaponless.

He seemed, indeed, at the mercy of his pitiless foe.

Abdullah smiled a cruel smile as he again raised his sabre.

But that smile was his last.

A lance-head gleamed past Jack, and transfixed Abdullah through the chest, so that he was borne down among the trampling hoofs of the horses.

"Yah, yah ; dat's one to me, Massa Jack," exclaimed Tinker, for he it was who had thus saved Jack's life.

Jack caught up Abdullah's sword, and, by a desperate charge, cut through the opposing Turks, now " demoralised " by the loss of their leader, and regained his Bedouin and English friends.

By this time the heat was very great.

The sky was like a dome of steel.

The sands of the desert burnt under the fierce sun.

The dust flew in clouds, save where the blood of the wounded and dying had soaked into the arid soil.

Taking advantage of the confusion that now reigned in the Turkish force, the English and Arabs made a last desperate effort to escape their foes.

With a yell of defiance, the fierce Bedouins, led by Kara-al-Zariel, dashed through the ranks of the enemy, dealing destruction right and left.

Taking advantage of the disconcerted state of the foe, Jack and his friends were enabled again to join their Arab allies, and the retreat of the whole party towards the shore began in good earnest.

They would soon have distanced their now exhausted foes, but, ere the English vessel could be reached, another large body of Turks came up to the attack.

This force was led by no less a personage than the Pasha Ibrahim himself, whose fierce grey eyes glared beneath his shaggy brows at those who had slain his vizier.

Beside him rode the officer in command of his squadron, and another young man, in whom, although dressed in red *fez* and Turkish uniform, Jack recognised Herbert Murray.

He was attended by his servant Chivey, also dressed as a Turk.

They were all splendidly mounted : their horses fresh, and their troops well-disciplined.

As the two parties approached, the pasha's eyes were fixed upon Thyra.

"It is the Pearl of the Isles," he exclaimed, "who was stolen by these infidels from the harem. She shall yet be mine. One thousand piastres to the man who will capture her."

A dozen of his men instantly started in pursuit of Thyra, who was a little in advance of her companions.

Her beautiful Arab steed seemed to have taken a sudden fright, for it started off at lightning speed, independent of Thyra's attempts to turn him, for she wished to die or escape by the side of her companions.

Separated from them, and pursued by a dozen well-armed men, her position was indeed perilous.

The speed of her horse seemed her only chance.

But the noble creature had been very hard worked that day, and after the first "spurt," showed signs of exhaustion.

The Turks, upon their fresh and fleet steeds, began to gain upon her every minute.

At length she was at bay, resolved to die defending herself and defying her enemies.

She placed her lance in rest as the foremost Turk came up.

Despite his efforts to avoid the weapon, she thrust it through his shoulder.

He fell, desperately, if not mortally wounded, and full of rage at being defeated by a woman.

His nearest companion now faced the beautiful amazon, who rapidly drew her revolver —the one Jack had given her—and fired.

The ball took effect, for the Turk reeled in his saddle and fell to the ground, dead.

The others now approached.

But Thyra discharged one, two, three shots from her revolver, and the last killed the officer's horse, which staggered and fell, bringing the rider to the ground.

Thyra urged her steed again towards the sea.

Herbert Murray and Chivey now pressed forward, resolved to try and gain the pasha's reward and the glory of achieving her capture.

Away went Thyra on her gallant steed.

She was near the sea now.

The murmur of its waves upon the sands resounded in her ears.

The British cruiser was seen about a mile away in the offing, and on the shore stood about half a dozen sailors, taking charge of the boats in which the armed force had come ashore.

They were anxiously watching for their companions to return, and on perceiving Thyra's peril, two of them went to her assistance.

And they arrived not a moment too soon.

Herbert Murray had ridden up to her.

Grasping the bridle of her steed, he thought he had effected her capture.

But at this moment a voice beside him cried out in English—

"Hands off there, you lubber !"

This showed that Thyra's call for help had been heard and responded to.

Murray turned, and saw the two stalwart British tars standing beside Thyra.

"Look here," continued the sailor, "if you don't leave this here young lady alone, and be off instanter, we'll take you aboard and let our captain deal with you."

Herbert Murray looked around, and seeing that the sailors were in a position to carry out their threat, angrily relinquished the chase, and turning his horse, rode off with Chivey, who had not approached quite so near.

CHAPTER LXXXVIII.

END OF THE CONTEST—DEATH OF THYRA.

THYRA was securely protected by these gallant tars until the rest of the party came up, which was not long, for after a slight skirmish, Jack and his friends managed to cut through the new force of opposing Turks, and made their way towards the ship.

Ibrahim Pasha, enraged at being thus defied, still pressed on, followed by all his force, but they only arrived at the shore in time to see Jack and the others embarking in the boats.

He now had recourse to threats.

"In the name of His Imperial Majesty the Sultan," he said to the officer in command, "I command you to give up to me these Englishmen, who have escaped from justice."

"They are British subjects," returned the officer, "who have sought the protection of their flag."

"Shall British subjects commit crime and yet go free ?" inquired Ibrahim.

"What crime have they committed ?" asked the officer.

"Murder—the assassination of his highness, Moley Pasha."

"What evidence have you to show to connect them with his death ?" asked the officer. "If you have but sufficient evidence, they shall be tried before a proper tribunal. Where the English flag floats, justice shall be done to all."

The pasha bit his lip.

He knew that his evidence against these Englishmen was very slight, being in fact only the assertion of Murray and Chivey, and that any mistake on his part would bring on political trouble that might be his ruin, so he began to draw in.

"At least," he said, "you cannot refuse to give me back my own property, stolen from my palace."

"That's a reasonable request enough," answered the lieutenant. "Point out your property, and you shall have it."

"There it is," exclaimed Ibrahim, as he pointed to Thyra.

"That your property, eh ?" said the astonished officer. "Well, a very nice property too. But how was she stolen ?"

"Stolen from my harem by that son of Eblis !" cried the old pasha, pointing to Jack.

"Ah, young man, I see how it is," said the officer, gravely shaking his head ; "you've been going it rather too fast, and brought on this trouble all on account of this Greek girl."

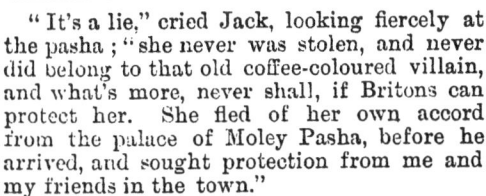

"It's a lie," cried Jack, looking fiercely at the pasha; "she never was stolen, and never did belong to that old coffee-coloured villain, and what's more, never shall, if Britons can protect her. She fled of her own accord from the palace of Moley Pasha, before he arrived, and sought protection from me and my friends in the town."

"In that case," said the officer, "we cannot give her up, for the British government does not recognise slavery, domestic or otherwise. Under our flag she is free."

A cheer of defiance from the group of English sailors greeted this speech.

"By the soul of the prophet," fiercely exclaimed the pasha, "am I to be defied by a bop, and an infidel—a son of Sheitan, to boot?"

"Boy as I am, I defy you," retorted Jack.

This was a bold, but foolish and incautious speech, destined to be disastrous.

The pasha, goaded to madness by Jack's words and defiant manner, drew his pistol and discharged it pointblank at our hero.

The action was a rapid one—so rapid as to take Jack unawares, but not so rapid as the love-quickened perceptions of Thyra.

She saw the pasha's movement, and throwing herself forward, seized Jack just in time to draw him aside.

By so doing, she saved his life, but at the expense of her own.

The bullet lodged in her breast, and with a cry she fell wounded into Jack's arms.

The disaster had come so quickly that our hero scarcely comprehended what had happened.

The pasha frowned darkly when he saw Thyra fall.

Some remorse was awakened, even in his iron heart.

He had intended to take a life, but not hers, and now indeed the Pearl of the Isles was lost to him for evermore.

"'Tis you now, pasha, who have committed crime," said the leiutenant, "and for this I call you to account. Surrender to answer for this deed."

"Surrender to Christian dogs! Never," answered the fierce Ibrahim.

"Then, men, fire upon these Turks," said the officer.

The rifles of the sailors were accordingly brought to cover upon the pasha's force.

Ibrahim immediately recognised a fresh and imminent danger, and resolved on a retreat.

Turning his horse, he gave the signal to his followers, and the whole body marched off rapidly, pursued by the fire of the English.

During this parley, Kara-al-Zariel and his Arabs had taken advantage of the preoccupation of their foes, to withdraw to the range of rugged rocks near the shore, which would at once shelter them from the attacks of the Turks and give them the advantage of being near their English allies in the ship.

But the pasha, now that the main objects of his expedition had escaped him, did not make any further attempts to pursue the Bedouins.

He and the remnant of his forces made the best of their way across the desert to the town.

And now all attention was drawn towards Thyra.

All perceived, with the deepest regret, that her hours were numbered.

She had been that day in the thick of more than one deadly conflict.

Hundreds of bullets had passed her, but this one, aimed at another, had only too successfully performed an errand of death.

Terrible indeed was the grief of Jack Harkaway.

"Oh Thyra," he exclaimed, "my brave, dear girl, he has killed you."

"I know it," she replied with a mournful resignation, "but thank Heaven you, dear Jack, are saved."

"I have not deserved this devotion from you," said Jack, in broken accents, while the tears fell from his eyes, "but you must not—shall not die thus. Can nothing be done for her?" he asked, looking round at the others.

"I fear not," replied the lieutenant, "but she must at once be taken on board, and placed under the care of the surgeon."

Thyra had been lifted up and her wound staunched with her scarf.

"Here, Harry," said our hero rousing himself from his grief, "help me to carry her to the boat."

But ere his friend could fulfil his request, a tall, wild form interposed between them, a brown, sinewy hand convulsively clutched Jack's arm to draw him away.

"No hand but mine," cried a voice broken by intense grief, "shall bear the Pearl of the Isles to yonder boat."

It was the Arab chief, Al-Zariel, his face haggard with grief, his dark eyes gazing mournfully at the pale but beautiful face of her he loved.

He raised her tenderly, this wild warrior of the desert—tenderly as a child, and disdained all aid, and bore her in his strong arms to the boat.

The others drew back; no one at that moment had the heart to say him nay.

Even the rough sailors, and the still rougher Arabs, were touched by the mournful scene before them.

It was indeed a solemn procession to the boats, almost a funeral *cortege* for they bore one, who, though not yet dead, would never see another day's sun arise.

Kara-al-Zariel gently deposited the dying girl in the boat.

"I have known her but a day," murmured the Arab chief, "and during the day she has shone upon my path like a gleam of sunshine from the gates of Paradise. From the first instant I saw her I loved her as I have loved no other, and as I shall love no other to my life's end."

He stooped and imprinted a passionate kiss upon that marble brow, pressing as he did so the lifeless hand, gazing into the fast-fixing eyes, and murmuring "Farewell" in his native tongue.

She understood him, and with a smile of gratitude answered him in the same language.

The boat put off.

Kara-al-Zariel, standing on the sands watched it for some moments, and then, as if unable longer to bear the sight, turned away, knelt upon the beach, and covered his eyes with his hands.

It was not grief alone that made him kneel beneath the open vault of Heaven.

In that terrible moment he registered to Heaven a vow of vengeance against the pasha who had slain the Pearl of the Isles.

The sturdy tars bent to their oars, and the boat left the murmuring waters of the sunlit Mediterranean.

Arriving on the ship, Thyra was placed with all care and tenderness upon deck.

The doctor examined the wound, and shook his head gravely.

"I can do nothing here!" he said, in subdued tones.

None answered him; only they saw too plainly that his words were final.

Poor Jack Harkaway! If ever in his young life he had felt grief, it was now, when he saw one who had so hopelessly loved him, dying through that very love.

"I am not afraid to die," said Thyra, in her low, faint voice, "and to die in this way is the best of all ; for my future life might have made both you and myself unhappy."

"Unhappy! How could that be, Thyra?" asked Jack, as he knelt beside her, his hand clasped in hers, her dying eyes looking upwards into his face.

"Because your love is given to another," she sighed, "and therefore, mine is hopeless ; but oh, may that other—whoever she may be—be now and ever happy in your love."

"You have died for my sake!" he said, "and can you think I can feel anything but the deepest gratitude, the most tender feelings, towards you? No, dear Thyra, I love you now, if I have not before."

"To hear that from your lips," she murmured, "is to die happy. All I ask now, is that you will always remember the little Greek girl who loved you, and—and who was unhappy in her life, and happy in her death."

"Remember you!" said Jack, "remember you, my noble Thyra! after what you have done? Always! always! Do not pain me by fearing that I may forget you."

"Then I am happy still ; listen. Here are a chain and a cross of gold ; keep them in remembrance of me, and when I am dead, have me conveyed, if it is possible, to the land of my birth, the beautiful island of Naxos, where my parents still live. Bury me there."

Jack promised this, and the old captain of the ship declared that he would have her last request fulfilled.

Thyra's strength was now almost exhausted, but, with a last effort, she raised herself from Jack's supporting arms, and addressed those around her.

"Friends," she said, "I give you many, many thanks for what you have done for me, in protecting me and aiding my escape. I can but give you thanks and my farewell. Farewell!" she added, " to the bright blue sky. the golden sea, and the beautiful green island where I was born and where I hope to rest when I am no more."

Here her voice died into a murmur, and the rest was inaudible to all but Jack.

Jack stooped as the Arab chief had done, and impressed a fervent kiss upon the fair young face, still bent lovingly towards him. At that moment he felt an electric thrill convulse her frame, followed by a complete stillness. In that last fond embrace her spirit had fled.

Thyra's troubles were over.

Two days afterwards the ship, whose captain had undertaken to convey Jack and his friends from those turbulent shores, touched at the Greek island of Naxos. There Thyra's parents were found, and the sad news of their child's death communicated to them.

She was buried in the little cemetery close to the shore, and amid groves of cypress and gardens of flowers, where sweet bird sing and sea breezes softly murmur, lies the beautiful Greek Girl who loved and died for young Jack Harkaway.

And all hearts were heavy with grief when, after the funeral, they hoisted sail, and steered in a westerly direction.

CHAPTER LXXXIX.

MARSEILLES—MR. MOLE AS A LINGUIST—AN UGLY CUSTOMER AND HIS ENGLISH CONFEDERATE—A COMPACT OF MYSTERY—MR. MARKBY PLAYS A VERY DEEP GAME—THE SHADOW OF DANGER.

OUR friends had been some days at sea.

The weather was fair, and their progress was for a time slow.

At length one day there was a cry—

"Land ho!"

"Which?" said our hero, who was anxious for anything that would make him forget his great sorrow for Thyra.

"I remarked 'Land ho!' Jack," said Mr. Mole, for he it was who first detected it.

"And I observed 'Which?' sir," said Jack.

"And why that unmeaning interrogation?" demanded Mr. Mole.

"Your speech is an anomaly, Mr. Mole," responded Jack, mimicking the voice of his tutor in his happiest manner.

"Why so?"

"You say my question is unmeaning, and yet you ask an explanation of it. If there is no meaning in it, how can I explain it?"

"Ahem!" coughed Mr. Mole. "No matter. You are too much given to useless arguments, Jack. I believe you would argue with the doctor attending you on your deathbed—yea, with the undertaker himself who had to bury you."

"That's piling it on, sir," said Jack, in a half reflective mood. "I dare say I should have a shy at the doctor if he tried to prove something too idiotic, but we must draw the line at the doctor. I could'nt argue with the undertaker at my own funeral, but I'll tell you what, Mr. Mole, no doubt I shall argue with him if he puts it on too stiff in his bill when we put you away."

"Jack!" exclaimed Mr. Mole, inexpressibly shocked.

"A plain deal coffin," pursued Jack apparently lost in deep calculation ; "an economical coffin, only half the length of an ordinary coffin, because you could unscrew your legs, and leave them to someone."

"That is very unfeeling to talk of my funeral, dreadful!"

"You are only joking there, I know sir," returned Jack, "because you were talking of mine."

"Ahem!" said Mole, "do you see how near we are to land?"

"Quite so, quite so."

"Go and ask the captain the name of this port."

It proved to be Marseilles, and the captain knew it, as he had been sailing for it, and moreover, they were very quickly ashore.

Mr. Mole was especially eager to air his French.

"You speak the language?" asked Jack.

Mr. Mole smiled superciliously at the question.

"Like a native, my dear boy, like a native," he replied.

"That's a good thing," said Jack, tipping the wink to Harry Girdwood; "for you can interpret all round."

* * * * *

France was then going through one of its periodical upsets, and a good deal of unnecessary bother was made along the coast upon the landing of passengers.

Passports were partly dispensed with, but questions were put by fierce officials as to your name and nationality, which all led up to nothing, for they accepted your reply implicitly as truth, and while it inconvenienced the general public, the Royalist, Republican, Orleanist, or whoever might chance to be of the revolutionary party for the time being, could chuckle as he told his fibs and passed on to the forbidden land.

M. le commissaire confronted Mr. Mole, and barred his passage to interrogate him.

"*Pardon, m'sieur veuillez bien me dire votre nom?*"

"What's that?" said Mole.

"*Votre nom, s'il vous plait,*" repeated the commissaire.

"Really, I haven't the pleasure of your acquaintance.

"*Sapristi!*" ejaculated the commissaire to one of his subordinates. "*Quel type!*"

"Now, Mr. Mole," said Jack who was close behind the old gentleman, "why don't you speak up?"

"I don't quite follow him."

"He's only asking a question, you know. You polly-voo like a native."

"Yes; precisely Jack. But I don't follow his accent he's some peasant I suppose."

"*Votre nom!*" demanded the official, rather fiercely this time.

"Now then Mr. Mole," cried a voice in the rear, "you're stopping everyone. Get it out and move on."

"Dear, dear me!" said Mole. "What does it mean?"

"He's asking your name," said Jack, and you can't understand it."

"Oh!"

"I'll tell him for you, as you don't seem to know a word," said Jack. "*Il s'appelle Ikey Mole,*" he added to the commissaire.

"*Aïké Moll,*" repeated the commissaire. "*Il est Arabe?*"*

"*Oui, monsieur. C'est un des lieutenants du grand Abd-el-Kader.*"

"*Vraiment!*" exclaimed the commissaire, in a tone of mingled surprise and respect. "*Pissez, M'sieur Aïké Moll.*"

They went on, and Mole anxiously questioned Jack.

"I'm getting quite deaf," said he, by way of a pretext for not having understood the conversation. "Whatever were you saying?"

"I told him your name was Isaac Mole, sir," returned Jack.

"You said Ikey Mole, sir," retorted Mole, "and that is a very great liberty, sir."

"Not at all. Iké is the French for Isaac," responded the unblushing Jack.

"But what was all that they were saying about Arab?"

"Arab!" repeated Jack, in seeming astonishment.

"Yes."

"Didn't hear it myself."

"I certainly thought I caught the word Arab," said Mr. Mole, giving Jack a very suspicious glance.

"You never made a greater mistake, sir, in your life."

"How very odd."

"Very."

* * * * *

The Cannebière is the chief promenade in Marseilles, and the inhabitants of this important seaport are not a little proud of it.

Two men sat smoking cigarettes and sipping lazily at their *grog au vin* at the door of one of the numerous cafés in the Cannebière.

To these two men we invite the reader's attention.

One was a swarthy-looking Frenchman from the south, a man of a decent exterior, but with a fierce and restless glance.

He was the sort of man whom you would sooner have as a friend than as an enemy.

A steadfast friend—an implacable foe!

That was what you read in his peculiar physiognomy, in that odd mixture of defiance and fearlessness, those anxious glances, frankness and deceit, the varied expressions of which passed in rapid succession across his countenance.

This man called himself Pierre Lenoir, although he was known in other ports by other names.

Pierre Lenoir was a sort of Jack of all trades.

He had been apprenticed to an engraver, and had shown remarkable aptitude for that profession, but, being of a roving and restless

---

* "He calls himself Ikey Mole," says Jack to the commissaire de police.

Aïké Moll!" repeats the commissaire, pronouncing the incongruous sounds as nearly as he can. "Why, he must be an Arab."

To which Jack, with all his ready impudence, replies—

"Yes, sir, he is an Arab. He was one of Abd-el-Kader's lieutenants."

We need scarcely remind our readers that Abd-el-Kader was the doughty Arab chief who made so heroic a resistance to the French in Algiers.

This satisfied the commissaire, who respectfully bade Mole pass on.

disposition, he ran away from his employer to ship on board a merchant vessel.

After a cruise or two he was wrecked, and narrowly escaped with his life.

Tired of the sea, for awhile he obtained employment with a medallist, where his skill as an engraver stood him in good stead.

From this occupation he fled as soon as his ready adaptability had made him a useful hand to his new master, and took to a roving life again. What he was now doing in Marseilles no one could positively assert.

How it was that Pierre Lenoir had such an abundant supply of ready money, the progress of our narrative will show—for with it are connected several of not the least exciting episodes in the career of young Jack Harkaway.

So much for Pierre Lenoir.

Now for his companion at the café.

He was called Markby, and, as his name indicates, he was an Englishman.

Being but a poor French scholar, he had scraped up an acquaintance with Pierre Lenoir, chiefly on account of the latter's proficiency in the English language.

There is little to be said concerning Markby's past history, for reasons which will presently be apparent.

What further reason he may have had for cultivating the friendship of the rover, Pierre Lenoir, will probably show itself in due course.

*   *   *   *   *

"I have disposed of that last batch of five-franc pieces," said Markby. "Here are the proceeds."

"Keep it back," exclaimed Lenoir hurriedly.

"What for?"

"It is sheer madness for us to be seen conversing together," replied Lenoir, casting an anxious glance about him from behind his hat, which he held in his hand so as to shield his features, "much less to be seen exchanging money—why, it is suicidal—nothing less."

"Is there any danger do you think."

"Do I think? Do I know? Why, this place is literally alive with spies—*mouchards* as we call them here. Every second man you meet is a *mouchard*."

"Do you mean it?"

"Rather."

"That's not a pleasant thing to know," said Markby.

"I don't agree with you there," replied Lenoir. "'Forewarned, forearmed,' is a proverb in your language. But now tell me about this friend and countryman of yours."

"He's no friend of mine," returned Markby. "I know him as a great traveller, and one who has opportunities of placing more false—"

"Hush, imprudent!" interrupted Lenoir. "Call it stock. You know not how many French spies may be passing, or how near we may be to danger."

Markby took the hint given him, and continued—

"Well, stock. He can place more—he has probably placed more than any man alive. He travels about *en grand seigneur*—lords it in high places and disposes of the counterf——"

"Stock."

"Stock, in regular loads. But he's as wary as a fox—nothing can approach him in cunning."

"The very man I want," exclaimed Lenoir.

"This fellow could, with my aid, make a fortune for himself and me in less than a year —a large fortune."

"You are very sanguine," said Markby, with a smile.

"I am, but not over sanguine. I speak by the book, for I know well what I am talking of. You must introduce me."

"You are running on wildly," said Markby.

"Did I not tell you that he did not know me —that he would not know me if he did? So careful is he that his own brother would fail to draw anything from him concerning the way in which he gets his living."

"*Dame!*" muttered Lenoir, "he seems a precious difficult fellow to approach."

"Yes, on that subject," responded Markby; "but he's genial and agreeable enough if you introduce yourself by accident, as it were, and chat upon social topics generally, without the vaguest reference to the subject nearest your heart."

"How shall I ever lead him up to the point?"

"Easily, for instance, talk about art matters. Allude to your gallery of sculpture. Ask him, is he fond of bas reliefs? Tell him of your skill as a medallist."

"Medallist might put him on the scent, if he is so dreadfully wary," said Lenoir.

"No fear. He would never dream of such a thing. Medalling being a sort of sister art to what most interests him, he would be sure to bite at the chance. You lead him to your little underground snuggery, and once there all need for his wonderful caution will be at an end."

"I see," said Lenoir, rubbing his hands. "But stay"—and here his face grew a bit serious—"this fellow is faithful?"

"True as steel," responded Markby.

"That's right," said Lenoir, with a look that caused a twinge of uneasiness to be felt by his companion, "for woe betide the man that plays me false."

"No fear of this man—man, I call him, but he is in appearance at least little more than a lad, although he has travelled all over the world."

Here Markby arose to move away.

"Stop a bit," said Lenoir. I have forgotten to ask rather an important detail.

"What is it?"

"The name of this fellow?"

"Jack Harkaway," was the reply.

CHAPTER XC.

MARKBY'S MISSIVE—ON THE WATCH!— "SMART FELLOW, MARKBY!"—MARKBY'S MYRMIDON—THE SPIE'S MISSION.

THE Englishman Markby was gone before Pierre Lenoir could question him further.

"Jack Harkaway," exclaimed Lenoir; "I have heard that name before. Of course; I remember now. But Markby speaks of him as a lad. Why the Harkaway that I remember must be a middle-aged man by now; besides, what little I knew of Harkaway then

would not show him to be a likely man for my purpose."

Not long after this, as Lenoir was upon the point of rising and leaving the café, a commissionaire or public messenger came up at a run with a note in his hand.

"M'sieu Lenoir."

"*C'est moi.*"

He took the note and found it to contain the following words, scribbled boldly by Markby—

"They are now coming along in your direction. You will easily recognise them—two youths in sailor dress. Follow them, and if they stay at any of the cafés, I leave you to scrape up an acquaintance with them.—M."

"Markby has been upon the *qui vive*," said Lenoir to himself. "Smart fellow, Markby!"

Glancing to the left he saw the two young sailors approaching; so Pierre Lenoir made up his mind at once.

He stepped into the house, intending to let them pass and then follow them, and, if by chance they should, on their way, stop at either of the cafés, he could drop in and seek the opportunity he so much desired.

But while he was waiting the young sailors came up, and instead of passing the café they dropped into chairs at the door and called for refreshments.

This was more than Lenoir had bargained for.

However, it was no use wasting time.

He desired to profit by the opportunity, and so out he came and sat at the next table to the two young Englishmen.

*   *   *   *   *

"What's your opinion of Marseilles, Jack?"

"Nothing great."

"Ditto."

"Nothing to see once you're out of sight of the sea, and the natives are not very interesting. They only appear to be full of conceit about their town without the least reason for it. I should like to know if there is really anything in Marseilles to warrant the faintest belief in the place."

This was Pierre Lenoir's opportunity.

He stepped forward.

"Excuse me, gentlemen," said he. "Englishmen, I presume?"

"Yes, sir," responded Jack; "are you English?"

"I haven't that honour," replied Pierre Lenoir.

"You speak good English. You have resided in England, I suppose, for a long while?"

"No, only a short time. Long enough to get a desire to go back there."

"That's very kind of you to say so. Your countrymen, as a rule, don't speak in such flattering terms of *la perfide* Albion."

"And yet they are glad enough to find a refuge there."

"True."

"Are you a native of Marseilles?" asked Harry.

"No."

"Then you are not offended at our remarks?"

"Not a bit," replied Lenoir, heartily. "The Marseillais are absurdly conceited about their town, and after all it contains but few objects of interest for a traveller."

"Very few."

"There are some, however, and if you will accept my escort, I shall be very happy to show you them."

They expressed their thanks at this couteous offer which, on a very little pressing, they were glad to accept.

"Thanks; we will go and tell a friend, who is waiting for us down by the quay, that he must not expect us for an hour or so."

"Very good."

*   *   *   *   *

Markby must have been pretty keenly upon the look-out, for no sooner were they gone than back he came.

"Well, what success?"

"Just as I wished," returned Lenoir, with a great chuckle; "they are coming back directly."

"That's your chance; you have only to take them up to your place. Once there, you will do as you please with them."

"There is no danger?"

"What can there be?"

"Only this—suppose that you were mistaken?"

Markby was visibly offended at this.

"If you think that likely after all I have told you, take my advice and have nothing whatever to do with them. I don't want to expose you to any risk that you think you ought not to run."

Lenoir appeared to waver momentarily.

Markby eyed him anxiously for awhile, until Lenoir, with an air of resolution, exclaimed—

"Hang the risk. I'll go for it neck or nothing."

"And you will take them there to-night."

"I will."

"Good! You'll have no cause to repent your decision. They'll do you a turn that you little contemplate."

"Right! Now off with you."

"I'm gone."

And away he went.

"What a strange fellow that Markby is," thought Pierre Lenoir, looking after him. "What an odd laugh he has."

Alas! Pierre Lenoir had good reason to bear that laugh in mind.

But we must not anticipate.

*   *   *   *   *

As soon as Markby was fairly out of sight, he beckoned over to a young man in white blouse and a cap, who had walked along on the opposite side of the way, keeping Markby in view all the while without appearing to notice him.

The fellow in the blouse ran across at once.

"Well, how's it going?"

"Beautiful," returned Markby, "nothing could be better. Already have Harkaway and his hard-knuckled companion, Girdwood, been seen in Lenoir's society. But before the day is over they will be seen in the Caveaux themselves, where proofs of their guilt will spring up hydra-headed from the very ground."

"And what will it end in?" asked the other, eagerly.

"The galleys," returned Markby, with fierce intensity.

"Beautiful!" exclaimed the man in the blouse, with unfeigned admiration. " You always must have been a precieos sight downier that I thought. Why, your old man was no fool. He made a brown or two floating his coffins, but he was a guileless pup compared to you."

" You keep watch," said Markby, hurriedly ; "and be ready for any emergency, It is a bold stroke we are playing for. Lenoir is a desperate ruffian, and the least mistake in the business would be something which I for one don't care to contemplate."

" Lenoir be blowed," replied the man in the blouse ; "the only people I care about if we should go and make a mess of the job is, firstly—Jack Harkaway, and secondly, his pal Harry Girdwood, which a harder fist than his I have seldom received on my unlucky snuffer-tray."

And he was gone.

CHAPTER XCI.

MARKBY'S NEXT STEP—THE PREFECT OF POLICE—THE PLOT THICKENS—A GLIMPSE OF MARKBY'S PURPOSE—A DOUBLE TRAITOR—DEADLY PERIL.

MARKBY went off muttering to himself.

" Wish that scamp could only share the fate I have reserved for that accursed Harkaway. However, I can't manage that, so I must be thankful for small mercies."

*   *   *   *   *

A short walk brought this Markby to the office of the prefect of police, and his business being of considerable importance, he was fortunate in soon obtaining an interview with that great man himself.

" This is an excellent opportunity," said the head of the police, " if your informatien is thoroughly reliable, although I confess that it almost sounds too good to be true."

" Pardon me, monsieur," said Markby, " the expression you use sounds as though I had got information second-hand ; I am a principal, On the 10th, you will please to remember. I have to be of the party."

" It is a very important matter," said the prefect, " that I will not attempt to disguise from you. This Lenoir is evidently at the head of a gigantic conspiracy. We have been long seeking to discover how he disposed of his counter——"

" Stock," said Markby, interrupting the prefect, with a smile. " He is the quintessence of caution, sir, and he never alludes to it by any other term."

" You really think that these English people are their confidants ? "

" The chief confederates ; yes. They are the heads of the English part of our scheme,"

" How many men should you require ? " demanded the prefect, changing the subject abruptly.

" A dozen fully armed, in plain clothes. These can descend into the *caveaux* to make the capture."

" A dozen ? "

" Yes."

" So many ! "

" You don't know Lenoir," said Markby ; " he's the very devil when he's aroused. A dozen will have all their work to do. As for the two Englishmen—— "

" They are young," exclaimed the prefect.

" They are young fiends. I have seen them fight like devils. They are just as dangerous as Lenoir. They are as cunning as the evil one himself, and will gammon even you, by their plausible tales."

" Let me see," said the prefect, thoughtfully. " I will take note of the names which you tell me they are likely to assume."

" One has been calling himself Jack Harkaway."

" And the other ? "

" Harry Girdwood."

" Good—and you can prove that both the persons whose names are assumed are in Turkey ? "

" I can."

" Very good," said the prefect rising, to intimate that the intercourse was over. " Our men shall be there in force for their capture."

CHAPTER XCII.

THE HARKAWAY'S GUIDE—LENOIR'S MUSEUM —THE CAVEAUX, AND WHAT THEY SAW THERE—THE MEDALS—THE TRUTH AT LAST—A COINER'S TRADE—AN ALARM— A DESPERATE FELLOW.

"HERE we are again, sir," said Harry Girdwood, stepping up to Pierre Lenoir; "but fear we are taking a great liberty in asking you to *cicerone* such a large party as we muster here."

Lenoir smiled.

It was not a free, frank smile.

To tell the truth, he was a bit annoyed, for besides the two boys there was Mole, and the attendant darkeys with them Tinker and Bogey.

Lenoir was a cautious man, and he did not care to run risks.

" Are they friends and confidants of yours ? " he asked, rather pointedly.

It was an odd speech to make, but as he smiled slightly, they took it for a sought of joke.

" Oh, yes, they are our confidential friends," returned Harry Girdwood, smiling.

" Very good, let us begin our look round. We will walk along the quays if you like, and thence past the Hotel de Ville. I shall show you several objects of undoubted interest," said Lenoir significantly.

He led the way on.

Jack fell back a few paces walking on with Harry Girdwood.

" He's a very odd fellow," whispered the latter.

" Very,"

Lenoir led them over the town before he ventured to approach the Caveaux.

" I have a little museum not far away," he said.

" I am afraid we shall be intruding," began Jack.

" Not a bit," protested Lenoir.

The snuggery in question was situated at

some little distance from the town, and away from the main road.

The cottage was only a one-story building.

"His museum is not very extensive." whispered Harry Girdwood to his companion, " if it is that cottage."

Lenior was remarkably quick-eared.

"My museum is cunningly arranged," he said to Jack, looking over his shoulder as he walked on ; " you don't get all over it at once. Here we are."

They had reached the threshold, and opening the door, he led the way in.

It was a neat little cottage interior, with nothing about it to attract attention.

Passing through the first room, Lenoir conducted them to a sort of out-house beyond.

Here they came upon the first surprise.

He opened a door which apparently shut in a cupboard, and this, to their intense astonishment, revealed a flight of stone steps which seemingly led into the very bowels of the earth.

"Hallo!" exclaimed Jack ; " why, what's this?"

"I thought I should astonish you, now," said Lenoir, with his same calm smile.

"What is this place?.'

"There is a whole series of caves below these, apparently natural formations. The only way I can account for them myself is that at some time or other some experimental mining operations have gone on there. Would you like to go down and see the place?"

"With pleasure," returned Jack, eagerly.

"Allow me to lead the way."

When they had descended a few steps, Jack half repented.

This man was a stranger to them, and he had brought them to a very wild and out-of-the-way place.

Had he any evil purpose in bringing them there?

Jack stood wavering for a few seconds—no more.

"We are four," he said to himself, "four without counting Mr. Mole ; they must be a pretty tough lot to frighten us much, after all said and done."

So saying, down he went.

The others followed close behind him.

At the base of the flight of steps they found themselves in a spacious vault that was unpleasantly dark.

"Allow me to lead the way now," said Lenoir, passing on. "Follow me closely ; there is no fear of stumbling, there is nothing in the way."

So saying, he conducted them through this opening, which, by the way, was so low that they had to stoop in passing under, and found themselves now in a narrow cave, which reminded young Jack forcibly of the dungeon and its approach of Sir Walter Raleigh, in the Tower of London.

"What do you think of this place?" demanded the guide.

"A very curious sight," was the reply. "You put all this space to no use?"

"Pardon me," said Lenoir ; " I practice my favourite hobby here."

"Here!"

"Yes—or rather in the next cellar beyond."

"And what may be that favourite hobby?"

"Medalling," was Lenoir's reply.

And again he shot at his questioner one of those peculiar glances which had so astonished them before.

"I should like to see some of your work," said Jack.

"I thought you would," said Lenoir, with a quiet chuckle.

Lenoir led the way into the next cellar or cavern, and here they came suddenly upon a complete change of scene.

Here they saw a furnace, with melting pots, bars of metal, moulds, files, batteries, and all the necessary accessories for the manufacture of medals.

Upon a flat stone slab was a pile of medals, all of the same pattern precisely.

"Just examine those, Mr. Harkaway," said Pierre Lenoir, " and tell me what you think of them."

Jack put his fingers through the glittering heap, and they fell to the table with a bright clear ring that considerably astonished him.

"Why, they are silver?"

Lenoir smiled.

"Very good, aren't they?"

"Very!"

Jack here made a discovery, upon examining them more closely.

"They are five-franc pieces!" he said, with a puzzled expression.

"Of course they are—and beauties they are too!"

"There's not much risk in getting rid of those, I should say?"

"Risk!" iterated Harry Girdwood.

"Aye!"

"Why risk?"

"I mean that no one could detect the difference very easily. "Why, they deceived you," he added, turning to Jack, with an air of conscious pride.

"Upon my life, I don't understand what you mean," said Jack.

Lenoir looked serious for a moment.

Then he burst out into a boisterous fit of merriment.

"You are really over-cautious, young gentleman," he said.

"Over-cautious?"

"Why, yes—why, yes. Wherefore this reserve? Why should you pretend not to understand? Don't you see," he added, with a cunning leer, "that I can make these medals as perfectly as they can at the Hotel de la Monnaie, our French Mint?"

"So I see," said Jack.

A faint light began to dawn upon Harry Girdwood—not too soon, the reader will say.

"It is rather a dangerous pastime, Mr. Lenoir, this medalling fancy of yours" he said.

"No," said Lenoir, pointedly, " the danger is not there ; the danger of this pastime, as you call it, is in disposing of my beautiful medals."

"Dear me, sir," said Mr. Mole. "Do you sell them?"

"Yes."

"How much?"

"The five-franc pieces two francs and a

half," replied Lenoir, "and so on throughout until we get up to the louis, the twenty-franc pieces ; those I can do for seven francs. You can pass them without risk."

This told all.

Jack and his friends were astounded.

"Are you making us overtures to join you in passing bad money?" demanded young Jack.

"Not bad money," returned Lenoir, "very good money—all my own make."

"It is very evident that you do not know us," said Harry Girdwood, "and so are considerably mistaken. Why you have brought us here and placed yourself in our power, it is utterly beyond me to understand."

Lenoir stared.

"What !"

"The position is most embarrassing," said Jack. "To do our duty would be to repay by great ingratitude your kindness in guiding us about the town, for we ought to denounce you to the police authorities."

This speech partook of the nature of a threat, and Pierre Lenoir was up in an instant.

"The worst day's work of your life would be that," he said, fiercely. "No man plays traitor to Pierre Lenoir a second time."

"Traitor is a wrong term," said Jack ; "we are not sworn to share such confidences as yours. We shall leave you now, but——"

"Stop !"

They were moving towards the entrance. when Lenoir sprang before them, and whipped out a brace of revolvers.

The position grew exciting and unpleasant.

"Stand out of the way, and let us pass," exclaimed Jack, impetuously.

"Don't come any nearer," said Lenoir, with quiet determination, "for I warn you that it would be dangerous. You can't move from this place until you have made terms with me."

"I for one will have nothing whatever to say to you," said Jack, haughtily. "I don't care to bargain with a coiner."

With his old foolhardy way he was stepping forward, in peril of his very life.

Lenoir was a desperate man, in a desperate strait.

His finger trembled upon the trigger.

"Stand back, on your life."

"You stand aside," cried Jack.

"Another step and I fire ! " cried Lenoir.

"Bah ! "

Jack pushed on.

Lenoir pulled the trigger.

Bang it went.

But the ball whistled harmlessly over Jack's head, and lodged in the slanting roof.

A friendly hand from behind the coiner had knocked up his arm in the very nick of time.

At the self-same instant some eight or ten men, fully armed, burst into the vault.

One of them, who was apparently in command, pointed to Lenoir, and said to the others—

"Arrest that man. He's the leader of them."

And before the coiner could offer any resistance, they knocked his weapons from his hands, and fell upon him.

But Lenoir was a powerful fellow—a desperate, determined man, and not so easily disposed of.

With wonderful energy, he tore himself from them, and, producing something from one of his pockets, he held it menacingly up.

"Advance a step," he exclaimed, "and I will blow you all to atoms, myself as well. Beware ! I hold all our lives in my hand. Now who dares advance ? "

CHAPTER XCIII.

LENOIR'S FLIGHT—MURRAY THE TRAITOR— HIS PUNISHMENT AND FLIGHT—A LONG RUN—THE AUBERGE—A STRANGE DISAPPEARANCE.

THERE was a pause.

Pierre Lenoir looked liked mischief.

His position was desperate, and they judged and rightly judged, that he was a man not likely to stick at a trifle.

The men looked at their officer, and the latter, a man of intelligence and prudence, albeit no coward, reflected seriously.

Several terrible calamities, accidental and intentional, had of late opened the eyes of the public to the destructive properties of dynamite, and to that his thoughts flew.

He wavered.

The coiner saw his chance, and quick to act as to think, he made for the exit.

"Stand back ;" he cried, fiercely, to the men who made a faint show of barring his passage. "I'll finish you all off at a stroke if you attempt to oppose me ? "

They fell back alarmed.

Lenoir darted on through the inner vault, and so on until he gained the flight of steps.

Reaching the top, he darted through the cottage, and reaching the open, suddenly found himself in the midst of about a dozen men.

The first person upon whom his glance rested was the doubly-dyed traitor who had betrayed him solely to serve his own ends. by entrapping Jack Harkaway—the Englishman, who must have been recognised by the reader, in spite of his assumed name, as Herbert Murray.

Instinctively Lenoir divined that his betrayer was the young Englishman.

No sooner did his conclusion force itself upon him than all thought of personal danger vanished from his mind, and he was possessed by one sole idea, one single desire. Revenge !

He lost sight of the peril in which he ran, but with a cry like the roar of a wounded lion he sprang upon the traitor.

A brawny, powerful fellow was Pierre Lenoir, and Herbert Murray was but a puny thing in his grasp.

"Hands off ! " exclaimed Murray, in desperation.

Lenoir growled, but said nothing, as he shook him much as a terrier does a rat.

Before the police could interfere in the spy's behalf, Lenoir held him with one hand at arm's length, while with the other he prepared to deliver a fearful blow.

The energy of despair seized on the hapless traitor, and wrenching himself free from the coiner's grasp, he fled.

"MOLE TOOK THE DOCUMENT, AND OPENED IT."

Pierre Lenoir stood staring about him a second.

Then he made after him.

Away went pursuer and pursued.

The terror-stricken Murray got over the ground like a hare, and although the coiner was fleet of foot, he was at first distanced in the race.

It became a desperate race between them.

Lenoir tore on.

He would have his betrayer now or perish.

But before he had got more than two hundred yards the pace began to tell upon him.

He felt that he would have to give in.

"I must go easier, or I shall fail altogether."

So reasoning, he slackened his pace, and dropped into that slinging trot that runners in France know as the *pas gymnastique*.

If your strength and wind are of average quality, you can keep up for a prodigious time at that.

Murray flew on, anxious to get away from his furious pursuer.

He increased his lead.

But presently the pace told upon him likewise.

He collected his thoughts and his prudence as he went, and rested.

Glancing over his shoulder, he saw Lenoir come bounding along, a considerable distance in the rear.

"Savage beast!" thought Murray. "He means mischief."

Murray meant tiring him out.

This, however, was not so easily done.

The Englishman was a capital runner, and had been one of the crack men of his school-club.

But his *forte* was pace.

The Frenchman, on the contrary, was a stayer.

It looked bad for Murray.

On they went, and when a good mile had been covered, Murray, on glancing back, felt convinced that it was only a question of time.

He must tire out the Frenchman in the end, he thought.

He believed that an Englishman must always be more than a match for a Frenchman at any kind of athletics.

He reckoned without his host, for while he (Murray) was getting blown, Lenoir swung on at his *pas gymnastique*, having got his second wind, and being, to all appearance, capable of keeping on for any length of time.

"I shall have to give it up," gasped Murray, when, at the end of the second mile, he looked over his shoulder again.

An unpleasant fact revealed itself.

While he was faltering, the Frenchman was rather improving his pace.

Yes.

The distance between them was lessening.

And now he could hear Lenoir's menaces quite plainly as the coiner gained upon him.

"I shall have you directly, and I shall beat your skull in!" the Frenchman said.

Murray's craven heart leapt to his mouth.

Already he felt as if his cranium was cracked by the brutal fist of the savage coiner.

Fear lent him wings.

He put on a spurt.

"Oh, if I had but a pistol," thought Murray; "what a fool I was to come unarmed on such a job as this."

He partially flagged again.

The distance between them was still decreasing.

This he felt was the beginning of the end, but just as he was thinking that there was nothing for it but to turn and make the best fight for it he could, he sighted a roadside inn—a rural auberge.

And for this he flew with renewed energy.

Dashing into the house, he pushed to the door and startled the aubergiste by gasping out in the best French he could command—

"*Un assassin me poursuit. Cachez-moi, ou donnez-moi de quoi me défendre!*"*

The landlord took Murray—and not unnaturally—for a madman.

He did not like the society of madmen.

To give a weapon to a furious maniac was out of all question.

And the landlord had nothing handy of a more deadly nature than a knife and fork.

Moreover, he would not have cared to place a dangerous weapon in a madman's hands.

So he met the case by humouring the fugitive with a proposal to go upstairs.

Murray wanted no second invitation.

Up he flew, and locked himself in one of the upper rooms just as Lenoir hammered at the door below.

"*Où est-il?*"† demanded the coiner, fiercely.

"*Qui?*"‡

"*Ne cherchez pas à me tricher*," thundered Lenoir. "*Il m'appartient. Où est-il, je vous le demande?*"§

The coiner's manner made the aubergiste uneasy, and thoughtful for his own safety.

So he pointed upstairs.

Up went Lenoir, and finding a room door locked, he flung his whole weight against the door and sent it in.

This was the room which the fugitive had entered.

But where was Murray?

Gone!

Vanished!

But where?

CHAPTER XCIV.

THE COINER AND THE SPY—A REGULAR DUST-UP, AND WHAT CAME OF IT—THE CHASE—AN ODD ESCAPE—HUNTING IN THE HAY—A ROUGH CUSTOMER DONE FOR.

WHEN Lenoir had puzzled himself for some time over the mysterious disappearance of Herbert Murray for awhile, he made a discovery.

The window was open, a circumstance which he had until then, in the most unaccountable manner imaginable, overlooked.

But when he got to the window and looked out, there were no signs of the object of his search.

---

* "I am pursued by an assassin. Hide me, or give me something to defend myself with."
† "Where is he?"
‡ "Who?"
§ "Seek not to deceive me." thundered Lenoir. "He belongs to me. Where is he, I ask you again?"

He had followed so sharply that Murray could not have had time to get off.

He looked up and down the road eagerly.

The only thing in sight was a waggon load of hay drawn by a team of horses, at whose head plodded a waggoner in a blue cotton blouse, whip in hand.

"*Hé, la bas!*" shouted the coiner from the window.

The waggoner turned and looked eagerly up.

"*Qu'avez-vous?*" demanded the waggoner. "What's the matter?"

"Have you seen anyone jump out of window?" shouted Lenoir.

The waggoner responded tartly, for he fancied that his questioner was trying to chaff him.

"I've seen no one mad enough for that; in fact I've seen no one madder than you since I've been in this part of the country."

"*Espèce de voyou!*" cried the irritable Lenoir, "*je te ficherais une danse si j'avais le temps pour t'apprendre ce que c'est que la politesse.* I'd dust your jacket for you if I had the time to teach you politeness."

"You're not likely to have time enough for that, as long as you live, *espèce de pignouf.*"

"Idiot!"

"*Imbécile!*"

This interchange of compliments appeared to relieve the belligerent parties considerably.

Lenoir was obliged to give it up for a bad job.

Suddenly a singular idea shot into his head.

The hay cart!

What if Herbert Murray had got into it unseen and was there now, without his presence being suspected by the waggoner?

Lenoir reflected for a moment.

Then he darted down the stairs in pursuit of the waggon.

"Hullo, there, driver!" he shouted.

The waggoner looked over his shoulder and recognised Lenoir.

So he whipped up.

The best pace that even a stout team of horses could put on, with a big load of hay behind them was not to say race-horse speed, so the coiner soon caught them up.

The waggoner awaited his approach, grasping his whip with a nervous grip that foreboded mischief.

On came Lenoir.

"I say, my friend," he called out, "I think you have a man concealed in the cart!"

"*Va-t-en!*—get out!" retorted the waggoner.

"I am serious. Will you oblige me by pulling up and looking?"

"Not exactly."

Lenoir had a very limited stock of patience, and he soon came to the end of it.

He ran to the leading horse and pulled it up sharply.

The waggoner swore and lashed up.

But Lenoir, turning his attention next to the shaft horse, pulled the waggon up to a standstill.

And the waggoner, furious at this, lashed Lenoir.

The whip caught him round the head and shoulders, curling about so that the man could not get it free.

Lenoir caught at the thong, and with a sudden jerk, brought the waggoner down from his seat.

Now began as pretty a little skirmish as you could wish to see.

The waggoner fell an easy prey to the furious coiner at first.

He was half-dazed with being jerked down to the ground.

But he soon recovered himself.

Then he set to punching at Lenoir with all his strength.

Then they grappled fiercely with each other.

A desperate struggle for supremacy ensued.

At length Lenoir's superior strength and science prevailed, tough as the waggoner was.

The latter lay under the coiner, whose knee pressed cruelly upon his chest.

"Now ask my pardon," said Lenoir.

"Never!" roared the defeated waggoner, stoutly.

"I shall kill you if you don't," said Lenoir, threateningly.

"Mind you don't get finished off first," said the waggoner, significantly.

As he spoke, he was looking up over his conqueror's shoulder.

Lenoir perceived this, but thought it only a *ruse* to get him to shift his hold.

So, with a contemptuous smile, he raised his clenched fist to deal the luckless waggoner a blow that was to knock every scrap of sense out of his unfortunate cranium.

"Take that!"

But before the waggoner could get it, Lenoir received something himself that sent him to earth with a hollow groan—felled like a bullock beneath the butcher's pole-axe.

Somebody had after all been concealed in the waggon.

That somebody was Herbert Murray himself.

The English youth had heard the scuffle, and seeing his opportunity, he slid out of his place of concealment and joined in the fight at the very right moment.

*   *   *   *   *

The waggoner shook himself together.

"That was neatly done, *camarade*," he said.

"I was just in time," said Murray; "look after him. He is wanted by the police; a desperate customer. They are after him now."

"He's very quiet," said the waggoner, with a curious glance.

"He's not dead," returned Murray; "he has his destiny to fulfil yet."

"What may that be?"

"The galleys," was the reply.

The waggoner stared hard at young Murray.

"I don't like the look of you much more than that of the beast lying there," he thought to himself; "mind you don't keep him company in the galleys."

An odd fancy to cross a stranger's mind.

Was it prophetic?

CHAPTER XCV.

PLANS FOR OUR FRIENDS' RELEASE—MUR-RAY'S COUNTERPLOT—THE LETTER, AND HOW IT WAS INTERCEPTED — HERBERT MURRAY TRIUMPHS—CHIVEY WORKS THE ARTFUL DODGE.

"WELL," exclaimed the unfortunate Mole, "this is a nice go !"

"I'm glad you think it nice," said young Jack, bitterly.

As they spoke, they were being led through the streets of Marseilles, handcuffed and two abreast, with a brace of gensdarmes between each couple.

The people flocked out to stare at the "notorious gang of forgers, which"—so ran the report—"had just been captured by the police, after making a desperate resistance."

The first impulse of Jack Harkaway himself had been naturally to resist his captors.

But he was speedily shown the uselessness of such a course.

When they were brought up before the judge for examination, they protested their innocence, and told the simple truth.

But this did not avail them.

Herbert Murray had prepared the way for their statements to be regarded as falsehoods.

By this means, when Jack protested that his name was Harkaway, it went clearly against him, inasmuch as it corroborated what Murray had said.

So they were remanded, one and all, and sent back to the cells.

Mr. Mole's indignation could not be subdued.

"These people are worse than savages !" he exclaimed ; "but we'll let them know. They shall make us ample reparation for this indignity."

He talked threateningly of the British ambassador, and made all kinds of threats.

But he was poohpoohed by the authorities.

Harry Girdwood was the only one of the party who kept his coolness.

He put forth his request with so much earnestness, to be allowed to see the English consul, that his request was granted at once.

He drew up a letter and entrusted it to the gaoler, who promised to have it forwarded.

Now this became known to Herbert Murray, and he then saw that he had still a task of no ordinary difficulty before him—that it was not sufficient alone to have his hated enemies arrested.

The greater difficulty by far was to keep them now that he had secured them.

In this crisis he once more consulted with his worthless servant and confederate, Chivey.

"Our next job," said Chivey, doubtfully, "is to get at the gaoler, and stop the letter he has received from reaching its destination."

"How would you set to work ?" demanded his master.

"You do what you can inside," said Chivey, "and I'll lay in wait for the messenger with the letter outside in case you fail."

"Good."

"You can buy that gaoler," said the tiger.

"I will."

"Do so. Your task is the easier of the two. Ten francs ought to square him."

"It ought," said Murray ; "but I question if it will."

*   *   *   *   *

Murray was doomed to a sad disappointment in his operations, for do what he would, he could not "get at" the man charged with delivering the Harkaways' letters.

But he contrived to ascertain who the man was, and to give a description of him to the tiger.

Chivey saw the man come out of the prison, and he thought over various plans for getting hold of the letter which he knew that he must be carrying.

His first idea was to go up to him and address him straight off upon the subject ; but this would not do.

The messenger would in all probability take the alarm.

He next had an idea of following up the messenger, and after giving him a crack on the head, rifling his pockets.

This idea he abandoned even sooner than the first, and this for sundry wholesome reasons.

Firstly, the man's road did not lead him into any sufficiently quiet places for such an attempt.

Secondly, the man was a tough-looking customer, and an awkward fellow to tackle.

And thirdly—but the second reason sufficed to send Chivey's mind away from all ideas of violence.

No ; deeds of daring were not at all in Chivey's line.

He had a notion, however, and this was to go as fast as he could to the British consul's, and there to be ready for the messenger when he came.

His plans were not more matured than this ; but chance seemed to very much favour this precious pair of youthful scamps—for the time being, at any rate.

*   *   *   *   *

Chivey timed his own arrival at the consul's residence, so as to be there just a few minutes in advance of the prison messenger.

The servant who admitted him was an Englishman, and told Chivey that his master was particularly engaged just then, and would not be visible for some considerable time.

"Be so good as to ask when I can see your master," said Chivey, with an air of lofty condescension.

"I must not disturb him now," said the servant.

"He will be very vexed with you if you don't," returned Chivey, "when he knows my business."

The servant being only impressed with this threat, went off at once to obey the insidious tiger, who of course was not in livery.

Barely had the consul's servant disappeared, when the messenger from the prison entered.

Chivey recognised him instantly.

"*Une lettre pour Monsieur le Consul*," said the messenger.

Chivey held out his hand, and the man,

taking it for granted that Chivey belonged to the consular establishment, gave it to him.

"*Il y a une réponse*—there is an answer," said the messenger.

"It will be forwarded," returned Chivey, with cool presence of mind.

"I ought to take it with me," said the messenger.

"I can't disturb his excellency now," replied the tiger; "those are my master's express orders, which I can't presume to disobey. He will send the answer on immediately it is ready."

The man paused.

"The consul was expecting this letter," said Chivey, moving towards the door, "and he told me particularly that he would send the answer on."

"*Puisqu'il est ainsi*," said the man, dubiously. "Since it must be so, I suppose I had better leave the letter."

"Of course you had," returned Chivey, closing the door. "I daresay you will get the answer within an hour."

At that very moment the servant returned with a message from the consul to the effect that in half an hour he could be seen, if the applicant would call again.

"Very good," said Chivey, in the same patronizing manner; "you may tell your master that I will look back later on."

"Very well, sir."

Chivey walked out, chuckling inwardly at the success of his mission.

"What could be easier?" said the Cockney scamp to himself; "shelling peas is a fool to it."

But before he could get fairly over the threshold, the servant stopped him with a question that startled him a little, and well-nigh made him lose his presence of mind.

"The man who called just now, sir, he left a letter."

"Eh? Oh, yes!"

"For you, sir!"

"Yes," added Chivey with the coolest effrontery. "My servant knew that I had come on here; thinking to be detained some time with his excellency the consul, I left word at my hotel where I was coming, and he followed me here with a letter."

"Oh, I see, sir," returned the servant, obsequiously, "quite so, sir, beg pardon, sir."

"Not at all, my good man, not at all," returned Chivey, superciliously; "you are a very civil, well-spoken young man—here is a trifle for you."

He passed the servant a large silver coin, and walked on.

The servant bowed again and examined the coin, in the process of bobbing his head.

"Five francs," said the consul's servant, to himself; "he's a real swell, anyone can see."

One word more.

The five-franc piece which had in no slight degree biassed the servant's opinion of the visitor, was one of Pierre Lenoir's admirable manufacture.

*   *   *   *   *

"Let's have a look at the letter, Chivey," said Herbert Murray, as soon as his servant got back.

But Chivey seemed to hesitate.

"Come, come," said Murray, "we shall not quarrel about the terms."

"We oughtn't to," returned the tiger, "for it's worth a Jew's eye."

Murray tore the letter open and read it down eagerly.

As it throws some additional light upon the actual state of affairs with the Harkaway party, possibly it may be as well to give the letter of young Jack to the consul verbatim.

It was dated from the prison.

"SIR,—I wish to solicit your immediate assistance in getting released from the above uncomfortable premises, where, in company with a party of friends and fellow-travellers, I have been by a singular accident carried by the police. From scraps of information I have gained while here, I believe I am correct in asserting that we have fallen into a trap, cunningly prepared for us by an unscrupulous fellow-countryman of ours, who has cogent reasons for wishing us out of the way, and has accordingly caused me and my friends to be arrested as coiners. The person in question is named Herbert Murray, but I am unable to say under what *alias* he is at present known in this part of the world. I mention this that you may be able to keep an eye upon the individual pending our release on bail, for I presume that bail is a French institution. My signature will serve you for reference on me, as it may readily be identified at my father's bankers here, Messrs. B. Fould and Co.

"Your obedient servant,
"JACK HARKAWAY."

Herbert Murray pursed his brows as he read on.

"What do you think of that?" demanded Chivey.

"Queer!"

"Precious queer."

"The one lesson to be learnt from it, Chivey," said his master, "is to stop all correspondence between the prisoners and the consul."

"And push forward the trial as much as possible."

"Yes, and get together as many reliable witnesses as we can——"

"Buy them at a pound apiece," concluded Chivey.

"Right," said Herbert Murray, with a mischievous grin; "forewarned, forearmed; we hold them now and we'll keep them——"

"Please the pigs," concluded Chivey, fervently.

CHAPTER XCVI.

OUR FRIENDS IN DURANCE VILE—A STROKE FOR LIBERTY—THE PRISONERS' PLOT—MOLE IS PRESCRIBED FOR—A FRIEND IN NEED—HOPES AND MISGIVINGS—"OLD WET BLANKET."

"IT's very odd."

"Very."

"And scarcely polite," suggested Mr. Mole.

"Well, scarcely."

"That makes the fourth letter I have

written to him, and he doesn't even condescend to notice them."

"Very odd."

"Very."

But while all the sufferers by the seeming neglect of the consul were expressing themselves so freely in the matter, old Sobersides, as Jack called his comrade, Harry Girdwood, remained silent and meditative.

Jack had great faith in his thoughtful chum.

"A penny for your thoughts, Harry," said he.

"I'll give them for nix," returned Harry Girdwood, gaily.

"Out with it."

"I was wondering whether, while you are all blaming the poor consul, he has ever received your letters."

"What, the four?"

"Yes."

"Of course."

"I don't see it."

"But, my dear fellow, consider. One may have miscarried — or two—but hang it! all four can't have gone wrong."

"Of course not," said Mole, with the air of a man who puts a final stop to all arguments.

"There I beg leave to differ with you all."

"Why?"

"The letters have not reached the consul, perhaps; they may have been intercepted."

"By whom?" was Jack's natural question.

"Can't say positively; possibly by Murray."

"Is it likely?"

"Is it not?"

"I don't see, unless he bought over the messenger."

"And what is more likely than that?" said Harry. "And if they have bought over one messenger, it is for good and all, not for a single letter, but for every scrap of paper you may send out of the prison, you may depend upon it."

This simple reasoning struck his hearers.

"Upon my life!" exclaimed Jack, "I believe Harry's right. We must tackle the governor."

"So I think."

"And I too," added Harry Girdwood; "but how?"

"I'll write him a letter."

"Yes; and send it to him by the gaoler," said Harry.

"Yes."

"The gaoler who carried all the other letters? Why, Jack, Jack, what a thoughtless, rattle-brained chap you are. What on earth is the use of such a move as that?"

Jack's countenance fell again at this.

"You're right, Harry I go jumping like a bull at a gate as usual. What would you do?"

Harry's answer was brief and sententious.

"Think."

"Do so, mate," returned Jack, hopefully again; "do so."

"I will."

He pressed his lips and knit his brows with a burlesque, melodramatic air, and strode up, and down, with his forefinger to his forehead.

He stopped suddenly and stamped twice, as a haughty earl might do in a transpontine

tragedy when resolving upon his crowning villany, and exclaimed in a voice suggestive of fiend-like triumph—

"I have it."

"Hold it tight, then."

"One of us must sham ill so as to get the doctor here. Once he's here, we shall be all right."

"Hurrah!" cried Jack Harkaway; "that's the notion. We shall yet defeat the schemes of that incarnate fiend, Murray."

"That is a capital idea," said Mr. Mole. "You have suggested quite a new idea."

"Now stop; the next thing for us to think of is who is to be the sham invalid," said Jack.

"I would suggest Tinker," said Harry.

"Or Bogey," observed Mr. Mole.

"Why?"

"Because it would not be easy to tell whether they looked in delicate health or not."

"There's something in that," said Jack, "but there's this to say against it."

"What?"

"They might not be able to keep the game up so well as one of ourselves, so I think——"

Here Jack paused, whilst Harry and he exchanged a meaning wink unobserved by the old gentleman.

"I think that it ought to be Mr. Mole," continued our hero.

"Why?"

"Why, sir; can you ask why? You are such a lovely shammer."

"Come, I say," began Mr. Mole, scarcely relishing it.

"He's quite right, sir," said Harry Girdwood, "you are inimitable as a shammer."

"I?"

"You can pitch it so strong, Mr. Mole," said Jack.

"And so natural," added Harry Girdwood.

"Life-like," said the two together, in mingled tones of rapt admiration.

Mr. Mole was but human.

Humanity is but frail, and ever open to the voice of flattery.

What could Mole do but yield?

Nothing.

He gave in, and shammed very ill indeed.

Well, the result of this was that the gaoler made his report, and the doctor came.

"*De quoi se plaint-il?*" demanded the doctor, as he entered the cell.

"What does he say?" asked Mole; "I'm as deaf as an adder."

"The doctor asks what you complain of?" said Jack, in a very loud voice.

"Oh, anything he likes," returned Mole, impatiently.

They were on the point of bursting out laughing at this, when the doctor startled them considerably by saying in broken (but understandable) English—

"What he say—anything I like? *Singulier!*"

"Ahem!"

Harry Girdwood gave the word; a glance of intelligence went round.

They, to use Jack's expression, pulled themselves together, and looked serious.

"It is headache," said Jack. "Violent headache, he says."

"Yes," said Mole.

"Show your tongue."

Mole thrust it out, and then the doctor felt his pulse.

"Very bad ; you have the fever."

"What ?" ejaculated Mole, aghast.

"You have the fever."

"What sort ?"

The surgeon looked puzzled.

"Typhus or scarlet," I should say, suggested Jack.

"What is that ?" demanded the French doctor, curiously. "*Je ne suis pas très fort*— I am not very strong in English."

"Then, sir," said Jack, "pray accept my compliments upon your proficiency ; it is really very remarkable."

"You are very good to say that," returned the surgeon ; "*mais*—now for our *malade*— what is *malade* in English ?"

"Patient."

"Patient ! Well, I hope that he will justify ze designation. What do you feel ?" he added to Mr. Mole.

"Rush of blood to the head," said Mole, thinking this quite a safe symptom to announce.

"Yes, yes—*sans doute*—no doubt," said the doctor, looking as wise as an owl. "We can make that better for you quick—a little *sinapisme*."

"That's what you call a mustard plaister, isn't it ?" said Harry.

"*Sinapisme*—mustard who ?" demanded the French doctor of Jack.

"Plaister."

"*Merci*."

"I'm not going to have any mustard plaister on," said Mole.

"*Comment !*" exclaimed the doctor ; "*il n'en veut pas !* he will not ! *Morbleu !* Ze prisonniers have what ze docteur ordonnances."

"Will he ?"

"Yes. You are quite right, doctor," said Jack, in French. "Where is he to have on the plaister ?"

"On his legs, at the back of his ankles," replied the doctor ; "it is to draw the blood from his head."

"Very good, sir."

Jack translated, and the patient singularly enough grew reassured immediately.

"It won't hurt much on the back of your legs, Mr. Mole," said Harry.

They enjoyed a quiet grin to themselves at this.

The prison doctor then sent the gaoler for writing materials for the purpose of writing out a prescription.

Then was their chance.

"Doctor," said Jack, "I want to see the governor."

"Why have you not asked, then, through the gaoler ?"

"I prefer some other method."

"Why ?"

"Because I don't know whether the gaoler is safe."

"I don't understand you," said the doctor.

"I have written four letters to the British consul," returned Jack, "and no answer has come."

"Well ?"

"Well, sir, I am afraid he has never received the letters."

"Why ?"

"Because my name is well-known to him, and he would have replied. I have referred him to the chief banker of the town, who can readily identify me through my signature. I wish them to communicate with my father, and, in a word, to show the authorities how utterly ridiculous and preposterous is the charge against us in spite of appearances."

Jack's earnestness caught his attention.

"They would never dare to keep letters back."

"Money has tempted them, I feel assured."

"Whose money ?"

"The money of a spy—a fellow countryman of ours, who has interest in keeping me out of the way."

"His name ?"

"His real name is Herbert Murray, his assumed name is Markby."

"Markby ; I know that name. Of course ; he is the principal witness against you. You say his assumed name ?"

"Yes."

"Can you prove it ?"

"Easily ; if I can get at the means of establishing a defence. It is to effect this that I have addressed myself to the consul, but he does not reply, so that, monstrous and absurd as this charge is, we are unable to disprove it, simply because here we are tied hand and foot."

"This is very strange."

The doctor, as he spoke, shot them a dubious glance, which did not escape Jack.

"I tell you, sir, that my father is rich and influential. Moreover, he is exceedingly liberal in money matters with me. I have not the slightest need to add to my income by any means whatever, much less dishonest courses."

"What proof can I offer to the governor ?"

"Plenty," returned Jack, eagerly. "Here is my father's address in England ; let him be communicated with immediately. This Markby is an unscrupulous rascal. He has forged my name to several cheques, and robbed me. He fears detection, and has built up a cunning plot, using the coiner, Lenoir, as his catspaw, and while we are caged here upon this ridiculous charge, he can get off to another part of the world."

This convinced the prison surgeon completely.

"I will see the governor at once," said he ; "meanwhile, see that your obstinate old friend attends to my instructions, and he will soon be well."

"Excuse me, doctor," said Jack, "but the honest truth is that he is not ill at all."

"Not ill !"

"No. We doubted the gaoler's honesty, and, fearing he was bought over by our enemy, adopted this ruse."

"To see me ?"

"Yes."

"Ha, ha ! I see it all now ; very ingenious on your part. Well, well, my young friend, I will see the governor at once, and you shall not be long in trouble."

"You will earn my eternal gratitude, and

that of my fellow prisoners, as well as the much more substantial acknowledgment of my father."

"*Bien, bien,*" said the surgeon smiling. "*Au revoir!*"

And bowing pleasantly to the prisoners generally, the doctor left the cell.

* * * * *

"There," said Jack. "You may look upon that as settled, so comfort yourselves."

"He has gone to the governor?" asked Mole.

"Yes."

"Hurrah!"

"I hope it will go all right now," said Harry Girdwood, who was scarcely so cheerful as his companions.

"You wretched old wet blanket!" exclaimed Jack, gaily, "of course it will."

"Of course," added Mole.

"You may consider yourself as good as outside the prison already."

"I do, for one," said Mole, quite hilarious at the prospect.

"Humph!" said Harry.

CHAPTER XCVII.

THE DOCTOR AND THE GOVERNOR—HOW THE PLOT WORKS IN FAVOUR OF JACK'S ENEMIES—UNLUCKY PRISONERS!

"*Sapristi!*"

Thus spake the governor of the prison.

The occasion was within a few minutes of the doctor's entrance into his private cabinet, to which the medico had gone immediately after quitting the English prisoners.

"*Sapristi!*"

"Well, what they say is very easily verified," said the doctor, rather tartly.

The fact is that he was somewhat nettled at the doubting expression with which the governor met his account of his interview with Jack Harkaway and his fellow prisoners.

"My dear Doctor Berteaux," returned the governor, with the most irritating smile, "this youth is a notorious young scoundrel. Just see how clever he must be, too; he has actually imposed upon the astute Doctor Berteaux, who has such a vast experience amongst criminals."

"But, sir——"

"I tell you, doctor, I know all about this young scoundrel from A to Z. His real name is Herbert Murray."

"Why, that he said was the real name of the agent Markby," exclaimed the doctor.

"The deuce he did. Egad! doctor, that's beautiful."

And the governor chuckled rarely at the idea.

The doctor began to look a little uncomfortable.

"Do you mean to say——"

"That you have been egregiously humbugged? Yes, that's exactly what I do mean. Why, doctor, doctor, at your time of life consider."

"But——"

"Come, come, get rid of this silly fancy, old friend."

"At least," insisted the doctor, "do me the favour to communicate with the consul."

"Indeed, I shall do nothing of the kind. You can see the British consul if you like, and a rare laugh he'll enjoy at your expense when he sees how you have been duped by this young scoundrel."

"Ahem!"

* * * * *

Well, the doctor did not communicate with the consul after this, and Jack Harkaway waited with his companions, Mole and the "wet blanket," Harry Girdwood, and the two faithful darkeys, and waited in vain.

Waited until they grew heart-sick with hope deferred.

CHAPTER XCVIII.

JOE DEERING AT HOME AGAIN—ON THE LOOK-OUT—NEWS AT LAST—JOVIAL CAPTAIN ROBINSON IN DANGER.

WE must cross the Channel to England again.

But not for long.

One character in our drama of real life has not appeared upon the scene for some time.

We allude to the skipper of the "Albatross," Joe Deering.

Captain Deering had finished his course and returned to his native land.

He was anxious to get home, for he had a purpose in view.

He wished to rout out two men to whom he owed a very deep grudge, which he was fully determined to pay off.

One was Mr. Murray, the treacherous owner of the ill-fated "Albatross," for Captain Deering, it should be borne in mind, was ignorant of the wretched man's well-merited fate.

The other was that traitor friend of his, the accomplice of the elder Murray—jovial Captain Robinson.

Joe Deering was in earnest, and he pursued his inquiries with the utmost diligence.

The jovial captain was not to be heard of anywhere at first.

But Joe Deering, baffled here, like a skilled mariner as he was, set out on another tack.

He made his inquiries for Mr. Murray alone.

"Where one thief is," said Joe, to himself, "the other murdering scoundrel is sure to be not far off."

For some time his search proved unavailing again; but he was presently rewarded for his perseverance by the first gleam of good luck.

He learnt the late address of Murray senior.

"This is a step in the right direction," said Joe Deering, with a chuckle.

So with renewed hope he went to the house.

"Mr. Murray ain't been home for many months, sir," said the housekeeper, in reply to Deering's inquiry, "and I haven't any news of him since goodness knows when."

"You don't mean that?" said Deering, aghast.

"Indeed, but I do, and I hope that you're not going to misbelieve me like that Captain Robinson, that calls here every——"

"What?" ejaculated Deering. "Avast there. Captain Robinson, did you say?"

" Yes."

" Do you know him ?"

" I can't very well be off knowing him, seeing as he's here about twice a day, and I know he never wished my poor master no good."

" What makes you think that ?" asked Joe Deering.

" Master used always to try to avoid seeing him, poor old gentleman," replied the housekeeper.

" Why do you call him 'poor old gentleman ?'"

" Because I know he suffered dreadfully, and I think he was worried by that Robinson into doing something dreadful."

" How dreadful ?"

Joe Deering's curiosity was excited now by the housekeeper's manner, and he pressed her for further information.

" That Captain Robinson worrited him to a skeleton, sir," she answered; " he was always here nag, nag, nagging night and day. At last my poor master bolted, sir."

" Bolted !"

" Ran away."

" Where to ?"

" I don't know; but he bolted from here, and from Captain Robinson."

" But Mr. Murray was surely not in fear of Captain Robinson ?"

" Indeed, he was. Captain Robinson knew something about my poor master that oughtn't to be known, so it was said, and he was always trying to force Mr. Murray to give him money."

" The deuce he was !" said Captain Deering. " This throws a new light on the scoundrel and his cursed good-natured-looking figure-head."

" A deceitful beast !" said the housekeeper, warmly. " You would have thought that he couldn't hurt a worm to look at him, and yet I do believe that he's drove poor Mr. Murray to make away with himself."

" You don't think that ?"

" What else can I think ? He hasn't been seen or heard of for months and months. But if I wasn't so heavy at heart over that, sir, I could laugh for joy to see that beast of a Captain Robinson's disappointment every time he comes."

" So he comes often ?" said Joe Deering, eagerly.

" Every day; sometimes twice a day," was the reply.

Deering thought this information over quietly.

" Would you like to serve him out ?" he asked presently.

" Who ?"

" Captain Robinson," responded Deering.

" That I should, indeed," said the housekeeper, eagerly; " only show me how to do it."

" I will."

Joe Deering did.

He made himself known to the woman, and convinced her that he had ample reason for wishing to repay the grudge.

And they plotted together to wreak a well-merited vengeance upon that falsely jovial Captain Robinson.

The nature of that vengeance you will learn if you have patience to wait till the next chapter.

CHAPTER XCIX.

HOW CAPTAIN ROBINSON CAME TO APPLY HIS LEECH AGAIN—WHAT CAME OF IT—THE SEA GIVES UP ITS DEAD—A FEARSOME SIGHT—THE TRAITOR'S TERROR—JOE DEERING WIPES OFF AN OLD SCORE.

CAPTAIN ROBINSON was more jovial than ever.

His honest-looking, ruddy face was beaming with smiles, and he appeared as hearty as the most honest, upright and plain-sailing fellow in the world.

Captain Robinson was like **most** sailors in one respect; he was remarkably superstitious.

Instinctive presage of good luck to-day put him in rare spirits, as he made his customary call.

" I feel as if I was going to land him to-day," muttered the jovial captain to himself.

And his face was actually beaming with smiles, as his hand rested on the knocker.

" Oh, good morning, Mrs. Wilmot," he said, heartily; " how are you this bright morning, Mrs. Wilmot ?"

" Better, thank you, Captain Robinson," returned the housekeeper, giving him an odd glance.

" That's hearty. Why, you are looking more yourself."

" Better in health, because better in spirits," said the housekeeper, insidiously.

The captain pricked up his ears at this.

" Any better news by chance, Mrs. Wilmot ?" said he.

" Ah, that there is indeed," said she.

" About the master ?" asked he.

" That's it," said she.

" You don't mean to say that he's coming home again ?"

" I don't mean to say that he's coming," said the housekeeper, with wondrous significance.

" Why, whatever are you driving at ?" he said.

" I'm not a-driving at nothing, Captain Robinson—leastways, not that I am aware of. All I know is, that Mr. Murray ain't likely to be coming home, for he ain't in a position to come home, seeing as——"

She paused.

" What ?"

" Guess what."

" Hang it all, I can't."

" You must."

She laughed outright, and clapped her hands in regular kitten-like joy.

" What on earth do you mean, Mrs. Wilmot ? I hate such palavering and beating about the bush. If he's coming home, say so; if he ain't coming home, tell me where I can see him, or where he's hiding."

" Why, he can't be coming home when——"

Here she stopped short in the most aggravating manner in the world.

The jovial captain grew black and threatening.

He was just going to burst out into a noisy fit of abusive language, when she stopped him short with a remark which quite startled him.

" There, there, what an impatient man you

are, surely, Captain Robinson. Go upstairs and see for yourself why he ain't coming home."

The captain could only infer one thing from her words.

Murray was back.

Yes, he was not coming home, because he had already come.

This explained the housekeeper's joyous spirits, which seemed to bubble over in her.

"She's a nice old gal," said Robinson to himself, as he mounted the stairs, "and I'll stand her a trifle after I have applied my leech to her master again. Ha, ha, ha!"

The jovial captain laughed at the quaint conceit.

He rarely enjoyed the prospect of once more gloating over the miserable Murray writhing under the moral pressure.

"I'll make him bleed handsome for keeping away so long," thought this jovial mariner. "I wonder how he'll enjoy the leech after such a long while?"

His hand rested upon the handle of the door.

What a startler it would be for Mr. Murray.

"I'll knock," thought the jovial Captain Robinson; "he'll think it's Mother Wilmot again. Such larks!"

He knocked.

"Come in."

How changed the voice sounded.

"He's caught cold," thought the practical joker.

He opened the door.

Closed it carefully behind him to guard against intrusion.

Then he turned and faced—Joe Deering!

* * * * *

Jovial Captain Robinson stood aghast.

The sight of his old friend literally petrified him.

Deering stood facing the jovial scoundrel, his hands leaning on the table.

Not a muscle of his face moved.

A cold, settled expression was in his eyes.

So fixed, so steady, that they might have been set in the head of a dead man.

The jovial Robinson was tongue-tied for a time.

* * * * *

"Joe!"

This monosyllable he faltered after a long while, and after a very big effort.

But Joe Deering said never a word in reply, nor did he move a muscle.

"Joe."

Deering stared at him with the same fixed, glassy eyes, until jovial Captain Robinson had a hideous idea flash across him.

Was it really a living man there?

He fastened a fixed, fascinating look upon the figure of the friend he had so villanously betrayed, and retreating a step, groped about behind him, for the handle of the door.

At last he got hold of it, and turned it.

"Stop!"

Deering had spoken, and with a jerk the jovial Captain Robinson turned round.

"Joe!" he gasped, again, "did you speak?"

Now Joe Deering saw by the traitor's pallid cheeks, and frightened look, what was passing in his mind.

So he was at no pains to destroy the illusion.

"I did. Your ears did not deceive you."

"I thought not," faltered Captain Robinson, plucking up in a faint degree, however.

"You marvel to see the ocean give up its dead," began Joe Deering, in a hollow voice.

Jovial Captain Robinson sank against the door for support, while a delicate green tint spread itself over his face.

We have said that he was a superstitious man.

This huge lump of humanity—nay, rather of inhumanity—was worse than a schoolgirl in point of courage.

The very word ghost frightened him, if he saw it in print.

He was sure that Joe Deering was dead.

Certain was he that Joe Deering had been decoyed into that floating coffin, and sent to a watery grave by himself.

Here then was the betrayed man's ghost come to reproach him with his crime.

The strong man turned heart-sick, and was like to faint.

Joe Deering looked at the fear-stricken traitor in silence.

He enjoyed his terror keenly indeed.

No feeling of pity at the abject terror of the wretched man crossed him.

For his thoughts went back to those fearful days and nights they passed on board the doomed "Albatross."

Jovial Captain Robinson had been pitiless before, and the sufferings gone through in that terrible time had hardened Joe Deering's kind heart.

A genial, generous and soft-hearted fellow as a rule, he could not pardon this infamous wretch who had lured him into such a trap, even while professing the most affectionate friendship for him.

No!

This was Joe Deering's chance — his long looked-for opportunity, and no weak emotion should spoil the revenge which he had waited for so patiently.

* * * * *

Jovial Captain Robinson essayed to speak.

In a faint, faltering voice, he managed to pronounce Joe Deering's name.

"Well, murderer!" returned Joe Deering; "what is it you want?"

"I want you to shake hands with me, Joe," responded the other, almost inaudibly.

"Assassin!"

"I—I—I don't mean you any harm," gasped jovial Captain Robinson.

"Liar!" thundered Joe Deering; "you dare make that statement, hovering as you do, between life and death!"

"No, no, no, no!" shrieked the jovial captain; "not that, Joe, not that."

"Yes, I say; for you are not long for this world."

"You are not sent to tell me that, Joe," said Robinson, his voice dying away in spite of a desperate effort to make it audible.

"I am."

YOUNG JACK HARKAWAY AND

204

"Ugh!"

And with a half groan, half grunt, he sank upon the ground prostrate.

Before his senses had fairly fled, Joe Deering strode over to him, and delivered him a heavy kick behind.

This brought him round in a wonderful way.

He knew that it was a material foot that had given that kick, and the conviction was a marvellous relief to him.

He scrambled up.

As he got to his feet, Joe Deering fixed him by the throat, and shook him.

"You plotted to accomplish my murder," he said; "but now my turn's come, Robinson, and I mean to punish you."

Jovial Captain Robinson was a coward, an arrant cur, yet he infinitely preferred having to tackle flesh and blood, to battling with a ghost.

He turned upon his assailant.

But Deering was not to be denied.

Before the jovial captain could do anything to help himself, Joe Deering hammered his face into a jelly.

Half dazed, stunned, and blinded, Robinson fought it out, and struggling fiercely, he shook himself free.

And then he fled like a beaten cur from the house.

Joe Deering did not attempt to follow him.

"There," he said, calmly enough, considering what had gone before, "that's done. Thank goodness it's off my mind. Mr. Murray must have my next attention."

He little thought that the wretched shipowner had already paid the penalty of his crimes.

* * * * *

Jovial Captain Robinson was never the same man again.

Whether it was the physical or the mental punishment he had had, we cannot possibly determine, but certain it is that something broke him up from that day, and he lingered on a miserable life of two [years or more, and died in abject want.

CHAPTER C.
A DOSE OF PALM OIL.

HAVING settled the hash of jovial Captain Robinson, we now proceed to the pleasant task of measuring out justice to others.

Messieurs Murray and Chivey are the persons we mean.

Those gentlemen, having taken such excellent precautions to cut off young Jack Harkaway's communications with the outer world, fancied themselves tolerably safe.

Yet every now and then Murray's nerves were shaken as he thought of the vindictive Lenoir.

What had become of that dangerous individual?

The police had gone to the spot where Murray told them he had left the coiner senseless, and there they certainly found traces of a severe struggle, but Lenoir had disappeared.

The peasant also had done his duty as a French citizen by reporting the affair to the first gendarme he met on his road.

But though Marseilles was thoroughly searched, no trace of the man could be found, either in the town or the surrounding rural districts.

"There's one consolation, guv'nor," observed Chivey, "he won't dare show his ugly mug in Marseilles any more, so you're safe enough here."

"He's desperate enough for anything."

"It's galleys for life if he's collared, and he knows it well enough."

"Galleys?—ugh!"

And Herbert Murray gave a convulsive shudder, in which he was sympathetically joined by Chivey.

"Ain't it 'orrid to see them poor devils chained to the oars, and the hoverseer a walkin' up and down with his whip, a-lashin' 'em?" said Chivey.

"'Tis, indeed."

Murray again paused and shuddered, but after a moment, he continued—

"But it would be jolly, though, to see Harkaway and his friends at it."

"Crikey! and wouldn't I jest like to see that old beast of a Mole pulling away on his stumps. D'ye think they'll all get it?" asked Chivey.

"Yes, unless they manage to communicate with their friends or the consul."

"Then I had better just stroll up and see if our old pal the gaoler has stopped any more letters."

"Yes, go by all means, for if we don't call for them, he's likely enough to give them up to——"

Murray hesitated, but Chivey instantly supplied the word.

"The rightful owners, you mean, guv'nor."

"Cut away!" sharply exclaimed Murray, who was annoyed at the liberties taken by his quondam servant.

Chivey strolled up towards the prison, and was just in time to meet the gaoler coming out.

"Mornin', mossoo," he said, with a familiar nod, "rather warm, ain't it? What d'ye say to a bottle of wine jest to wash the dust out o' yer throat?"

The Frenchman did not comprehend a fourth part of this speech, but he understood that he was to partake of a bottle of wine, and at once signified his willingness.

"Vid moosh plaisir, m'sieu."

And he led the way to a cabaret where they sold his favourite wine.

"Now have you got any letters for me?" said Chivey, when they were comfortably seated at a table, remote from the few other customers, who were engaged in a very noisy game of dominoes.

"No understand," said the man, shaking his head.

"Any letters—billy duxes?"

The man made a gesture to indicate that he did not understand.

"Thick-headed old idiot," muttered Chivey; then calling in pantomime to aid his lack of French, he produced the first letter Jack had written to the consul.

"Letter, like this."

The gaoler's eyes twinkled; he nodded and

half drew from the breast pocket of his uniform the very document Chivey was so anxious to get hold of.

"Hand it over, old pal," he said, holding out his hand.

The gaoler smiled as he again concealed the letter.

Then he in turn held out his hand, and made signs that he required something to be dropped into it.

"Old cormorant, wants more palm oil," muttered Chivey, and most reluctantly he drew from his pocket one of the gold pieces Herbert Murray had given him for the purpose of bribing the gaoler.

But the Frenchman shook his head.

"Two; I cannot part with the letter under two," he said, in much better English than he had hitherto spoken.

"Well, I'm blest! Why couldn't you speak like that before? We'd have come to business much sooner."

"I thought Monsieur would like to exhibit his extensive knowledge of the French tongue, but here is the letter."

"And here's the coin. I will buy as many as you can get at the same figure."

"You shall certainly have the first chance."

Chivey helped himself to another glass, and asked—

"When is the trial to be?"

"The judge, unfortunately, has been taken ill, and the prisoners will have to wait about three weeks for an opportunity of proving their innocence."

"That's unfortunate. What do you think they'll get?"

"If found guilty, twenty years at the galleys."

"What, old wooden legs and all?"

"The gentleman who has lost his limbs will be probably sent to some other employment."

"What a pity. Well, good-bye, old cock; keep your weather-eye open."

"*Au revoir, monsieur.*"

Cocking his hat very much on one side, Chivey stalked out of the place.

CHAPTER CI.

HOW THE PURLOINED LETTER WAS LOST— AND WHO FOUND IT.

"THAT 'ere frog-eating swine gets two quid for bonin' the letter, so I think I'm entitled to one. Can't let all the coin go into old Frenchy's pocket."

Thus Chivey muttered to himself as he neared the place where he and Herbert Murray were staying.

Chivey evidently intended putting the screw on Herbert.

"Look here, guv'nor," said he, as he entered the room; "I ain't much of a reading cove, but I see once a book called Jessop's fables."

"Æsop's fables, I presume you mean, Chivey?"

"It's all the same. But there's a yarn about a monkey what made the cat pull chestnuts out of the fire; and I'm jiggered if I'm going to play the cat."

"I am not aware that anyone wishes you to do so," responded Murray, in his blandest manner.

"Well, you are a-trying it on, at any rate."

"How so?"

"Why, supposing it's found out about our stopping these here letters?"

"Which letters, Chivey?"

"The one I've got in my pocket, and——"

"Oh, you've got one, then. Hand it over, please, Chivey."

"Not so fast, guv'nor. You jest listen to what I've got to say first?"

"I am all attention."

"Well, supposing this game was found out, who do you think would get into trouble?"

"Why, you would, undoubtedly; and your friend the French gaoler."

"And don't you think it's worth your while to come down very handsome, considering the risk I run."

"It does not strike me in that light; but I do think it would be a good plan for you to get rid of the stolen letter as soon as possible; for if anything is found out, and the gaoler says he gave you the letters, it is not likely that his word—the word of a man who acknowledges himself a thief—will be taken against yours, unless the documents are found in your possession."

"That's all very well."

"Then if it's all very well, just hand over the letter."

And Murray held out his hand.

Chivey, very reluctantly, passed over the letter, muttering as he did so—

"Well, I'm blest if I don't think you would whistle a blackbird off the nest while you stole the eggs."

Herbert Murray took no notice of this speech; he was too deeply engrossed with the letter which he found read as follows—

"*To Her Britannic Majesty's Consul at Marseilles.*

"*SIR,—I have already addressed several letters to you on the subject of the incarceration of myself and friends in the prison of Marseilles, on a charge of counterfeit coining. I also explained how we were led, by the artful devices of a person calling himself Markby, to be actually in the coiner's house when the police entered it, and, therefore, appearances are certainly against us. To all those letters you have made no reply, which I think is certainly hard, and not quite right, as I imagine the duty of a British consul includes looking after the interests of British subjects in the town or district he is stationed at.*

"*Now, sir, in my former letters I requested you to communicate with the bankers in this town, and also with my father, whose address I give below, and who placed money in their hands for my use. If you will do so, you will see that all the statements in my former letters are correct; but if you do not, a number of British subjects will probably be condemned and heavily sentenced, entirely through your neglect.*

"*Therefore, I beg of you at once to communicate with those who can identify me and my*

friends, and in the meantime to use your influence to postpone the trial till that communication can be effected.

"*Your obedient servant,*
"J. HARKAWAY, JUNR."

"My eye!" said Chivey, when Murray had read the letter aloud, "ain't he getting his back up?"

"No matter. They are all of them safe enough, and if they get out, I'll forgive them."

"But they won't forgive you."

"Perhaps not; but ring the bell, Chivey. We'll have some wine after this, and just hand over the cigar box."

The ex-groom gave a tug at the bell-rope and ordered wine.

Then he took up a cigar-box and, giving it a vigorous shake, ejaculated—

"There ain't a blessed smoke in it, guvnor."

"Well, I'll just put on my hat and stroll up to the shop of Monsieur Cretineau-Joly and order a fresh stock. I must have a few minutes' exercise before it gets dark; shan't be ten minutes."

Herbert left the apartment, while Chivey muttered—

"He's afraid of meeting that Lenoir if he goes out after dark."

And Chivey was quite right.

Herbert Murray walked briskly up the street till he reached the tobacconist's, where he paused a moment, to look at the numerous varieties of the nicotian herb displayed in the window, along with pipes and cigar tubes of every shape and pattern.

As he looked, several others looked, and one of the lookers, while removing his pipe, was so unfortunate as to allow some of the tobacco ash to blow in Murray's face.

"Curse you, for an awkward Frenchman," growled Murray, while the other politely apologised for the mishap.

Herbert coughed, and sneezed, and drew out his handkerchief to wipe his face; but neither he nor anyone else noticed at the same time he drew out young Jack Harkaway's letter, which fluttered slowly to the pavement, where it lay with the address downwards.

Murray bought his box of cigars, and returned to the hotel where he resided, but still the letter lay unheeded beneath the tobacco shop window, till darkness had settled over the town of Marseilles except where street lamps and shop lights pierced the gloom.

Then there came up to the shop an old man, who apparently had been a soldier, as he dragged one leg very stiffly, and had his left arm in a sling.

But although his hair was white, his carriage was upright and martial.

He looked in at the door, then entered, and purchased some tobacco, after which he stood outside and filled his pipe.

"I might have taken a light inside," he muttered, when that operation was finished, and seeing a scrap of paper on the pavement, he picked it up, to use as a pipelight.

But the writing on the outside caught his eye.

"A letter to the British consul!" the old man

ejaculated. "It may be worth a franc or two, if I restore it to his excellency."

So he thrust it into his pocket, obtained a light, and hobbled away in the direction of the consulate.

But presently he paused in a retired spot, where only a single lamp illumined the surrounding houses.

"I wonder what the letter is about," he said; "I can make a better bargain, perhaps, if I know the contents."

And without more ado, the man pulled out the letter, and read it carefully.

Although it was written in English, the old French soldier seemed to understand it thoroughly.

"That cursed villain's name again," he hissed, through his teeth, when he had read a few lines. "But I'll pay him yet."

Then he continued the perusal, steadily, till he came to the end.

"It looks like truth," he said, as he returned it to his pocket. "I will restore it to the consul. Ha, ha! it will be sport indeed if I, Pierre Lenoir, the proscribed criminal, can defeat the schemes of that villain."

With a subdued chuckle the coiner departed on his way, revelling with delight at the thought that he would yet be avenged on his perfidious friend.

He reached the consul's residence, knocked, and was admitted by the same servant who had formerly opened the door to Chivey.

"Is his Excellency the Consul at home?"

"Yes, but werry much engaged," replied the flunkey.

"I do not particularly wish to see him, but I have found this letter in the street, and it may be something of importance."

"Right, my good feller; 'ere's a franc for you."

And the door was closed on Lenoir, who hastened away.

*   *   *   *   *

Two hours later the governor of the gaol and the consul were engaged in an important conversation.

But their plans must, for the present, remain a secret; nor did Jack and his imprisoned friends know that their last letter had produced a better effect than the first.

CHAPTER CII.

A SORROWFUL HOUSEHOLD—NEWS AT LAST.

CHANGE we the scene to England, and to that particular part of the island where old Jack and his friends were living.

Though surrounded by every luxury that money could procure, they were not happy.

"No news yet?" was the first question that Mrs. Harkaway would ask her husband in the morning, and he with a shake of the head, would respond—

"None yet, my dear; but do not despond."

But the fond mother vainly endeavoured to hope against hope.

Little Emily, too, went about in a most listless, melancholy manner, wondering why it was that Jack did not write, and Paquita, too, was quite despondent at not hearing anything of Harry Girdwood.

Dick Harvey did all he could to cheer up everybody, but it was a hard task, for he was working against his own convictions, which were that the youngsters had got into some trouble from which they were unable to extricate themselves.

Letters had been written to young Jack at Marseilles, but these had never reached him, having fallen into the hands of Herbert Murray, who had applied at the post office, in the name of Harkaway, for them.

Paquita and little Emily, though still firm friends, were not in each other's society so much as formerly, as they both preferred to endure their sorrows in solitude.

Paquita, in particular, was fond of a sequestered nook in the grounds, where, half hidden by shrubs, she could command a view of the long straight road leading from the nearest railway station.

She had a notion that she would be the first one to see the absentees, and had chosen that as a place of observation, where she would sit for hours watching and trying to hope.

Harvey found out her retreat, and employed the photographer who took Emily's portrait, to give him a good likeness of the southern beauty.

Paquita knew nothing of this, so absorbed was she in her own meditations, till a few days afterwards Uncle Dick, as she had learnt to call him, gave her some copies of it.

She thanked him, and, hurrying off to her own room, enclosed one in an envelope, which she addressed to Harry. There was no letter with it, but underneath the portrait she wrote—

"*With Paquita's dearest love. As she waits for one who comes not.*"

This she posted herself, registering it for extra safety.

* * * * *

Still came no tidings, as day after day passed, till one morning the postman brought a large official-looking letter, addressed in a strange handwriting, and bearing foreign postmarks.

Despite all his hardihood, Harkaway's hand trembled as he took it up, and, eager as he was for news, it was some seconds before he could nerve himself to break the seal.

His wife sat watching with breathless expectation, feeling convinced that at length there was news.

"Are they safe?" she asked, when she had followed her husband's eye to the conclusion of the lengthy epistle.

"They *are* safe, for the *present*."

"Thank Heaven!" she exclaimed, giving way to woman's great relief—tears.

"But *where* are they?" she continued a minute afterwards.

"At Marseilles, where they have been for some time, so the British consul tells me, and where they are likely to be till we go to release them."

"Release them! What do you mean? Don't keep back anything from me, dear husband."

"Well, if you must know the worst, they are in prison, on a charge of coining."

"What an infamous charge to make against them!" exclaimed a couple of indignant femi-

nine voices, belonging to little Emily and Paquita, who had just come into the room.

"Husband, you don't believe our boy to be guilty of such a crime?"

"No ; but——"

"But what?"

"Appearances are very much against them, the consul says. The great thing is to establish their identity, as the boy is supposed to have assumed the name he bears."

At this moment Harvey appeared, and the news was instantly imparted to him.

"It is a very serious affair, and it is certain we must go at once. But really it is ridiculous to fancy old Mole and those black rascals accused of coining."

"It will not be ridiculous, if they are condemned and sent to the galleys, pa," said little Emily.

"True, little girl, therefore we will see about starting at once. You see about packing my things, while I run up to town to get passports for the lot of us."

"Passports are not required for travelling," said Emily.

"Certainly not for travelling ; but what can establish our identity better than passports signed by the British Secretary of State for Foreign Affairs?"

There was no answering this question ; so Dick started off to London, while the rest busied themselves with preparations for a Continental trip.

Within forty-eight hours they were crossing the Channel ; six hours later they had entered Paris, where they took a brief rest, and then continued their journey towards Marseilles.

For just as they were starting Harkaway received a telegram from the consul at Marseilles—

"Come as soon as you possibly can, or you may be too late."

Need it be said that, after such a message, they lost no time in speeding to their destination?

CHAPTER CIII.

MONSIEUR HOCQUART CLERMONT DELAMARRE —THE COINER AT HOME.

BUT what had the consul and the governor of the gaol been doing all this time?

When the consul first called upon the governor of the gaol, that official tried to laugh off the matter.

"Surely," said the governor, "you don't believe the tale these young fellows tell?"

"I am more than half inclined to do so, if only from the fact that the writer of this appears to have written several other letters which have miscarried. But why, may I ask, was I not informed that some of my countrymen had been arrested?"

"Well, my dear sir, their story seemed to me so absurd, that I did not think it worth while to trouble you."

"But they asked to see me."

"True."

"And I fear as you did not forward their request, I shall be obliged to mention your name to our ambassador in Paris."

"For Heaven's sake do not! If such a thing

were known to the minister of justice, I should lose my situation at once."

"Then if I am silent on this matter, you must render me every assistance in finding out the truth about these prisoners."

"Willingly. What can I do?"

"I should like to see the youth who calls himself Harkaway; but first of all, where is the gaoler who usually has charge of these prisoners?"

"Gone to his home, monsieur. The ordinary officials are, as you are doubtless aware, replaced by a military guard, between sunset and sunrise."

"Good, then oblige me by bringing him here."

So young Jack was brought into the presence of the consul, who closely questioned him as to what he had been doing in Marseilles.

He told the truth, and, in spite of the severe cross-examination by the governor and consul, stuck to his tale.

"Humph!" said the consul. "You are consistent, at all events. Well, for the present, you may return to your cell, but don't tell even your friends that you have seen the British consul."

"I won't mention it, sir."

And Jack returned to his cell, escorted by the governor himself, as the consul did not wish anyone to know of the interview.

But when the governor returned, the consul said—

"Now, Monsieur Hocquart Delamarre, what do you think of the affair?"

The governor did not reply, but there quietly glided from behind a screen, which probably had concealed him during the interview, a man of middle age and height, with nothing at all striking in his appearance.

He might have passed for a clerk, a second-rate shopkeeper, or a superior artisan; anyone passing him in the street would have taken no notice whatever of such an everyday kind of a man.

Yet, after all, a very close observer would have noticed something very peculiar about him. His eyes!

One moment they seemed to pierce the inmost recesses of your very soul, yet when you tried, through them, to find a clue to their owner's thoughts, you were utterly defeated, for they became misty and expressionless.

"What do I think of the affair, monsieur?"

"Yes."

"Well, so early in the case, it is difficult to pronounce a decided opinion," said Delamarre.

"That is very true, Monsieur Delamarre," said the consul.

"But as your excellency has sought my professional assistance in this case, I feel my reputation is at stake, and shall exert myself to the utmost."

"Monsieur Delamarre is one of the cleverest gentlemen we have in his line of business," said the governor.

The middle-aged gentleman bowed.

"You are kind enough to say so, sir."

"You have made a good selection, Monsieur le Consul. In the detective police Monsieur Delamarre has few equals."

Again the detective bowed, and addressing the consul, said—

"When shall I next have the honour of waiting on you again, monsieur?"

"As soon as you have learnt anything you think of sufficient importance to tell me."

"At the consulate, of course?"

"Will it be safe for you to be seen there?"

"Monsieur, I stake my professional reputation that, when I call on you, you shall not recognise me till I choose to reveal myself. There is an extremely artful person mixed up in this affair, but I shall prove still more artful than any of them; take the word of Hocquart Clermont Delamarre."

With another bow the French detective made his exit.

He proceeded in the first place to his own temporary residence, where he made a considerable alteration in his personal appearance.

Then making straight for the quarter of the city mostly inhabited by the respectable working classes, he made a friendly call on Pierre Lenoir the coiner, who, as it will be remembered, the police had been unable to trace since his encounter with Herbert Murray and the waggoner.

A friendly call we have termed it, and so it seemed at first, for the detective and the criminal shook hands in the most friendly manner.

"Hullo, friend Clermont," exclaimed Lenoir, "what brings you from Paris?"

"Why, it was too hot for me there."

There was a pause.

"And you, too," continued the detective. "I have heard your name mentioned very much of late. How did that affair happen?"

Pierre Lenoir told his friend, whom of course he did not know as a detective, but merely as an associate with coiners and such like people, how he had been tricked by Markby.

"But I'll have his life, though!"

"Doubtless. It will be a bad day for him when he falls into your hands."

Lenoir growled a fierce oath.

"He has escaped me for the present, but if I wait for years, I will have my revenge. Pierre Lenoir never forgives."

Unheedful of the coiner's anger, the detective stroked his moustache, and continued—

"But how about the prisoners up at the gaol yonder?"

"They are innocent."

"Innocent!"

"Undoubtedly."

"Then why are they in prison?"

"Because the only persons who can clear them are Markby and myself."

"Ah, I see!"

"And Markby for some reason or other won't clear them."

"Some old grudge, I suppose."

"Yes. However, they are innocent; when I tried them, they flatly refused to have anything to do with the game."

"Well, they are in a nice fix; but how did you manage to escape after that little affair with Markby and the peasant?"

"Crawled into a bush as near as possible to the scene of the fight."

"Ah!"

"If I had gone half a mile away, the police

YOUNG JACK. HARKAWAY AND HIS BOY TINKER.

" 'OUT OF THE WAY, UNCHRISTIAN DOGS!' CRIED MOLE."

would no doubt have found me, but the thick-headed rascals never thought of looking only half a dozen yards off. Ha, ha, ha!"

The detective smiled grimly.

"They are thick-headed rascals."

And after a pause occupied in listening to sounds in the street, he repeated—

"And the English prisoners are entirely innocent then?"

"Entirely."

"Now listen to me, Pierre Lenoir," continued the detective, rapping the table smartly as though to command attention. "But what a curious echo you have in this old room."

"I had not noticed it; but to continue."

"These English refused to have anything to do with your business, you say?"

"Yes; and showed fight when I would have used force to detain them."

"Then if the judge knows that, the young fellows will be released?"

"Yes; but, my dear friend, it is not likely I shall go to the court to give evidence in their favour."

"You will."

"Nonsense."

"I shall take you there."

There was something in his visitor's manner that made Lenoir first start from his seat and make a hasty movement towards the table.

But he recoiled when Hocquart Clermont Delamarre thrust a revolver in his face and exclaimed—

"If you make another movement towards that drawer where your pistols are, I will send a bullet through you. Keep your hands down by your side."

"What in the fiend's name does this mean?" gasped the coiner.

"It means that you are my prisoner."

"Prisoner!"

"Yes."

"Then who are you?"

"You have known me as Clermont, but my real name is Delamarre."

"The detective?"

"The same."

The coiner gave a hasty look round the apartment, and then made a step towards the door.

But it instantly opened, and there appeared a police officer in uniform, who said—

"If you attempt to pass this door, you are a dead man."

The window!

It was not very high above the roadway, and one bold leap might yet bring liberty.

But, as if reading his very thoughts, Delamarre gave one of those peculiar raps on the table, which was again echoed from without, and instantly the figure of a policeman armed with a revolver was seen filling the casement.

The chimney!

That he knew was crossed by strong bars. No exit that way.

"Sit down, Pierre Lenoir."

The detective was provokingly cool, and the coiner gnashed his teeth with rage.

"Sit down, man; why, you ought to feel proud at being taken so neatly."

"Curse you!"

"Never mind. I have the finest and easiest pair of wristbands any gentleman in your line of business ever wore. Let me try them on."

Lenoir for a moment contemplated resistance, but two revolvers were close to his head, so second thoughts prevailed.

He was firmly handcuffed.

"Now, Pierre," said the detective, "listen to me, and I will quickly prove that I am a far better friend than you think me."

The coiner smiled a bitter smile.

"Of course it doesn't look so; but listen."

"I am compelled to," replied Lenoir.

"You can clear these English prisoners."

"If I choose to speak."

"If you choose to speak, the English consul will exert all his influence to procure a mitigation of your sentence—whatever it may be."

Lenoir nodded.

"But if you do not, why, the whole force of the British Embassy will be exerted against you; so I fancy your choice will soon be made."

Lenoir sat silent for some minutes.

"Have you made up your mind?" asked the detective at length.

"I don't see why I should speak; they belong to the same cursed country as that Markby."

"Well, don't you see how nicely things come round? You clear the prisoners, and by so doing incriminate Markby, alias Murray."

"Aye; but where is he?"

"In Marseilles. I am only waiting for a little more evidence before I lay my hands on him. He is a slippery customer, and it won't do to arrest him until the case is complete."

"Then, curse him, I'll tell all—nay, more, if you look in that drawer, where the pistols are, you know, you will find a note from him to me. That will be quite as good evidence as my word."

"Good, Lenoir. I can't promise you a free pardon, but I fancy you will get off lightly."

"I hope I may be sent to the same galley as Murray, alias Markby, has to serve; and if I am only chained to the same oar I shall be happy."

"Why."

"I will find an early opportunity, and then I will kill him."

"No, Lenoir; that will not be the way to shorten your sentence."

"I'll kill him."

"No; lead him a life of misery and dread while he is chained to the oar. What you do when you are both released is a matter I have no present concern with."

"March, then; let us be going."

And the coiner walked gaily away, his anger at being captured having been replaced by joy, at the hopes of avenging himself on the treacherous Markby, alias Murray.

Hocquart Clermont Delamarre himself walked arm-in-arm with the coiner, and the good people of Marseilles knew not that he had been taken.

Even in the gaol he was entered under an assumed name.

The gaoler, who had been in attendance on the English party, could not understand why his prisoners wrote no more letters to the English consul or their relatives in England, and Herbert Murray almost suspected the truth when he chanced, the day after losing the letter, to look for it.

But Chivey reassured him.

" I went all over your clothes and my own this morning afore you was up, guv'nor, and burnt every one of the letters I could find."

" What for ?" demanded Murray.

" In case of accidents. It would not do us any good to have them things found on us ; and nobody ever knows what is going to turn up."

CHAPTER CIV.

THE ESCORT—THE TRIAL.

" MARSEILLES at last !" exclaimed Dick Harvey, as the train came to a standstill.

" I thought we were never to end our journey," said little Emily.

However, they quickly got clear of the railway station, engaged apartments at an hotel, and then, without waiting to eat or drink, made their way towards the gaol.

" I wonder what house that is with the Union Jack flying over it," said Mrs. Harkaway, as they passed along a street near the harbour.

" The British consulate very likely," said her husband. " We had better call there."

But the consul was not at home.

" Do you know where he is gone ?" asked Harvey of the servant.

" Why, sir, there are some Englishmen to be tried to-day for coining, and he is gone to watch the case."

" To-day ?"

" Yes, sir ; in fact, the trial will commence in ten minutes," replied the man, after consulting his watch.

" Where does the trial take place ?"

" The second turning on the left, sir. The hall of justice is a large building just round he corner."

" Come along, then," said Harkaway ; "there is no time to lose."

They hurried along the street at a rate that made the French people stare.

Paquita was the first of the party to turn the corner, and she had no sooner done so than she exclaimed—

" There they are."

And running between a file of soldiers, threw her arms round Harry Girdwood's neck.

Little Emily would have followed her example, but the officer in charge of the escort would not permit any such irregular conduct, and Paquita was compelled to rejoin her friends.

" Hurrah, dad !" exclaimed young Jack ; " I knew you would turn up in time. And, mamma, how pale you are looking."

" Can you wonder at it, my boy, considering the anxiety we have all suffered ?"

" Mr. Mole, Mr. Mole." exclaimed Dick Harvey, shaking his head. " I am surprised indeed to hear that you have taken to counterfeit coining."

" Harvey, this is really no joking matter," replied Mole.

" No, it will be no joke when you are chained to the oar in one of those galleys down in the harbour."

" Stand back, ladies and gentlemen, if you please," exclaimed the officer commanding the escort. " I cannot allow any communication with my prisoners."

So they were obliged to keep at a distance.

At that moment a portly, elderly gentleman, who had been watching the scene, came up, saying—

" Have I the honour of addressing Mr. Harkaway ?"

" That is my name, sir."

" I am the English consul."

Our old hero at once seized him by the hand, saying—

" Sir, words are powerless to express how grateful I am for your interference on behalf of my boy."

" Don't mention it, sir, I only did as I am instructed to do in all such cases."

" But about the trial ; what chance does that young scapegrace stand ?"

" There is very little doubt that he will be acquitted, as we have the best of evidence in his favour. But come along, sir, let us get into court."

The consul led the way into the hall of justice, and placed the Harkaway party among the audience in such a position that they could see all that was going on, without being conspicuous themselves.

Then they waited patiently till the judge arrived.

*   *   *   *   *

While our young hero's father and friends were thus entering Marseilles, two people were trying to leave that city.

These were Herbert Murray and his friend Chivey.

" There ain't no use in stoppin' 'ere, guv'nor," the latter had said. " We can see by the papers what they gets."

" You are right, Chivey ; we will get away for a time."

" We can come back an' see 'em when they are fairly fixed, you know."

" Well, pack up, and we'll just take a trip to Paris for a week."

Their portmanteaus were quickly got ready, and a vehicle was engaged to take them to the railway station.

But when they alighted, and were about to take their tickets, a very polite police officer tapped Murray on the shoulder, and said—

" I much regret to have to ask Monsieur to postpone his journey."

" What ?"

" I must request Monsieur to defer his visit to Paris till after the trial of the English coiners."

" What has that to do with me ?"

" The judge may desire your presence, monsieur ; he may wish to hear your evidence."

" Nonsense !"

" It may be ; but I am compelled to say that I cannot permit you to leave Marseilles to-day, and I must request you to accompany me back to the hall of justice."

"We are prisoners, then?"

"By no means. Only the law requires your presence, and the law, you know, must be obeyed, monsieur?"

Chivey had not taken part in the conversation, but had been looking round for a good chance of escaping.

"You, of course, will accompany your friend?" said the detective, tapping him on the shoulder.

"Must, I suppose," responded Chivey, who noticed several other policemen were loitering about the station.

So, with a very bad grace, the two intending excursionists walked back to the hall of justice.

The English prisoners had already been brought into the hall, and the trial had commenced.

It certainly seemed at first that our young hero had got himself into a bad fix, for the evidence was much against him.

The police had captured them in Lenoir's workshop.

They had been seen in conversation with him not only there, but at the café the police had been warned of their nefarious doings and so forth.

"Have you any witnesses to call, prisoner?" asked the judge, addressing young Jack.

"Yes, Monsieur le Juge; and the first of them is Pierre Lenoir. Let him be called."

"What folly is this?" demanded the judge, sternly.

"I ask that Pierre Lenoir shall be summoned to give evidence," repeated young Jack, who had been told by Delamarre what line of defence to adopt.

"Do you think he will respond if called?"

"If he does not respond, I shall derive no benefit from his evidence."

"Let Pierre Lenoir be called," said the judge, rather angrily.

And Pierre Lenoir was called by an officer of the court.

"Here!"

The answer was clear and distinct.

And the next moment Pierre Lenoir, escorted by two gensdarmes, marched into the court room.

Chivey touched Murray on the arm, and both had an idea of sneaking away.

But the polite and attentive officer who had brought them back from the railway, stood in the doorway, and was evidently watching them.

In fact, he spoke to them.

"Things are getting interesting, gentlemen," said he; "it was worth losing a train to see such a dramatic trial as this promises to be."

"Interferes with our business, rather."

"Not so much, monsieur. But hush!"

The evidence of Pierre Lenoir was then taken.

The public prosecutor objected at first to his evidence; but it was urged by the counsel for the defence that although accused of many offences, he was at present convicted of none, and therefore was entitled to full credence.

"Your name is Pierre Lenoir?" asked Jack's counsel.

"It is."

"Do you know the prisoners?"

"But slightly."

"Say when you met them."

"I met them at my own house where they came by invitation to see some specimens of my skill as a medal engraver."

"Did those Englishmen assist you in any way to pass counterfeit coin?"

"Neither of those Englishmen; but that man did."

And turning half round, he pointed at the wretched Murray, alias Markby.

And at the same time the affable police officer drew nearer, smiling more blandly than ever.

"'Tis false!" shrieked the wretched Murray.

"The public must maintain silence in the court," said the judge.

"It's a base lie!" exclaimed Murray.

"The officers of the court will arrest the disorderly person."

The smiling gendarme at once swooped down on his prey.

"That man," continued Lenoir, "not only passed bad money for me, but he persuaded me that the prisoners would do so also. But when I introduced myself and tried to get them to join me, they absolutely refused."

The public prosecutor tried in vain to shake his story, but he positively adhered to every word he had spoken.

Then Harkaway senior was called upon, and he in conjunction with the banker proved that there was no need whatever for the prisoners to commit such an offence, as by simply signing his name young Jack could draw far more francs than the judge's yearly salary amounted to.

The counsel for the defence then challenged the prosecution to produce any evidence that the prisoners had passed bad money, and the public prosecutor was obliged to confess that he could not do so.

Whereupon the judge remarked that the prosecution had utterly failed, and directed the prisoners to be discharged.

But Lenoir and Murray were directed to be kept in separate cells till they could be tried, and Chivey was ordered like accommodation.

And having now plenty of time for reflection, Herbert Murray sat with irons on his arms and legs, thinking dolefully over the past, and thinking whether, after all, honesty would not have proved the best policy.

CHAPTER CV.

A LAST VIEW OF MURRAY AND CHIVEY.

"HURRAH, dad!"

"Hurrah, my boy! Now, then, one and all. Hip, hip, hip——"

"Hurrah!"

The peal that burst from the throats of the reunited English party fairly astonished the assembled crowd of citizens who were flocking out of the hall of justice.

And then such a shaking of hands and kissing

The latter form of insanity at length became infectious, and the two black imps Tinker and Bogey insisted on pressing a chaste salute on Mr. Mole's coy lips, to the intense amusement of the bystanders.

"Get out, you black devils!" exclaimed he.

"Why, Massa Mole, we been good friends dis long time in dat 'ere ole prison ; you isn't a-gwine to turn round on de poor niggahs now we's got out."

"Get away. Never mind, don't get away; I'm not proud—hurrah !"

In his excitement Mr. Mole threw his battered hat a great height into the air, but slipping while so doing, he sat down upon the pavement rather violently.

"*Sac-r-r-r-ré !* seize that old villain !"

The indignant command came from a mounted officer in charge of a considerable body of soldiers.

While directing the movements of his men, drawn sword in hand, down came Mole's *chapeau* on the point of the deadly weapon, which went through the crown, and the lining getting entangled with the hilt, it could not be very readily removed.

And, of course, the French spectators at once began laughing to see the rather absurd situation of the officer.

Mole would certainly have been dragged off again had not the British consul once more interposed.

"Monsieur le Colonel, I hasten to assure you that it was an accident," he said.

"I will not be insulted by accident ; arrest him !"

"But consider, sir, you have no crime to urge against him."

"Bah, what care I ?"

"He will apologise."

"Of course he will," said Harvey, thinking it time to interpose. "Here, where are you, Mr. Mole ?"

"Down here, sitting on the other end of me," responded the ex-tutor in very doleful accents.

"An apology !" said the excited officer, who had dismounted, and was brandishing his weapon as though about to sacrifice Mole.

But poor Mole seemed altogether too confused to say the soothing words required, so the consul again interfered.

"Really, Monsieur le Colonel, this poor gentleman seems to have sustained some severe injury. You will see he has lost both legs in a series of heroic actions, the particulars of which I have not time to give you, but accept my assurance that the affair of the hat was entirely an accident."

"Lost legs in action ! Ah, then it becomes my duty to apologise for the hasty language I have used to a brave soldier."

As things were changing a little, Mole thought it time to become conscious, and with the aid of Tinker and Bogey, he struggled to his feet.

"Monsieur," continued the officer, "I withdraw my words."

"Enough said, my dear sir," responded Mole ; "let the matter drop, I pray."

The officer gave a military salute, restored the perforated hat to its owner, and rejoined his men.

"Really imprisonment seems to have no effect on you, Mr. Mole," said Harvey ; "you begin your old pranks the moment you are released."

"What do you mean ?"

"Why, you pass yourself off as an old soldier."

"No, it was our good friend the consul."

"Well, you allowed the colonel to deceive himself."

"It's all the result of my really martial aspect, my dear boy."

And Mole hobbled on, trying to sustain his military appearance.

* * * * *

Our friends did not at once leave Marseilles.

They were informed that perhaps they might be required to give evidence against Murray, so they took up their residence in the best hotel of the place and waited, the elders of the party being perfectly content now that the youngsters had regained their liberty.

However, as events turned out, they were not called upon to attend the trial of the ship-owner's son, as Monsieur Hocquart Clermont Delamarre and his assistants managed to pile up quite sufficient proof to convince the judge of Herbert Murray's guilt.

He, Lenoir, and Chivey, who certainly was not so deeply involved as his master, were sentenced to serve ten years each in the galleys.

Lenoir's original sentence was fifteen years, but the promised intercession of the consul was effectual in shortening it to ten.

There was, however, another trial, at which young Jack and Harry Girdwood were requested to attend, and the prisoner in this case was the gaoler to whom they had entrusted their letters to the consul.

He being clearly convicted of receiving bribes from prisoners, was sentenced to two years' imprisonment, and so retires from the scene.

Young Jack, his parents, Harry Girdwood, Harvey, little Emily, and Paquita were taking a walk in the neighbourhood of the harbour one morning, when they became aware of a very dismal-looking procession coming down the road from the prison.

First of all came half a dozen soldiers, trailing their rifles, which were evidently loaded and ready for instant use.

Then, in single file, about a yard behind each other, and every man with his right leg attached by a ring to a long chain that extended the entire length of the party, came ten men clad in garments of very coarse serge, and with closely-cropped heads.

The instant he saw them in the distance, young Jack guessed what it meant, and pointed the gang out to the others.

"Let us get away if we can," said he.

"Why ?" asked Harvey.

"Because it will look as though we came here simply to gloat over their disgrace," replied Jack.

"Right, my boy."

But there was no way of avoiding them, as there was no turning out of the street, and all the house doors were closed, so they were compelled to see all.

First of all came seven of the lowest-looking ruffians in creation, villains whose countenances were expressive of nothing but brutality and vice; the eighth was Chivey, whose cheeks bore traces of tears, and the ninth was Pierre Lenoir, who walked erect and proud as Lucifer, except when he made a half turn about as though he would like to strangle Herbert Murray, who walked with tottering steps at the end of the chain.

"Poor fellows!" said Mrs. Harkaway.

"They deserve it," exclaimed her husband and Harvey, simultaneously. "They tried to get our boys the very punishment that has overtaken them."

Our friends, however, had seen enough, and did not care to witness what followed.

If they had gone inside the harbour gates, they might have seen three or four very long sharp-bowed vessels moored to the quay or lying at anchor a little way out.

Neither mast nor sail had these vessels, but from each side projected a dozen or more of gigantic oars larger than those used by Thames bargemen.

Had they gone down to the harbour they would presently have seen chained up, two of them to each oar, but with their feet so far at liberty that they could move backwards and forwards three paces.

Then they would have heard the word of command given, and would have seen the poor slaves tugging away at the oars till the huge craft was sweeping rapidly out to sea, while the galley-master walking up and down between the two rows of oarsmen, gave blows of his whip on the right hand or the left when he saw a man flagging, or an oar that did not swing in unison with the rest.

Such was the fate to which the career of crime had brought the son of the once respected shipowner Murray.

Slavery from morn till night, beneath a broiling sun, or exposed to cold, rain, and hail, the coarsest of black bread and lentil pottage, formed his scanty meal; his associates the lowest type of humanity.

And even over and above such a hard lot there fell upon his heart the craven fear some day that Lenoir, who was chained to the next oar, would break loose and kill him.

Many would have preferred death to such slavery, but Herbert Murray feared to die.

"Hollo, Englishman, faster!" the galley-master would shout. And then his whip or cane would sharply visit poor Murray's shoulders.

And the chuckling voice of Lenoir would be heard, exclaiming—

"Ah. traitor! this is nothing to what you will suffer when I have my chance for revenge."

CHAPTER CVI.

TERRIBLE RAILWAY ACCIDENT.

THREE days after Murray and Chivey embarked on their dreary voyage the Harkaway party quitted Marseilles.

The waiter and the diver, so long young Jack's companions in adventure, preferred remaining at Marseilles.

They had no home ties, and had so long been accustomed to a wandering Continental life, that they had no great desire to settle down quietly in England.

However, Harkaway senior made them a handsome present each, and he also presented Monsieur Hocquart Clermont Delamarre with a very substantial proof of his esteem and gratitude, and the detective was further gratified by receiving from the two young ladies, Paquita and Emily, a handsomely-mounted *carte de visite* portrait.

"And now for home!" exclaimed our young hero.

"You will be sorry when you get there, won't you?" said Emily.

"No, dear; why should I be?"

"Because in England you can't go on as you have been doing, running away with fair Circass——"

There was nobody looking, so Jack took the liberty of cutting the reproach short with a kiss.

"You must not say anything more about that, dear Emily; and, after all, I don't think you would have approved of my leaving her to the mercy of those Turks."

"That I should not, Jack."

The youth then handed his young sweetheart into one of the vehicles in waiting, and off they started for the railway, where they found they had to wait ten minutes.

To occupy the time they strolled up and down the platform.

Suddenly Harry Girdwood exclaimed—

"Why, where is Mr. Mole? Did he come in your carriage, Jack?"

"No; I thought he was with you."

"Left behind, by Jove!" exclaimed Harvey.

"Serve him right if I left him behind entirely," said Harkaway senior, rather angrily.

He was on the point of sending one of the porters back to the hotel, when Mr. Mole appeared.

Now there were two things that had delayed him.

One was that on the very morning Mr. Mole had mounted a new pair of artificial legs made by the very best surgical instrument maker in Marseilles.

Some time had been taken over the proper adjustment of these.

For the second reason—Mr. Mole had discovered that the hotel cellars contained some excellent brandy, and he had been taking a parting glass with the Irish diver before commencing his journey.

And as he now made his appearance on the railway platform, he was anything but steady on his new legs.

"Better late than never, Mr. Mole," said Harvey.

"I am not late."

"Yes, sir. Two minutes more, and the train will be here."

An engine was in fact at that moment shunting some carriages which were to be attached to the train.

Mr. Mole turned on hearing the noise of the approaching locomotive.

But being, as aforesaid, slightly unsteady on his legs, he fell.

Fell right across the metals.

"Oh! help!" he cried.

But before anyone could stir, the engine was upon him.

The porters shouted, the ladies screamed with fright.

"Oh, Heaven! is it not horrible?" exclaimed a Frenchman. "Did you not hear the bones crash as the wheels went over his legs?"

"Over his legs," shouted Harvey. "Ha, ha! if that is all, it does not matter much."

The engine stopped, and Mole was rescued from his perilous position.

He had fainted, but a glass of water restored him.

"Are you hurt, old man?" asked Dick.

"No; I think not. It's only my legs, nothing else."

"Great Heaven, what a narrow escape!"

"So it is; but here is a nuisance, both my legs cut clean off, six inches above the ankle."

"Here, porter, put this gentleman in a first-class carriage," said Harkaway senior.

"But, monsieur, he must be taken to the hospital; the surgeon is close at hand."

"Doctor be hanged! This gentleman must go to Paris by the next train."

The porters, being evidently unwilling to touch Mr. Mole, Harkaway said—

"Here, lend a hand, old man.".

"All right." responded Harvey.

The pair of them immediately hoisted Mr. Mole into the carriage, the others took their seats, the engineer blew his whistle, and off they went.

To complete the horror of the spectators, who admired Mole's fortitude, and loathed the apparent barbarity of his friends, as the train was moving off, Harvey was plainly seen to cut off the old gentleman's shattered limbs, and pitch them into some empty goods waggons that were going in another direction.

"What horrid barbarians!" was the general exclamation of the bewildered spectators of the strange scene.

"A pretty object you have made of me certainly," grumbled Mole, looking down at his curtailed legs.

"Your own fault, Mr. Mole," responded Harvey.

"Lucky it was not your head, Mr. Mole," said young Jack.

"You are all against me, I see, but it does not matter."

So saying, Mole took out his pocket flask and was about to refresh himself.

But Harkaway senior, stretching out his hand, took the flask.

"No, Mr. Mole; if you have any more, I fear we shall have a more serious accident. So not a drop till the first time we stop."

"Why, this is a mail train, and only stops about every two hours."

"And I am quite sure you can exist without brandy for that little time."

"Well, I suppose I may smoke then?"

"Certainly; you shall have one of my best regalias."

Mr. Mole took the weed, and puffed away rather sulkily.

They had got about eight miles from Marseilles when suddenly the engine slackened speed, and the train drew up at a little roadside station.

"What does this mean?" said Harvey. "We ought not to stop here."

"This is our first stopping place, however, so I'll trouble you for my flask, according to promise," said Mole, with a beaming countenance.

Harkaway handed it over and was settling back again when he heard a police official asking—

"Where is the gentleman who was run over at Marseilles?"

"Here," said Harkaway.

The gendarme ran to the spot, and to his intense surprise saw the victim of the accident in the act of taking a hearty drink from his brandy flask while his left hand held a lighted cigar.

"What do you want?" demanded Mole.

"The officials at Marseilles, unable to stop the train, telegraphed to me to see that you had proper medical attendance."

"Ha, ha, ha! look here, old boy; I always carry my own physic. Taste it."

The officer took the flask, and finding that the smell was familiar, applied it to his lips.

"The fact is," said Harkaway, "the gentleman was wearing wooden legs, and they only were damaged."

"Indeed; then you think that you are able to proceed on your journey, sir?"

"Yes, if you will leave me some of my medicine."

The gendarme bowed, handed back the flask, and the train rolled away.

CHAPTER CVII.

A DUEL.

"PARIS at last," exclaimed Harvey.

"That's a good job, for I am tired of sitting, and want to stretch my legs; don't you, Mr. Mole?" said young Jack.

"Don't be ridiculous, Jack," replied Mr. Mole.

Harkaway senior, who had been looking out of the window, drew in his head and said—

"Well, Mr. Mole, you are in a nice fix."

"How?"

"I don't see any——"

"Any what?"

"Any cabs."

"The ——"

"Don't swear."

"My dear Mr. Harkaway, now if you were without legs, would not you swear?"

"Can't say, having the proper number of pins."

"You'll have to walk," said Harvey. "There's not a cab in the station."

"But how can I walk?"

"Don't you remember the hero in the ballad of Chevy Chase?"

"Who was he?"

"The song says Witherington, but we will call him Mole.

"'For Mole, indeed, my heart is woe,
    As one in doleful dumps;
For when his feet were cut away,
    He walked upon his stumps.'"

By this time the train had stopped, and all the party got out, except Mole.

As Harkaway had said, there was no vehicle in the station nor outside of it, so Mr. Mole was obliged to remain till his friends could hit upon some plan for removing him.

A porter was the first to make a suggestion. "An artificial limb maker lives opposite, monsieur," said he.

"Ah!"

"If I carried Monsieur over, he might have some—ah—substitutes fitted on."

"A capital idea!" exclaimed Harvey; "over with him."

And before Mole could remonstrate, he was hoisted to the porter's shoulders, and trotted across the street.

Great was the joy of the Parisian *gamins* at having such a sight provided for their amusement.

Mole, however, bravely bore the chaff, half of which he did not understand.

The maker of artificial limbs soon fitted poor Mole with a pair of legs.

But alas!

No sooner had he stood upon them than his friends burst out in a loud laugh.

"What is the matter with you?" demanded Mr. Mole, who felt inclined to stand on his dignity as well as on his new legs.

"Ha, ha, ha!"

"I wonder you don't remember what Goldsmith says," continued Mole.

"What does he say, Mr. Mole?"

"Don't you remember that line about 'the loud laugh that speaks the vacant mind.' I fear your mind must be very vacant, Mr. Harvey."

"He had you there, Uncle Dick," said young Jack.

"Pooh! But look at his legs."

"Ha, ha, ha!" laughed young Jack in turn.

Mr. Mole's trousers, it will be recollected, had been cut away below the knees immediately after his railway accident, and now he stood in a pair of nicely-varnished boots, above which could be seen the various springs and hinges of his mechanical limbs.

The trouser legs were not longer in proportion than a small boy's knickerbockers.

By this time, however, a cab or two had turned up, and, the ladies having been fetched from the railway waiting-room, the whole party proceeded to one of the many good hotels Paris possesses.

* * * * *

The third evening after their arrival, young Jack and Harry Girdwood strolled out together.

They no doubt would have enjoyed the company of the two girls, but little Emily and Paquita had been roving about the town all day long, and were too tired to go out that evening.

"What is this place, Jack?" asked Harry, as they both paused in front of a narrow, but brilliantly-lighted doorway.

"A shooting gallery, I fancy."

"Shall we go in?"

"Certainly; but I don't fancy the French are very great 'shootists,' as the Yankees say."

"All the more fun, perhaps."

And without more talk, the youngsters walked in.

It was a long room, divided by slight partitions into four different galleries, and at the end of each of these was a target in the shape of a doll.

After watching others for a time, Harry took half a dozen shots at one of the figures, which he struck four times.

Young Jack then tried, and was equally successful.

"Good shooting, young gentlemen," said one of the spectators, an Englishman; "but if you want to see real pistol practice, look at this Frenchman."

And he pointed to a tall, dark man who was just preparing to fire.

The target he had before him was not a little doll like the others, but a full-sized lay figure dressed in black, closely buttoned up, and holding in its hand an empty pistol pointed towards the live shooter.

"He is a noted duellist," said the Englishman, "and has killed more than one adversary."

Jack and Harry looked at him with considerable curiosity, with which was mixed a tinge of loathing.

The duellist had brought his own pistols, one of which he carefully loaded, and having placed himself in position, rapidly aimed and fired.

Instantly the lay figure showed a spot of white on its black coat, which, after all, was only made of a kind of paste or varnish, which chipped off when struck by the bullet.

"Straight to the heart," said the Englishman.

"That's good shooting," exclaimed Harry Girdwood.

The Frenchman fired again, making an equally good shot.

When he had fired ten, young Jack for the first time broke silence.

"I don't believe he could do that in the field with a live adversary and a loaded pistol opposite him."

The Frenchman again pulled the trigger, but the eleventh shot flew wide of the mark.

Almost foaming with passion at having missed his aim, he dashed the weapon to the ground.

"I must request the gentleman who spoke to stand the test."

"With great pleasure," responded Jack, coolly.

The Frenchman stared at the speaker.

"Bah! I don't fight with boys."

"Then I shall proclaim to all Paris that you are a cur, and try to back out of a quarrel when your challenge is accepted."

"Very well, then, you shall die in the morning. Henri"—this to a friend—"arrange with the English boy's second if he has one; if he has not, find him one."

The Englishman who had previously spoken at once stepped forward and offered his services.

"Although," said he, "I should much prefer to see this affair settled peacefully."

"I am entirely in your hands, sir," responded Jack.

And he retired to the other side of the room.

"Jack, Jack! what demon possessed you to get into such a mess?"

"No demon, Harry, but some of my father's hot blood. He was always very prompt to accept a challenge."

"He will not let you fight."

"He will not know till it is settled. Listen to me, Harry, if you tell him or anyone else, or try to stop the plan that my second may propose, I swear I'll never speak to you again."

"But you stand every chance of being killed."

"Harry, we have both of us faced death many times, and I am sure I am not going to turn my back on a Frenchman."

Poor Harry could say nothing more.

The Englishman rejoined them.

"I can't get that fellow to accept an apology ——"

"That's right," interposed Jack.

His second looked surprised at the youth's coolness, and continued—

"So I must parade you in the Bois de Boulogne at sunrise. It's about an hour's drive."

"Where shall we meet you?"

The second hesitated, and then named a time and place.

"Now," said Jack, "I will go and have a little sleep; not at home, but somewhere in this neighbourhood."

They went to a respectable hotel close by, and Jack, having made a few simple arrangements (including a message to Emily), in case of being killed, laid himself on his bed, and was soon slumbering peacefully.

*　　*　　*　　*　　*

About a quarter of an hour after the sun had risen, they were all upon the ground.

Jack and Harry with their second, and the Frenchman with his.

There was also a surgeon present.

Little time was lost.

The pistols were loaded, according to previous arrangement between the two seconds, with a lighter charge than usual, so that Jack might possibly escape with only a flesh wound instead of having a hole drilled right through him.

The combatants were then placed half facing each other, fifteen paces apart.

"There is a grave suspicion afloat that your adversary has an ugly knack of pulling the trigger half a second too soon," whispered Jack's second, "so I am going to give him a caution."

A pistol was placed in the hand of each, and then Jack's second spoke.

"Listen, gentlemen. You will fire when I give the word three. If either pulls the trigger before that word is pronounced, it will be murder."

He looked at the Frenchman, and then counted—

"One, two, three!"

But before the word "three" had fully passed his lips, the Frenchman's pistol was discharged.

Young Jack, however, prepared for such a trick, had just a moment before turned full towards him and stared him in the face.

This manœuvre was entirely successful.

The Frenchman's unfair, murderous aim was disconcerted, and his bullet whistled harmlessly past our hero's ear.

Jack then deliberately levelled his pistol at the Frenchman, who trembled violently, and showed every symptom of the most abject terror.

"I thought so," exclaimed Jack. "A vile coward as well as a murderer."

And he discharged his own pistol in the air.

"Why did you not shoot the villain?" exclaimed Harry Girdwood, the surgeon, and Jack's second simultaneously,

"It would be doing him too much honour, gentlemen. I leave him to the hangman."

"You should have killed him," growled the surgeon, glancing after the discomfited duellist, who was sneaking off, unattended even by his own second.

"I don't feel bloodthirsty just at present, and I have proved the words that gave rise to the challenge."

"That is true, but some other poor devil may not be so lucky."

"I fancy after this morning's *exposé* anyone may refuse to go out with him without fear of dishonour."

"True; that is one good thing."

They re-entered their carriage and returned to Paris.

Just as young Jack alighted from the vehicle, he found himself seized by the collar and shaken violently.

He turned hastily.

"Dad!"

"You young rascal!" exclaimed Harkaway senior, "where have you been all night?"

"Why—I—I arranged to go out early in the morning for a drive with this gentleman and Harry, so I took a room here at this hotel so as to be close to the rendezvous."

"That is the truth, but not all the truth. Sir, may I ask you the object of your very early excursion with my son?"

"Well, sir, the fact is, this young gentleman became involved last night in a little dispute which necessitated an exchange of pistol shots, and your son, I must say, behaved in a most gallant manner."

"Not touched, Jack?"

"No, dad."

"Did you shoot t'other fellow?"

"No, father; I only shoot game—human or brute. I leave gamekeepers and hangmen to exterminate vermin."

"Well, now, cut along home. Your mother is in no end of a funk about you."

*　　*　　*　　*　　*

So Jack went home, and, having explained the reason of his absence, was soon forgiven by all, except little Emily, who boxed his ears, declaring it was evident he did not care about her, or he would not have risked his life in such a manner.

Then she refused, for a whole hour, to speak to him; at the expiration of which time she kissed him, and asked his pardon for having shown such bad temper.

"All right, Em. You're a brick."

"Don't talk slang, sir."

*　　*　　*　　*　　*

That same evening they left Paris, and at an early hour the next morning were in London.

CHAPTER CVIII.

"LAST SCENE OF ALL, THAT ENDS THIS STRANGE, EVENTFUL HISTORY."

"JACK."

"Yes, father."

"What do you think you are going to be? I mean what business or profession?"

This conversation took place about a week after their return to England.

"Would you like to be a doctor or a lawyer, or become a great financier in the City?" continued Harkaway senior.

"Neither of those, thank you. I have been too much used to plenty of fresh air and exercise to settle down to an indoor occupation; the sea is my choice."

"It is not your mother's choice, so you may just give up that notion at once and for ever."

"Well, next to that I should like to have a nice compact farm of about six hundred acres in a part of the country where there is good shooting, hunting and fishing."

"Ah, that's better."

"Then we'll consider that settled, dad."

"Yes; but you must finish your education first; that has been much neglected."

So the result was that both young Jack and Harry Girdwood were sent to reside for a year with a clergyman, who was also a farmer, and who undertook, while improving their general education, to give them a practical knowledge of agriculture.

* * * *

The year passed away, and the two young men returned home for a brief holiday before settling down, for Harry was also to be a farmer, Dick Harvey having undertaken to put him into a farm.

They were sitting at breakfast one morning when two letters were brought, both with foreign postmarks.

Harkaway senior opened them.

"This concerns you, my dear," said he to Paquita.

"How so?" asked the girl.

"It is from your father. And you must prepare to hear bad news."

"He is dead! he is dead!" she exclaimed, bursting into tears.

When some time had passed, she was calmed sufficiently to hear the letter read.

It was a deathbed letter, in which the writer stated that remembering the noble-hearted Englishman, Harkaway, he appointed him sole trustee of his wealth, to be given as a marriage portion to Paquita.

Documents were enclosed to put Harkaway in possession of the writer's riches, and he concluded by praying Heaven to bless his daughter.

A postscript was added in a different hand.

"*The writer of this died on the 4th of April last, the day after he signed this letter and the enclosed documents which are witnessed by me.*"

"ANTONIO DELAVAT, *Surgeon.*"

Paquita's grief at the death of her father was great, but in little Emily and Mrs. Harkaway she found two comforters, who did their best to assuage her sorrows.

* * * *

But the other letter.

"Why, this is from our old Australian friend, Rook!" exclaimed Harkaway.

"Rook!"

"Yes. And this is what Rook has to say for himself.

"'*If ever a man had reason to be grateful to another, surely I have cause to bless the day I met you. For thanks to you, I am no longer an outcast, but have atoned for the past—aye, and refunded with interest that sum of money which was the cause of my being sent here. Through your kindness I was enabled to go into business as a farmer, and I have prospered so that I am now one of the richest men in this part of Australia; but I owe all my prosperity to you, so I will not boast of it. Being better educated than many of the settlers, I have been appointed magistrate for the district; but whenever I can be lenient without being unjust, I humble myself, remember what I once was, and try to give the culprit another chance. Heaven has greatly prospered me, and I pray that Heaven's blessings may rest on you and yours.*'"

"Bravo, Rook!" said Harvey and Harry Girdwood.

* * * * *

"What are you thinking about, Jack?" asked Harry, a day or two after.

"About old Mole."

"What about him?"

"Why, we haven't had a good lark with him since we left Marseilles."

"True."

"The old man will get rusty if we don't wake him up a little."

"Well, what is your idea?"

"Haven't any at present; but something will turn up."

And something did turn up that very day.

Now it should be known that Mole, although he passed the greater time with his old friends, had taken a small cottage close by so that he might not entirely wear out their hospitality.

He generally slept there, but spent his days with the Harkaways.

Jack and Harry called upon the old man, and were admitted to his presence, as he was putting the finishing touches to his toilet.

This consisted in anointing his bald head with some wonderful fluid, warranted to produce a luxuriant growth of hair.

This gave the youths an idea, and having invited him to dinner, they departed to carry out their joke.

All passed off pleasantly during the evening, but Jack and Harry were absent about an hour. During that time they procured access to Mole's premises, and having emptied his bottle of hair restorer, filled the phial with liquid glue, after which they returned to the house.

"I must go early," said Mr. Mole, rising. "I have to attend court as a juryman in the morning."

"Then you won't be able to dress your hair properly," said Jack.

"Oh, yes; I shall put on a good dose before I leave home, that will last till evening," replied Mole.

He went home, but overslept himself, and had to dress in a hurry.

Mole had got to the door, when he remembered the hair restorer, and going back, applied a plentiful dose with a sponge.

He reached the court very hot.

By that time the glue had set, and he found he could not remove his hat.

"Isaac Mole!" shouted the official who was calling the jury.

"Here!" replied Mole, as he rushed to the box.

A murmur of astonishment was heard.

"Hats off in court!" shouted the usher.

"Really, I——"

"Everyone must be uncovered in court."

"But, I assure you, I can't——"

"Are you a Quaker?" demanded the judge.

"No; but I wish to explain that I kept my hat on because——"

"I cannot listen to any excuse except the one I mentioned. Take off your hat instantly."

"But I say I kept it on because——"

"This is intolerable. Do you mean to insult the court? Take your hat off instantly, or I will fine you for contempt."

"Well, I must say it's hard I can't say a word."

"You are fined five pounds, and if you don't remove your hat——"

"I want to explain."

"Officer, remove that man's hat."

The tipstaff approached Mole and hit the offending hat with his stick, but it did not move.

Then he struck it harder, and the crown went in.

"This is too bad!" screamed Mole.

But the tipstaff was wrath, and picking up a large law book, smashed it flat.

This was too much for Mole.

"You mutton-headed idiot, if you and the judge had a particle of sense, you would know that I did not remove my hat, because I couldn't. It is glued on."

Mole, however, was led away in custody, and a fresh juryman sworn.

But Jack and Harry, who had been highly-amused spectators, thought the joke had gone far enough, so they tipped a solicitor through whom an explanation was made, and Mole was released. He also got off serving on the jury.

They left the court together.

But another surprise was in store for them.

"How are you, gentlemen?" said a very familiar voice, and, lo! Figgins the orphan stood before them.

Figgins had not remained in Marseilles like the others, and, therefore, had escaped being arrested for counterfeit coining.

He reached London in safety, and having taken the upper part of a house within half a mile of St. Paul's Cathedral, resolved never more to trust himself beyond the City boundaries.

Yet, in his retirement, his conscience pricked him for having left so hurriedly the friends who had rescued him from many a danger.

And Mole, too, his own particular travelling companion.

"I must go and see him once more," thought the orphan.

So one fine day he plucked up courage to venture a short journey on an English railway, and knowing where the elder Harkaway lived, was speedily instructed how to find Mole.

So now behold him shaking hands all round.

"I thought I must see you once more," said he, "but it is a great undertaking, you know, for my travels made me more timid than ever I was."

"Timid?" ejaculated Mole; "why, on one or two occasions you displayed bravery almost equal to my own."

"Mildly, Mr. Mole," said Jack.

"Ah, Mr. Harkaway, you three gentlemen are brave men, but I am only a poor timid orphan."

"That need not make you timid."

"But it does. So I have resolved never to trust myself out of London again."

"Then I am afraid we shall not meet very often, Mr. Figgins," said Mole, "for I, you know, hate town life."

"If you do come to town, though, you will call?"

"Certainly."

"Then, gentlemen, I will wish you farewell. I am deeply grateful for all you did when we were abroad——"

"Don't mention it."

"Mr. Mole, farewell. You know I feel more like an orphan than ever now I am parting from you."

"Don't talk like that, Figgins," said Mole.

"I can't help it, indeed, I can't. Farewell, my dear friend, farewell!"

And Figgins retired to his City home, where he still lives, though he is getting very feeble.

Still, he brightens up whenever he speaks of his old friend and travelling companion, Mole.

*   *   *   *   *

It is hard to part with old friends, but the decrees of fate cannot be avoided, so we must conclude our story.

It will be hardly necessary, we fancy, to inform our readers that young Jack eventually married little Emily, and Harry Girdwood led Paquita to the altar.

And as weddings are very much alike, we will not describe the ceremony, but content ourselves with saying that as much happiness as this world can afford was and is theirs.

Jack and Harry have extensive farms near each other, and are wealthy country gentlemen.

They are fond of outdoor sports, and have recently established a pack of harriers, Tinker and Bogey being respectively first and second whips. In each establishment there was formerly a room kept always ready for Mr. Mole, who went from one to the other as it pleased him, sure of a hearty welcome always.

But, alas! poor Mole is now no more.

Age preyed on his shaken body, and at length laid him on his deathbed.

Even then he could not help referring to the matrimonial portion of his life.

"I have been too much married, Jack. I am 'a wictim to connubiality,' if I may be allowed to quote Sam Weller; but never again, dear boy."

And when only half conscious, he would re-

peat—"Never again, dear boy," expressing his firm determination not to marry again.

Poor Mole!

After all, he ended his days in peace, and died regretted by all his friends, who, if they had laughed at his failings, also remembered his kindly disposition.

He left behind him sufficient of this world's goods to enable his faithful Chloe to give the twins a good education.

They are now rollicking schoolboys, but will have a fair start when their guardians, Jack and Harry, fancy they are fitted to begin their battle with life.

* * * *

Old Jack—he is getting old now—lives with Emily not far from his son, and with them, of course, is Dick Harvey.

Often on a fine day Old Jack will lead his grandchildren to the village churchyard, and while the youngsters deck poor old Mole's grave with flowers, will relate to them the best incidents of the old man's life.

Not far from poor Mole's grave is another tomb, in which rest the earthly remains of Monday, Prince of Limbi, who had grown grey in the service of Mr. Harkaway.

A much severer winter than usual laid the seeds of a complaint which speedily carried him off.

Sunday, whose head is fast becoming white as snow, took his death much to heart, and even now frequently strolls into the quiet churchyard to indulge in pensive recollections of his old friend by the side of his grave—aye, and perchance to reflect on his own end, which he knows full well must be fast approaching.

Monday had been thrifty, and when the days of mourning were over, his widow retired to Oxford to pass the remainder of her days with many good presents from Jack Harkaway, given in remembrance of his faithful servant Monday, the Prince of Limbi.

* * * * *

Readers, our tale is told; and we leave Harkaway to the repose he has so well earned.

But if you would prosper as he has done, be like him, truthful, brave, and generous.

In bringing to a conclusion the long series of Harkaway stories, Mr. Edwin J. Brett cannot let the occasion pass without thanking the readers for the patience with which they have followed the hero's career, and the praise they have always bestowed upon the story or stories.

To invent the plot and incidents has been a labour of love on the part of Mr. E. J. Brett, and it seems now like parting from old and intimate friends, to say adieu to all the characters whose lives have been the subject of the story. But there must be an end to all things, even to Harkaway.

THE END.